'A blockbuster . . . an excellent reading experience' *Literary Review*

'The mix of suspense, romance, humour and good old heart-tugging pathos is irresistible'
Elizabeth Buchan, *Mail on Sunday*

'A blockbusting story of romance and intrigue'
Family Circle

'The perfect beach book' *Marie Claire*

'Sharp . . . wickedly funny' *Mail on Sunday*

'Ambition, greed and manipulation add up to a great blockbuster' *New Woman*

'You won't be able to put it down'
Good Housekeeping

'A well-written contemporary story that has all the necessary ingredients to make a great read – and it is!' *Oracle*

'Anita has the storyteller's gift' *Daily Express*

'Sinister and avaricious forces are at work behind the pious smiles . . . Gripping!' *Daily Telegraph*

'A sure-fire bestseller' *Prima*

Anita Burgh was born in Gillingham, Kent, but spent her early years at Lanhydrock House in Cornwall. Returning to the Medway Towns, she attended Chatham Grammar School, and became a student nurse at UCH in London. She gave up nursing upon marrying into the aristocracy. Subsequently divorced, she pursued various careers – secretarial work, as a laboratory technician in cancer research and as a hotelier. She has a flat in Cambridge and a house in France, where she shares her life with her partner, Billy, a Cairn terrier, three mixed-breed dogs and three cats. The visits of a constantly changing mix of her four children, two stepchildren, six grandchildren, four stepgrandchildren and her noble ex-husband keep her busy, entertained and poor! Anita Burgh is the author of many best-sellers, including *Distinctions of Class*, which was shortlisted for the Romantic Novel of the Year Award.

By Anita Burgh

Daughters of a Granite Land 1: The Azure Bowl
Daughters of a Granite Land 2: The Golden Butterfly
Daughters of a Granite Land 3: The Stone Mistress

Distinctions of Class
Love the Bright Foreigner
Advances
Overtures
Avarice
Lottery
Breeders
The Cult
On Call
The Family
Clare's War
Exiles

Tales from Sarson Magna: Molly's Flashings
Tales from Sarson Magna: Hector's Hobbies

ADVANCES

Anita Burgh

ORION

An Orion paperback

First published in Great Britain in 1992
by Macmillan Publishers Ltd
This paperback edition published in 1997
by Orion Books Ltd,
Orion House, 5 Upper St Martin's Lane,
London WC2H 9EA

Reissued 2001

Copyright © 1992 Anita Burgh

The right of Anita Burgh to be identified as the
author of this work has been asserted by her in accordance
with the Copyright, Designs and Patents Act 1988.

All rights reserved. No part of this publication may be
reproduced, stored in a retrieval system, or transmitted, in
any form or by any means, electronic, mechanical,
photocopying, recording or otherwise, without the prior
permission of the copyright owner.

This novel is a work of fiction.
Names and characters are the product of the
author's imagination or are used fictitiously and any
resemblance to actual persons, living or dead,
is entirely coincidental.

A CIP catalogue record for this book
is available from the British Library.

ISBN 0 75280 931 8

Printed and bound in Great Britain by
Clays Ltd, St Ives plc

For Suzanne Baboneau,
with love, and thanks for having
such wonderful ideas

ACKNOWLEDGEMENTS

I should like to thank my friends in the worlds of writing and publishing who helped me with this book, even if sometimes they were not aware of it.

In particular: Alison Samuel, Gail Lynch, Billy Adair, Suzanne Baboneau, Tom Burns, Philippa McEwan, Martin Neild, Jane Wood, Vivienne Worldly, Mic Cheetham, Marina Oliver and the many others too numerous to mention. And especially Billy Jackson for his constant support and patient Carol Slater who typed it all.

part one

chapter **one**

The white fog clung damply to the window. Julius Westall moved the heavy brocade curtain to one side and peered out, remembering other fogs, other days. Fogs which had billowed without warning across the square, blanking out man and buildings with their great swirling yellow clouds. Fogs sulphurous in their density. Fogs in which anything could happen, untold adventures could begin . . .

He turned from the window abruptly. An old man losing touch with reality in daydreams, that was what he was becoming. Senility lay that way and life was already complex enough without giving in to advancing age.

On his desk lay last year's audited accounts. He stood, a tall, patrician figure, looking down at the glossy black spiralled folder. His thick hair, once blond, was silver now, the once-piercing blue eyes were faded and with the aureole of age around the iris. But the figure was upright, that of a man who looked fit even though he knew he was not.

He was tired, that was his problem, nothing more ominous he was sure. Tired of fighting against the odds, of hoping to balance books which never would, of losing money, of responsibility, of family relationships which he could not heal, of every damned thing. He had to cling to the idea of normal fatigue: if he didn't he was afraid what lack he might find in his mental resilience.

From a cabinet at the side of his desk – a fine marble-topped desk with outspread golden eagles at either end for legs – he took a glass and a bottle of Glenfiddich and carefully poured a large measure.

'Give up the whisky and cigars for a start, Julius,' Sir Archibald McKinna, his socially smart and elegant Harley Street physician, had said that morning. But Sir Archibald had been known as 'Baldie' in his schooldays, and it was difficult for Julius, remembering the snotty-nosed fag Archibald had once been, to take anything he said seriously. Or was he using those memories as an excuse? Had he known, even as his old friend lectured him, that he would take no notice – could not face the consequences of doing so?

Did he want to live what was left of his life without the drink, the cigars, the rich food he loved? For what? An extra year, maybe two. Extra time to worry about the business, to war with his children and be ignored by his wife.

Certainly he should slow down. He might even learn to enjoy it. There were his roses, after all, he would like to spend more time pottering among them. Odd how he had come to gardening so late in life. He had never before felt any inclination to garden, could never understand those of his friends whose passion it was. Gardens had been places for others to tend and for him to sit in occasionally. And then, quite suddenly, just after his sixtieth birthday, he had the notion to plant his rose garden and for the past five years he had lavished his love, spare time and money on it. He realised now that the roses had taken over when Gemma, last of a long line of mistresses, had left him for someone younger and richer. In the past he would have sallied forth and quickly found a replacement except, after Gemma, he found he really could not be bothered – hence the roses.

It was ironic after sixty-five years of life, years packed with amorous adventures, to find himself thinking of his love for the flowers. But then, what else, who else was there to love?

Certainly not his family. Jane, his wife, six years and two children into their marriage had coldly announced that there would be no more sex as if, by producing the children, she had done her duty and would now rest on her laurels. Not that Jane had referred baldly to 'sex', she was far too genteel even to acknowledge the word existed let alone the practice. No, she had met him one evening on his return from work to inform him that is things had been moved from *her* room, that he now had a room of his own. The implication of such a move did not even need to be discussed between them. He understood. He was not surprised. A considerate lover, whatever he had tried had failed to awaken any passion in his otherwise perfect wife. He had felt sorry for her – then. How bleak never to know the fulfilment and relief of a good physical relationship. If he was honest he was relieved, as if her frigidity was no longer his

4

responsibility. Julius had not liked the sense of failure her lack of response gave him – it made him feel that he had let her down – but then, in his defence, he doubted if there was a man alive who could rouse Jane.

After the night of his dismissal from her bedroom, he'd been unfaithful for the first time. He felt he had every right to; she did not. And as mistress followed mistress he had watched Jane's pretty face turn thin-lipped, bitter and shrewish. She had loved him once but Julius had seen that love turn to hatred, ice cold, polite, but hatred none the less. Jane had the final revenge – she refused to divorce him.

Divorce. In this day and age divorce would have been automatic, and no one would have thought the less of him – a modern Julius would have had no qualms about it – but he had been brought up in the old ways and divorce was out of the question. Appearances had to be maintained and now it was too late to bother. He had accepted the ground rules of their relationship – the façade that all was well – but when he contemplated the lost and empty years, he wondered why and for whom he had done so.

Inevitably his liaisons became known and he had acquired the reputation of a roué. Unfair, when all he had ever wanted was a happy, loving marriage. Jane, on the other hand, while not much liked – she was not an easy woman for anyone to like – received sympathy as the wronged wife. Julius had never explained the true situation to a living soul, not even his army of mistresses. It was not his way.

And his two children? He did not even know them, did not even want to now. John, his son and heir, had rejected publishing for banking and was now nearly forty, suitably pompous with a large enough gut to proclaim to the world how successful he was. Caroline was a bigot who lived in the country with her minor 'landed gentry' husband who tried to lord it over a community, which these days refused to cower satisfactorily.

He had once overheard someone say that it was possible to dislike your children but nothing could ever stop you loving them. Well, he could put the lie to *that* theory, he thought, as he poured another whisky, raised his glass and silently toasted Sir Archibald.

All he cared for was this room, the company and his roses.

Julius leaned back in the high-backed wing chair and looked with satisfaction at his office, as he often had over the thirty years since he had inherited it from his father. He had always worked long hours – invariably the first in and the last to leave – and from the very beginning he had resolved that if he was to spend more time here than in his home, then he would make this room as beautiful and comfortable as it could be. Hence the valuable desk, and the two enormous George III breakfront bookcases, containing every book he'd ever published, bound in best Morocco leather, the Chippendale library steps, the fine Amritsar carpet and the pictures. Ah, the pictures, his pride and joy. Sutherland, Hitchens, Bacon, Spencer, each purchased with love, each now worth a small fortune.

The company Westall and Trim had been founded by his great-great-grandfather in 1859. Each generation that followed had taken up, with pride, the running of their 'house'. Trim's descendants had long ago faded from the scene, bought out one by one by Julius's predecessors. By the time he had joined the firm, the name was merely part of the logo. Westall was a name to be proud of in the literary world, a name anyone would care to follow – all, that is, except his son who, with his ruthless accountant's eye, had scanned the balance sheets and opted for what he saw as the safer world of banking.

On that score Julius had to admit John was right: there could be no arguing with such a conclusion. Working at Westall's would not have bought him the fine house in Ebury Street, the small farm in Sussex, the bolt-hole in the Dordogne. But banking could never provide John with the excitement that publishing had given Julius all his working life. He was convinced there was nothing in the world to compare with finding a new writer, taking that first gamble on an unknown. Nothing could match the satisfaction of nurturing him or her, supporting, persuading, cajoling, sympathising, dealing with the tantrums and the self-doubt, having the patience of Job, all for that end product – *The Book*. A book that might sink without trace, but at the same time a book that might, just might, be lauded, awarded and sell. The authors thought it was they themselves who were important but for Julius they were a means to an end – the production of that precious volume. Where in banking could he find the pleasure of having an idea and matching it to the right author – the next best thing to being a writer himself? It never palled. Each time a new book arrived from the printers, encased in the dust jacket over which the designers had argued and laboured, Julius always felt the same sense of excitement and pride.

He had taken many gambles – books that, in the end, he realised only he and the author loved, and others that he had known would never return the outlay but which he had still gone ahead with because he was a publisher and he felt they *should* be published. Publishing to Julius was about books, not profit, and that, in the 1990s, was where the problem lay.

All his predecessors had had other means – share portfolios, property with which they had been able to cushion their lives against the ups and downs which had always been the way of publishing – but Julius had none of these. After death duties, what had been left had gradually been eaten away by the necessary injections of cash that this insatiable monster – his 'house' – required to stay afloat.

In the old days, once an author joined you, they stayed until they wrote no more or died – Julius had found the two usually came together. But that had all changed. He still had that precious asset which made him a good and highly respected publisher, the ability to spot talent – often when others had passed it by. He would do his part of the job to perfection but invariably the great conglomerate sharks lurking out there in today's murky waters would strike, offering enormous advances which his firm could never match. Author loyalty was long dead. He did not blame them and always sent them on their way with his congratulations and wishes for their good fortune ringing in their ears. For who but the richest could turn their backs on such seducers?

Those advances! He hated the word, loathed the lengthy negotiations they invariably involved with rapacious authors hiding behind equally rapacious agents who did the dealing for them. Time was when an author accepted a couple of hundred pounds as a loan against future royalties – a modest sum to tide him over. Once that couple of hundred had been earned he was paid his royalties. Now there were authors whose advances were so high they never earned a penny in royalties. Advances so huge – half a million pounds, a million, anything was possible – that the publisher could never hope to earn the money back. It was madness, all of it.

Of his own authors he could rely on only two: Gerald Walters, knighted now for services to literature, Nobel Prize winner and doyen of English writers whom Julius had first met at Cambridge and whose first book Westall's had been proud to produce. Every three to four years a chaotic manuscript would arrive on Julius's desk. Gerald, he often thought, must be the only author alive who was allowed to present his work like that rather than neatly typed.

Then there was Sally Britain – crime writer *extraordinaire*, winner of the Golden Dagger award, who each September, for fifteen years, had presented him with yet another beautifully crafted thriller. A sweet woman and one with whom he had enjoyed a happy summer affair soon after she had joined them. Sally did not strike one as a romantic but as the years went by and she still stayed with him, he often wondered if it was for old times' sake.

Each year Julius was anxious, knowing that both these writers would be approached by the larger publishers with promises of untold sales and promotion but, luckily for him, they had always refused. But then, both were in that small band of successful writers who were content with the money they made and could afford the luxury of loyalty.

The others, one by one, had left what, he supposed, they saw as a sinking ship. And new blood, initially sycophantically grateful, was, once Westall's had done the groundwork on their careers, seduced away by offers which, to Julius, resembled telephone numbers.

It wasn't as it used to be . . . There he went again, that's how old men thought and talked . . .

The solution was easy. He had only to hint he wanted out and the bargaining from the conglomerates would be deafening, the cheque books would flash, the piranhas would strike, and Westall and Trim would never be the same again.

His family was as aware of this as he and there had been many discussions, usually slipping into arguments, as they pointed out what a selfish fool he was. Maybe so, but he could not sell out. He'd rather die in harness. But he needed new blood in the company, sympathetic blood, someone who could look at the dear old lady and drag her, screaming if necessary, into the new decade.

Not Crispin, though. Never! He still rued the day he'd

listened to his sister, Marge, and agreed to take on his nephew, cocky and fresh from Oxford, as a junior editor. Now he was financial director – from ability certainly, Julius wasn't a total fool and certainly not where staff were concerned. But Crispin, with his thrusting arrogance, his streak of ruthlessness, his greed, was not a person Julius could ever like and certainly not the person to entrust with this love of his life. If he did, Crispin would sell out within twenty-four hours he was certain.

He supposed he had to listen to old Archibald, though – if not for himself at least for the firm. He was not ready to give up yet, he still had things to do. He needed help, he realised that now. Someone younger, but someone who thought as he did. He had a number of ideas stored away in the back of his mind. Perhaps it was time to bring them out, dust them down and mull them over seriously.

The clock on the mantelshelf chimed the hour. Julius checked it against his watch. Ten. Hardly worth going home. He closed the ledger he should have been studying and locked his safe. Carrying his bottle of Glenfiddich and with a typescript under his arm, he mounted the stairs to the attics where, years ago, he had created a small flat for himself, the scene of many of his conquests.

Stupid old goat! He laughed at himself. All that was over and thank God it was. As a young man he could never have imagined a day would dawn when he would be grateful that the hormones had quietened down. Now he felt it was one of the greatest advantages of age, even the memories did not bother him any more.

He opened the small refrigerator to see what Roz had bought for him just in case he slept over. The perfect secretary, Roz. Pity she had blotted her copybook, in his eyes, by having an affair with Crispin – not that he was supposed to know.

chapter **two**

Like many housebound women, Kate Howard had a moment in the day that was more special than any other. Before it could be reached, however, the chaos of the early morning had to be surmounted. First, she had to sort out her family ready for work and school. She had winkled them reluctantly out of their beds. She had searched for and found a vast range of things they could not find – items of clothing, satchels, briefcases, last night's homework, dinner money – all of which were invariably in the place she had suggested. She had mediated in an argument that had erupted from nowhere and over nothing. She had fed and watered them, arguing with her dieting daughter about the need to eat and reprimanding her son whose bolting of his food was putting his future digestion at risk. Long ago she had resigned herself to her husband hiding behind his paper, loftily impervious to the noise. As usual she had waylaid the morning post, secreting away the electricity or telephone bill knowing, from experience, that such matters were better received at the end of the day rather than at the beginning. She had kissed them goodbye and waved them on their way. Then the front door slammed on the last of them and a silence descended upon the house, a silence like no other, a moment like no other.

Kate now sat at the table in the kitchen and looked with distaste at the dirty breakfast crockery which littered it. She leaned back in her chair and let the quiet wash over her, calm her and set her up for the rest of the day. She felt the peace of the house seep through her as if it was flowing in her veins.

Kate was not a morning person and never had been. When the alarm clock rang it was a rebirth for her, and an agonising one too. She always rose first and had a quick shower, cleaned her teeth, brushed her hair and, these days, avoided looking in the mirror over the pampas-green basin with its gold-plated taps. Then she padded quietly down to the kitchen to put the kettle on.

She was always first down, too, not out of any sense of duty but rather because it gave her half an hour before she had to speak to anyone. If it was necessary for her to speak before then it invariably emerged as a snap which put the whole household out for the rest of the day.

For years she had thought guiltily that it was only *her* family who faced such chaotic mornings, that in some way they were all her fault, for she had made the mistake of comparing them with the calm of her mother's house where everything worked like clockwork and no one ever had a cross word with anyone. She knew better now. From friends she had learned she was not alone, that the behaviour in this household was the same as in a million others. Her mother's house was the odd one out.

When the family had gone Kate ate, or not, depending on whether she was dieting, or whether she had given up on the latest one, the latter being the more common. But first she cleared the offending dishes from the table, loaded the dish-washer, wiped the cooker down and then made her tea and toast. When she thought of the amounts of food her son and husband consumed without putting on an ounce, she resented bitterly the guilt she felt as she ate her toast and put a spoonful of sugar into her tea. Then she lit her first cigarette of the day, the one she enjoyed most, and finally was at comparative peace with the world.

She could not enjoy a total peace for Kate had reached the point in her life where she had begun to feel as confused as she had as an adolescent. As her hormones thrashed about in their dying phase, she found her moods swinging alarmingly. If she felt happy and elated she could not rely on it to last for she knew full well that a dark feeling was always lurking ready to take hold. When it came she tried to fight it, to make it go away, for she knew that if she allowed it to linger long, it would sneak into the centre of her soul, and the consequences could be disastrous. It had crept stealthily over her, so slow and subtle its onset that neither she nor those around her were aware of the change in her.

Kate called it a feeling because, in fairness to herself, it wasn't a true depression, not a medically diagnosable condition. Rather, she felt as if the joy had departed from her life and much of her spontaneity disappeared with it. She felt herself becoming, by insidious degrees, empty and colourless and the more she felt this the more rapidly she began to look as she felt – so much so that a passer-by in the street would no longer notice her, would pass the insignificant woman she had allowed herself to become without a second glance. Even her walk had changed. These days she walked with eyes downcast, not wanting to glance up to meet the blank stare of a stranger, knowing that in the uninterested glance was the proof that her youth had gone once and for all, that she was middle-aged.

She was surprised by her reaction to the loss of more youthful looks. She had not expected it. She had assumed that only beautiful women cared. Kate had never been beautiful and had imagined that she would be able to shrug off advancing years when her skin lost its elasticity, the wrinkles appeared, her waist thickened, when she would meet men and see that they were not attracted.

She found she thought constantly about that lack of interest. She had never played around, had not wanted to – but now that it was all too late, she found a reservoir of regret within her that now she never would. A sadness that she would never know what it was like for another man to make love to her.

Discontent, unknown to her before, had begun to infiltrate her life. Yet the life she lived had not changed, only herself. Her routine was the same as it had been for nearly twenty-four years – a routine she had not questioned, had been too busy even to think about. But now she found she was beginning to resent it, and sometimes felt as if her home was becoming a prison from which there was no escape.

That was when the guilt began to surface, for what had she to be so discontented about? She had everything that a woman could want – or, rather, what her upbringing had taught her a woman should want. Tony, her husband, worked hard for them all – too hard, in fact, for she would have preferred him to spend more time with them than he did. He did not drink excessively, he was not a womaniser, all his free time was spent at home and many of her friends, with husbands who strayed, envied her. Lucy and Steve, their children, were healthy and good-looking. They had never been a problem, there had been no unsuitable friends, no drugs and she and Tony had even been spared political views alien to their own, which, she knew, in other homes had led to rows of volcanic proportions. They were ideal children. Lucy, bright as a button and about to finish her A levels, had opted for a career in law just like her father, which had pleased him immensely. Steve, a bit slower than his sister but with far more charm and about to take his GCSEs, wanted to be a landscape gardener. Tony could not understand this ambition and, Kate felt, found it somewhat *infra dig*. Of the two she was most at ease with her son.

Kate's life had been predictable. She had lived with her parents – solicitor father, housewife mother – in their large semi-detached Victorian villa in a good part of Bristol. She had done moderately well at school and if, in her teens, she might have dreamed of travel and adventure, she had known these were only dreams. She had been brought up to marry a suitable man and have children, the best role for women – she should know, her mother had told her often enough.

Her only time away from home had been at teacher-training college where her speciality had been domestic science. Most weekends she returned home and took little part in the college's social life for by then she had met Tony, articled to her father's firm. She had never taught for as soon as she had her diploma she married him. Her life was pre-ordained. It was to be the same as her mother's, and rightly and gratefully so, Kate knew that.

The young couple had lived for a happy year in a small flat in Bristol until one day when Tony returned in a high state of excitement with the particulars of this house, then in need of repair and restoration. It would be an expensive and long-term project and the only way they could afford it was by delaying the family they planned. There was no question of Kate working to help, Tony would never have countenanced such an idea.

It was hard for Kate not having a baby when she so wanted one and as much as she loved the house she felt she would rather they had bought something cheaper and she be allowed the children she wanted. But Tony had set his heart on it and Tony always had his own way. He expected it and she accepted it, for had not her own father always decided everything?

They had worked on the house for nearly five years – Tony regarded her decorating skills more as a hobby than as work. When the second bathroom had been fitted the news she longed for came – Tony said they could start a family. First Lucy, followed a couple of years later by Steve. They were a perfect family in their perfect home.

It was a gem of a house, old and built in beautiful Cotswold stone and standing in a village which nestled in the folds of the Mendip Hills. Nothing here had changed in centuries if one discounted tarmacadam, electricity, telephone, TV aerials and running water. Kate had an *en-suite* bathroom, an Aga in the kitchen, a lovely garden and her own car, even if it was secondhand, in the garage. She had the best of the old world and the new. She had everything.

So why had she begun to question it, to feel that she had missed out in life and that, in some way, everything was over?

At night in bed, when she felt so hot she couldn't sleep, she knew the answer. She wanted to do something, to be someone, not just a wife and mother but important to others, too. The thought would give her hope, make her feel that all was not lost. But in the morning it became no more than a dream and the 'feeling' would take hold of her for the rest of the day.

Breakfast over, her second cigarette alight, Kate read the *Daily Mail* from cover to cover – the only time she felt was hers alone to be so self-indulgent.

There were times when she dallied with the idea that if they were richer she might not be feeling the way she did. Her husband must be earning a good salary as the middle partner in a firm of solicitors in the nearby town of Graintry. She did not know since Tony had never told her what he was paid, only that there was never enough and she must be careful.

For years 'being careful' had been a challenge that she had taken pride in meeting. She worked hard at domesticity, wrote 'Homemaker' with pride on forms. And the reputation she had acquired among their circle for being a good manager had filled her with a sense of purpose.

Lucy, cleverer than Kate at manipulating Tony, had recently acquired a dress allowance from her father, which Kate, tired of asking for money for her own clothes and often having to make them, had to admit she envied. But when she had *wondered* if she should not have one too, the request was met with a look – there was no need for words. *Wondering* was Kate's way of asking. Early in her marriage she had discovered that she got nowhere with Tony by asking outright for something. It appeared to irritate him and his 'no' was virtually automatic.

Kate would wander round Debenhams and look at the make-up, the moisturisers, the anti-wrinkle creams. She could have bought them, the housekeeping allowance would stretch to the occasional treat, but she did not. She could never quite bring herself to spend that sort of money on herself, feeling it would not be right and certainly unfair to Tony. The supermarket was her main beautician. She had her hair permed twice a year and managed it herself in between times. Her only extravagance was shoes, in that she only ever bought good quality, expensive ones, but that had been drilled into her by her mother, so it was not really her decision.

She made all the curtains, lining them, stiffening the pelmets, making a job of them that a professional would be proud of. She had never opened a can of soup in the whole of her married life and her pantry was a joy to enter with its rows of home-made jams, chutneys and bottled fruits lined up neatly on the shelves.

Kate was a paragon of a housewife. But recently in her quiet moments, she had looked about her immaculate kitchen with loathing and would sit and dream of hair appointments and manicures in expensive London salons, of throwing out all her carefully hand-made clothes and shopping for new in the expensive boutiques in Graintry, of buying face creams that cost a whole week's housekeeping, of going to a health farm and being cosseted for a week. She would imagine herself in some exotic island location, the warm tropical wind riffling through her newly streaked hair. In this dream there was always a shadowy figure in the background – male, of course. And, although she had not put a face to him, she knew it was not Tony.

Kate was at a dangerous age. An age made more dangerous because she could see no way out of the domestic trap in which, at forty-five, she found herself, and where she dreaded remaining for the rest of her life.

chapter **three**

Crispin Anderson had not meant to enter the restaurant quite so surreptitiously, thereby attracting far more attention than he had intended, but, in the circumstances, it was difficult not to look shifty. Fearful of being overheard he had made the appointment from a call box; he had lied to his secretary, telling her he was going shopping; he had ordered a taxi for Harrods and there had changed cabs, knowing that his destination would appear on the taxi firm's account. By the time he arrived at the restaurant, situated far away from any prying eyes in Bloomsbury, he felt quite elated and sure he knew how a spy must feel. The venue he had chosen was in the nether regions of Battersea. He had felt like an intrepid traveller crossing the river – rather like crossing the Rubicon, he thought, and chuckled quietly at his own joke. He rarely joked and even more rarely understood the witticisms of others – hence his inordinate pleasure in this one.

He rejected the first table he was shown to, in the window, and asked for one at the back conveniently hidden by a large potted palm. He looked about the less than half-full room to make certain he knew no one there, and relaxed. But then, who would travel this far for lunch? And, as far as he was aware, he knew no one who lived in this district.

Crispin resided in a tall white-painted house in Chelsea, generously bequeathed him by his paternal grandmother. Even with what he and his wife earned they would never have been able to afford such a prestigious address from their own resources. They claimed the house was Regency, which it certainly looked. He kept secret, even from his wife, the fact, gleaned from the deeds, that it was Victorian. Everything about the house was perfect and nothing in his and Charlotte's lives could mar it. They had no children and no intention of having any, and Charlotte's wish not to procreate had been the deciding factor in his marrying her. They had no dog, cat or even gerbil to shed hair, puke, pee or fart.

They had searched painstakingly to find the right fabrics, wallpaper, furniture, objects and paintings. All were in period – if one ignored those irritating few years that placed the house in the wrong era. They ate off bone china and drank from glass made before the mid-nineteenth century. Both would have died rather than have plastic in the house – even their toothbrushes were tortoiseshell, the bristles of which were restored at regular intervals.

Such electrical equipment that, given their busy lifestyles, they needed – washing machine, drier and the vacuum cleaner their cleaning lady adamantly demanded – was relegated to the basement so that their sensitive eyes need not be offended and they could pretend the intrusive gadgets did not exist.

Among their small group of closest friends, all of whom lived in identical houses, they were famous for the exquisite dinners they gave, the whole house lit by candle-light, coal fires glowing – they had refused to install central heating. Crispin had a fine line in embroidered waistcoats and cravats while Charlotte nursed a collection of antique dresses. It pleased him to watch her prettily fussing about their guests in her sprigged muslin, which allowed him to fantasise that he was about to screw Jane Austen.

In reality the house was their own private dream world. Neither of them took their fascination with the past into the outside world of business: Crispin was always impeccably suited by Savile Row, Charlotte by Catherine Walker. It fascinated him that, in effect, Charlotte was two people, the soft, daintily adorned woman inside the house and the other suitably dressed outside for her powerful position at Phipps and Secton, one of the largest advertising agencies in the Western world.

Peter was late, for which he was glad. It gave him the chance to study again the figures in his briefcase. He had no need to do so, he already knew them by heart, but Crispin was meticulous where business and figures were concerned.

He ordered a Perrier with a slice of lime. Crispin never mixed alcohol with business, he had seen too many fail that way. His uncle Julius was a prime example, taking pleasure and pride in his long, heavy, alcoholic luncheons. Probably a contributory cause to the mess he was in right now. Crispin had no patience with such people or such behaviour.

He looked with satisfaction at the neatness of the rows of figures. Roz had done him proud this time. One of his most sensible decisions in the ten years he had been at Westall and Trim was the one made, nearly a year ago when he first started seriously to plan his future, to seduce Julius's personal secretary.

It was his uncle's fault that he was having to act like this: Julius had a romantic, stupid attitude to publishing that for some time had been driving Crispin mad with frustration. There was money to be made, big money – he saw it happening in the go-ahead firms unencumbered with a dreaming old fool at their head – but not with the independents. They'd had their day. Crispin had every intention of joining the ranks of the rich conglomerates as soon as possible.

That day was moving nearer now that he had all the information he needed. At first he had had all manner of wild plans to oust his uncle from control but thanks to Roz's help he had not made such clumsy errors. He had learned he would have to wait but, it transpired, not for too long. Now was the time to begin to put out serious feelers within the industry so that the minute the old man died he would know which course to take.

There had been times in the past year when the expense of a mistress, coupled with an expensive wife, had made him wonder if the outlay was ever going to be worthwhile. In the beginning, his main stumbling block had been the inconvenient discovery that Roz was infuriatingly loyal to Julius. It had required enormous patience and self-control on Crispin's part to bide his time with her.

Not that it had been difficult to recruit her in the first place. Crispin was handsome, smart, and could turn on that easy charm which, all his life, those women he had selected fell for. It was one of the reasons he despised women as much as he did, for Crispin was fully aware how superficial it was. He regarded it as just another useful tool, like his intelligence and his good looks.

Using charm, it had taken him just six months to get Roz to dig out the share register of Westall and Trim – since it was a private unlimited company it had been impossible to find out any other way. His mother held shares but, typical of her, she had refused to tell him how many.

He should not have been surprised at her attitude: all his life his mother had been irritatingly secretive, almost pathologically so, he thought. The result was that after thirty-three years he did not know her at all. She had been a widow for six years and although he had tried to find out her financial standing and whether she had any followers she might marry, he had failed – as he always did where she was concerned. Sometimes he had the feeling that it was only with him she was secretive, that she did not like him. He did not mind in the least since he felt nothing for her. If he thought about his father these days it was to feel sorry for him for having shared his life with someone like Crispin's mother. He did not know what her attitude was towards her brother Julius, which made planning more difficult than it need have been. He had once thought of soliciting her help, confiding his long-term plans to her, but when she had told him to mind his own business over the shares he had resolved not to rely on any maternal feelings.

Knowing who held which shares, however, had not helped him one iota. Julius owned 49 per cent, his brother Simon – a painter of little distinction, in Crispin's view, and less success – held 20 per cent, as did Crispin's mother, Marge. Julius's wife Jane held 9 per cent and the Lepanto Trust held the remaining 2 per cent.

In the unlikely event of Crispin being able to persuade his mother, Uncle Simon and Aunt Jane to go along with him they would still only equal Julius's 49 per cent. The key, therefore, to a majority holding would be the trust. What or who this trust was had beaten both his own and Roz's investigative abilities. The last dividends had been paid into an account at Hoare's Bank, no address available. At this rate he'd have to acquire another mistress, at Hoare's, to find out.

He had been despondent until last week, unable to see any way of gaining control of Westall and Trim. What had changed the whole scenario was discovering from Roz that the old boy had been to see his doctor in Harley Street. Crispin had been unable to do any work that day, he was so excited about the possible implications of his uncle's appointment. At first Roz had refused to tell him anything, pretending she knew nothing. But Crispin knew that if the old boy had told anyone anything it would have been Roz – he was ridiculously fond of the girl in Crispin's eyes. He had not pushed the issue but had invited her out to dinner and cleverly manipulated the conversation so that she thought she had brought up the subject herself. At first she had wittered on about promising not to tell a soul, that she could not break a confidence. He had pretended to respect her wishes, changing the subject, talking about a mythical happy childhood in which his uncle had played such a loving part. It did the trick, she burst into tears and spilled the works. It appeared that Julius's heart was in bad shape and that the doctor had told him that unless he gave up drinking and smoking and went on a strict low-fat diet, he could die at any time. Crispin was suitably distressed, an act difficult to maintain when Roz, crying even more, told him how worried she was since Julius seemed to be drinking even more in a crazy act of defiance. To get her to commit the final treachery he had had to promise her the ultimate – that he would leave his wife for her if only she would open Julius's private safe and photocopy his will.

It never failed to amaze him, in this day of sexual equality, the power men could exert just by promising marriage. Not that he had meant it. He would never leave Charlotte for anyone, least of all Roz. She was a nice enough girl and far more enthusiastic in bed than Charlotte had ever been, but she was not right for him. Once or twice he had been horrified to notice she wore clothes blended with man-made fibres, and she had the most vulgar collection of earrings. But she had believed him and last night, in bed in her small flat, she had presented him with the longed-for copy of the will.

The will was the other key. It had always worried him what Julius would do with his shares. Julius had never made any secret that he loathed his children so Crispin had feared he might leave his shares divided among old, loyal employees or to Battersea Dogs' Home or whatever.

His relief when he read the document was total. Julius was just like all the others of his generation: he had left the lot to his children – all except his flaming paintings which he'd bequeathed to the Fitzwilliam Museum, Cambridge. Crispin did not mind that. They were a load of rubbish, as far as he was concerned, even if they were worth a small fortune. Crispin much preferred a nice understandable still-life or landscape. All the same, it might be useful to dig in the accounts and find out how they had been paid for – they might belong to the firm, one never knew.

With this information he could really begin to plan. He knew his cousins John and Caroline. Neither had any interest in publishing and both needed money, John because he collected the stuff like other people collected stamps or butterflies, and Caroline because her small estate in the country was always needing money – the place devoured every penny she and her husband could raise. Both would be only too happy to sell to the highest bidder – and bidders, he knew, there would be aplenty. Westall and Trim was a distinguished name and half a dozen firms, both English and American, would be only too happy to acquire such a house.

'Sorry I'm late.' Peter Holt slipped into the seat opposite. 'I know you said discretion was essential but isn't this going a bit far?' He grimaced.

'I'm told the food is surprisingly good.'

'I hope you're right,' Peter said with feeling. 'Double gin and tonic,' he instructed the hovering waiter. Crispin's lip curled ever so slightly with disdain. 'I presume, with all this skuldug- gery, you've something secret to tell me?' he went on, as he flicked his napkin across his knee and opened the menu.

'Wine?' Crispin asked, delaying any business since he knew he was going to enjoy this interview.

'But of course – red, if it's all right with you.'

Crispin studied the wine list. He would like to have chosen a cheap house wine since he wasn't drinking but, realising he must have Peter on his side, steeled himself to order a particu- larly expensive Burgundy and a bottle of Perrier for himself.

'What's the news, then?' Peter asked as he ripped his roll to pieces, crumbs flying all over the place.

Crispin had to force himself to ignore such brutishness. 'I phoned you, Peter, for as you know I've always had the greatest respect for you and value our friendship greatly.' Peter said nothing to this since it was all news to him. He smiled instead, he hoped graciously. 'I've approached you – and only you, I hasten to add – since fairly shortly I shall be looking for interest from a larger firm.'

'You're leaving Westall's?'

'No.' Crispin hoped he did not sound too irritated. 'I mean I shall be in control of Westall's. Let's face it, Peter, the day of the independent is over. I've always respected what you and Phillip have done with Shotters. You're *the* success story *par excellence* in postwar publishing. We, the family, shall be selling up and all of us would prefer you to be the buyer. I shall, of course, have one or two expectations – a seat on the board, Westall's to remain as an imprint with me in control . . .'

'And a sack of money,' Peter laughed.

'Of course.' He tried not to lean over, tried not to appear too desperate.

'The old boy retiring, giving you the whole bang shoot, then?'

Crispin shrugged, thereby saying nothing.

'When?'

'I'd rather not say at the moment. And I'd prefer it if you didn't mention this meeting to a living soul. I just wanted you to know, for when it happens there will undoubtedly be a rush. I wanted you to be in a position of strength.' He dug into his briefcase and slid a black folder across the table. 'Those are the firm's figures for the past ten years, plus projections, plus details of business in hand.'

'You're taking one hell of a risk giving me all this.'

'I trust you implicitly, Peter.' Crispin smiled his most charming smile.

'Well, thanks.' Peter stuffed the folder into his own briefcase. 'Right, where's that wine? I've one rule, Crispin, I never mix food and business.'

Crispin had to agree, he had no choice, but he was disappointed. Peter could have been his uncle Julius speaking.

After lunch, Crispin took a taxi to Harrods. He purchased two Sea Island cotton shirts, some silk socks and a box of Irish linen handkerchiefs. Then he went to a phone booth and made three calls. The first was to the managing director of Tudor Holdings UK, the English arm of a large American publishing conglomerate, the second to the chairman of Pewter, the largest of the English publishing empires. Then he called his cousin, John Westall.

chapter **four**

Peter manoeuvred his Mercedes into the space reserved for him in front of the large office block of Shotters. He collected his papers together, strode rapidly across the pavement and into reception, nodded pleasantly at the girl behind the desk, and stepped into the lift which shot to the top of the building and the wide, white-painted lobby of the executive floor. At sight of him there was a flurry of activity as his secretary collected memos and Ben, his personal assistant, walked quickly to open the large double mahogany doors at the end of the hallway. The green suit Ben was wearing today was more lurid than usual, and Peter disliked his hairstyle – extravagantly quiffed in the front, and flat as a board on top, as if he spent the night standing on his head. He supposed he should speak to him about his appearance but, even as he thought it, he knew he would not. He would have resented such criticism at Ben's age and he liked the young fellow – besides, he was the brightest assistant he had ever had.

Several people had been sitting in large comfortable dark blue leather armchairs, which matched exactly the blue of the carpet woven specially with the Shotters logo of a small pistol in gold. Peter had had doubts about the carpet at the drawing-board stage and had voiced them, but the combined sulks and cajoling of his wife and the epicene designer had finally persuaded him. Anything for a quiet life. Too often he gave in for that reason and then despised himself. It didn't help that he had the satisfaction every day, as he walked on the thick carpet, of knowing he had been right: it was unbelievably vulgar. He smiled, as if in apology, to those waiting as he hurried past. He looked at his watch, he was running late again.

He walked through the door, still held open by Ben, and into the vast room which was his office.

'You know, Ben, I'm quite capable of opening a door,' Peter said, with an unusual flash of irritation.

'Sorry?' Ben said, puzzled.

'Oh, never mind. Who's out there?' He nodded curtly towards the hallway, annoyed at himself. That was twice this week he had snapped at Ben, plus shouting at Em and reducing her to tears. It was not like him. Maybe he needed a check-up, a holiday, or something.

'Your two-thirty and your three-fifteen appointments. The three-fifteen is bloody early.'

'Must be keen,' Peter said with a grin, hoping the grin would excuse his earlier bad manners. He threw his document case on to the desk, which was so large that although the black leather case skimmed across its surface it did not slip off. He shrugged out of his jacket and took from his secretary, Em, the sheaf of telephone messages. He glanced quickly through them. 'Anything important?'

'Your wife telephoned to remind you about the opera tonight. She says she'll meet you here at seven. Joyce Armitage insists on speaking to you personally. She refuses to discuss whatever it is with Gloria, who thinks it's probably something to do with the new artwork,' Em said apologetically. Peter rolled his eyes with exasperation at authors who thought they knew better than the art department. 'And a producer from BBC Bristol called. They want to know if you'd be interested in appearing in a programme they're planning on publishing. I said you wouldn't be free to return his call until late afternoon, he said he'd be there until seven. The rest can wait.' Em closed her notepad.

'I hate doing TV,' Peter complained.

'Think of the free publicity. Perhaps they'll want to do it here – you could have all the latest books lined up behind you,' Ben said, excitedly, already arranging the books and posters in his mind's eye.

'I think you're wonderful on television, Peter.' Em smiled her shy smile.

'Thanks, Em – you and my mother.' He laughed. 'Would you be an angel and rustle up some coffee? I've just had one of the foulest lunches of my life. So, Ben, who's waiting?'

'Stone, from Stone and Solomon, with the layouts.'

'Who?'

'They're doing the hoardings for Bella Ford's new one.'

'Oh, yes, I remember. She's becoming a sticky bitch – too demanding.'

'Her sales on the last one are up.'

'I could almost wish she'd fail, and then the pleasure I'd have rejecting the next book. I loathe the woman. You'd best get the art director up. Bella will hit the roof if we get it wrong this time. Who else?'

'Your three-fifteen is Marsh – they're a public-relations firm, specialising in book promotions, poor bloke's probably touting for business. And there's a young fellow, Chris Gordon, he's looking for a job.'

'Then send him to personnel.'

'He says his mother met your wife at a charity lunch and she suggested he drop by. Apparently she said you wouldn't mind.' Ben smiled to himself.

Peter loosened his tie with exasperation. He wished Hilary wouldn't do that sort of thing, but it just wasn't worth the ensuing row not to see the fellow – there he went again, giving in. 'Very well, but he'll have to wait until after I've seen the others and made my calls. And get some info on him – look at his CV. Phone Lorna, ask her what jobs are going, if any. Right, tell Em I'll have the coffee in five minutes.'

As Ben let himself silently out of the room, Peter threw himself lengthwise on to the six-seater sofa. He levered off his fine black leather loafers, closed his eyes and, concentrating on his toes, made himself relax. He lay so for four minutes then stood, refreshed. It was a trick he had learnt from a hypnotist who had lectured the Parapsychology Society when he was a student and it always worked, even though he knew it had led to a host of jokes in the outer office. He crossed the wide room, opened a concealed door in the mahogany panelling and entered the small shower room. He splashed his face with cold water, brushed his hair, noting a few more silver hairs in the faded blond, now bordering on mouse. He inspected his nails, put on his jacket again, pressed the button on his desk and was half-way across the room, hand held out in greeting, as his two-thirty nervously entered the room. An assistant followed him, weighed down by the large leather portfolios that were the stock-in-trade of advertising men, designers and the like.

'Stone – a million apologies – the traffic . . . Now, let's see what you've got – I've been waiting all day to see ... Bella Ford is so excited ...'

It was gone six before he had completed all his appointments and calls – early for once. From the document case he removed the folder Crispin had given him, laid it out on the desk and began to study the figures.

'So, what was the mystery lunch about?' Phillip Stern, his partner, had popped his head round the communicating door of his office.

'Come in, Phillip. Crispin, up to no good ...' He pointed to the open folder.

Phillip loped across the room on his long, thin legs and glanced down.

'Is this for real?' He slumped down on a chair, looking quizzically at Peter.

'It would seem so. He claims he's tipping us off first – that it'll be up for grabs shortly. Wants a seat on the board, etc, etc ...'

'That creep comes in the door, I walk out. I'm serious.'

'Don't worry. I have to admit he's bloody good at his job, for all his old-fogey ways, but who could work with a shit like that? You'd be spending all your time watching your back.'

'I can't believe old Julius is retiring.' Phillip shook his head in disbelief.

'Neither can I. Undoubtedly he knows nothing about this.'

'Is he ill?'

'It's the only explanation I can think of.'

'And the figures?'

'Grim.'

'What's he asking?'

'We didn't get that far but from the odd hint dropped I should say he's thinking in the region of twenty million.'

'You have to be joking. He's mad!'

'Crispin's a greedy little fart. He's putting too big a value on the name – maybe it had it in the eighties but not any more. The money's not around.'

'And what is it worth?'

'I've only glanced at these.' Peter pointed to the folder. 'Of course they've got the freehold and they've Gerald Walters and Sally Britain. The rest?' Peter rested his chin on his hands. 'What else is there? Honourable literary losses. I'd say in the region of five million. It needs revamping, more staff, more authors, more money – lots of money. It's a creaking dinosaur. It's a miracle it's survived this long.'

'Julius must have been funding it with his own money. Fatal. But it won't be the same without him around, will it?'

'No, it won't. Poor Julius. I'd put money on it that Crispin's already lined up three or four of us. Offering it to us first, my eye!'

'Bet he's been on to Tudor Holdings then. Who else? Sovereign?'

'No, my guess is Pewter's. I'm seeing Mike Pewter tonight, I'll see what I can fish out. Drink?'

'No, thanks, I've got tickets for the Stones. Milly's waiting for me downstairs.'

'Philistine.'

'That's right, mate, that's me and proud of it. Enjoy your Verdi or whatever . . .'

As Peter showered he was thinking. He never stopped thinking and planning: he'd long ago resigned himself to the fact that he couldn't even take a holiday without his mind still whirring away. Even when he slept he was likely to dream about business.

Wrapped in his bathrobe, he padded across to the drinks cupboard and poured himself a large whisky. He took it to the sofa, selected a small cigar and lit up. He sat staring into space.

Poor Julius indeed, he thought. One of the last. It was a dreadful indictment of the business he was in that there was no longer room for the gentlemanly, creaking approach to publishing which was Julius's style. If the old boy went it would be everyone's loss, that was the tragedy. But then, was he not himself one of those to blame?

It was Julius who had given him his first job when, against parental advice, he had insisted on going into publishing. He smiled to himself as he looked about his palatial surroundings with the plate-glass sliding doors which opened out on to the huge terrace. He'd certainly come a long way from the small chaotic office at Westall's – more a cupboard, really. He knew which one he preferred. He still felt uncomfortable in this place, almost as if he were trespassing. It was like a set for a Hollywood film on big business and he sometimes felt like an actor and at any moment a director would shout, 'Cut.'

He looked gloomily into his glass. Great days they had been. Julius listened: that was his great strength. It did not matter how junior you were, he always had time to listen to your schemes and ideas. He had listened when Peter had pounded into his office, breathless with excitement, with a typescript he had taken off the slush pile, the large heap of unsolicited manuscripts that plagued every publisher. At Westall's, when they had time on their hands they had been duty bound to take from the slush pile. At weekends, evenings, Julius expected them to read from it. 'Who knows what gems lie in there?' he would repeat time and again to his frequently bored and exasperated staff, the cynics among them snorting behind his back with derision. But at least when Westall's returned a manuscript with a rejection it had been honestly read, not like some publishers – or his present operation if he was honest.

Once, though, he knew he had found the gem that Julius was convinced lurked there and Julius had agreed. That had been Tain Ross's first novel. It had gone on to win the David Higham Prize for Fiction. His second novel had been shortlisted for the Booker. Then Tain had gone, left poor old Julius, ungrateful sod, but for ever more, Peter was famous in literary circles for discovering him. Give Julius his due, he always gave credit to those who had earned it. Peter took a sip of his whisky.

But that was exactly what he had done too – left Julius. He had been seduced just as the authors had, bribed away to Freehold's with a salary Julius could not match, let alone top, and with promises of more responsibility. A disaster, that move had been. He should have realised that a megalomaniac like Bartholomew Freehold with his huge business conglomerate would know nothing about publishing and would, consequently, interfere unmercifully. That's what being a megalomaniac was all about, he supposed. Julius had warned him and he had chosen to ignore the warning. As the books they published became seamier and seamier, Peter became ashamed of the list and resolved to quit. Luckily for him that was the precise moment his father had died leaving him a tidy sum, so with Phillip, his friend from Cambridge, equally suddenly endowed by a departing grandfather, they had started Shotters. 'Let's have a shot at it,' one of them had said, they could no longer remember which. Hence Shotters.

Now those really had been the happy days. Toiling away all the hours God gave in those cramped offices off the wrong side of Tottenham Court Road, as close to the magic of Bloomsbury as they could afford.

Even Hilary had cared then and had worked long hours as an unpaid secretary. Come to think of it, with the pittances they paid themselves, they were all virtually working unpaid. Now she did not care a jot about the business so long as the money kept rolling in.

He had poached too. He had taken writers from Julius just like everyone else. Julius never appeared to mind, but he must have. He would shrug his huge shoulders, smile, wish everyone luck and plunge back looking for fresh writers to nurture. What the hell would they all do without Julius and his unnerving ability to spot talent? Find their own, and about time too.

Peter had known right at the beginning that his father had been wrong, he only wished he had lived long enough to see the success his son had become. Peter and Phillip were the whizz-kids of publishing. Their rise had coincided with the City's discovery that publishing was 'sexy'. They had grabbed at the opportunity long before anyone else had woken up to what was happening. From taking on board small houses which were in difficulties they had moved up the scale, gobbling up the middle ones, absorbing them like an insatiable amoeba. Now they were there up at the top with Sovereign, Tudor's, Pewter's. Up there with the big boys.

From two cramped uncomfortable rooms to this fine purpose-built office block, purveyors of dreams. Bah! He drank deeply.

He sighed. He knew why he sighed. He had been sappy then and now he was not. He was no longer a publisher, he was an accountant and administrator. Too often recently, he would dream of jacking it all in, of selling. He would come out with a fortune, his family would be safe. He wanted to go back to the heady days of a two-roomed office, the excitement and the despair, the fear of the bank breathing down his neck. How Julius must feel, he supposed, every working day . . .

He could get out if he wanted. He had only to hint that Shotters was up for grabs: two American firms and one German had already indicated interest. He knew Phillip, the dreamer of the two, would not mind. He would be the first to admit that the power was Peter's, and the ability too. Provided Phillip had his state-of-the-art sound system, his cannabis, his tumbledown house in Shropshire and Milly, his flower-power wife, whose petals had never wilted, Phillip would be happy. What would they get? Clear of outstanding debts? He stroked his chin as he calculated figures. He could set up a trust for the kids, pay off the mortgages and start again with the rest – far more than he had started with last time. He stretched his legs and wiggled his toes at the joy of the dream . . . but a dream none the less.

'Good God, man, aren't you even dressed? I told Em seven.'

The door had opened and there stood Hilary, his beautiful, expensive wife. He got slowly to his feet.

'I needed to think.'

'We'll be late,' she snapped.

'No, we won't. We'll leave the car here, Em will have called a cab.' He crossed the room to the small dressing room. As he slipped into his dinner jacket he sighed again. Out there in the main room was the biggest obstacle to his dream of turning back the clock. Hilary would never countenance his risking everything he had made for the sake of a dream. She enjoyed being the wife of one of the most powerful publishers in the country. He was no longer sure how much he enjoyed having her as his wife.

chapter **five**

Michael Pewter's father had been knighted for services to publishing. Mike wanted a life peerage. 'One up on the old bastard,' he was fond of saying to anyone who would listen. That his father was dead and would never know if his son succeeded in getting one was neither here nor there: the hatred of the son for the father was so deep-rooted that ambition had become obsession.

It puzzled Mike that he was not elevated already. He had done, and did, all the right things. He had married well – Lady Lily, insatiable worker for charity, and daughter of a Duke – he gave more than his tithe to charity each year, he knew everyone of importance and entertained right royally, quite literally. He should have been ennobled years ago but as he read in each honours list the names of lesser mortals, he would slump in his chair, his large brown eyes filled with tears, his hurt awesome to witness.

Mike Pewter did not have an enemy in the world. He did not need one for he was his own worst. Mike was big and loud and lovable, like a giant brown bear. No one took him seriously. He had become a joke, the court jester and, sadly, he was unaware of it.

Six feet four and a good twenty stone with a large, ruddy face, he boomed and chuckled his way through life. His appetites were as gargantuan as his size. Many a society hostess's heart quailed, fretting that her cook might have miscalculated on quantities, as she watched the food pile on to his plate. He drank with equal enthusiasm and a night with Mike always ensured everyone else under the table as he called for yet another bottle of port. He adored women and they him, despite his size. Lady Lily turned a blind eye to his many infidelities, for he was always discreet and she had long ago tired of his stupendous weight crushing her into the mattress. Not that he did that any more – that was too athletic by far –

but women without number were willing to sit astride him and make them both happy.

He should have been dead, of course, and it was a constant puzzle to his doctors that he was not. But each annual medical showed his blood pressure low, his organs in tip-top shape, and even his lungs, assaulted daily by the smoke from forty cigarettes and a minimum of three fat cigars, still functioning without a wheeze or an obstruction. Carouse as he did, he had never had a hangover in his life. His appetites had never cost him a day's work. He could drink all night, grab three hours' sleep, and still be in the office on time, bright-eyed and bushy-tailed. And everyone adored him – everyone, that is, except the Honours Selection Committee.

Pewter's was, with Westall's and a few minor firms, one of the last entirely family-run publishing houses left in the country. But Pewter's did not have Julius's problems. Founded a hundred years ago, backed by a fortune amassed from steel-making, Pewter's had never had a liquidity problem. They were so wealthy and successful that failures were easily absorbed, cushioned by an enormous technical and educational list. It was a rare child who did not have one of Pewter's language dictionaries in their school satchel. Few motor mechanics, engineers and plumbers would have qualified without Pewter's handbooks. And Pewter's had been first to lead the field into the computer-manual boom. In addition, there was Pewter's Book Club, the largest, and moving rapidly into Europe.

Mike was rich, but in the way of the really rich he had not the least idea how rich he was. He was happy, for he was of that lucky band who love their work, so that it had never been irksome toil but always pleasure.

At Covent Garden, Peter and Hilary were shown up immediately to the Pewter box. Peter was relieved. Hilary had strong views on the state of dress of the majority of the audience and was quite capable of saying so, loudly.

Peter greeted Lily with enthusiasm. He liked her and found her an honest woman. If pushed to explain what he meant by this description he would have said it was her naturalness. He liked the way, at fifty, she was growing old gracefully – not like Hilary who waged a bitter, expensive and, he was sure, painful war against flab, cellulite and wrinkles. Lily never whined, nagged or cajoled. If she wanted something, or something upset her, she said so outright and expected a discussion and a solution to the problem immediately. She was kind and thoughtful and there was a calmness about her that made one aware that here was a natural confidante. She did not give a fig for fashion and wore what was comfortable. Invariably she was the most feminine woman in the room.

Peter did not like *Cosi Fan Tutte*. He would have been quite happy to explain he preferred something with a good tune, but rarely did so – it would have given Hilary apoplexy. He sat in the darkened box and from the lights of the stage could see Hilary sitting just in front with Lily. He looked at her with sadness and wondered what had happened to them.

When they had married – she at twenty and he at twenty-four – she had been so different, sweet and fun. God, he had loved her then, could not get enough of her, wanted her every day, several times. Looking back he supposed they'd been happy for ten, maybe twelve years. She had supported him in his plans, had faith in him, worked with him. And then success had come and the money with it and everything had changed.

Suddenly the comfortable but slightly shabby place in Battersea was not good enough and they had crossed the river to Chelsea to a fine Georgian house and a mortgage which had given him nightmares. He had become used to the house and the mortgage eventually, he even enjoyed living there, until five years ago when it no longer suited Hilary and she had demanded they buy a manor house in the country. He had sold the Chelsea house, bought a flat in the Barbican, gritted his teeth and negotiated an even larger mortgage which even now, rich as he was, made him sometimes wake up in a cold sweat. The country house was a source of embarrassment to him still. It had become a cliché these days: it seemed that everyone they knew who had made some money scuttled off to play at being country folk. Hilary had thrown herself into the country life, nurturing suitable friends, hunting, doing good works. It bored Peter stiff: he loathed riding and he found their neighbours bigoted and unattractive. And the rows he had endured with Hilary because the one thing he would not do 'for a quiet life' was to take up shooting. She was in a sulk at the moment because she wanted a swimming pool. When Hilary wanted something she wanted it immediately. The beautiful

Elizabethan stone manor house and a swimming pool just did not seem to go together in his eyes.

He would not mind so much if everything he did for her, and bought for her, made her happy. But it did not. He was watching her becoming more bitter with each year that passed as if she was angry with him. Yet he did not know what it was he had done to make her so.

'Fancy a smoke?' Mike hissed in his ear. He thought it was a whisper, but Mike's whispers never worked and he was rewarded by a spate of shushing from those close by.

Peter followed as quietly as possible as Mike knocked his chair over and inadvertently slammed the door.

'I hate bloody Mozart,' Mike said with feeling, stripping the band off his cigar and searching in a cavernous pocket for his cigar cutter.

'I must admit I'm not too keen on his operas,' Peter took out his more modest cigar. He rationed himself to two small cigars and three cigarillos a day. He had once smoked cigarettes with the best of them and had given up ten years ago. At least he told himself he had given up, but he often wondered how true this was when he watched others smoke and found himself wanting to tear the cigarette out of their mouths. He supposed the longing might go eventually.

'If you don't like Mozart what are you doing here?' Peter asked.

'Something to do with one of Lily's charity dos. Didn't you realise? She'll be worming a cheque out of you before the night is out.'

'No, I didn't. Hilary sees to all that sort of thing.'

'Quite right too. So, what do you think about Crispin?'

Peter coughed on the smoke of his cigar. 'Sorry?' he said, playing for time. He had meant to decide on what strategy to use with Mike and instead had been mooning about his relationship with Hilary.

'You mean he hasn't been in touch? He's carting Julius's figures around, touting them for anyone to see. Fellow should be shot.' For someone as good-natured as Mike this was serious talk.

'Yes, I have seen him. I was going to talk to you about it but, of course, I didn't know if you'd want to say anything.'

'Bloody right I do. This isn't the normal cut and thrust, this is treachery.'

'What did you make of the figures?'

'Right mess – in fact, with interest rates as they are, more like a bloody disaster. Julius can't be having fun any more with that lot slung round his neck. You've got to be able to make mistakes in this game or you might just as well give up.'

'What are we going to do about it?' Peter asked, since a solution entirely escaped him. He was disappointed to hear Mike's reply.

'I don't see what we can do. Crispin's obviously got some shares. I'd always been led to believe he had none. That's a complication. And Crispin's no fool. If Julius is giving up, then Crispin will sell to the highest bidder. I presume he's been in touch with Tudor's – they're acquiring like crazy at the moment.' Mike puffed thoughtfully on his cigar and then smiled slyly. 'We could make it so that no one would want it.'

'How?'

'I'll take old Walters on – he'd slot in nicely. You can have Britain – more your imprint than mine.' Mike waved his cigar airily. Peter smiled at the implication. He had never made any claim to being a literary house: commercial fiction, DIY, cookery, hobbies generally were his strength. The others might make the odd snide remark but everyone these days had to do more popular books. If he let his guard slip for a moment, he would have to defend his properties with an axe in the stampede to sign up Bella, Heather Gardens, Shiel de Tempera or Grace Bliss, any of Shotters' stable of incredibly successful female writers.

'Walters and Sally Britain wouldn't leave Julius.'

'They might if they knew what was afoot.'

'I don't think I could do that to Julius, it would break his heart.' Peter paused. 'Anyone else but not him.'

'I'm glad you added that rider, thought you were getting soft, that would make things boring.' Mike guffawed and the laugh rumbled around his huge chest, escaped and bounced off the flock-covered walls of the corridor.

'I think we've got to talk to Julius,' Peter said.

'I hoped you'd say that.'

'I'll arrange a weekend. Do you think we'll be missed?' Peter nodded towards the door of Mike's private box.

35

Mike shook his large head vigorously. 'No. They're both in seventh heaven – mystery to me. Let's go to the bar, they'll know where to find us.'

Across London Crispin was just being let into his cousin John's house in Ebury Street. He was agog with curiosity. He had never been here, they were not a close family, and he had never had anything in common with John – until now.

The servant showed him into the study where John waved at him and mouthed apologies that he was on the telephone. It was a long call and obviously to someone in the States; figures were being rattled around as if he was discussing his shopping list. Crispin was certain the call was being made on purpose to impress him. He carefully set his features into a bored expression.

John finally and, Crispin was sure, reluctantly put down the receiver.

'This is a surprise, Crisp. What couldn't wait? Whisky?'

'I'd prefer white wine. I never touch spirits.'

'Fine, Crisp. I'll have to ring for my man.'

Crispin managed not to shudder or show by the twitch of a muscle just how annoyed he was at the use of his childhood nickname. No wonder he had never bothered with John.

'So?' John asked once the drinks had been dispensed, the servant had withdrawn and polite but uninterested enquiries had been made as to the health of respective wives.

'Do you like your father?' Crispin asked, deciding not to employ his usual subtlety.

'An odd question,' John answered, and looked thoughtfully at Crispin as if deciding how to reply. 'As a matter of fact, we've little in common.'

'I didn't ask you that. I asked if you liked him. It's important.'

'Well, I wouldn't want it repeated, but, no, if you must know. We've never been close.'

'He's dying.'

'My mother hasn't said anything,' John replied in the tone of voice used for discussing the weather.

'She probably doesn't know.'

'Then how do you know?'

'I found out.'

'I see.' John smiled in a particularly unpleasant way. At that

36

point Crispin would have liked to tell him to get stuffed, but he needed him. So he smiled back.

'By accident. His secretary was less than discreet – the poor girl was devastated, you realise.'

'Ah, ha . . .'

'The point is, John, the company is going down the chute and fast. We had the audited accounts last month. He lost £400,000 last year.'

Crispin had the satisfaction of seeing John's discomfort at this information.

'I hate to tell you this, John, but your father is behaving most oddly. I'm concerned about his will and to whom he might leave the business.' Crispin spoke in a soft, caring voice, as if his cousin's future was of the utmost importance to him.

'He's left it to me and my sister. I know. He consulted me about it.'

'Really?' Crispin failed to keep the cynicism out of his voice. In view of the relationship between John and Julius, well known within the family, it was more likely that John had been doing a bit of judicious snooping himself. 'He could change it, though. I told you he's very odd at the moment – people can go funny when they get old. I want to ensure the future of the company. I want a proper stake in it.'

'When it's losing as much as it is?'

'I love the company, John. It's my family too, remember. I've worked nowhere else, it's my life. Without a Westall and Trim, publishing would never be the same again.' Crispin was proud of the feeling that he had put into that little speech. Quite moving, he thought.

'My sister and I had decided to sell when he goes. I'm reliably informed I can get quite a tidy sum for the name and, I think they called it, "the backlist". And, of course, there's the freehold.'

'Would you mind telling me how much?'

'My friend said confidently five million.'

Crispin could have sighed with relief. He'd thought a banker would have been better informed.

'A little on the high side, I'd have said, more like three million,' he lied effortlessly, with all the assurance of a financier who bandied these sums around daily. 'But there's no need to sell. With the right management, a more go-ahead approach, a fortune could be made. And I'm the man to do it. But I need the security of a holding in the company.' Crispin was amazed at how easily lying came to him once he had started.

'But whose shares?'

'That's the point. As you know, I'm sure, your father has forty-nine per cent. If I can buy in, then, with the backing of everyone else, I can get him to move with the times. You need someone who knows the ropes there and who's loyal to the family. If he dies and, God forbid but I think we should look at the worst eventuality, if he left it outside the family, then we would have control of the company over the beneficiary.'

'Whose shares? My mother has her nine per cent. Julius needed some money some time back and sold them to her. I advised against it, but she wouldn't listen.'

Crispin tutted sympathetically. So that's how she'd got her hands on the shares, he'd presumed as much.

'I'd want more than the nine.'

'What about your mother?'

'My mother?' Crispin snorted. 'She'd never help me, you can bet on that.'

'That leaves Uncle Simon.'

'Exactly.'

'What would you offer him?'

'Three hundred thousand.' Crispin spoke quickly, as if by doing so the sum would diminish.

'And you have that sort of money?'

'Yes,' Crispin said, staring steadily at his cousin. He had, almost. The bank he had approached was impressed with his figures. They were deciding right now; he should hear next week. They would have preferred Julius to die, of course, but it seemed they were willing to gamble with Crispin. He was going to have to put his house up as security, that was painful, but it would be worth it in the end.

'I'd recommend him to sell to you for that. He's old and, as you know, not too successful with his painting. It will help all the family if he's cared for now rather than later.'

'That's settled, then?'

'He's away at the moment – painting trip to Italy, odd time of year, isn't it? I presume you would like me to give him a buzz in a couple of weeks when he's back, tell him you want to see him. You do realise that a special meeting would have to be called, all the shareholders given twenty-one days' notice, and they would have to agree by a majority for any shares to change hands other than to another member of the board – which, of course, you are not, Crisp, even if you're called financial director.'

'I can't see any problems, can you?' Crispin smiled his most charming smile, ignoring his cousin's gibe.

'Well, there is your mother.' John laughed. He actually laughed. Crispin was amazed.

'Oh, I don't think she'll mind so long as it doesn't cost her anything. If you could speak to Uncle Simon, I could then visit him with your blessing?'

'Of course, Crisp, old chap.'

Crispin stood up to leave, amazed that it had all gone so smoothly. It wouldn't matter now if Julius lived or died, he had a stake. And his £300,000 could grow rapidly to four million when he persuaded the others to sell up. It made his mind reel.

John showed him to the door, his arm about his cousin's shoulders, which Crispin did not enjoy. He did not care for physical contact with virtual strangers, but for the sake of his plans he accepted the comradely gesture. The door was just about closing and Crispin was having to fight himself not to leap down the steps, when John called out.

'Tell me, Crisp, what about the Lepanto Trust? That could be a sticking point. Julius has always had its proxy vote. We've never managed to get out of Julius who, or what, it is.'

'The Lepanto? Oh, no problem there,' Crispin said brightly – he hoped not too brightly.

chapter **six**

Kate looked up from the sink where she was peeling the potatoes for the evening meal. In the window she could see her reflection – lank dull hair, spectacles slipping down her nose, overweight, dowdy, done for ... She had got to pull herself together, she told herself for the umpteenth time that week.

The door of the kitchen burst open.

'Mum, have you seen my grey blouse anywhere, the one with the high neck?' her daughter Lucy asked.

Kate continued to gaze at the window. But forty-five was no age, she thought. How had she let herself get like this? Look at Joan Collins, how attractive, how desirable she still was but, then, she had had the courage to grab at life by the throat, live it to the full, not like Kate, cruising aimlessly along, getting nowhere, endlessly feeling sorry for herself.

'Mum, coo-ee!' her daughter shouted, standing close to her.

Kate jumped. 'Lucy, you did give me a start. I'm sorry, were you speaking to me? I was miles away.'

'I'm looking for my grey blouse.'

'Is it in the laundry room?'

'Oh, Mum, no! Does that mean you haven't done it for me? I did ask.' Lucy ran out, slamming the door behind her, and Kate could hear her noisily opening and shutting the doors of the washing machine and drier in the laundry room. She returned to the kitchen, the damp blouse hanging limp in her hand looking like a drowned cat.

'You did promise,' Lucy said accusingly.

'Well, I forgot. Wear something else.'

'But I wanted that blouse.'

'But you can't have that one, can you, not if it's wet. Be sensible.'

'I asked you ages ago. I told you I wanted this blouse for tonight. You don't seem to remember anything these days!

Nothing gets done around here any more,' Lucy whined in an aggrieved tone.

Kate looked at the anger in her daughter's face, the discontented expression, and would have liked to slap her hard. She found herself wondering, quite dispassionately, if it was possible to love someone even when one thought one was beginning to dislike them.

'Maybe it's about time you did your own washing for a change. At seventeen I'd have said you were old enough,' she said.

'That's right, make me sound in the wrong.'

'I didn't mean to. It was just a suggestion so that at least one reason for the unpleasant scenes we keep having would be removed.' Kate spoke calmly and with exaggerated patience.

'And when am I supposed to have the time to do this Widow Twanky act? Tell me that.'

Kate leant against the sink feeling an intense wave of anger surge over her. 'Make time!' she shouted, throwing the vegetable knife into the water, splattering the front of her own blouse as she did so. 'I'm sick to death of this family and its endless demands on me. I'm fed up with being regarded as the hired help around here. I'm a person too, you know, or have you not realised?'

Lucy stepped back, an expression of shocked surprise on her face. She looked as if she was about to argue but, apparently thinking better of it, turned on her heel. At the door she swung round. 'You're really getting menopausal, you know.' And before Kate could answer had slammed out again.

Kate searched in the muddy water for her knife, aware that she was shaking. She forced herself to peel the potatoes again. She wondered how many she had peeled in twenty-four years. Laid end to end would they girdle the earth? Fiercely she concentrated her thoughts on the potatoes, knowing that if she did not she would want to cry. This crying was a new thing come to join the feeling of despair she so loathed. She resented the tears. She played a game: if she could peel this one in a complete piece, everything would get better. Slowly and carefully she peeled, the skin curling below her like a snake. She cheated, digging hard into the potato flesh, but despite her care and her cheating the peel broke off. She watched it sink into the water in the bowl and, as she watched, knew that, despite

41

herself and the games she played, she was going to cry, and that she would despise herself for doing so.

She was not crying over Lucy, they argued too often for that. In fact this evening she was feeling rather pleased with herself for shouting back. Usually she tried to understand her daughter's frustrations. Not any more, she had enough of her own.

Lucy's 'menopausal' taunt puzzled rather than hurt. She felt it bordered on treachery coming from one of her own sex, and from one so much younger. She wondered if it was the female equivalent of a young stag taunting an old one. But, then, over the years any mood she had, any irritation she had shown, Tony had invariably blamed on her hormones. Just recently he, too, had taken up the menopause cry instead of pre-menstrual tension as explanation for her behaviour. It was as if women could not be like the young, or men, but were expected to live on a saintly plateau of calm, emotionless equanimity. It seemed never to have struck Tony that there could be any other cause for her changes of mood.

Now the menopause, which had taken the blame when it did not exist, had finally come, and Kate wasn't enjoying it. Secretly she'd always looked forward to the 'change' as her mother coyly referred to it, doing away with all that monthly mess, getting her moods on the level everyone expected of her. Her mother had made such a drama out of her own menopause, making the whole family's life hell, but Kate had resolved she wasn't going to be like that – it was a blessing to look forward to, not misery. The reality was different: her hot flushes were mild, but the aching joints were more of a problem, especially first thing in the morning when she was certain she would never move easily again. She wished someone had warned her about the unsightly bristle which suddenly appeared on her chin and which, with each plucking, grew longer, stiffer, blacker – like a walrus's tusk, she told her friend Pam. She would also like to have been warned that it was wiser to cross her legs when she sneezed. Nor had she realised that her waist would thicken quite as quickly as it did. Still, her skin had not dried out yet: she had few wrinkles. And she didn't have hysterics – but sometimes she wondered if she wasn't going mad.

She hated shopping now. She found – in the street, in the car, in the middle of Sainsbury's, anywhere – that she would, without warning, suddenly panic, certain the car was about to crash, whole buildings were about to collapse and kill only her. She thought about her death a lot, she would even admit to becoming obsessed by it. Yet it was a subject she had preferred not to think about. She had trotted out the old clichés – 'we've all got to go some time', or 'when your number's up', that sort of thing – but now 'some time' seemed uncomfortably close. Then there was this fight not to cry. She cried not because she was unhappy, but simply because her tear glands produced fluid that squeezed out of her eyes and trickled down her cheeks of its own accord – it was rather like having a runny nose from a bad cold – she had no control over it at all.

Tony appeared, kissed her cheek, asked what was for supper and disappeared into his study to work until his food was ready. Lucy banged out of the house without a goodbye, and Steve would not be home from the camera club until ten. It was just Tony and herself, an evening alone. Once they would have been excited by that prospect, now it meant nothing, she thought, as she laid the table.

When they sat down to eat, she automatically asked about his day, though she rarely listened to the answer since he did not often have anything of much interest to say. Graintry did not go in for juicy divorces or murders.

'Lucy tells me you were horrible to her this evening,' he said instead.

'Did she? She shouted at me, I shouted back, that's all.'

'A trifle undignified, wouldn't you say?' he asked in his measured tone.

'She asked for it. She treats me like a servant and I've had enough of it.'

'She works hard at school, she can't be expected to work at home too.'

'Well, that's where we differ. I think it's about time she did help more. In fact, I think it would be nice if everyone did a bit more to help me.'

He did not respond but continued to eat. The rhythmic click of his knife and fork made her want to scream.

'This is a good bit of meat. Did you get it at Flitch's? Damn good butcher, Flitch.'

'Do you realise, Tony, that of every piece of meat you have ever eaten in this house, you've made that self-same remark?'

She spoke brightly enough as if she believed she was camouflaging her annoyance.

'Have I? Well, it's true.' He looked up at her, slightly puzzled.

'It's also bloody boring,' she said defiantly.

'I beg your pardon? And what do you mean by that?'

No sooner had she said it than she began to regret it. It was such a pointless conversation and one that could lead to an argument if she was not careful. Or was that what she wanted? she suddenly thought. A row? Just to relieve the tedium?

'I'm sorry, that was unpleasant of me.' She looked down at her plate.

'I should think so.'

'I said I was sorry.'

'If you hadn't said it there would have been no need to apologise, would there?'

She did not reply, thinking she had better not, afraid of what else she might say, feeling she was teetering on the edge of something and not knowing what it was. She put down her knife and fork.

'Tony, I don't want you to take this as any form of criticism of you. I don't know what's wrong, but I feel so discontented these days.'

'Do you?' He looked up from his plate with as much animation as if she was talking about the electricity bill. Come to think of it, she thought, he would have been a lot more animated if she had been.

'I feel so restless. Unhappy inside . . .

'Perhaps you need a check-up.'

'I've had a check-up. There's nothing wrong with me. The doctor was his usual helpful self,' she said with an irony which was completely lost on her husband. She certainly was not going to go into the useless interview she had had with old Dr Plaistow, whose reaction, when she had plucked up the courage to ask about hormone replacement therapy, was a shocked lecture on unnecessary chemical interference. He had not said that when he'd put her on the pill, she had thought. It was tempting to think there was a male conspiracy against women, just to keep them down because of their biological differences.

'I sometimes feel, Tony, that apart from producing two children which, let's face it, any healthy woman could do, I've done nothing with my life – '

44

'Oh, God, Kate, not this again.'

She looked down at her plate. 'I'm sorry. It's just that I feel everything is passing me by. I . . .' She jumped at the clatter of his knife and fork on the plate, and looked up to see him staring angrily at her.

'What's so special about you? Don't you think we all feel like that sometimes? Do you think I'm happy with the routine of my life? It's life, that's all. Grow up, Kate, for goodness sake.'

'I was just wondering if we couldn't do something – go away for a weekend without the children, just take off . . .' Her voice trailed off lamely at the irritated expression on his face.

'Don't be stupid.'

'But we seem to spend so little time together. You're always working.'

'That, Kate, is how the bills get paid, or didn't you realise?' he said sarcastically.

Kate stood up and collected the empty dishes.

'It's apple crumble. Do you want cream with it?' she asked equably, as if the previous conversation hadn't taken place.

'Please.' He picked up his book, he always read between courses. She frequently thought he would prefer to read throughout the meal rather than have to talk to her. She wished she had the courage to pick it up and hit him over the head with it.

As soon as they had finished Tony took his coffee and disappeared once more into his study. She often wondered what he did in there. He said he worked but they only had his word for it. He could have a woman or the biggest collection of pornography in the world secreted away, or he might just sit and twiddle his thumbs, she wouldn't know. She began to load the dishwasher. Well, that was a pointless exercise, she thought to herself. Where had it got her? Nowhere. The telephone rang.

'Kate, have you ever heard of a Felicity Marchmont?' She heard the confident voice of her friend Pam Homerton who never announced herself but blithely presumed that whoever answered the telephone would recognise her immediately.

'No, I can't say I have. Should I?'

'I haven't either. She's a writer. She runs a writers' circle, they meet every Wednesday morning over at Little Moreton. Let's join.'

'I don't write.'

'Neither do I, but we can learn.'

'Oh, I'm not sure . . .'

'Come on, Kate. It could be fun. I don't know any authors and I'd like to see inside her house – there are some lovely houses in Little Moreton, and I bet she lives in one of them. It would be something different to do, something to relieve the bloody boredom of our lives,' Pam said in a dramatic tone and then laughed. Pam was never bored, she was one of those lucky ones who always found something to amuse her even in the most mundane of circumstances – but then, Kate thought, she wasn't menopausal yet. It would be interesting to see what Pam would be like when she was.

'All right. I don't promise to stick at it but we could give it a whirl.'

They chatted on for a while about the happenings in their locality. They were just like schoolgirls who rush to the telephone on returning home to talk to the friend they have just left. They had seen each other only yesterday, but they still found plenty to talk about.

As she finished her conversation, Steve clattered in from his club. She smiled at the noise he made: when he was trying to be quiet he invariably made even more noise than usual. She looked up with affection at the tall and gangly youth who, at nearly sixteen, had reached the point of accelerated growth where no part of his body seemed to match any other.

They spent a few minutes together while she admired the latest batch of photographs he had developed. It was not hard to do, for they were good and she found herself wondering whether Tony would regard photography as a more acceptable career than landscape gardening. She told him of her and Pam's plans.

'That's a wonderful idea, Mum. Take you out of the house, and doing something interesting instead of looking after us lot.'

She smiled at him and not for the first time thought how much easier it was to love her son than her daughter.

Ten. She poured the two whiskies that she and Tony always had as a nightcap, knocked on his study door and waited for his reply. Tony hated anyone to enter without knocking, hence her fantasies as to what he got up to in there.

'Was that Pam?'

'Yes.' She handed him the glass.

'Anything interesting?'

'They've definitely decided to go to Provence this year to look for a holiday home.' This she said rather wistfully, for she knew Tony's views on how unproductive was the use of capital invested in a second home. 'She thinks Carol might have a new boyfriend.' Tony was yawning. 'And we're both enrolling in a writers' circle. A local novelist has set one up.'

'You've what?' Tony looked at her with incredulity. 'You don't write.' He laughed.

'I've always wanted to,' she lied.

'News to me.' He snorted. 'Maybe it will cheer you up, make you less neurotic.'

The look she gave him was a mixture of hurt and loathing but it was a waste of time, he had returned to his papers. She turned to leave the room.

'Oh, by the way,' Tony said. 'I forgot to tell you at dinner. We've been invited to a party the Saturday after next. You'd best splash out on a new dress and get something done to your hair.'

Involuntarily she patted her hair. 'Whose party?' She knew she sounded surprised, but for Tony to tell her to buy a frock was rare indeed.

'Sir Barty Silver's,' he announced, grinning at her, waiting to see her reaction.

'Barty Silver?' she repeated. 'I didn't know you knew him.'

'I don't. He's thinking of buying some property in the Bristol area. He wants someone in the vicinity involved, not his London solicitors, and he wants to meet one of us. Tom's away visiting his daughter in Australia, Freddie's tied up, so that leaves me. Apparently he likes to do business at his parties.'

'Barty Silver,' she said again in a dreamy voice. He was one of the people she read about in Nigel Dempster over her toast and marmalade when everyone else had left the house. He was not someone she had ever dreamed of meeting. 'I wish I'd known earlier, I could have told Pam.'

'No doubt you will tomorrow, pushing up the telephone bill . . .'

That night in bed Tony made love to her. At least, that was what he called it. She wondered if he had done so to try to make her feel better about herself, for he did not often deviate

47

from his Saturday and Wednesday routine. No doubt he would be shocked and hurt if he knew it made her feel even more depressed. She sometimes thought that Tony, when taking her, had a chart in his head – like painting with numbers. She certainly could have reeled off the order of his caresses for it never varied. A kiss on the mouth, then a nuzzle of her ear. First he rubbed one nipple between thumb and finger, then the other, just as if he was fine tuning a radio. A quick grope between her legs, a little heavy breathing and then he was on top of her and in her and it was over in minutes.

Not that she wanted him to prolong the act, it had become so irksome to her. She wondered if the same had happened to him. Now the closest she got to an orgasm was reading about it in *Cosmopolitan*. She'd heard that sex improved the longer one knew a person, which certainly had not happened to them. She supposed she had enjoyed it once, she could not be sure for she could no longer remember. And then she wondered if she did not remember because she no longer wanted to. But as she lay in the dark looking at the ceiling she could not help wondering what it could be like.

chapter **seven**

From her kitchen Kate heard the faint throaty roar of Pam's car as she approached the village. She looked quickly about her making a last-minute check. She unlocked the cat-flap, moved the tea-towels from the bar in front of the Aga for safety, picked up her handbag and the spiral-bound notepad she had bought, and was standing by the gate as Pam screeched to a halt.

'You must be psychic, you always know when I'm arriving.' Pam was smiling as she leant over and opened the passenger door for Kate.

'No, just good hearing – and this car's roar would be difficult to miss.' Kate kissed her best friend in welcome.

'Roar? My darling purrs, positively purrs, don't you my sweet?' Pam patted the fascia of the E-type Jaguar, her current pride and joy. 'Are you excited? I am,' she said as she put the car into gear.

'I'm a bit nervous. I mean, I've never written a thing in my life apart from school essays and letters. I don't really know why I'm going and I certainly shan't know where to begin.'

'Oh, go on, don't be such a wimp. It'll be a laugh if nothing else,' Pam said with her easy confidence as the sleek red car with its long snout sped quickly through the lanes towards Little Moreton.

Pam loved to drive and did so with far more panache and expertise than most men. Kate enjoyed being driven by her for she herself was one of those women who saw motoring as merely a means to get from A to B. She could not have cared less what she drove provided it was reliable and not too big to park easily. Pam, on the other hand, always had high-performance cars which she changed with extraordinary rapidity. This red Jaguar was the only one that Kate had known her to keep more than six months. She had nearly died of shock when Tony had told her how much these old cars cost. It had been a birthday present from Pam's husband and Kate did have a frisson, not exactly of jealousy – she would not have wanted such a car in the first place – no, it was more of longing and curiosity to know what it must feel like to have a husband so rich that such a present was a normal thing.

The Homertons lived, for the moment, in a large imposing mansion, near Graintry, about ten miles from Kate's village. They had two hundred acres. The heated swimming pool was in its own custom-built house which looked like a giant Victorian Gothic gazebo. There was a tennis court, horses in the stable – not that Kate had ever seen any of them ridden – and a four-car garage. Their son was at Marlborough and their daughter at Benenden. Pam did not have a wardrobe for her clothes, she had a whole room. Their *en-suite* bathroom was so huge and plush that Kate always felt she was slumming when she returned to her own more than adequate one.

They had lived in this house for three years which for them was a long time. In the eighteen years she had known Pam and Doug they had moved at least seven times, always to a place bigger and grander than the one before. 'Trading up', Doug called it but Kate thought it must be a dreadful way to live, like nomads forever packing up, never settled. Pam joked that it was the only way that she kept her cupboards tidy but Kate often wondered if she was really as happy with the arrangement as she made out.

The talk among their group was that this time the Homertons were finally settled, for where could they 'trade up' this time? They had the most imposing house in the area, to get anything bigger or grander they would have to move further away from Graintry and everyone was certain that was something Doug would never do.

Doug was the true 'local lad made good' of people's dreams. He had left school in Graintry at sixteen with two O levels, in metalwork and technical drawing. He had started working for a local builder when a lucky, but modest, win on the football pools had enabled him to set up on his own. Six years later he had bought out his previous employer who was retiring and then bravely borrowed a fortune and built houses, in the process making himself a fortune. He had stayed in building but had also diversified into so many other ventures that Kate was never sure how many there were. She knew of a bingo hall, a carpet warehouse, several pubs and a string of video-hire shops but was aware there were others. So, when recession came and the building trade was inevitably sorely hit, Doug was safe and could ride out the storm while others collapsed. More often than not it was Doug who bought up the bankrupt businesses at rock-bottom prices. He was unpretentious, funny, kind, generous and Kate admired him.

Tony had been in the vanguard of those who had prophesied that he would fail. Even now, eighteen years later, when Doug appeared fire-proof, Tony could not bring himself to admit he might have been wrong and still tutted and frowned and said, 'Wait and see.' Kate had the horrible idea that Tony would be pleased to see Doug fail. Further, she had reached the conclusion that her husband was riddled with envy, which did not, however, stop him accepting Doug's hospitality, frequently.

'Doug's going to buy me a word processor,' Pam said as the car climbed the hill out of Kate's valley.

'What on earth for?'

'To write on, of course. All writers have them these days.'

'Do you know how to work one?'

'No, but everyone says it's easy.'

'Rather you than me. Tony has horror tales about the one in the office.'

'I looked at it this way. If that thick cow in Doug's office can get the hang of it, so can I. You can come and use it any time.' Pam smiled across at her.

'Thanks, but I think it's unlikely I shall be needing one.' Kate laughed and looked at her friend with affection. That was the endearing thing about Pam, she always wanted to share everything. 'Doug's pleased you're going to this writers' circle, then?'

'Ecstatic. He thinks it'll keep me out of his hair for a while.'

'Tony just laughed. He thinks the idea of my writing anything is a joke.'

'Then prove him wrong,' said Pam, not pausing in the conversation as she overtook a surprised septuagenarian on a particularly difficult stretch of road.

That was an approach Kate had not thought of but, as they sped along, and the more she considered it, the more she thought, why not? Why did she automatically think she could not do it, could not write, would fail? Because Tony had implied it, that was why.

'Thanks, Pam,' she said. 'I might just try to do that. It would be nice to prove him wrong for once.'

'I never understand why you snipe about Tony like that. He's such a nice man, a wonderful husband. You don't know how lucky you are, that's your problem,' Pam said quite sharply. 'And at least he still makes love to you,' she added for good measure.

If you can call it making love, thought Kate, but said nothing, for loyalty would never allow her to discuss Tony's sexual inadequacy, not even with Pam. Pam herself suffered no such inhibitions.

'I sometimes think if I was a balance sheet then Doug might screw me again,' Pam said, as if reading Kate's mind. She was laughing but Kate knew her well enough to know that it was a laugh to mask the hurt and frustration that was her sexless marriage. 'We had a row last night. I told him straight that, at forty-two, I was not ready to give up on the nooky.'

'You're not forty-two.'

'I am next April. I said if he didn't get his act together then I was going to look for a lover.'

'What did he say?'

'Not much. He shrugged and asked me if I'd like a word processor. I ask you! Am I supposed to shag that? It's guilt of course, that's all. I know how his mind works. Give the nagging bitch another pressie and she'll shut up.'

'Poor Doug. Maybe he can't any more – look at the pressure he works under. Have you thought of that?' Kate said, and thought how strange it was how she was always defending Doug while Pam was Tony's best advocate.

'Poor Doug, my arse! He never has been one for it. It's a bloody miracle to me that I managed it twice and got two kids.'

Pam's rather lurid turn of phrase was totally at odds with her appearance for she was lovely and had the fragile beauty of a Dresden figurine. Kate was always aware of what an odd couple they made. She spent her time fluctuating from eleven to twelve stone while Pam was always striving to stay at seven. Kate was always dressed sensibly and, although she tried to be neat and tidy, after half an hour she always looked a mess. Pam dressed immaculately, designers' initials proclaiming the cost. And she looked as good at the end of the day as she had at the beginning. Her nose never shone, she did not eat her lipstick and her thick red hair, once combed, obliged by staying in place.

Pam's eyes were dark brown, soft like a puppy's and Kate envied her for she loathed her own grey ones. She had once had blue contact lenses made for her short-sighted eyes in the hopes of jazzing them up a bit. She quite liked the effect even if it meant her world was permanently tinted slightly blue. But one day, while gardening, she had sneezed and one lens had flown out never to be found. When Tony discovered that, in the interests of economy, she had not insured them, he had refused point blank to give her the money to replace it. She regretted its loss, she felt she had looked better without her spectacles. Not that Tony had said so, but she was almost sure she did.

The two women had lapsed into the companionable silence that is allowed in a long friendship. Kate looked out at the passing scenery. It was one of those crisply cold autumn mornings which Kate sometimes thought she preferred to spring or summer, until, that is, those seasons came in their turn. As they broached hill after hill, down in the valleys small hamlets nestled. They were all alike, a collection of old houses clustered around the church, as if for solace, built in the same bleached Cotswold stone. Only the names were different. Smoke was rising from several of the chimneys in straight white columns and the air was full of the distinctive sweet smell of burning wood. The pale golden stone houses seemed to be hiding in the gauze-like shroud of the morning mist which still lingered. An early frost was painted on to plants and grass making them stiffly sculptural. The hedgerows glistened with the frozen dew on a thousand webs. Rooks called noisily to each other and the barking of a distant dog was so clear it could have been alongside the car.

Such a village was Little Moreton, its claim to fame being that it had rather more than its fair share of small but architecturally important Elizabethan houses.

'God, just look at those wonderful houses. I've always wanted one of those ones with flagstones and a panelled cross-passage hallway. Lovely.' Pam sighed.

'You on the move again?' Kate asked with a smile, recognising the emergent signs of another Homerton decampment.

'They must be so convenient, not like our mausoleum,' Pam replied.

They were disappointed as they followed the instructions Pam had been given to find that Felicity Marchmont did not appear to live in one of them as they had expected. The car finally slid to a halt outside a cottage that evidently had once been two. It was old and pretty but not in the league of the houses they had so admired.

Kate hauled herself out of the almost prone position required to sit in the E-type, and was glad that there were no men around to see the expanse of fat thigh she exposed as she did so. Pam slid effortlessly and elegantly from behind the steering wheel.

They rang the bell, and pulled their coats around them against the chill as no one answered.

'You sure you took the address down correctly?' asked Kate. She knew it was an unnecessary question: Pam might appear vague but in fact was highly organised.

'The Grange, that's what I was told.'

'It doesn't look much like a Grange to me, more like two artisans' cottages knocked into one.'

'Try the bell again. I'll go round the back and see what I can find.'

Kate was stamping her feet with cold when Pam reappeared.

'There's a tray of cups and saucers laid out in the kitchen so someone's expected. It's probably us.'

They both spun round as the gate creaked and a small, dowdily but neatly dressed woman with the under-nourished look of a vicar's wife, scuttled almost apologetically towards them.

'Are you Felicity Marchmont?' asked Pam in the tone of voice which implied she could not believe she was Felicity and, if she was, that Pam was sorely disappointed.

'Me? Good gracious no. I'm not nearly clever enough to be Felicity. I'm Mavis Crabtree. I live over there.' And she pointed to by far the largest and grandest of the houses they had so admired. 'Silly question, but have you rung?' She tittered nervously.

'Twice.' Pam and Kate answered in unison.

'Oh dear, I do hope Clarissa hasn't forgotten us again. She leads such a wonderfully busy life, the house always teeming with people and children and dogs – it's all so jolly. And she's so clever with her hands, restoring and painting and making things. I don't know how she manages with it all, clever young thing.'

At which a bedroom window opened and the 'clever young thing's' head appeared.

'Hello? If that's the baker just leave me a bloomer will you?' A voice of brittle accent called down.

'It's us, Clarissa. It's your turn for the circle . . .' Mavis twittered again but almost admiringly at such vagueness.

'Golly, gosh! I'd completely forgotten. Crikey, you've caught me completely on the hop. Everything's in the most unholy mess. Hang on . . .' The window slammed shut and Mavis, Kate and Pam smiled inanely at each other. As they were wondering how long they would have to wait outside in the freezing cold, an MG sports car screeched up out of which stepped a tall, slim, smartly dressed young woman whom Mavis introduced as June Fleming. She lived, she told them, close by on an executive housing estate which Doug had built – not that Pam mentioned it.

'Clarissa isn't claiming to have forgotten again?' June said with a sigh of exasperation.

'The poor dear has so much on her plate,' Mavis fluttered.

'My eye. Filthy manners more like,' June muttered.

'You said, June dear?'

'Nothing.' June angrily rang the bell again.

'Oh Christ, she's not up to her stupid tricks again is she? It's too bloody cold to stand about, freeze the brass knobs . . .' an even younger woman in a lurid cerise and lime-green shell suit said as she joined them and was introduced as Tracey Green. At last they heard a bolt being drawn and the door being unlocked. 'About bloody time,' Tracey said for them all making Mavis wince.

'Come in, my dears . . .' A dark, long-haired, perfectly made-up though barefoot Clarissa ushered them in with no apology for making them stand and wait.

The sitting room covered most of the ground floor of the house. It was tidy, a log fire crackled in the inglenook fireplace. The room was a brave attempt to disguise that they were hard up: the shawls artfully flung over the sofas were undoubtedly to hide holes. And Kate dreaded to think of the state of one chair which was completely covered in a white sheet. The coffee table was an old door, painted gloss green, balanced on a pile of books.

There was the fusty smell of furniture from secondhand shops. Most of the ornaments were Victorian bric-à-brac and the paintings were nondescript watercolours of the sort that Kate always imagined were done by impoverished relations of grand families who took them in out of duty not love.

'You see the fearful mess. Golly . . .' Clarissa trilled as she busied herself taking coats. 'I'm Clarissa Steele-Greene – with oodles of 'e's.' She giggled. 'And you two must be Kate and Pam and which is which or who is who?' She laughed, a forced little-girl laugh as if a bolder, louder one might be being kept in check. Who was who having been sorted out, they were told to take their seats while Clarissa just had '. . . to fly into the kitchen, just for a second, and get the coffee ready. Such mundane things . . .' And she whisked away.

Kate and Pam looked significantly at each other and while both were fully aware of the social games some people played they were both flummoxed at what conclusion to draw from Clarissa's alleged absentmindedness.

Clarissa swept back, talking non-stop, saying nothing really but leaving sentences hanging with no end to them like smoke trails disappearing in the air.

'Money . . . I really think . . . don't you?'

'Yes, of course. How much?' Kate asked.

'It's Felicity . . . money . . . she finds it all so vulgar . . .'

'My arse!' Pam whispered but not softly enough.

'She's artistic,' Clarissa said sharply.

'Of course,' the friends replied.

'Well, now . . .' Clarissa explained about the joining fee and each week's subscription. 'And a little extra for the coffee and things . . . that's for me, coffee, you understand . . . so expensive.' The false laugh tinkled. 'If you're paying by cheque make it out to Doris Miller – that's her real name, not that she ever uses it . . . well, one doesn't, does one?'

'Of course.'

Kate was opening her handbag and wishing it was the last week in the month rather than the middle and was already juggling menus in her mind.

'I'll get this.' Pam was already delving into her handbag

which, as always, was overflowing with money and had settled the bill before Kate had even found her pen.

Kate had never met a writer before and was not sure what to expect. In the event she was somewhat disappointed by the stout grey-haired woman, in a tweed skirt with a voluminous navy jumper over her ample breasts and a voice of deepest profundo. She reminded Kate uncomfortably of her old head-mistress and she felt frightened of the bright brown eyes which stared intently at her as if reading her thoughts.

'So pleased to see our little circle growing,' Felicity boomed. 'You're not the Mrs Homerton who lives at Felix Park?'

'Yes, that's me.'

'Such a lovely house. I used it for the setting in my Regency *Feud of the Soul*.'

'Really, how exciting,' said Pam, politely if a bit vaguely. 'Regency? I'm afraid I don't understand.'

'It's a *genre* term, my dear, for a period novel.' Felicity rolled the word genre around her mouth as if enjoying the sound of it immensely.

'But the house is mainly Victorian,' Pam said, sweetly.

'Artistic licence, my dear. Tell me, you must know dear Peter and Hilary Holt, they live your way.'

'I've met her, at a gymkhana, that's all.' Pam forbore to say that she had found Hilary stuck up, and that upon discovering Pam's husband was a builder Hilary had lost interest in Pam immediately.

'You must look her up. Contacts, my dear, so important in publishing.'

'Hilary's a publisher?'

'No, but dear Peter is, why he *is* Shotters. Let's to work, ladies,' Felicity called, making them all jump and obediently begin to sort out their notepads and pencils with a flurry of clicking handbags and briefcases – all except Tracey who carried everything in a Tesco carrier bag. Felicity waited until everyone was settled. 'Now, with newcomers we must all explain ourselves and our plans and strategies. Shall I go first?' which she did since she was not the sort of woman anyone present was likely to argue with.

'I started writing nearly twenty years ago. I have written over a hundred short stories, I've lost count of my articles and eleven of my books have been published. I am presently at work on my twelfth book, a saga set in medieval England at the court of Mathilda. So you see, both of you, I think I can honestly say that I am well qualified to lead our little group, don't you?' She beamed, for the first time displaying a fine set of dentures with bright pink gums.

'Such a lot of books. You must be very proud,' Kate said with admiration. Felicity bowed her head graciously.

'I don't know how to say this, Felicity – I read the most massive amount, but I've never read any of your books. Have you, Kate?'

Kate, greatly discomfited and wishing Pam was not always so forthright, agreed she had not.

'You'll find them in libraries.'

'Not in shops?'

'My publishers – Drummond and Lock – specialise in library books not for sale to the general public.' This was said as if there was something not quite nice about selling to the public.

'That explains it, then,' Pam said brightly. 'I never go to libraries. I never want to return the books.'

'We shall have to rectify that, won't we, Pam?' The pink gums were flashed again but Kate was concerned to see it was not a happy smile.

'Do you make as much money selling to libraries?' Pam asked, apparently all innocence, and Kate wished she would drop it.

'You must not believe everything you read in the papers about money paid to authors, it's mainly all lies,' Felicity announced airily. 'Now, Clarissa . . .'

One by one they listed their successes – not many – and their ambitions – numerous.

Clarissa was writing a novel of the destructive love of a man for a woman as his soul descends to hell. But, importantly, she wanted there to be another main character in the book, the moorland where the two lived. Kate sensed that Pam was about to blurt out that it had already been done but managed to press her thigh against Pam's with sufficient pressure to warn her off.

Mavis admitted she attended more for the company and found it a help in compiling her nature notes for the parish magazine and then, almost as an afterthought, told them that the magazine *Hearthside* had, just yesterday, confirmed they were buying a short story.

'That's wonderful,' Felicity said rather stiffly, and the others went wild with excitement and congratulations for Mavis who became quite pink.

June said she wanted to learn to write, something she had always wanted to do, and in any case she was bored with housework. Tracey said she had had two stories taken by *Teen Life* and wanted to be published by The Paradise Club, make a fortune and retire to the Isle of Man.

'And you, Pam?'

'I want to write a bestseller – you know, the ones you see at airports – and appear on chat shows,' Pam answered, much to Kate's surprise. It was the first she had ever heard of it.

'Quite.' Felicity smiled in a very superior way. 'Wouldn't we all? And Kate?'

'I'm not sure,' Kate said, feeling flustered and unprepared. 'I've never written anything. I don't know what I could or couldn't do. Perhaps I'd be best starting off with a short story or two.'

'Short-story writing is a particularly difficult genre, you know.'

'Is it?' Kate asked, wondering why Felicity seemed so intent on putting people down.

'Remarkably so. Now, first things first. I repeat this every week and shall continue to do so. Market trends,' she spoke these two words as if they were in capital letters, 'market trends are the key to everything. Once you've identified your market then you'll know what to write.'

'Can't one just write whatever is inside one?' Kate asked.

'Not unless you're a second Iris Murdoch. Not if you want to sell you can't,' Felicity told her sharply.

There then followed a bewildering list of books to buy on how to write, magazines that must be read – not the magazines in newsagents but the trade press – *Publishing News* and *The Bookseller* – and two for aspiring authors. 'And there's no harm at this stage in getting Macmillan's *The Writer's Handbook*. Our bible, isn't it, girls?' She beamed at her little flock, who not only hung on every word but wrote it down as well.

What followed next Kate found awful and she doubted if she would ever have the courage to participate. One by one they read out passages they had written on the subject Felicity had set them the previous week. They then proceeded to criticise each other's work. What was most surprising was that the sad-eyed, depressed-looking Mavis was the most vicious critic of them all. And soon, sleek, confident June was sobbing until Felicity told her sharply to 'Pull yourself together, June,' and proceeded to lecture them that this was good for them, that professional writers must be used to criticism for how else would they cope with unfavourable reviews?

Tracey held her own magnificently and shrugged off her critics as of no importance.

'But you kept repeating the same words,' Clarissa pointed out gleefully, for she had just, thin-lipped with exasperation, absorbed an attack from Tracey on her use of pretentious words.

'I did it on purpose.'

'Why?'

'For emphasis, and it works.'

Clarissa's lips went thin again, and Kate found herself agreeing with Tracey, it had worked, and of them all she thought it was Tracey who could write.

By the time they broke for coffee, Kate felt as exhausted as if she had been writing herself. The sharpness and envy had all disappeared and everyone appeared to be friends again.

'There's a writers' weekend just before Christmas, which, if you're quick, you might just get on,' Felicity told Pam and Kate. 'It's essential to meet other writers. Cross-pollination, I like to call it.'

Kate found it was a nice feeling to be referred to as a writer even if she had not written anything. And another even stranger thing was happening. As Felicity set their project for next week – three hundred words on 'A Winter's Romance' – Kate found that ideas were flying about in her mind, like small black birds beating at the inside of her skull in desperation to be let out.

'What did you think?' Pam asked when they were eventually driving away in the direction of Graintry.

'To be honest I feel oddly elated.'

'Me too. It's exciting, isn't it?'

'I'm not too sure of Felicity, though,' Kate said. 'She strikes me as a bit of a bossyboots if you let her get away with it. Mavis is intriguing, isn't she? Such a quiet, unassuming little thing and yet she was quite bitchy. Maybe she's led a hard life.'

'Mavis? Don't see how. She's married to Crabtree's Cough

Lozenges – they've loads of money. Doug built their gazebo, cost an arm and a leg. Why don't we go to Smiths, get all these books?'

They had driven back to Kate's after buying the books and magazines – or rather Pam had bought them for there was no way Kate could have afforded all of them. It was not until they got to the house and were sitting over coffee and sandwiches at the kitchen table that she discovered Pam had bought everything in duplicate.

'Pam, I can't take them.'

'Of course you can. Don't spoil my fun. We've got all this bloody money. I don't know what to do with it half the time.'

'You're always so kind to me, but I'm paying for my subs,' Kate said getting out her cheque book.

'What about this writing weekend?'

'Oh, I don't know. I don't think Tony would like me away all the weekend.'

'Sod the men. Let's do it. I'll pay.'

'No, you won't. I'll talk to Tony about it. Here's my cheque. Now bank this one, not like the last.'

'Maybe I will, or maybe I'll keep it as a souvenir when you're a famous author.'

'You've a long wait, then.' Kate laughed.

Once Pam had left Kate sat with her pile of women's magazines, flicking through them reading a story here and there.

She learnt one thing. She did not think that writing romantic short stories was what she wanted to do. And then she realised she had learnt something else. This morning, she thought, she had listened to the others and she knew she could do better. It was not conceit, it was something inside her that told her so.

chapter **eight**

It had been a pig of a day, Gloria thought, as she pushed open the small gate with her hip. Such an awful day that she felt it inevitable that the hinge of the gate should choose this evening to grind painfully and the gate, in slow motion, swing back at a drunken and broken angle. It had been wobbly for months and she should have had it mended. She could just hear what her mother would have said: 'A stitch in time . . .' At that thought she turned round and kicked the gate with irritation. The pile of books and papers she was carrying slipped in the crook of her arm and slid to the ground. She lunged to save them and dropped her keys. The strap of her large, cumbersome handbag slewed across her chest and the bag banged against her knees, tripping her, so that finally, as a *coup de grâce*, she knocked the bottle of milk flying from the doorstep. Elephant, still clutched safely under her other arm for he was the last thing she would ever drop, yapped excitedly as if laughing at her.

'It's all right for you, you can smirk.' She chucked the little Yorkshire terrier under his chin and began searching in the dark for the keys. She cursed mildly as she did so. She was not cursing the keys but her own clumsiness, for this clattering of her possessions down the small garden path was an all-too-common occurrence these days.

Once she had located the keys, she undid the mortice lock and then the Yale and as the burglar alarm whined she sprinted for the box in the fifteen seconds allowed before the neighbours and police complained yet again. This frantic daily race was her own fault. It was she who had insisted on the ugly box of the burglar alarm being hidden away, so that instead of being conveniently situated in the hall, it lurked under the stairs in a cupboard containing all the things she didn't know what else to do with.

Elephant jumped from her arms and raced for the kitchen.

She returned to the steps and retrieved the scattered papers and books, dusting them down – at least it had not been raining, she thought, as she added them to a precarious pile already sitting on her desk. Then she did what she always did, ran around the small house, switching on all the lights. It always made her feel better, safer somehow.

An imperious bark from the kitchen informed her that Elephant was not prepared to wait much longer for his food. Dog food! 'Oh, Lord,' she mumbled, burrowing in the cupboard, Elephant looking accusingly at her as if about to say, Not again! Right at the back she found a small tin.

'See, you're wrong. There was one,' she said to the dog, who was excitedly leading the way to the drawer where the tin-opener lived. The cat-flap rattled and Mog appeared, sliding sinuously through. Elephant looked at the cat and then at the tin-opener and decided to stay with the food.

By the time she had fed both cat and dog, emptied the rubbish bin she should have dealt with that morning, taken supper, enough for two, out of the freezer and made herself a cup of tea, she felt exhausted as she settled on the sofa, kicking off her shoes and wriggling her toes in liberation. On days like this she thanked God she did not have kids or a husband. There were other times when she came home from work and the house depressed her with its emptiness. Then, she would dream of what it must be like to have a family waiting for her. But today she marvelled at how some of her friends managed, those who, after a disastrous day in the office, had to return to demanding children, their chatter and noise, help with home-work, fulfil demands for fish fingers and baked beans, wash their clothes, see them to bed. They would be followed by husbands who wanted sympathy for the day *they* had had and who were quickly sniffing around wondering what was for dinner. Letitia did it, and Jenny – how? She shook her head in wonderment at the organisational abilities and strength of character of others, so lacking in herself, and pressed the playback button on the telephone answering machine.

There were several messages. First was her mother complaining that Gloria never phoned, not that she actually complained, she was far too subtle in her dealings with her daughter for that. The long message was punctuated with the odd strategically placed sigh, and the wistful tone of her voice was a complaint in itself. Gloria was left feeling riddled with guilt, which was what her mother, no doubt, had set out to achieve. Next was the service engineer about the washing machine – she had missed him again. That would mean another week at least that she would have to lug her washing to the launderette. She had recently edited a book about all manner of happenings in a London launderette, including the heroine falling in love. No such adventures had happened to her; she found the place depressing in the extreme. Then there was a call from a woman desperate to sell her a new kitchen followed by another equally keen on double-glazing, and two calls from people who had chickened out and left no message – the most infuriating of all. But the call she wanted, and all the way back in the car had almost prayed for, was not there. Were everyone's messages as relentlessly boring as hers? Surely other people returned to urgent, exciting messages, not tele-sales people and their mother!

Elephant, having finished his supper, barked to go out into the garden. Patiently she unlocked, unbolted and unchained the back door. These security precautions irked her daily, making her a self-imposed prisoner in her own home. Some days she hated London and longed to be in the country again, where front doors could be left unbolted. The feeling never lasted though. She loved the city and now wondered why she had not gone mad with the tedium during all those years of her youth in her parents' house in Cornwall where the routine was always monotonously the same.

'Why can't you use the cat-flap? You're small enough,' she complained, opening the back door. With great dignity Elephant ignored her question and sallied forth into the night.

She prodded the packages she had taken from the freezer – of course they were still solid. She peered at the backs of the outer wrappers, wondering why the makers of frozen food always wrote the instructions in the smallest print possible and often in green or red ink, always the hardest to read in artificial light. 'Not suitable for home freezing', she read on one of them. 'Oh sod it,' she said aloud. Probably won't hurt, Gloria thought hopefully. She could just imagine her mother's hysterics if she saw that lot, followed by a lecture on price and nutrition. Replacing the packets on the worktop she picked up a glass, opened the fridge door, took out the ice tray, did futile battle with it for a minute or two, then threw it into the sink. She picked up a bottle of vodka, returned to the sitting room, and poured herself a stiff measure. She wondered whether to rerun the tape in case she had missed his message, and then told herself not to be so stupid.

Still, she thought, he might just turn up, he did not always telephone. From the pile of papers on her desk she took a typescript off the top, rearranged its pages in order, settled down under the reading light and tried to concentrate on what she should have finished days ago. She quickly scanned the reader's report and found when she got to the end that she could not remember what it had said at the beginning. With exasperation she threw the typescript onto the sofa, and took a sip of her vodka. She never used to be like this. In the past the most reliable member of staff at Shotters had been Gloria Catchpole: give it to Gloria – it got done. Ask Gloria – she'd have an answer. 'I can't find it' – Gloria could.

But in the past six months things had changed. Her once tidy square of office, in which she had known exactly where everything was, had become, to say the least, untidy. The floor was littered with Elephant's toys. Unread manuscripts stood in piles, the curling of their paper an indication as to which had lain there the longest. Her in tray was full and the out was empty. The rubber plant on the windowsill had died of neglect. Compared with the other offices, glimpsed over partitions, and through the potted plants of the open-plan office, hers was a disgrace.

Without doubt one of the reasons for this state of affairs was the environment she worked in. She hated the vast room, close carpeted, and the large windows that never opened. It was always too chill in summer from the air conditioning and too hot in winter, as if a mad engineer controlled their working temperature. A no-smoking policy was in force and although she had never smoked herself she would think with longing now of the fug in past offices. There was little clutter, camaraderie was sorely lacking. It was as if the building made everyone, crouched over their VDUs, anonymous within it.

Gloria had worked in publishing since leaving university fourteen years ago. She had begun as a junior secretary at Westall and Trim and had been there only a month when Julius had called her into his office and suggested that she might like to try her hand as assistant to the publicity manager. In the years she had spent with Julius he had nurtured her career with as much care as he took over his authors. She had worked in every department, even having a short stint on the road as a rep. Consequently there was little about the business she did not know. For the last two years with Julius she had been what she had always wanted to be – an editor.

Then she had left. She always frowned when she thought of that, her act of betrayal. But she had been invited by Peter Holt to join Shotters which he had recently started up and which he had been running on a shoestring ever since. She had gone for the challenge and excitement and she had received both in spades. Life at Westall's had been satisfying, at Shotters it was knife-edged excitement tinged with terror most of the time.

The general women's fiction list had been her responsibility. She was proud that, without doubt, her efforts had helped Peter reach the position he was in now. It was she who had discovered Bella Ford and Shiel de Tempera. It was she who, working subtly and patiently, had poached Heather Gardens and Grace Bliss from other publishers. These four were in the vanguard of women's literature, their sales enormous. The writers she had garnered had helped in the upsurge in Shotters' fortunes. And when Peter had bought Blades, about to expire but once famous for its mainstream fiction, Gloria and her writers had become part of it, and she had been instrumental in nursing it back to health and viability.

Sometimes, though, she wondered if she had done Peter a favour. There were days she had serious doubts. As Shotters became more successful, as it bought in other ailing publishing houses and grew larger and larger, she had watched Peter change from brilliant publisher into astute businessman. But was he happy?

In the old days, in the cramped offices off Tottenham Court Road, he had been different. Then he seemed charged with electricity as he bounced ideas about, excited at the challenge ahead of him. Then he was approachable on any problem. Now she sensed a dullness about him, he even seemed to walk differently. These days, although she kept an eye open for him, she rarely saw him, stuck away as he was on the top floor in that ludicrous suite of offices.

She had been in love with him then. Sometimes she thought

he was the only man she had loved. Not that he ever knew how she felt for he was married, and if there was one rule Gloria had it was that she did not mess with married men. In any case, at the time she had liked Hilary. But Hilary had changed too. Once she had been one of them, but now, with Peter's success and money, she had become grand and detached. Gloria could not remember the last time she had seen her, and now, if she did, she would not be in the least surprised if Hilary cut her dead.

As the firm leapt up the ladder of success one set of offices was exchanged for another. Each move was into premises more convenient and spacious than the last but they had all been offices where the intimacy remained, where the feel of books was in the air. All that had gone with this last move. Now, when at work, Gloria could imagine herself anywhere – an insurance company, a broker's.

There were days when Gloria had begun to think the unthinkable – that she was in the wrong job. But what else could she do? This was all she knew. She had toyed with the idea of setting up as an agent, which was what most discontented editors did. Certainly she had the contacts and the push needed to succeed. But then she would not be doing what she was best at. How could she bear to find an author and then hand him or her on to somebody else to tend and prune and polish?

It was not just the office though, she had to be honest. The problems of the past six months had begun when she had been passed over for promotion to editorial director, a post which she was not alone in regarding as hers for the asking. Instead it had gone to that wimp Norman Wilton whom she could have wiped the floor with: he lacked her intelligence, experience, and certainly her instincts. Once she would have rushed to Peter with her anger and disappointment but not any more. He was too remote, and since the senior management structure had mushroomed to include a small army of people with grand-sounding titles, she doubted if the decision would have been his alone.

She had become despondent and the 'couldn't care' attitude towards work was spilling over into her home, once her pride and joy. She just could not seem to be bothered about anything.

The restlessness inside her was as physical as any itch on the outside.

And then there was Clive. He was the latest in a long line of romantic catastrophes. The men Gloria knew she should have gone for – sensible, hard-working, reliable types – just did not interest her. Time and again it was the drifters, often artists, writers, actors, all handsome, virile and usually younger than herself, who excited her.

Clive Renshaw was typical of them. At twenty-five he was ten years younger than her. He was handsome, intelligent and without doubt the best-endowed man she had come across – and he knew how to please her. She did not love him nor he her. He was a good lay. There had been a time when she would have congratulated herself on her luck but, just recently, she found herself longing for something more than sex.

She never knew when he would turn up. They had a relationship of sorts but it was strictly on his terms. Such behaviour was normal with the men in her life, and it was an attitude she had encouraged. 'No commitment' could have been her motto. But she had changed, she would have liked to know where she stood with him, she wanted a normal life.

What was different with Clive from the other affairs was that until him she had not felt hurt; each had used the other. But with Clive she felt used and almost angry that she did not love him, as if it was his fault.

Even Jenny, her friend, did not understand. At least, she had been her friend until last week, and then they had rowed – over Clive, what else?

Gloria had been having a moan about Clive, trying to express how empty she felt when Jenny had gone too far. 'It's your own fault, Gloria,' she'd said, standing by Gloria's desk and smiling as she spoke. 'You enjoy the drama, you enjoy being badly treated. You search these men out on purpose just so that you can be hurt. You're a mental masochist. The good sex that comes from it just isn't worth the pain . . .'

The ensuing row must have been heard all over the editorial floor – certainly people seemed to have been looking at her in an odd way ever since. She and Jenny passed each other without speaking and Gloria now regretted ever confiding one word to her. What a thing to say. Gloria shook her head as if to blot out the memory. She looked at her watch. Eight-thirty.

If she had a long bath, maybe he would arrive in the middle of it – then they could bathe together. That is what she would do.

During the following hour she shaved her legs, removed her nail varnish, plucked her eyebrows, washed her hair. Still he had not come. She dried herself, perfumed herself, changed into her new Marks and Spencer pyjamas that looked and felt like silk and took ages over painting her nails. Still he had not come. She stood studying herself in the mirror as if the image could give her the reason for his absence. It did not. She liked what she saw. She might have problems but not about her looks, she had always been confident of them. She was a tall woman with a face more striking than beautiful; her hair was her best feature, dark, almost black, thick and naturally curly. Her brown eyes were sharp and intelligent. With her strong bones she had a forceful face which she was aware frightened some men away – but that was all right, she supposed, she would not have been interested in such wimps, anyway.

Maybe she was not meant to find a man, maybe this was how her life was to be led. Jenny was wrong, she hated being hurt like this, loathed the humiliation. This time she had not heard from Clive for ten days – that was too long, even for him. He would not change, she realised that: if she had learnt anything from the past it was that no man ever changed his ways. Maybe she should try to forget him, maybe she would have more luck with someone nearer her own age. She sighed at that thought. 'Fat chance,' she said to the mirror. She knew from the experience of her other friends that men her own age were, if unmarried, either weird or gay. And the tales she had heard of divorced men riddled with guilt, pining for their children and with never enough money, were enough to put off a woman for life. She let herself out of the bathroom. Elephant was sitting on the landing.

'I'm better off with you, aren't I, Heffalump?' She bent down and patted the small dog who licked her hand excitedly. 'Shall we go to bed or go and have some supper?' The dog looked up at her, head on one side, and turned to the top of the stairs. 'Yes, you're right, I should have something to eat.'

Back in the kitchen her meal was still partly frozen. She rinsed the carton of *moules* under the hot tap, then knocked the contents sharply on the bottom of the box into a non-metal dish. She placed this in the microwave and gave it an extra few minutes for the icy bits. She looked with disgust at the resultant over-cooked mess and scraped it into the bin, then she threw the other packages after it. She wondered how many dinners she had got out, just in case he came, that had ended up ditched like this.

'Bed, then.'

She settled Elephant in his basket covering him with his blanket and kissing him. Even as she did so she knew it was no way to treat a dog, knew that she was making the little dog a substitute for the emptiness of her life. She knew she should not, but she could not stop now.

Gloria climbed into the large and very empty bed. She did not even bother to wind the clock. Saturday tomorrow, she could have a lie in. Tomorrow was Barty Silver's party. She had meant to surprise Clive with that – it would have been an important party for him to attend. Goodness only knew which important actors and producers he would have met there, any one of whom might have offered him work, let alone Barty himself. Serves him right, she thought, as she turned off the light. She would not answer the telephone tomorrow, she would go by herself, let him suffer for a change.

On Saturday evening Gloria dressed with extra care. She might, last night, have thought she was destined never to find a man, but she wasn't willing to give up trying yet. Tall and with good legs, the short Hempel dress in dark blue taffeta suited her. It had cost her several months' salary – she didn't care, no matter what her mother would think. She liked good clothes and, thanks to a grandmother and two great aunts all dying at nearly the same time and leaving her money, she had no mortgage to pay, so she could afford the odd splurge.

She checked her make-up one more time and kissed Elephant, locked the kitchen door, had a moment of panic about her car keys and finally set out into the night.

'Aren't you going too fast?' Kate craned her neck to see the speedometer but, in the cluster of spinning dials, she was not sure which one it was. He ignored her question. She fumbled with the cigarette lighter, unfamiliar with its position in this new Rover speeding up the M4 to London.

'You smoke too much,' Tony replied, waving his hand in the exasperated way of a non-smoker. In the darkness Kate rolled her eyes with aggravation and inhaled deeply in defiance.

'You didn't answer my question,' she said.

'We'll be late. And don't smoke there, Sir Barty abhors smoking.'

It had all the makings of a strange evening, she thought. First, this unexpected invitation to such exotic circles. Then he had told her she didn't have enough make-up on. And then, biggest surprise of all, he had shyly given her a small box containing a pretty pair of gold earrings. Now he was driving too fast. Tony never speeded, never got tickets, in fact he frequently embarrassed her with his sedate pootling along, annoying other motorists and, no doubt, causing all manner of accidents in his wake.

She hoped the dress was all right. She had bought it in a small shop in the local town, feeling unable to cope with the crowds in Bristol. She was not used to attending smart London parties and it had been difficult to know what to buy, having no idea what women wore outside her own small circle. She had opted for a safe black crêpe one, loose to cover up the bulges she knew she had but never seemed to have the will to do anything about – like most things these days.

'You're quiet . . .'

'I was just thinking.'

'You think too much, that's half your problem. Look in the *A to* Z. It must be close to here . . . Clarendon House, Silver Street. Found it?'

chapter **nine**

Joy Trenchard sat in the white, gold and beige drawing room of her elegant house in Holland Park.

With her sleek head of short-cut straight blonde hair, her pale skin, the expensive beige silk dress she wore with a large gold Butler and Wilson lizard snaking across it, it was difficult to tell if the room had been decorated to suit her or she to go with the room.

She was reading a book. At least, it looked as if she was reading but for the past half-hour she had been looking fixedly at the same page. She did not read, she could not, for the words were blurred from staring at them for too long and the book was of no interest to her. It was a prop in case someone should come into the room and find her still sitting and waiting.

She looked up at the sound of whispering outside the door.

'Come in, Hannah,' she called, her sad expression disappearing immediately, her face transformed by a beautiful smile.

Hannah, her four-year-old daughter, entered, closely followed by her nanny, Sheila. The child's hair, as fine and blonde as her own, freshly washed, hung loose and long, spread on the pink of her pyjamas. She clutched a small and almost bald teddy bear.

'Do you like the new pyjamas?'

'I like the Snoopy dogs on them, Mummy.'

'I wish I had such lovely ones. None of mine have dogs on them.'

'Why don't they make grown-ups' pyjamas with Snoopy on them?'

'I really don't know, my darling. Kiss?' Joy held up her face to be kissed, Hannah scrambled onto the sofa beside her to be able to reach her. 'Ready for bed?'

'You will read to me, please.'

'Not tonight, darling, Mummy's going out in a minute.' She did have time to read, it was just that she could not, she knew she would not be able to concentrate. 'I'll read you two stories tomorrow and that's a promise,' she said, at sight of her daughter's look of disappointment. 'Off you go.' She gently patted her daughter's small rump. Joy stood up and faced the nanny, a woman she loathed but who was super efficient. Sheila was so reliable that Joy could never find any reason to sack her, especially when Hannah adored her. 'Sheila, Mr Trenchard has been delayed in chambers. I'll wait a few minutes more but then I'll go on to Sir Barty's on my own. I've written the number on the pad in the hall should you need me.'

'Yes, Mrs Trenchard,' Sheila said as she began to usher her charge towards the door. 'Shall I tell Mr Trenchard that's where you are when he comes home?'

'That won't be necessary, he'll probably go straight on to the party.'

'Of course, Mrs Trenchard,' Sheila said with such an expression of disdain that Joy had to look away quickly, as though it could scald her. Once the door was closed she crossed to the drinks tray and poured herself another gin and tonic. This was her third so far in the last hour. She knew she should not drink so quickly, not with Barty's party to go to, but she could not help herself. It was Charles's fault if she got drunk – at least, that's what she told herself. Where was the bastard?

From a table beside the sofa she picked up the telephone and dialled his chambers. She listened to the monotonous sound of a telephone ringing in a deserted room. She did not think it was her imagination that telephone rings sounded different when there was no one there to answer – like the way one could always tell when a house was empty. Five more rings she would give it, she told herself. Three, four, five. Reluctantly she replaced the receiver. She did not know why she had bothered, she had been phoning at regular intervals since six to remind him of the party. There had been no reply before, so why should there be one now?

No sooner had she replaced the instrument on its cradle than it rang. She virtually dived for it, spilling her drink in the process, but mercifully on the sofa and not her dress.

'Yes?' she said breathlessly.

'Joy, it's me, Betty. I'm in a fix, I don't know which way to turn.'

'Tell me about it,' Joy replied patiently, managing to disguise her deep disappointment that it wasn't Charles.

'It's gone – totally. I can't write,' Betty said dramatically in her husky, smoker's voice.

'What do you mean, you can't write? Of course you can, you write beautifully.' Joy was using her most professional and soothing tones.

'I can't, Joy. The stuff that's coming out isn't me at all. I've lost my style, I've lost my voice.' Betsy Farmer sounded virtually hysterical.

'Betty, try to calm down. Tell me what it's like.'

'Short sentences, staccato almost.'

'What are you reading?'

'Reading, what do you mean?'

'What book are you into for relaxation.'

There was a long pause. Joy smiled to herself. When she had been an editor she had had this conversation on more than one occasion with an hysterical author. Whatever it was she was reading, Betty didn't want her to know.

'Well, there's my research . . .'

'No, Betty, I need to know what novel you're reading.'

'The latest Jackie Collins, actually.' Betty's deep voice was ripe with embarrassment.

Joy laughed. 'That's it, then. Collins has a particularly strong style and you're catching it, it's easily done. Good read, isn't it?' Joy was laughing again, but silently, for Betty Farmer liked to think of herself as something of an intellectual. Her books were far from being so, but Betty did not see it that way and took her writing far more seriously than the content warranted.

'I think one should keep abreast of trends,' Betty said defensively.

'Essential,' Joy replied soothingly.

'And that's all you think it is?'

'I'm sure, Betty. While you're writing stick to encyclopaedias or *Whitaker's Almanack*, anything but Jackie Collins or other writers with such distinctive prose.'

'You're such a pet, Joy. Always so good-natured and understanding.'

'It's what I'm here for, Betty.' Odd, she thought as she spoke, how normal she could make herself sound when she was cracking up inside – she did it all the time.

The call eventually over, she raced out to the small cloak-room and dampened a hand towel. With it she worked quickly, mopping up from the sofa the spreading damp from her drink. She was in a panic. She had had such a fight with Charles when she had chosen this expensive white slubbed silk covering, she could imagine his fury if his worst fears had materialised and the sofa was ruined. She stood back and looked carefully at it from all angles. She had been lucky, it had not stained.

Poor Betty, she thought, as she replaced the dirty towel with a clean one and checked her face in the mirror over the basin. It must be hell to be a writer, always so insecure – far better to be an agent. She wished she was an agent with an office, though, then she would not have to field that sort of call when at home, often when it was the last thing she wanted to do.

She did not have the capital to set up an office, that was her problem. She had asked Charles to help but he did not take what she did seriously enough to invest any money in her. He had suggested she try the bank. She had no luck there either; it transpired that her manager had known more than one client like herself, bored, married to a rich man, who had set themselves up as a literary agent, thinking all that was needed was a telephone and a typewriter. They all gave up within the year when the money did not come in as they anticipated, and the outgoings became far more than they had ever dreamed possible.

Despite these setbacks she had carried on, using her dress allowance to finance herself so that Charles could never com-plain about the telephone bill. She had asked for an electric typewriter for her birthday and was now about to ask for a fax machine for Christmas. She was determined to succeed, to show him that she could do it. She needed one writer who would earn her a substantial commission, a deal which would make people sit up and take notice. It would come, she was sure, for she loved the work, loved the excitement that each new writer could be the one.

She had not had much luck in the six months she had been in business. There were plenty of writers out there, she had advertised only twice in writers' journals and after that it was a rare day that new work did not arrive. But out of the piles of manuscripts she had waded through – some almost indecipher-able – she had found only two she thought might have the spark, if she could persuade them to revise certain parts. There was Betty. If she reworked a couple of sections, Joy was convinced she could sell her book to Wallers who specialised in women's lightweight romantic fiction. But she knew the sum they would get was unlikely to be as much as Betty dreamed of, nor would they be the publishers she hoped for. And, unfortunately, Betty took the trade press and knew exactly what sums some authors were getting.

She had had one success with Brian Hoskins – he was thirty, a journalist – who with his first novel showed great promise. He had been accepted last week but the sum which she would eventually get as her commission would not even cover the amount she had spent on lunching likely editors, on telephone calls, and photocopying the manuscript. She had been so elated, almost as if she had written the book herself, but Charles had been unimpressed. She had, with aggrieved irritation, pointed out to him that she had to start somewhere. His reaction only fuelled her determination to prove him wrong.

Back in the drawing room she looked at the carriage clock on the mantelshelf – eight-thirty. She would give him another fifteen minutes. She poured herself another drink. She had spilt the last so that did not really count, she told herself. She sat again on the sofa, stroked the telephone and debated whether to call again or not. Her hand fell to her lap – what was the point?

She would often say, always with a laugh, that in the fourteen years of her marriage to Charles she had lost count of the times he had been unfaithful. This, of course, was a complete lie. It was the sophisticated, throwaway remark she made to her friends to cover up her hurt. In fact Joy remembered every one of them, their names, ages, what they looked like. She remembered every ounce of pain, every lonely evening she had spent. The humiliation of keeping appointments without him or, worse, not keeping them and lying to her hostess, saying she was unwell, had become a sickening repetitive routine. Especially as she knew that none of them was taken in for one moment. The whole of London knew about Charles.

She loved him, that was her curse.

She had loved him the moment she had set eyes on him at a May Ball in Cambridge when she had been with someone else – his friend, in fact. She had seen him, tall, blond, blue-eyed with his long-legged elegance, and had known she did not want to marry anyone else. It had taken her six months to get him and a further six before he proposed, and only six months into their marriage he was unfaithful for the first time. That time, since she was pregnant, she had told herself was understandable. Poor Charles must have been put off by her lumbering body. She had lost that baby. They never spoke of it, but she sometimes wondered if, like her, he blamed that particular affair, with the stress it had caused her, for her miscarriage. He was wonderful to her for some time after that. He was contrite. He loved her, he told her a dozen times a day. But then the signs came again that another affair had started – the lateness from work, the truncated telephone calls when she walked into a room.

Over the years, she had tried to rationalise the problem. He was like an alcoholic really, except it wasn't booze with him, it was the constant renewal of fresh pussy he was addicted to. Her pain at his rejection of her had often goaded her into confronting him. They had had scenes without number when she had angered him by threatening to leave. Then he would hit her. But it was almost worth it for then he always said he was sorry, he would promise her, swear to her that he would never do it again, that she was the one he loved, and she the one he would stay with until his dying day. That said, he would sally forth for another fling as if his promises to her exonerated him – until the next scene.

The one thought she would not allow herself to dwell on was the one that told her he should never have married in the first place. She supposed she should have become used to it, but she had not. What she had become adept at was hiding her feelings, burying the pain so that all their friends, while amazed at her relentless cheerfulness, her apparent understanding of her husband, could only assume that she condoned what he did.

But this time was different and this time, on top of all the usual emotions of rejection and unhappiness, she felt fear.

In the past she had been able to convince herself that the women were transient. There was a form of comfort in the sheer volume of turnover. She had also met most of them – it appeared to give Charles pleasure for her to meet his mistresses. Doing so had, in a way, removed fear. They were all young, vacuous, women he was certain to tire of quickly and come back to her as he always did.

Penelope Hawkins was a different proposition, however. Charles's affairs usually lasted, at most, three months. But this one had been going on for over six. Penelope was older than they usually were, more beautiful and, most worrying of all, she was highly intelligent. Like Charles, she was a barrister and so they had much in common. Had he been a criminal barrister, Joy herself could perhaps have been interested in his work. But a tax expert? It was not a subject she could get excited about nor could she cobble together a great deal of small talk on the subject for use over the dinner table – but Penelope could.

She realised now that she had always been waiting for someone like Penelope to enter his life. Now it had happened and she did not know what to do. She had nothing to offer him that Penelope had not more of. While beautiful herself she could acknowledge, in that cold calculating way in which women assess each other, that Penelope was more so. Undoubtedly she was better company for him and, at thirty, was five years younger than Joy. In her mind, each day since the start of this particular affair, Joy had made herself feel more and more inadequate so that in the end she felt there was nothing of value about herself at all.

Previously she had always comforted herself that her position was inviolate, for Charles loved their daughter as much as she did – he would never risk losing the child. But this year, for the first time ever, he had missed Hannah's birthday party. His love for the little girl was no longer an assured comfort to her.

Her marriage was over. That's what she thought, in those long sleepless hours, in the depth of night when everything is blackest. Usually one can laugh at such night-time notions when daylight dawns. Except Joy couldn't this time, the idea persisted night and day.

She knew she should fight back and despised herself for not doing so. If she could only find a lover for herself, maybe Charles would be beside himself with jealousy, begging her to return to him, vowing never to stray again. It was something she was never likely to put to the test. The problem was, if you loved someone as Joy loved Charles then no one else held any attraction for you, the very thought was anathema. She could not bear the thought of anyone else kissing her, stroking her, inside her, no, she knew for certain there was no other man for her. Who else could give her the pleasure in bed that Charles could? Those times when she knew he was with another woman caused her physical pain. She wanted him, needed him, was fixated with him.

She looked at her watch. Ten to nine. She tried the phone one more time. No answer. She really had thought he would turn up for Barty Silver, an important client. This time she would not telephone with an excuse, this time she would go alone. She needed a big book to establish herself, to make the publishers, as well as Charles, take her seriously. She planned to try to have a word with Barty Silver tonight. She wanted to suggest he write his memoirs and she act as his agent. She knew a dozen publishers who would fight to publish them. She also knew that many before her had badgered Barty and failed. Difficult though it might be, she was going to have to find the courage to speak to him.

She got up and collected her handbag. She stood up straight as if steeling herself to go alone. In the hall she slipped into her coat and let herself out into the night, hoping she would pick up a taxi quickly.

chapter **ten**

Sir Barty Silver was a master in the art of party-giving. He should be, he had had enough practice. He gave more parties than anyone else in London; it appeared to be his favourite hobby. In fact it was not, it was how Barty liked to do business. Just as well, for Barty's hours did not fit in with most people's idea of a working day. He never woke before noon, having rarely got to bed until dawn. He then had a leisurely breakfast, served by his Mexican manservant, followed by an equally leisurely bath; by the time he had changed into freshly laundered silk pyjamas – his chosen mode of dress for this part of the day – one and a half hours had passed. His secretary would come to take down letters and to deal with any business in hand, for which he allotted a further hour, not a minute more. He would then deal with his tailor or his shirtmaker, his masseur, herbalist, hypnotist or take a swim in his sumptuous indoor pool. This he called his maintenance hour. He then spent the next two on the telephone, calling business contacts in all corners of the earth, with scant regard to which time zone they were in. At five-thirty he would nap until six, when he would change again.

On the dot of six-thirty his aides arrived, all young men, all noticeable for their extraordinary good looks, charm and elegance. They were male for, if the truth were told, Barty was uncomfortable in the presence of all but a few women friends. The aides were handsome for Barty liked to surround himself with beauty. At this point, his day could go in two directions.

On those he called *drudgery* days he would have a stiff martini, check the figures and the weekly ticket sales sent over from the various theatres where his shows were on. He would then sally forth to one of those theatres selected at random and inspect his show. The knowledge that he was 'out front' put fear into the heart of even the most famous actor, for after the performance there would be a lengthy backstage post-mortem, which had been known to go on for hours. Such discussions could, and frequently did, result in Barty cold-shouldering those who had not reached his demanding standards – Barty expected perfection. He dined late, at a supper club he had founded simply so that he would always have somewhere to eat at any hour of the night. There, he did business into the small hours over several bottles of claret while those about him tried to stay awake. These nights he would go home early, for him. In bed by three o'clock, he would then speed-read scripts that were sent to him by the sackload. Those who had written plays or musicals chosen by him for further consideration were, if the work was finally selected, assured of a golden future. Barty's touch was infallible. It was a mystery to all the other impresarios in town, who worked far harder than he and at more conventional hours, how Barty could be the runaway success he was.

The other days he called his *relaxation* days – not that anyone else in his entourage would agree with the description. Such evenings would begin with his usual stiff martini followed by a light supper. Then he would go to a party – he never went to a party without setting up some deal or other. His interests were vast, not just the theatre, but a stage school, real estate, several night clubs, the supper club, three pop groups, two public houses, an Italian restaurant. These were his visible assets, but they alone could not explain his extreme wealth. In addition, he dealt astutely in all the markets of the world – his portfolio was a treasure chest.

The hostesses at these events knew that when they invited Barty they would have to invite one of his aides as well, which, when it was a dinner party, vexed them dreadfully. But Barty was so socially powerful that no one ever dared to refuse him. It did not matter if he had been to a dinner party, a party or a reception, he would always end up at his supper club and, to everyone's amazement, would have another meal.

But the relaxation days he liked the best were when he gave his own parties, two or three times a month. These he preferred for the simple reason that his parties were always the best. And they were the only nights when he did not go to the supper club – he had no need, for at about two in the morning his chef always served a late supper.

One of the secrets of the excellence of his parties was that there was never that awkward hiatus period when the party was not yet under way, when few people had arrived and those who had just stood about unsure what to do or say, waiting for something to happen. If the invitations said eight, it was certain that a number of people, chosen for their extrovert characters, would arrive extra early so that a small party was already under way before the main one had even begun.

And Barty set great store by champagne cocktails.

'Get the buggers tiddly-poo the minute they arrive, then it'll go with a swing – sober 'em up later.' He said this so often that people said it should be carved on his tombstone. The first two cocktails he offered were extra strong on the brandy. There was then a subtle lessening of the potency of the drinks so that the euphoria was judiciously kept topped up, but it was rare for anyone to get legless at his dos. How his staff knew who was at which drinks stage was one of the wonders of London society.

Barty was also adept at juggling his guest list so that the widest cross-section of people was invited. It was possible at any of his parties to meet someone you might need in your passage through life. There was always a sprinkling of the beautiful and young so that the possibility of romance hung heavy and excitingly in the air. A bishop, monsignor or rabbi was invariably present should the possibility of marriage arise. Estate agents from the larger establishments were usually there, brains packed with information on desirable residences. Barty took an inordinate interest in his health so a smattering of Harley Street specialists would be on hand, and if an obstetrician was not among them they would be only too happy to recommend one. The world of finance was represented by bankers, stockbrokers, financial advisors in droves. Lawyers abounded for pre-nuptial agreements, divorce and wills. Actors, writers, painters, musicians – classical and popular – were on hand to amuse. One person who was a more frequent guest than most was Sir Hugh Morangie – the most famous gerontologist in the land – for Barty was taking as much care of his future as he did of his present. And, of course, the bishop, monsignor or rabbi were also there to arrange a nice burial or memorial service and so complete the circle.

Barty's house was a dream. Many had offered to buy and all had been refused. Large, white and imposing, built by a courtier at the time of Charles II, it stood in a small street in Chelsea shielded from the noise of the city by ten-foot walls and a huge wooden gate that thumped shut after each arrival so that the casual passer-by only ever caught the tiniest glimpse of the huge gardens with their immaculate lawns and fountains, the graceful sweep of the driveway.

Only royalty and the lame were allowed to drive through the gates to the front of the house. Everyone else, without exception, was made to park elsewhere and walk, for Barty hated his front drive cluttered with cars. This had led to frequent altercations with the gate-keeper by those who did not know better. Many were the threats to his occupation, many were the tossed heads, the fury, and the declaration that they'd never been treated like this before nor so insulted. It made no difference, either they accepted the rule or they did not come. The majority did. Those who had fallen by the wayside were an American female singer of stunning vulgarity and wealth, a particularly pompous, and newly created life peer, a High Court judge who everyone knew had a propensity for child pornography and the exclusion of these three was generally welcomed.

The house contents were worthy of a museum. Looking about it people shuddered at what the insurance premiums must be.

Barty's study was the room where his parties took place, spilling out if necessary into the adjoining drawing and dining rooms, when the double doors were opened and the three huge rooms interlinked. But the core, and where the cognoscenti gathered, was the study. Told to go there, new guests were not prepared for what was in store. It was a vast room, which had once been a ballroom. Long sash-windows opened on to a balcony that wound round the ground floor of the house. At one end, on a dais, was Barty's desk, threateningly wide and heavy, behind which were french windows and steps leading down into the beautiful garden. It was decorated in lush Pompeian red, the mouldings and cornices picked out in white, gold and black. Rich, wild silk curtains, which matched the walls exactly, hung heavily pelmeted and swagged at the windows. On the highly polished oak plank floor were scattered priceless Persian rugs. Against the walls were ebony bookcases, the books all re-covered in black, red and white bindings of finest kid. Upon black plinths, set at intervals around the room, were marble busts of Roman emperors. On the many tables were Barty's collections – lapis lazuli, jade, gold, silver, crystal. And everywhere were photographs of Barty with royal persons – only the more important ones – and presidents – from only the major powers.

Very few people had ever ventured as far as Barty's private apartments. There, they would have been even more impressed, for stepping into these was like moving into an Arabian Nights of colour. His bedroom was decorated as if it was a Bedouin tent, the opulent wall hangings spread across the ceiling in a graceful arch, caught in the centre by a solid gold sculpture of two cupids. His low bed was covered with a counterpane made from the fur of thousands of mink throats, the antique tapestry cushions scattered about it seeming to glow with the richness of their colours. Here there were no paintings, as in the other rooms, except opposite the bed where hung a discreetly lit Russian ikon for which the Russian government would happily have paid millions. At the touch of a switch the rich hangings on one wall parted to expose his computers, faxes, telephones, all the hardware that kept him in touch with the rest of the world.

Everything about the house, and the man, was rich, exclusive and amazing. Not bad for an ex-Dr Barnardo's boy, deserted at birth by his Cockney mother who would not divulge the name of his father. Amazing for one who had started his working life selling, from an attaché case, doubtful items of jewellery outside Selfridges in Oxford Street.

He was ready for his party and excited. He always was – another reason why he was such a successful host. The day he did not feel this excitement would be the day he gave his last party. He was dressed in a dark green suit of the softest French velvet, his cream silk shirt was finished at the neck with an equally fine silk cravat. On his feet were matching green slippers, his initials finely embroidered in gold. It was a vulgar outfit which, on Barty, lost its vulgarity. It would have been fashionable in the sixties but without doubt, by tomorrow, copies would be being made for sale in the shops by the end of the week.

He was short, and surprisingly muscular. His hair was white, thick and luxuriant. There was much debate as to whether his hair was his own or a wig, and the question of whether he had a face-lift was of great interest to many. He had a smooth, round face with deep-set grey eyes and an unblinking stare with which he observed everything.

How old he was nobody knew, and he never said. Forms of any description requiring his birthdate were left blank, so that consulting *Who's Who* was of no use. His passport, when travelling, he kept strictly on his person, while at home it was locked safely away in his personal safe. He looked to be in his mid-forties but had been famous for too long to be anything but in his sixties.

The majority assumed he was a homosexual – his exotic house, his obsession with the minutiae of entertaining, his style of dressing, his coterie of beautiful young men, his unmarried state, were all given as proof of his sexual proclivities. The truth was a long way from this. Barty wasn't homosexual, bisexual or heterosexual: he had no interest in men or women, never had. He had not experienced love as a child, and never in his whole life had he been hugged or kissed. He had survived, and could see no benefit to be gained from physical contact with another human being. Or from any emotional entanglement. Perhaps a psychiatrist would have said he was an incomplete person, a damaged individual, but Barty would have scoffed at such a notion. He genuinely could not understand all the fuss about sex and felt quite strongly, from observing his friends, that it invariably led to grief.

His excitement was gained from making money. He loved the stuff, or rather the buzz it gave him, with a deep passion. Money to him was life, without it he would not have wished to continue living.

Now he stood at the door to his study, a glass of champagne on the table beside him, and waited to welcome his guests with that inner feeling of delicious anticipation at wondering what deals, what ideas he would be given tonight.

chapter **eleven**

Kate had not even reached the large wooden gate and already she was feeling sick with apprehension. They were in Silver Street, part of a long queue of people edging along. She wondered if Sir Barty had bought his house because of the name of the street or whether the street had been named after him. The crowd was noisy with excitement and there were frequent shrill cries of recognition from the women. They reminded her of the parakeets in the zoo calling to each other. She was amazed at the number of fur coats she saw, and even more amazed that people were still brave enough to wear them. But, then, the women wearing them looked so groomed and sleek that, apart from this party, it was unlikely they walked anywhere at all. Certainly she could not imagine them shopping at Tesco or doing the school run – such an idea was ludicrous. These women would be protected, by chauffeur-driven cars and exclusive, guarded shops, from the more extreme of the animal-rights people. They had such an air of superiority that she found them frightening. But then, she told herself, they were women just like her, they must have the same worries and fears. Undressed, they had two boobs and no doubt worried about the passage of time, as she did. They might all be smiling and appearing happy, but were they? Did they find their husbands irksome? The routine of life restricting? And she found herself wondering what they did with their lives, how their days were filled. Was it fun being rich, never having to worry about the bills? Or could luxury become boring? Was it possible they were as discontented with the lives they led as she was with hers?

Those women who weren't in furs wore evening coats or swirling capes in silks and satins. Kate pulled her serviceable tweed closer to her and knew with a sinking certainty that her dress was not going to do at all.

This was confirmed in the ladies' cloakroom. It was more

like the cloakroom of a hotel or a smart restaurant than a loo in a private house. There were four lavatories for a start, each behind doors painted with wonderful *trompe l'oeil*. Four basins with gold-plated taps were set in a vast vanity unit; over each hung a fine Chippendale mirror. On the marble surface, and at each basin, was a full set of make-up by Charles of the Ritz and a selection of perfumes in the largest size bottles that money could buy. Beside them lay silver-backed brushes and combs. On a table was a stack of gleaming white hand towels. Comfortable armchairs were scattered about the white marble floor, marble which appeared to be veined with gold, and on a low coffee table were copies of all the latest magazines. In attendance was a maid, in uniform black dress and crisp, starched apron, who was taking the coats and wraps through to an adjoining room.

Her coat taken, Kate felt even worse as she saw herself in the long mirrors that covered one wall. She looked like a fat black crow in the midst of a flock of exotic birds. If Pam were with her she could have told her which designers had created the dresses about her. Everyone was expensively clothed, made-up and coiffed – everyone, that is, except Kate. She glanced quickly into one of the mirrors, peering at herself over the head of a particularly sophisticated woman in crimson silk, whose body did not appear to have an ounce of fat on it and whose face, though rigid from a face-lift, looked as if it had been painted by an artist. Kate would like to have picked up one of the bottles of perfume – she'd spied Joy, a smell she adored and could never hope to afford – and have a quick dab, but no one else was doing so, and she did not like to. Her Estée Lauder would have to do.

In the hallway the men waited for their women, milling about confidently, greeting each other far more quietly than their female counterparts. It was all right for them, thought Kate, in their dinner jackets. They did not have to suffer the humiliation of not being smart enough. And their middle-aged spread was counted a sign of success, not a sign of neglect. It was an unjust world, she thought, as she looked about for Tony and tried not to gawp at some of the famous faces around her.

Sir Barty Silver looked exactly as he had in the copy of *Hello* magazine she had picked up in the hairdresser's – what a fuss they had made of her when she had shyly said she was going to his party. Never one to boast, she had quite taken herself by surprise at even mentioning it. But she was so excited and so proud that it had just slipped out.

They edged slowly towards him in the receiving line, slowly, since Sir Barty seemed to have a word for everyone. She noticed that as each guest approached a young man surreptitiously whispered in his ear – so surreptitiously that it was barely noticeable.

'Mrs Howard, thank you so much for coming to my party.' She found her hand being firmly shaken, and noticed with surprise that he spoke with a pronounced Cockney accent.

'Thank you for asking us,' she said. She knew it sounded inane but she felt almost weak-kneed as if in the presence of royalty.

'And the children, are they well? Steve and Lucy, isn't it?' He looked straight at her and Kate found the unblinking stare disconcerting.

'Very well, thank you.' She was aware that she looked half-witted in her astonishment that he even knew she had children.

'And Mr Howard. I'm so looking forward to our chat, say in . . .' He turned towards the young man hovering behind him, who without even glancing at the paper in his hands, whispered again. 'Fine, nine-thirty, in the small library. We'll talk then, Gervase here will show you the way.' And they found themselves standing the other side of Barty, ushered there by the gentle pressure of his hand, as he turned to the next guest. A waiter was hovering with a tray of glasses. Kate took one, smiling her thanks.

'Don't drink too much,' Tony hissed in her ear.

'How did he know about Steve and Lucy?' she asked, curtly.

'He obviously does his homework.'

'Then what else does he know about us?'

'There's not a lot to know, is there? We've hardly got any dark secrets.' He laughed.

'You can say that again,' Kate muttered into her glass. This really was a lovely drink, cool, bubbly and yet giving one an instant lift.

'What did you say?'

'Nothing,' she replied, and wondered how often women said that little word to their men. She used it all the time. Saying the word gave her a measure of satisfaction when irritated by him, as well as avoiding a full-scale row.

'We ought to circulate,' he said, looking about the room with a smug, self-satisfied expression on his face.

At sight of the half-filled room, Kate knew she would never have the courage to do that and she took a huge gulp of the comforting drink. 'I can't,' she hissed back at him. 'I just couldn't. I feel shy.'

Tony looked at her with undisguised irritation. 'Don't be so feeble. Well, I'm going to,' he said, and plunged into the nearest group.

Kate stood on the sidelines and watched. She had to admit to a degree of smugness herself as she noticed the blank looks on the group's faces as Tony, a shade gushingly she thought, introduced himself.

For a while she was occupied in studying, with genuine interest, the tables holding Barty's collections of *objets d'art*. She accepted another drink gratefully and longed for a cigarette. She looked about her but, Tony had been right, no one was smoking. She wished it was not winter, then the french windows would be open and she could have escaped on to the balcony and had a quick puff out there. Everyone knew everyone else, except Kate who knew no one, and, it appeared, was of no interest to anybody else. It looked as if she was in for a boring evening.

And then she recognised, in a corner of the room, sitting regally in a chair, wearing a dress of cobalt blue which made her eyes look even bluer, a mass of white hair framing her fine face and observing the scene with an almost cynical smile, Joyce Armitage.

Kate clutched at her throat with excitement. Joyce Armitage! Kate had read every book she had written. Read was the wrong word for the pleasure they had given her, devoured would have been a better description. Everyone knew about Joyce – she was the sort of woman who gave other middle-aged women hope. At the age of fifty-eight she had had her first book published, never having written a single word before, not a short story, a poem, nothing. Her husband had left her for a younger woman, her children, grown-up, had left home, and Joyce, instead of crumbling into a self-pitying heap, had put pen to paper and written the whole sorry tale – beautifully.

Fame had not come immediately, that was another lovely part of the story about her, she had become successful by word of mouth. Out in the country, women told other women of this new writer, keen to share their discovery with others. Her publishers had had to reprint six times – it was all part of the legend. Now her novels, one every other year, five in number, leapt straight into the bestseller list.

Here was someone Kate wanted to talk to, someone she knew she would get on with, she knew that from the books, for what Joyce wrote was what Kate so often thought. She grabbed at the sleeve of a passing waiter, and took another glass. Silly of her, she thought, she did not need courage to speak to this woman who, from the way she wrote, was already a friend, but she drank it all the same. She approached Joyce.

'Mrs Armitage?' she began.

Joyce Armitage swung slowly round to face her and Kate found two bright blue eyes looking at her unquestioningly.

'I was sure it was you. I do hope you don't mind me approaching you?' Kate found she was clutching her hands together tightly. There was no response from the writer. 'Only, it's just that I find your books such a joy – totally. I can't tell you the pleasure they give me and my friends . . .' Kate realised she was prattling but found, now she had started and with no response from Joyce, she did not know how to stop. 'I've all your books. I wish I'd known you would be here, I'd have brought them with me – got you to sign them . . .' She giggled stupidly.

The blue eyes stared at her with an expression which lacked any interest at all; Kate felt herself begin to panic. 'I'm sorry,' she said, miserably. Suddenly Joyce smiled, her face transformed. Kate sighed inwardly.

'Peter, I hoped you'd be here,' Joyce cooed in a soft and very attractive voice.

'Joyce, my dear, and how's my favourite author?'

Kate swung round to find two men standing behind her. She stepped to one side, flustered.

'I'm sorry to interrupt your conversation,' the younger of the two men said to Kate.

'You aren't interrupting anything. Peter, sit here with me, I insist.' Joyce patted the arm of her chair and Kate wished the ground would open up and swallow her.

'Hello, Joyce, I'm glad to see you looking so well.' The older man spoke.

Joyce looked at him, and through him, and turned her attention towards the man she had called Peter. The older man shrugged his shoulders expressively and turned to Kate.

'Your glass is empty, let me get you another.' He attracted the attention of a waiter, took two glasses from the tray, handed one to Kate and took a step away from Joyce. Kate followed. 'My name's Julius Westall.' He held his hand out to her.

'Kate Howard.'

'Are you a writer?'

'Me? Good gracious, no.' Kate laughed at the very idea.

'You should be with a name like that – it's perfect.'

'Is it?'

'I can just see it on the spine of a book – short, neat, memorable.' He was laughing now.

'Are you one? A writer, I mean?' she asked.

'No, a publisher.'

'Of course, how stupid of me ... Westall and Trim.' Kate felt confused again at not making the connection. 'It's funny, though, you asking me that, I've just joined a local writers' circle. Just for fun,' she added hurriedly, for she did not want this nice man to think she was being pushy. He might go and then she would be alone again.

'I've known many writers who have started that way. I wish you luck. You know Joyce?'

'No. I think I might have just committed a dreadful gaffe. I'm a fan of hers, but she didn't want to know me. I expect she gets fed up with all the adulation.'

'It's not that, she's just a very unpleasant woman and, to compound it, a crashing snob.'

'You know her well?' She was shocked by his assessment but at the same time the gossip in her wanted to know more.

'I know her, she'd rather not know me,' he said, smiling. 'I was her first publisher, you see.'

Kate did not see, but was saved from having to comment by the arrival of the younger man whom Julius introduced as Peter Holt.

'Are you a writer?' he asked. 'With a name like that ...'

Both Julius and Kate began to laugh.

'We've been through that, Peter,' Julius explained.

This was the point where, if she took Felicity Marchmont's advice, she should make herself known to Peter as someone living in the same area, interested in writing. Only she could not do it. She was amazed at the prospect of anyone being able to advertise themselves, it was against everything she had been taught.

'Kate's a writer,' Julius said, smiling kindly at her.

'Oh, hardly, Mr Westall.' She laughed nervously. 'I've only just begun.'

'Really?' said Peter in such an uninterested voice that she was glad she had not mentioned where she lived, or anything about the circle.

'Peter, have you noticed how many publishers are here? You, me, I saw Mike Pewter, Anthony's over there.'

'I know. I've just been talking to Martin and he said that there's four or five from Tudor's. What's our friend Barty up to?'

'I trust he's not thinking of going into publishing. With his track record of success we'd all be bust by the end of the year.'

'There's something I want to talk to you about, Julius.'

'Here?'

'Excuse me, I think I should go and find my husband,' Kate said, feeling that she was suddenly in the way. Since neither man made a move to ask her to stay she turned away, just as the younger man invited the older one to his home for a weekend. But in turning, Kate knocked the arm of a man standing closer than she realised. The drink in his glass slopped dangerously close to the rim as he held it away from him with both hands, balancing it carefully.

'I'm so sorry,' Kate blurted out.

'Nothing to be sorry about. See, not a drop lost.' He laughed. He was grey-haired and with the kind of deeply lined face – more crevasses than wrinkles – that implied a life led to the full. He was tall and large and well padded and he shambled, reminding her of a bear. His laugh was deep and rumbling, which for some reason made her think of molasses – if molasses could laugh, she told herself.

'Stewart Dorchester,' he said in introduction holding out his hand to her.

'Kate Howard and clumsy.'

'Not at all. I like Barty's party but he will invite too many for my taste. You can't really talk to people.'

'I know what you mean,' she said with feeling.

'Do you know Barty well?'

'No, not at all. And you?'

'I've known him for years but I don't *know* him but, then; I don't think anybody does. A man of mystery.' He smiled this time and Kate noticed deep crow's feet around his eyes, sign of one who smiles often.

'Are you a publisher too?'

'No, a mere journalist.'

'Really?' Kate's voice perked up with interest. 'That must be such a fascinating career.'

'Not as glamorous as it seems. Everything becomes routine in the end.'

'But there's routine and routine. There's mine which I wouldn't wish on anyone but then a brain surgeon has a routine but he's . . .' She didn't finish the sentence. A young woman in a skimpy skirt, thick make-up and long heavy earrings, which threatened to distort her ear lobes for life, had sidled up and put her arm through his.

'Stewart, the very man. You simply must meet Sylvan, she's *the* face of the future,' she said confidently, completely ignoring Kate, and tugging at Stewart to follow her.

'Excuse me, Kate. These pushy PR people!' He pulled a face of apology. 'See you later?'

'Yes, I'll be around.' She found herself giggling and wondered why on earth she was.

She watched him go with regret. She liked him, he seemed warm and sincere. There were so many things she would have liked to ask him about his work. Tony often told her she should not get people to talk shop, that it was boring and insensitive of her. Yet she always found that people talking about what they knew best were always fascinating. 'Stewart Dorchester,' she said to herself. Of course, she had only been talking to one of the leading journalists in the land famous for his in-depth interviews. What an ignorant fool he must think her, not even realising. God, what she would do for a cigarette. Perhaps there were ashtrays in the ladies.

*

Gloria had been round the room twice and her feet were killing her. Professionally it had been a good evening. She had met two highly successful authors, more than discontented with their present publishers, and had invited both to lunches to talk about the possibilities of their moving. She had chatted up Marina Smallwood, the international model. Over the hill now, perhaps, but with the life and lovers she had had, from politicians to pop stars, not to mention a stretch in Holloway on a drugs rap, she was ripe for a ghosted autobiography which could be a smash hit. And, Marina had confided to Gloria, she could do with the money. She was so keen that Gloria had been able to arrange an office meeting. That would please the accounts department for a change, they were always querying her expenses. She gossiped with several publishers and agents. Much could be gleaned from a party such as this. Secrets, which it would have been impossible to find out in working hours, were freely whispered when alcohol had loosened tongues. Serious secrets, such as who had paid what for whom, projects hoped for, where discontents lay, some of no interest, others to be stored for future use. She had managed to avoid Joyce Armitage, whose editor she was and wished she was not. The woman was impossible, arguing over every changed comma let alone phrases. To get her to cut anything needed all the skills of a diplomat – skills Gloria felt she was sadly lacking these days. Yet they were crucial to her job. On a personal level it had been a success too. She had given her card to one young man who had taken her fancy – so much for her lecture to herself last night to find someone more suitable. But, she thought, if she did not get out of these shoes, she would hit someone. Gloria was used to the cocktail circuit and always brought a second wellworn pair with her to change into once she had made her entrance and that all-important first impact.

Joy was late arriving, she had walked miles before picking up a taxi. She had looked a mess when she arrived and had spent ages repairing her make-up and thawing out in the cloakroom. She knew the maid, Sylv, from past parties and the woman had kindly got her a large brandy.

Barty was no longer receiving when she finally joined the party. He was moving slowly about the crowded room, his aides picking out the chosen with whom Barty wished to have a further word. Butterflies were careering about in her stomach as she joined the crowd hopefully trying to catch the attention of Barty or one of the aides. Barty moving about his guests always reminded Joy of the Queen at a Buckingham Palace garden party.

She didn't have to jostle long for Barty himself saw her and moved towards her.

'Joy, my love.' He approached her with hands held out in expansive greeting, took hers and squeezed them tight. He did not kiss her, everyone knew that Barty never kissed anyone. 'Where's the old man?' He looked around.

'He was delayed at the office, an important case,' Joy lied loyally.

'Oh, yeah?' Barty smiled kindly at her. She looked away, knowing he probably knew more about Charles's affairs than she did. She took a deep breath, it was now or never.

'Barty, might I ask you a favour?'

With a nod of his head, Barty indicated that they should move away from the circle about them to the relative privacy of the dais on which stood his desk. 'What's that, ducks?'

'I'm a literary agent now – it means I can work from home. I'd love to represent you, Barty.'

'Me? I don't write. I don't even write me own letters.' Barty laughed.

'You wouldn't have to. We could find a ghost, who'd do the writing. I'm talking about your memoirs, Barty. They'd sell like a bomb.'

'I'm sure they would, girl. But I'm not about to tell nobody nothing. I think me memoirs will have to wait till I'm in me box – I know a little bit too much about too many people.' He tapped the side of his nose with a forefinger.

'I suppose you're always being asked to do them.' Joy tried to keep the disappointment out of her voice.

'You could say that,' he answered kindly, and then as he saw her begin to sway, 'You all right, love?' he asked, concerned, but looking about him wildly for someone to support her should she fall.

'Yes, I'm fine,' Joy laughed, holding on to the side of the desk. 'Probably drank your bloody champagne cocktail too quickly.' Her laugh was brittle and false. Barty looked about him. At the end of the long room he saw what Joy had seen –

Charles with Penelope beside him standing in the doorway, relaxed and smiling.

'Joy . . .'

'Excuse me, Barty. I need some water . . .' And she slipped away from him, her lovely face white and wraith-like.

Kate was sitting behind the locked door on the lid of the lavatory seat, deeply inhaling the smoke from a cigarette – at last. The maid was no longer here, having a break, Kate assumed. She had looked about the luxuriously appointed room but saw nothing that she could be sure was an ashtray. There were several pretty bowls but they looked too valuable for stub ends. She was sitting in a cloud of her Estée Lauder, she had sprayed the air just in case someone else walked in and smelt what she was up to. She stiffened as she heard the clatter of high heels on the marble steps leading into the room.

'Sylv, you there?' A voice called out. 'Sylv, it's me Gloria Catchpole, I need my other shoes. Sylv? Sod it, where's the woman got . . .' The door of the cubicle beside Kate slammed shut. Kate lifted her feet so that they stuck out in front of her and tried to hold her breath. The cistern flushed. The cubicle door banged. Gingerly Kate lowered her legs, and began to breathe normally again as she heard the woman washing her hands across the room. A further clatter of heels announced the arrival of another. Oh, Lor', thought Kate, how long was she going to be stuck here? She lit another cigarette from the end of the first one, raised the seat, threw the stub in the pan and winced at the hiss it made. Might as well be hung for a sheep . . . she decided, settling back on her perch with difficulty as she curled her legs under her, the less likely to be seen under the gap at the foot of the door. There she crouched on the lavatory lid for all the world like a black, bespectacled gnome on a toadstool.

'Joy, darling. You look bloody awful. What's happened? Sit down . . . come on, come over here. There . . . Now what's the matter, tell me,' the voice called Gloria said, brimming with bossy concern.

'I can't, I'm too mortified.' Joy was obviously crying.

'You stay here, darling. I'll be back. You look as if you need a drink.'

Kate sat, wondering whether to slip out quietly, but when

she heard the remaining woman begin to sob noisily, she felt she could not. Something very bad must have happened to upset her so much, and Kate's presence might make matters worse.

'Here you are. I met Sylv. She got me a bottle of champagne. I told her to try and head other people off – there's another loo along the corridor. Now, you drink that.'

'I want a smoke.'

'I don't have any, I don't.'

'In my bag . . . there . . .' Joy spoke through her tears. Kate, in her cramped prison, rolled her eyes with exasperation. So she could have smoked after all and need not have got into this stupid situation.

'Was it Charles?'

'Yes. The bastard's out there with that whore Penelope.'

'No!'

'He's done it to humiliate me. Nearly everyone I know is here.'

'But why?'

Kate sat trapped and could not help but listen to the sad tale Joy was blurting out between sobs and large gulps of champagne. Normally she would have found it riveting. As it was, she was acutely embarrassed to be eavesdropping in this undignified manner. The right thing to do would be to make a noise, flush the loo, brazen it out – but she could not. She had been too quiet for that.

Gloria made sympathetic noises at intervals until Joy stopped, obviously talked out.

'You should leave him, Joy. He's only going to get worse. Women are like a drug to him, you must have learnt that by now.'

'I love him.' Joy sniffed loudly.

'How can you? He's a bastard, he obviously doesn't love you or he wouldn't do this to you.'

'Don't say that!' Joy wailed.

'Well, someone's got to, darling. He's going to make you ill. Get out, take Hannah, make a new life for yourself.'

'How can I? I've no money. I can't even make any.'

'Go to a lawyer, get a settlement. He'll have to pay you, support the two of you.'

'Bah!' Joy managed to laugh. 'Have you ever heard of a

barrister whose wife came out on top in a divorce? They close ranks, it happened to a friend of mine. She couldn't find a lawyer for love or money who'd give her the right advice. The legal profession is famous for sticking together.'

'Shop him then, I would. Write to the Lord Chancellor. He can say goodbye to silk then, the law doesn't like divorce in its midst.'

'He is a silk already.'

'Then perhaps they'll take it away,' Gloria said hopefully. 'You know what, Joy? I bloody loathe men, they're nothing but grief.'

The two women were silent for a while and to Kate's horror she realised she had got cramp in her leg. In the constricted space she tried to twist her leg round, to ease the pain. She was hot now and her spectacles had slipped down her shiny nose. As she grabbed at them before they fell her handbag slid to the floor with a clump.

'What was that?' Gloria said. 'Is there anyone in there?' There was a pause and then she was banging on the door. 'Are you all right?' she shouted.

Kate stood up, straightened her skirt, took a deep breath, opened the door and emerged blushing furiously.

'What must you both think of me? I can't apologise enough. I didn't mean to listen. I was desperate for a smoke and locked myself in there. Then I heard you two and I was so scared at being found out, I got stuck in there. Oh, Lor' . . .' She felt the blush deepening and longed to leg it quickly out of the room.

Gloria looked at Joy, and Joy at Gloria, and both burst out laughing.

'Are you a journalist?' Gloria asked, suddenly straight-faced.

'Me, no. I'm a housewife.'

'That's all right, then. Have a drink.' Joy was waving the bottle at her with one hand. 'And a smoke.' She held out a packet of cigarettes with the other. 'Could happen to anyone. Sit down, join the party.' Her speech was markedly slurred.

Kate, not sure what to do, decided that perhaps it would be best to join them, perhaps she could explain better. They did not seem too cross with her. 'Thanks,' she said, taking a glass and a cigarette. She looked about her guiltily before bending her head over Joy's wavering lighter.

'Barty doesn't mind you smoking here, it's banned in the

study with all those lovely rugs and only at the big parties. He once saw someone stub one out on a particularly precious rug,' Gloria explained.

'How dreadful,' Kate said with genuine shock. 'You can't blame him, then, can you?'

'There's a lot of creeps around,' Gloria said sagely, pouring herself another glass and topping up Joy's as she did so.

'And my husband's the chief creep out there,' Joy announced. 'Is your husband a bastard?' She looked closely at Kate as if trying to focus.

'No, he's not a bastard, but . . .' and to her utter astonishment she heard herself say, 'but he's a dreadful bore.' Having said it aloud, Kate felt a wonderful and strange feeling of liberation as if saying that had peeled the scales from her eyes. She saw it all now, understood everything, knew why she was so fed up. She had been blaming herself when all the time it was his fault. This ladies' loo was her road to Damascus. 'Boring as hell,' she said loudly and gleefully, as if testing that it wasn't all a dream.

It appeared that holding such sentiments about her husband made her an immediate member of this circle. The other two held their glasses aloft.

'Down with boring men,' Gloria toasted.

'Let all the bastards rot in hell,' Joy added.

And Gloria thrust another glass of champagne at Kate. To her equal astonishment she found she was telling them about her discontent, her menopause and how she loathed being overweight and middle-aged – all things she had not even discussed with Pam. In return she learnt that Joy was a literary agent and she was filled in with more of Charles's misdemeanours and an insight into the life of the rich which, it seemed, wasn't nearly as good as Kate had presumed. And Gloria had a good moan about her young men and her own dissatisfaction with her love life, her career as an editor, with everything.

'We should all meet up again, this is fun. It must be the ambience.' Joy was giggling. And Kate agreed, she'd never normally have chosen a lavatory for such confidences, she said. Joy was reduced almost to hysteria and in attempting to give Kate another drink managed to pour it straight down her dress. This upset Joy out of all proportion to the act and she burst into tears again.

'Poor bitch,' Gloria said over her head to Kate. 'I think I'd best get her home.'

'You're not thinking of driving?' Kate asked, concerned.

'God, no, I'm way over the top. I'll get a cab.'

They stood up and Kate helped Gloria get the very unsteady Joy on to her feet, a now very maudlin Joy who was slurring her way through, of all songs, 'Stand By Your Man'.

'I'll pay for the dry clearing,' Joy stuttered.

'It doesn't matter, honestly.' Kate was not lying, she had felt so ugly all night that she had vowed never to wear this dress again.

'It's the least I can do. Gloria, in my bag ... my card ... give darling Kate one ... Such a lovely woman. She understands, Gloria, she understands everything ... Now, you send me the bill, you promise.'

'All right, then,' Kate said as she took the card.

'Nice meeting you, let's hope we meet up again some time.' Gloria shook her hand. 'Come on, Joy, old girl. Let's find Sylv, get our coats, I'm taking you home.'

Kate felt strangely lonely after they had gone. As she walked up the steps to go back to the party and find Tony her legs felt dramatically unsteady.

'Where the hell have you been?' Tony snapped on seeing her.

'I've been in the ladies' loo,' she said with total honesty and dignity.

'You sound drunk.'

'You know something, Tony? I think I am.'

'That's disgusting, I loathe drunk women.'

'Do me a favour, Tony. Sod off,' she said, before she passed out on Barty's favourite rug.

chapter **twelve**

The consequences of Barty's party reverberated like the rumblings of a distant summer storm.

Tony virtually frog-marched Kate down the steps of Barty's house and along the street to their parked Rover. He slammed shut the door of the car, crashed the gears noisily, then mounted the kerb, knocking a dustbin flying, and did not even bother to get out to see if his precious vehicle was damaged. Kate leant back in the seat and closed her eyes, thinking that silence might be best in the circumstances. However, she found that closing her eyes was an unpleasant experience: something had happened – everything was whirling out of control.

'You do realise you've probably cost the firm a very valuable contract?' he eventually said in a tight-lipped way.

'Um . . .' replied Kate, finding that if she turned her head slightly to the left the whirling was a little better. In fact, if one allowed it to take one over it was quite a pleasant sensation, like being on a fairground carousel.

'If this gets out we could lose other clients.' He then began a monologue of her faults until well past Reading. Not only was she a disastrous wife and mother but she was a social catastrophe. Her behaviour would undoubtedly lead to Tony's partner's children being removed from their fee-paying schools, and their lives ruined by contact with the hoi-polloi in the state system. The senior partner's wife would no doubt have to give up her horses and God alone knew when anyone would have a holiday again. When she did not react to that threat he finally looked at her. Kate was snoring contentedly, a tiny whiffling sort of snore. So enraged was Tony that he pressed his foot down hard on the accelerator. The Rover, feeling itself liberated at last, kicked itself into action and leapt down the M4.

They had almost reached their junction turn-off when he heard the chilling wail of a police siren. Dutifully he pulled over on to the hard shoulder. He smilingly apologised for his speed, quickly explaining he was a solicitor and that it was the first and last time he had ever exceeded the speed limit. It would never happen again, he promised. Tony's attempts at charm had little effect on the constabulary who insisted on breathalysing him. He failed.

Kate eventually woke up as the car, driven by a strange policeman, pulled into the police station car park.

'What happened?' she asked, fear clutching at her. Was Tony ill? Had she been kidnapped?

'Your husband's up ahead, in custody.'

'In custody? Tony? I don't believe it . . .' And she began to laugh drunkenly at the ridiculous prospect.

They eventually took a taxi home in sullen silence. It cost nearly thirty-five pounds, an amount that neither could raise between them and the driver was none too happy at the prospect of accepting a cheque. Guiltily Kate slipped into the house leaving Tony to deal with him. In the kitchen she put some coffee on.

'I'm sorry,' she said, shamefaced, when Tony eventually appeared.

'Sorry? You think you can stand there and say "sorry" and I'm going to forgive you?'

'I didn't make you get drunk,' she said defensively.

'Drunk? You were the one who got drunk.'

'I wasn't the only one, according to the police.' In the circumstances she felt quite pleased with such a sharp retort.

'I was only just over the limit, if you must know.'

'*Just* is quite sufficient.' She knew she smirked, knew she was being unpleasant when she had set out to be sympathetic. She knew she was rousing his anger.

'Look at you, you look dreadful. I'm ashamed of you. You of all people. Well, Madam, you are going to have to live with the consequences of your gross behaviour, I can promise you that.' He was shouting at her. She found herself stepping backward until the Aga prevented her going further. He's going to hit me, she thought with alarm.

'Coffee?' she asked, in as normal a voice as she could muster.

'I want nothing from you. I'm finished. I'm sick to death of you and your bloody moods, your whining, and now this.'

'And have you ever wondered why I get moods? Has it ever crossed your mind that I might be bored to tears with you, this house, my life, with everything?' She spoke firmly now, anger sobering her long enough to enable her to argue.

'You ungrateful bitch. After all I've done for you – the hours I work, the money I lavish on you.'

Kate laughed, a short, sharp and mirthless laugh. 'Why, Tony, you sound just like my mother. You never did, or gave me, anything that you didn't want to. Everything here, everything you've ever done has been for your own ego, for your self-satisfaction. I'm just a possession to you, not a person in my own right.'

'In your own right? You're nothing without me. And just look at you – you've no style, you look a permanent mess. Do you want to know the truth? I was ashamed to be seen with you tonight.' His head was thrust forward, his eyes bulging.

Kate stood silent as if absorbing his words. She threw her head back and laughed. 'And who are you? Adonis? Have you looked in the mirror recently? Seen your gut? Counted your chins? Noticed your hairline? If you don't fancy me any more, that's fine by me. You know what you can do about it.' She was shouting now, saying things she did not mean, things she did not want to say, but did not seem able to stop.

'And what's that?'

'Try and find someone else who'll put up with you and your nasty little habits as I have done.'

'What habits?'

'You pick your nose when you think I'm not watching. Your feet smell and you slurp your soup.'

'This is childish. I'm going to bed. I'll speak to you when you are in a more dignified condition.'

'Good, I can hardly wait.' She was close to tears now, and turned back to the Aga. 'And you scratch your balls!' she managed to shout before the kitchen door slammed shut. The coffee was heated, Kate poured herself a cup, black, with plenty of sugar. Angrily she wiped a tear away with the back of her hand. No, she was not going to let bloody tears get in the way this time, she'd show him. 'Pompous twit,' she muttered to herself as, with exaggerated care, she carried her cup to the table. She slumped down on a chair and gazed morosely into space. She wondered why it was that people, when arguing, always ended it by announcing they were going to bed. She sat at the table and thought about this for some time and then realised that the amount of effort she was having to put into its contemplation could only mean one thing – she was still drunk.

'I'm going to bed,' she said to the cat, not to be outdone.

Upstairs she wavered outside her room. That was another thing about rows with one's spouse, it always seemed bizarre to end up lying together in the same bed. Ah, well, she thought, maybe he'll have calmed down in the morning. But even as she thought it she doubted it would be so.

The bed was empty, Tony's pillows missing. He must be in the guest room. She took off her dress, crossed to the bathroom, cleaned her teeth, looked at her reflection and laughed – she certainly looked decidedly blotto. She never got drunk, rarely drank to excess, only at Christmas. It must have been such a shock for him to see her in that state. That was what had made him fly off the handle at her, shock, she reassured herself, preferring to draw a discreet veil over her finale at Barty's. She turned the light off – her face would have to wait, she had not the energy. Similarly she couldn't be bothered with her bra and tights, so she crashed into bed half-dressed.

When Kate awoke it was eleven and pouring with rain.

'Oh dear,' she said in the time-honoured way of the morning after the night before. She turned and looked at the empty space beside her. She put out her hand and touched where he would normally lie. They had never slept apart because of anger before. She stretched – she enjoyed the freedom of the large bed to herself, always had in the past if he was away overnight on business. She wondered if he would return to it and found this morning she did not mind if he did not. Certainly she would not miss what passed for sex between them. She did wonder if her disinterest in him sexually was because she no longer loved him, whether it was what to expect at her age – a slowing down of desire. Desire? She laughed. Had she *ever* desired him? No, she did not think so. Maybe when she was very young, but that was where her memory let her down again. But then, *if* it had all been wonderful once, surely she would have remembered?

She turned restlessly in the bed. Had she lost all interest in sex? The truth was, no. She fantasised, and when she did she was ashamed, feeling it was almost a betrayal of Tony even to think of herself with another man. She consoled herself with the thought that perhaps Tony did also which made it a bit better.

It would be easy to allow herself to dream of that man Stewart she had met last night. He was not conventionally handsome, nor was he young, but all the same there had been something about him, and a quickening of her pulse when he spoke to her, and the way she had felt quite skittish. But she had not seen him later and probably wouldn't again. And what conceit made her even dream that he had felt awakened by her?

She sat up, thumped her pillow, and shook her head as if to rid herself of such thoughts. She looked at the window and watched the rain lashing the glass, the greyness of the sky mirroring her mood. She should not have said what she had, though, about his paunch and his hair, it had been spiteful. But, then, she thought, he had been the first to make personal remarks – he'd asked for it.

She raised herself with effort on to the pillows. He had certainly told her straight last night. 'I'm finished,' he had said. What did he mean by that? She had to admit she had been so obsessed with her own problems and feelings it had never crossed her mind that he might be thinking the same. It was a shattering prospect. She would never have regarded herself as arrogant, but certainly she had been over this.

Was he thinking of leaving her? She felt a frisson of panic at the prospect. She hugged her arms about her for comfort. What on earth would she do? She had no career to fall back on, all she knew how to do was homemaking. He managed all their affairs, decided how to invest their money, paid the big bills. She knew nothing about organising her own life. Could she learn? Could she cope? Loads of other women did, she told herself, she knew of three within their own circle. After the initial shock they seemed to have settled, to have come to terms with the new situation. In fact two were positively jolly in their new freedom. Freedom. What an odd word to spring to mind for such circumstances. She sat up straight, she was feeling less panicky now.

She looked about the room on which she had lavished much love and thought over the years. A room furnished bit by bit as they could afford it, everything in it chosen with care. If he went, what would she be left with? She could not afford to run this house on her own. Would he buy her another, smaller, cheaper to manage? She would have more time for herself with a smaller house to run, that was for sure. Had he met someone else already? Well, last night she had given him permission to go to her . . .

She shook her head, puzzled. She should be feeling terrified, but the panic had subsided and she was beginning to feel a strange sense of excitement and anticipation. What did that mean?

All the same, she was going to have to face him. Goodness knows what she was going to say. She owed it to him to apologise – sober this time. It had all seemed funny last night, but he had been right, she had behaved badly. If he hadn't been so angry with her he would have driven home at his normal sedate pace and the police would not have stopped him. In his position – a solicitor, governor of the local school, respected freemason – a court case would be a disaster. It was unfair on him, he was normally so careful, so law-abiding. It was mainly her fault, there was no question about it.

Gingerly she slipped her legs over the side of the bed and stood up. She deserved to feel dreadful but in fact she felt fine. She showered quickly, scrubbing off the remains of last night's make-up, disgusted with herself for being such a slut. She dressed quickly in skirt and jumper, brushed her hair, put on a little make-up – she felt she should try to look as attractive as possible. But she had to hurry, they would all be starving by now.

The kitchen was deserted. Dirty breakfast plates stood on the table. Kate pushed back her hair and tried to smother the feeling of irritation that they had not bothered to put them in the dish washer for her. Propped against the milk jug was a note.

Who's been a naughty mummy, then? Tut, tut. Dad's gone to see Freddy to discuss a 'limitation exercise' he said. He is FURIOUS. I'm spending the day at Mandy's. Steve's gone to Tom's. There's a note from Pam in the hall. How's your head?
Lucy.

He need not have told the children, she thought with annoyance. That was a mean thing to do, she would have covered up for him. In the hall she found Pam's note telling her that she had enrolled them both in the writers' weekend, that it was all paid for and it was to be Kate's birthday present. Kate smiled to herself. Her birthday was not until next June and, no doubt, by then dear Pam would be giving her something else.

She went back to the kitchen. She stacked the dishes in the dishwasher, wiped the kitchen table down. She put on an egg to boil and found she was going back over everything again, the thoughts whirring around trapped in her skull. Abruptly she turned, crossed to the dresser and collected pen and paper which she put on the table. She stood a moment, looking down at the pristine white paper, deep in thought, until the pinger sounded and she collected her egg.

Breakfast over she pushed the dishes to one side and sat, pen in mouth, gazing out of the window at the pouring rain. She began to write. She began slowly. When she had covered a quarter of the page she stopped, read what she had written, screwed it into a ball and started again. Four false starts she had, but on the fifth she began to write with speed. She was thinking so quickly now that her writing could barely keep up with the flow of words tumbling about in her mind.

Once the dishwasher had finished she was unaware of any noise in the kitchen apart from the scratch of her pen on paper. She was so absorbed that she did not hear the clock ticking, the low hum of the refrigerator, the sibilant hissing of the Aga, the occasional swish of a car's tyres on the damp road outside. When she finally laid down her pen it was past three and beginning to get dark. She had covered sheets of paper. She collected them together and laboriously began to count the words – she had written three thousand five hundred and forty-two!

She put the kettle on, made herself a mug of tea, switched on the light, lit a cigarette, realigned the papers in front of her and, taking a deep breath, began to read.

She sat back in the chair and smiled. She was surprised, she liked what she had written. What was more she had enjoyed doing it, it had been such fun. She realised she was not depressed, she had not wanted to cry once, and she wanted to go on, and on . . .

She took a clean sheet, thought for a moment and then printed, A WINTER'S INTERLUDE by KATE HOWARD. She held the page up and studied it. She preferred this title to 'A

Winter's Romance' and that nice man Julius had been right, her name looked beautiful.

Sylv, the maid who had supplied Kate, Joy and Gloria with the champagne, was summarily dismissed by Barty. No pleading on her part would make him change his mind – she knew the rules about the supply of drink to guests and she had broken them. Dismissal was to be expected, the housekeeper had informed her. She was given two hours to pack her bags and leave.

Gloria was woken by the telephone ringing. Immediately she looked at the pillow beside her – he had gone. She had to cough several times before she could get her voice to work properly.

'Gloria Catchpole,' she rasped.

'Gloria, my dear, did I waken you?'

'No, no,' she lied, frantically trying to put a name to the familiar voice.

'I wondered if we could have lunch one day soon?'

'I'd love to,' she replied, and immediately realised she had left it too late to ask who was speaking.

'I don't want anyone to know I'm talking to you. Sorry to be so cloak and daggerish about it, but you'll understand when I explain everything. But say the Gay Hussar, next Thursday?'

'That would be lovely,' she said, still racking her brain for a clue to her caller.

'See you, then.' And the phone went dead.

Gloria replaced the receiver, turned and stroked the pillow beside her. She lay down burrowing her head into it, searching for his smell. She had done it again. Fool, she told herself.

Clive had been here waiting for her when she had returned from the party. She had found him lying on her sofa fast asleep. She had stood for a while looking at him, fuddled with drink, not sure which emotion to grasp hold of. She was angry with him for his neglect and for his assumption that she would be pleased to find him here. She could not continue to drift like this, she must finish with him to maintain her own self-respect. She should waken him, tell him to go, instead she watched him, trying to memorise exactly how his long black lashes appeared to lie on his cheek. She put her hand out wanting to touch the hollow of his cheek, outline the fullness of his lips. Her hand hovered. She did not touch him. Not this time. This time she was going to finish with him for good. And then he had opened his eyes and he smiled his lazy smile. 'Sorry,' he had said. And she was in his arms, lost once more, instead of reading the riot act to him.

He had said he could only stay an hour. She had argued with him for where was there to go at this time? He would not tell. Still, she had thought, once in bed he would forget, he would stay.

She knelt beside the sofa and with agonising slowness unzipped his jeans, all the time watching him, her eyes sparkling with anticipation, the tip of her tongue moistening her lips. He was already hardening as she held him in her hands, stroking gently, enjoying as she did the almost miraculous velvety texture. But she was enjoying even more the feeling as it became rigid in her grasp. And she could see the expression of lust in his eyes.

'Like it?' she asked.

He did not answer but took her head in both hands and guided her to where he wanted her to be. Her mouth felt full of him as she sucked at him like a greedy child. His hands found her breasts and he began to play with her erect nipples. She was writhing with pleasure. He groaned. She let go of his penis and pulled him down towards her on the floor and quickly, almost desperately, she pulled down his jeans and as quickly pulled off her own pants. She searched in the pocket of his trousers and found what she knew would be there. Gently and so slowly that he began to groan, she slipped a condom over his huge throbbing member. Then she was astride him and he jerked upwards and easily into her and she was riding him. As he thrust deeper into her she cried out. She lifted her hands above her head, breasts thrust forward, dark curly hair falling about her face. She lifted her head, looked down at him. She was happy, so very happy. And then she climaxed and her body jerked as her orgasm seemed to explode within her. Then he came and it was over and she slumped on to his body; that fleeting moment of happiness had slipped away, again.

'Hand me my fags,' he said, flexing his body under her to make her get off him, ridding himself of the condom.

'You bastard,' she said.

'After that?'

'You don't understand, do you?' She rolled off him and leant across the floor for his cigarettes and lighter.

'What more do you want?' he asked, putting a cigarette in his mouth.

'Oh, nothing,' she replied. She would have liked him to say he loved her, even if it was not true. But he never did. But it would be nice to hear, she thought, hunching her knees up, putting her arms round them and hugging them.

'Women!'

'Men!' She smiled.

He did not go immediately, instead they had a glass of wine and then he led her to bed and there they made love again.

She must have fallen into a deep sleep, and he had quietly left her bed, avoiding her pleas to remain the whole night.

She sat up and thumped the pillow feeling wretched. She could not blame him this time, it was she who had instigated it. She pushed her hair back. Why did she do it? Why did she so often allow her pussy to rule her head?

'That, my girl, was the last time,' she said aloud, pleased with the conviction in her voice. She climbed out of bed and walked out of the room naked. An annoyed Elephant was sitting on the landing waiting for her. 'Sorry, my darling. That's the last time. That particular one won't be back to banish you.' She entered the bathroom, the little dog with her, who, once her bath was run, took up station on the bathmat as if guarding her.

In her bath Gloria made herself puzzle over the voice to stop her thinking of Clive. It was familiar, obviously someone who knew her well enough to be confident of being recognised, and someone she liked enough to have given her home telephone number to. It was also the voice of an older man, so it could not have been the young man she had met at the party. It was an annoying habit, not announcing yourself like that, arrogant really. Still, she would go. For a start she was intrigued and, secondly, just to eat at that restaurant once more would be nice. She would not eat the day before and then she would have the wild cherry soup and the chicken-stuffed pancakes with paprika. She used to eat there often, now rarely. Hopefully she'd remember the name to go with the voice before then.

*

Joy Trenchard woke with a fearful hangover and felt very sorry for herself. She lay in the bed in her large white and pink bedroom, looked about the room, which contained everything a beautiful woman could possibly want, and felt she had nothing.

She covered her face with her hands at the memory of last night. Her thin shoulders shook under the silk of her nightdress as she began to cry. Was she doomed to spend the rest of her life weeping? Looking up she caught sight of herself in the mirror opposite. She saw a thin, bedraggled woman, her face blotched from her tears, slumped pathetically in the huge bed. She loathed the sight.

Angrily she felt for a tissue in the box on her bedside table and wiped at the tears and blew her nose noisily. God, what a mess she looked. What if he came back and found her looking like this?

'So what?'

She looked up abruptly. That was the sort of thing Gloria would have said, not her. But Gloria was not here, so had she said that? Or was she hearing things?

'So what?' she said aloud. Yes, she *had* said it, and yes, she meant it. 'So what?' She tried it again and she smiled, admittedly a rather wan smile, but a smile none the less. Two little words that made her feel better, two words out of all proportion to their size.

She slipped from the bed, crossed to her bathroom and ran herself a bath. She lay a long time soaking and thinking. She forced herself to return to last night and to go over in detail what had happened. She made herself remember who was there. This time Charles had gone too far. How could he have humiliated her by arriving at Barty's with his mistress, to a party where he knew there would be many of their friends? Not only did he not love her any more, he did not respect her. She had done nothing to lose it except to acquiesce too easily to his previous indiscretions. She had been a fool, a weak despicable fool. Now she was in danger of losing her self-respect. The loss of that would be far greater than the loss of Charles's for her, she decided. She was going to have to change. She did not know how, but change she would.

An hour later she emerged from the bathroom and she was angry, very angry.

She took a long time dressing and doing her face but as she worked on her make-up she suddenly realised she was taking care for herself and not for him. The thought made her calmer, gave her confidence and she saw herself smiling in the mirror.

In the kitchen she found Hannah and her nanny having a mid-morning mug of hot chocolate.

'You look pretty, Mummy.'

'Why, thank you, my darling, and so do you.' She bent and kissed her daughter's cheek.

'I assume you'd like some black coffee, Mrs Trenchard?' Sheila asked. It was the tone of the question that made Joy's hackles begin to rise.

'No, thank you, this chocolate looks delicious.' She took a mug from the cupboard and helped herself to some – the last drink she wanted, but she forced herself to sip it.

'Mr Trenchard didn't come home before I went to bed, last night, so I couldn't give him your message.' Sheila persisted in the cold, clipped voice which had always irritated Joy.

'No. We met at the party.'

Sheila's disbelieving smile made her wish she could slap the supercilious bitch. She sipped at the chocolate, looking hard at the nanny, enjoying the thought.

'Daddy said we could go to the zoo this afternoon.'

'He's had to go out on business.'

Joy knew it wasn't her imagination that Sheila smiled again with the expression of one who knew that Charles hadn't come home at all last night. It was an almost triumphant look. Sheila didn't respect her either, that was patently obvious now. She wondered what it was about last night that had suddenly made her see everything so much clearer.

'It is my afternoon off,' Sheila said petulantly.

'Of course, Sheila. Am I likely to forget? If Mr Trenchard is held up, I shall take Hannah myself.' She plonked the mug, barely touched back on the table. 'I've got to go out. I'll be back by one, Sheila, don't worry.'

'I've an appointment – '

'I said I'd be back.'

'There are a lot of promises made in this house – ' Sheila began, and then as if thinking she might have gone too far, shut her mouth tight like a clam shell shutting.

'And what does that comment mean, Sheila?'

'Nothing.'

'It had better not,' Joy said sharply. She kissed her daughter again, let herself out of the kitchen. In the hall she slipped into her white cashmere coat, checked herself in the mirror over the console table, picked up her car keys and let herself out of the front door and raced through the rain to her car.

She found a florist open and spent so much on flowers that she had to use a credit card to pay for them. As she watched the girl slide her American Express card into the machine the thought crossed her mind that perhaps she should use her cards with enthusiasm during the next few weeks – hit him where it hurt. On a small card she scrawled two words. *Sorry, Joy.*

'We can deliver if you want, we've a Sunday service.'

'No, thanks. There'll be someone there.'

She drove towards Chelsea and wondered why she was doing so. She could have written, could have telephoned even. She could have had the flowers sent. But she felt she had to do this in person. Even if she did not see him, taking the flowers herself, hopefully, would make the apology appear truly sincere, all the other ways were too easy. She felt certain he would understand the gesture.

Barty was in and although he did not normally receive people without an appointment he made an exception for Joy. He was impressed, she had courage, there were not many who would face his anger the next day.

'Barty, I can't apologise enough,' Joy stepped forward her face half concealed by the huge bouquet. 'You can see how embarrassed I am, I wouldn't normally buy such a vulgar profusion of flowers.'

'They're lovely, Joy. My favourites, all of them.' He grinned as he relieved her of the huge bunches of flowers and laid them carefully on a table. 'I'll arrange them myself.' He nodded.

'Apart from letting you know how ashamed I am at my behaviour last night, I felt I had to come, I didn't want the maid, Sylv, to get into trouble. I know your strict rules.'

'I've dismissed her.'

'Oh, Barty, no. Oh, how awful. That makes everything worse. She's worked for you for years. We made her get the drink, you know.'

'She needn't have.'

'But you know Gloria when she wants something, no one

can resist Gloria's powers of persuasion.' She laughed a tiny, useless laugh. 'And we were only a little tiddly.' She rushed on recklessly. 'I mean no harm was done, was it?' There was an anxious tone to the last question since her own memory of the end of the night before, and her part in it, was vague to say the least.

'You know why I control the drink the way I do? Let you all get a bit sozzled so as you enjoy the party and then sober you all up before you go?'

Joy shook her head to show she had no idea.

"Cause one of my best mates killed himself drunk driving.'

'I'm sorry.'

'He had every right to kill himself but not the poor little bird with him. He got drunk in my house, and I vowed I'd never have anything like that on my conscience again.'

'Oh Lord. I'm sorry. It was my fault entirely. I was fed up.' An awkward silence descended. Joy could not think what else to say.

'You got off a bit better than your friend Kate,' he said suddenly.

'Kate?'

'Kate Howard – dull little mouse of a woman. She passed out after telling her duller husband to "sod off".' Barty laughed loudly at the memory and Joy, sensing his anger was long over, managed to join in.

'What you going to do about that bastard of a husband of yours, then?' Barty had stopped laughing as abruptly as he had started and his expression was serious now.

'I'm going to divorce him,' Joy heard herself say, to her complete astonishment. 'Yes, divorce would seem the only sensible action,' she added trying to inject a confidence into her voice she was far from feeling.

'That's my girl, and about time too. Stay to lunch, talk about it with me if you like.'

'Barty, I'd love to but I promised my little girl I'd take her to the zoo. Charles had promised to take her but I can't rely on him turning up.'

'I like that.' Barty nodded his head sagely. 'Never let the nipper down, that's how it should be. Tell you what . . .' he paused and looked at her with a strange expression, almost as if he was shy. 'I wouldn't mind joining you both.' He grinned, sheepishly.

'Barty, we'd love you to come. Two-thirty, at my place?'

'Right on.' He nodded his head with satisfaction.

'Then I'll know I'm really forgiven.' She smiled at him.

'I wasn't angry with *you* in the first place.' He laughed, putting his arm under her elbow and guiding her to the door. Even as he did so Joy realised it was the first time she had ever known Barty touch anyone, other than a handshake. At the door he paused.

'You like Gloria, don't you?' he asked.

'Why, yes.' She looked at him curiously, wondering why he asked. 'She's a good friend to me.'

'And what makes a good friend?'

'She's loyal and loving, she gives you her time. And I admire her enormously.'

'Why?'

'Mainly, I think, because she doesn't give a damn about what anyone thinks of her. I don't think Gloria knows what fear is.'

'And you do?'

'Don't we all?' Joy laughed nervously, surprised by the intensity of Barty's expression.

'You trust her?'

'I'd trust Gloria with my soul.'

'You're lucky. I think I could do with a mate like that.' He was smiling as he opened the door for her.

As soon as Joy had gone Barty went to his study. He rang for his butler and told him to send Sylv to him. Within five minutes Sylv was reinstated. He took a call from Gloria who was sufficiently apologetic also to be forgiven. Then he faxed Charles's law firm announcing he would be dispensing with their services in future. He made a note for his personal assistant to inform all his contacts of what action he had taken – where Barty went everyone else would follow.

Wandering about the zoo, a place he had not been to in years, Barty could not remember when he had enjoyed an afternoon so much. To Joy's embarrassment he insisted on thanking her time and again for permitting him to come. It was raining and cold and they only had a short time before it was dusk and the zoo closed. They returned reluctantly to Barty's Rolls-Royce, all excitedly planning another visit when the weather was better and they could stay longer.

Joy never knew why she asked him back for nursery tea, but she did, and he accepted with surprising alacrity. As she watched him playing snap with Hannah, after sausages and chips followed by jelly which he had eaten with gusto, Joy wondered if she was not watching a lonely man who, although he might declare he disliked children, deep down wanted a family just like this but knew it was something he could never have. He was like a hungry child in a Dickens novel who, having been found looking through the window at a happy family, had been allowed in.

He had kept saying he must go and did not, but finally he was putting on his coat. He turned to her.

'My autobiography – you're on, girl.'

'I beg your pardon?' She knew she looked astonished.

'You heard.' He was grinning.

'Wonderful, but why?'

'I don't like bastards who walk out on their kids,' he said simply, and quickly slipped out of the door as if he was saying too much, allowing too much of himself to be known.

chapter **thirteen**

It was as well it was Sunday. Crispin rarely drove and consequently his ideas of road management did not necessarily coincide with those of other road users. Crispin's policy was to set off in the direction he wished to go – and just go. He did stop at red lights and junctions; he was fully aware of the danger if he did not. But roundabouts were a different matter: he went into them without pausing, oblivious to the mayhem he invariably left behind him. Neither he nor Charlotte possessed a motor since neither of them fully approved of them – they took taxis and relied on other people. He had borrowed this 2CV from an artist friend. He felt less revulsion for this particular brand mainly, he thought, because it was so unlike a normal car.

He wished it wasn't raining, driving was hazardous enough because of road hogs without the addition of rain, he thought, as he drove the little car off the slip road on to the motorway, totally ignoring the large articulated lorry which was already in the lane he chose.

Perhaps when he was a millionaire he might have to have a car – he shuddered at the thought. Perhaps a vintage Bristol would not be so vulgar, he would have to discuss it with Charlotte when he returned.

He was in a very good mood. Last night at one of their dinners, not only had Charlotte excelled herself with the food, but an old friend had asked permission to bring a friend who turned out to be the banker of Crispin's dreams. Everything was set up over the port and cheese, no having to wait for decisions. He knew Charlotte would have liked to have accompanied him but he had resisted her requests. He wanted to do all this alone – she was too clever by half and might hijack the proceedings. He could only rely on Charlotte being sweet and submissive inside their house. Outside it she was, he knew, far more hard-headed than he would ever be.

He glanced at his watch. Ten-thirty. With luck he would be at his uncle's within the hour – reluctantly he had to admit that motorways had made travelling so much quicker. He had planned on an hour to persuade the old codger and then he would be out of the house by lunchtime. He wished his uncle lived in Oxford rather than Cambridge, there were better restaurants there, but he'd try the Blue Boar. He had many a good lunch there as an undergraduate when he visited on union business.

In fact he was later than he had planned: as always when in Cambridge, he found himself seduced by the beauty of the Backs and the chapel of King's College rising mysterious and ethereal from the hazy mist of the drizzle. He saw a car moving out from a parking space and, neatly, he thought, swung the 2CV over the road and slipped in. A burly man driving a Mercedes, who had been waiting patiently for the place, banged his fist on the steering wheel and stuck two fingers in the air at Crispin. Crispin acknowledged the gesture with a gracious inclination of his head, slipped on his coat, locked the car and walked quickly over the bridge towards the college.

He stood for a moment, oblivious to the rain, and breathed in deeply, as if inhaling the sheer beauty and magnificence of the place. Two Fellows emerged from the chapel and, with gowns billowing, stalked self-importantly across the lawn in the centre of the court. Crispin watched them with admiration as they walked across the grass from which all others were banned. What a life they must lead, rooms in these stunning buildings, High Table, civilised people to talk to, time to think. That is what he should have done, instead of rushing into trade. He should have stayed on at Oxford as an academic, become a Fellow and undoubtedly have ended his days as the Master of a College, a life far more suitable to someone as sensitive as himself. And then the thought came to him, hit him, made him suck in his breath with the sheer beautiful simplicity of it. Of course he could now! Once he had all those millions, he could return to academe. He wondered how Charlotte would react to the prospect. Even if she did not like the idea of living in Cambridge, it would not matter. They would have so much money they would be able to have a home in London and one here – he would have the best of both worlds.

Crispin had never visited his uncle at home but he knew Cambridge well enough to find the house off the Madingley Road with ease. He had anticipated that his relative would live in one of the solid, large Edwardian houses that were common in this part of the city, a period of architecture that he could appreciate even if he never wanted to live in one. When he pulled up in front of the address he shuddered visibly. He had never contemplated the thought that anyone he knew, let alone was related to him, might choose to live in such a monstrosity.

'What an abortion,' he said with horror as he looked at the offending house. In fact, the house was famous as a prime example of thirties' architecture with a preservation order on it, something Crispin would never have believed. It was built of concrete, painted white. There were no sharp edges to its profile, all was a symphony of curves. Even the windows, large and steel-framed, swept gracefully around the sides of the house. To appreciative eyes the house looked like a liner, docked in a wild garden where shrubs had been allowed to grow in unchecked profusion. To Crispin, it should have a large stash of Semtex placed under it.

'My dear Crispin. It is Crispin, isn't it?' Simon Westall stood in the doorway, towering over his nephew – Crispin had forgotten how large his uncle was, how the sheer bulk of the man had frightened him rigid as a child. He remembered how in the night when he could not sleep and his sadistic nanny would not let him have a night light, he had convinced himself that this particular uncle was the giant who ate Englishmen. He had not expected him, as an old man, still to be larger than himself.

'Yes, it's me, Uncle. Did Cousin John tell you I'd be calling?' He spoke briskly, endeavouring to quell such childhood fears.

'Yes. Such a surprise hearing from two of my nephews in such a short space of time. Dulcett, come here, it's my nephew. Such excitement . . .'

Crispin had the grace to feel guilty at the genuine warmth of his uncle's welcome.

'Come in, dear boy, come in.'

Crispin found himself in a surprisingly spacious hall, white-painted like the outside, an uncarpeted, well-constructed oak staircase leading off from the end, and with good, sturdy, oak doors.

Crispin approved of the excellent carpentry – he might like the interior if only he could forget the exterior. The paintings on the walls he could never like however, far too abstract and modern for his choice. He preferred not to look at them, feeling they assailed his fine senses.

A dark-haired woman with large breasts on a slim frame, fine bone structure, huge luminous eyes and, despite her fifty-odd years, considerable beauty, smiled shyly at him.

'Whatever you do, don't call me Aunt Dulcett,' she laughed with a delightful low chuckle as she held out her hand to be shaken. Surprisingly Crispin found himself stirred by her – unusual, for he did not normally find himself attracted to older women. But he could just imagine the comfort and security he would feel with his head cradled on those fine breasts, white they would be and finely marbled . . .

'Dulcett . . .' His voice was husky as he spoke. She laughed at him and he realised in one appallingly embarrassing instant that she knew what he had been thinking. 'How do you do,' he said, and the danger passed. For Crispin was appalled at the rough, calloused hand he found himself offered and he let go of it as quickly as possible. There was no way he would allow such hands to touch his tender body. No woman should have skin like that, like a navvy, he thought, as he smiled his most winning of smiles.

He was ushered into a large room which, in a normal house, would have been a drawing room but in this house was a mixture of sitting room, studio and dining room judging by the table already set for a meal. Crispin could not stop his lip curling with disapproval at the heavy, chunky, gaudy china on the table. The whole room was a mélange of objects of the cottage-industry type, rough rush matting on the floor, books cluttering every surface and the unmistakable smell of turpentine in the air. Crispin, who worshipped order and neatness, was doomed to feel an alien in it.

'You'll lunch with us?' Simon was smiling broadly at him.

'I wouldn't dream of imposing, Uncle. I just meant to stay for five minutes, have a chat.'

'We wouldn't hear of such a thing, would we, Dulcett? We shall have so much to catch up on after all these years.'

'I've cooked for three,' Dulcett said moving away, presumably to the kitchen. Despite her hands, Crispin once again found himself admiring her: he liked the way she walked, head held high, an almost regal walk.

'Beautiful, isn't she?' Simon was grinning proudly. 'When I met her I thought she was the most beautiful creature I had ever set eyes upon, I never dreamt that she would get more beautiful as the years passed – and did you note her knockers? Lovely, aren't they?'

Crispin found himself blushing for his uncle. What a disgusting way to talk! In Crispin's view old men did not notice women's breasts, let alone comment upon them. 'I didn't even know you were married, Uncle,' Crispin said stiffly, his mind racing, wondering if she might make things more difficult for him, trying to gauge how intelligent she might be. He knew he need not worry about Simon's level of intelligence, it was well known in the family that he was not very good at anything – particularly painting, Crispin thought as he avoided looking at the lurid pictures, in various stages of completion, scattered about the room.

'I'm not. Never have been.' Simon laughed loudly at the shocked look on Crispin's face. 'Dulcett and I have lived together for twenty years now. You wouldn't want me to be unconventional, would you?' He threw his head back and Crispin averted his face from the display of ugly fillings as his uncle roared with amusement.

'Unconventional? I'm afraid I don't understand,' Crispin said limply.

'I believe in conventions, as an artist I toe the line, you see. It would be too unconventional of me to be married.' And he was laughing again, at what Crispin hadn't the least idea – as always jokes were a mystery to him.

'Is this your work?' Crispin tried to inject enthusiasm into his voice, knowing he was going to have to talk about the pictures sooner or later.

'Yes, but the sculptures are Dulcett's.'

'They're wonderful,' Crispin said insincerely, forcing himself to look at the strident colours of his uncle's paintings and the large, lumpen, ugliness of Dulcett's sculptures, which at least explained the state of her hands. He was puzzled by the paintings. Julius had several examples of his brother's work, but they were not like these. Crispin had always thought them rather poor imitations of Augustus John. 'You've changed your style quite dramatically,' he said.

'I still do the old potboilers, but this is the real work.' Simon waved his hands at the large canvases, all of which, as far as Crispin could make out, were of the same subject, a tree of life or some such allied theme, he assumed.

'Potboilers?' Crispin asked, innocently, he hoped. This was a good indication, serious artists who stooped to such work were seriously hard up, he thought.

'Still lifes, odd portraits, that sort of stuff. I've got to keep the shekels coming in somehow, now your publishing house rarely pays a dividend.'

'Not my publishing house, Uncle.' Crispin smiled but in his haste it wasn't one of his more charming ones but emerged rather unctuously.

'What's gone wrong, Crispin? Whenever I ask Julius I don't seem to get anywhere.'

'Ah well, it's rather a long story,' Crispin said apologetically, hardly able to believe his luck. He had expected an uphill struggle to get Simon to listen and here was the old boy asking to be told.

'Sherry?'

'Thank you.'

Crispin, once started, was soon in fine form explaining Westall and Trim's problems, in depth, to his more than receptive audience. They were soon joined by Dulcett with their meal. All through lunch Crispin continued, patiently answering the many questions showered upon him. He really had to congratulate himself on how well he was doing. He never once blamed Julius – blood was a funny thing he knew from experience. No, instead he gave a masterly dissertation on the state of publishing in Britain in the nineties, and the hopelessness of Westall's position. It was just as well he was so engrossed in his own cleverness, for otherwise he would have had problems consuming the nettle soup, the vegetable cutlets, and the execrable parsnip wine.

'What's the solution, then, Crispin?'

'Please don't think me ungrateful, Uncle, for what I'm about to say. I love Uncle Julius, I owe him so much, but – ' He paused dramatically. 'We need younger blood, we need a big injection of capital.'

'Well, don't look to me for it.' Simon gave one of those laughs which Crispin was finding increasingly unpleasant on his ears. 'Dulcett and I haven't two halfpennies to rub together, have we, my darling?'

'But we're happy.' Dulcett put out her hand, took hold of her lover's and squeezed it. 'And we've this beautiful house.'

'And a bloody great mortgage . . .' Simon said gloomily, helping himself to another glass of parsnip wine which Crispin hurriedly refused, using the need to drive as an excuse.

'But I thought . . .' Crispin began delicately, and coughed, thus indicating that he was treading on ground far too personal.

'The potboilers don't pay the bills, old boy. I had to raise money on the house about ten years ago. The point is, Crispin, we're getting on, Dulcett and me. It's always been my dream to settle in Tuscany, better for the old bones.' Crispin flinched, prepared for the raucous laugh, but for once it wasn't coming. 'Your cousin John hinted that you might be interested in buying me out?'

'Well, yes.'

'How much?'

Crispin's mind was scudding about. The old boy had said that John had hinted, did that mean John hadn't mentioned any exact sums? What if he said £200,000 instead of the three he'd planned, or knocked the odd fifty thousand off? He stroked his chin, he always felt the gesture added a certain gravitas to his persona when he did so. Best not risk it, not when everything was going so well.

'Three hundred thousand,' he said quickly, before he could change his mind.

'Yes, that's what John said.' It was Uncle Simon's turn to stroke his chin as he studied his nephew carefully from under his bushy eyebrows. 'I think I might consider it for another fifty thousand.'

'That's more than your share is worth.' Cripin spoke quite sharply. How dare the old codger ruin it when everything was going so smoothly?

'Now, but not if you get bought out by some American multiple with more money than you and I can ever imagine.'

'But none of us would ever let that happen to Westall and Trim.' Crispin injected a fine degree of emotion into the sentence, only to be rewarded by a cynical snort from Simon.

Perhaps the family was wrong, perhaps they had misjudged Simon's ability all these years.

'What I don't understand, Crispin, is, if things are as bad as you say, why are you risking such a lot of money? A young chap like you could lose everything.'

'I'll be straight with you, Uncle. It's the young blood and expertise that's needed. With me as a shareholder I can get capital, I know I can. I've banking friends, you see . . .'

'I don't, but I suppose I have to take your word for it. It wouldn't be nice to lie to your old uncle now, would it?' Simon leant across the table at him, menacingly, Crispin felt like he was a little boy again and Uncle was frightening him . . .

'Could you imagine me doing anything so dastardly?' Crispin's perfect white teeth flashed. 'There's just one thing, I'd prefer you not to mention anything to Uncle Julius, not just yet, not until we're sure. He's not been too well recently, I don't want the dear man unduly worried.'

'Ill? Nothing serious?' Simon leant forward anxiously.

'No, no. Just a nasty bout of flu he's had difficulty shaking off. You know Julius, fit as a flea.'

'I'll think about the offer. I won't worry Julius.'

'But I need a decision,' Crispin said.

'Then you're going to have to wait, young man. It's not every day I have to contemplate selling my heritage.'

'When would you let me know?'

'I'd like a few days to think about it. Now, tell us all about your wife. Any children?'

Crispin had to endure another hour of their company before he thought courtesy could allow him to take his leave. The initial guilt he had felt upon meeting his uncle had completely disappeared, destroyed by boredom and irritation that he was not going home with a decision.

Crispin's 2CV had not cleared the outskirts of Cambridge before Simon was on the telephone. Dulcett could have told Crispin that Simon had never felt it necessary to honour a promise.

'Julius? It's me. Odd thing's just happened . . .' And he told Julius of Crispin's visit and his offer.

'I'm not surprised,' Julius said calmly. 'Don't take it. When I croak they'll sell the whole bang shoot and your share will be worth millions.'

'Crispin said they would never sell.'

'Don't you believe it, Simon. My dear son and daughter will be in the marketplace before I'm cold.'

'But your own son advised me to accept, said they would never sell.'

'Did he, now? When?'

'A couple of days ago. It was he who telephoned to say Crispin was coming and to advise me to accept. But I've asked for more.'

'Very commendable, Simon.' The irony in Julius's voice was completely lost on his brother.

'But if you're right, I could be an old old man before I saw anything. You're as fit as a fiddle, fitter than me, aren't you, Julius? Crispin said you'd been unwell, nasty attack of flu or something? You are all right, aren't you?'

At the other end of the line, Julius frowned. He should be straight with his brother, should tell him what the doctors said. But he couldn't. If he said it, it might happen even sooner. And Simon's concern, what was it for? Concern for him, or concern that he might be making the wrong decision? He didn't blame him. Why shouldn't he look after his best interests?

'I'm fine,' he said shortly, suddenly feeling very weary.

'So you don't think I should sell then?'

'No. You'll regret it.'

'Thanks, Julius, then I won't, that's a promise. Fancy buying any pictures?'

Julius laughed, he already possessed going on for fifty of his brother's works, all purchased for double their value, all purchased with love and, if he was honest, a sense of guilt that the company didn't pay Simon more. 'I'm a bit strapped myself these days, Simon,' he said apologetically.

'These are hard times, Julius, old boy, hard bloody times.'

Julius slept soundly that night, Simon didn't. He and Dulcett sat up long into the night with several bottles of parsnip wine, and one of elderflower, as they went over the best course of action.

'But Julius could live for ever,' Simon kept repeating.

chapter **fourteen**

Gloria had long ago decided that if she had been God she would never have created Monday. No matter how she planned, how organised she thought she was on Sunday evening, by Monday morning everything had gone to pot. And this morning was to turn out to be a cracker.

The traffic was heavy as she slowly edged her way across Albert Bridge towards her office. It would have been faster by tube but Elephant did not like public transport. People assumed it was because he was small and was easily frightened, but Gloria knew better. Her dog was a snob. So, each morning she braved the worsening traffic chaos of London while Elephant sat grandly beside her barking instructions at other road users.

Gloria drove her Golf down the ramp to the cavernous underground car park beneath Shotters, and into her allotted bay. She might not be happy working in this huge publishing house but this car park and her parking privilege, she knew, saved her a small fortune each year in parking tickets and fines.

In reception she stood waiting for the lift, clutching Elephant close – he did not like lifts either – and pushed her way into the next one that stopped. There was no need to say which floor she wanted: at this time of the morning it stopped at every floor. No one spoke, everyone stood in that dazed manner of office workers returning after a weekend, like battle-fatigued soldiers in the frightening lull before the next assault.

On the fourth floor she got out. Immediately outside the lift, on the deep red wall, was the gold shape of a scimitar, Blades's – this particular branch of Shotters – logo. As she walked into her office, the telephone was ringing.

'This will not do, Gloria,' a voice screeched at her without preamble.

'Belle! My, you're up bright and early.' Gloria tried to sound pleased but Bella Ford was nobody's favourite author, certainly not first thing on Monday morning.

'You have to be up early to stay ahead of the rats in this game,' Bella said unpleasantly, and Gloria's heart sank. Trouble!

'What can I do for you, Bella?'

'Have you seen the latest *Publishing News*?' Bella demanded. Gloria sighed. Monday was the day when this type of call was common, when those authors who bothered to take the trade press had read something over the weekend that displeased them.

'Yes,' said Gloria, already on the defensive and racking her brains for anything in the last edition about Shotters and Bella that might have offended her.

'Did you see what Pewter's are laying out in publicity for Philomel Greensward's next book?'

'No, I didn't.' Gloria did not ask how much. She knew she need not bother, that Bella would quickly tell her – which she did.

'Philomel's useless, written out. I sell more than her but I don't get a budget like that.'

'You mustn't believe all you read, Bella. There's a lot of lies told and exaggeration in this business. Why, only the other day I saw an author, who shall be nameless, claiming she had sold over a million worldwide and I know for a fact her book is about to be remaindered.'

'Don't try and be smart with me, Gloria.'

'Belle, your own publicity budget hasn't been decided yet. As soon as it is I'll let you know,' Gloria said, lying through her teeth. If there was one rule in publishing it was never to let the author know what the publicity spend was to be – it was never enough for them. Not unless, as Pewter's had done, the sum was so vast that it was worth banging the drum to awaken interest early from the booksellers. 'Peter Holt is taking a personal interest in all the artwork for your publicity,' she said in a soothing voice. 'And we're all so looking forward to you coming to the sales conference. You know you're everyone's favourite author.' Gloria pulled a face at this bare-faced lie. Bella was to be at the sales conference because with her fruity vocabulary and her ability to consume copious amounts of alcohol and still stand up, she was a favourite with the reps – the only people she was ever nice to.

'I'm looking forward to the conference too. At least with the sales force one is meeting fellow professionals,' Bella snapped. Gloria chose to ignore that thrust. 'And I'm glad Peter is condescending to take an interest. But I can't be soft-soaped or distracted from my original point. I'll expect an equivalent sum, Gloria, I'm warning you.'

'It's not up to me, Bella.'

'Then make certain those people who decide know my strong feelings.'

'I will, Bella . . . I will – '

But the line had gone dead without even a thank-you. 'Grasping, ill-mannered, cow . . .' Gloria muttered to herself.

As if she had been waiting for the call to end, her secretary Rachel popped her head over the top of the partition.

'Now or later?' Rachel grinned apologetically.

'Now – why not? After Bella, what could possibly be worse?' Gloria laughed.

'Production are screeching for dates for Heather Gardens' – '

'Sod . . . I haven't finished the line edit. I thought we had a good two months to play with,' she said, turning to the shelf behind her desk and manhandling a large typescript off it. 'I've still a third to do, then Heather has got to have it back. She works fast but . . . we need one month at least. Why the sudden panic?' she asked as she riffled through the pages of typescript as if hoping to find she had done more than she thought.

'They've had to bring the publication date forward a month. Apparently Grace Bliss is having trouble getting the end of her book right, so the whole list is being shuffled.'

'Again? That bloody woman is incapable of delivering on time. Production should realise that, make allowances. Why wasn't I told?'

'You were, Gloria. Last week.' Rachel pulled her funny face again, the one she always used when apologising or when she thought the going might be getting rough. It was an expression which was unnecessary, working for Gloria. Rachel was envied by the other junior staff for having Gloria as her boss. She was not one of those women, abundant at Shotters, who found it necessary to prove their seniority by behaving like Attila the Hun. Responsibility sat lightly on Gloria's shoulders. If she shouted it was only to equals and those senior to herself, never the juniors.

'Was I?' Gloria's voice was resigned.

'I put the memo on your desk myself.'

They both looked at the paper-strewn desk, a desk which looked as if no order could ever be achieved from it. Gloria grimaced and shrugged her shoulders at the muddle. 'I'm sure you did, Rachel, my fault entirely.' She smiled up at Rachel. 'Be a love, make me some coffee?'

'Sure? Dieting or not?'

'Not.'

She hung up her coat, checked Elephant's water bowl, sharpened four pencils and was straightening the typescript when Rachel returned with her coffee.

'Bless you. Hold all my calls, say I'm in a meeting. All that is except – '

'Clive?' Rachel asked, laughing.

'Yes. I know what you're thinking but don't say it and ruin a perfectly good relationship, will you?' Gloria said good-naturedly.

'Don't forget you've got to see the art manager this morning over Bella's stuff and Adam in production would like a word and – '

'For God's sake, what else?'

'Top floor want you. Logan has summoned you.' Rachel rolled her eyes heavenward.

'Give me an hour of peace with this. I might go home with it this afternoon and work on it there.'

She chewed the end of her pencil looking abstractedly out of the window at the blank side wall of the building opposite. What could Logan want? He was the chief accountant in charge of overall finance and a person one rarely saw unless it was bad news. But her sales figures were up this year, not like most. She had no idea what the summons was for.

Gloria turned her attention to Heather Gardens' *Dawn Chorus*. Six hundred and fifty pages of double-spaced A4, four hundred and fifty edited, another two to go. As she read Gloria's attention was total. This was what she loved to do best. Her only regret was that she was being harassed and this type of editing needed to be done slowly, patiently. Other editors eagerly farmed this work out to juniors, not Gloria. She did not do it for all her authors – there was not time. But someone like Heather, whom she had discovered, whose hand she had held through various writing crises, numerous writer's blocks, whose book she was nursing through every stage of the process – Heather's she insisted on doing. Some authors resented this process, argued over each comma altered, but Heather wasn't one of those. She saw the edit as Gloria did, a polishing process. Taking the book line by line, ferreting out the disorderly syntax here, the repetition there, improving, honing the whole way, making it perfect without removing Heather's voice. It was a challenge, and ideally one over which author and editor worked in unison. For an hour Gloria worked steadily.

The art manager, Bart Friars, was dealt with quickly. He had wanted her to see the proofs of the jacket for Bella's new book. As usual there was a rush on – there always was. Publishing dates, ideally, should be fixed a good year ahead – the publisher's catalogues had to be produced, the sales team needed time to whip up interest with the booksellers. But it was not an ideal world. Too often dates had to be altered: frequently it was the writers themselves not finishing on time, occasionally the legal department stepped in, unhappy with a possibly libellous passage in one book which sent the whole list of books into a reshuffle. In this case, Bella's new book, due out next June and one which they were promoting heavily, would, they had discovered, coincide with a mega-seller from Tudor's by the American writer Tympany Fox. This news had sent publicity into a spiral of hysterical despair. With Tympany, all slink, sex and seductiveness, in town to promote it, Bella's fluffy faded prettiness would not get a look in with the profile writers and chat shows. Hence this rearranged schedule to get her out in May. It would not have been so bad if Bella and her agent had not rejected the first two jacket roughs. There had once been a time when an author was presented with a jacket design and if they did not like it they had to lump it. Now, any self-respecting agent inserted a clause in their contracts demanding the right of consultation in all aspects of the production process.

'If the old bitch doesn't like this one, I'll murder her personally for you, Bart,' she promised as she slipped from the art department and next door into production.

Adam Preston presided over his domain in a permanent state of dyspeptic confusion. It was he who selected and bought the paper, sometimes buying tons in advance, like a futures broker on the market. He chose the typeface, decided on the design of the book. He haggled with the printers to get the best deal. He checked the artwork and liaised with the sales force. He pulled together all the various strands that went into producing a book. Nothing ever went smoothly no matter how hard everyone tried. As she had suspected he, too, was in a Bella panic.

She listened to his anguish over the number of changes Bella had insisted upon making to the proofs. Gloria apologised for her inability to control this author, and commiserated with him over the row that was now brewing with the printers about who was to pay for the changes. She tutted patiently. Bella was one of the worst at having second thoughts, she explained. Now he was worrying what they would do if she did not like the latest jacket design.

'Don't worry, Adam, I'll take the artwork over personally and I'll make her like it.'

'Sales are screaming for jackets. What else are they to sell on?'

'Her charm perhaps?' Gloria smiled sweetly. 'Maybe not,' she snorted.

She grabbed a quick coffee before taking the lift to the top floor and the senior executives' offices. Compared with the bustle downstairs it was a bit like entering a church up here where silence reigned and the most beautiful of the receptionists smiled charmingly but blankly at her.

'Gloria Catchpole for Logan Perriman.'

'Oh, yes, Gloria. Logan is expecting you,' the girl said in a soft sing-song voice as she picked up the telephone. 'Pandora? India here, Gloria Catchpole for Logan.' She smiled up at Gloria as she spoke, as if including her in some sort of conspiracy. It was an odd thing in publishing these days, Gloria thought, everyone had such daft names. She could only presume that these were the latest crop of débutantes' names. Publishing paid such lousy salaries that only girls with a daddy who would help out could afford to work here in the junior positions. Pandora, tall and willowy with an abundant mane of hair and dressed from head to toe in St Laurent, sashayed towards her.

'Gloria Catchpole?' she queried, smiling an empty model's smile. Gloria longed to snap, 'Yes, I am, Senior Commissioning Editor for Blades, with Shotters from the beginning and important.' She did not, of course, merely followed dutifully like a little dog along the wide swathe of blue carpet to the large mahogany door of Logan's office.

'Gloria, great to see you. How's things?' Logan, all six feet and ten and a half stone of tightly coiled energy, sprang across the huge expanse of office and was taking her by the hand and pulling her into the room as she shook it. 'Coffee? Perrier?'

'Gin and tonic, please, ice no lemon,' Gloria said with malicious satisfaction. Logan, she knew, never drank and disapproved strongly of those who did, especially during office hours. But a summons here could only mean bad news so Gloria reckoned she needed something strong.

'Well, if that's what you want,' said Logan, looking pointedly at his watch.

'Make that a large one,' said Gloria to Pandora as she swayed towards a bookcase, pressed a concealed button and a drinks cupboard appeared. How naff, thought Gloria.

Logan waited until Gloria had her drink and Pandora had silently let herself out of the room. Bet she listens on the intercom, thought Gloria.

'As I was saying, Gloria, how are things?'

'Apart from the normal Bella panic, fine,' she lied.

'I wish I could say the same. Times are bad, Gloria, couldn't be worse.'

'Don't worry, Logan. You know publishing as well as I do. There are always these ups and downs. What specifically? Christmas orders not looking so good?'

'Disastrous.'

'It'll pick up, it always does. All those last-minute shoppers panic-buying and before you know where you are the twenty-four-hour ordering lines will be glowing.'

'I hope you're right.'

'And it always gets better come spring and summer. Remember what old Gladys Hellman used to say? "Get the bums on the beaches, only time the buggers read."' Gloria hooted with laughter at the fond memory of Gladys who had worked as Peter's assistant and general factotum for years until she had been run over by a number 39 bus which, given the scarcity of buses on that route, was an achievement in itself.

'It's more complicated these days, Gloria, as well you know. Too many books, that's what I keep telling Peter.'

Gloria clutched her glass tightly. No editor liked to hear

those words. It was true, of course. The number of new titles every year was reaching monumental proportions yet the size of the reading public remained static. But it was always others' lists that should be cut, never one's own.

'I've been looking at your sales figures, they're good.'

'They are, aren't they? Better than most, well over target,' she said pointedly. The target system had been brought in a few years back and everyone hated it. Now they all had goals to reach. Each editor had a set amount of money they were expected to earn the company each year and woe betide them if they slipped below this mark. Their projected sales figures, on what they anticipated each book to make, were critical rather than the hit-and-miss affair they once had been. Gloria would frequently be over-optimistic on some but had never once slipped below her target, using the expedient of always downgrading projected figures of the Bellas of this world just to be on the safe side.

'Yes, they are good, but rather by manipulation than judgement, wouldn't you say, Gloria?' Logan smiled his icy smile, sitting bolt upright and rigid opposite her. Gloria found herself wondering what he would be like in bed. She could not imagine one part of his anatomy, even the most important part, being warm to the touch.

'I don't know what you mean,' Gloria said, smiling, because she was still distracted by the thought of the doubtful body heat of his penis.

'Look at these figures on Bella. You know damn well she'll sell almost double that. Come off it, Gloria. You write her down to puff the others up. It doesn't make sense and you know it.'

Gloria sat silent, she was not smiling now. It did make sense, if not accountancy sense. She knew that if she did not inflate the figures on some of her books they would never get published in the first place. No new author, unless well known to the public in some other field, ever sold thousands. It was her way of keeping her stable supplied with fresh talent, writers she would coax along so that by the third or fourth book the figures were becoming respectable and she could leave them to survive on their own.

'There's dead wood here, Gloria.'

'There's what?' Gloria slammed down her glass, splattering

its contents on the desk's leather surface. She hastily began to mop it up with a Kleenex. 'I'm sorry about that, but I can assure you there's no dead wood in my list,' she said angrily.

'For a start I can see a couple, if not more, we have got to drop. Concentrate on the earners.'

Gloria sat aghast as Logan in his dry, lifeless voice quoted figures of her authors who were in the various stages of beginning on the treacherous road of writing. If Shotters dropped them, their chance of being picked up by the others, especially now with publishing in one of its periodic doldrums, was remote. Logan was not exaggerating, times were harder but hardest for those writers who did not sell in mega-figures.

'Look at it this way, Logan,' Gloria began, fighting to keep her sense of outrage from her voice. 'What if Bella fell off the twig – now there's a pleasant thought . . .' She laughed, he did not. 'Seriously. If Bella and Shiel and all the big earners suddenly stopped writing, or were all killed in a bus on a writers' day out, say, where would we be? We need to be bringing on others to take their place.'

'Actuarially it's unlikely they'd all die or get writers' block together,' he said stiffly.

'They could move, go elsewhere to be published,' she said, with a sense of glee at the scenario that shot fear through the heart of all financial directors. 'I was over at Tudor's the other day. I could swear I recognised one of Shiel's typescripts on the senior fiction editor's desk.' Gloria had seen no such thing but it was worth a try, she reasoned with herself.

'And how could you possibly know it was hers?'

'Because I do, that's how. The first thing you learn as an editorial assistant is to read a manuscript upside down on somebody else's desk.' She was grinning, he was not.

'We look after all our top earners and they know it. They're loyal to us,' Logan said staunchly.

'If you think that, Logan, then you're naive and know bugger all about publishing. They're an egotistical bunch who'll leave at the drop of a hat if they think the pickings and the ego-massage will be better elsewhere.'

'I'm sorry, Gloria. This is getting us nowhere. Your list must be shortened. I know it's hard. It's always hard telling a writer their next book isn't good enough.'

'I won't say that to them, not one of them. It wouldn't be

true and imagine the damage it could do to their confidence. You want to know what I think, Logan? I think a few less ludicrous advances to some of our writers would sort out a lot of our problems. First novels are notoriously difficult to sell, as well you know. But those you picked out are getting there. Next time their figures will double and so on.' Logan moved uncomfortably in his chair. 'Look at that bloody awful book last year by Gail Storm. OK, the publicity generated good sales but remember the obscene advance we paid her? That will never be earned back. We need the good, reliable workhorses of writers to bring the money in for mad flights of fancy like Gail, who is unlikely to write another thing – if she wrote the last one,' Gloria said darkly. She had not liked Gail's book, in fact had refused to edit it. She had not come into the business to work with pornography, she'd said, and, give him his due, Peter had accepted her objection. She was not sure but she believed the damn book was taken on simply because the ex-model Gail was Hilary Holt's best friend – she knew Peter, anything for a quiet life.

'You don't seem to understand, Gloria. This is not a matter open to discussion. I asked you here to tell you, not to argue the toss with you.'

'We'll see about that.' Gloria was standing now and very angry. There were two things Gloria was passionate about: Elephant and her authors. 'You'll be hearing from me.' She turned, stormed from the room and into the reception hall. India stood up to greet her but Gloria swept past in the direction of Peter's office.

'You can't go in there,' India wailed, tripping down the hallway on her Manolo Blahnik shoes. 'Peter's in conference, he's not to be disturbed.'

With a defiant flourish Gloria opened the double doors to Peter's office.

'Gloria, what a nice surprise,' Peter said, looking up from the *Beano* he was reading.

At sight of her chief executive's reading matter, Gloria burst out laughing. 'Some conference,' she spluttered.

'What can I do for you?' Peter grinned back, threw down his comic and leant back in his chair. He was always pleased to see Gloria. She was so straight in her dealings and never played games. She was lovely too, she always had been, but was one of those women who, he thought, was improving with age – confidence suited her. 'What's the problem?'

'Either my list stays my way or I'm resigning.'

'Who have you been talking to? Logan? Ah well, I might have guessed. How about lunch? I'm free if you are. We'll thrash it out over a good bottle of claret. Always makes everything clearer, a good claret.' He grinned at her.

'Yes, I'm free.' She found herself calming down. 'I'll just go and tell Elephant.'

He took her to the Caprice. They ordered and he asked for the claret to be served as they waited for their food. Gloria did not waste time but went straight into the attack. Peter sat silent listening to her tirade, watching the emotions flit across her honest, expressive face. How he envied her, he thought, as he sipped the wine he had promised them both. This was how he had once been. There had been books he had felt so passionate about he sometimes used to wonder if he would kill for them.

For a good fifteen minutes Gloria spoke non-stop and then stopped suddenly, embarrassed as she became aware that their starter had arrived and she had not noticed and that Peter had not said a word.

'That's it.' She slumped back into her chair.

Peter looked at her for what seemed an age.

'God, Gloria, you're so lucky. You're still in love with it all, aren't you?'

'Yes, I am. But I'll be honest with you, I hate Shotters as it is now. I wish we could put the clock back, have it as it used to be.'

'You're not the only one. But this is progress.'

'How can it be if it stops new writers coming forward?'

He laughed. 'Tell you what. Just for twelve months don't take on anyone new, keep the Logans of the world happy.'

'We can't do that. If the agents twigged that, we wouldn't see anything worthwhile when we were ready.'

'We could prevaricate. Anything you find keep them dangling.'

'No, I won't do that. Who suffers when we hold back on typescripts for months at a time? The poor bloody authors. I've always prided myself on making quick decisions. Well, I used to, I've got a bit sloppy with my reading these past few months. No, I can't do that.'

'Enough publishers do.' He rubbed his chin with his hand. 'You win.'

'You mean my list stays?'

'Yes.'

'And I can still take on new talent?'

'Let's ration it for twelve months – say, two new writers, if you can find them.'

'Peter, thank you, thank you.' She grabbed at his hand and squeezed it but she noticed he did not smile. Still holding his hand she looked closely at him. 'You're not happy, Peter, are you?'

'Not very.'

'Do you want to talk?'

'There's not much to say, Gloria. I'm probably being stupid, I just feel discontented and what have I to be discontented about?'

'Quite a lot,' she said. And it was true. She knew he felt as she did about publishing, this conversation had proved that, and there was Hilary. How could he still be in love with her as she was now?

'Oh, it's nothing.' He shook his head and looked away embarrassed.

'Well, if you ever want to talk, I'm always around, you know that, don't you?'

'Yes, Gloria, I know. Thanks. We haven't been fair to you recently, have we?'

'Promoting that prat Norman Wilton over me annoyed me, yes,' she said, shaking her head defiantly.

'It wasn't my choice,' he said apologetically.

'Quite honestly, I don't see the point in owning a company if you are not in total control,' she answered sharply.

'Point taken. It's just that everything has become so large . . .' He leant forward. 'Look, Gloria, I understand why you're unhappy but don't do anything rash, not at the moment, will you?'

She looked at him with a puzzled expression, taken back by the intensity of his stare. 'No, all right, I won't.'

'Promise?'

'What is this?' She laughed. 'OK, I promise – Brownie's honour.' She joked. It was not necessary – even after all this time she knew she would promise him anything.

'How about some more claret?' He managed a smile.

'That would be lovely. Why not? Blow the office.' She grinned and removed her hand from his and he found he was disappointed that she had.

chapter **fifteen**

Each day of the following week involved a mish-mash of drama for all concerned.

Crispin, not having heard from his uncle Simon if the deal was on or not, had worked himself into a lather of fear and apprehension. Meeting Roz on the stairs he had snapped at her most unpleasantly. It was unnecessary but then, he felt, it was equally unnecessary of her to burst into tears. The sight of her mascara rolling unbecomingly in black rivulets down her cheeks was so unappealing that he marvelled that he could ever have gone to bed with her in the first place – he certainly did not want to again. He had begun to apologise for his behaviour when it struck him that he already had most of the information he required from her and, since she was as much in the dark about the Lepanto Trust as everyone else, now might be the best time to divest himself of her – and he told her so.

He returned to his own office feeling quite satisfied with his morning's work. He felt good for the first time since the weekend when he had seen Simon. But the feeling did not last and within the hour he was back to tearing out his hair with frustration.

His hand hovered frequently over the telephone receiver but he fought a battle of wills with himself and refrained from calling his uncle. He must not appear too keen or concerned or the old fool would smell a rat.

For the past two days he had resisted telephoning his cousin also. He did so on two counts: he so loathed the man that he couldn't bear to talk to him even at a distance, and he did not want John to know that anything was awry with his plans. He could just imagine the toad smirking at him if he sensed that Crispin's grand plan was about to fail.

Frustration finally won, however, and he called John at his bank. He was told that his cousin was in a meeting and could not possibly be interrupted. He had to wait two miserable hours until his call was returned.

'Meeting go well?' Crispin said airily.

'Meeting?' John answered, and Crispin smiled to himself, he had caught him out. Or had he? Was John making sure he knew there had been no such appointment? 'Fine, yes of course. Money rolling in,' John chuckled. 'So Crisp, what can I do for you?'

The knuckles of Crispin's hands whitened as he clasped the receiver with pent-up anger at the use of that name.

'I suddenly realised the other day that we had never had you and dear Poppy to our place. I thought perhaps a light dinner, say tomorrow?'

There was a self-important rustling of a diary's pages.

'Sorry, Crisp, no can do. New York beckons, I'm afraid.'

'Perhaps when you return?' Crispin tried to sound as pleasant as possible, hard in the circumstances.

'Hang on. I've just remembered. I have a cancellation – a client flying in from Japan has got himself held up in Bombay with engine trouble. I could manage tonight.'

'Tonight?' Crispin's mind was racing. If he said yes it implied he and Charlotte had no social life. If he did not, he might have days of this agony. Charlotte would not be happy, normally she liked several days to prepare for a dinner party. 'Why not? Wonderful.'

Five minutes later he was not so self-satisfied. Not once he had spoken to Charlotte.

'What the bloody hell do you mean? A dinner party tonight! It's out of the question, can't be done.'

'But, Charlotte, my sweet one, it's important to me. I must find out what Simon's about. This is the only way.'

'No.'

'Charlotte, please.'

He winced at the language as Charlotte harangued him. It was strange how forceful and coarse her language could become when away from their delightful home and ambience, he thought, as he held the telephone away from his ear.

'Very well, my darling. You're right, I should not have been so inconsiderate. I do understand. I'll get one of those catering Sloane types to come in and do it – save you the bother.'

'You'll do no such bloody thing!' Charlotte shrieked, just as he had known she would. If there was one thing his wife would never countenance it was someone else in her perfect kitchen, messing about with her precious *batterie de cuisine*.

Crispin had only met his cousin's wife once, at their wedding. The creature who stood on his doorstep at seven-forty bore no relation whatsoever to the sweet, fresh-faced bride he had remembered. This Poppy was hard-faced, Knightsbridge-chic and bored before she had even crossed the threshold. What was even worse, she smoked. Since none of their friends indulged in the disgusting habit this was a state of affairs that had never happened before. He saw the strained face of his wife as Poppy lit up without even the courtesy of a 'Do you mind?' He prayed she was not a chain-smoker. She was.

At such short notice, Charlotte had surpassed herself. The lightly seasoned consommé was masterly; the turbot in a gentle coating of subtly coloured sauce nantua was sublime; the crisp sorbet of peach was delicious; the rack of lamb, so moistly pink with its vegetables moulded into pretty castle shapes, was accompanied by a rowan sauce of such delicacy that Crispin could have wept at its excellence. Charlotte had arranged the salad that followed with such an eye for colour and design that he could have fallen in love with her all over again. Her cheese board was famous. And the flim-flam that followed was a delightful surprise.

It was a feast of taste, smell, colour – and Poppy left practically everything, being that abomination at a dinner party, a woman on a diet. John ate with such disgusting and noisy relish that it quite spoilt his compliments.

By the end of the meal, when Charlotte rose prettily and suggested that she and Poppy should withdraw, she was ashen-faced with despair.

Crispin placed several knobs of coal on the fire while the maid they always employed for dinner parties cleared the dishes. He collected the port decanter and walnuts and leant back in his chair. He was suddenly aware that John was looking anxiously about him.

'Something wrong, old chap?' Crispin asked.

'No, nothing,' said John, and slipped his hand into his jacket pocket and brought out a cigar case.

'No, thank you, I don't.' Crispin waved his hand at the offensive object John was offering him.

'Mind if I do?'

'No, no, carry on,' Crispin said almost hysterically. But then, he told himself, fighting to calm down, Poppy had done so much damage with her weed what was a bit more?

'I spoke to Uncle Simon. I told him we were coming here tonight.'

Crispin choked on his port with surprise and a dribble landed on his waistcoat, a particular favourite. He dabbed miserably at the stain.

'Sorry, didn't mean to startle you, Crisp.' John smirked at him.

'I wasn't startled. The damn port went down the wrong way. How is the dear old chap? I had a wonderful lunch with him and Dulcett. Quaint couple, aren't they? I've been meaning to get hold of him but, with one thing and another, I've been too busy.'

'Really?' John smirked again and Crispin marvelled at the paucity of facial expressions the man possessed. He noisily slurped from his port glass so that Crispin was made aware it was empty. 'You wouldn't have got hold of him,' he said once he had refilled his glass. 'He's in Tuscany.'

'Tuscany?' Crispin asked lightly, unsure of the significance of this news. 'He said nothing on Sunday.'

'Went as soon as he'd seen you. He's gone away to think what he should do, he says. I've got his number, of course. I think he's looking at property. Working out how much more he should screw out of you.'

'I couldn't go higher. I agreed top price with him.'

'Think you might have to, old boy. The old cove isn't nearly as stupid as he appears.'

'What do you think he'll do?' Crispin loathed himself for asking the question but, on the other hand, nothing could have contained his anxiety.

'Take it and hop off to Italy with his fat and horny-handed whore, no doubt.'

'Let's hope you're right. Some Stilton, John?'

At least Crispin bored John as much as vice versa so it was only half an hour later, after a tisane in the drawing room where they had found Poppy sitting with a tumbler of lemon barley water in her hand and a surprised expression on her face that she had not been offered a brandy, that they left.

Their car had barely started before Charlotte was rushing about the rooms opening windows and lighting a month's supply of scented candles.

'How could you, Crispin? How could you have invited such crass and vulgar people to our little nest?' Her pretty eyes brimmed with tears. Her pert white breast swelled becomingly over the top of the forget-me-not-sprigged Empire line dress she wore. Crispin could feel himself hardening at the sight and at the thought of the night ahead. She looked so distressed and agitated that he thought they should definitely play the virgin-bride-on-her-wedding-night ravished by her dastardly-brute-of-a-husband game. They both enjoyed that one immensely.

'I'm sorry, my sweet one. But it was business.' He leant forward and gently touched the white, marbled flesh so temptingly displayed.

'But we promised each other, Crispin. We promised never to let the horrible twentieth century into our home. You've let me down so badly.'

'Dearest heart. It's over. The bad man's gone away. You've only this bad man now. One who's going to bruise those pretty little breasts of yours.'

'Oh, Crispin, fuck you – and your stupid bloody games!' she shouted raucously, hit him hard across the face and rushed from the room slamming the door with such force that two particularly sensitively executed watercolours smashed to the floor.

Crispin fumbled towards the nearest chair and slumped into it, his face white with shock. What had gone wrong? What was happening? Why had she spoken to him like that? It was not allowed, not here. He could cope with most things but not that, not the loss of his wonderful, delicate, sweet world. And he put his face into his hands, as if to shut out the confusion.

chapter **sixteen**

To say that Charles Trenchard was surprised to find his bags packed and in the hall when he eventually returned home was something of an understatement.

He prodded a case with his foot and it fell on its side heavily. It was full. Joy was not playing games. It looked as if she meant business. Surely not?

'Oh, Lord,' he sighed, and scratched his head. If she was serious, why? She knew him, knew he always came back to her. She had forgiven him enough times in the past; it was reasonable for him to think that she would continue to forgive him. Of course, he thought, peering at his face in the hall mirror, it had been stupid of him to turn up at Silver's party with Penelope. But he had been drinking champagne, and Penelope had begged him to take her. He had never been able to resist a pretty woman's pleas.

What the hell had changed? He did not understand women. Joy had everything she could wish for – just look at this house and the lifestyle he gave her. She had known what he was like when they had married: he had never made a secret of his predilection for women. His mother had never complained about his father, so why should Joy? Indeed, she was more fortunate than his mother for he had hinted, broadly enough, that he did not mind in the least if she took a lover – provided she was discreet.

He looked again at his cases and wondered what she had forgotten to pack. In a strange way he felt a sense of relief. He had to admit this fling with Penelope was different from all the rest for she *was* different – intelligent, on his wavelength and beautiful, too. He had even begun to think he might be in love with her. But then, even taking into account Penelope's virtues over the usual bimbos he chose, he doubted if it would last, they never did.

It was not his day, he thought ruefully. The accountancy firm for whom he acted as consultant were none too pleased with him in view of the amount of suddenly cancelled business. This morning he had endured a painful interview with the senior partner. Charles had offended Barty Silver and, he was told, only a bloody fool did that. He could only assume the self-righteous poofter objected to him with Penelope. He aimed a kick at another case. Interfering bastard! No doubt he was behind this too. Joy would never have done it without someone goading her into it. How was he to handle her? He liked his women, but he loved Joy, this house, Hannah and, no, he had no intention of losing any of them – not even for Penelope. He would talk to Joy, calm her down, buy her a new piece of jewellery – that usually worked. Maybe they could go away for Christmas. He had always won her over in the past but, then, she had never packed his bags before. Best face her, he thought, get it over with, and he bounded up the stairs two at a time.

Joy was on the telephone and barely looked up as he entered the room, intent on listening to whoever was on the other end.

'Why are my bags in the hall?' he asked, in such a reasonable voice that this might have been an everyday occurrence. 'Am I going somewhere I don't know about?' He smiled, knowing it always made him look more handsome.

'Do you mind? I'm busy,' his wife said, looking at him coldly and placing her hand over the mouthpiece. She deliberately turned her back on him and continued with her conversation.

It was that action that made Charles lose his temper. He was not used to being ignored, and never by women. 'I'm talking to you.' He raised his voice.

'Excuse me a moment, Barty. Something's turned up . . .'

Charles wrenched the receiver from her hand. 'The "some-thing" is me, her husband, you jumped-up oik!' he shouted into the telephone before slamming it back on to its cradle.

'How dare you! That's my most important client.' She stepped back from him, rubbing her wrist which he had hurt.

'I want to talk to you – ' The telephone rang, Charles bent down and wrenched the socket from the wall. 'What are you playing at?' he demanded angrily.

Joy laughed, a shrill, ugly laugh. 'You have the audacity to ask me that? I'm not playing at anything, Charles. I've woken up at last. Woken up to the true bastard you are and the realisation that you're sick. You can't keep your prick in your pants, it's like an obsession with you.'

'My, my. The perfect, cool Joy talking dirty. I like that.' He threw back his head and laughed. 'There's hope for you yet!'

'Yes, there's certainly that. I've seen a solicitor and I want a divorce.' Joy faced him squarely and although she was speaking calmly it was a forced calm, for she was shaking with emotion. 'I've talked it over with her, and she says – '

'Her, did you say?'

'Yes, I thought I'd get a fairer hearing from a fellow female. I know you lot and the way you stick together.'

'Don't be paranoid, Joy, it doesn't suit you.'

'I don't want to make any trouble for you so I won't be suing you for unreasonable behaviour. I'm happy to wait the two years and we'll go for irretrievable breakdown of marriage.'

'I don't want a divorce.'

'Well, I do. Have it whichever way you want. But I want this house.'

'Don't be naive, Joy. How the hell do you think you can continue to live here? I can assure you that I would so arrange my affairs that your alimony wouldn't cover the cost of running this place, let alone the shopping and the clothes you so love.'

'I don't want any money from you, just this house.'

'Good God, woman, what do you think this house is worth? You needn't think I'm going to give you a fortune in property without a fight.'

'I've a right to a roof over my head.'

'Yes, but not this one.'

'All right, then. I agree, we sell this and you buy me something smaller.'

'That was not an invitation to an agreement.' Suddenly he smiled. 'And how are you going to eat if you're so proud that you won't take an allowance from me?'

'I can work.'

'You? It would interfere too much with your social life, the trips to the hairdresser's, lunching with your vacuous friends.'

'My friends are *not* vacuous! They filled the long hours.' She ignored him as he played an imaginary violin. 'With my work I shall be satisfied, it will fill my days.'

'You'll starve before you become a success. Why, what have

you done? You've just been playing at being an agent, the reality is far harder.'

'I'll succeed. I've Barty Silver as a client now. The interest in his memoirs is already monumental and they aren't even written.'

'Oh, yes, dear Barty. You realise he is trying to ruin me? Since that bloody party the firm's lost a stack of business.'

'You don't know it's him,' she said, but her voice wavered – it was just the sort of thing Barty would do. He was a wonderful friend but a fearsome enemy. 'Why should he bother with someone like you?' she asked, for if it was true, then she was in serious trouble with her husband.

'I don't know, I haven't worked it out, but I'll get to the bottom of it, one way or another. Maybe he fancies you.'

'Don't be so stupid.'

They had been standing facing each other like combatants. Suddenly Charles turned and walked to the drinks tray. 'G and T?' he asked, his voice once again normal and pleasant after the shouting and sneering.

'Why, yes, thanks . . .' she said, caught off guard. He often did this when they were arguing, switching moods so that she did not know where she was, making her feel like one of Pavlov's dogs.

'I can't believe we're having this conversation. I just don't believe it's happening to us,' he said with feeling as he handed her her drink. She sat down on the sofa.

'It has to be done, Charles, if we are ever to find any peace,' she said, getting the strength from somewhere to stand her ground. 'You're obviously not happy with me. If you were you wouldn't need these mistresses. It makes me unhappier than I can describe. And then there's Hannah to think of. Our relationship will eventually begin to affect her. I know you love her, and we must handle this so that she is not damaged in any way. I shall make no difficulty over access.'

'No – ' he started to say. The word burst forth, then he was silent, looking into his drink. She watched him anxiously, trying to fathom what he was thinking. His mind was whirling; the one thing he could not argue about, at this point, was his daughter – his one vulnerable spot. He would have to move cautiously, he could not put his possession of Hannah at risk. If Joy went ahead with this divorce one thing was certain, he swore to himself, she would not get his daughter. He had not been handling this right, he told himself, best not to shout at her, best to watch it. He looked up at her, the expression on his face changed to one of pleading.

'Tell me why, Joy? You've always understood my little peccadilloes in the past.'

'I didn't understand, Charles. I put up with you. But no more.'

'Please, Joy, I don't want us to end.'

'It has to.'

'No. You don't understand, I love you.'

'I'm sorry.' She looked away from the pain she saw in his eyes, she dare not look at him lest he made her change her mind.

'Please, darling . . .' He put out his hand to take hers but she moved away from him, to the corner of the sofa, knowing only too well the effect his touch might have on her.

'I won't let you do this to us,' he said softly.

Joy looked at him, her expression a mixture of pity and disbelief. 'Oh, Charles,' she said. 'Just listen to you. I'm not doing anything to us – it's you, don't you see that? You're unfaithful not just to me but to those other women also. You screw around and never think of the consequences, the pain you're inflicting. You never stop to think why you are as you are. What's wrong with *you*? If you did, maybe you'd finally grow up.'

'Joy forgive me. I do think, honestly. I know I've hurt you. But I promise, my darling, I won't stray again, I promise. Tell you what, let's get away for Christmas – somewhere warm, just you, me and Hannah.'

'I want my freedom. You have no choice. My solicitor says – '

'Shut up about your bloody solicitor!' He was yelling, his temper, which he had always had difficulty in controlling, slipping away from him again. 'So you think I have no choice. Well, you're wrong. I've got a choice.' And he stood up, moved quickly towards her and before she could escape he had grabbed her by the arm, was pulling her up from the sofa and marching her, she protesting, towards the door and up the stairs.

He kicked open the door to their bedroom, pushed her in

front of him into the room and slammed the door shut. He took hold of the bodice of her dress and deliberately and slowly ripped it to the hem. She stood rigid, making a strange mewing noise of fear, desperately scrabbling at the torn cloth, trying to clothe herself with it.

'See. This is my choice,' he said his eyes glinting dangerously.

'Please, Charles, I don't want to,' she pleaded, pulling away from him. 'I beg you – please . . .'

He scooped her into his arms, virtually threw her on the bed and, pinning her down with one hand, began to unzip his trousers with the other.

'This is my choice and you love it, always have, haven't you, ice-cool Joy? The best times have always been when I've just come from another woman's bed. Admit it.'

She lay still, imprisoned by his legs, as he straddled her. She remained silent.

'Admit it!' he shouted and slapped her hard across her face.

'Yes,' she whispered.

'Louder.'

'Yes.'

'Tell me you like it,' he ordered, his hand raised ready to strike her again.

'I like it,' she sobbed.

His mouth was crashing down on her. She tasted the salt of her own blood, and felt she would suffocate as his full weight was upon her and, with no concern for her or the pain he was inflicting, he was ripping what little remained of her clothing from her.

As he entered her, involuntarily she groaned. Rhythmically he began to thrust, back and forth, his large penis seeming to grow inside her. She felt her body betraying her as it rose in time with him.

'No!' she shouted, attempting to push him from her. 'No!' Her mind tried to resist him but her senses won. She arched her back allowing him to penetrate deeper, and she screamed as she climaxed, her whole body shaking with the intensity of it.

When he had finished with her he rolled away, raised himself on his elbows and looked down at her.

'Better now?' He smiled, raising one eyebrow quizzically. 'You never could resist a good fuck, could you?'

Her blue eyes were dark, almost black with emotion. She

pulled herself up in the bed. 'I hate you. Hate you!' she screamed, but who did she hate, him or herself for enjoying it? And as if her hand had a life of its own it lashed out, hitting him across the face. He did not pause for a second but hit her back, far harder.

'Want some more? Want it rougher?' He was laughing.

Sobbing, Joy made to get off the bed, but he grabbed her. She fought against his hold and abruptly he flung her from him. She fell against the side of a chest, banging her head. She was past feeling pain and it was almost with surprise that she felt the warmth of blood trickling down her forehead. She picked herself up and stumbled towards the bathroom, locking the door behind her.

She slumped against the basin, shivering, retching with shock. She looked in the mirror. The cut was deep, her face ashen and where he had hit her the skin was already discoloured.

'Joy, Joy, I'm sorry.' He was banging on the door. She clutched at her throat with fear. 'Darling, I'm sorry. I shouldn't have done that. I was angry. When you spoke of Hannah and taking her this red mist came. I don't know what came over me.'

Like all the other times, she thought sadly to herself. She splashed water on to her throbbing face. 'Not any more. He's never going to treat me like that again,' she told the reflection in the mirror. In her dressing room, she put on a loose dress, grabbed a raincoat and, throwing some night things into a bag, unlocked a door on to the landing that was never normally used. She looked nervously over her shoulder, afraid he would remember there was another way out, but she could still hear him banging impotently on the bathroom door. She raced down the stairs. As she reached the hall the front doorbell rang. She opened the door wide and with a little cry pitched headlong into Barty Silver's arms.

'Well, now,' Barty said holding her awkwardly, nodding frantically at his assistant Gervase to come to his rescue. 'What's all this, then?' he said, pushing her gently away from him. He saw her bruised and bleeding face. 'A fine kettle of fish and no mistake, you'd best come home with Barty, ducks.'

Barty, who never liked to become involved with the lives of others, was inadvertently becoming heavily involved with Joy's.

Even as the Rolls carried them from Charles's house to his mansion Barty realised he had made a tactical error. For a start, what was he to do with a bleeding, near hysterical, woman? And secondly, even a bachelor such as he knew that she should never have left the matrimonial home. He, by stepping in, had undoubtedly made matters worse.

'Who'd ever've thought it?' he kept saying as the large car purred along, 'a smart, sophisticated, cool-as-a-cucumber geezer like Charles behaving like a raving monster. Who'd ever have thought it?'

Back at his house his personal physician was summoned and photographs were taken of Joy's face, despite her protests.

'Evidence, my girl. You never know when you might need it.'

'I couldn't admit to this, I'd be too ashamed.'

'Why should you be ashamed? It was him did it.'

'I can just hear everyone talking. "Why did she stay with him? She must have liked it," you know the sort of things people say.' She accepted the glass of brandy which the doctor had said she should not have but which Barty thought was essential.

'You mean this isn't the first time?'

'No.' She shook her head and then winced because it hurt. 'And if I stayed it wouldn't be the last time.'

'Bloody animal,' Barty growled. 'Who'd ever have thought it?' he repeated. 'And him appearing so nice and respectable – amazing. Why?'

'I used to think he couldn't help it – he's always had a short temper. I thought it must be my fault, that I annoyed him so much I made him do it. I know better now. I know he enjoys it.'

'Joy. I'm sorry.' He shook his head in disbelief, for if there was one thing Barty could not stand or understand it was physical violence.

'I'm sorry too, Barty, landing you in it like this.' She was curled up in the corner of the large sofa in his study.

'You look like a little girl, sitting there like that,' he said softly.

She tried to smile but it would not come.

'Look, love, I don't think you can stay here.'

'I know, Barty, I'll go to a hotel.'

'Looking like that? What if some mucky reporter sees you?'

'I'll risk it.'

'No, you can't do that. Tell you what. You stay here tonight – I was going out anyway. I'll just stay out all night – we've got your reputation to think of,' he said seriously.

At that Joy did smile, for the very idea of anyone thinking that she might misbehave with Barty was just too silly to contemplate.

'I've got a little service flat you can move into tomorrow, till you get yourself sorted out, see your brief, that sort of thing.'

'Barty, you are so kind.'

'I've got to look after my agent, now, haven't I? Who wants me book, then?' he asked, more to distract her than to hear the outcome.

'I've only floated the idea so far and it's had a wonderful reception.' Barty had the satisfaction of seeing Joy brighten up considerably as she talked about their project and the reactions provoked during the past two days by her talks with various editors. 'When I've found a ghost-writer you feel you can get on with – I've several in mind – I think we should auction it.'

'Me? Being auctioned? Now there's a funny idea. How's that done, then? Haul me along to Christie's?'

'No. We offer it around to a selected group of publishers and invite them to bid within a set deadline. They can do so by telephone or by sealed bids. It's up to you which way. Then you choose which one you want. In a case like this it's a way of seeing, right away, what the highest bid will be.'

'Sealed bids, I like that idea. But I don't want Shotters to have it.'

'But they're likely to be one of the highest bidders. Such a book is just right for them, they would market it beautifully,' she said feeling disappointed.

'Let them bid, we don't have to accept them.'

'But why, Barty?'

'Secrets, Joy,' he replied, winking at her and tapping the side of his nose with his finger. 'Know what I mean?' he said with a jerk of his head. 'An auction, I'm tickled pink. I'd like to know me price.' He laughed, and Joy was laughing too even though it hurt. But she realised she suddenly felt safe.

chapter **seventeen**

Tony had not spoken to Kate since the night of the party three days ago. He was still sleeping in the guest room and had moved more of his stuff into it. She found that his silence did not make a great deal of difference to her. He had always been taciturn at breakfast, and spent so much time in his study, that it was only at supper and when she was undressing to go to bed that she missed conversation.

But it was far from an ideal situation. The atmosphere in the house was unpleasant, the rancour between her and Tony almost a physical thing. While she could enjoy the lack of nagging on his part it was ludicrous and childish to be relaying messages through the children, and goodness knows what it was doing to their authority with them.

She had made use of this to her advantage, however.

'Lucy, would you tell your father that I am going away for the weekend with Pam?' she said, as they were eating yet another meal in uncomfortable silence.

Lucy grinned broadly as if enjoying the situation immeasurably. 'Mum says – '

'I heard. I'm not deaf,' Tony growled.

'So?' Lucy spoke with her mouth full, a habit Kate had never been able to break and doubted if she ever would now. Though she sometimes wondered if Lucy only did it to annoy and ate perfectly normally when with other people.

'Do you have to eat with your mouth open?' her irate father asked her.

'Yes,' Lucy said, masticating even more noisily. 'You didn't answer.'

'Answer what?'

'Answer Mum.'

'Your mother can do what she flaming well likes,' Tony said, standing up and flinging his napkin down on the table with a dramatic gesture.

'Good,' Kate said with equanimity, and began to clear the dishes. Tony slammed from the room and Kate sighed at the damage all this bad temper must be causing to the house. Much to her surprise Lucy followed her into the kitchen with a tray of dirty dishes and began to help her clear up without being asked.

'Why are you two behaving like spoilt brats?' Lucy asked, picking up a tea-towel.

'Your father blames me for his getting breathalysed.'

'That's not fair. You didn't pour the drink down his gullet, did you?'

'No. But I'm afraid I laughed. Unforgivable where men are concerned, Lucy.'

'Where are you going this weekend or is it a deadly secret? I won't tell if you don't want.' Her daughter grinned at her.

'It's no secret.' Kate was smiling. So, it was nosiness that was making her daughter help, not a reformation in her character. 'Pam has booked us in to a writers' weekend. We go on Friday to Weston and I'll be back on Sunday evening. I'll leave food organised and notes to tell you what to do with it and – '

'A what?' Lucy stopped drying the saucepan lid in her hand and stood stock still like a statue.

'It's a weekend arranged for people who want to write. There are lectures by well-known writers – Bella Ford is coming to this one.'

'Bella Ford? Wow!' Kate was pleased to register that Lucy was impressed.

'Then there are workshops, seminars, we get tips on being published, that sort of thing. And we discuss each other's work . . .'

'You're having me on, aren't you?'

'No. Of course, it might be dreadfully boring. But Pam and I thought we ought to find out. Well, the truth is more that Pam decided, I had nothing to do with it.' Kate smiled.

'I don't believe it.' Lucy was laughing. 'It's just too silly. You, a writer!'

'Why?' The smile disappeared from Kate's face and she felt herself becoming defensive.

'I suppose there's no reason why not, except you're not, are you? A writer, I mean. You can't be taught how to write, Mum. You're born one. I mean, you haven't done any. Or have you?'

'As a matter of fact I have. I've written the start of a novel. Pam and I joined a writers' circle in Little Moreton, I'm sure I told you.'

'Can I see what you've done? Go on, let me.'

'Well . . .' Kate paused and, seeing the blatant amusement in Lucy's face, turned away and rapidly wiped down the draining board.

'Come on, Mum. Get it out, let's see it.'

'No, I'm sorry, Lucy. I couldn't. I know it's silly but, well . . . I feel shy about it.'

'But you just said you'll be discussing your work with these other so-called writers.'

'Yes, but they'll be different. They'll know what it's like, they'll understand. At least, I think I'll show it to them. I'm still not sure. It's mine, you see, precious to me.' She swung round, her face alight with excitement. 'Oh, Lucy, it's such a wonderful feeling to know I'm creating something which is all mine. I'm so thrilled about it and what's happening to me. Do you understand what I'm trying to say?'

'Nope. You haven't got any spare tights, have you?'

'Top drawer of my dressing table,' Kate replied automatically and began vigorously to wipe down the work surfaces, trying to ignore the disappointment she felt. She had wanted to share her feelings with Lucy, to try to explain the importance of it, but there was no point. Lucy would not understand. Why should she?

She finished tidying the kitchen quickly and laid the breakfast table. She had been doing everything fast since Sunday because, once started on this book, she did not know how to stop. She certainly knew she did not want to. She squeezed her writing into any available moment. When not doing it, she was thinking of what she would be writing next. Tony's sulk had helped her enormously. She had taken to getting up in the morning and preparing everyone's breakfast, putting it in the warming oven of the Aga and then going back to bed. She did not go there to sleep, instead she sat up, all the pillows puffed up behind her, and wrote. She had discovered that this was the best time of day, when the ideas came pouring out, so that her pen had difficulty in keeping up with them. It was as if she had her own private cinema in her head. She would sit on the bed, start the film and write down the images, the scenes, the conversation that was taking place on this personal screen. At night, without Tony to consider, she worked into the small hours. When she eventually put out the light she lay in the dark, thinking about what she had just created, working out ways to improve it in the morning. She found now that she was even dreaming her plot.

The three hundred words that Felicity had told them to write on 'A Winter's Romance', had, in Kate's hands, become nearly ten thousand words on 'A Winter's Interlude'. Her excitement at what she was doing was so overwhelming, such a surprise, that Lucy was the only person she had told – even Pam did not know.

A novel. The very thought made her sigh. It was all so impossible – and yet was it? And to her! The book, her book, had, in this short space of time, taken over her life completely. She, who had always been such a good housewife, in the past few days had become slipshod. She hoovered and dusted quickly, skimming over the surfaces, only bothering with the bits that were seen. She was behind with the washing and ironing. She cooked only meals she could knock together as rapidly as possible and the store cupboard was emptying fast as she had delayed her weekly trip to the supermarket. She found that she resented anything that interfered with her book. And as she got out her paper and pens, she paused and smiled. She had not realised until now, but that stupid crying had stopped.

Kate read what she had done this morning in bed and the little she had managed this afternoon, and the pages she had ripped through while watching the vegetables cook for supper. They all joined together neatly. Her fear had been that working in this haphazard way the writing might be disjointed. She wanted to know what progress she was making. How long should a novel be? Was there an easier way to count the words than one by one? She should study *The Writer's Handbook*, that might clarify things. It would have to wait though, she could not do it now, she had words desperate to be put down.

Kate's euphoria vanished smartly at the next meeting of the circle. When it was her turn to read her work she explained that she had got somewhat carried away and had written thousands instead of hundreds of words. She smiled, expecting an avalanche of congratulations.

'The whole object of the exercise is discipline, Kate,' Felicity said, standing four square on the carpet, reminding Kate even more forcefully of her late headmistress. 'We could all write on and on, there's nothing special in that. I asked you for three hundred words for a reason – to teach you to write to a specified number. The Paradise Club is not interested in writers who write on and on. They want fifty thousand words and they expect fifty thousand words.' Kate felt herself redden as she saw Clarissa begin to smirk. 'What if you wrote a short story for *Hearthside* and instead of one thousand submitted two? What would happen? I'll tell you, rejection.' The last word boomed out.

'But I know now I don't want to write short stories.'

'Maybe, Kate, it would be a good idea for you to learn to walk before you can run. Now let us hear the first three hundred words of this opus, shall we?'

Kate began to read, diffidently at first, and then as the pleasure in what she had written took over, with growing confidence. She stopped after two pages.

'Well, yes,' Felicity started, after what seemed an age. 'As I said, you must be prepared to learn – there's plenty of room for it.'

Kate clutched her exercise book to her, horrified to find that she wanted to hit Felicity over the head with it.

'Bit purple in places, wasn't it?' Clarissa asked as she smoothed a piece of ancient material on the arm of a chair which she had just acquired. She was inordinately proud of it, but Kate had noticed it stank of cats.

'I can't put a name to it right away but I'm almost sure I've read that piece somewhere before,' Mavis said, smiling innocently at Kate.

As the criticisms mounted Kate felt hurt – not for herself, she realised, but for the book. She wanted to run out of the room, shut these horrible words out of her ears. She had believed she could take criticism but she could not. This was different, this was painful.

Later, as she and Pam drove away, she asked her friend if it had been that bad.

'Well,' said Pam, serious-faced. 'I think it was a bit wordy, if you know what I mean. It could have been condensed.'

'I don't see how,' Kate said despondently.

'That's why we joined. As Felicity said, we've a lot to learn – if we're willing to listen,' she added pointedly.

'At least they liked your piece,' Kate said. She had been surprised by that, she had not liked it herself but she had not said so, for she would not have put Pam through this agony.

'Yes, they did, didn't they? Mind you, I was as nervous as hell. I shan't be next time. It's so constructive, all of it, isn't it? I tell you, Kate, I really like this writing lark.'

Pam pulled up outside the house. Normally Kate would have invited her in for a snack lunch and a gossip. She did not, she had no time for gossip now. She excused herself, pleading too much housework. A rather stiff-faced Pam drew away from the kerb.

Once in the house Kate decided the ironing could wait; she would get something out of the freezer for supper. She would reread her work and see where she had gone wrong, where she could alter and improve it. It was childish and counter-productive to react to criticism as she had done. Pam was right, she must listen to others. She did not even bother to take off her coat. She sat down at the kitchen table, pushed aside the breakfast dishes that she had not had time to clear away this morning, and concentrated.

An hour later she looked up from her task. They were wrong, she was sure. All her misery was dispelled. This was good. It was not perfect yet, it could be improved – anything could be. But it had pace and interest. She could write!

The kitchen clock showed two. She had planned to go to Sainsbury's. Never mind, she would go tomorrow. This was more important. If she worked on until four she would still have plenty of time to clear up before Tony returned.

When she heard the front door slam she expected one of the children to come in. With a shock she saw it was dark outside. She looked up at the clock – it was five-thirty and the voice that called out from the hall was Tony's. She looked wildly about the chaotic kitchen. Hurriedly she began to load the dirty breakfast plates into the dishwasher, which was full of unloaded clean plates.

'Drat it,' she muttered as she squeezed the dirty ones in among them.

'What on earth have you got your coat on for? Is there something wrong with the central heating? Has the Aga gone out?' Tony was standing in the kitchen doorway.

'No, no, I've been out, just got back,' she half lied. 'I didn't realise it was so late. Where are the children?' she fretted.

'It's Wednesday or have you forgotten? Lucy's got drama and Steve's got football practice.' He stepped into the kitchen and glanced about him. 'Good God, what an unholy mess.'

'I know, I'm sorry, I stayed out too long . . .' she said, riddled with guilt. She flung a tea-towel on the table in a vain attempt to cover up her exercise books.

'You're not still doing that scribbling? I hope that doesn't mean we're all destined to starve?'

Kate began to relax. Something had happened, he was speaking to her and laughing as well.

'You're in a good mood,' she said and immediately regretted saying it, the implication was obviously that he normally was not.

'Yes, I am. And so will you be. Get changed, I'm taking you out, let the kids fend for themselves. We're celebrating.'

'Celebrating what?'

'My drink-driving charge. I had a phone call from the police today. They're dropping the charges. It would seem their equipment was faulty. They're confirming by letter tomorrow.'

'Tony, that's wonderful.'

'It is, isn't it? Leave all this, take a bath and we'll try that new Italian in Graintry. Fred says it's very good.'

'Shall we take a taxi?' she smiled up at him slyly.

'Perhaps we should,' he said, patting her on the rump. 'Cheeky!' But all Kate could think about was the worrying idea that he would want to return to her bed. How would she keep up her work?

chapter **eighteen**

Gloria was early for her appointment at the Gay Hussar. She had thought it the best tactic. This way, whoever had invited her would have to approach her, and it would be less embarrassing all round. She ordered a Perrier water while she waited, feeling it would be presumptuous to order a drink since she did not know who her host was. One only did that sort of thing with a good friend.

Several heads were raised in appreciation of the smart attractive woman seated by herself. She had gone to a lot of trouble to look right for this mysterious assignation. In fact she had even shopped especially for it – or that was what she told herself. She had on a short black dress by Jean Muir she had had some time, and her pride and joy, her new classic Armani jacket in pale yellow which she had been promising herself for years, and which she resolved to hide should her mother come to stay, as she often threatened. The truth was that she had not bought the Armani jacket just for this meeting, it had been a consolation too, something to cheer her up because Clive had not rung – but she preferred not to dwell on that sign of weakness.

She opened the menu and, to avoid the curious eyes of the others lunching, studied the choice intently. Maybe she would not have the soup, maybe she would have the boar's head brawn in aspic instead . . .

'Perrier, Gloria? Whatever next? Don't tell me you're on the wagon, that will never do.'

'Julius!' Her voice rang with pleasure and surprise. 'It was you!'

'Yes, it's me.' He shook his head, puzzled, as he took the chair opposite.

'I didn't recognise your voice, I should have, I know it well enough. But I was still groggy with sleep when you telephoned.

I've been agog all this week wondering who it would be.' She laughed.

'Then I hope I'm not a disappointment?'

'Good gracious, no. I can't think of anyone I'd rather be with.' It was true, it was a rare woman who could resist Julius's particular charm. Charm that could make even the plainest woman think herself, for a moment, a raving beauty and the most important woman in the world. But even as she spoke her sharp mind was wondering why he had invited her. They were old friends but not lunching friends – that was business. Supper she would have understood.

Julius ordered them both dry martinis. He took a long time discussing the menu with her, consulting the waiter, before deciding what to order. He then took an even longer time pondering upon which wine to drink. He finally handed the menus to the hovering waiter, leant back in his chair, sipped his martini with appreciation, and smiled at her.

'You are so beautiful, Gloria. The colour of that jacket becomes you.' He was that rare creature, a man who could compliment a woman without it sounding sickening, false, or a come-on.

'Thank you. It's a consolation present to myself.' She laughed with pleasure.

'And why on earth have you need of consolation?'

'Men.' She shrugged her shoulders.

'Then they are fools. If I were only a few years younger . . .' He smiled and made a Gallic gesture of despair with his hands.

'I wish you were too,' Gloria said with more heartfelt expression than she had intended.

'You're unhappy?' he asked with concern.

'Not really. Nothing changes with me, Julius, still making silly mistakes where my heart is concerned. I'm feeling rather stupid, that would be a better description.'

'Still choosing the bad ones, then?'

'All the time.' She laughed.

'It's strange that some women always go for the wrong ones, time and time again, as if they never learn. Oddly too, I've noticed, it's invariably the more intelligent ones who do. It makes me think that maybe what we are led to believe is the ideal relationship isn't in fact too boring for words, and only bright women like yourself have gathered this.'

'Somewhere in there is a compliment – I think. And what were you, Julius?' She smiled at him.

'Me? I tried to be good but you know, Gloria, it's a very hard thing to do. I never meant to hurt anyone, but, unintentionally I always seemed to land up doing just that.'

'We'd have been made for each other.' Her laugh was a delight to hear. 'I get masses of advice – go for someone older, more settled. I try. But they never excite me, Julius. There'd be no challenge.'

'I understand totally, my dear. But I would not be your friend if I did not warn you that our way leads to much loneliness when you get to my age. But such philosophical talk is for after midnight and too much wine. Not lunchtime. It has earned us another martini, though, wouldn't you say?'

Julius ordered and they talked of little until the waiter had served them their drinks.

'Are you lonely, Julius?'

'I think I am, but I do begin to wonder if I say I am because the adventures are over, or whether, in truth, I might have been lonely all my life.'

'I can't believe that,' she said, but at the same time she shivered at how close to her own truth he was.

'You're not like most women. You haven't yet asked me why I invited you.' He changed the subject, sensing her discomfort.

'I presumed you would get around to telling me.'

'I asked you to find out if you would be interested in coming back to Westall's.'

'Me? But you don't publish what I'm good at. Westall's is too literary for my sort of list.'

'I'm planning a new imprint – popular women's fiction. You would have total editorial and budgetary control. Whatever Shotters is paying you and the rest. Car. No interference.' He leant back in his chair, smiled across the table and watched her absorbing this information that he had rattled at her like grapeshot.

'Popular women's fiction? Westall's? I can hardly believe it.'

'We should have gone along that path a long time ago. I've been too pigheaded to see it. Crispin has warned me time and time again. My ostrich attitude, my hoping always that we could go along as before, is why we are in the doldrums now.'

'They'll crucify you, Julius. Westall's publishing schlock?

The heavens will fall in. It would be like a bishop becoming a pimp.' She shook her head at the very idea.

'I've never regarded what you do as producing schlock, Gloria. Women's fiction has always had an honourable place in English publishing. You're being over-sensitive to the literati and their sniping. Who's to say what is schlock and what isn't? And, in any case, I don't think a generation can judge what will and will not last. I've always said it takes the hindsight of at least fifty years to sort out the sheep from the goats. Look at Emily Brontë, none of her contemporary critics, who lambasted *Wuthering Heights*, would have dreamt it would now be regarded as a masterpiece, would they?'

'I know what you mean but I can't see anything written by Bella Ford being a set book in schools in fifty years' time.' She chuckled at the very idea.

'Maybe not her but who's to say that out there somewhere, scribbling away, there is not another Brontë?'

'Darling Julius. Always the dreamer. I remember you and your slush pile, each day certain you were going to find a priceless piece of literature in there.'

'I still do.'

'My genre is not so easy. The manuscripts come in droves but to find anything . . .' She shrugged at the endless frustrations of her work, the many disappointments when something that looked as if it might be good on page one had petered out by page fifty.

'You must keep faith, Gloria. Look at du Maurier, never out of print since thirty-eight. If you had been around then you would have stood as good a chance as any of discovering her.'

'You're preaching to the converted, Julius. It won't be me you'll have to persuade. It'll be the rest of the board, the booksellers wondering if Westall's is being serious and can really produce the bestsellers the public will want to buy, the reviewers who will tear them to shreds – simply because it is you doing it. Why, even your reps are going to hate it. They've always regarded themselves as a cut above everyone else for selling your books, or didn't you know?' She looked at him slyly: it was well known that the Westall's sales team behaved very much like the members of an exclusive gentlemen's club – for of course they had no women on the road, all the reps would have resigned *en masse* at the very suggestion. They did not use the hard sell with the booksellers like everyone else these days. Rather, they graciously dropped in for a chat about books, preferably over a glass of claret or a good sherry. The talk was that they were part of the reason Westall's was in the mess it was now.

'Revamping the sales team is the first of my priorities,' Julius said a shade defensively. He knew full well what they were like, but how could he complain when he felt very much the same? Bookselling should be a leisurely occupation, not the rat-race of pushiness it was becoming. He mentally shook himself at such an idea: thinking like that was why he was here, his resistance to change had caused all his problems.

'I could never work with Crispin. I'm sorry, I realise he's your nephew – '

'You wouldn't have to. I said this would be totally autonomous, an imprint within an imprint. You can choose the name for it, if you like.' He leant forward eagerly.

He was deadly serious, she realised. She began to feel excited. Back with Julius. No more committees, no more interference from jumped-up accountants. Lovely offices, total control . . .

'Julius, I can't.'

'I don't expect you to make your mind up here and now. It is obviously something that needs a lot of thought. I can assure you I'm not speaking about this to anyone else.'

'Julius, I think you should. It's a marvellous offer and one I would love to jump at. But, you see, I promised Peter Holt something the other day. I don't think I could go back on it, not to Peter.'

'Look, Gloria. Let's leave the offer on the table. Odd things happen in publishing. Well, that's over. Business out of the way. Did you order the wild cherry soup?'

'Yes. I starved all yesterday so I could have it.'

'Thank God I'm not a woman.' He laughed fondly at her.

chapter **nineteen**

If there was one thing Hilary Holt could not be faulted on, it was her style of entertaining. An invitation to a weekend at the Holts' country retreat was always welcome.

On this particular cold and wet early December evening, the house, standing in its own parkland, glowed with welcoming light from every window so that from a distance it looked like a giant doll's house lit up. Two cars, carrying the Pewters and the Westalls, had barely halted on the neatly raked gravel drive before the large imposing oak door opened and more light poured out onto the arriving guests.

A housekeeper ushered them into a large hall with a flag-stoned floor on which were scattered antique rugs whose colour was intensified by the warm grey of the floor. The fine collection of highly polished oak furniture reflected the logs blazing in the ten-foot-wide fireplace. Large vases were full of out-of-season blooms and the air was scented with the sweet smell of burning wood and the lingering scent of lavender polish.

Hilary raced into the hall, hands held out in greeting, slightly breathless as if she had been running. She was dressed for riding, her slim figure made sexier than usual in the tight-fitting riding breeches and beautifully cut hacking jacket. There was much social kissing of the air in the vicinity of the guests' cheeks and cries of pleasure at their arrival. She showed them to their respective bedrooms where their luggage had already been stowed away.

The bedrooms were elegantly furnished. Fires glowed, flowers bloomed, fruit waited, polished, to be eaten. This month's magazines lay in serried, unsullied ranks. The drinks trays were complete down to ice, lemon, olives and the latest fashionable bottled water. The newest books from Shotters were on the bedside tables.

'Good God, this bang shoot must cost Holt a fortune,' Mike

Pewter said, as he eased his bulk into an easy chair and began with one foot to ease the shoe off the other.

'Lovely curtains,' Lady Lily said.

'Bloody fortune,' he repeated. 'I don't see how he does it,' he added, with the puzzled air of one whose fortune is based on old money and, unable to comprehend the new, feels an illogical resentment towards it.

'You're not the only successful publisher, Mike my dear,' said his wife. 'Don't be so catty. Fortunes have to start somewhere.' Lily had an unnerving way of reading his mind

She opened one of the doors to find a bathroom containing an imposing Edwardian bath encased in shiny mahogany with brass taps burnished to reflect the bather. 'Just look at this bath, and we had all ours torn out. Now they're back in fashion again, how confusing. And so much Floris . . .' she exclaimed happily.

'It's her, I reckon. Not Peter. I can't see him wanting all this high-falutin' living,' Mike announced. 'It's a bit like one of those damned chintzy and oh-so-genteel country-house hotels, where you can't fart and it costs an arm and a leg to pretend you're a nob for a day.' Mike hauled himself out of the chair and in stockinged feet lumbered across the room to inspect what drinks were available. 'Laphroaig. My favourite.' And he poured himself a tumblerful, ignoring the ice and the water.

Lily was still exploring her quarters. 'It's so exciting, sleeping somewhere different, isn't it? Reminds me of when we were children and went on holiday, and finding everything new and strange.' She opened a second door to find that she and Mike had been allotted adjoining bedrooms. 'How very thoughtful,' she said. When staying with friends it always worried her that she might be expected to share an uncomfortable night with her overlarge husband. 'Are we here for any specific reason or is it purely social?'

'Julius is in a mess.'

'Again? Oh, the poor dear man. He deserves to succeed. You can always rely on one of his books to be all right – nothing nasty, if you know what I mean.'

'No fucking in them, you mean,' Mike bellowed. 'Soft porn makes money, though, that's the dilemma, or not, whichever way you look at it.'

'And you and Peter want to help. That's nice.'

'His greedy nephew is up to all manner of tricks. We thought he should be told.'

'Do you think that's wise, Mike? It's not a good idea to get involved with family problems. It only leads to trouble. You could get hurt.' Others who thought they knew him would have been surprised by this conversation, but few were aware that the loud rumbustious Mike was as sensitive as a shy maiden at times. Lily knew.

'I know there are risks, Lily. But we can't just stand by and see the poor old boy shafted. Especially by that slimy bastard Crispin.'

'It's not only the nephew you should be concerned about. His wife is greedy too, and more dangerous . . .'

Across the upstairs hallway Jane Westall was also exploring her room. But she did so in a far more ruthless manner than Lily Pewter. The curtains were inspected, the quality of their fabric, their linings, whether they had been correctly weighted with lead shot. She lifted the bowl of fruit to see its maker's mark. She pinged the glasses to check if they were crystal. She fingered the flowers to make sure they were not silk. She seemed almost disappointed that she could find nothing false.

'It's nice to see some publishers know how to make money,' she said icily.

Julius, inured to years of his wife's carping, poured himself a large Glenfiddich and thought how kind it was of Peter to remember his particular favourite.

'If you had had the courtesy to ask, I would have said I'd like a dry sherry.'

'I'm sorry. I didn't think you would want one – a bit too early for you,' Julius said pointedly, measuring out the sherry.

'It's not too early for you so why should it be for me?' she said sharply. 'It's all desperately *nouveau*, don't you think? A little too perfect.' She waved her hand to encompass the beautiful room.

'I think it's all very nice. They have gone to a lot of trouble.' His voice had the resigned quality of one who had had this conversation many times before.

'He can afford to.'

'Then good luck to him.' Julius downed his drink, poured another and, noting the disapproving expression on his wife's face, topped it up making it even larger. Such little victories gave him inordinate pleasure, he had discovered.

'Did you notice Hilary didn't smell of horse at all? She hadn't been near a horse, that's what I reckon. She was just dressed up like that to impress.'

'Really?' Julius did not even bother to argue with her. What was the point?

'Why are we here?' she asked, taking the sherry.

'Does there have to be a reason?'

'Hilary would not be wasting her time on us if there was not a reason. We're not rich or important enough for her.'

'I'm sure it's just social,' he said. He went into the bathroom and turned on the taps. 'Mind if I bathe first?' he called. He did not really want or need a bath, having showered in his flat before they had left London. But in here he could get away from the sound of her voice and the bitterness that dripped on him like a Chinese water torture.

He began to lay out the silver-backed brushes given him by his godfather at his coming-of-age and rebristled so many times he had lost count. Of course it was not purely social. Pewter and Holt had something up their sleeves. They had been approached by Crispin, after he had had access to the share register, after he had heard of Julius's visit to the doctor, before he had approached Simon. He knew all that – a tearful and repentant Roz had confessed to him. He had reassured the girl, for what could Crispin do for the moment . . . He shuddered at 'for the moment' and then put the thought of his own death to the back of his mind. Crispin had no shares and his brother was unlikely to ignore Julius's advice and sell to him. Simon had always listened to Julius even when they were young. He lowered himself into the warm water, his glass of Glenfiddich close at hand. After all, there was always the Lepanto Trust, his own personal defence.

In the master bedroom Hilary was sitting at her dressing table staring vacantly into her looking-glass, displeasure writ large on her face.

'If you have to invite your publishing cronies you could at least have invited someone interesting.'

'I thought you liked the Pewters – you accept their hospitality often enough,' Peter said, twisting to right and left, trying to see around her and into the same mirror, to check his bow tie was straight.

'Mike is a buffoon with the manners of a pig and Lily talks only about her charities, her flaming garden or her smelly dogs. You should keep anything to do with publishing in London. I don't mind helping you out there – it's my duty – but not here.'

'But why, Hilary? I can't switch off just because it's the weekend.'

'It bores me rigid.'

'It didn't bore you once . . .' Peter began, and then thought better of it. 'It pays for everything,' he said, equably enough.

'But why couldn't I have had a big dinner tomorrow? Invite an interesting mix?' She was wheedling now. 'We still could. I could phone up, say there had been a change in your plans – the Websters wouldn't mind, nor the Flynns – they're always good for a laugh. What do you say?' She had brightened up at this idea and was already reaching for her fat Filofax. Peter laid his hand over it to prevent her from picking it up.

'No. I want a quiet weekend with my two friends discussing business. I don't want the Websters here, let alone the Flynns. To tell you the truth, Hilary, your friends bore me as much as mine obviously do you.'

'Well, we know where we stand then, don't we?' she said, turning round abruptly and looking at herself in the mirror again.

'What does that mean?'

'I'll hostess for you this time but it's the last. So don't repeat it, not unless I can have my friends too.' And she concentrated on her make-up. 'And one other thing,' she said, as Peter moved to leave the room. 'No business tonight, I'm sure the other wives don't want it. I'll take the women to Graintry tomorrow, look at the shops or something. You can talk then.'

'Thanks, Hilary. And about tomorrow evening, if that's what you really want, invite who you like.'

'There. I knew you would see sense in the end. Gracious, the others might be bored to tears too. What a silly you are.' Already she was picking up the telephone.

On the Saturday morning with the women away on their shopping trip to Graintry, Peter would normally have suggested they take a walk. But, knowing Mike's aversion to exercise of any description, he suggested they meet in his study for a mid-morning coffee. He had grinned at them as he suggested this, knowing full well the coffee would only be drunk by himself. How the other two could drink mid-morning and still function was a mystery to him.

His guests were now settled in comfortable wing chairs, glasses in hand with whisky bottles close by. Peter stood with his back to the fire. He had worried about what to say to Julius, but decided that the truth and no prevarication was the best approach.

'Julius, I invited you here under false pretences. Mike and I want to talk business with you – your business.'

'Oh, yes? Can't say I'm that surprised.'

'Business is bad at the moment for everyone, but Mike and I know that you've been harder hit than most.'

'You could say that.' Julius smiled good-naturedly.

'The truth is, Julius, we have both been approached by Crispin with an offer to sell Westall and Trim.'

'I know. Bloody little fool . . .'

'You know?'

'Yes.' Julius did not explain further.

'And you've spoken to him?' Mike asked, leaning his considerable bulk forward in his chair.

'No.'

'Don't you think it would be wise to?' Peter was sitting now.

'Why? There's nothing he can do.'

'Well, he must think he can, or he wouldn't be bothering, would he?' Mike asked logically.

'He approached my brother Simon, offered to buy his twenty per cent shareholding. I advised him not to sell – Simon will listen to me. I told him that when I pop my clogs those shares will be worth a fortune to him, but not now.'

'You're not thinking of retiring, then? It was the only reason we could think of for him moving now,' Peter said tactfully.

'You're not ill, are you? Been given the proverbial life sentence?' Mike, lacking Peter's finesse, jumped in.

'I'll die in harness.' Julius side-stepped the question. 'I'm resigned to the business being sold when I'm dead – I can only protect it so far. But while I'm alive it continues. I've got the odd plan.'

'Look, Julius, we both want to see Westall and Trim last,

even when you're no more. I know I'm a fine one to talk, the way Shotters gobbles up other publishers. But your firm is different. It's always been there, one of the last of the old-time independents. It's a part of everyone's heritage really, like the Crown Jewels.'

'It's a nice sentiment, Peter. But I don't see how.'

'Peter and I were wondering if you would sell us your shares,' Mike began. 'We could have it all tied up, no funny business, so that we, in turn, could not sell – maybe set up some sort of trust just so that it remains independent.'

'And who would run it?'

'Now? Why, you, of course, just carry on as you are.'

Julius looked long and hard into the fire. He closed his eyes so that the others could not see how close to tears their offer had brought him.

'It's a wonderful offer and a tempting one. But, gentlemen, I can't. Westall's is my responsibility and I could not let anyone else own it – even if it was token. And in any case how could I let such good friends risk their money?' Julius laughed.

'The offer's there, Julius.'

'Thanks, Mike. I've got my plans though. Maybe they'll work, maybe they won't. But I've got to give them a try. And as I explained, there's no panic at the moment. Crispin can't do anything – my family knows which side its bread is buttered on.'

'There is one thing you don't seem to have thought of, Julius,' Peter said kindly. 'He's trotting around all over London. We know for certain now that Tudor's have seen the figures. Who else has he shown them to? If it got out how bad things were you could begin to lose your best authors and then what would you do?'

'Tudor's too? I didn't know that. I thought it was just you two and I knew neither of you would do anything without consulting me. You're right, though, I shall have to talk to them – especially Sally Britain and Walters. If they went then the game would well and truly be up.'

For the next couple of hours they talked of publishing, the love of all their lives and a subject which never palled. Before lunch Julius went for a solitary walk.

He might be being stupid but he couldn't help himself. It had been a generous offer, but would it have worked? Fine while those two were alive but what then, what would their heirs get up to? He had been in business long enough to know there was not an agreement made that a clever lawyer could not find a way round. He could not, after all this time, run Westall's, worry about it, and it not be his. No, that was not the way.

Hilary's Saturday evening party was a success, as far as she was concerned. The others were not so sure. Her friends were a noisy crowd, especially Pinkers Flynn. Peter had disliked Pinkers the moment he had met him. There was that stupid name for a start, given because pink gin was his favourite tipple. But there was an oily charm about the Irish bloodstock dealer that irritated him. He did not know if he was successful or if he was a con-man – he was not sure why but he sensed the latter. But the party hat put Hilary into a good mood and she appeared to be almost sad when they said goodbye to their guests after Sunday lunch.

Jane was mostly silent on the drive home but Julius felt elated at the good friends he had in Mike and Peter: discovering something like that gave one a lift never to be forgotten. But once in the house he was tired with a tiredness that was new to him. Last night had been noisy and late and his days of loud parties were long since gone. There were two urgent messages for him, left on the pad beside the telephone by the cleaning lady. His life had been full of such calls and it was one reason he refused to have an answering machine in his home: experience had taught him they were never as urgent as the caller implied, and certainly not on a Sunday. He needed to sleep, if only for half an hour – he felt he could barely stand.

'I think I'll take a short nap,' he said.

'As you please. It will be cold cuts for supper.'

'I don't think I want anything – too bloody tired.'

'You must eat,' Jane said sharply.

An hour later, refreshed from his sleep and before his supper, he called the first of the numbers, his brother Simon, back from Tuscany.

'Julius. I'm glad you called. I've done it.'

'Done what, Simon?'

'Decided to sell my shares to Crispin.'

Julius had been standing holding the telephone. He felt

blindly behind him for a chair. The room, momentarily, had become foggy and seemed to be listing to one side. He took a deep breath.

'Why, Simon?'

'Dulcett and I are getting on. We've found this wonderful house in Tuscany. And, well . . . we fell in love with it.'

'You haven't told him?'

'Yes, I have. I couldn't get hold of you. No answer when I rang – and I did, Julius, all Friday evening and yesterday. Yesterday a cleaning woman answered, said she had popped in to feed the cat and she didn't know where you were. You see, the problem was urgent, the owners of the house had other people interested – they had to know I was definitely on by this weekend. I promised, you see.'

'Didn't it strike you, Simon, that people selling houses often say things like that?'

'I know. But it could have been genuine. So I got hold of Crispin. John told me to. When I couldn't get hold of you I rang him. John said I would be a fool not to accept. He is your son, after all. I could not imagine him advising me in any way that would damage you.'

'I could,' Julius said, but so softly Simon would not have heard. 'You do realise there has to be a special meeting to confirm that the other shareholders agree – there has to be a majority in agreement?'

'Yes, I knew all that. And it's all right. I called Marge and I spoke to Jane an hour ago – she said you were tired and having a sleep. You should watch yourself at your age, Julius. They've all agreed. What's more they think it would be a good idea for Crispin to be on the board. That only leaves you, Julius. You won't let me down, I'm certain of that.'

'I wish, Simon, that for your own sake you had listened to me. The company would be worth a fortune if sold outright.'

'I know that, Julius. I'm not totally stupid – could go for millions of pounds. But would I ever see a penny of it? That's what I had to ask myself. Don't forget I'm older than you. You could live for ever.' Simon laughed.

Julius was too fond of his brother to tell him the truth. He listened while Simon babbled on about his farmhouse, the plans he and Dulcett had for it. He even heard himself accepting an invitation to go and stay. When the call was finally over he did not stop to collect his thoughts. All he felt was betrayal and anger and a growing fear for the firm he loved.

'You stupid, arrogant woman,' he shouted at his wife when he eventually found her in the conservatory tending her plants. Julius, who never normally shouted and so rarely lost his temper, was shaking with the violence he felt growing inside him.

'What do you mean, raising your voice at me in such a way?' Jane said with indignation.

'Why didn't you wake me? Why didn't you discuss this with me?' He was pacing the conservatory, hitting one hand into the palm of the other with impotent rage when it was his wife's face he longed to strike.

'Because I already knew what your answer would be,' Jane said, stepping behind a table, putting it between her and this uncharacteristically furious husband. 'Your brother is fast becoming a liability,' she added quickly. 'You don't think that dreadful gypsy creature he lives with would have stayed with him much longer in view of the financial mess he's in? She would have been out searching for another mate before it was too late . . . before what's left of her looks – '

'Shut up, shut up!' he yelled. 'Why do you have to denigrate everything? Dulcett's a good woman, she truly loves him . . .' He sat down on a bench and put his head in his hands, feeling the energy draining from him, feeling defeated.

Jane squared her shoulders, taking control again.

'You and I would have ended up supporting Simon, something we can ill afford to do. He might even have hoped to move in here with us. Well, no thank you, Julius. Not if there's an alternative, as there is. This way he is set up for the rest of his life, and no doubt Dulcett will stay with him in the hope of getting something out of it when he eventually dies. I think we owe Crispin a large thank-you. What's more, I did it for your own good. You might not see that now, but you will eventually.'

'God, how you must hate me.' He looked at her with horror. 'I knew you did, but not this much. I'm going to London.'

'When should I expect you back?' The question was asked with no interest, it was a mere formality, and she turned back to the flower she had been tending when he had first walked in.

'Never!' And he turned on his heel and walked from the

conservatory, walked out of the house he had juggled his finances so hard to keep for Jane. Tired as he was, he took the car out of the garage and drove round to the front of the house. He put the headlights full on and let them play on the carefully pruned and nurtured roses in his garden. He said goodbye to them and then, berating himself for being sentimental, swung the car round and drove at a furious pace down the long sweeping drive.

He had driven ten miles or so, his anger slipping away from him at every passing mile, when he pulled the car over on to the side of the road and switched off the engine. He sat, hunched over the steering wheel, staring into the darkness beyond. What on earth was he doing, hurtling off into the night, having a maudlin conversation with his roses? At his age, with so little time left, what was the point in running away? Nothing was different, Jane was behaving as she always did, jumping at any opportunity which might present itself to annoy him. He had lived with her long enough to be able to weather it until the end.

He switched on the engine again. In any case, why should he leave his roses? He turned the car round and headed home.

He met Jane in the hall. She ignored him, made no comment that he had changed his mind. That was the only moment he wavered, thinking how nice it would be to shock her out of her smug complacency. But no, it was not worth it, time was too short for stupid games.

He entered his study. And he called the second number.

'You left an urgent message for me, Roz?'

'Mr Westall, thank you for calling.' Roz, he was sure, was crying.

'What's the matter Roz?'

'Mr Westall, I've done a dreadful thing. I can't sleep worrying about it. I should have told you everything. You see, it wasn't just the share certificates I showed Crispin. Oh, Mr Westall, you'll never forgive me, I showed him the copy of your will.'

For the second time that night Julius sat down hard on a chair. He was conscious of his heart pounding painfully in his chest, and once again watched the familiar room become unstable.

'Mr Westall, are you there?'

'Yes, I'm here, Roz,' he managed to say, but fighting for breath.

'I'll resign, of course.'

Still he said nothing.

'He promised to marry me . . .' He heard Roz wail.

'Poor Roz. Your resignation won't be necessary,' he said and wearily replaced the receiver. Maybe he should have accepted her resignation, punished her for her treachery. But it would mean training another secretary in his ways and with so little time left he could not be bothered.

Once the call was over, Julius found he was no longer tired. He took pen and paper and sat a long time making notes and calculations. He then dialled a west country number, apologised for the lateness of the call and spoke on the telephone for some time.

chapter **twenty**

It was Tony coming back from work at lunchtime on Friday that made Kate realise he was not happy with her weekend plans. Since her announcement that she was going he had said nothing about it, not even when they had made up their quarrel. Nor had he commented when, after breakfast, she had kissed him goodbye. He never came home for lunch.

'How do I get in touch with you if there's an emergency?' he asked, as he watched her put her case in the hall, ready for when Pam came to pick her up.

'What emergency could there possibly be?' She laughed, she hoped encouragingly, as she moved briskly into the kitchen.

'Something might happen to the children.'

'Oh, Tony, don't even say such things!' This was emotional blackmail, she thought, touching wood all the same. 'I've left the number of the hotel. You'll call me just as I would if you were away on business. After all, you go away yourself often enough and the house hasn't fallen down, has it?'

'I go away for business. I don't go away for pleasure,' he parried.

She turned to face him. 'Please, Tony, don't spoil this for me.'

'I'm not spoiling anything. I'm just saying the truth. When have you known me do something like this?'

She could have reminded him of the time he had gone to Spain with Freddy to watch some golf, or the time he had gone to Liverpool with friends to see the Grand National. She did not say anything, she knew better, he would only claim that both outings had been strictly 'business'.

'If you're beginning to feel guilty about going away that's your problem, not mine.' He stood leaning against the Aga, arms folded, his bottom lip thrust slightly forward giving him a petulant look, something he did when he was not getting his own way.

'I don't feel guilty, why should I?' she said staunchly. She had not, but he was beginning to make her feel just that. 'Look, I've left instructions for everything, you can't go wrong between you.' She showed him the lists she had written out for when various dishes should be taken from the deep freeze, how long they would take to defrost, their cooking times. 'And I've put a beef casserole in the lower oven which will be ready by seven. Here's the hotel's number. Now, have I got everything?'

'What I don't understand is why you want to spend time with a load of catty women.'

'At least they're women, you've no cause to complain on that score,' she said, checking the contents of her handbag for the umpteenth time.

'Don't go, Kate,' he said softly yet urgently.

'Oh, come on, Tony. Why ever not? You're behaving as if I was going away for weeks. You'll enjoy yourself without me around. You can spend the whole weekend locked in the study.' She smiled brightly, aware it was probably too bright. She was rescued by the loud tooting of a car horn outside. 'There's Pam, best not keep her waiting.' She stood on tiptoe to kiss him but he averted his face. 'Have it as you want,' she said sharply. If guilt had begun to take root, such a childish action on his part had wiped it all away. 'I'll phone this evening.'

'If you can find the time.'

'Goodbye, then.'

'Goodbye,' he mumbled grudgingly.

Kate had never shut the door of her house with such a sense of relief before. She ran down the path almost as if she was afraid he would follow and persuade her back. Pam was waiting in their large Mercedes. Tracey, to Kate's surprise, was in the back, complete with her Tesco carrier bag.

'Poor Tracey was going to go by coach so I offered her a lift,' Pam explained, once all the hellos were over.

'You should have seen my kids' faces when Pam arrived in this. I tell you, my standing on the estate rose.'

'Have you been to one of these weekends before?' Kate asked her as Pam manoeuvred the large car round in a three-point turn.

'Only once, two years ago – I can't afford more often. It's fun, everyone talking books. I wanted to come this time especially because one of the speakers is an editor from The Paradise Club. I want to try and nab her, show her my stuff.'

'You and most of the others, I shouldn't wonder,' Pam said.

'Yeah, I know, that's the problem. I raided the electricity meter so I can buy her a couple of drinks in the bar.'

'Who's looking after the children?' Kate asked.

'My Sean. He's on the dole so it isn't as if he's got anything better to do.'

'How long have you been going to Felicity's circle?' Kate enquired.

'Couple of years. I used to go to the one at Ferrington, then a year ago she started the one at Little Moreton, so I joined that – it's nearer, saves on the bus fares.'

'How many circles does she run?' Kate asked with surprise, she had presumed that theirs was the only one.

'Five. One for each day of the week.'

'Good Lord. How does she find the time to write, then?' Pam asked, concentrating on the road and them at the same time.

'Evenings, I suppose, like the rest of us.'

Both Kate and Pam looked embarrassed at this. It was women like Tracey with no money and little hope who, more than anything else, made Kate despise herself for being discontented.

'But she's successful, look at the number of books she's had published,' Pam pointed out.

'Her? She's as poor as a church mouse. That publisher she's with, Perry Lock, is a bastard. Don't get into his hands whatever you do,' Tracey said knowledgeably.

'What's wrong with him?' The other two asked in unison.

'He pays peanuts for a book. Sure, he promises you royalties on top of the couple of hundred he gives as an advance. Trouble is, he never prints enough for you ever to earn any royalties and never reprints – smart, isn't it?'

'Then how does he make his money?' Kate asked, puzzled.

'Volume, sheer volume – hundreds of women like Felicity, desperate to see their name in print. It costs him bugger all to produce the book. He uses lousy paper and the covers are a laugh. So deduct the pathetic cost of producing the book, Felicity's pathetic advance and the rest is sheer profit. Multiply that by the number he's churning out every year and he's making a nice little bundle.'

'How do you know so much about it?'

'I try to find out. I've learnt one thing, if you want to make money you've got somehow to go mainstream publishing or The Paradise Club – there's bugger all else.'

'Are Felicity's books any good?' Pam asked.

'Crap.'

'And what's so good about The Paradise Club?' Kate asked. Like everyone else she had seen the books everywhere, not just in bookshops but filling stations, at the supermarket check-outs, even in chemists.

'They're a different kettle of fish altogether. For a start, they pay ten times what Lock does as an advance for a book the same length. They sell in thousands so you stand a chance of royalties once your name is known by the readers. And then they sell abroad, and you really can get rich. *Then* it's Isle of Man time.' Tracey laughed.

'I must buy some, read them, see how it's done.' Pam chuckled.

'It's hard to get accepted – everyone's trying. But once you're in, they look after you real proper and advise you how to look after your money. I've given myself five years to crack it. Then it's growing mushrooms or raising angora rabbits for me.'

'I think you'll make it. I think you're good, certainly the best in our circle,' Kate said, askew in her seat so that she could see Tracey better.

'Thanks, Kate, but I don't agree. I'd say you were the best by far.'

'Me?' Kate was astonished.

'Yes, didn't you know? Don't you feel it inside you? You should.'

'But the others, they said – '

'You don't want to take any notice of them. They're jealous. The worse they are about your work the better you know it is. If they like it, forget it. Mind if I smoke, Pam?'

'I'm surprised you can afford it if your husband's on the dole,' Pam said sharply, her pretty face marred by a shrewish expression.

'Ta,' said Tracey, blithely ignoring the tone of Pam's voice as she got out a tin of tobacco and began to roll a cigarette. Oh dear, thought Kate, poor Tracey had forgotten the praise heaped on Pam. And then she saw Tracey wink at her and she was not so sure.

'What about Clarissa?' Kate asked, hurriedly changing the subject.

'What a pseud!' Tracey rolled her eyes heavenward. 'She thinks she's a literary writer. That absentminded crap is all part of her image. Mind you, I think she could do it, but it's more likely to be along Felicity's path than a contract with Westall and Trim.'

'I met Julius Westall at a party the other week.'

'You did *what*?' Tracey shrieked.

'You never said,' Pam said accusingly.

'I didn't think. I mean, it's not as if any of us are going to be published by him, are we?'

'But he's a publisher. I'd sell my soul to meet a publisher.' Tracey sighed. 'Crikey. I know someone who's met Julius Westall!' Kate noticed Pam's hands tighten on the steering wheel.

'What did you think of Bella's book?' she asked in a somewhat irritated tone.

'Were we supposed to read it?' Kate swung round to look at Pam.

'I told you. I said she would be there, and we were to read *Troubled Nights* for group discussion.'

'No, I haven't. Oh, God, what's it about?' Kate felt herself beginning to panic – she remembered that feeling from years back when she had not done her homework.

For the rest of the journey in her precise and analytical way Tracey gave a complete rundown on *Troubled Nights* for Kate.

The seaside hotel had the sad and seedy air peculiar to such places out of season. Not even the rather garishly decorated Christmas tree helped to lift the mood of the place. It smelt of stale tobacco trapped in unaired rooms with an overlay of beer and cabbage. The carpet in the entrance hall was so brightly coloured and heavily patterned it gave warning of worse décor to come. The wall lights, with tasselled parchment shades, had hunting scenes embossed upon them which shed as little light as possible. A harassed receptionist was at a small desk built into an alcove decorated with plastic Doric columns. She was trying, single-handed, to sort out the requirements of twenty women who had all managed to arrive at the same time. She was not helped by the reappearance of half the thirty she had already dispatched to their bedrooms coming back to complain they were not satisfied.

Kate and Pam sat on their cases and decided to wait for the rush to subside. Again, Kate had that strange feeling of being back at school, but a new school for most of the others were shrieking at each other with tribal cries of recognition.

There was only a sprinkling of young women. Several of them had welcomed Tracey with open arms and she had long since disappeared. They glimpsed Felicity in the corner, standing beneath a niche with polystyrene Regency architrave, which held a rigid arrangement of plastic flowers. She was regally holding court. Mavis was standing beside her like an attendant unsure of her role in life and nervous that, not knowing, she might get everything wrong. Her face lit up when she saw Kate and Pam and she sidled over, apologising to everyone and even the furniture as she made her way. Clarissa had not come, she told them, a large house party was descending on her.

'I bet. Couldn't afford it, more like,' Pam muttered.

Everybody was in pairs as if they lacked the courage to come alone. But what impressed Kate and Pam most was how intelligent the women looked. And Kate pointed out how well dressed everyone was but Pam, more expert in these matters, could not agree.

'New girls?'

They both looked up to find a confident-looking woman with black hair pulled back dramatically into a severe bun and dressed in scarlet chiffon, which matched exactly the red of her lipstick. Red, that's the colour, Kate made a mental note. 'I'm Siobhan Appsley, course organiser. Welcome,' she said in the measured tones of an actress and held out her hand. Both Kate and Pam leapt to their feet. 'Any problems, any queries, you come to me. You promise?' she said smiling, and they both felt themselves engulfed in a great wave of charm.

'Promise,' they obediently said in unison.

'You'll find your folders in your rooms giving the times when you should be where. Please try not to be late, we've a tight schedule to get through.'

'Of course,' they muttered, before Siobhan whisked herself away to welcome the stragglers.

'It's all very professional, isn't it?' said Kate. It was dawning on both of them that everyone here was very serious about the business in hand.

As soon as they were in their room and had sorted out who was to sleep in which bed – decided finally by a toss of a coin since both were too polite to opt for the bed by the window – Pam had her case open and a bar set up on the dressing table.

'Doug doesn't mind what I spend but woe betide me if I use the mini-bar – they're a right rip-off,' she said, as she poured them both large gins and tonic in the plastic tooth mugs from the bathroom.

'There isn't one.'

'Good job I brought the booze, then, isn't it?'

They sat on the beds with shoes off and went through their folders. The party was to be divided into four groups and they had been separated: Pam was in the 'Catherine Cookson' section, Kate in 'Danielle Steele', Tracey was in 'Shiel de Tempera' and Felicity in 'Jilly Cooper'.

'You wait. One day they'll have a Kate Howard group.'

'Or a Pam Homerton.'

'Never. I shall use a *nom de plume*. I thought about Emma Peel.'

'You can't use that, she was in *The Avengers*.'

'You know, I thought it sounded familiar when I chose it. What about you?'

'I think I'll stick to my own name. After all, it's got a right royal ring about it.'

Kate fretted over what to wear – the others were so smart. Pam had brought two cases of clothes with her and it really did not matter what she chose, for everything in them was delectable. Kate finally, on Pam's advice, selected a dark green velvet A-line skirt, which helped make her hips look less bulky, and a black jumper. Pam lent her a large Paisley throw in bright reds, blues and greens which quite transformed the outfit.

'You should wear brighter colours, Kate. You always go for the mousy dull shades and with your good skin you can get away with the more vibrant stuff.'

'You think so?' Kate said, so pleased with the compliment that the implied criticism of her wardrobe went unnoticed.

Pam herself chose a stunning black silk tuxedo with a huge spider diamanté brooch on the lapel.

'You look a star!' Kate exclaimed admiringly.

'So do you, my sweet. Ready?'

In the bar their fears that no one would speak to them proved unfounded. Everyone was welcoming, and all the talk was of books, agents and publishers and how to get into mainstream publishing and see your books at airports and WH Smith. As novices they listened attentively, absorbing all this new information. They could both have been excused for believing that there was a conspiracy out there in the big book world to stop anyone ever getting published. They heard, wide-eyed, tales of manuscripts going missing and publishers denying they had ever been received, of manuscripts having to be chased up after months, if not years, of no news, of manuscripts that everyone else had said were marvellous being rejected twenty, thirty, forty times by stupid publishers. They even heard one poor soul tell how, having had her book accepted, the publishers went bust and she had not seen a penny. They listened to complaints that only famous people were ever asked to submit novels, taking the bread out of the mouths of honest hard-working writers like themselves. There were assurances that someone who knew someone who knew another who really knew had told them that the slush piles were never touched, the manuscripts in them were merely held for a decent time and then sent back unread. And, they were told, a publisher would not consider you unless you had an agent but, then, no agent was interested unless you had been published. Therefore, those still unaccepted appeared to be trapped in a hopeless circle of frustrated ambition.

If publishers were not popular, agents were given even shorter shrift. 'Cowboys', 'sharks', 'bloodsuckers' were the most common descriptions they heard. Even those who had acquired one of these selective and elusive creatures did not seem to have anything good to say about them.

Kate found it difficult to believe everything she heard. If it were so, she would not read in her newspaper of new writers and first novels – which she did, quite often. She was left with the distinct impression that should one of these 'parasite' agents appear, there was not a woman in the room who would not lie down and die for the privilege of being represented by him or her.

They had wrongly presumed that everyone was a professional writer: they were not alone in being unpublished, and several like themselves had never submitted a thing in their lives and were just beginning.

It was at this point that the secretary of the Red Rose Society invited them to become probationary members, apologising that only published writers were entitled to full membership. Kate had never belonged to any society in her life, apart from the PTA and that did not count since it was duty. She glowed with pride as she signed her application form. She was being taken seriously.

In the dining room a hush fell when Siobhan entered shepherding her party of guest speakers to a central table where the flowers, unlike all the others, were real.

Kate recognised Bella Ford from the times she had seen her on television and in magazine interviews. Though rather hippy she was smaller than Kate had expected and the red curly hair was less ginger than on TV. The prettiness was of the faded type – too doll-like to be compatible with wrinkles. To compensate she had used a touch too much make-up which accentuated the lines rather than minimised them. But she smiled all the time, such a warm smile that Kate felt herself respond to it immediately as if the smile was just for her. She was dressed entirely in lilac, scattered with sequins, and had several long toning chiffon scarves around her neck which floated behind her as she walked to her table.

'Bet she's got one of those crinoline ladies over her bog paper,' Pam whispered. 'And a fluffy toilet-seat cover. And hasn't she put on weight?'

'I wouldn't know. She looks very sweet,' Kate said, feeling quite defensive towards a woman she did not know.

'Sweet? That one?' Pam snorted. 'Those fluffy, oh-so-feminine types are usually as hard as nails.'

'Who are the others?' she asked Tracey, sitting the other side of her.

'The one in black is Faith Cooper, she's Bella's agent. Old dyke, if you ask me,' Tracey said, a shade too loudly for comfort.

Faith was also in a black tuxedo suit but, better endowed than razor-slim Pam, the effect was not nearly as successful. She was tall with hair cut strikingly short but more magenta than the deep chestnut one presumed she had aimed for. She strutted in and smiled at no one. Following her was a quiet-looking, neatly dressed woman in a plain pale blue wool dress, with a small stock-pin at the neckline and a pleasant intelligent face, who reminded Kate of a Sunday-School teacher.

'That's Ann Cuthbert, she's the senior editor at The Paradise Club. She looks approachable, doesn't she?' Tracey whispered.

'Very,' Kate assured her.

After dinner, a welcoming talk from Siobhan, a lecture by Faith on public lending and foreign rights, delivered at such speed it was doubtful if anyone understood one word, Kate was tired.

'If you don't mind, Pam. I've got to telephone Tony. I think I'll stay in the room and go to bed,' she said, as everyone headed for the bar.

'Party pooper.' Pam laughed as she followed the others.

She let the telephone ring and ring but nobody was at home. That's odd, she thought as she turned off the light but was too tired to think further about it.

By the middle of the following morning Kate was in the swing of things and thoroughly enjoying herself. The weekend had been divided into lectures followed by workshops when, in their groups, they worked on various exercises set them by Siobhan. The guest speakers moved about these groups in turn, sitting listening, offering advice and help when necessary. Kate was impressed by how helpful everyone was, those with most experience advising beginners like herself. So much for Tony and his 'catty women' remark. She would have pleasure in letting him know how wrong he was. Criticism here was constructive, not hurtful as it was at Felicity's and soon her notebook was half full of hints and suggestions. In the breaks groups gathered around the guest speakers, hanging on their every word.

They had just finished one seminar in which Kate had read a chunk of her work. Reading aloud at the writers' circle had been bad enough, but this was far worse. Professional writers had been listening to her, and the presence of Faith, the agent, sitting at the back of the room, apparently intent on every word, had not helped. She had been so frightened by the whole ordeal that when the session ended she headed straight for the bar and had a quick whisky, which she downed in one, before going to the lecture hall for one of the high spots of the whole weekend – the lecture to be given by Bella Ford.

Everyone sat tense and excited, notebooks open, pens poised, and Bella, as if sensing this, smiled at them, making them relax.

'It was only a few years ago and I was one of you, hoping, praying to succeed. If I can, you can. Believe in yourself . . .' Her lecture began.

The room was silent except for the scribbling of fifty pens and pencils as copious notes were taken, as if any word might, just might, be the one containing the secret of the Holy Grail: how to be accepted. And how to be as successful and rich as Bella, for those who had been published but were, as yet, earning only a pittance.

She spoke of plot, and 'hooks', and pace and 'page turnability', which made Kate feel more amateur than ever. She repeated constantly the importance of the first sentence, the first paragraph, the first page. She said how essential was research, she likened it to the hidden part of an iceberg in relation to a good book. She told of planning, of making in-depth character profiles before a word was written. 'Know everything about your heroine. Did she have measles as a child? Does she like champagne or does it make her burp? Does she like horses, dogs? What colours does she prefer? Build her up. Create her. Play God.' Bella lectured on with enthusiasm, eyes sparkling, scarves whirling, hands waving dramatically. She explained her own filing system as if imparting the secret of the runes. At length she made them privy to her working methods, the discipline, the necessary routine. And the whole lot made Kate slump with despondency. How on earth had she had the presumption to think that she could write a novel, given her slap-dash approach, her total lack of routine? How could her method of simply writing whatever came into her head, of not knowing what the next sentence would be, let alone the next chapter or the end, ever work?

Kate was the odd one out, the others poured out from the lecture rejuvenated, fired with hope and optimism, buzzing with excitement. The noise level, as they took their lunch, was deafening. Siobhan smiled at her flock knowingly. She had seen this so many times – an author's enthusiasm for her trade transferring itself to her listeners by mental osmosis.

Kate was helping herself to coffee in the bilious yellow

residents' lounge, overcrowded with tasselled gold Dralon chairs that did not quite tone with the walls, when she was joined by Faith Cooper, dressed today in grey pin-stripes.

'I liked that piece you read out this morning,' she said to Kate as she poured her coffee from the Cona machine.

'Thanks.' Kate could feel herself blushing to her roots.

'Have you any work finished?'

'Nothing. I'm trying to do a novel but after listening to Bella, I don't think there's much point.'

'Don't believe everything Bella says she does.'

'No?'

'In any case, every writer has her own methods. There's a lot of crap talked, you know.' Faith spoke in the deep and gravelly voice of a heavy smoker.

'I see.'

'So, how much of this novel have you written?'

'About twenty thousand words.'

'Typed?'

'Longhand.'

'Get it typed up – A4 double spaced – and send the first chapter to me.'

'Just one chapter?'

'I pride myself on being able to tell from the first page.'

'Thank you,' said Kate, fully aware of the importance of the offer but at the same time thinking she did not like Faith much and in any case, after Bella's lecture, she was worried about her own first page.

After lunch they all filed in for the second high spot, a talk from Ann Cuthbert for all those aspiring to be published by The Paradise Club. If Bella's lecture had seemed pointless to Kate, this one was even more so for the books published by this particular publisher were written to a prescribed formula, from length, to settings, to type of hero and heroine, their ages, hair-colouring, occupations, even the sort of ending – happy. Kate knew she could not write to such a strict set of rules, she was far too undisciplined for that and it would be like wearing a mental corset. She spent most of the lecture dreaming of her book and wondering if she would find the courage to send it to Faith. And then she remembered the woman she had met at Barty Silver's party. June, Joan somebody. The one who could not stop crying. Had she not said she was an agent? Surreptitiously Kate opened her handbag to see if she still had her card. She found it. Joy Trenchard. But would she even remember her?

If Bella had inspired everyone, Ann had made many of them burn with renewed ambition. There had been excitement before, now it was a real presence as, at the end, the women pressed round a rather harassed-looking Ann.

Kate, not wanting to write for The Paradise Club, went to the ladies' to wash her hands. Ann Cuthbert entered, looking agitatedly over her shoulder. She smiled nervously at Kate, who mumbled her thanks for the interesting lecture, and Ann quickly entered one of the cubicles and locked the door.

There was a commotion of raised voices outside and then the door flew open and Felicity marched in, followed by several other women. Her hair was askew, and there was a wild look in her eyes.

'Did Ann Cuthbert come in here?' She did not ask but demanded of Kate.

'Yes, she's in there.' She nodded at the cubicle door.

'Ann. Ann. It's me, Felicity!' Felicity bellowed, and bent down and peered under the door as if not believing Kate.

'I won't be a minute,' Ann called back.

'It doesn't matter. I'll give it to you now.' Felicity opened her voluminous handbag, took out a manuscript held together with an elastic band and, belly flopping on to the tiled floor, her large breasts squelching out on either side like squashed melons, she pushed the papers through the gap under the door.

Her action seemed to release her followers from normal restraint. One stood on the still recumbent Felicity and hurled her manuscript over the top of the door. One slipped into the booth next door and, standing on the lavatory, peered over the top.

'Ann, Ann, catch,' the woman called, dropping over her offering. Another two made for the booth the other side at exactly the same time and momentarily became stuck in the doorway. But then, like a champagne cork, they burst through, both clambering on the lavatory lid which creaked ominously. They jettisoned their manuscripts just as the lid gave way and two legs were wedged firmly into the bowl.

Kate stood open mouthed, and blinked. It had all happened so quickly she wondered if it had been real. Ann was screaming, accompanied, like a descant, by cries of genuine pain from the two women blocking the lavatory.

'What the hell is going on here?' Siobhan appeared, incandescent with rage.

'Siobhan. For Christ's sake, get me out of here,' Ann wailed.

'Ladies, ladies, this is so unseemly,' Siobhan was clapping her hands. 'Out, all of you,' she screamed. Felicity picked herself up, dusted herself down, collected her fellow conspirators around her like a fussy mother hen and, with great dignity in the circumstances, stalked out followed by those who could walk.

'I told you to get out,' Siobhan shouted at Kate.

'I haven't done anything,' Kate protested, wrongly accused. 'I only came in to wash my hands.'

'Siobhan, is it safe?' There was an anguished call from Ann who sounded as if she feared she had been forgotten.

'Ann, my dear. I'm so sorry. What can I say? What can I do?'

Ann stumbled out leaving behind a cubicle covered with scattered papers and fell sobbing into Siobhan's arms. 'They were like wild animals . . . I was terrified . . . What the hell got into them?' she gasped, between sobs.

'Was she one of them?' Siobhan pointed imperiously at Kate.

'No; no. You were washing your hands, weren't you?'

'Yes. I don't even want to write for The Paradise Club.'

'I'm not sure if I want to stay working there.' Ann moved gingerly towards the basin and began to splash water on to her face.

'Help us, please.' A pathetic voice issued from the booth with the broken lavatory.

'Kate, get the management. Get those stupid women out.'

As she passed the door she saw the two women, one leg stuck in the lavatory, clinging desperately to each other. In the hall she found a distressed-looking Tracey.

'What's the matter?'

'Ann won't talk to me now. She won't want to speak to anyone. She'll want to get the hell out of it.'

'You give me your manuscript when we get home. I'll get it seen for you.'

'You? How?'

'Trust me.' Kate smiled, thinking of Joy again.

The management were summoned, plumbers arrived and Siobhan called a meeting. A collection was taken for a bouquet for Ann as an apology from everyone. It was a subdued gathering. Of Felicity and her collaborators there was no sign, nor was Ann in evidence. The rest of the weekend passed quietly.

chapter **twenty one**

It would soon be Christmas and moving about London had become a nightmare with the crowds in town for shopping and to see the lights. Joy was fuming as her taxi was stuck in a monumental jam at Marble Arch, the traffic solid behind them and ahead down the length of Park Lane. She looked out of the window at the shoppers hurrying by in the drizzle and saw how, despite the weather, despite the crowds, they all looked happy. She, however, was dreading this Christmas.

She was fretting because she had an appointment with Barty in half an hour and at this rate there was no way she was going to get there on time. She knew Barty: if you were late you missed the appointment, he never allowed for excuses. Then when *would* she see him? He was flying out to Australia tonight for his own Christmas.

Barty, and his autobiography, were hot news; she had to be able to act now while he still was. Next week it could be someone else the publishers were all fighting over. What if Sean Connery finally agreed to write his autobiography, or a royal, or any of half a dozen gold-plated possibilities? It was very easy to become yesterday's news in this voracious profession. She opened her handbag and nervously lit a cigarette.

The sliding window between her and the driver opened. 'Look, love. It's miles round, but what say we nip up the back here, round to Holborn, sneak down to Trafalgar Square and through that way? Don't want you to think I'm cheating you.'

'Driver, to the moon and back if you can get me to Silver Street by three.'

For the umpteenth time she checked in her briefcase to make sure she had everything she needed. Her head was throbbing – it often did since the fall. To hide the scar on her forehead, she had had a fringe cut, which she knew did not suit her.

It had been a bad time. She had tried to see her daughter but had found the house with shutters closed and locks changed.

Where Hannah was she did not know. When she called Charles invariably his secretary said he was out of the office. Her mother-in-law had slammed the receiver down on her when she telephoned, desperate to find her child.

What was the cruellest was that Charles, somehow, by employing detectives, she presumed, had found her hideaway in Barty's service flat. He did not call, but every day flowers were delivered from him, with no message, no news, only his name on the florist's card. It was as if he was taunting her, punishing her, when she had done no wrong.

Finally she had refused to accept the flowers and the deliveries had stopped. Then her action made her wonder if she should have continued to take them, that he would eventually have contacted her, but that now she had angered him.

She made an appointment to see a solicitor; the games had to end. But last week, out of the blue, the telephone had rung and it was Charles, refusing to tell her how he had acquired the ex-directory number. The call had upset her dreadfully, especially when he told her Hannah cried for her each night. Then, she was almost sure, he began to weep himself, certainly his voice sounded strange. But that did not stop him refusing to tell her where Hannah was. The following morning she had cancelled her appointment with the solicitor. Far better, she thought, that they try to work things out between them, better for Hannah as well as for them.

He did not call again. The telephone rang constantly but it was always Barty or a publishing contact to do with his book. She had had to learn, immediately, at the sound of the wrong voice to make her own appear bright and efficient, as if she hadn't a care in the world.

Now she found she was longing, praying for him to call. Anything to have contact with him, and through him her daughter. That's what she told herself . . . or was she deceiving herself? Was she not also longing for the calls just to hear his voice?

At such thoughts she made herself concentrate on something else. She could not allow herself to think this way. She hated him, she told herself a dozen times a day. But then at night, the telephone silent, alone in the little flat, the thought she could resist in the daytime wormed back into her mind. She still loved him, still wanted him, missed his body so that at night she could not sleep for longing for him. Then she would permit herself to dream of them back together, a happy family, Charles changed for good. But dreams fade in the morning.

It had been a busy week too. Word was out that Barty's autobiography was to be sold. All those editors to whom she had floated the idea, and had sworn to total secrecy, had let the cat out of the bag. But the fault was hers – she knew well enough that nothing stayed secret long in the writing world, that publishing was a giant galleon on an ocean of gossip.

When the various editors, agents and even writers in person discovered she was not at her usual number they had contacted Barty.

'Suss them out good and proper. Only give Joy's number to those you're sure are *bona fide* – certainly not her husband. Get it?' Barty had instructed his staff. Hence her telephone never seemed to stop; at the moment all she could do was stonewall everyone while keeping the interest whipped up.

'We're going to have to set you up in a proper office, my girl,' Barty told her over dinner one night. 'This is ridiculous. Ten lines I've got, and half the time they're blocked with calls for you. You're costing me a small fortune in lost business.'

'Barty, I'm sorry. I promise, I'll fix something up soon, after Christmas,' she said, with no idea how she was to manage it.

'No, you won't. I will. When I get back from down under. We'll find you a nice little office, with a nice rubber plant and a girl to help and all the gizmos.'

'Barty, I couldn't afford an office, not yet. When I find somewhere of my own to live I'll work from there.'

'What on earth do you mean? Barty Silver's agent working from a bed-sit? Never! I'd lose all me street-cred if you did it that way. Enough said. Barty will see to it.'

She had kissed him when he had said that, right in the middle of his forehead. Immediately she was horrified at her temerity and he was amazed to find he had not minded.

Barty was to be her partner. She had not suggested it, had not mentioned it. He had insisted. At this moment lawyers were working on their contract.

If her personal life was in tatters her career life was working out wonderfully. Barty, as she had known he would be, was her big break. Now she was being approached with projects from other authors asking her to represent them. If she worked hard and was cautious in her choice of writers to handle she could be the success she longed to be.

To gain that success, Joy was aware, would be an uphill struggle. Hannah and the never-ending ache she felt to hold the child in her arms again; Charles and her longing for him; her future, or not, with her husband had somehow to be compartmentalised, separated from her working day. How this was to be achieved she was not sure. She had known men whose wives had left them, taking children with them, and they had not crumbled but had continued with their careers. They could not afford to throw in the towel and say they were too sad to work this week. If men could do it, so could she, she told herself several times a day.

Some days it was easier than others. Today seeing Barty would buoy her up – he always did – even if this morning she was going to have to be stern with him. Publishers were hungry for this book, banging on her door for it, and not one word was written. Barty could not agree on who was to ghost-write it for him. There had been no shortage of volunteers, several were famous in their field as biographers and a couple were household names. Barty had turned them all down though he had agreed to meet two; both, in Joy's opinion, would have been ideal.

'Nothing personal, mate. Just wouldn't work,' he had said to them, one by one.

When Joy had tried to find out what the problem was, in the hope she could find someone who would suit, all he would say was that the chemistry had not been right. Today she was sure she had the solution for him, the ideal person. If he refused Brian Hoskins, she was not sure what to do next.

She looked at her watch as the taxi raced along the Embankment. Her hopes lifted, they were going to make it.

Now there was also the problem of Christmas to face. She did not know what to do. She had thought of going to a hotel but each one she had called was fully booked. She could not go to her mother's, she had already been deluged with censorious telephone calls telling her what a fool she was to leave such a wonderful husband, and what was she thinking of? She had not told her mother the full story, she could not. Pride, she supposed, the same pride that had made her rush out of the house and not call the police to report her husband had raped her, and make Charles the one to leave. Pride and that stupid middle-class fear of making a scene, of the neighbours knowing. And look where that had got her – no home and no Hannah.

The taxi screeched to a halt. 'There. Three minutes to spare.' The driver grinned at her.

'You're a wonder,' she said, tipping him a fiver.

Anxious-faced Brian Hoskins, her most talented client so far, stood against the wall of Barty's garden.

'Joy, I can't do this. It's madness,' he said in greeting. 'I don't know anything about writing autobiographies.'

'Of course you can, Brian. Would I have suggested it if I wasn't confident of your ability?' she asked, concentrating all her energies on gearing up Brian's confidence. 'You did research at Cambridge for a year. Then there's your journalism – it makes you ideal.'

'But I'm not a ghost-writer. I write books about serious matters.' His face screwed up into a feeble attempt at a smile which failed. Joy grabbed him and hugged him.

'You can, you can. You'll like Barty. This really is a worthwhile project, and you need the money right now.'

'Yes. But Barty Silver? He's not my kind of subject.'

'You're the right person for him, the only one. I know it.'

Barty was waiting for them in his study. It was one of the things she liked most about him: as he expected you to be on time for an appointment, so was he. There was no waiting around in anterooms with Barty; if he said three, then at that time he would be ready and waiting for you. A rare thing in a man of such success and power.

'So you're Brian Hoskins?'

'Yes, sir.' Brian shuffled miserably and looked everywhere but at Barty.

'You written anything before?'

'A novel and lots of newspaper articles.' Joy answered for him.

'A journalist?' Barty said suspiciously.

'Not the sort you're thinking of, Barty. Brian's more an investigative journalist – he did a wonderful piece on one-parent families and the DSS in the *Independent*, didn't you, Brian?'

'Yes,' Brian mumbled.

'And why should I choose you to ghost-write this book of mine when I haven't even heard of you?' Barty peered at Brian.

'He's coming new to this, as you are, Barty. A fresh approach, not the usual pedestrian biography at all. And he writes like a dream. You may not have heard of him now but you will,' Joy said staunchly.

'Can't he speak? All I've heard are two yesses.'

'I can speak and if you want the truth, Sir Barty, I'm not sure I want to be your ghost-writer.' Brian appeared to have suddenly woken up.

'And why's that?'

'I'm a novelist for a start, a bloody good one and . . .' Brian looked about the opulent room. 'Quite honestly, I don't think we've anything in common and what is more I don't really think your life would be of the slightest interest to me.'

'Well, there's a thing!' Barty laughed loudly. 'Got spirit then, have you? So have I. Let's have a coffee, let's talk.'

'You've got a lot more in common than you realise,' Joy said, quickly picking up her handbag, lowering her head so that neither of them could see her smile.

'Like what?'

'I'll let him tell you that. I've got some shopping to do. When shall I come back to see how you've both got on?' Joy said.

'Give us an hour,' said Barty. 'See if I can persuade this young man differently.'

Joy had no shopping to do, instead she walked up to the Fulham Road and found a café where she sat smoking and drinking coffee. Now she was alone her mind switched gear and she sat thinking of Hannah, and the more she thought the angrier she became. Not just with Charles but with herself for allowing this situation to rumble on. She would go and see him, camp in the chambers if necessary, embarrass him – that's what she would do.

She looked at her watch. The hour was nearly up.

The butler let her into the house and, anxiously, she approached the study. As she opened the door she heard laughter.

'And that's not all, Brian me lad. You should have seen him the next morning . . . Joy!' Barty leapt to his feet. 'You're a genius. We got along famously.'

'I knew it. I just knew you would.' Joy laughed. 'At last!' she added with feeling.

'We're like bruvvers, aren't we, Brian? It's not just Eton has an old boys' network you know, we Dr Barnardo's boys work the same way. Sly minx. Why didn't you say?'

'I wanted you to meet each other. I didn't want either of you to feel you were being pressurised.'

'I wouldn't have thought that of you, girl. But, you just think of it, Joy, what this boy's done – Cambridge, with his back-ground. I'm proud as punch.' Barty was grinning from ear to ear as if he was talking about his own son.

'You haven't done so badly yourself, Barty,' she was sur-prised to hear Brian say. Few were the people allowed to call him by just his Christian name.

'Yes, but you're educated. That counts, Brian. That counts.'

'Now, to business. We must agree a fee . . .' Joy began trying to sound businesslike among all the euphoria.

'It's all done. I know, I know, it's your job.' He held up his hand as if to ward her complaints off. 'I'm sorry but we've agreed and it won't alter your firm's percentage, now will it?'

'Might I ask how much?'

'Brian's to get twenty per cent of whatever I get.'

'Oh,' said Joy, the wind taken out of her sails. With the sums Barty was likely to earn, and Brian's relative lack of experience, she would have asked for only five per cent. Brian would earn a small fortune this way.

'It's more than fair, Barty. But I think Brian is going to need some sort of subbing now.'

'All arranged. He's moving in, aren't you, Brian? Then we can work any old time. And he's coming to Australia with me for Christmas. We leave tonight, we can talk on the way out and back. Why don't you come, girl? Have a break.'

'Barty, I'd love to. But I can't. I'm determined to find a way to see Hannah.'

'Of course, wouldn't be right would it, you the other side of the world at Christmas, of all times? But you promise me one thing while I'm away and can't keep a beady eye on you. Don't go back to him. Understand?'

'Yes, Barty. I promise.'

Joy had intended taking Brian out for a drink either to celebrate or commiserate, but now, with packing to do, he did not have the time. There was no point in going to find Charles either – he would not be in chambers now. She returned to the flat and was running herself a bath when the doorbell rang.

Her heart lurched when she saw Charles standing in the hallway with a huge bouquet.

'Since you refuse to accept my flowers from the delivery man, I thought I'd best bring them myself,' he said, smiling at her. She stood rigid, holding the door as if in support. 'And I think we should talk, Joy, don't you?' he said quietly.

'Yes. Yes, we should.'

'Can I come in, then?'

'Sorry . . .' She stepped back, opening the door for him.

'Nice flat,' he said, looking around him and then pushing the flowers towards her.

'Thank you, they're lovely.' She put the flowers to her face, covering it so that he could not see her expression. 'Coffee or a drink?'

'Nothing. I need to talk to you, Joy. I won't say sorry again – there's no point is there? You can't forgive me my unforgivable behaviour, can you?' He said it in the beautiful voice which she had always loved to hear.

She did not answer.

'I've been thinking, Joy. You remember you said to me I never questioned my actions, the hurt I caused? Well, I have. I've faced myself and it wasn't easy. You were right.'

Joy laid the flowers on the table. 'Do you want to take your coat off? It's warm in here,' she said for something to say, afraid of the feeling of hope his words were giving her.

'I've been so selfish, my darling. I just thought I could cruise through life doing my own thing because you loved me and would never stop loving me. What a fool I've been. Now I've destroyed your love.' He looked at her sadly and her instinct was to rush into his arms and tell him she loved him still. She held on to the back of the chair to stop herself.

'Look, Joy. I know you can't forgive and all that but, well, it is Christmas and Hannah needs both of us. Come back just for that. I promise you I won't try anything – I'll sleep in the dressing room. Anything you want. But just for Christmas. What do you say?'

'Yes,' she answered simply. There was no other answer to

give, not with him here in the room with her ... so close ... and Hannah.

So it was that before Barty's flight had taken off, Charles was carrying her cases from the taxi into their own home.

chapter **twenty two**

The huge jet aeroplane lifted its nose and rose quickly above Paris. Crispin settled himself into his club-class seat, opened his briefcase, took out a stack of papers and sat reading none of them. What to do or where to go was occupying his mind.

He realised he could not permanently delay seeing Julius but he hoped that being away now would give the old boy time to calm down and come to terms with what had happened. Crispin had been taken by surprise to find that he felt quite a measure of guilt – he had not expected that. It was not unusual for him to travel about Europe in December – he usually did, it was a good time to visit foreign publishers. Few others bothered to go because Christmas was so close. This way he need not see Julius until the New Year.

But what to do with himself in the meantime? Things were not good with Charlotte. They had barely spoken since that dreadful dinner party. At first he had felt sorry for himself but then decided he was glad they were not speaking. His initial shock and pain had turned to anger towards her. He would never be able to forgive her lapse in their nest. She had let him down, betrayed him. He found now that whenever he thought of her, it was her face that night, ugly with anger, her mouth shrieking those appalling expletives at him, that came to mind.

Most certainly he was not willing to spend Christmas with her. In one of their rare exchanges she had announced that she was going to her parents and he had announced that he was not. Shortly after their marriage he had visited them once, and once was enough. Upon meeting them, and seeing where they lived, he had understood her reluctance to invite them to the wedding. A bungalow in Budleigh Salterton did not fit his idea of a suitable background for his parents-in-law. Budleigh Salterton he could manage – a delightful place with some good architecture remaining. No, it was the bungalow and the tasteless interior that he abhorred.

That visit, he had thought what a miracle it was that she had overcome such beginnings to become the sensitive soul-mate she was. And he had nothing but admiration for her – then. Of course he had loved her – then. He did not love her now. And that scene had shown her in her true colours, proving that blood would always out.

He ordered a drink from the stewardess and watched her as she sashayed back up the aisle of the aeroplane – nice figure, pretty face, almost Pre-Raphaelite, perhaps a little too much make-up but that was expected of stewardesses, he supposed.

He had to decide, and quickly, what he was to do about Charlotte and his marriage. It was over, there was no doubt about it, he could never play games with her ever again – she had spoilt everything. The point was how to get rid of her without having to pay out too much. If he dithered, Julius might die and he could end up paying out a fortune to her in divorce settlements. Better to do it, before she realised he had his shares. That had been a lucky break – her not speaking to him had made it possible to keep secret that Uncle Simon had agreed. The house would have to go – that was a pity, but then, he brightened up, he could always find something better when he had sold Westall's. Yes, that's what he would do. Once he was back he'd get on to his solicitors.

What about Christmas? Where could he go? He did not fancy being on his own, but staying with friends might be difficult, for it was early days, and until the dust settled he would not know which camp, his or hers, they might fall into. He did not fancy a hotel with all the false bonhomie. Maybe he should go right away – the Bahamas, or maybe Switzerland.

The stewardess returned with his drink. He smiled up at her and contentedly watched her reaction. Almost electric, he congratulated himself. Gently, very gently, he let his hand brush against hers.

'Any chance that you're free over Christmas?' he asked with no preamble, totally sure of himself.

'As a matter of fact . . .'

'Good. Where shall we go?'

Julius had not been looking forward to Christmas. This was nothing new, he never had enjoyed the enforced jollity that was his family's idea of fun. This year he was to be lucky. Jane's sister was suddenly taken ill. The woman was one of the few people his wife genuinely cared for.

'I must go to her, you do understand, Julius?' she had asked upon receipt of the news.

'But, of course,' he answered solemnly, while his heart lifted.

'I shall have to cancel the family coming here, but you must go to John's or Caroline's for the festivities. They will welcome you.'

'I don't think so, Jane. I don't want to put anyone out. I'll give Angus Fairley a ring. I'd quite like a break of a week or two up there.'

He called Angus. He had difficulty in extricating himself from Angus's immediate invitation to spend Christmas with them.

'You're very kind, Angus. And normally I can think of nothing I would rather do. But the point is, I need some time alone – I've one or two things to work out. I wondered if you had a cottage spare?'

It was not in Angus's nature to pry, so they decided on which of his numerous cottages was the most suitable and all mention of Christmas was dropped.

Julius, who in the whole of his life had never spent Christmas alone, was rather looking forward to the experience. He went to his wine merchant's and bought a selection of assorted malt whiskies. He went to Harrods and bought a Cumberland ham. He dug out his thermal underwear, his tweed plus-fours, packed his bags and caught the train for Scotland.

Kate had returned from her weekend to a frigid atmosphere. The reason she had not been able to get Tony on the telephone was simply because he was not there. She had returned to an empty house and a burnt beef casserole. He had taken the children to London. This had annoyed Kate. A few weeks back when she had suggested that she and Tony go away on their own for a weekend break, he had told her she was being ridiculous. It seemed a petty revenge on his part to punish her by giving the children the treat instead. However, she had tried to disguise her annoyance and felt she had succeeded. She had told him of her weekend, and the writing, and Faith's interest in her. He, by a blank look, a finger pointedly marking the place he had reached in the article he was reading, had told her he was not interested. If he thought this attitude was going to make her stop it had the opposite effect. It galvanised her into writing more and sowed a deeper ambition to succeed, if only to show him.

Kate was in a total whirl. She had set herself the task of typing her first chapter, double spaced, with two fingers, determined to send it off before the holiday period. If it had not been Christmas with its added expense she would have taken it to an agency to have it typed professionally – as it was she felt she could not afford to. The whole thing was taking so long to do that she was behind with all the other preparations.

On top of all this she had inadvertently upset Pam. She had declined a shopping trip to London and another one to Graintry; since they always did their Christmas shopping together, it was not surprising that Pam was upset. But then Kate had compounded it by saying she had decided to stop going to the meetings of the writers' circle.

'Why?'

'I thought sending only one chapter was silly so I'm doing two. I want to get it finished and off to an agent, and it's taking so long.'

'One morning won't make that amount of difference.'

'It will. To be quite honest, Pam, I can't see the point in going. Felicity isn't what she cracks herself up to be, and in any case I don't think I can face her after that fiasco in the loos. I think I'd probably be wasting my time, none of it's what I want to do.'

'And I'm not wasting my time?' The question was asked in a voice so frosty that Kate found herself looking at the receiver with surprise.

'I didn't mean that – you know I didn't. It's just that I'm not interested in writing sloppy short stories for *Hearthside* and I know I could never do anything that The Paradise Club would even want to look at.'

'Good gracious me. How long have you been writing? A month, six weeks? And already you're an expert.'

'Pam!'

'It was all such fun and now you're taking it so seriously and spoiling everything.'

'I admit I'm taking it seriously but I so want to succeed and Faith was so nice about – '

'One woman says she likes what you do and now you're imagining yourself in the bestseller list.'

'I think that's uncalled-for.'

'Do you? Well, I don't. When was the last time I saw you?'

'I've been so busy.'

'But not so busy that you could not find the time to drive over to Tracey's.'

'I only went to pick up her manuscript as I had promised – you know she doesn't have a car. This is silly.'

'It might be to you, it certainly isn't to me!' And the telephone went dead.

Kate sat for some time wondering what to do. She and Pam had never had a cross word before. She could not remember ever seeing her friend in a mood, let alone a temper. So what had she done wrong? If it had been Pam who had suddenly discovered what she wanted to do she would be happy for her, want to help her. 'Ah well,' she said aloud to the room. 'I've work to do.' And she set up the typewriter hoping to get another few pages done before the children came home from school.

The next day she had finished. She reread carefully several times, looking for errors. Then she could delay no longer. She crossed to the telephone. Despite Faith's encouragement, she'd definitely decided to approach Joy first.

'May I speak to Mrs Trenchard, please?'

'Speaking.'

'You probably won't remember me, but we met at Barty Silver's party – Kate Howard?' she said, unaware that had she called a few days earlier she would not have found Joy back in her home.

'Yes, of course I remember. Oh, what a disgrace that party was!' She laughed.

'Yes, I'm only just out of the dog-house with my husband, actually.'

'Your dress, I owe you for the cleaning bill.'

'Well, that isn't what I'm calling about, actually,' she said, and wished she could stop saying 'actually'. It sounded so gauche. She took a deep breath. 'You said you were a literary agent?'

'That's right.'

'It's probably rubbish, but . . . I started writing a book when my husband wasn't speaking to me . . .' She giggled and then regretted that as well. 'The point is, another agent overheard me reading a part of it and said she would like to see it.'

'Yes?' Joy's voice sounded interested. Kate felt bolder.

'But I wondered if I could send it to you first. I'm not sure I'd get on with her – bit bossy, if you know what I mean.'

'How nice. I'd love to see it!' Joy replied and would have liked to ask who the other agent was but stopped herself. She checked that Kate had her address and Kate explained that she had only typed the first two chapters and was that all right? Joy assured her it would be fine, at least it was a start.

'There's one other thing. I hate to be a nuisance, but do you know anyone at The Paradise Club? Only a friend of mine is desperate to be published by them. She works so hard and needs the money so badly.'

'It's an extremely difficult market to break into.'

'She knows that. They have rejected her twice already. But we learnt at this writers' weekend that it helps if you have an agent, and I was wondering . . .'

'Of course, pop it in with yours. And the dress, how much do I owe you?'

'Nothing.' Kate laughed. 'I threw the flaming thing away. I decided I looked like a pregnant crow in it anyway.'

Kate flew out of the house, clutching the large manila envelope to her. It was already sealed and addressed before she made the call. She drove into Graintry to the main post office – with the Christmas rush on she was not going to risk the local one. To make doubly sure she sent it by special delivery. Once she was home she poured herself a large brandy to celebrate having had the courage to call. She was astonished that she had done it – pushed herself. Amazing! A couple of months ago she would have shied away from doing any such thing. Now, she told herself, she had to pull herself together, forget all about the book until she heard from Joy, and start concentrating on Christmas and her family.

Undoubtedly it was finding his wife back in the familiar mould and the house spotless once more that must have convinced Tony he had won, for suddenly he was nice again. He even went as far as to apologise for his lack of interest and, as if to make amends, on Christmas Day the large box under the tree with Kate's name on it revealed a word processor.

Kate thought she was going to burst into tears. At last he understood.

'That should put a stop to all this nonsense,' he laughed. 'You'll never get the hang of the thing. I'd bet a month's income.' In truth, he'd bought the machine for himself and the children. He felt sure there'd be a return on his investment.

But his remark was to seal all their fates.

Gloria waited until Christmas Eve just in case Clive telephoned or turned up. Then, that morning, she put his present by the telephone, the cat in the basket, loaded all Elephant's toys and, with him beside her on the front seat, the cat complaining bitterly in the back, she set off for what she knew would be a dismal Christmas with her parents.

'Bet it rains,' she said to Elephant.

Peter Holt was in New York. Normally he liked its buzz and excitement and usually did well there. He liked Americans and their enthusiastic way of doing business and they in turn liked him. But this time nothing was working out as he wanted. He did not know what was wrong with him, for this trip he felt totally uninterested in everything. Physically he felt lethargic, and, oddly for one with so many friends here, he felt lonely. The city he loved and had always found welcoming suddenly felt cold and threatening. After one particularly unproductive and rather acrimonious meeting with a publisher – his fault entirely, he knew – he decided to cut his losses. He wanted to leave and quickly. He cancelled, with insincere apologies, the next two days' appointments and, thinking hang the extra expense, caught the evening Concorde home.

From the airport he stopped off at his office which, apart from the security men, was empty. He was not even sure why he had gone there. So close to Christmas it was unlikely anyone would still be working, but he wondered if he had come in the hope that someone would be here – Phillip, or Gloria preferably. But that was a forlorn hope: of all of them Phillip was always the first to scuttle away, and there was no sign of Gloria. Instead, on his desk, Em had left an urgent memo that he was to call Phillip the moment he arrived.

'We had a summons while you were away. Costas Carras

wants to see us, like yesterday.' Phillip's lazy voice answered his call.

'I've just got in from New York. I left early, suddenly got fed up.'

'I know, I tried to get hold of you there. Are you all right?'

'I think I must need a holiday, or a check-up, or something. Nothing seems to matter any more,' Peter replied, laughing slightly, feeling he should really be apologising to his partner.

'You're getting there, my old friend. Nothing does matter, that's the great gas! There's nothing wrong with you, mate, just that you're beginning to see sense. Join the club.'

'Did Costas say what he wanted that was so urgent?' Peter asked, trying to get back to business, not wanting to be like Phillip.

'No, but I've a shrewd guess, haven't you?'

'And?'

'Up to you entirely, mate. You're the one who does all the work, makes all the money. I'm the drone who spends it.' Phillip laughed.

'We could talk, it won't hurt. It would be interesting to see what he's got to say.'

'*You* can talk. I'm flying out to the Seychelles first thing. I made an appointment for you tomorrow at ten, Claridges, hope that's all right. I leave it all in your capable hands.'

'When do you get back?'

'A month.'

'Carras won't wait that long.'

'I meant it, Peter. Whatever you decide, you've got my power of attorney, you always have.'

'You'll be contactable?'

'Maybe. I've left a couple of numbers with Em. I don't promise to be at them, mind you.' Phillip laughed.

'Fine.'

'Keep on trucking . . .'

Peter collected together a pile of papers, half a dozen files and a ledger. He called the security man to help him carry them down to the garage and flung them in the back of the car. After all, he thought, there was no harm in being prepared. The powerful car slid up the ramp of the underground car park.

There was no point in going to the country with such an early appointment. In any case, Hilary would not be expecting him for another two days. He drove to the flat, let himself into the darkened hallway and once again felt that loneliness which had been bothering him in New York. He crossed to the sitting room and switched on the CD player. He turned the volume down slightly as the music of Mozart filled the room. He kicked off his shoes, poured himself a brandy and soda and sat in his favourite chair. What the hell was wrong with him? Peter was not one for thinking about himself, there had never been time, let alone inclination. He had always felt that too much introspection could be a dangerous thing. And yet here he was, several possibly lucrative appointments cancelled, mooning in a darkened room with Mozart for company and feeling sorry for himself.

He had meant to study his papers, be prepared for Costas in the morning, but even that he could not be bothered to do. Yet there had been a time when looking at the company's figures was his favourite occupation, one that gave him indescribable pleasure. There was no fun any more. No fun anywhere at work or home – that was half the problem. This would not do, he told himself firmly as he downed the brandy in one. A good night's sleep, that's what he needed. Everything would look better in the morning.

He switched off the light, left the CD to play itself out, crossed the wide hallway and down the corridor to his bedroom. Halfway along he stopped and listened. He was sure he had heard something. Silence. He began to walk and then stopped again. There *was* someone, he had distinctly heard a muffled cry. Gingerly he opened his bedroom door.

Peter was just in time to see Pinkers Flynn ramming himself into his wife, pink arse heaving up and down between Hilary's white splayed legs. He saw Hilary's body rise in the bed in orgasm and heard her cry out in the throes of her passion. 'Pinkers, I love you.'

He stood in the doorway, momentarily frozen. Then he turned and quietly shut the door.

In the sitting room he retrieved his shoes and found that he was shaking. He closed his eyes as if trying to blot out the scene he had just witnessed. He picked up his keys, left the flat, collected his car and left.

He did not know how long he drove or where, he just felt he wanted to keep moving. He was angry, so angry that he drove too fast, quite unaware of other road-users, until an articulated lorry, blaring its horn at him, brought him to his senses. He pulled into a lay-by.

The engine switched off, he lit a cigar – one over his allowance he reminded himself, and he smiled. Then he wondered how he could smile after what he had seen. And why had he just walked away? Why had he not made a scene? Why had he not tried to kill Flynn? That's what a normal man would do. And then he remembered Pinkers's pink arse pumping up and down and he began to laugh – my God, he thought, what a grim sight that was. So if he was laughing where was his anger? Then he realised that these days, in all matters, what Hilary did with her time was of supreme indifference to him. Why should this not be the same? When had they last made love? He found he had to think long and hard to remember. Months ago, and then it had been quick, something to be got over fast.

How strange, to be sitting in this lay-by, accepting the end of a marriage and not caring. Once, this would have been unthinkable. Once, he would have been suicidal with despair. Once, he had loved her like no other. But she had changed and no doubt he had too. Sad.

He restarted the car, turned it round, and headed back to London and his club. On the drive he felt strange. He was not aware at first what it was he was feeling and then he realised it was elation. He felt free and he found he was singing. Perhaps the answer was to free himself of everything.

Peter was shown into Carras's suite at ten the following morning. He had met the man maybe half a dozen times and always socially but he knew he was about to sit down and do business with one of the most astute brains in the Western world.

Costas Carras was short, fat and bald, with an oily complexion. One expected him to be as gross in his attitudes and speech as he was in appearance but, meeting him for the first time, people were always surprised at his old-world charm and his impeccable Boston accent.

'How kind of you to come at such short notice, Peter.'

'Not at all, Costas. It's always a pleasure to see you.'

They shook hands politely and Peter towered over the smaller man who, as if feeling at a disadvantage, sat down quickly on a sofa and indicated Peter should do the same.

'And your charming wife? She's well, I trust?'

'Very. She couldn't be happier.' Peter smiled faintly as he spoke.

For the next few minutes they exchanged social pleasantries, Costas all the time watching Peter with a shrewd expression as if assessing him.

'So Costas. Why am I here?' Peter asked.

'I've heard a rumour,' Costas said as he flicked his fingers at an aide who hovered at the side of the room. 'Coffee?'

'What rumour would that be?'

'That you wish to sell Shotters.'

'Sell? Me? I'm sorry, Costas, I think you've been misinformed. Why should I want to sell?'

'For a lot of money.' Costas grinned slyly.

'Well, they do say everything has a price but I doubt if what I regard as a *possible* price for Shotters would be the same that you had in mind – that is, *if* I wanted to sell, which, I'm sorry Costas, I don't.'

So, with such games, two days of negotiations began.

Peter summoned Logan, Em, his personal accountant and solicitor, who came with their assistants.

The arguments washed back and forth. The negotiations became heated, then calm, only to hot up again. They would take breaks, both men gathering about them their advisors, in select and secret huddles.

On Christmas Eve the deal was finalised. Shotters had a new owner.

As he shook hands on the deal Peter realised he felt almost light-headed with excitement. He had not known he wished to sell. But now it was done he felt a surge of relief, of happiness.

He was free. Free of a wife he no longer loved and free from a business that, without him realising, had become irksome to him.

part two

chapter **one**

The cottage stood high on a cliff. The Atlantic ocean far below pounded relentlessly and noisily at the shore. The house appeared to huddle in a slight fold in the land as if cowering from the ferocity of the wind which tore at the thatch on its roof, screaming through any available chink or gap in window or door. The rain, itself a victim of the wind, was not falling but being hurled in horizontal sheets against the granite walls. With sea and sky a dull gunmetal grey, it was impossible to see where the horizon began or ended. The tough grass, the bracken, were flattened by the onslaught and the one tree in the garden was bent low to the ground like a giant bow.

Gloria looked gloomily out of the window. She thought this holiday would never end and, not for the first time since her arrival, wished she had never come, and wondered how soon she could decently escape.

The weather was not responsible for her mood, the cause as always, was her mother. They had never got on, never would. Gloria was a straightforward person but her mother chose to mask her criticism of Gloria – of which there had been a lot – in a fog of innuendo accompanied by much loud sighing.

'It's my own fault, Elephant. We shouldn't have come,' Gloria said to her dog. She often debated with herself why she had when she knew all her visits ended this way. She realised there was an element of duty involved, for her parents had been good to her and the least she could do was to visit them occasionally.

'I suppose we had better go and offer to help, Elephant. Or that will be wrong.' She crossed to the door leading to the kitchen, the dog at her heels.

'Anything I can do?' she asked brightly.

'I suppose you could do the Brussels sprouts for me,' Mrs Catchpole said grudgingly. Gloria smiled to herself, aware that her mother was annoyed that she had volunteered, thus depriving her of a source of martyrdom.

Gloria had barely begun to prepare the sprouts when the back door flew open and her father appeared from his trip to the village, accompanied by part of the storm, his mackintosh dripping onto the spotless kitchen tiles.

'Graham, really! Just look at the mess you're making,' his wife fretted, leaping up to collect her mop.

'I think you should see this, Gloria,' her father said, completely ignoring his wife – but, then, he might by now be oblivious to her ways, Gloria thought, as she took the copy of the *Daily Telegraph* he handed her. She glanced idly at it, and then, in the way of words hidden in a thousand others, those relevant to her appeared to jump off the page, blacker, larger than all the others. 'SHOTTERS SOLD.'

'Good God . . .' Gloria smoothed the paper out on the table and bent over it reading the copy, her heart beginning to pound. 'The bastard!' she exclaimed.

'Gloria! Really, your language – ' her mother began but her husband took hold of her arm and shook his head at her in warning. 'What's happened? Tell me.' Mrs Catchpole grabbed at her throat with anxiety and craned forward, trying to see what Gloria was reading.

'I just don't believe it!' Gloria slumped back on the kitchen chair. 'The creep! I had lunch with Peter Holt only the other day and he didn't say a thing.' She looked up anxiously at her father. 'Or did he? I said I was fed up at Shotters and he said to me, "Don't do anything yet." He must have known then. He needed me there, didn't he, to sell on? It wouldn't have looked too good, one of his senior editors leaving. He had to make it appear a happy ship.'

'These takeovers often come completely out of the blue, Gloria. I shouldn't judge him too harshly. It's quite likely he didn't know himself,' her father counselled.

'He's just upped and sold us like a load of cattle and you say don't judge him, Dad? Oh, come on . . .'

'And to an American company! Why could he not have chosen a nice English company.' Mrs Catchpole sighed.

'Because no English company would have paid him what that greedy bugger wanted.' Gloria stood up. Her chair scraping painfully on the tiled floor. She picked up her Filofax from the dresser and began to look for Peter's home number.

'What will you do?' her father asked.

'Resign.'

'Gloria, you can't do that, not with the position you have. Why, you said only last night that you hoped to be made a director soon.'

'That's what I thought he meant when he told me not to leave.'

'Maybe he'll recommend you for a directorship to the new owners. I'd be so proud of you.'

'Mum, it's no great deal, you know. Some publishing companies make staff directors at the drop of a hat. It doesn't mean you've a seat on the board. It's a sop in lieu of decent wages.'

'You've become so cynical, Gloria.'

'No, Mum. I've become a realist.'

She picked up the telephone. 'Oh, no, I don't believe it. It's dead.' She shook the instrument with exasperation.

'It's the storm.'

'I've got to go. I've got to get home.'

'Not in this weather, Gloria, please,' her mother begged, but Gloria was already half-way up the stairs.

An hour later she was driving to London, through the scudding rain. Because of the weather conditions the drive took nearly twice the normal six hours. By the time she opened her front door Gloria was exhausted. Quickly she fed the animals and then took a bath and went straight to bed. But she barely slept; instead she tossed and turned with anger. In the morning she left early for the office, leaving Elephant, still sleeping, behind.

It was 28 December and the building should have been empty. Instead, in every office, in the corridors, even in the lavatories, clusters of anxious people were gathered, each with a different worry, a different snippet of gossip.

'Gloria, I'm so glad you made it here.'

Gloria swung round at mention of her name to find Peter's secretary, Em, standing behind her, clutching a sheaf of papers. She noticed Em's eyes were rather pink and puffy.

'Hi, Em. What a cock-up! Can you tell us what the hell is going on? Where's Peter? Is anyone getting the push?'

'I tried calling you in Cornwall yesterday but the lines were down – a storm, they said.' Em avoided Gloria's questions. 'Peter was very anxious to speak to you personally and was upset when we could not get through. He's called a meeting in the canteen in half an hour's time. He asked specifically that you should hang on for a few minutes after the meeting is over.'

'What for?'

'I'm afraid I've no idea. But if you wouldn't mind?' Em smiled questioningly before excusing herself to speak to Blades's design team who had just walked into the office.

The atmosphere in the canteen was charged with equal measures of anger and fear. Peter finally arrived with Logan Perriman and they both climbed on to the small stage that only a short time ago had been the scene of the annual pantomime. Somebody switched on the spotlights. Gloria was shocked at how exhausted Peter looked. He fiddled with his papers; a nervous man, too, she thought. She would have liked to rush up to the stage and fling her arms around him. And then she scolded herself for being a fool. It was his own fault if he looked like that, he need not have sold. He was not worthy of sympathy. She must remember that.

'Ladies, gentlemen, thank you so much for coming to this meeting. I apologise to you for breaking into your holidays . . .' Peter looked up from the papers in his hand and smiled but no one smiled back. 'I thought it was best that I should see you all as soon as possible and explain a thing or two, and try to pre-empt any gossip.' Gloria wished he would stop smiling at them. He coughed and people began to shuffle, becoming restless. As if sensing this, he squared his shoulders and appeared to discard his notes. 'I realise this has come as a shock to you all – ' Someone at the back snorted with derision. Peter looked about the jampacked room, not a seat free nor any standing space.

'You didn't have to bloody well sell,' a male voice shouted out.

'No, but it's better for everyone that we have.'

There was loud laughter at this but it was not caused by humour. It was derisory, bitter.

'Great, so you pocket millions while the rest of us can go to hell.' It was a member of the Blades art department on his feet, and shouting.

'Of course I've made millions. What do you want me to do, stand here and lie to you and say I haven't? But don't you be all pious and think you wouldn't have done the selfsame thing if you had been in my shoes. Be realistic, for Christ's sake.'

At last, thought Gloria, he's getting into his stride. His audience had sat up, were taking more notice. She even heard a few genuine laughs, and the odd murmur of agreement.

'It's a change of ownership, that's all, we carry on as before. Well, almost. Phillip is leaving, he wants to devote more time to his gardening.' At this there was a loud roar of approval: it was no secret in Shotters that Phillip's interest in gardening extended only to the fine crop of cannabis plants that he tended lovingly in deepest Berkshire. 'All those who worked for Phillip will be absorbed into other departments. There will be no redundancies, I assure you. Each imprint will continue with its own autonomy. We'll get what we need – a large injection of capital at a difficult time in publishing. I shall be staying on as chief executive. There will be one major difference. As some of you know, for some time I had been thinking of us starting up our own paperback house instead of selling paperback rights outside. Vertical publishing is the way forward, you don't need me to tell you that. This is exactly how Costas sees it, so we shall be looking to take on extra staff – not losing people. As from later this year we shall be starting Sabre, a completely new imprint that in three years, I predict, will be in the top four. I, for one, am very confident this is all for the best. Now does that make you all feel more secure? Any questions?'

Murmurs of approval greeted this, but, thought Gloria, if everything was so wonderful, why did Peter look so awful?

A junior editor stood up. 'This Carras person, what does he know about publishing?'

'Not a lot,' Peter said, joining in the laughter. 'He owns one of the largest private companies in America. He began in real estate, I think. He's recently acquired a publishing house in the States and one in Australia although nothing on this scale. But this is why I think he is a good person to sell to. He's interested in publishing but since he knows little about it he's going to leave it to us. Provided we are profitable, we'll be left alone.'

For a further hour Peter parried questions which, as time progressed, began to get more stupid, Gloria thought. Finally the meeting was over. Not that anyone said it was but it just fizzled out, having lost its momentum. Peter left the stage and once he was out of the room the noise in the canteen was deafening, as everyone went over again what they had just heard. Like Gloria, several were unconvinced and said they were resigning. Or was it just bravado on their part? Gloria wondered. And did she herself mean to? She was no longer sure.

Em appeared and reminded Gloria that Peter wanted to see her. She took the lift to the top floor.

His office was crowded with men, the majority of them strangers to her. Upon seeing her, Peter excused himself and came over.

'You've been with me the longest, Gloria. There's a couple of things I should explain to you.'

'I'd appreciate that,' she said seriously.

'Let's go next door, it's a madhouse in here.'

They went through the communicating door into the calm of Phillip's office. They sat opposite each other. She looked with concern at his haggard face, he avoided her stare.

'Look, Gloria, I'm sorry. You must be feeling very let down,' he said studying his hands.

'You could say that, Peter. Thanks to you, I turned down another job just before Christmas.'

'Might I ask who with?' He looked up.

'Julius. He wants to start publishing commercial fiction. I was to – '

'That would have been no good,' Peter interrupted. 'Poor old Julius is finished. He's clutching at straws. If you had gone your job wouldn't have lasted long.'

'And who are you to say that? Have you got a hotline into the future or something? Julius and I would have made it work,' she said with spirit.

'I'm sorry, Gloria. I put that badly. You're safer here, is what I was trying to say.'

'You reckon?'

'Yes, I do. Costas is all right. And just think, with our own paperback house every book you buy is guaranteed publication in soft covers.'

'You reckon?'

'Yes. From day one we'll have combined decisions. No book is bought unless both hard and paperback editors agree.'

'Come on, Peter. That's a Utopia you're imagining. It will be worse than it is already. All it will mean is more committees to persuade on your choice of book. And who's going to run Sabre?'

'That's why I wanted to see you. How about Gloria Catchpole?'

'Me?' She shook her head. 'I don't think so, Peter. I'm an editor, not an administrator.' Gloria did not even have to mull over this suggestion.

'You'd have been an administrator at Westall's.'

'Yes, but look at the scale of Julius's operation compared with here. I would still have been able to edit.'

'It would mean a doubled salary and all the fringe benefits.'

'I still don't think so. What's more, my appointment would be a disaster for you personally. I'd let you down. I couldn't organise a teddy bears' picnic let alone a new imprint.'

'Nonsense! You were once highly organised.'

'*Once* is the operative word there. Perhaps I'm getting old. Perhaps we both are.' She looked sad.

'I'm sure Julius's offer seems even more appealing at the moment. But you're wrong. I also think you're wrong to turn down Sabre. I need you, Gloria. Please don't resign.'

'Why should you need me?' she asked, a shade suspiciously.

'Because I respect you and trust you. Because you're good. Because – ' He stopped abruptly, stood up and crossed to the window.

'Because what?' She waited.

'Nothing.'

They were silent, looking at each other.

'You could tell me one thing,' she said. 'If everything in the garden is so wonderful why do you look almost ill?'

'I'm tired, that's all.' He pushed his hand through his hair. 'It was a hard round of negotiations.'

'It's not just that. Come on, Peter, I've known you a long time.'

He turned and looked out of the window. 'I've left Hilary,' he said with his back still to her.

'Oh, Peter, I'm sorry.' She blurted out the words automatically – she wasn't at all, but then what else could she say?

'Don't be. I'm not. I should have done it ages ago.' He turned and faced her.

'Which came first – Hilary or selling the company?'

He laughed. 'Clever Gloria . . . But, no, it's not what you're thinking. I found out about the two almost at the same time. They seemed to slot in together. No Hilary, I don't need Shotters. No Shotters, then I doubt if Hilary would have stayed.'

'But then . . .'

'Let's just say I've spent the last few days coming to terms with quite a few things. It's not much fun facing the fact that you've wasted so many years with the wrong person.' He looked at Gloria long and hard and stepped towards her as if he was going to say more but he didn't. Instead he took a cigarette from his pocket and lit one.

'You're smoking again. Peter, that's silly.'

'I know. I'll stop once everything is sorted out.' He smiled at her, pleased by her concern for him.

'If there's anything I can do . . . You know, if you want to talk or anything,' she said feeling awkward and looking at her shoes intently.

'Does that mean you'll stay?'

'Yes, for a bit to see how things go. I've blown it with Julius anyway.'

'I'm pleased, Gloria. I promise you everything will be fine.'

'I do hope so, Peter,' she said, and wished she had the nerve to cross the room and hold him.

chapter **two**

Christmas at the Trenchards' had gone surprisingly well. This was due, Joy was sure, to her having invited her parents to stay. She knew she was safe with them in the house for there was no danger that Charles would annoy her father – he was too rich and too important. She had changed, she had to acknowledge. Only a few short weeks ago she would never have admitted, even to herself, that this was so. Charles only bullied the weak, had been her unpleasant conclusion.

She explained nothing to her parents, allowing them to think she had merely had a row with Charles and had gone away for a few days' break and that everything was now fine. She could be a good actress when she wanted, she decided.

Over the holiday period Joy could not fault Charles. He had never been sweeter nor more considerate to her every need. She had lost count of the number of times, when alone, he had apologised for his unforgivable behaviour. He had swamped her with the most wonderful presents. He had vowed never to stray again.

Upon her return she had insisted he sleep in his dressing room – her parents need never know. But on Christmas Eve, although she blamed the alcohol she had drunk, she supposed it was inevitable that she would relent and take him back into her bed.

Charles was a consummate lover when he wanted to be. That night he had undressed her with an agonising slowness, all the time loving her with kisses and caresses which, by the time she was naked, had made her nearly desperate for him.

'I want you now,' she looked at him, her hunger blazing in her eyes.

'Don't be in such a hurry, little one. We've the whole night ahead of us.'

It was a night of exquisite, gentle torture as his mouth, his hands led her almost to climax and then he would turn from her, offer her a sip of champagne, all the time teasing her. So that when he finally took her she was screaming her passion and her need for him.

'Oh, why can't it always be like this?' she had said, as she lay cradled in his arms, totally relaxed after such intense love-making she thought that now would be a perfect time to die.

'It will be. This time, I promise you, my darling, nothing will alter.'

Now the holiday was over. Charles had returned to work and her parents had left that morning. After breakfast and a quick game of snakes and ladders with Hannah before she went for her morning walk with her nanny, Joy raced up the stairs and into her bedroom. There she picked up the Jiffy bag which had arrived by special delivery before Christmas. She had been longing to delve into it during the holiday but had forced herself to leave it until now. From inside she took two bundles – Tracey Green's complete novel and Kate Howard's two chapters.

She looked first at Tracey's. She was not a fan of The Paradise Club style of book, but from the first page she realised that this was very much what they were always wanting. In truth, it was better than most she had glanced at over the years. She skim-read, dipping here and there into the book to check that it stayed consistent with the first page. Half an hour later she telephoned Ann Cuthbert, senior editor of The Paradise Club.

Joy had known Ann for years, ever since they were junior editors in their first jobs. She liked it when she knew an editor quite well for she found it easier to talk to them, easier to convey her enthusiasm. It worked with Ann for she agreed to read the manuscript which Joy said she would send over by messenger. She hung up, anxious to get on with Kate's book.

She was only half-way down the first page when it happened. The hair on the nape of her neck stood up, her breathing was faster, her pulse raced, she felt butterflies in her stomach. She was almost too afraid to continue in case the magic of Kate's opening paragraphs did not continue.

She need not have worried. She read on with mounting excitement only to be deeply disappointed when she got to the end of the section and there was no more. She longed to find out what happened next. She leant back in the chair feeling elated. This was it, the book she had dreamt of finding. First Barty and now Kate. And a Kate she had met at Barty's, as if Barty held the key to her success. She did not hesitate but picked up the telephone.

'Gloria? It's Joy.'

'Are you all right?' Gloria asked anxiously.

Joy laughed. 'Couldn't be better.'

'You haven't gone back to him?'

'I have. I know what you're thinking, but – oh, Gloria, I'm so happy. I had the most wonderful Christmas. It's as if I've fallen in love with Charles all over again.'

At the other end of the telephone Gloria rolled her eyes with exasperation. There were times when she found her own sex frustratingly illogical but, then, who was she to criticise another woman? Wasn't she just as daft where men were concerned?

'And how's your love life, Gloria? Happy?'

'Don't even talk about it – non-existent. I've resolved to give them up.'

'That'll be the day.' Joy laughed, and Gloria thought how wonderful it was to hear her laughing again. 'You must come to dinner one day. How about next Wednesday?' Gloria accepted with pleasure: she had never been to Joy's house, or met her husband – she was curious to see what the big attraction was.

'I never expected to read that Peter had sold Shotters. I mean, it's his baby, isn't it? Will this new company work?'

'Of course, it's better all round. New capital, vertical publishing. New dynamism. The bigger the better in today's publishing world.' Gloria repeated the little pep talk she had been handing out to the authors and agents ever since business had started after the holiday. She had serious doubts, but it would be a disaster if they got wind of discontent in the office.

'I always thought Peter had got too big already. He's a publisher not an administrator. Now the firm will be even larger.'

'Oh, he loves it. He says he was born with the soul of an accountant.' Gloria forced herself to laugh. 'He's left Hilary,' she said, and wished she hadn't – she should not be gossiping but she was so pleased she wanted everyone to know.

'So I heard. And . . .?' Joy was laughing now, a small arch laugh.

'And what . . .?'

'I always thought you had a thing about Peter. Now's your chance.'

'Me? Don't be silly, Joy. He's just a very old friend. That's all.'

'Is that so?' Joy smiled to herself.

'What can I do for you?' Gloria asked, abruptly, wanting Joy's teasing to stop. It made her feel very uncomfortable.

'I've got the most marvellous piece of work for you to see. Two chapters and a rather vague synopsis. Honestly, I couldn't put the damn thing down. It's going to be wonderful. Mega.'

'Yeah?' said Gloria, unexcited, used as she was to the hyperbole of literary agents. Whatever they were selling was always the best, always unputdownable. One had to admire their tenacity.

'I know agents are always saying that about their books, but this time it's true. You remember that woman who was skulking in Barty's loo, having a quick fag? Well, it's her, Kate Howard. Marvellous name, isn't it? No need to alter that.'

'She was nice,' Gloria said, with more interest.

'It will be just up Blades's street. You'll love it. Bet you get as excited as I am. When I read it I knew you were the only editor for it and for Kate.'

'She didn't say anything about being a writer.' Gloria ignored the compliment. That was par for the course from agents as well.

'She wasn't then. That's the amazing thing. She tells me she has only just started and it's just pouring out of her.'

'I don't like buying first novels on so little. I prefer them to be finished. You know how it is, Joy. They start all fired up with ideas and enthusiasm and then it all peters out before they've got half-way and they run out of ideas or suddenly realise what hard work it is. I should think this nation is littered with wonderful beginnings of books stuffed away in drawers. Sorry, but I've had my fingers burnt once too often.'

'This is different, *she*'s different. I reckon she'll have finished it completely in six weeks if not less,' Joy said, mentally crossing fingers and toes. 'I'll bike it over to you,' she added emphatically. She had quickly learnt not to say 'Shall I?' to an editor.

'Do that, but I'm not buying, not until it's finished. I don't care how good it is. Anyone else seen it?' she asked, even though she knew it was a futile question. Half a dozen publishers might have thumbed it but the agent would always deny it. There had been a time when you could tell a typescript had been the rounds by its general tattiness, with thumb marks and coffee stains on the pages. These days, with word processors and fast, efficient photocopiers, scripts by the score could be churned out so that each publisher received a pristine one and there was no way to call the agent's bluff.

'No. I told you, I thought of you immediately. I've only just this minute finished it.'

'How are you doing on the Barty project? That was one hell of a coup, Joy. How did you manage it?'

'God knows. I'm waiting for him to return from Australia. I should have something to sell on pretty soon.'

'Well, let Shotters have a stab,' she said, loyal as always.

'I'll be auctioning this one. There's just one thing, Gloria. Don't tell Barty I'm back with Charles, will you?'

When she had put the telephone down she wondered what had made her say that; all she knew was that she did not want Barty to know – not yet.

She picked up the telephone again, not wishing to think too long about her motives for wanting him kept in the dark. As she dialled she thought this was the best part of her job, letting a writer know you liked their work. When she decided she didn't like a book enough to handle it, she never used the telephone but, like everyone else, hid behind the anonymity of a letter.

'. . . I just can't wait to read on. You do have more, don't you?' There was silence from the other end. 'Kate? Kate, are you there?'

'Yes, I'm here.' Kate's voice sounded faint and far away. 'I'm just overwhelmed.' And to Joy's horror she heard her burst into tears. 'I'm sorry.' Kate fought for breath.

'I loved it, absolutely. When can I see the rest?'

'I'm still struggling with my word processor but my son is helping me, it's not so puzzling any more. I'll get it to you as quickly as possible.' Kate gulped.

'Now, I'll tell you what I've done. Remember the other woman in the witches' coven at Barty's? Gloria. I've sent it to her. She's senior fiction editor at Blades who are part of Shotters.'

'I didn't know that.'

'It's always confusing. Publishers seem to buy and sell themselves faster than any other business. Even we get confused. And to confuse you even further Shotters has just been bought by Carras of New York. But don't worry, it doesn't affect the authors and Gloria is staying on. Anyhow, I've sent it to her.'

'Joy, I can't thank you enough.'

'Look, Kate, don't get too excited, it's early days yet. Blades won't buy an unfinished work – it's unusual unless you are a writer with a track record. But the important thing is we'll get feedback from her. She'll love it and her enthusiasm will make you want to finish it.'

'I don't need anyone to make me finish it, I can't wait to find out what happens myself.'

'Gracious, you are an unorthodox writer.' She laughed. 'So you'll send me the rest? We must have lunch one day soon. Oh, by the way, Ann Cuthbert's agreed to look at your friend's book personally.'

When Joy replaced the receiver she hugged herself with sheer happiness. What a wonderful career she had chosen, she told herself. When things were going well what better was there?

Joy dressed quickly in newly cleaned jeans, a sweater, flat leather pumps and a navy blazer and took a taxi to the flat Barty had loaned her. She made a point of going every few days to collect any mail that might be there for her. So it was that she happened to be in the flat when Barty rang. She accepted his invitation to go straight over to his house for a light lunch, but warned him she was casually dressed. What one wore mattered to Barty.

'You're back early, I didn't expect you until next week,' she said, as she entered his study.

'Too damned hot for my liking. Felt homesick for some nice drizzle.' Barty fussed over her, taking her jacket, ordering her a drink.

'Then you must be sadly disappointed.' She nodded to the window where the sun was shining brightly and unseasonally.

'It'll come. I missed you, girl,' he said, grinning broadly.

'I missed you, too. How did it go?'

'Like clockwork. Brian and me, we get on like a house on

fire. He understands me, Joy. I don't have to explain things to him, you see. He doesn't bore me.'

'I'm so glad. Getting on with your ghost-writer is so important. Do you know if he has written anything yet?'

'Love you, yes. We've mapped out a sort of synopsis, well, chapter headings really. And I know he's done the first chapter. That was hard that, things I didn't really ever want to think about again. But, there you go. I said I'd do it, and do it I will. And at least the first bit's over, the worst is done.'

Joy put out her hand and touched his gently. 'I'm sure it was hard. But you know, Barty, you've so much to offer people. When they read your story it will be an inspiration to so many.'

Barty produced a large white linen handkerchief and blew noisily into it.

'Did you know that Shotters has been sold?' Joy said, hurriedly changing the subject, embarrassed by Barty's obvious emotion.

'I told you, didn't I?'

'No.'

'Yes, I did, when I said I wouldn't sell my book to Shotters. Remember? You'd be no good in business, my girl, if you couldn't pick up on a hint like that, especially one from Barty.'

'How did you know? I don't think even Peter Holt knew until it happened.' She laughed.

'Costas and I go back a long way. He's wanted to get into English publishing for some time. I kept an ear open for him, advised him. I felt Peter was restless, ready for something to happen. Told Costas to act now. I was right, you see.'

'A wonder!' she teased him.

'So's Costas. You think I've got a story to tell, why his would make your hair stand on end. Orphaned at five . . . now one of the richest men in the world.'

'Obviously the rest of us were at a disadvantage not losing our parents.' She laughed gaily.

'Never say that, Joy. Never.' He had swung round and was facing her, his expression sad and serious.

'No, I'm sorry, it was tasteless of me,' Joy said quickly.

'I've got your new office for you,' Barty announced brightening up. 'All signed and sealed. Bloomsbury, that's the proper place for you. And there's a nice little flat above it, so your business and housing problems are solved in one, There's a garden for Hannah to play in and . . .'

'Barty . . .' She paused.

'Yes, girl?'

'Oh, nothing. You're too kind to me.'

'For a moment there I thought you were going to say you'd gone back to that bastard. I wouldn't like that.'

'No. I know you wouldn't,' she said, wondering what on earth she was doing by not telling him the truth.

After lunch, with Gervase in tow, they went to inspect the new office. It was in a house in the maze of streets behind Tottenham Court Road, that elegant and relatively peaceful part of London with its Georgian terraces, lovely squares and its literary past.

Barty had acquired the whole house, though whether bought, leased or rented he was not saying. The basement he had promised to a friend, he explained to her as he let them in to the main part of the house. Reception and the secretary's office were on the ground floor. Joy chose the largest room on the next floor for herself. Once the drawing room, it had fine mouldings and two large windows that stretched from the ceiling almost to the floor and the room was filled with the January sun. The other room on this floor they earmarked for another agent, when they expanded. They giggled happily at the idea. The flat above was on two floors. A huge sitting room, a small study, three bedrooms and a compact beautifully fitted kitchen which opened on to a small balcony at the back.

'Barty, it's wonderful.'

Barty was grinning at her, Gervase appeared with a bottle of champagne and two glasses.

'New beginnings, always exciting,' said Barty, raising his glass. Joy wished she had not lied to him but could not see any way out of it now, and she raised her glass to him in return.

chapter **three**

Kate looked at the kitchen clock. It was half past twelve. They were giving a dinner party tonight. The senior partner of Tony's firm and a new client, both with their wives, were the guests. Kate did not mind giving dinners but she loathed not having met two of her guests, it always put her on edge. She sat at the kitchen table and looked at her tattered manuscript and stroked it gently. She still could not believe the conversation she had just had with Joy. She leafed through it. Nearly a hundred thousand words written, she guessed, and of that only the first two chapters were typed. But she had printed out the last two she had written, now that she was managing to cope with the word processor, though she was far too slow to do it all herself. When could she get it into town to be typed professionally? What about now? No, she told herself, she had too much to do. But still, she had made the puddings . . . how long would the starter take? She looked at the recipe she had cut from one of the colour supplements. She had wanted something different from the usual hot chicken liver salads or quails' eggs that everyone was serving at the moment. That was why she was about to break the rule of a lifetime and serve guests a dish she had not tried on the family first. She read it through: a timbale of puréed vegetable and smoked fish. No, it would take ages. If she made something else, if she got the ingredients in Graintry, then she would have time to get the typing into the agency. She would think what to cook in the car.

She hurriedly slipped on her coat. It was putting the manuscript in a Tesco's bag that must have reminded her that she had not telephoned Tracey to tell her her good news too. She went back to the kitchen. Tracey's reaction was the same as Kate's had been – she burst into floods of tears. Kate had to calm her down, and try to make sure she was not too excited, so she reiterated that it had only been sent to be read. And then Tracey insisted she tell her all over again what Joy had said.

It was not until she was in the car and heading, at last, for Graintry that she realised she had not cleaned one piece of silver and she still had the tablecloth and its matching napkins to iron – a pure linen one with drawn thread work, which was a work of art and a horror to iron. She felt herself beginning to panic, so much so that she misjudged a corner and narrowly missed an oncoming car by inches. The driver blared his horn and made obscene signs at her and she forced herself to slow down.

She parked on double yellow lines and raced to the typing agency, only to find it closed and due to open at two. She returned to the car in time to accept a parking ticket from the traffic warden which she stuffed into her handbag. That would make Tony happy, she thought with a grimace. She had to queue to get into the multi-storey car park and by the time she arrived at Sainsbury's she could not remember what it was she had gone there for. Pudding, that was it. She had to change the pudding, she finally decided. She wandered the aisles with her trolley, her mind on Joy not on shopping. Unsure what she would prepare she selected some kiwi fruit, a punnet of strawberries, flown from God knew where, and bought a lot more cheese from the delicatessen counter just to be on the safe side.

At the typing agency the fact that she had a novel to type caused a great deal of excitement. 'A4 paper, double spaced,' she repeated like a mantra. The cost came as a shock. Even more of a shock was the news that it would be ready the week after next. Her pleas that she needed it sooner than that met with the smooth suggestion that if she was prepared to pay extra then that, too, could be arranged. She steeled herself to write the cheque. At least, she reasoned with herself on the way back to the car, they were putting it on disc for her so that it would work in her own word processor. It was a one-off cost. You had sometimes to lay out money to make money, she remembered Pam's husband saying often enough. That would be the tack she would take with Tony when she had to explain the severe depletion of her allowance.

Her car refused to start. The AA were quick, but even then it was past five when she finally returned home. Steve was sitting at the kitchen table reading a comic and eating a peanut butter sandwich of such proportions that she feared for the safety of his jaw.

'You look in a bit of a tizzy, Mum.' He grinned up at her from behind the wedge of bread.

'I am, I am.' She flopped down on the seat opposite him. 'You'll never guess what's happened. An agent loves – not likes but loves, she said – my book and, I can hardly dare to believe this, she's sent it to a publisher.' She sat back, her turn to be grinning from ear to ear.

'Mum, that's absolutely brill. Just think of it, my mother a famous author.' His grin was even wider.

'There's a long way to go yet,' she said, trying to suppress her excitement, which refused to be suppressed. 'I'm so lucky. It can take years to get this far. Getting an agent is one of the hardest parts.'

'Hardly, Mum. Writing it is, more like.'

'Yes, well, after writing it ... Gracious, I must telephone Pam, I haven't told her yet. Oh, Lord.' She stood up. 'Look at the time. Why, oh, why, do we have to have guests tonight of all nights?'

'I'll help.'

'Would you? Would you really? If you could buff up the silver that would be wonderful. Now starter, starter,' she muttered to herself as, without bothering to take her coat off, she began to unpack the bag of groceries. 'Oh, my God, I've bought for puddings not starters. I'm going mad.'

'Not surprising, Mum, it's been a big day. Who gives a damn about starters on a day like this?'

The back door opened.

'Hi,' said Lucy as she breezed in. 'Mum, Christine and I are going to a disco, is my pink skirt clean?'

'Guess what, Lucy? Mum's book is being looked at by a London publisher,' Steve said excitedly.

'That's great, Mum. You know the pink one I mean, don't you?'

Kate had been burrowing in the depths of the refrigerator looking for inspiration for the wretched start to the meal. 'No, I don't. I doubt it, though, I haven't done any washing for days,' she said, straightening up.

'Oh, Mum, really.'

'I thought we had agreed that you do your own washing now. I don't have the time.'

'All you think about is that flaming book. Dad was right – ' Lucy stopped mid-sentence.

'Oh, yes, and what was your father right about?' Kate stood, hands on hips, between the door and her daughter.

'Nothing.'

'I want to know, and you, madam, are not going out until you tell me.'

Lucy flounced, flicking her long hair over her shoulders as she did so. 'Very well, if you must know. Actually, Dad said you were being selfish, but that it was only a passing fancy and that you'd get back to normal sooner or later.'

'Well, *actually*, what your father thinks of my writing is of no interest to me whatsoever – and you have my permission to tell him that.' It was not strictly true but she congratulated herself on how well it sounded. 'And what is more, Lucy, do you think that you and I are destined to spend our lives having conversations about the state of your laundry? If so, I can think of nothing more pointless or more tedious. Sort yourself out, Lucy, I'm not doing it, not any more,' Kate said icily, and returned to her fruitless search of the fridge.

'Well . . .!' pouted Lucy. 'God, why can't things be like they used to be?' she cried dramatically and stomped across the kitchen but at the door turned and poked her tongue out at Kate's rear.

'Childish brat,' sneered her brother.

'It'll have to be soup. Your father won't like it but he's going to have to lump it,' Kate said emphatically, collecting onions and potatoes from the vegetable rack. 'Bread!' she suddenly exclaimed, making Steve laugh as she raced across the kitchen.

'You're like a demented hen, Mum.'

'I've no rolls and the village shop will be shut by now. I can't give them soup without bread.' She ran her fingers through her hair.

'Croûtons,' said Steve, simply.

'Steve, you're a genius.' Kate dived into the large earthenware bread pot. 'Steve, you've eaten all the fresh, this bit's got mould on it.'

'Cut it off,' Steve said, 'it won't hurt them. Sorry about the bread, I was peckish.'

For the next hour Kate was running round in circles. The soup was bubbling. Luckily, looking at the bottom of her near-empty freezer, she had found an unlabelled bag of stock. She offered up a prayer that it was chicken, as she slid it, hissing, on to the gently sautéing onions and potatoes. She trimmed the pork fillet, cut it open and bashed it flat with the rolling pin. Into her Magimix she threw some prunes, apples, cooked rice and offered up another prayer of gratitude for progress. Deftly she stuffed the fillet, rolled it, tied it and browned it quickly in butter and garlic. She assembled the ingredients for the lemon and white wine sauce she would make at the last minute, using the pan juices. She parboiled the potatoes, sliced the leeks – they were too big to cook whole – and puréed the spinach, which she put into buttered ramekins to cook in her *bain-marie*. Was there enough? She would do parsnips in orange juice and brown sugar cooked in the oven – everyone always loved that. And then she fretted that perhaps the whole meal was going to be too sweet. She checked her tangerines stuffed with ice cream in the freezer and realised they were uncomfortably close to the parsnips with their orange juice. But then, she told herself, there was nothing she could do now. And what was more, she suddenly realised, she did not care. She had poured herself a large gin and tonic and was just starting to iron the tablecloth when Tony walked in.

'What on earth have you got your coat on for? This is always happening these days.'

'I've been in a rush.'

'You look like a peasant.'

'Good,' she said defiantly, and took a deep swig of her drink.

'Is it wise to start so soon?' he said, placing two large clinking carrier bags on the table.

'Mum's got the most amazing news,' Steve said from his station at the sink where he was carefully washing and drying the silver.

'What's that?' Tony asked absent-mindedly as he unpacked his wine bottles. 'I got one white and two red and a Sauternes for the pudding, that should be enough,' he said, without waiting to hear the answer and stood back to admire his purchases.

'It's pork. I told you it was.'

'You didn't.'

'I did. I asked you, shall I do the prune-stuffed pork and you said yes, you liked it.'

'If you had, why should I buy red?'

'I haven't the foggiest idea. But it doesn't matter, lots of people drink red with pork.'

'Well, I don't. Christ, Kate, you're useless, now I'll have to go back into Graintry.'

'There's an off-licence in Malt Lane,' Steve said helpfully.

'At Malt Lane prices, young man. No, I'll go to Peter Dominic's. What's the starter, we haven't messed that up have we?'

'It's soup.'

'Soup! Can't you do better than that with such important guests? What will they think?'

'Mum's soups are wonderful,' Steve chipped in.

'I ran out of time, Tony, I'm sorry. I had the most wonderful news, you see . . .' And excitedly, her eyes shining, she told him what Joy had said.

'You mean to say you've messed up this important dinner party because of that damn book of yours?'

'I had to get to Graintry to the typing agency.'

'Christ, how much will that cost?'

She told him in little more than a whisper.

'You're mad, bloody mad, do you realise?'

'Joy wanted it next week. I'm still quite slow on the word processor,' she added quickly to pre-empt him.

'I don't understand you, Kate. You used to take such a pride in everything – this house, yourself, dinners. Now everything's going to pot. You're being selfish, Kate, I hope you're aware of that.' And he slammed out of the back door.

Kate felt her face stiffen. It was one thing to hear Lucy repeat what he had said about her, but actually hearing him say it, that hurt.

'Here you are, Mum.' Steve handed her the glass of gin and tonic she had poured. 'Sit down and drink this. He didn't mean it.'

'Yes, he did.'

'Well, I'm proud of you. Even if the publisher turns it down, how many people get this far? Don't take any notice, Mum. The dinner will be lovely, they always are. Don't let him stop you, Mum. You do it. You show him. Tell you what, I'll give you another lesson on the word processor this weekend, show you all the short-cuts, shall I?'

'Thanks, Steve,' she said, giving him a hug, but all the pleasure of this morning had gone.

Although Tony was barely speaking to her – a state of affairs that was completely lost on their guests since he still appeared to be – the dinner was good, even if the company wasn't. Fred, the senior partner, was not one of her favourite people though she quite liked his wife, Philly, who made Kate laugh – Silly Philly they all called her behind her back. But the stumbling block was John Premier, the important client. He was pompous, loud and constantly putting down his wife.

The food, although good, was, as she had feared, unbalanced with too much fruit and too many sweet tastes. It was a mistake she would never have made in pre-writing days. But all the guests ate with gusto and much appreciation, especially, she was amused to register, for the soup.

Pre-writing days, everything had changed since then, she thought as she sat through the long dinner and watched her husband at the other end of the table. She would show him. She would succeed without his support, she did not need it.

'And what else do you do, Kate, other than produce food fit for the gods?' John Premier, sitting at her right, asked her.

'I write,' she said loudly and confidently.

'Kate, I didn't know you were a writer, how exciting,' Philly said, face alight with interest.

'Kate can hardly call herself a writer. You can only do that when you're published by someone,' Tony added from his end of the table.

'I didn't say I was a writer, I said I write.' She looked at Tony steadily.

'I'd love to be able to do that. You are lucky,' Margaret Premier said, totally unaware of the tensions building up around her.

'And have you a publisher?' John asked.

'My book is with one now. Blades, a part of Shotters.'

'My, the big-time. I thought you were going to say The Paradise Club.' John threw back his head and laughed. 'Right load of rubbish they are. Margaret spends all her time reading the drivel.' His wife looked embarrassed.

'In fact those books are very hard to write, it's a very special technique. I know I couldn't do it, I lack the talent,' Kate said.

'Oh, come on, Kate, any fool could do them,' John persisted.

'No, I mean it.'

'Well, their success is beyond me. Sell millions, don't they?' John asked.

'Yes. No doubt their success is due to the fact that they fill a very necessary void in many women's lives.' Kate said quietly, smiling at Margaret and ignoring the looks of fury being semaphored down the table from Tony. She stood up. 'Cheese everyone?' she asked with a smile.

chapter **four**

Julius, alone in Scotland, could not remember when he had enjoyed himself so much. To find a time he would have had to return to the days of his youth, when, as an undergraduate, working for exams, he had rented an isolated cottage in Wales for a few days. In the intervening years he had always been surrounded by other people, bothered by their noise and problems. He had forgotten how pleasurable solitude could be. So great had been his pleasure in his own company, and with Jane still away at her sister's, he had prolonged his stay in the cottage in the wilds of the Northern Highlands for several weeks.

With no telephone there was no one to bother him. With no newspapers to read, no doubt the world was carrying on in its usual cruel, hysterical way, but without him having to worry about it. With no company and no television he had reread *Bleak House*, *War and Peace* and *Vanity Fair* plus a handful of easily consumed thrillers. His supply of malt whisky had been diligently depleted. If he had a complaint it was that he was a little tired of eating Cumberland ham or salmon and he had resolved it would be some time before he bothered with them again once he was back in what fools called civilisation.

Every couple of days or so he wrapped up warm and trudged across the snow-covered fields and through a wood of magical winter icicles to his friend Angus Fairley's improbably turreted castle. There he picked up mail forwarded by Roz. He had told her not to telephone unless anything crucial cropped up. To his delight, nothing had, apart from the notification of a directors' meeting of Westall's to be held at the end of January, to vote on the proposal that Crispin be appointed to the board and be allowed to acquire Simon's shares. The resolution was proposed by his brother and seconded, he noted with wry humour, by his dear wife.

He liked Angus, and Flora, his wife, friends of such trust and long-standing that explanations for his behaviour were not asked for, nor expected. They all delighted in each other's company and they all respected each other's need for privacy. Shortly after his arrival he had confided in Angus his death sentence and then wished he had not as he saw the pain and distress the news had caused this dear friend of a youth long gone. He had begged him not to tell Flora and resolved never to tell another living soul.

Sometimes he stayed with them and their guests for lunch – the invitation was always forthcoming. At other times he thanked them and scurried back to the small crofter's cottage beside a burn which flowed so swiftly it rarely froze even in the extreme temperatures here. At night it was to the sound of this water that he drifted off to sleep. When he first arrived he had thought what a wonderful sound it would be to die to. And then there were nights when he found he wished he would not wake up. But, to his sadness, the mornings came.

Such morbid thoughts were at the beginning, now he had changed. Whether it was the peace, the beauty of the place or the sheer magnitude of the scenery, he did not know, but now when he woke up it was with joy at the prospect of another day. He no longer wanted to die. He was so happy he had even tinkered with the idea of letting everyone have their way and selling up Westall's, giving Jane the house and retiring up here. But if he did that the years of work and worry would be for nothing. There had to be another way.

The day of the meeting approached and it was time to leave this idyllic spot. He felt immeasurably sad as he packed his few belongings and waited for Angus to come in his Range-Rover to drive him to Inverness to catch the night sleeper. He gave his friend the last full bottle of whisky, a Laphroaig. On the station platform he had to look away as he saw Angus's eyes fill with tears. He listened to the invitations to come back soon, to regard Burn Cottage as his whenever he wanted, or to stay with them, whichever he preferred. He accepted with gratitude but even as he did so he knew he would never return, and realised that Angus, too, knew he would not.

He climbed on to the train, waved goodbye, and settled himself in his sleeping compartment, unpacking the half-full bottle of whisky he had saved for the journey. He changed into his pyjamas and lay back on the narrow British Rail bed. He wondered how he would readjust to living with Jane after his enjoyable solitude. Once or twice he had wondered if they should not part. Jane might find someone else, someone capable of making her happy – but, then, with his prognosis, what was the point? She would be a widow soon enough. It would be an expensive and pointless exercise.

There was also the company to think about, Crispin and Simon, and what to do. Could he let his brother down? His thoughts zigzagged around. Whichever way he turned them he did not like the conclusions he reached. This was one decision that refused to be resolved.

Crispin had had a strange time recently. Parts had been good and others bad. Confident that his deal with his uncle was finalised he was somewhat put out when the greedy old codger had asked for more – not a little but a lot. And Crispin had the devil's own job raising the extra. It was not in his nature to go cap in hand to anyone, least of all the banks, and to be turned down like a nobody was painful. He had finally raised the money, by the skin of his teeth, but to do so had been forced to sacrifice six paintings, some silver and a rug to the various dealers from whom he had originally purchased them. He knew he had been cheated; when money was needed quickly it was unseemly how rapidly the value of possessions fell. But there was no time to wait for an auction or to find that rarity, an honest dealer. He had accepted their money and vowed never to do business with them again. But nothing could assuage the loss of these objects, their absence would always leave a void in his heart.

Charlotte was being rapacious in a way he would not have thought possible. She was behaving like a shopkeeper with her interminable lists of what she regarded as hers – rapidly becoming the majority of the house's furnishings it seemed to him. The house was on the market – something he had not told the bank yet. Of course they would have to know eventually, since it was their security against his loan, but it was one of those irritating details he preferred not to think about for the moment, just as he preferred to ignore what was to happen when Charlotte discovered this fact. It had probably been unwise of him to forge her signature on the bank documents but, there, it was done now. It was not his fault, he had not known he was going to fall out with Charlotte, it had seemed safe at the time. And what was to happen if the bank insisted on their money the minute it was sold? And who had first priority, banks or greedy, divorcing wives? Unpleasant thoughts best not dwelt upon. The happy thought was that if everything was taken from him then there would not be enough money for the bijou mews residence Charlotte had set her heart on and had found with what he regarded as indecent haste.

His holiday in the Bahamas with the air hostess, Carol, had started off badly when she had insisted they go to a disco, of all places. He had enjoyed three nights of her body, though. She was at first delightfully insatiable, and was one of those rare women who did not mind what was done to her. But three nights was enough. He felt exhausted and was quite relieved that she had to leave to return to her job. He said he would look her up when he was back in London – something he had no intention of doing. She was disappointed that he was not travelling with her but by a piece of good fortune, he had bumped into an old Etonian chum, in real estate in Miami, with a holiday home on the island, who had most hospitably invited Crispin to stay. And then, at a party given by this friend, he had met a gem.

Brenda Benton. He had almost been put off by the name – Brenda was not a name conducive to a great passion, he thought. But, luckily for him, he had registered her surname just in time to give her the benefit of his full charm. Benton: the mass-market jewellers, hoteliers and fast-food chain. He had accidentally found himself a pretty, gentle, well-educated and docile heiress to millions.

He had returned to England with Bee-Bee, as he now called her, madly in love with him, desperate for him to meet her parents and sweetly hinting that marriage to him would make her happy. What to do? While divorce would cost him dear, marriage to Bee-Bee would quickly refill the coffers. Sex was likely to be a problem, however. From their nights in bed, he had learnt that Bee-Bee was a traditional girl – him on top and strictly no fellatio. She might change, of course, and he could have a mistress, but it was annoying.

Before he took such a step as matrimony, however, there were one or two things he would have to sort out with her father. There was still the extraordinary meeting at Westall's to go through. He had not had time to find out more about the Lepanto Trust – his foolish trip to the Bahamas had seen to that, and had he not found Bee-Bee, he would now be kicking himself for an indolent fool. But meeting her had, possibly, changed everything.

He had formulated a second plan. If Julius should dig in his heels over the shares, and Lepanto remain a mystery, he must not miss the opportunity that meeting Bee-Bee had given him. He had ingratiated himself with her father and had interested him so much in the world of publishing that he was pretty confident he could get old man Benton to finance him to buy all the shares he wanted, maybe even the company itself – once Julius was dead. But Crispin would want definite assurances before he went ahead with any nuptials. And if this was to be the outcome he was going to have to teach himself patience. Difficult, but important.

Today was the meeting. Crispin was in his office trying to appear as though he were working at the same time as his future was about to be decided two floors above. Even with the money arranged for the initial plan, even with his secondary plan incubating in his mind, he had an uncomfortably churning stomach. For who knew better than he did how quickly things in one's life could change? What if Bee decided not to marry him? What if her father were not as amenable as he had thought?

So he had plan three – a shot in the dark but all that was left to him. He could not imagine Julius voting for him so he had asked his mother, should Julius vote against his inclusion and use the Lepanto vote to scupper his plans, to insist upon seeing the authorisation papers for Julius's proxy. She would have the right and there was a faint chance the mystery might be solved – if the beneficiary of the trust was named on the proxy. Then he would be able to approach whoever it was, work on them to vote for him, and try again later. The problem with this scheme was that he did not know if his mother would act for him – he never knew with his mother. He bent his head over the papers in front of him, he had done all he could. Now he was going to have to wait.

The large boardroom at Westall's had been set ready. There were four ordinary chairs with blotter, pen and paper, water carafe and glass before them on the table. A larger chair stood at the head for the chairman – Julius.

Julius entered the empty room and crossed to the window. No matter which window he stood at in this building the sight of the square, unchanged since these houses were built, always pleased him, whichever the season. The room was called a boardroom but, with so few directors or shareholders, it was rarely used. The art department had long ago purloined it, using the large mahogany table to great effect for layouts of jacket and poster designs. Today their paraphernalia had been stacked on side tables and propped up against the walls.

He watched his sister Marge and his wife greet each other across the square. Even from this distance it was possible to see, from the stiff way they stood, the perfunctory handshake they gave each other, the careful distance between them as they began to cross the road, that here were two people who had no time for each other. He wondered if Jane was complaining about him. If so, she would get scant sympathy from Marge, who had loathed Jane from the minute Julius had brought her home to introduce to his family. Marge had liked him then, loved him even, and so close had they been that it was inevitable that no one would be good enough for her brother. Caring for him as she did then, it had always been one of life's greatest puzzles to Julius why, when he had gone ahead with his marriage to Jane, his sister had turned her enmity on him too. Enmity that had lasted to this day. It was extraordinary, he thought, just how long the female of the species could maintain a feud.

He turned as the door opened and Simon entered the room, crossing it immediately towards Julius, arms held out, in expansive greeting, which he wrapped around his brother in a huge hug. If pressed, Julius would admit to loving Simon alone in the family. But it would be hard not to, for the large bear-like man exuded such affection and was basically honest. And Julius was aware that, in all probability, Simon was the only one who truly loved him and would be scarred and saddened by his death.

The two women clattered into the room on immaculate high-heeled shoes, both equally expensively suited and scented. Both were unnaturally thin with the twig-like slenderness of the late middle-aged woman who has dieted too harshly and too long.

Marge greeted him pleasantly enough and he was glad she did not find it necessary to kiss everyone welcome. Jane nodded curtly.

'So you're back? How kind of you to let me know,' she said coldly.

'I'm sorry, Jane. I travelled down on last night's sleeper. I called but you had already left. How's your sister?'

'Fully recovered, thank you.'

Julius mumbled how pleased he was and then thought how little it would matter to Jane if he had left her. If the cook handed in her notice it would upset her far more.

At two he called the meeting to order by taking his seat. The others slid into theirs where Roz had placed their names. There was much straightening of blotters and realigning of glasses, which Julius presumed indicated that none of them was as relaxed as they appeared. Quietly Roz took her place at the side of the room at a small table as secretary. Julius glanced down at the agenda.

'As always I have Lepanto's proxy on all matters, should any point arising necessitate holding a shareholders' meeting after this one.'

'So yet another year goes by and are we still not to be privileged to know who Lepanto is?' Marge smiled.

'Should anyone query my proxy they are at liberty to inspect the necessary documents.' He smiled. He had often wondered if this would ever be raised. He could smile, for he knew that only the solicitor who dealt with the administration of the trust had signed the document, on behalf of the trustee. Anyone studying it would get nowhere in discovering his secret. The Lepanto secret had always been a game with him but it was now turning into far more than that.

'I might,' Marge said, tightly.

They raced through the business but then, he was fully aware, none of them wanted to hear his financial report which was nothing but failure and gloom. In the past he had witnessed animated interest on their faces in the good years when the profits were high. He reported on his acquisitions, mentioned his plans for the future, none of which was of the slightest interest to them.

Finally they reached the all-important minute. The proposal

that Simon be allowed to sell his shares to Crispin and that Crispin be elected to the board.

'Is anyone opposed to Crispin's becoming a shareholder?' Julius asked. There was silence. 'I would like it put on record that I, as chairman, am none too happy with Simon selling his shares and that I have indicated to him on several occasions that this is a course of action he might come to regret.'

Roz's pencil skimmed with speed across her shorthand notebook.

'Why?' asked Jane.

'Because my brother would do better to wait. When I'm dead this firm will realise a lot of money, that's why.'

'Why, are you thinking of dying, Julius?' Marge asked, her husky, heavy-smoker's voice full of humour.

Julius ignored his sister.

'They are Simon's shares to do with as he wishes. I don't think any of us has the right to stop him selling at this point if he wishes,' Jane said in her oh-so-reasonable voice. 'It will give him much-needed security,' she added, looking pointedly at her husband.

'I do need the money now, Julius, old chap. Not some vague date in the future.' Simon laughed nervously.

Julius rested his head on his hands and looked at the face of his brother. He could not let him do it, it would not be fair. Think how Simon would feel when he died and he realised how much he had lost. 'It's like this . . .' he began.

'Hold on, Julius.' Simon held up his hand. 'No need to do the protective brother act with me.' He laughed, nodding at the others around the table. 'When we were young he was always like this, never letting me get a word in edgeways, interrupting me when I had something important to say,' he explained, smiling fondly at Julius. 'It's my turn to speak up today, Julius. What I wanted to say . . . It's like this . . . I'm fully aware that if Julius dies I'd receive a lot of money from the sale of the firm – far more than Crispin is willing to pay me. But for a start I don't like all this talk about when Julius dies – he's my brother and I love him.' He coughed, his voice thick with emotion. 'Apart from that, if, and God forbid it does – if anything happened to Julius and everyone wanted to sell up, well, to be honest I wouldn't want a penny of the damn stuff. Selling would be a betrayal of Julius and everything he's worked for all his life. This way – selling to young Crispin – I can buy my house in Tuscany, have money enough to see me out, something to leave Dulcett and, most important of all, a clear conscience.'

It was Julius's turn to cough and to find his voice was husky too. 'Thank you, Simon, I appreciate that.'

'Of course, there is another matter.' Everyone looked at Marge who appeared totally unmoved by her elder brother's speech. 'Crispin is loathsome, driven by pure self-interest. Do we really want him on the board?'

'Really, Marge, what a dreadful thing to say about your own son,' Jane admonished.

'It's the truth. Tell me, Julius, do you like him?'

'No,' Julius answered.

'See,' Marge said pointedly to Jane.

'Who *does* Julius like in this family?' Jane snapped back.

'Certainly not you, if he's got any sense left,' Marge countered quickly.

Jane sat even more stiffly in her chair, turning her back slightly in haughty dismissal of her sister-in-law. 'He's good at his job, Julius has said that enough times. He knows the financial side of publishing inside out.'

'I'd like to cut the cackle and put it to the vote, if you don't mind.' Simon was getting restless, dreading the thought of his farmhouse in Tuscany disappearing, dreading the legal implications if he did not buy, since he had already signed the initial documents.

'Should I strike those last comments of Mrs Anderson's from the minutes?' Roz asked politely.

'No, keep it on the record,' Marge ordered. 'He knows what I think of him, I don't care if he reads it.'

'This whole voting is a waste of time, this meeting is a waste of time. We all know how Julius, with his proxy giving him fifty-one per cent, will vote, don't we?' Jane gestured with a thumb pointing downwards.

'Right. Those in favour of resolution five, please raise your hands,' Julius said smoothly.

Every hand around the table shot into the air – including Julius's.

chapter **five**

Although she had known Joy professionally for years, Gloria had never met Charles. She had several married friends in the business whose husbands she did not know. When two people involved in any aspect of publishing met socially, it was rare that anything other than books was discussed. Consequently it was not unusual for people to keep their family and work lives separate. Gloria was curious to be meeting a man who from many talks with Joy she felt she knew personally but whom she had not yet seen.

She parked the car outside the large, imposing white house in Holland Park. A wrought-iron and glass canopied porch stretched from the door, down the steps, along the path to the gate. Gloria was most impressed: these places cost a fortune. Maybe that was why Joy had returned to him – money. Then, as she locked the car, she chided herself for such an uncharitable thought. Money did not matter to Joy, but then it need not, she had never in her life been without it.

The inside of the house was even more impressive. Gloria was shown into the hall by an incredibly handsome blond butler. He was far too young to be a proper butler, and Gloria presumed he was an out-of-work actor hired for the evening. The hallway was laid with black and white marble. Over a gilt Regency console table, with legs so slender it seemed a miracle they could support the heavy marble top, hung a large and very fine Chippendale mirror with candles lit in the sconces at its side. Gloria made a point of checking herself in the mirror for experience had taught her that the more expensive the mirror the more becoming the reflection in it.

The butler led the way to the wide sweeping staircase. He walked in such a stately manner that she was convinced she had been right in her original assessment of him. As he mounted the steps ahead of her she had an almost uncontrollable urge to pat his delectable buttocks. Gloria adored men's bottoms, the perter and tighter the better. She always claimed that it was going to school in Plymouth and, at a young and impressionable age, seeing *matelots*' buttocks in their tight bell-bottom trousers that had left her with this particular fixation.

Joy was waiting for her at the head of the stairs. Without waiting to welcome Gloria she grabbed hold of her arm.

'Barty's here. Please don't breathe a word about my being back with Charles,' she whispered urgently.

'But if Barty's here and Charles is here, won't he guess?' she whispered back, gesticulating questioningly with her hands, palms held upwards.

'Charles is in New York. Barty thinks I'm here to look after my daughter while he's away and that I'm borrowing the house for this dinner,' she said, speaking normally now that the butler had reached the foot of the stairs and was crossing the hall to answer the door again.

'If you don't mind my saying, Joy, aren't you in the process of creating the most awful muddle in your life?'

'I know, I know. But what else can I do?'

'Tell the truth for a start. It's hardly Barty's business if you go back to your husband, is it?'

'But it is, you see. Barty loathes Charles – he's even trying to ruin him. And if he finds out, he could do anything – cancel the book, break up our new agency.'

'But . . .' Gloria was about to point out that if Joy loved her husband, being in business with someone intent on his ruination seemed an odd way to show affection, but she thought better of it. 'Don't you think if Barty finds out from other people he's likely to be far more furious?' she asked reasonably.

'He won't, though, will he? Unless people tell,' she said, staring pointedly at Gloria.

'Rather you than me.'

'Ian, Peggy, hello.' Joy beamed at the new guests ascending the stairs. 'Be a darling, Gloria, go and talk to Barty while I welcome my guests.'

The drawing room into which Gloria stepped was a wonderful, light and airy room with the kind of flower arrangements that took hours of supreme patience to achieve – that or horrendous florists' bills. Elephant could efficiently have wrecked the white silk upholstery in five minutes. She was glad she had not asked Joy if she might bring him. But, for all its perfection, the room was cold and soulless, a bit like a too-perfect woman, Gloria thought. For her, rooms had to have a bit of human clutter to make them real.

Barty was in deep conversation with a young man over by the window. Rather than interrupt, Gloria studied a painting over the mantelshelf. It was of a man, so handsome and perfect of feature that he was beautiful. He had a pleasant smile, which told of immense charm, but the eyes that looked at her from the painting – blue and icy – told Gloria it would be of a smooth and superficial variety. Like the room, he was too perfect and what size ego did a man have who had a portrait of himself hanging in his drawing room?

'Cold-looking cove, wouldn't you say?' Barty was standing at her elbow.

'A bit surprising. I had imagined him dark, not blond. And with far more passion about him. It is Charles, I presume?'

'Yes, it's him all right. He's got the passion, too. Problem is he can't keep it in his trousers.'

'Poor Joy.'

'Not any more. She's made the right decision at last. She'll be OK now. She thinks a lot of you, by the way. I was very pleased about that.'

'How nice,' said Gloria, but was unable to find out why Barty should be so pleased, for Joy had come in with her other guests.

Ian, sleek and rather pleased with himself, was a banker of decided opinions. Judging by Barty's reaction to him he must have been quite important too for one could always gauge Barty's assessment of someone by the way he greeted them. Ian's wife, Peggy, was beautifully dressed with immaculate hair and fine jewellery. Every time she spoke she looked nervously at her husband before starting and then even more nervously when she had finished. A wife-beater, Gloria decided, and liked him even less.

She was then introduced to Ferdie, something in the City, early forties and affluent-looking but with a pleasant smile and an infectious laugh. And lastly there was Brian, Barty's ghost-writer, who was unkempt, somewhat ill-at-ease but with a rather wild expression in his eyes which intrigued Gloria. She wondered which of them had been invited specifically for her. She knew Joy of old and like so many friends when happily married, or, as in this case, enjoying a happy interlude in an otherwise turbulent marriage, liked to matchmake. Was she supposed to make a play for Ferdie or Brian? Of them all she fancied the butler most.

'How do you enjoy working for my friend Costas?' Barty had rejoined her, drink in hand.

'It's all right. It's really too soon to tell,' she answered, bestowing a dazzling smile on the butler as he handed her the vodka and tonic she had asked for in preference to a champagne cocktail which always made her legless.

The butler moved on to the next guest.

'He's not your sort, love. Eton and Christ's and his father's a viscount,' Barty whispered conspiratorially, his sharp eyes never missing a trick.

'Then why's he a butler?' she whispered back, glad that it took a lot to make her blush these days.

'For laughs, I should think. So why don't you like working for Costas?'

'Did I say that?' She spoke defensively.

'I would hardly think that "all right" means you're happy in your job.'

'The job's OK, it's the building. He's turned it into Fort Knox – passes, security guards.'

'Costas doesn't like industrial espionage. He's been caught before.'

'But this is publishing.' Gloria laughed at the very idea.

'So?' said Barty. 'In my experience if something's worth paying good money for then there's always someone who would like to nick it off you.'

Gloria sipped at her drink and to her horror found she had already finished it. 'By the way, I heard about the book. I hope Joy stitches up a good deal for you with it.'

'No worries there. With my Joy in charge it'll be the sale of the century. Clever little thing, isn't she?' He lifted his glass to Joy across the room and smiled a soft, gentle smile. Joy waved back. A thought so bizarre entered Gloria's head that she had to shake her head to rid herself of it, but she could not stop staring at Barty who, aware of her gaze, raised his eyebrows quizzically, so that she had to say 'sorry' and quickly turn away.

The dinner was wonderful but, then, that was what one would have expected from a perfectionist like Joy. Gloria was placed between Ian and Ferdie and had a difficult time deciding who was the most boring. Ferdie spoke only of shooting and money, while Ian's interests extended only to fishing and money. It was evenings like this that confirmed her belief that the ideal marriage her mother envisaged for her, with a successful monied husband, would be mental suicide.

At the pudding stage Joy made everyone change places. With relief Gloria now found herself between Joy and Brian while Barty had taken on the money men with relish. They were free to talk about what they liked best – books.

Looking across the table Gloria saw that the shamefully ignored Peggy, who throughout the meal had successfully semaphored the state of her empty glass to the butler, was sitting bolt upright on her chair fast asleep without making a hint of a whiffle.

'What a talent, I wish I could do that,' Gloria whispered to Joy nodding to the sleeping woman.

'Oh dear,' said Joy with a little laugh. 'I'd best say it's time we withdrew.' In the ensuing hubbub as chairs were pushed back and the men stood and the women looked for their handbags, Joy was able to wake Peggy without her husband noticing.

In the drawing room, large iced vodkas in their hands, Peggy already asleep again in the corner of the sofa, Gloria and Joy could get down to what they had been longing to discuss all evening.

'Well? What did you think of it?' Joy opened the proceedings.

'What?' Gloria replied with, she hoped, a good air of vagueness, because one of the first things she had been taught about her job was never to show too much enthusiasm – it could be costly.

'You know what I meant' Joy pushed her playfully.

'Do I?' Gloria grinned.

'Yes. Have you read it or not?'

Gloria paused before answering and studied her shoes intently. 'I did.'

'And?' Joy leant forward.

'There's not enough to go on.'

'There's enough, you know there is.'

'A lot of work needs to be done on it.'

'Come on, it doesn't, editors always say that about every book.'

'I'd need to see a lot more.'

'She's lunching with me next week, would you like to meet her again? She'd love to see you.'

Joy crossed to the desk and took her bulky Filofax. 'Here we are. Tuesday, one, Panakies.'

'My, my, you're pushing the boat out for her, aren't you? One you say?' Gloria opened her Filofax.

'I expect great things from Kate, I believe in spoiling a good author.'

'What did you think of the other guests?' Joy changed the subject, her face alight with curiosity.

'Not a lot. I was surprised about them more than anything else, I'd have thought they were more up Charles's street than yours.'

'They weren't my friends. Barty asked me to invite them, I was hosting for him, you see.'

'Ah,' said Gloria, understanding a soupçon more.

At eleven-thirty she made her farewells even though there was talk of moving on to Barty's supper club. In the hall she managed to slip a note to the butler suggesting he meet her in an hour at the Groucho Club.

Barty had been right. He was not her sort at all. Polite and gentle in the extreme, he spoke of the metaphysical poets and Zen Buddhism until, to her shame, she had nodded off.

Now she was looking at herself in the bathroom mirror, wishing it had the kind reflection of Joy's Chippendale, and wondering what on earth had made her do that. And then she looked at herself sadly and wondered how many times she had asked herself that question and how many times in the future it was likely to be repeated. And what the hell to give him for breakfast with the fridge empty and the corner shop shut?

chapter **six**

Kate had been so absorbed with her writing and the battle to master the word processor that it was some time before she realised she had not spoken to Pam on the telephone for days, let alone seen her.

She dialled Pam's number.

'Pam? I need your help desperately. Joy Trenchard, my agent . . .' She paused, she had not meant to, but those two words were like a dash of cymbals in her head. 'Joy has invited me to lunch at Panakies. That's a very posh place, isn't it? What kind of thing do you think I should wear?'

'I don't know, I've never been there in my life.' Pam's voice was distant and chill.

'But you're always going out to lunch in super London restaurants, please help.'

'Wear a suit, the blue one. Is that all you wanted? I really must be going . . .'

'Pam, what is it? You sound so cool with me.'

'Well, what do you expect?'

'I'm sorry?'

'If you must know, I was rather hurt to hear, from Tracey Green of all people, that you had found yourself an agent. In my book, that's big news. Something I could reasonably have expected you to share with me. After all, I am supposed to be your best friend, at least that's what you were always telling people.'

'Pam, I'm sorry. I just don't seem to have the time any more to do half the things I should. When I first heard from Joy, we had a dinner party that night, and I got into such a flap that telephoning you went quite out of my head. I do apologise.'

'You didn't manage to remember after that either, did you?'

'It's the book, I just can't seem to think of anything else. The next day I went back to the writing and well, you know what it's like, everything else goes by the board.'

'Felicity says you're probably being taken for a ride.'

'Really? Does she? Why?'

'She says London is full of so-called agents – cowboys, actually. Women setting up with a telephone, typewriter and fax, knowing bugger-all about publishing. She says that you're only really safe in the hands of the proper large agencies.'

'I don't think that's necessarily so. Joy's a lovely person and obviously knows the publishing world. I don't think that's a fair comment when Felicity hasn't even met her.'

'I'm only telling you what Felicity advises, but then you don't like Felicity, do you?' Pam's normally sweet voice sounded quite hard.

'It's not that. I'd rather be handled by a person who's working in a small way and can spend time with me, rather than a huge organisation which must be more impersonal.'

'You're the one who would know, of course, with all your experience.' There was no mistaking the venom behind the remark.

'Pam, please. Don't be like this. How can I make amends?'

'Perhaps, in future, it would help if you told me first hand what was going on.'

'I promise faithfully I'll call you next Tuesday – soon as I get back from London – and tell you everything. What I want, though, is for you to come shopping with me tomorrow. You know how hopeless I am at putting clothes together.'

'Sorry, no can do. Out of the question. I have to stick to *my* writing routine, you should understand that. There's just one thing, Kate, it's not very attractive only calling on friends when you want something.' The line went dead and Kate was left looking at the receiver with a surprised expression. It was her fault, she had been thoughtless and totally self-absorbed. In the past she had always been available, at the drop of a hat, for Pam. No wonder she was hurt and upset. Once she had finished the book she would try to make it up to her. Not yet, though, she was not going to allow anything to impede the book's progress.

'Tony, might I have a word?' she asked. There was an irritated rushing of the newspapers, Tony hated to have his Sunday-morning read interrupted. 'My agent wants to take me out to lunch on Tuesday.'

'How very nice for you,' Tony answered, and she was almost sure he was not being sarcastic.

'Yes, isn't it? The thing is, would you mind taking my typescript into the office tomorrow and getting your secretary to photocopy it for me? I need two copies.'

'But I seem to remember you spent a fortune last week having it typed.'

'They only made one copy and I need two.'

'Run it off on your word processor,' he said reasonably.

'I haven't got enough paper and I won't have time tomorrow to get more.' She did not look at him as she said this for it was an out-and-out lie, she had a large box of paper and another unopened in the cupboard, but she had already worked out that if she shopped in the morning, she could work in the afternoon and add another couple of chapters to what she already had ready for Joy.

'I suppose so. I don't promise anything, it depends on how much work the girl has to do. Leave it by my briefcase.'

'Thanks.' She let herself out of the drawing room and went straight to the kitchen where she quickly knocked up a chocolate mousse, Tony's favourite, rather than the shop-bought treacle tart she had planned to serve. That made and chilling in the refrigerator, she raced back upstairs to the spare bedroom. This room was rapidly metamorphosing into her study with paper and books littering the bed, and the word processor on the dressing table by the window for the light. She was soon tapping away. But she had learnt a thing or two and now she typed with an alarm clock beside her, set to ring when the potatoes needed to go into the oven.

Tony was somnolent after his roast-beef lunch and two large helpings of mousse. He was sprawled in his favourite chair, legs stretched out in front of the fire, looking as if he was about to fall asleep.

'You look very content.' She smiled at him.

'I feel it.' He patted his stomach.

'You have a nice sleep. I think I'll do some more writing,' she said, standing up. She paused in the doorway. 'Oh, by the way, I thought I'd go to Graintry tomorrow and get a new outfit for Tuesday – give me confidence.'

'You do that, Kate,' he said, yawning mightily.

Kate did not like using such ruses to get what she wanted.

When she had first married she had despised any woman who stooped to such feminine wiles. But that was a long time ago, and experience and disappointments had taught her that it was often the only way with her husband. What if her book was accepted, what if she made some money, what would it be like to be able to buy what she wanted when she wanted and never to ask again?

'No!' she said firmly and aloud, back in her study, and purposefully switched on the machine. This was a silly way to be thinking. It was sure to lead to disappointment. She turned back to her work.

Kate felt almost sick with apprehension as she approached the restaurant.

'Madame?' A waiter welcomed her. Joy had not arrived. For a moment she managed to work up quite a good panic, convinced Joy had forgotten, but then, glancing at her watch, she saw that she was early. Joy had asked her to be there for twelve forty-five. It was only twenty to. She declined to be shown to the table immediately and asked for the ladies'. She had already spent ten minutes in the toilets at Paddington station, fiddling with her hair, her make-up, her clothes. She stood once again staring at herself in the mirror and for the umpteenth time wondered if she had not made a ghastly and expensive mistake. If only Pam had been willing to come shopping with her, to advise her, she would not be so worried and flummoxed now. At the same time she loathed herself for being such a wimp.

The black patent shoes with gold buckles were all right, so was the handbag, but that was about it. The rest of her, she felt, looked a disaster. The three-quarter length, fine wool, red coat was all wrong. It was too bright. And what on earth had made her listen to the shop assistant who told her she looked wonderful in the red and pink, swirling-patterned silk two-piece that matched the coat. She never wore such bright colours, and certainly not ones that clashed as much as these did. Looking at herself now, she looked like a child's kaleidoscope. She peered at her chin line and round her ears, checking there was no tidal rim of make-up – she never normally wore so much. And should she have worn her hair quite so loose at her age? God, she looked a mess, she thought mournfully. Would she ever wear any of it again? She doubted it.

The door swung open and Joy Trenchard, elegant in taupe and white silk, drifted in, short blonde hair straight and gleaming, make-up so discreet as to be almost invisible.

'Kate!' she cried out with genuine pleasure. 'Are we destined always to meet in the loos?' She chuckled.

'Hello,' said Kate, feeling huge and awkward.

'Yum, I love the outfit. Where did you get it? I'd die for that silk suit,' she said, as she glanced at her face in the mirror and then looked enquiringly at Kate.

'Graintry, a small shop,' she said, realising that Joy meant it, she really liked what Kate was wearing.

'Did you bring the rest of the book?' Joy asked eagerly.

'Yes, it's here, two copies as you asked.' Kate pointed to the rather shabby old briefcase of Tony's which was the only thing she could find big enough to hold two copies of her typescript.

'Wonderful. Let's go and order drinks.'

They were settled at one of the central tables and Kate, feeling happier now that Joy had said she liked her outfit, was looking around surreptitiously just in case there was anyone famous to tell Pam about. But they were the only customers, it was still too early for most people. Kate ordered a spritzer, primarily because that was what Joy ordered.

'I asked you early because I wanted time alone with you before Gloria comes.'

'Gloria? She's coming here?' Kate asked feeling all the anxieties rushing back.

'Don't look so frightened.' Joy patted her hand. 'She absolutely adores your work.'

Kate felt the room reeling and her skin burning and had to hold on to the edge of the table for support.

'There is a slight problem.'

'Of course,' said Kate, sinking back into her chair. Of course there would have to be, wouldn't there? she thought.

'As I warned you, Blades don't give advances on first novels until they're completed. Nothing to do with your work, it's company policy. It's in case the rest does not come up to standard and they will have thrown money away.'

'I could always give it back if they did not like it,' Kate said helpfully.

'Oh no! No one ever does that. Most authors I know spend their advances immediately. They're nearly always in debt, you see. Goodness, don't even suggest it, you'll start a revolution.' Joy laughed at her. 'But that was why I was so keen for you to bring more, keep Gloria on the boil until you can finish it. How far along are you, do you think?'

'I had some typed professionally, and now I'm much quicker on my word processor, so I was able to print out another chunk. I must be about three-quarters of the way through.' Kate plucked this figure out of the air because she had no way of knowing where she was in her tale. Since she had planned and plotted nothing it was difficult for her to say how far away the end was.

'Three-quarters!' Joy shrieked, and then covered her mouth with her hand to stop herself. 'You're amazing. You've only just started, how do you do it?'

'I don't know. The words just come out so quickly and I have to write them down in case they all escape.'

'How many words do you write a day, for goodness sake?'

'It varies, depending on what else I have to do. I have to squeeze it in. I managed seven thousand one day, but my husband was away, and the kids were out. Most days I hope to get three or four thousand words down.'

'Unbelievable.' Joy looked at her with admiration.

'The house has suffered and the garden is a shambles.'

'What do they matter? Someone else can always do them,' Joy said grandly, in the manner of someone who has such things done for her. 'It's the book that counts.'

'Yes, it is, isn't it?' Kate beamed, basking in this conversation with someone who obviously understood her compulsion.

'The thing is, Kate, don't be down-hearted if Gloria says little about it, will you? And if she does, and if – it's unlikely to happen, of course – but if she starts talking money, don't say a word. Understand? Oh, and by the way, if she does, you need the money.'

'Well, of course I do. Doesn't everyone in this day and age?'

'Good. I'm glad. If they think the money is unimportant to you and that they can get something for nothing they will. Gloria, over here . . .' she called.

'Kate, lovely to meet you again.' Gloria shook her hand and smiled at her. She sat down, slipped off her jacket, plonked her handbag on the floor, ordered a vodka and tonic and sat back and smiled again at Kate. 'I have to tell you, I liked the little bit of your book Joy allowed me to see. It promises to be good.'

'Thanks.'

'Guess what, Gloria.' Joy was leaning forward eagerly. 'Kate's already over three-quarters through the book. She writes at the most amazing speed. She'll have finished in a matter of days, won't you, Kate?'

'Hopefully, domestic crises permitting.' She grinned and felt herself blushing though she did not know why. Since they were talking about the book, was this the time to give it to Gloria? Or should she wait for someone else to make the move?

'She's brought you a copy, haven't you, Kate? Go on, dig one out for Gloria,' Joy encouraged her.

'Yes,' said Kate, covered with confusion, and she burrowed into the briefcase to remove one copy. It was an odd feeling handing it over to Gloria. She had posted the first section with excited glee. This was different. There was far more of it. Last time she had not expected much to happen, but now that so much hung on Gloria's opinion Kate felt almost loath to let it go. As Gloria took the large wodge of paper she felt suddenly bereft, painfully so.

'I'll look after it, I promise,' Gloria said. 'It must be an awful wrench giving it to me, like giving your baby to someone else to criticise.'

'Yes, it is.' Kate smiled at her, happy that she should be so understanding.

'I'll be straight with you both. I know we don't normally buy ... The thing is, I'm in two minds on this one.' She paused, looking at the typescript, flicking through as if to see the number of pages. 'Tell you what. I'll read this and if it's as good as the rest then I'll talk to Joy straight away. I can't promise you more than that, can I?'

It would have been difficult to judge whose grin was the wider, Kate's or Joy's. Gloria put the typescript into her own case. She did not know what had made her say that. She did not normally let herself fall into any of the traps invariably set up by agents, nor even half promise things. But there was something about Kate she liked, a shy enthusiasm, a bewilderment at what was happening, almost. And she realised she felt keenly that she did not want to let her down. She always hoped a book was right, this one she longed to be so. She could wish Kate was a bit younger and wore contact lenses – publicity always wanted them glamorous today and only literary writers got away uncriticised for looking frumps. Still Kate looked better than the last time she had seen her, much smarter and prettier.

'I love that suit,' Gloria said. 'I love clashing colours, don't you?'

Kate mumbled, not sure if this was a compliment or not, as the waiter took their order.

On the train back to Graintry, Kate was certain it was not just the afterglow of the wine she had drunk that was making her feel so euphoric. A tiny bit of her was beginning to believe that the impossible was possible: she was going to be published. But then the other, more sensible, part of her squashed flat such a notion. Best not to think about it. Logically, what were her chances? Nil. She knew already the heartbreak suffered by other writers far more experienced than she. What right had she to think that she could possibly be that much luckier than everyone else? Ah well, she thought, if nothing happened, if she heard no more, she had lost nothing. She had had a lovely lunch, it was all a little adventure, really. And she had a super new outfit – she liked it now, she told herself, seeing her reflection in the train window as they entered a tunnel. One thing was certain, though: if no one wanted this book, it would not stop her, she would carry on with the next one. In the last few days new ideas had begun to float into her mind, like small motes which, each day, grew bigger.

Joy returned home to be met by the nanny who, with the greatest pleasure, told Joy that her husband had telephoned and would be late home.

Joy did what she always did when upset: she poured herself too large a gin and tonic and took a long bath.

Gloria had not bothered to return to the office. The three of them had shared two bottles of wine and work was out of the question. She returned home to a furious Elephant, not best pleased at not being taken to work, and she called Rachel to say she would be at home reading. She did not intend to do any such thing. She meant to have a bath and then to sleep until she woke up. She looked in her briefcase for some Nurofen – lunch-time drinking always gave her a headache. To find it she removed Kate's typescript. She glanced at it idly. Three hours later she was still reading it.

chapter **seven**

Gloria showed her security card to the uniformed guard, the barrier was raised and she drove down the ramp into the car park. She took the lift to reception, and joined the queue of employees waiting to sign the large book on the desk and to enter their time of arrival – they would be putting in a time clock soon, was the current joke among them. Here, again, she had to show her pass to the security officer on duty. These new procedures, introduced by the Carras organisation, were ridiculous, she thought, as she had thought every day since they had been instigated. She knew each officer by name and they her, but every time she entered the building the same ritual had to be gone through.

Getting into Shotters was like getting into a prison, she had decided, though friends who had odder friends assured her prisons were easier. She supposed Peter Holt and Costas Carras were the only people allowed in without this rigmarole. Even then, maybe Peter was in the same boat. She must ask him what he thought of all these ludicrous new regulations when she next saw him. She was sure he had not instigated them, he was far too casual a person for that. It would probably be a long wait: she saw him even less these days. She often wondered what the authors thought about it all when they visited but, then, they were no longer particularly welcome here. A memo had been sent to all departments pointing out that authors should not be encouraged to call at the office. It was only a matter of time before the authors were banned altogether as an unnecessary nuisance. A day would come when her authors would be voices at the end of a telephone, or senders of fax messages, or images on a video screen; people who would only be trotted out to appear at a launch party and to face the press on publication day, like performing puppets. This high security added to the atmosphere of paranoia which was now rampant here.

She stuck out her tongue at the TV camera which swept back and forth filming the crowd in the reception area. Pointless really since it certainly would not be Costas at the other end – he was in New York, only his aides remained. But she liked to imagine Peter might be there. She would like him to know just what she thought of him and what he had done, what he was allowing to happen.

He had lied to everyone. The promises of no redundancies had been empty. A massacre had taken place here and that was no exaggeration.

In mid-January a team of men from across the Atlantic had entered Shotters. Who was who was difficult to tell since they all wore identical grey suits, button-down shirts, and understated ties. Even their haircuts were the same. For a week some had pored over the bookkeeping while others prowled around the building with clipboards in their hands and, although they did not have stop-watches, they looked as if they should. Round and round they went, observing. It had been an unnerving experience for everyone.

The feelings of relief when they closed their notepads, packed away their clipboards, shut their briefcases and boarded their Boeings back to New York were enormous. Everyone had relaxed, blissfully thinking that they had passed some test, that now they would be left alone to get on with what they were good at doing.

There was peace for a couple of weeks and then the telephone on one editor's desk had rung with a summons to Peter Holt's office. Ten minutes later she emerged looking ashen and, with everyone in the office watching in horror, she silently began to pack her things – the first to be made redundant.

The others huddled together, reassuring each other, confiding one to the other that this editor had not been much good anyway. Dead wood should be cut out, they rationalised. But word filtered through from the other sections of Shotters that editors were falling like ninepins.

For the next week there was a strange stillness about the building. Where before there had been jokes and laughter and the constant buzz of conversation and discussion, now there was nothing. Sombreness permeated everywhere even down to the boiler room where the maintenance staff had been decimated. Telephones frequently rang for a long time: people were becoming afraid to answer them for fear of the summons.

Then attention was turned to the other departments. First publicity, then production, followed by the art departments. Teams were pruned. Then the announcement that everyone half expected, and although they might think it a logical step, it still frightened them – individual departments working on separate imprints were to be amalgamated into one, servicing all the various imprints within the group. What had been pruning became ruthless and radical surgery.

It was not over. Marketing and sales were finally confronted. Whereas each house within Shotters had its own sales team, now they, too, were to be joined into one large one. Large it might be, but not large enough, and reps who had been with Shotters from the beginning were shed as unfeelingly as the newcomers.

The whole huge building was now a frightened hive of rumour, the occupants like bees whose nest had been disturbed after the winter slumber. Heads of department walked about with the look of hunted animals, badgered as they were by staff for information that they themselves did not have but which everyone else believed they did. People slipped quietly about the building as if trying to make themselves invisible in case they reminded the powers that be of their presence.

Gloria had lost count of the tearful farewells, the attempts to cheer up with warm white wine those who had been sacked, the piles of Kleenex they were getting through. Redundant they were called but, at the end of the day, they had been sacked. It did not matter a jot what cosmetic words the bosses used. Sacked with a pay-off. What was there to say to them? Assurances that they would get other work were misplaced, for this could not have happened at a worse time. Business was slow in the book world and other publishing houses were also shedding workers – if not on the massive scale at Shotters. The bleak truth was there were no jobs to go to.

The survivors felt exhausted. Living with this amount of tension began to take its toll. Tempers became short, ailments that doctors could find no cause for affected many, marriages were under strain and colleagues had become rivals.

Blades's office space had been rearranged. Where she once had three editors Gloria now had one – Letitia. Editorial assistants, those who traditionally were being trained to become editors in time, were all gone. Secretarial staff had been cut ruthlessly. Rachel now worked for both Gloria and Letitia. The only good thing to happen was that Gloria had been given a private office, quite grand and large, and glassed off from the main floor. There had not been space before, but that was one thing Shotters had plenty of now.

The 'list' was now on everyone's mind. How long before cuts were to be made there? With this depleted staff there was no way they could continue to produce the number of books they had been, and which made Blades viable. As word went out and journalists picked up the story, so anxious authors began to telephone, worrying about their contracts, their options, the chances of their next book being picked up.

During this period, although she kept a sharp look-out for him, she rarely saw Peter. Then one day they had shared an uncomfortable journey in the lift. Neither had known what to say to the other. He seemed unable to look at her and spoke only of the weather. She knew she should have told him exactly what she thought. She could not, for she felt she was looking at a man who, from the loss of weight she noticed, the puffy eyes from drinking too much and the harassed expression, was facing the fact that he had made the worst decision of his life. But nor could she bring herself to put out a hand and touch him and tell him she understood and did he want that shoulder to cry on? She wanted to but something – shyness, perhaps – stopped her. After that encounter he seemed to be avoiding her.

If Gloria had started to become disillusioned with Shotters before, it was nothing to how she felt now. She had begun to dread entering the building, afraid of what the day might bring. She was trapped. How she rued the day she had honoured her pledge to Peter and turned Julius down.

On this day, as she made her way through the huge open-plan office, she had promised to write a reference for a wan creature who asked her even before she had reached her own door. Once inside she shut the door quickly as if she could shut out the misery outside it.

The telephone trilled. It was Lorna Willington's secretary from personnel asking for her immediate presence. In the past a summons from personnel usually meant some silly problem with tax or national insurance. Not any more. Her heart seemed to plummet.

'Lorna will have to wait,' she said, with a courage she was far from feeling.

'I'm sorry, Gloria, but she said it was important.'

'Half an hour,' she said, more out of bravado than anything else.

She sat and forced herself to think logically. She was too senior to be given the boot by personnel, only the junior staff had been told that way. People like her had been summoned to the top floor and given a stiff drink before hearing the news. So why was she being called? After her job her next greatest worry was for Blades itself: she had a nasty idea its days were numbered. How long before all the middle-market books produced under the various imprints were put under the editorial directorship of Tatiana Spence of Shotters, and the Blades logo was no more? When that happened Gloria was leaving, she had promised herself, with or without a job to go to. She loathed Tatiana. There was nothing wrong with the woman as an editor – she was one of the best, Gloria was the first to admit. No, she disliked her superciliousness, her perfection, her neatness, her organisation. In her presence Gloria always felt she was back in the Lower Fourth and being interviewed by the head girl.

She berated herself for getting worked up. Such a major decision would be told her by Peter, not by washed-out Lorna in personnel. She looked at her watch, the half-hour was up.

'Now, Elephant, you be a good boy. Mummy won't be a minute,' she said, and picked up her commodious handbag. That was another unpleasant change about this place, one couldn't leave anything of value lying around: someone was sure to nick it if you did. But she could leave the dog with confidence. Provided she told him she would be back he would stay patiently waiting for her; he never roamed and would bite anyone who tried to steal him.

'Morning, Lorna, what can I do for you?' Gloria said with breeziness to the head of personnel whose office was on the second floor. Lorna, a thin-lipped and dyspeptic-looking woman, was head of personnel for the whole group: at least here was one department that had not altered much.

She might manage to sound breezy but, for all her logical thinking, Gloria's heart was pounding.

'Gloria, thank you for coming so promptly.' Lorna smiled her wintry smile. From anyone else such a remark would be sarcasm, something beyond Lorna.

'I've an editorial meeting at eleven.' Gloria looked pointedly at her watch which showed a quarter to.

'I'll get straight to the point, then,' Lorna said, but instead of doing so began to shuffle papers about her immaculately tidy desk. Gloria was not surprised, Lorna was incapable of getting straight to the point of anything. She had always felt sorry for the woman, sensing she had strayed into a job that was way above her capabilities and was now doomed to a life of constant worry.

'So?'

'This is very difficult . . .'

Gloria waited, attempting a bored expression.

'I've had a complaint, well, several in fact.'

'What about?' Gloria's forced boredom continued in her voice.

'Your dog.'

'Elephant?' She did not pretend to be bored now, she was alert and on the defensive. 'What and who?'

'There are some who think it's unhygienic for you to bring that animal to work as you do. Not healthy at all.'

'What the hell do you mean?'

'I've received instructions to ask you to desist from bringing it.'

'*It*, as you call it, is a dog, *my* dog. Peter Holt gave me permission to bring him with me. I only work here on the understanding he comes too. No dog, no me.' She spoke clearly and coldly, not feeling at all sorry for Lorna now.

'It's the health risk. Certain matter has been discovered. It's not nice, Gloria, not nice at all.' Lorna was twisting her hands as if washing them in unseen water and soap.

'What "matter"?'

Lorna put her head on one side like a weary bird and lowered her voice. 'A motion,' she whispered.

'A motion? What the hell's a motion? Do you mean a crap, or a turd? If so, why can't you say so?' Gloria's voice was beginning to rise.

'You know exactly what I mean, Gloria, and it's not my habit to use the language of the gutter.'

'Elephant's been set up. He'd never crap indoors, he'd burst rather than do that. Whoever said that is a bloody liar. Who was it?'

'Gloria, calm down do, you're sounding paranoid.' Lorna was beginning to flutter.

'Paranoid? Me? Don't be so bloody patronising.' Gloria's voice was raised, and heads began to lift and peer towards the glass partition behind which the two women were now standing, glaring at each other. 'You know what you can do with your instructions, Lorna? You can stuff them. I've a meeting to go to.' Gloria picked up her bag and swept from the office.

'Well!' Lorna sat down heavily on her chair, not for the first time wondering if she was in the right profession.

Gloria returned to her office. She looked about the outer office with a hurt expression: she had thought these were her friends. She had been certain that everyone loved Elephant as much as she did. It was unbelievable that any of them would lie about the little dog. She reassured the dog loudly, for everyone to hear, that no one was going to besmirch his name like that again. People looked upset; it crossed her mind that it might not be anyone here. It might have been the blank-faced men from New York who had objected.

Her mood was not improved by being unable to find the reports she had prepared last night on two novels she had to present this morning. Now she was going to have to do it off the cuff. These presentations were new to Shotters, something the editors were learning to approach with nervous apprehension. Having found a book they liked and believed in, it was then their job to persuade the rest of the staff that it was good enough for the house to publish, and the book passed or failed on a vote.

In the past when Shotters had belonged to Peter, Gloria had had her own budget to work within. Any book she liked, up to a certain sum, she could purchase without consultation with anyone. What had usually happened, however, was that she solicited other people's opinions anyway, but from choice, it had not been a rule. Above that sum she would consult with Peter and Logan and they had always sanctioned what she felt strongly about. Then, editorial meetings had been held to report on books that had already been accepted for publication, reports on work in progress, discussion of ideas each editor might have had. But now everything, it seemed, was to be decided by a committee.

When she arrived it was to find Tatiana sitting in on Blades's editorial meeting.

'Tatiana,' Gloria said coldly.

'Do hope you don't mind me sitting in on this meeting.'

'Why?' Gloria asked the question everyone else in the room had been longing to ask but had lacked the courage to do so.

'Just interested in what Blades's spring list for next year might hold.' Tatiana never smiled as other people did. Her face was a rigid, perfect mask. One theory going the rounds was that, like some models and actresses, terrified of facial lines forming, she never smiled for fear of inflicting them upon herself. The other theory was that she was so devoid of humour she never found anything to smile about. As it was, for politeness' sake her lips, with bright red lipstick that never smudged, never seemed to be eaten, were stretched a millimetre or two, showing just the tips of her perfect teeth.

'Sure it's not to see what we've got that might fit an amalgamated general list?'

'Oh, Gloria, what on earth gave you that idea?' Tatiana laughed, but, with mouth almost closed, it emerged somewhat false and tinny.

Gloria found the meeting tedious and endless. She nearly nodded off as Peregrine Phelps, ex-Wykhamist with a personality problem, droned on about the biography list. She fantasised about the joy of strangling Jill Case as she twittered on about some new cooking star she had found and *longed* to sign. Jill always 'longed', never asked, demanded or wanted, and Gloria loathed her silly little-girl voice, so at odds with the body of a fat middle-aged woman.

'Gloria?'

Gloria looked up. Norman Wilton, her editorial director, was smiling encouragingly at her. She had forgiven him for being promoted over her and quite liked him now.

'Sorry, dozed off, I can't cook.' She grinned in apology thus upsetting Jill who was frequently hurt at the best of times. 'I had a rush, I'll have to send my reports round.' There was a shuffling at this – it was quite common for Gloria not to have her reports ready.

'Right. I've two completed works. *Revenge* title self-explanatory, by a new writer, Primrose Cooper, she lives in East Anglia. And *The End is Nigh* a modern romance, saga length, by Serena von Hohenzohe.'

'I hope it's not a medical with a title like that,' someone joked.

'That can't possibly be her name?' It was Jim Field from marketing. Gloria did not know him well but resented him, unfairly she realised, for he had replaced Chris Bootle. Chris, in her eyes, had been the best marketing manager she had ever worked with.

'It is. She's a lovely woman and as glamorous as her name, and lives in London. She used to freelance for several of the women's magazines, this is her first novel. The advantage with both of them is they are new and hungry writers, we'll get them cheap. Only Serena has an agent, so we'd get world rights, America, TV, the lot with Primrose. I've received from Joy Trenchard an historical saga by a Betty Fammer – I've not had time to do a report on it for you but I like it and if you would trust to my judgement? Joy is keen to hear since she's thinking of sending it to Wallers. She's certain they'll buy but at least we would get away with Wallers' rock-bottom advances.'

'Joy Trenchard – another rich woman playing at being an agent,' Tatiana drawled.

'She's not playing, she's highly professional. She signed up Barty Silver, after all,' Gloria said sharply. She then began her synopsis of the works in question, trying to convey in the too few minutes allotted to her the excitement and the pleasure she had felt upon beginning to read the typescripts, imparting to others the enthusiasm that never left her when she found a book she believed in and wanted.

The Betty Farmer went through on the nod – at that price they could take the risk on Gloria's word alone. Everyone was excited about Serena, especially when Tatiana announced that she knew her and confirmed what a glamorous, vibrant person Serena was. Copies were to be sent around; if the majority liked it they would offer on the lowish side but be prepared to double if necessary.

But on the first book she had talked about, and Gloria's

favourite – *Revenge* – they stuck. It wasn't the plot, a searing tale of jealousy and revenge between twin sisters, well plotted, good characterisation, wonderful use of words. No, the sticking point was Primrose Cooper herself: she was fifty-four and a grandmother. She was too young to be published under the 'isn't she marvellous for her age, writing about sex in her seventies' school of thought. And she was too old to be a sex symbol herself.

'But it's a wonderful book.'

'Fifty-year-old grannies are hell to publicise. The chat show hosts want glamour,' Coco from publicity wailed.

'Not everyone watches chat shows,' Gloria snapped.

'Has she led an interesting life?' Jim asked hopefully.

'Her husband's a civil servant.'

A collective groan went up around the large boardroom table.

'You know the problem, Gloria,' Norman said kindly. 'Look at the number of these novels published each year. You've got to have a publicity hook. I'm sure it's a wonderful book – your instincts are always right, Gloria. But we need a personality, your Primrose sounds about as exciting as a ham roll.'

'And, after all, Gloria, we are stuck with the Kate Howard you bought before this new system was introduced. She's problem enough without another middle-aged frump to add to my troubles. I mean they're always so lacking in confidence. They dry up on radio, are worse than useless on TV.' Coco did not so much speak as whine. Gloria gave her an irritated look, which was completely lost on her, as she concentrated on the complicated doodle she had been doing.

'If I could be of help,' Tatiana said smoothly. 'Our list over at Shotters is already full for next spring. I know that Ann Cassell is keen to do a novel, I could get her agent to call Gloria.'

'I'm quite capable of calling her agent myself.' Gloria glared. She felt sick, she wanted Primrose's book badly. She had met the woman, she had already told her how excited she was by the book, she had probably said too much, cruelly raising her hopes – but she'd been so sure on this one. Now she felt she had failed her.

Around the table everyone was talking excitedly about Ann Cassell. Ann was a journalist who wrote a regular column on one of the Sunday papers, cross between a social diary and social comment. She was often to be seen on television, was young, beautiful, slim and articulate. Her novel would be a bestseller just on her name alone.

'You'd have to move fast, she only approached me first because we were at college together. Of course, with her readership each week she'll be looking for a hefty advance,' Tatiana continued smoothly.

Suddenly Gloria saw very clearly the way things were going. Tatiana knew already they were to be shifted – she wasn't going to let a catch like Ann slip through her fingers. She was offering her to them purely and simply because, by the time the book was published, Blades would be no more. It would be part of Shotters' general list and run by Tatiana. Blades would do all the work and Shotters' imprint would publish it and get the acclaim. Worse, the woman would be her immediate boss! Gloria sat silently, listening to the others, hearing the words she loathed – media interest, hype – and suddenly spoke up.

'God, this sort of publishing makes me feel ill,' Gloria said, loudly interrupting the hum of general euphoria over Ann Cassell. 'We don't even know if Ann can write a novel. Primrose has – a wonderful unputdownable book. My instincts are screaming – buy, buy. Handled and marketed well this book could be a megaseller. It's nearly as good as Kate Howard's and, admit it, you all loved hers. And yet you'll let Primrose slip through our fingers. You're all getting your knickers in a twist about a self-opinionated journalist whose idea of a long piece is a thousand words when we are in the market for at least two hundred thousand. To cap it all, you are willing to give an unknown quantity a stupid advance. I just don't believe what I'm hearing.'

'But Ann would be so marketable.'

'If she pulls it off. Look at all the journalists getting on the bandwagon. I'm sick to death of having to put heart into their books for them, that's *when* they deliver them. Never on time, I'd like to point out. That's what it comes down to. Primrose has written with feeling and with love, not for money. Writing for money doesn't work, you land up with a sterile nothing,' Gloria said.

'But they sell.' It was Jim again.

'But can she write a second? Answer me that. Primrose is

halfway through her second,' Gloria said triumphantly. 'And with an advance for Ann of that size, what sort of publicity budget are you into? Word of mouth still works out there, Jim, with the great reading public. You know it does, it happens time and again. And the public isn't so daft, it can recognise a book hype at a mile. What do you say, Norman?' Gloria appealed to the editorial director of Blades.

'I'm afraid I'm with the others, Gloria. There are just too many fifty-year-olds out there already. Now if she was seventy – ' He stopped, obviously thinking better of it upon seeing the expression on Gloria's face. He coughed. 'And you know how sticky first novels are to sell. The booksellers loathe them, the reviewers never bother with them. Let her go elsewhere, we can always offer for her next when someone else has had the mammoth task of building her up.'

Gloria sat silent for a moment and looked around at the faces of the others. One or two had the decency to look shamefaced, no one liked a book they felt strongly about to be turned down. Tatiana's lips moved. It was probably that version of a smile that did it.

'That's it, then.' Gloria suddenly felt oddly lonely and very tired. She stood up, picked up her handbag and faced them all. 'I quit. This isn't a publishing house any more, it's a sausage factory.'

'Gloria, you can't. Sit down, let's talk this through.'

'No thanks, Norman. We've talked it through. I'm through. I'll return the car in the morning.'

As she left the room, head held proudly high, she had the satisfaction of hearing a buzz of consternation behind her. She was a good editor, she knew she was. She loved her job, the real part of her job, getting her hands on a book, working with the author, coaxing out of her the book she had meant to write in the first place and hadn't. She knew she would be sorely missed, not just by the house but by her authors too.

Back in her office she picked up the two typescripts she had been working on, walked into the outer office and dumped them on to the surprised editor's desk.

'There you are, Letitia. It's all yours and there's a rush on – I've quit.'

She did not wait to hear Letitia's comments but went back to her desk, emptied two boxes of computer print-out paper onto the floor and began to load her dictionaries, reference books, and signed copies of novels into them. She picked up a black bin-bag and emptied the contents of her drawers direct into it. By now there was a ring of concerned faces peering around the door frame, watching her.

'Gloria, you can't – '

'Gloria, stop it – '

'Gloria, calm down – '

Gloria swung round and faced them. 'I can do it. I'm not stopping and I'm perfectly calm, thank you. If you'll take my advice you'll quit too – before you're all axed. Anyone willing to help me with these?'

Staggering under the weight of the bag and boxes, it was a subdued procession that accompanied Gloria and Elephant to the lift and down to the car park. By the time she kissed her goodbye, Rachel was crying. The others looked white-faced with shock.

Gloria gunned the car, and defiantly turned the stereo up so that Elvis blared out, echoing in the cavernous car park. She felt excited and elated. The tyres howled in protest as she shot up the ramp.

At the top she slammed on her brakes, her way blocked by a large Mercedes whose driver was reversing into a reserved parking bay. Gloria, leaving her engine running, jumped out and crossed to the other car and began, angrily to bang on its roof. The window purred down.

'Gloria . . .' Peter smiled pleasantly up at her.

'You big creep!' she yelled.

'What have I done?' He looked nonplussed as he climbed out.

'You don't know, do you? Still you don't understand. How long will it take for you to realise you've sold loyal colleagues down the river? That you have ruined a wonderful publishing house. And for what?'

'But, Gloria. Let me . . .'

'Money!' she shouted, unable to stop. 'You're just like everyone else. Greedy. And I – ' She gulped for breath. 'And I was the fool who thought you were different.' She wiped her eyes with the back of her hand, horrified to find she was beginning to cry. She turned abruptly. 'I've quit.'

'Gloria, please, let's talk . . .'

'Don't give me that rubbish. What did you say? "Stay Gloria, I need you . . ." Bah! What for? When do I see you? When have you consulted me? We've nothing to talk about. Nothing. You're a Judas, Peter Holt!'

'Gloria . . .'

But already Gloria was stalking to her car. She opened the door and swung round to face him.

'But I'll give you one piece of advice for old times' sake. Watch your back. Watch Tatiana – she wants your job, Peter. Maybe then you'll understand . . . I do hope so.'

She slammed the door shut and, with foot down, shot out of the car park, past a white-faced Peter. Far too fast, she drove down the street, tears of anger and disappointment rolling down her cheeks.

chapter **eight**

One of publishing's curses, though in this case one of its blessings, was that gossip spread through London at the speed of a forest fire. By lunchtime Julius knew that Gloria was out of work and, what was more, every detail of her departure from Blades. By two he was on the telephone offering her the job he had planned for her. By one minute past she had accepted.

Julius replaced the receiver on its cradle and was smiling. He was pleased to be proved right. He could have offered the job to many editors, but he had chosen to wait, certain it was only a matter of time before someone as individual as Gloria would walk out of Shotters and into Westall's.

'Come in,' he called in answer to the knock on the door and felt his smile disappear. The knock would be Crispin. Julius had an open-door policy in his office, people were encouraged to pop in and out with ideas and problems at all times. Only his nephew knocked. It irritated Julius out of all proportion, probably since there was nothing he could do about it, for Crispin was only appearing to be polite after all. 'Appearing', for Julius was sure that Crispin knew that his knocking annoyed him and continued to do it on purpose.

'I don't know how many times I have to tell you, Crispin, but there's no need to knock. If the door is open it's because I'm available.' Julius sounded querulous.

'I know, Uncle. I just couldn't do that, it would seem so wrong. I have to knock.' He smiled his oleaginous smile.

Julius looked down at the papers on his desk to get away from that smile. He loathed the bugger more with every passing day. And, what was more, he hated Crispin calling him 'uncle'. It only reminded him of a relationship he would have preferred did not exist. But, again, there was nothing he could do about that, either.

'What can I do for you?'

'It's the Barty Silver autobiography.' Crispin placed the folder he had been carrying on the desk.

'It's good, isn't it? I don't know the young journalist who's writing it but he's got the sound of Barty, the feel of the man, just right.'

'It will be the autobiography of the year, undoubtedly. But I don't understand, Uncle. These figures here, they're in your handwriting.'

'Yes?'

'But with these figures we won't stand a hope in hell of getting it.' Crispin tapped at the top page with his perfectly manicured fingernail. 'I mean, Uncle. Really! The advance you're suggesting is almost an insult to the man. And the publicity and marketing budget, that's more than the advance. Have you made a mistake? Have you got them the wrong way round? Even if you have, it's still too low, far too low.' He flashed his teeth but his eyes were cold. The old fool's going ga-ga, at least he could do the decent thing by everyone and die, he thought dispassionately. He placed another piece of paper on the table. 'Look, I've done my own costings, presuming a first print-run of ten thousand and a major paperback deal – I suggest Thistle's. With serial rights and subsidiary rights, we should be looking at – '

'There's no mistake, Crispin.' Julius looked calmly at his nephew. 'You're getting carried away. We can never hope to match what the big boys will be offering for this one. I've heard that Mike Pewter's determined to get it and he'll keep upping his offer until he does. We don't have that kind of money. But what do we have to offer Sir Barty?' Crispin looked blank. 'We have our name and our reputation, that's all, that and what we can honestly afford to offer. Barty's no fool. If we offer a ludicrous sum he'll know we've nothing left in the piggy-bank to market it properly.' Julius waited for a reply but none was forthcoming. 'I agree with you, we don't stand a cat in hell's chance of getting it.'

'Then why offer?'

'Courtesy, I suppose. Barty will be in on every stage of this book – he's like that. No doubt he gave his agent the list of publishers he wished it sent to. I've known him for years, I'd hate him to think we weren't interested.' It was Julius's turn to smile at the look of total frustration on Crispin's face.

'I despair, Uncle,' he said.

'I know, I know. But these things can't be helped.' He returned to the papers on his desk as Crispin turned to leave. 'Oh, Crispin. One piece of good news. I've just heard that Gloria Catchpole is to join us.'

Crispin stopped dead in his tracks and stood still as if caught in a child's game of statues. He turned slowly. 'Gloria? What on earth for?' His lips were curled with disdain: he had little time for the popular fiction that was Gloria's speciality.

'We're going into women's mainstream publishing. Of course we shall have to start in a small way and build. It might take time, but if we're lucky and find a couple of blockbusters it won't. Hence Gloria – she could be the saviour of us all.'

'I don't believe you.' Crispin sat down sharply without being asked, something he would never normally do. 'I've never heard of anything so stupid.' The shock he was feeling had, for once, stripped him of his impeccable manners.

'Thank you for your judgement.' Julius laughed. 'I'm sorry you've taken it this way, I thought you would be pleased. You're always saying there's money to be made and we're not making it.'

'Yes, but not with schlock. We've our reputation to consider. Why, you'll be a laughing stock.'

'No one will laugh if we're successful. It's not part of human nature to scoff when money's being made. Gloria's good. Don't fall into the trap of thinking just because a book is popular it's rubbish.'

'I'm sorry, Uncle, but I never expected to hear you talk in this way.' Crispin frowned. 'I really think you should have discussed this with me first. This is a major change in policy,' he said stiffly and, he thought, with dignity, but only managed to look pompous.

'The policy of this company is my responsibility, not yours, not yet. In any case, there was no time. I only heard at lunch from Mike Pewter. Gloria would have been snapped up by mid-afternoon – no doubt by Mike himself.'

'The market is awash with out-of-work editors at the moment.'

'Ah, yes, but they're not Gloria, are they?'

'Our other authors are not going to like this one little bit. For a start, we risk debasing our name and reputation.

Secondly, the advances some of these so-called writers demand will anger the literary ones with their more modest ones.'

'Then they'll have to be told the facts of life, won't they? If we can't generate more sales, then there won't be money for them to be published at all.'

Crispin snorted disdainfully to cover the anger he was feeling. Everything his uncle was saying was correct and something he had long thought necessary. Success now might push the selling price of Westall's up marginally, and that would be fine. But what he feared most was, if the miracle happened, and Gloria succeeded, and dividends were paid out – and the rake-off could be substantial there was no denying it – then, he feared, his family might find themselves suddenly becoming sentimental about the old firm, suddenly finding they like the kudos of owning a publishing house once more, and refuse to sell. He had too much at stake for success to befall Westall's at this late hour. With a few judicious dinners here and the odd whisper or two there, he had already set in motion his plans to return to an academic life. What was more, Bee-Bee was thrilled with the notion of life as an academic's wife. The dear girl, insulated all her life by the abundant rewards of trade, had a healthy snobbish dislike of where her money came from. This could ruin everything.

'So, Crispin, here's your chance to ask one of our literary authors. Sir Gerald is, if I'm not mistaken, about to walk through that door. He's due here at two-thirty and I've never known him be a minute late.'

Crispin swung round just as Sir Gerald Walters walked in carrying his Tesco shopping bag containing his latest manuscript. Crispin swooped on it like a bird of prey. It was everyone's fear at Westall's that vague, partial-to-his-drink Sir Gerald might one day leave a masterpiece on a London bus.

Sir Gerald was only half-way across the room and Julius was already pouring him a glass of Madeira. Sir Gerald drank Pernod in the morning, Madeira after lunch and port in the evening. A habit which his resplendent nose, swollen, red and pockmarked, proclaimed, but a habit which had never interfered with his writing.

'My dear Gerald. Here we are again. And what is this one called?'

'Julius, my dear boy, looking fit as always. This one? *To*

Whom the Bird Has Sung – good title, don't you think?' He was already drinking as he spoke.

'Can't be, my dear friend. Don't you remember, we once published a book with that title by Ulrika.'

'Shit!' said Sir Gerald, doyen of the English language. 'It's been bothering me where I got it from. How is the dear old girl?' He stuck his nose into his glass and sniffed appreciatively. 'How about *Last Song*?'

'Agreed. I like it,' said Julius topping up the glass of Madeira. 'Well, Crispin, should you ask Gerald what he thinks of my plan?'

'Yes, Uncle, I think we should.' Crispin looked very serious. 'Sir Gerald, my uncle has come up with a plan that I feel I cannot endorse. I fear for the reputation of the house. I fear giving offence to our prestigious authors such as yourself . . .'

Crispin stood with hands folded, a pious, smug expression on his face. Just like a church acolyte, Julius decided. He had had to pause while Sir Gerald had a coughing fit, brought on by smoking one of the shortest, blackest, most evil-smelling cheroots it had been Crispin's misfortune to get a whiff of. The attack over, Crispin took a deep breath and relaunched himself.

'I believe you would wish to find another publisher, sir – '

'Good God, Julius, what on earth are you planning?'

'I want to make some money by moving into general fiction with those large, saga-type books for women,' Julius said, smiling.

'What, those big things you see in airports and stations, all covered in glittering letters in gold and silver?'

'Exactly, sir . . .'

'Full of sex and ripping bodices?'

'Undoubtedly, sir . . .'

'Splendid. I like a bit of soft porn myself,' Sir Gerald said, holding his glass up to his smiling publisher. 'I'll drink to that.'

Peter Holt felt his day could not get worse. He was still reeling from his encounter with Gloria in the car park. She had looked as if she hated him and that had hurt – God, how it had hurt.

She was right, she had not seen him to talk to, he had not confided in her. How could he? He was too ashamed to face her, of all people. She had been with him the longest, she was an important contributor to his success. No wonder she was bitter.

She was wrong that he did not understand. He had fought to help her in the past few weeks, when his masters from America like grim reapers were cutting back his staff. The men from America had adjudged Gloria too individualist for the corporate image – nor had they gone too much on the dog. Her leaving was the worst, for it was almost as if a part of his past was chipped away from him.

He should have stopped her. He should have grabbed hold of her, made her listen to him. Apologised to her, begged her to stay. Anything, rather than this awful emptiness he was feeling now that he knew she was no longer in the building.

He remembered how, in her anger, she had managed to look even more beautiful. Her dark eyes flashing, her fine-boned face arrogant with hurt pride. And he had caused that anger.

As if all this was not enough, he had had a lousy session with his lawyers over his impending divorce. It took divorce, he had decided, really to get to know who you were married to. As his lawyer had pointed out to him, unnecessarily since he was no fool, he could not have chosen a worse time for a divorce: having sold the company he was vulnerable to a large settlement.

'Give her what she wants,' he had said wearily at the start of their session together. He had changed his mind sharply when he had heard what it was she wanted. Now he was determined to fight such unreasonable demands. Why should he shell out millions for that pimple-arsed Irish creep, Pinkers, to enjoy? He had always prided himself on his liberal outlook and he had always thought the divorce laws fair. Now involved in the whole sorry business, he had changed his opinion.

He had had a long and lousy transatlantic conversation with the American financial controller, who had informed Peter that the cuts made at Shotters were not enough, that further savings had to be made in overheads. When Peter had pointed out that he could see no way of saving another penny, the fool had queried whether soft bog paper was necessary and how about using lower wattage bulbs? Was this what publishing was about? He had slammed the telephone down in exasperation and refused to pick it up again when the man called back.

Catastrophes seemed to be multiplying when he was told

that Shiel de Tempera was moving publishers. After years of building her into a top-ten writer, the ungrateful woman was taking her wares elsewhere – to Mike Pewter with whom Peter had had lunch only yesterday. And Mike had sat through the lunch, which Peter was paying for, without giving a whisper away.

He picked up his telephone and asked Em to get him Faith Cooper, de Tempera's agent.

The connection was made.

'Peter, nice of you to call,' Faith's deep voice said. 'But I'm sorry, don't even ask, Shiel won't change her mind.'

'I don't expect her to, and even if she did I wouldn't have her back. I just wanted to know why she left.'

'She felt in need of a change.'

'Oh, come on, Faith. There's more to it than that. We paid her handsomely, we looked after her well, she's been happy here.'

'OK, Peter. I've known you a long time, maybe I owe it to you to tell you. Shiel was happy at Shotters until the last couple of years. She felt it was getting too big, the attention paid to her less. This sell-out of yours was the last straw. She doesn't like the idea of swimming in the pool with a crowd of other big fish. You've become very author-unfriendly, Peter. She was beginning to feel insecure. Too many changes, too fast.'

'Thanks, Faith. I'll remember that.'

He replaced the telephone and ignored the flashing light that told him another call was on hold. That conversation with Faith put it all in a nutshell. He could not blame de Tempera, nor could he blame Gloria. What was happening here was the total destruction of everything he had worked for. His American masters were playing accountancy games with something that such games could not be played with. Every book and every author was different. Publishing was not like any other manufacturing process. Publishing was about people, their sentiments, their fears, their egos. The end product was, in a sense, manufactured, in that a book was produced. But there was an ephemeral quality to it all which his new master was incapable of understanding. Where creativity was concerned, such ruthless accountancy should really fly out of the window.

He hated his job now. He dreaded the faxes and telephone calls from across the Atlantic. This firm was his baby and he was committing infanticide. He could do nothing about it either: he was a puppet and Costas's minions were pulling the strings. All the negotiating he had done, the watertight contracts he thought he had pulled off, were not worth the paper they were written on. Except one, his own contract. He could see no way of breaking out of it, certainly not with an expensive divorce on his hands.

He stood up abruptly. He had to get away from this place.

'Em, cancel all my appointments,' he said into the intercom.

'You've got Bella Ford at four.'

'Sod her. Get someone else to see her. Tell Tatiana. Tell Bella I've got a sudden attack of myxomatosis or something.

He picked up his briefcase, looked at it, threw it back down on his desk and walked out of the door, ignoring the jangling of his telephone.

chapter **nine**

Gloria opened her front door to find the normally immaculately dressed Peter somewhat dishevelled, standing on the step. His hair flopped forward over his blue eyes, his generous mouth was grinning at her, but in a rather sheepish manner. He carried, awkwardly, a cheap bunch of flowers. She was surprised to see him there, but at the same time suspicious and a shade defensive.

'Peter, what on earth are you doing here?'

'Might I come in?'

'I'm not coming back if that's what you're here for.'

'I wanted to say goodbye to you properly and to set the record straight, that's all.' He spoke so matter-of-factly, she felt it might be the truth.

'I warn you, Peter, nothing will persuade me to come back.'

'I wouldn't even dream of asking you to.'

'Well, thanks.' She laughed. 'That's hardly complimentary.'

'I didn't mean it like that. I don't blame you for leaving as you did, Gloria. I just wish I could do the same.'

'Oh,' she said, nonplussed. 'Come in, then.' She held the door wide open for him, feeling ashamed she had been so discourteous.

'I shall miss you dreadfully,' he said, as they walked along the hall.

She turned and looked at him closely to see if he had been drinking, but he looked sober and steady enough. 'Come on, Peter, don't give me that rubbish.' She opened the door to her sitting room.

'But you were *there*, that was the point. Now I feel completely alone in the salt mines. Elephant, and how are you?' He bent down to stroke the little dog who, at sound of his voice, had come rushing in to welcome him for Peter was someone of whom he had always approved.

'Sorry about the mess, I wasn't expecting visitors,' she

apologised, and began to tidy the piles of paper which were littering the floor and furniture. 'I've been sorting out what stuff is mine and what is Shotters'. This for a start.' She hauled a large typescript from the sofa. 'This is a marvellous novel. For God's sake, back it now I've gone, Peter. Those charlatans might let it sink without trace, might even not go ahead with it. I only wish she had not signed the contract otherwise I would have taken her with me. Add it to that pile there. Perhaps you could take them with you when you go.'

He took the heavy pile of papers from her and glanced idly at the title page. The name rang a bell. He frowned, trying to place it. Then he smiled. No wonder it sounded familiar, it was the name of a Queen of England, after all.

'You've got another job already? That was quick.' He sounded hurt. 'Where are you going?'

'Westall's. Julius said he'd been waiting for me and hadn't even advertised the post. Said he knew it was only a matter of time before I left Shotters.' She laughed. 'I said he must be a warlock to know.'

'What's he up to?'

'There's no harm in telling you. He's already organised an interview for me with *Publishing News* to coincide with the announcement of his plans. He's going to build a middle list – women mainly.'

'You'll have an uphill task there. I often wonder if that particular market hasn't reached saturation point.'

'Thanks for cheering me up,' she said.

'De Tempera's left,' he said, taking a seat on the sofa from which she had cleared the papers.

'She's what?' Gloria turned round sharply. 'Why?' she asked with amazement.

'Something I should have thought about, been aware of. It's certainly something the new owners won't even begin to understand. It was all too big and impersonal, even someone as successful as de Tempera was beginning to feel insecure. "Author-unfriendly", is how her agent put it.'

'Where's she gone?' Gloria asked with genuine concern. She liked Shiel, a rare creature who had not let her success go to her head. Hadn't turned from a pleasant, co-operative writer into a demanding ego with a pen as did so many of the others.

'Pewter's.'

'She'll be safe there. Liz Baker's a good editor, I'm sure they'll get along.' She was standing in the middle of the room, clutching a pile of papers. She looked at Peter and saw how tired and dejected he was. 'Is it too early for a drink?'

'Is it ever?' He laughed, and suddenly realised how little he had laughed recently. 'It's good to see you.' He smiled up at her.

'Mutual,' she said, finding she had to turn away from the intensity of his stare which, for some reason, embarrassed her. 'Whisky, gin, wine?' she said hurriedly to cover up.

'Wine would be lovely, but only if you have any open.'

'Open and not drunk? Don't be daft! In this house?' She went into the kitchen, took down two glasses from the cupboard and a bottle of Australian Chardonnay from the refrigerator. When she turned round it was to find Peter standing in the doorway. She did not know how long he had been watching her, he might just have appeared, but his being there made her feel ham-fisted. 'Would you do the honours?' She handed him the bottle and opener.

'This is a nice house,' he commented as he uncorked the wine.

'Thanks, I like it. I've got all sorts of plans for it but they never seem to materialise. Of course, you haven't been here before, only to that tiny flat I had in Clapham – God, that seems like a hundred years ago.' She smiled, accepting the glass of wine he gave her.

'This is an improvement on that flat. More than three people and you had a serious case of overcrowding.'

'Do you remember that night when you came with Milly and Phillip and the three of you sat on my put-you-up and it collapsed, just as I'd given you your plates of spaghetti? I was finding bits of dried spaghetti in my bed for weeks after.'

'And the time you decided to give a fondue party and the burner under the doo-da blew up.' He was laughing again.

'I'd forgotten that. And that time when Phillip and Milly came with their new baby and swanned off totally forgetting the brat?'

'Yes, and we were all rushing down the road screaming at them to come back?'

'Poor kid, it was a good half-hour before they realised they'd forgotten him. Something like that could have marked him for life. How's he turning out?'

'You wouldn't recognise him as Phillip's son. He's a very serious young boy, highly intelligent and he wants to read law when he leaves school and eventually go into politics.'

'Heavens! An MP with a father growing the biggest crop of cannabis in the UK – what a hoot!' She was nearly crying with laughter. 'I mean, he can't, can he? Either the son gives up his ambition or Phillip burns his crop.'

'I think Phillip would leave the country, plants and all.'

'Dear Phillip.' She sipped the wine feeling the contented happiness that talking about good memories can give one.

'You know this house reminds me so much of Hilary's and my first house, the one in Battersea.'

'It's very similar. Not surprising, London is full of these little Victorian terraces.' The feeling of contentment passed, she did not want to be reminded of his wife.

'Nice garden?'

'Lovely. Do you want to see?' She unlocked the back door and, preceded by Elephant, they went out to the small court-yard garden she had created, full of pots and creepers climbing the wall she had whitewashed. 'Actually, it's bigger than you think.' She led him out into the main garden. 'There's not much to see at the moment, but come spring this will be a blaze of colour right through until late autumn.'

She was surprised at the interest he showed and his knowledge of the different plants – not so easy to identify with only their early foliage on, but he did.

'I didn't know you were interested in gardening,' she said when they eventually made their way back into the house.

'I love it. Mind you, now . . . well, the gardens we've got are so huge and formal, they have to have gardeners who would not appreciate me grubbing around in the flowerbeds.'

'You can always come and grub in mine, another weeder would be greatly appreciated.' She laughed gaily, began to put the table lamps on in her sitting room and selected a Chris de Burgh compact disc to put on the machine.

'I might take you up on that. May I?' He indicated the bottle and his empty glass.

'Help yourself. Where are you living now, since . . .?' She

288

stopped, wishing she had not said that. For all she knew they might be back together again.

'I'm at our flat – no garden unfortunately, just some indoor plants. But I'm going to start looking for a small house. Something like this, I think. Get back to basics, shed some of the paraphernalia.'

'So you didn't enjoy the life of a country squire?'

'Me? No. That was for Hilary, really. She loved it, the social life, the horses. It bored me to tears to be quite honest. I've always been a bit of a Philistine where the country is concerned. To me it's for visiting, not living in.'

'I know what you mean. When I go home to my parents', at first I love it, the wind, the wide skies, the sea, and I think, how the hell do I survive in the smoke? And then – it usually takes a week – I'm longing to get back, longing for the noise and the bustle. So, is Hilary going to stay on in your house in the country?'

'Not if I can help it,' he said shortly.

It was a chill March and, although the central heating was on, it did not seem to be enough. She leant forward and lit the gas under the coal-effect fire.

'Bit naff, I know,' she said, and even as she did wondered why she should be apologising for something she had chosen herself.

'I think they're marvellous, no mess, they look so realistic. Of course – ' he began then stopped.

'Hilary wouldn't contemplate one.' She finished the sentence for him and smiled at him.

'I'm sorry, I didn't mean to come here and talk about her.' It was his turn to sound apologetic.

'Why did you come?' she asked, suddenly serious.

'Maybe I shouldn't have.' He began to stand up.

'Don't go. I didn't mean to sound rude.' She, too, had jumped up.

'The truth is, Gloria, I don't know why I did come. I just suddenly felt so depressed and trapped. I had to get out of the offices. I felt . . .' He stopped again and looked at the flickering flames. He was going to say 'lonely', but something stopped him. It did not seem the right thing to say to her, somehow. 'I wanted you to know that I understood your going. I wanted to say sorry for the way things at Shotters have turned out.' He had sat down again.

'Why did you sell?' She, too, had taken her place in her chair again. She refilled her glass and, kicking off her shoes, curled her long, shapely legs up under her.

'Why?' He shook his head. 'It was no longer right. We had already got too big for comfort, the intimacy had gone, there were employees whose names I did not even know. And there were certainly books we were producing that I had not even read. You yourself had picked up that I was fed up with it, felt I wasn't a publisher any more.'

'But this is worse. You're even less of one. I could have understood you selling up and starting again in a small way. Gracious, I'd have jumped at the chance of going with you.'

'I had to stay. My continuing as chief executive was one of the conditions of the deal.'

'Can't you leave?'

'It might be difficult. Before I came here I went to see my lawyer to see if there's any way out of my contract.'

'There must be. I bet Costas had a loophole built in in case he wanted to get rid of you. You can rely on that.'

'That's what my lawyer said. He said that a clever lawyer can always find a way out of a contract. I just hope he's clever enough.'

'If he isn't, find another one. But why Costas? I don't understand that, either. I know you said it was because he didn't know much about publishing, but surely that's why everything is in the mess it is now?'

'Do you want to know the truth?' He looked at her, she nodded. 'I found my wife in bed with a creep the very evening I found that Costas wanted to buy. Suddenly, there really seemed no point in carrying on with Shotters. Phillip didn't care one way or the other, so I thought, "Sod the lot of them," and rushed straight into the arms of Costas when I wasn't really thinking straight. I can see that now.'

'Oh, Peter, that must have been awful for you. I'm so sorry.' She felt a surge of anger that Hilary had treated him in this way and wished she could help.

'I'm not. I regret selling to Costas, of course, it was the act of a fool in a slough of self-pity. I don't regret finding Hilary out. Our relationship had been dead for years. I was just too lazy to face up to it.'

'And the kids?'

'They appear to have taken it quite well. They're used to their parents arguing and not being particularly loving to each other. I suppose only time will tell how affected they are. Josh is happy at school and at eighteen was already starting to drift away from us. In any case he will be away at university later this year. Rose, I don't know. She doesn't get on that well with her mother – I gather it's quite common for girls to have stormy relationships with their mums.'

Gloria smiled at him. 'Yes, I'd agree with that,' she said with feeling.

'I know I shall miss her. You know, daddies and their daughters.' He tried to smile but only succeeded in looking sad.

'Couldn't she live with you?'

'It wouldn't be fair, would it? She likes the horses and all the country crap. You know what sixteen-year-old girls are like.'

'Yes, I can still remember that far back,' she joshed him. 'At sixteen I'd have given anything to live in London. The horses by then were most definitely becoming a secondary interest.'

'But do you know what hurts me most, Gloria? It's the idea of that Irish bastard taking my place in Rose's life.'

'She's too old for that. No one will replace her dad, not now. I promise you.'

'Really?' His face lit up. 'I do hope you're right.'

'Shall we have another bottle of wine? I don't know about you but I reckon there's a government plot that's making the bottles smaller, they never seem to last as long as they did once.' She was laughing, hoping to cheer him up.

'Good God! Look at the time. Gloria, I'm so sorry, I'd no idea . . . I do apologise for boring you with my problems . . . I must be going, I'm keeping you . . .'

'Sit down. You're doing nothing of the sort. I've nothing to do but feed the cat and Elephant. I've not much to eat, mind you – some cheese, or we could get a take-away?'

'Let me take you out to dinner.'

'I'd love to.'

'You feed your zoo, I'll book a table.'

*

They went to the local bistro Gloria had suggested, chosen since it was unlikely that anyone they knew would be there. She had felt in his present mood he would not enjoy a too-sociable evening. But also she suggested it because she knew she wanted him all to herself.

They talked and Gloria could not remember the last time she had opened up to someone quite as honestly as she did to Peter. It was almost a relief to be with someone she trusted well enough to confess her loneliness and how unsatisfied she was in her personal relationships. Gloria was cursed in that to the world she seemed a sophisticated, confident, slightly hard woman. But Peter knew her far better than she realised. He was aware of the kind, vulnerable, rather frightened person she was inside. Had he not known he would have been most unperceptive not to realise it that night. She told him everything from her past, things she would prefer to have forgotten but which, strangely, she felt impelled to tell him.

'Good heavens, Peter. I can't imagine why I'm unburdening myself to you like this. Sorry.'

'Don't even think of apologising. I'm honoured you should trust me.' He smiled and, even though the light in the restaurant was dim, she could see the kindness and understanding in his eyes. He put out his hand and covered hers. She felt a pleasurable jolt at his touch. 'We all need friends, Gloria.'

She smiled back, feeling different, as if her confession had cleansed her. She looked at him with longing, wishing he needed more than a friend, and then felt quite taken aback by the thought.

'Isn't it odd how with some people it's easy to pick up the thread of true friendship, and with others it's impossible? They belong in a time and a place in the past and can't come with you into your present or future.'

'Takes a very special sort of friend.' Peter smiled at her, slightly lopsidedly, over his glass of brandy.

Then it was his turn and, in depth, he told her of what he now regarded as his empty years. He spoke of love and the lack of it in his life and in turn he talked of his loneliness.

They only left the bistro when the waiters noisily began to stack the chairs on the tables.

Though cold, it was a lovely evening with a clear sky and,

they both agreed, a definite smell of spring in the air. When he took her hand she felt ridiculously happy.

As they walked along she knew she wanted to invite him in, knew she wanted him to kiss her, knew without doubt that if he did she would want to go to bed with him. 'Not this time,' she told herself. This time she would not make the mistake she had so often made in the past. She would be courted. She wanted him to wine and dine her, shower her with flowers and little presents, with notes and telephone calls. This time it had to be perfect as it never had been before. She wanted to try to recapture her youth.

'That was a lovely evening, Gloria. Thanks,' he said, as they stood on the pavement outside her house.

'It was.'

'We must do it again sometime.'

'Yes,' she said fighting the longing to hold him.

'Shall I call you?'

'Yes,' she repeated, wondering what his kiss was like.

'Right. Yes, well, I'd best let you get to bed.' He turned away and began to walk down the street.

She watched him go and although she had won her fight with herself she still felt let down. She kicked her gate open and its hinge finally broke and crashed to the ground.

chapter **ten**

Having signed her contract, Kate had banked her first advance cheque from Shotters. To do so she had opened a new account. She had not done this to keep it from Tony but, rather, she had decided to use it for the things she needed for writing, any new clothes that her lack of confidence demanded, and – the most revolutionary idea of all – to buy ready-prepared meals from Marks and Spencer that she could put in the freezer. Then, when she was writing, the family would still eat well. She had heard good reports about the food from Pam who rarely cooked if she could help it. If she was careful in disposing of the packets, Tony need never find out. It was not a lot of money but she hoped it would tide her over until the next tranche came when Shotters had accepted the final manuscript. They would pay her the last instalment when the book was published by which time, hopefully, she would have finished the second book, with which she was already tinkering. She had not meant to start on it so soon, she wanted to have the first one completely finished before she did, but her brain had other ideas, and with a new plot, and characters in her mind, she had found it necessary to begin.

It was as well this was so for things were not going too smoothly in her life at the moment. Steve had found himself a job, miles away in Yorkshire, working in the garden of a stately home.

'I've got to take it, Mum. These jobs don't come up that often.'

'But it's so far away. Could you not find something nearer?'

'Mum, you don't understand, these gardens are world famous, I'll learn so much there. The head gardener is well known. I'll get a job anywhere with him having trained me. Will you tell Dad?'

She had agreed to, not that she had looked forward to it. Predictably Tony was furious.

'What about his GCSEs? He can't give up on those.'

'He says he doesn't need them.'

'That's ridiculous. Of course he needs them – everyone does these days. He should go to horticultural college if he wants to go ahead with this crazy plan.'

'He says, quite honestly, that he wouldn't stand a chance of getting into one, that he's too thick.'

'He's not thick, he's idle.'

'Tony, I know it's hard when it's your only son, but Steve isn't very bright academically. If only you could face that, not dream impossible dreams for him. Isn't his happiness more important? Anyway, I'm rather proud of him, taking the initiative like this. Taking control of his own life.'

'Kate, you talk such twaddle at times. I know there's nothing we can do. But at least we should try and stop him, the boy need not think he'd have my blessing. Thank God we have Lucy.'

'Yes, dear, thanks for Lucy.'

He looked up when she said that and glared suspiciously, as if he had caught the shadow of sarcasm in her voice. But he said nothing, for she was smiling sweetly at him.

The atmosphere in the house had been difficult since this bombshell from Steve. There had not been a row but everyone was aware that one was brewing just under the surface. As she bought clothes for him that she felt he would need, and washed and packed for him, Kate felt such a weight of sadness. It had all happened so quickly. One day Steve was a toddler and now she was packing his case ready for him to leave, probably for ever. She had known it would come one day, but she had every right not to expect it so suddenly.

She had tried to persuade Tony to drive up with them, but he stolidly refused. His only concession, that showed he might be upset, was the cheque he had given Steve the morning he was leaving. 'For emergencies,' he had said, somewhat gruffly.

Kate knew that Steve had really wanted to travel to Yorkshire alone. He was afraid people would think him a wimp arriving with his mother.

'Let me, Steve. If I know where you are, what it looks like, it will be easier for me to imagine you there,' she had pleaded. When it came to the day, she sensed that he was relieved the arrangements had been made this way. She was not the only one who was tearful when it was finally time to say goodbye.

'Think, Mum, you'll have a lot more time to write with one less of us.'

'You were never any trouble.'

'You will carry on, won't you? You won't let Dad stop you, will you?'

'What an odd thing to say. Why should he stop me?'

'Because I think he's jealous of it, he'll hate it when you're a success – I shan't, I shall boast to everyone.' He smiled and let her kiss him farewell.

They had stopped off overnight on the way up to Yorkshire, so that Kate could get away early. It was a long drive back and, with no one to share her misery, a lonely one. Hence, instead of going straight home when she arrived in Graintry, she decided to make good her promise to herself and to go to Marks' and stock up with food.

She enjoyed the next hour as she ambled around the aisles of the large foodhall. She often bought clothes here, but had never bothered even to look at the provisions section. It was wonderful. Dishes she had often thought of making but had felt were beyond her, and dishes that were old favourites of everyone. Slowly and surely her trolley filled up.

So engrossed had she been with reading the packaging that it was not until she had almost finished that she became aware of the funny looks she was getting from the other women. She could just imagine what they were thinking: 'Look at that lazy bitch ...' '... What a dreadful wife and mother ...' and worst, 'No wonder she's so fat ...' All the guilt that Kate was normally fighting rose up in her and engulfed her and she almost put everything back. Then she saw a man, about her own age, with a trolley even more full than hers and totally unselfconscious, laughing and joking with the woman at the till. If he can, why can't I? she thought, and proceeded to unload the trolley on to the conveyor belt before she changed her mind again, but resolved even more firmly to stick to her diet.

It was seeing the café she and Pam often had a snack in, and the old coaching inn where they sometimes treated themselves to a proper lunch, and passing Pam's favourite dress shop, that made Kate long to see her friend. She wanted to tell her how miserable she was about Steve, she wanted them to be like they once had been.

Instead of driving home, she took the turning that led to Pam's. It was weeks since she had seen her. She had telephoned upon her return from her lunch with Joy and Gloria as she had promised. She had begun to tell her all about it but Pam had sounded so bored that she had stopped. She had kept her in touch with every development – all through the nail-biting days of waiting for confirmation that Shotters wanted her book, through the days of Joy's financial negotiations. She had done all that but there were times she wondered why she bothered because Pam was always so cool about it. She needed Pam and she was going to get to the bottom of the trouble between them.

Pam was surprised to find Kate standing unannounced on her doorstep. By no stretch of the imagination could her welcome be called warm.

'We're going out to dinner,' she said somewhat sharply.

'I just want to see you for a moment.'

'I suppose you had better come in,' Pam said ungraciously.

They played conversational games as they asked each other about their families, Kate finding herself wanting to delay anything deeper. They were in Pam's drawing room, a room of great opulence. Portraits hung on the walls – nothing to do with their families and, to give them their due, they never claimed they were. But Kate often felt sorry for the faces in the pictures for they were like orphans having lost their real families and unlikely ever to be traced.

This was ridiculous, Kate told herself. This polite enquiring was not why she had come. 'Look, Pam, I think we're being silly. I thought we had sorted everything out. I've telephoned you often. There's something else that's annoying you and I want to know what it is. And right here and now I'll say sorry, whatever it is.

'Oh, Kate, I've missed you so,' Pam said standing in the middle of the room like a small exquisite doll and looking as if she was about to burst into tears.

'And I you. What dumb clucks we are.' Kate was laughing. 'What happened?'

'I don't know.' Pam shook her head. 'You remember what it was like at school and suddenly your friends were doing something else and you weren't included? It's been like that. I've felt so left out as if you were going away from me.'

'It's not just you, it's everything – the whole of my routine has gone by the board. This writing is like a drug.'

'Don't laugh at me, will you, but, I feel silly even saying this – I felt jealous of the book. Does that make sense?'

'Pam, I'm so sorry.' She put her arm around her friend's thin shoulders and hugged her. How strange, she thought, that Steve should say the same thing about his father, but she decided not to mention that to Pam.

'And there's something else . . .' Pam said looking anxiously at her.

'What, Pam?' Kate suddenly felt uneasy.

'I . . . it's nothing. It can wait. Don't look so worried, it's not serious.' And Kate relaxed as Pam laughed. 'Gin?'

'Please. Have you heard from the Red Rose Society?'

'Yes, last week. Shall we go?'

'Let's. It'll be fun seeing everyone again. I've got to have lunch with my publishers that day. We could meet up and go to the meeting together.'

'There you are.' Pam's shoulders slumped with dejection again. 'You're in a different world already.'

'No, I'm not. We're both in the same one. I'm just a step ahead of you, it'll be your turn next.'

'I doubt it,' Pam said morosely. 'Did you know Tracey's been accepted by The Paradise Club? Felicity is furious.' She managed to smile as she imparted this piece of gossip.

'I'm not surprised. Poor Felicity, all those years of trying and then Tracey and I have such good luck. How's your book coming along?'

'Slowly. No one takes me seriously. If I say I'm a writer people just grin. You have to be accepted before anyone will respect you and leave you alone to get on with it.'

'You must be firm and insist no one interrupts you when you're working. Make the family understand it's important to you. Think about yourself for a change. You've got to, to get anywhere.'

'You will help me when I've finished it, won't you? Like you helped Tracey?'

'Of course I will. You're my best friend, aren't you?'

'You wouldn't read what I've done? Take it with you, let me know what you think next week?'

'Of course I will,' she said as Pam rushed off to get her manuscript for her.

Later, back home, she wondered if it had been a wise decision. Pam had not written much, only fifty pages, but as Kate read them her heart sank. She did not understand it or what Pam was trying to do. She could not see it selling, she certainly would not buy it. It was as if Pam could not decide what sort of book she wanted to write or for whom. It slipped from a fantasy world and then back to a more normal one even in the same paragraph.

Once she had finished it Kate sat for a long time wondering what to do about it. Should she be straight with Pam and tell her truthfully what she thought about it? No. She could not bring herself to destroy something someone else had toiled over, nor risk ruining Pam's confidence in herself. Should she advise her, tell her where she thought the writing could be improved? No. What if Pam resented her interference? Should she lie and say it was wonderful? No. It would be cruel to lie. She would not like this herself, so why should Pam be different?

What then? Maybe she could ask Joy, as a favour, to read it. Let her do the dirty work for her. Joy did not know Pam, it would be easier for her. Yes, that was what she would do, she thought, as she slid the papers carefully back into their envelope.

chapter **eleven**

The following week an edgy Kate, in a new skirt, blouse, shoes and jacket, stood in the reception hall of Shotters to keep her appointment. She knew she would have felt better if she was waiting to meet Gloria. Her call to tell Kate that she had left had been a shock. Although, apart from buying manuscripts, she was unsure what the role of an editor was, she had felt convinced that she would be able to work with Gloria. Now she was going to have to get to know new people.

She wished she had worn her red silk, with its matching coat, instead of this much safer navy-blue outfit. She knew she looked better, having lost weight, but she wished she had worn something with a bit more panache. She did not want to look too middle-aged.

She looked up at the photographs of Shotters' star authors hanging on the walls and inwardly laughed at the silly idea that one day she could be there in their hall of fame. On another wall were posters of all their latest books – those by the most famous, she noticed, were awash with embossed gold and silver lettering. In a locked cabinet were the books themselves, laid out on black velvet like priceless exhibits in a museum.

'Kate. So wonderful that you could get here.'

Kate looked up to find a young girl dressed entirely in black: black mini-skirt, large baggy black sweater, thick black tights that reminded Kate of her grandmother, and smart, suede ankle boots.

'I'm Cressida, Tatiana Spence's personal assistant. She's upstairs waiting to meet you – everyone is. We can't wait to get to know you.'

Kate stood up, far too fast she realised – it made her appear over-eager and she dropped her handbag in doing so.

'Oh, what absolutely scrummy shoes, I'd die for them,' said Cressida as she dived at the same time as Kate to retrieve the handbag. Kate wished she hadn't noticed them – black patent pumps from Bally with gold bows on them – for she was sure to have spotted Kate's ankles, swollen from the heat of a surprisingly warm April. They squeezed into the already crowded lift.

'I just adored *Winter's Romance*. Couldn't put it down, page-turnability in spades,' Cressida gushed, and Kate knew she was blushing as everyone in the lift turned to look at her.

'It's *Winter Interlude*, actually.'

'Yes, of course, silly me. Well. Never mind. Ah, here we are.'

The lift doors hissed open on to another large reception hall, close-carpeted in deep red, with matching red walls. Right opposite them two men, on ladders, were unscrewing what looked like a large gilt scimitar from the wall. Of course, Blades's logo, she remembered.

They walked at speed through an open-plan office towards a glassed-off section at the end of the large room. Kate did not think it was her imagination but she was sure people were staring at her. It made her feel uncomfortable.

Waiting for them was a tall woman with impeccably groomed blonde hair, perfect make-up, and a smart yet fashionable suit in navy blue, the skirt barely skimming her knees on which were sheer black tights. She too had black patent leather shoes on, but she did not look middle-aged at all. Beside her stood a younger woman in the shortest mini-skirt that Kate had ever seen, more like a pelmet in her opinion. Under them she wore tights of a mind-numbing complexity of colour and abstract shapes, and on her feet were boots that would have looked well in the Lake District. Her jumper was thick and white, scattered with embossed knitted fruits and Kate could not help but notice that on one nipple was a cherry and on the other a raspberry and she wondered if they were there by accident or design. At the sight of both of them Kate felt she had aged a good twenty years.

'Kate. *Wonderful* to meet you at last.' The older of the two women had stepped forward, hand held out in greeting. 'I'm Tatiana, your editorial director. It means I'm the boss.' She laughed her constrained laugh. 'This is Coco, your publicity manager. And here is Bart, your designer. Come in, Bart, do, meet dear Kate.' Kate was shaking hands with a young man with dreadful acne, wearing a rather grubby T-shirt with something on it in French, but her French had never been up to much so she did not understand it.

'How do you do?' she said stiffly.

'We all just know you're going to be one of our favourite authors,' Tatiana gushed, and Kate wondered what she put on her lips to keep them so shiny and glossy. Lipstick on Kate lasted a matter of minutes. 'And here's Letitia, she will be your editor, the one you liaise with the most. Letitia, meet darling Kate.'

Letitia was tall and thin, too, everyone was, which only made Kate feel more gross. Her earrings did not match. Kate wondered if it was a mistake but then, upon noting she was dressed in black and white spotted trews with a black and white striped sweater, she presumed that the one black and one white earring was on purpose. But she had a gentler expression than the others and Kate hoped that here was someone she would get on with.

'Kate, I just loved *Winter Romance*. I couldn't put it down, read it in one sitting. Page-turnability in spades.' Letitia smiled and Kate felt a jolt of *déjà vu* and wondered why everyone seemed to speak in italics and why no one could get the title right.

'We decided on a working lunch, Kate, hope you don't mind but we've so much to talk about. Coco, be a pet, tell Cressida to ring the canteen and rustle up some sandwiches.'

Kate said it was fine even though she felt disappointed. Lunch with one's publisher sounded so grand when one said it, and she had read of the extravagant hospitality of some famous publishers.

Chairs were pulled up and they settled around Tatiana's desk.

'There's just one tiny little thing, Kate. It doesn't affect you at all – not in the slightest. But, you see, Blades is no more. You're to be published by Shotters – far more prestigious, of course, than small Blades ever was. It's just an internal little thing, a rationalisation. We didn't want you to be confused.'

'Thank you,' said Kate, unsure if it was significant or not. The door opened and Cressida appeared with a tray of sandwiches and several glasses of Perrier water. Tatiana signed a docket with a flourish, Cressida took it and left the room shutting the door behind her.

'Now, Kate. Tell us *all* about yourself.'

'There's not much to tell you, really,' Kate said, voice heavy with apology as she launched herself rather tremulously into telling them about her very ordinary life. There was silence when she finished and she found herself looking at four blank faces and four sandwiches poised, half eaten, in the air.

'That's it,' she added, to make sure they knew she had finished, and she took a large draught of the Perrier and, finding she was no longer hungry, refused a sandwich.

'And you've done nothing else? Travelled, any interesting or unusual hobbies?' Coco asked after a pause that seemed to have gone on for ages.

'None, I'm afraid. I mean, cooking and sewing, well everyone does those, don't they?' She laughed but no one else joined in. 'Sorry, I'm not a murderess, an embezzler, or adulteress – nothing. Just me.' She smiled wanly.

'How did you start writing?' Tatiana asked, dabbing her mouth where there were no crumbs and where, miraculously, the lipstick still shone.

'It just happened, like a dam breaking. I mean, one day I started and I can't stop, it seems.'

'How many times were you rejected?' Coco enquired, her frown deepening.

'There's only been you.'

'Submitted to one publisher, that's very unusual.' Tatiana studied her nails.

'I know. I realise I've been very lucky,' she mumbled, and cursed herself for sounding so humble.

'How long have you been writing?'

'Let me see, this is April.' She began to count the months up on her fingers. 'Six months,' she concluded.

'Six months?' they all said in astonished unison. 'Good God!' they all added for good measure.

'But you must have written something else, short stories, articles?' Coco put her head on one side and one earring fell off. She scrabbled for it on the floor.

'Nothing. This is the first thing.'

'That's got to be your angle, Coco,' Letitia said.

'There's nothing else is there? Well, if that's that, if you'll excuse me, Kate, I've got *masses* to do – Bella Ford's new one is out next week.' She stood up, checking she had both earrings on. 'It's been just *wonderful* getting to know you. I'll be in touch. I need you to fill in one of my *dreaded* author profiles – everyone hates them. And I think we should talk about you having an author piccy taken.'

Coco slid out of the room.

'We've pencilled your publication date in for February,' Tatiana said, ostentatiously leafing through a large desk diary. 'It's one of the best months without doubt. You pick up sales with the book tokens after Christmas – everyone is too weary to cash them in January. And there are no big names for you to clash with. You'll have the field to yourself.'

'I see,' said Kate, and would have liked to ask why, if it was such a good month, no big names were published in it. But she thought it politic to keep quiet at this stage and in any case was far too scared to query anything.

'Oh, yes, Feb's a fab month for you,' Bart spoke for the first time. 'I've done some rough sketches for our catalogue – it goes out to the bookshops and some members of the public are on our mailing list. It'll be a bit of a rush job to get it in but with luck we'll manage.'

He showed her a rough outline of a book jacket. It showed a simpering blonde of chocolate-box prettiness, in her early twenties, against the background of a seascape.

'What do you think?'

'It's very nice,' she said doubtfully. 'It's just that my heroine is forty and there's no sea in the book at all. And the title's wrong – it's *Winter Interlude* not *Winter Romance*. Apart from that it's very nice,' she repeated for something to say as the others shuffled in an irritated way. 'But you've got my name right,' she added with a little more spirit.

'That's OK then.' Bart stood up. 'Wonderful to meet you, Kate. I just know we're all going to work wonderfully together.'

'The thing is, Kate,' Tatiana began once Bart had left, 'we really want to angle this book seriously at the women's market. Now, our research shows us that if you put the word love or romance into a title we sell double the amount, at least.'

'Yes, but – '

'It really is a better title, you know.' Tatiana flashed a smile at her and Kate wondered why she reminded her of a head girl at her school whom she had particularly loathed. It was strange how all through this writing process the comparison with school kept coming up. 'We do know what we're doing,' Tatiana added and Kate thought there was an unmistakable sound of annoyance in her voice.

'But, Tatiana, if you don't mind me pointing out to you, I haven't written a romance. Why, the end is sad, you couldn't have a sad end to a romance now, could you?'

'Yes, well, that was something I wanted to talk to you about. Sadly . . .' she looked pointedly at her watch, 'I've an appointment and must rush. But Letitia here will explain everything. Use my office, darlings. Finish up the goodies.' She pointed to the tray of curling sandwiches and the by now flat Perrier and in a rush and a cloud of expensive-smelling perfume she was gone.

'Right, Kate. With that lot out of the way we can get down to the serious business.' Letitia had taken Tatiana's place behind the desk. She opened a file and took out a sheaf of papers. 'I've had these photocopied for you so that you can take them home to mull over. Now, Kate, you must understand they are only my little suggestions. You must do just what you want. I'm only the boring old editor who will drive you mad on the commas and semi-colons and the syntax.' She laughed gaily, turned, and from the shelf behind her manhandled on to the desk what Kate recognised as her typescript. It was no longer the pristine one she had submitted, there were pencil marks all over it. Letitia laughed again when she saw the horrified expression on Kate's face. 'I know just what you're thinking. What have they done to my lovely manuscript? It's only pencil, Kate, can be rubbed out in a trice. Now . . .' Letitia bent over her notes and when she looked up it was with a very serious expression. 'I take your points about the cover rough. I know there's no sea in your book and, at the moment, the jacket design is all wrong. But we've talked about this at the highest level and well, Kate, it would be a help if you could alter the setting. Regional novels are so strong, you see, and this one isn't really set anywhere, is it? We thought Cornwall would be nice. Cornish novels always sell well – especially in Cornwall.' She giggled. 'Do you know it there? If not, why not take a holiday, take some snaps of the coves and *delicious* cliffs, absorb it.'

'I could, I suppose,' Kate said doubtfully.

'Of course you could, Kate. Anything's possible. Now the

age of the woman.' She studied her hands intently as if searching for inspiration and looked at Kate even more seriously. 'It's a difficult one this, Kate. She's so old. We'd much rather she was young.'

'But – ' Kate attempted to interrupt.

'I know *just* what you're about to say – that you wrote her that way because you, well, forgive me, but that's your age. Please, Kate. Have a try. Knock twenty years off, that would be wonderful.'

'I don't think I can remember how it was to be twenty. And if I did, none of the rest of the book would make sense.'

'You'd have to tinker about a bit here and there. But try, Kate, you'd be amazed at how easy it is. And then there's the horny problem of sex. Oops,' she clapped her hand over her mouth. 'Unfortunate choice of words there.' And she laughed but Kate felt it was at a joke she had used many times. 'What we would love to have, Kate, and what would help your sales enormously, is, well, if you could put in a lot more sexual *frisson* – there's a dear.'

'I can't write sex, it makes me embarrassed.'

'Really? How riveting! Do try, though, won't you? Now the end, Kate. I mean it's wonderful and tight and dramatic – delicious. But an unhappy ending? Oh, dear Kate, our readers will *hate* it. And I can tell you now America won't touch it – they hate unhappy endings more than we do.'

Kate could not stop herself from slumping back into the chair.

'Come, come, Kate, it's not as bad as all that, these are just our little suggestions. We want to make it perfect, don't we?' Letitia stood up. Obviously the meeting was over and there was to be no discussion.

'Have you far to go?'

'No, I'm going to a meeting of the Red Rose Society.'

'The RRS – wonderful women. Several of our authors are members. Bella Ford is – do you know her? A wonderful woman. Tell me,' Letitia said, not waiting for Kate's reply as they walked towards the lifts. 'Any ideas on number two?'

'I have, actually. I've been working on some ideas for two women, set in the last war.' Kate began to perk up at this.

'Oh, no, really?' Leeitia pursed her lips. 'Difficult, Kate, the market's awash with books on the last war. Historicals are getting so difficult to sell. Best stick to moderns, there's a dear.' The lift whined to a halt. 'Now, Kate, any worries, any problems, you just give me a ring.' She kissed her on both cheeks, which Kate felt was a bit much since they had only just met and she had torn her book to pieces. 'I just know you're going to become one of our *favourite* authors. Absolutely!'

Kate took a taxi feeling far too demoralised to take the tube. She quickly flicked through the pages of her precious typescript. She could not find one page which was not covered by pencilled crossings out, corrections and lengthy suggestions in the margins. And with it were the four foolscap pages of more detailed instructions. She felt she wanted to cry. She stuffed the pages back into the large Jiffy bag that Letitia had given her and felt like hurling it out of the window. What was the point in her going on? They obviously did not like what she had done so why should any reader? But as the taxi progressed towards her destination there was a change in Kate and by the time she arrived, she was fuming.

She was late and the meeting had already started. She was shown the hall by a porter and although she opened the large, heavy door as quietly as possible it still made a noise and an even louder one when it slipped from her hands and swished shut behind her. She tiptoed down the long hall towards the group of chairs but the plank floorboards squeaked at every foot fall. Faces turned at her and glared and there was much shushing.

'Sorry,' she mouthed exaggeratedly as she slipped into a vacant chair in the back row. A chair of canvas and steel which rasped as she sat on it. 'Sorry,' she mouthed again.

Bella Ford was on the platform, introducing the guest speaker, in place of the chairman who was in the midst of a writing crisis. She was in lilac silk again, without the sequins but still with two long chiffon scarves about her neck, and paused pointedly in her opening remarks, drummed her fingers on the lectern and waited for Kate to settle. Unfortunately the interruption had made Bella lose her momentum and the rest of her introduction tended to ramble so that soon the whole of the hall was full of the noise of other chairs creaking under restless bottoms.

'So, it's my pleasure to introduce James Truelove. Really, Mr Truelove, with a name such as yours you, too, should be a romantic novelist.' Bella smiled louchely at him and fiddled with the scarves, flicking one over her shoulder in what was evidently meant to be a carefree, girlish gesture but succeeded only in appearing arch.

James Truelove began to speak. Kate went over the morning's interview in her mind and the fuming became a rock-solid anger.

'Where did you get to?' Pam rushed up to her even as the audience was applauding Truelove's efforts.

'What on earth was he talking about?' Kate looked up, startled, realising she had not heard a word.

'Copyright or something, I wasn't really listening. It hardly affects me, does it? So what did you think? I've been desperate for your call.'

'Sorry?' Kate said vaguely. 'What do I think about what?'

'My book,' Pam said, standing dejectedly in front of her. 'You haven't bothered to read it.'

'Pam, I'm sorry. Of course I've read it. I had such a wretched morning, forgive me. I've sent it to Joy and I've asked her to look at it and comment. You should have professional advice,' Kate said breathlessly, fearful Pam might register that she had not given her reactions, and feeling totally wretched about the whole affair.

'Kate, you're an angel. I love you so.' And Pam kissed her enthusiastically which only made Kate feel worse. 'So, tell me, how did it go?' Pam asked taking the seat beside her.

'It was bloody awful . . .' And Kate launched into the tale of her first experience with her publishers.

'That's dreadful. They can't make you do that!' Pam exclaimed.

'Oh, yes, they can.' A grey-haired woman in front turned to face them. 'Excuse me, but I couldn't stop myself listening. When you've been in this business as long as I have you'll have heard this tale time and again.'

'It's not that I didn't expect criticism and that there would be things that would need changing. I'd prepared myself for that. But this . . . this is something else. If I do everything they want then it won't be my book any more.'

'If you don't, though, they'll say the manuscript is unacceptable and refuse you the next payment of your advance,' the woman said kindly and introduced herself as Emma Scott, someone Kate was relieved to find both she and Pam had read and enjoyed so there was no embarrassment between them all.

'The worse thing is it wasn't the person who bought my book. Now, I think I would have got on with her. I don't think she would have asked for such draconian alterations.'

'Who was that?'

'Gloria something . . .'

'You should talk to Bella. Bella's livid, she's got a thing or two to say about Shotters at the moment, I can tell you.'

'I couldn't bother an important author like her with my problems,' Kate said, flustered, and dreading to talk to the woman after making so much noise in entering the hall and putting her off her stride.

'Every member of this society is important to the others. It's why it was formed, to give each other support and help. I'll introduce you.' Emma took hold of Kate's hand in a no-nonsense grasp and led her through the knots of women who were now slowly making their way to the next room where tea was to be served. Quickly Emma explained Kate's plight to Bella.

'Of course, I've heard a lot about you from the people at Shotters. A wonderful success my dear, your first book – the society is proud of you.' Bella smiled sweetly. 'And weren't you at the weekend at . . .?'

'Yes. Oh dear, what a weekend!'

'Everyone's laughing about it all now, even dear Ann Cuthbert, thank goodness. But this Shotters business isn't funny, is it? Gloria was my editor and a good one too. But my dear, this is dreadful for you, such a worry.' Bella led Kate to a chair and sympathetically coaxed out of Kate how she was feeling.

'What shall I do?' Kate looked appealingly at Bella.

'Don't do anything if you don't want to. They can't make you. Don't let them bully you,' Bella advised. 'Do you know what promotional plans they have for you, author tours, that sort of thing?'

'No one has said.'

'Insist. They'll fob you off if they can. You can always tell where you stand with your publisher depending on what tour they give you. Someone from publicity to attend you, aeroplane, first-class everywhere, five-star hotels, TV – you're a star. On your own, but first-class British Rail, four-star hotels, national radio – they've got hopes and plans for you. An Inter-City supersaver and local radio – you're sunk,' Bella rattled off knowledgeably.

'Really? Oh, thank you, Bella, you've been so kind.'

'Not at all, we fellow writers have to stick together. Now I'm gasping for some tea, aren't you?'

Kate glowed at being referred to as a fellow writer by someone so successful, and looked about for Pam. They enjoyed the tea: several women from their weekend at Weston were there and all, somehow, had heard of Kate's luck. Everyone congratulated her and she did not feel a tinge of envy from anyone.

On the drive home Kate thought that Pam was very quiet, but she did not mind, she was tired and she had a lot to think about.

Bella, upon returning to her flat, was quickly on the telephone.

'Tatiana? Sorry bothering you so late but I thought I'd best let you know. You're likely to have trouble with a new writer you've just taken on. Problem these days is they buy themselves a word processor and they think that's all there is to it.'

'Really? A new writer, you say? How kind of you to bother, Bella.'

'Not at all. I must look after my publishers' best interests, after all – you've all been so good to me.' She laughed.

'Who is it?'

'A Kate Howard. Silly woman thinks she knows it all.'

chapter **twelve**

'I haven't heard from Kate, Tatiana. I'm sure if she was bothered about anything she would have been in touch with me.'

'I do hope you don't mind me contacting you, Joy, but as her agent I thought you should know,' Tatiana cooed into the telephone.

'It's kind of you, I'll have a word with her.'

'I mean, it's best to nip this sort of thing in the bud, isn't it? We see the problem time and again here – I'm sure you do too. The poor dears think they know best and, of course, you and I know they know nothing.' Tatiana laughed but laughing on the telephone is a dangerous occupation for the instrument only accentuates falseness.

'But you all got on well with her?'

'Everybody absolutely adored her. She's just so sweet, made us all think of our mothers. Of course, it's a pity about the spectacles and she could lose some weight. You don't think she'd agree to trying contact lenses, do you? And what about a health farm?' The false laugh trilled forth.

'It's rather personal, isn't it?' Joy sounded as shocked as she felt.

'I agree, it's terribly difficult but, then, it is for her own good, isn't it? The competition in her particular genre is so fierce and to be quite honest with you, Joy, publicity are a little bit in the doldrums about her. Perhaps if you had a teeny weeny word?'

Joy heard herself agreeing and sighed deeply as she replaced the receiver.

'Problem?' asked Barty from the other side of her desk.

'Do you remember that nice woman Kate Howard at one of your parties, the one, to our shame, that Gloria and I got squiffy? I've sold her first novel to Shotters. Now it seems they want to change bits and Tatiana the new editorial director has just been on the line saying she's been tipped off that Kate is going to refuse to do it.'

'Can't say I blame her. That's one hell of an achievement, writing a novel. I couldn't, and could this here Tatiana?'

'No, but one must be able to listen to criticism, especially as a novice, and be prepared to act upon it.'

'Depends upon the criticism and what you think of the person giving it, surely?' Barty countered reasonably.

'Yes, I suppose so. But now they don't like the way she looks and expect me to talk to her about it.'

'And will you?'

'How can I? She's pretty unsure of herself as it is. Still, you're not here to discuss my problems with Kate.' Joy pulled a pile of large envelopes to her. 'They're all here, the last one was biked over with two minutes to spare to the deadline.' She patted the pile, smiling excitedly at Barty.

'Looks a fat heap.'

'I told you everyone would want you.'

'Tell you what, let's go up to the flat and have a nice cosy cup of tea while we sort through them.'

'As you wish,' Joy said, and buzzed her secretary to say where she would be and to field any calls until she returned.

Barty held the door open for her and bowed her through courteously. She led the way up the stairs to the flat. She could never be sure when Barty would drop in, and he always seemed to want to talk in the flat and not the office. Joy was finding that making the flat look occupied was harder than she had imagined. She always put the newspapers up there and first thing each day she dampened the soap in the bathroom, ran some water in the kitchen sink, left some washing up on the draining board and made sure the tea-towels were slightly damp, all to make it seem she was living there. But for all that, the flat, to her, had the air of unused space.

She went first to the kitchen and put the kettle on, then laid the tea on a small tray.

'It's still very sparse, isn't it?' said Barty, standing in the doorway and looking at the sitting room behind him. 'That husband of yours is being dead mean with you. You need more ornaments, paintings, that sort of thing.'

'I don't want anything of his,' Joy said, not looking at him.

'You're a brave woman. I can't tell you how much I admire

you.' Barty coughed as if embarrassed by this statement. 'I'll have to get you a few things.'

'No, Barty, I couldn't allow that, you've done too much for me already. I'll never be able to repay you.'

'Who's asking?' Barty coughed again. 'So, to business,' he said as she completed making the tea. He walked back into the sitting room, sat down on the sofa and pulled the coffee table towards him.

Joy was ripping open the large padded envelopes, and piling them in order. Once finished, she handed him the top one. 'You see I didn't even peep at one. That took some doing, I can tell you. I asked them all to give us an idea of their marketing and publicity budgets and how they envisaged selling into the bookshops. That top one's Tudor's.'

'Well, I never. Haven't they done me proud?' Barty was grinning as he removed the glossy, spiral-bound brochure that Tudor's had produced to persuade them both that they were the best, the only ones, fit to handle Barty's book.

Soon the coffee table was full and they moved on to the floor and the rug was quickly covered with similar brochures. Some had included artwork for proposed covers and posters. Every major London publisher was represented.

'We should have had Brian here, it's so exciting,' Joy said, looking up, eyes glowing with satisfaction at this, her first major publishing coup.

'I didn't think it was a good idea. He might have been seduced by money and that's not everything is it, gal?'

'No. But it's a big factor. If a publisher pays dearly he's got to spend on marketing to recoup his advance. Still, I'd never let you go to Merrytown – they're hopeless, all talk and no action.'

They began to weed the unsuitable ones out. Joy was about to put Westall's on the rejected pile.

'No, leave them in,' Barty held up a restraining hand.

'But their offer is derisory.'

'Do you think so? Maybe it's all they can afford.'

They debated and argued until the brochures were whittled down to four. Pewter's with the largest bid, followed closely by Tudor's, then Shotters and lastly Westall's.

'Westall's it's got to be,' Barty finally said.

'But I don't understand. Their offer is the lowest on every-thing – advance, marketing and publicity budgets. They haven't even bothered to do any artwork – the others all have. Quite honestly, Barty, I think you would be making a serious mistake. They really don't have the marketing expertise – '

'I wouldn't say they had done badly over the years,' Barty said, sharply. 'I like it because it's honest. We all know they're in a mess. Julius could have offered millions and we would know that he was lying. Look at Dewridge here . . .' He pushed one of the booklets across to Joy. 'Ridiculous. Bloody liars. They're on the slide and everyone knows it and yet look what they're promising me. Mark my words, if they're not taken over in the next six months they'll be bankrupt and where would that leave us?'

'Agreed.' Joy was disappointed, she felt thwarted.

'I'll tell you another thing, Joy my girl. Westall's is the best, isn't it? Me? I likes the best.' He nodded.

'I think Brian might be disappointed with his advance.'

'Don't you worry about Brian. He's as happy as a pig in shit. I'm looking after him. Right, I'm off, then. Highly satisfactory.'

Joy followed him down the stairs to the front door where Gervase stood waiting.

'We should celebrate this.' He turned as he was about to leave. 'Have dinner with me tonight, with champers, of course.'

'Why . . .' she paused a second, her mind racing, trying to remember if she and Charles had anything planned. She could not remember. She would have to risk it. 'That would be lovely, Barty,' she said.

'I'll pick you up here.'

'No, not here if you don't mind. I've appointments until late. Say the Groucho, will that do?'

Back in her office she felt exhausted. It should have been easy enough pretending to Barty since she was here every working day and she had bought timers to switch the lights on and off of an evening, just in case he should drive by. One thing she had not thought of was that he often telephoned her in the evening. She had got round the problem neatly by having an answerphone and calling it several times each evening, replaying the messages with her bleeper. She had explained the answering machine always being on by saying that it was safer, for a woman living on her own, to be able to intercept calls. Barty had accepted this as being eminently sensible. But now that he had taken to popping in, it was only a matter of time before she was going to have to explain why she was always out.

But then, it was *her* life. Why shouldn't she return to her husband?

She looked at the telephone on her desk. Who should she call first, Kate or Julius? One a nasty call and one a lovely one. She decided to deal with the problem of Kate first. Kate's problem was not new; when Joy had been an editor one of the first things she had learned was how to tell a writer tactfully that what he or she considered perfection could be improved. But there was no answer from Kate's telephone.

Calling Julius to tell him he was the successful bidder for Barty's autobiography was one of the nicest things she had ever had to do. She laughed at the total disbelief in Julius's voice as he asked her to repeat what she had just said. She might think Barty was mad for selecting Westall's lowest bid, but on a personal level she could not be happier. Because for this, the first major deal of her new professional life, she would be dealing with the straightest, the most honest man in the business.

Kate was not in because she was on her way to London to see Joy. She had tried telephoning all morning, but no one seemed to arrive in the office before ten. Joy was not in, and on calling again later, Kate was told she was in a meeting and could not possibly be disturbed.

Kate had had a sleepless night, too, tossing and turning, wondering what she should do. She had finally got up before dawn. Not being able to speak to Joy had been too much of a frustration so she had collected her handbag, the typescript, the suggestions, and set off for London. She could not have endured another hour of twiddling her thumbs and seething at not being able to do anything.

She called Joy from Paddington. Joy could not see her until six and suggested that they meet at the Groucho Club. Kate spent the afternoon window-shopping and in the National Gallery, but both activities failed to divert her mind from the problem of her book.

Kate sat in the vestibule of the club in Soho, waiting for Joy, and watching the people who were breezily clattering in through the revolving door, depositing their mobile telephones at the desk like cowboys handing in their guns in a Wild West movie. She waited and waited. An anxious look at her watch told her it was twenty past six. God, she thought, people have such filthy manners these days. A door swung open and there was Joy.

'Kate! I'm so sorry. I was waiting for you at the bar. How silly of me not to check if you were here.'

Kate would like to have agreed with her but instead followed Joy back into the bar.

'Look, there's a free sofa,' Joy said, pointing across the room. 'Grab it quick, I've got to go to the loo.'

Kate inadvertently beat two young men to it, unaware that a sofa here was a prize. She sat down, burrowed in her handbag for her cigarettes and with one lit, looked about her.

The room was large, crowded and noisy. People were talking loudly, waving and shouting across the room at each other. She was reminded of the members at a Hunt Ball she and Tony had mistakenly gone to once. They had bayed at each other, just like these people. The bar was long and people were crushed around it two deep, desperately trying to attract the barman's eye. A pretty girl made her way calmly about the room, taking orders from those sprawling on the sofas. Such confident-looking people, Kate thought.

Each time the door opened people looked up to see who was entering. Those with well-known faces received sly but lingering looks. Nonentities were immediately ignored. No one seemed able to concentrate on their companions, instead they were looking about them constantly, as if searching for better company.

While she waited for Joy to return, Kate amused herself picking out famous faces so that she could tell Pam. She would be riveted by this, she thought, seeing a celebrated and titled writer sitting among a fawning group and noting with uncharitable satisfaction that she looked older than on television.

'Sorry about that. Drink?' Joy asked, as she flopped down beside her in the evidently approved fashion. Kate asked for a gin and tonic and assured Joy she was having a wonderful time just rubber-necking.

'Now, I gather you've got a few problems with Shotters?'

'You know?' Kate said with surprise.

'Yes, Tatiana called me this morning – someone tipped them off.'

'But I haven't spoken to anyone . . . apart from . . . but . . .' Kate looked thoughtful, remembering her conversation with Bella. But surely she, a fellow writer, would not have welshed on her? 'Who?'

'I haven't the foggiest but I wish you had called me. It's my job to sort out any difficulties for you.'

'I did. I couldn't get hold of you.'

'I'm sorry. It's just that . . . I've been so busy recently. It won't happen again, I promise.' Joy smiled at Kate who was quick to notice it was with effort. Joy would like to have confided in Kate, told her of the strain of juggling her two lives so that she felt her nerves jangling with the effort. But she resisted. It would not be professional she told herself. 'Now, what's the problem?'

'They want me to change the book out of all recognition. I don't want to be difficult or anything but the problem is I can't do it and that's all there is to it.'

'Of course I understand you feeling a bit disgruntled, but everything can always be improved, that's all they want to do. Present your book to the public the best way possible,' Joy said patiently.

'But it's not an improvement. I think they are going to ruin my book.' And Kate launched into a lengthy description of her interview at Shotters.

'That's not on. I'll speak to them for you, sort it out. Perhaps you'd get on better with another editor?' Joy said soothingly.

'No, I've made up my mind. I don't want to go ahead with it, Joy. I'll give them their money back, cancel the contract. We can do that, can't we?'

'Oh, Kate, I know how frustrated you must be feeling but don't act too hastily. So many writers would give anything for your good fortune.'

'I know all that. I know what I'm risking. But you see, Joy, the book is more important to me than anything else. I'd like you to find another publisher for me.'

'I'll do everything I can, but I must warn you, Kate, once this gets out it is likely to prove harder than you think. You'll be labelled a difficult author, and no one wants a problem writer on their books.'

'They were being difficult publishers,' Kate countered.

Joy, who had been smoking, quickly lit another cigarette. She could understand Kate's annoyance but it didn't alter the fact that she was asking almost the impossible. Not only would she damage her own reputation, but by association Joy's also. It was hard enough to get first novels published and now this. Still . . . she sat up straight.

'Well, the problem to surmount is your contract.'

'You don't think they'll hold me to it? They can't make me write,' said Kate, voice rising with panic.

'Don't worry. In law they could but it is unlikely they would insist.'

'What about Gloria? She loved it,' Kate said, brightening up at the sudden idea.

'Gloria's at Westall's now and, Kate, I know, I understand how wonderful you think your book is but a house like Westall wouldn't even read it. They publish only literary fiction. But . . .' Certainly it was an odd career move for Gloria, famous for her editing of popular fiction, Joy thought. She hadn't heard any gossip on the grapevine of a change in Westall's publishing profile, but it might be worth talking to Gloria. 'Leave it to me . . . I'll sort something out.' Joy slumped back on to the sofa, suddenly feeling exhausted.

'What sad-faced ladies.'

They both looked up to find Barty Silver with his entourage standing by their table. A hush had fallen on the room and everyone was looking at them with envious expressions.

'Kate Howard, isn't it?'

'Why, yes,' she said, amazed that he should remember her.

Barty sat down and Gervase ordered champagne. At first Kate said she must go but Barty insisted she have a glass.

'So why the despondency?' Barty wanted to know, so Joy explained. He invited Kate to join them for dinner. She would have loved to, but she had just remembered she had not left Tony a note explaining where she was. She must get to a telephone and then home as quickly as possible.

'Thanks, but I must go.'

'Pity,' said Barty. 'Remember one thing, Mrs Howard. Listen to your instincts and you can't go wrong.' And he winked broadly at her.

chapter **thirteen**

By the time Kate put her key into the lock of her front door, it was nearly ten and she was tired.

'I've been worried sick wondering where you were.' Tony was standing in the doorway of his study as if he had been waiting for her.

'I did telephone as soon as – ' She stopped at that, uncertain how to continue, how to explain her lapse without hurting him more.

'As soon as you remembered me. Was that what you were going to say? Thanks a lot.'

'Tony, it wasn't like that – honestly. I can't tell you the state I was in. I wasn't thinking straight. I just knew I had to get to London, see my agent and ask her to sort out the problems with the publishers for me.'

In the kitchen, Kate heaved up the lid of the Aga and scraped the large kettle across to the hotplate. She decided that the best thing was to try to appease him. She crossed to the dresser, took down two mugs, and got the instant coffee out of the cupboard.

'Coffee?' she asked, in a reasonable tone.

'I just don't know what's got into you, what's changed you, Kate. We used to have such a wonderful, happy life together.'

This was too much. Kate slammed the mugs down on the table. 'Wonderful for who? Who was happy? Certainly not me. I did everything just as my mother and you expected me to. And what was the result? I suddenly realised I'd become a cipher, nothing more. You didn't even notice what I did until the day I stopped doing it and your quiet, orderly, life was remotely disrupted.' Angrily she spooned the coffee into the mugs. 'You don't care one iota about me as a person. You don't give a damn about my book. Any normal husband would be pleased with what I've achieved, be proud of me. But you?

What's your reaction? To whine and complain because, for once, I'm not here.'

'I do care. Didn't I say the minute you walked through the door that I had been worried sick wondering where you were.'

'Ha!' Kate's laugh was short and cynical. 'Worried that there was no supper on the table, more like.'

'That's unfair, Kate. I wasn't to know you were in this state.'

She turned slowly and faced him. 'But that's the whole point, Tony. You didn't know because you never listen to me. Ever since I began to write I've tried to involve you – but you haven't wanted to know. I tried talking to you last night. I told you the editor at Shotters had upset me. I knew you weren't really listening.'

'Not interested? Who bought you a word processor? And that wasn't cheap, I can tell you.'

'Fine, but do you remember what you said? I'll remind you. You said that the word processor would put an end to all this nonsense.'

'It was a joke.'

'My eye. For years I've endured hearing about your work, even when I didn't want to, even when it bored me or I didn't understand. But can you do the same for me? No. I'm warning you, Tony. I've got this far and nothing is going to stop me getting to the top. Not you, not the children, not this house nor your flaming suppers!' She was shouting and shaking and as she poured the now boiling water on to the coffee she slopped some of it on the Aga. She watched it hissing and steaming and forming into little balls shining, looking almost like mercury, as they scurried about the hotplate as if trying to escape. She felt like one of those balls of water.

'It's not just me. I saw Pam the other day. She said much the same, that you didn't care any more, that she hardly ever saw you.'

'Pam is playing at writing. I'm not. I know I don't see her so much, I don't have the time. If she was serious about it she wouldn't have the time either.' She placed the mugs of coffee on the pine table.

'We used to have real coffee once,' Tony said mournfully.

Kate looked at him, eyes blazing with fury. She picked up the mugs and hurled both of them across the kitchen where they smashed on the furthest wall. The cat leapt with a yell and rushed for the cat-flap as the broken china flew to right and left while the coffee trickled down the tiled wall, forming puddles on the floor.

'Then make it yourself.' She walked to the door, choosing to ignore the mess. 'Oh, by the way. I'm going to London again on Monday, you'd best make arrangements to eat out.' And she slammed the kitchen door shut behind her, ran up the stairs and into her workroom, shut the door and switched on her word processor.

Joy had lied to Charles when she telephoned to say she was having dinner with a client he did not know but, she reasoned, he had lied to her so many times that this little untruth hardly counted.

It had been a pleasant evening. Usually when one dined with Barty there were up to a dozen other guests. But tonight he had dismissed his entourage and it had been just the two of them.

It did not seem to matter where they went, Barty was always known and the management made an inordinate fuss of him and thus her. It was rather enjoyable and something one could easily get used to, she thought, as they left the bar he had taken her to after the Groucho. Dinner was to be a surprise, he had said, as the Rolls-Royce hummed along, out of central London, across the river and into the East End into suburbs where she had never ventured before. They stopped at an eel and pie shop where, once again, Barty was treated like visiting royalty.

Joy had looked at the plate of mashed potatoes, swimming in a sea of green juice from the mushy peas, with suspicion. Tentatively she forked a little into her mouth, only to find to her surprise, and Barty's delight, that it was delicious.

They had then gone to a pub and watched a drag show. Unsure at first if this was what she wanted to sit through, Joy was in for another surprise. It was one of the funniest things she had ever seen, made funnier by the wit of the audience of locals hurling remarks at the performers, who lobbed back retorts at such speed it was difficult to believe it was spontaneous. She told Barty it was like listening to a verbal tennis match.

From there they had travelled back up West to a jazz club where she had discovered that Barty's knowledge of jazz music was formidable. Once she had confessed she did not know a trombone from a saxophone, Barty set himself the task of educating her.

It was nearly four when they finally drew up in front of the office and the flat where Barty fondly thought she was living. The chauffeur opened the door and she slid out. Barty followed her. She stood on the pavement feeling awkward, not knowing how to proceed, feeling a little like a teenager on a first date.

'Barty, I'm so tired. Forgive me if after such a wonderful evening I don't invite you in for a drink,' she apologised with a weary smile.

'I wouldn't dream of accepting. Why, at this time of night, with a lady on her own? Good Lord, Joy, what do you take me for?'

She would like to have kissed him for his thoughtfulness, but knowing how he felt about human contact, she did not like to. Perhaps the biggest surprise of the whole evening was when, to her astonishment, Barty leant across and kissed her gently on the cheek.

'Night, little lady,' he said and climbed back into his car. Joy stood waiting but the car did not move and then she realised he was waiting to see her safely into the building. She unlocked the door, stood in the doorway – but still the car stood motionless. Sighing, she closed it, and climbed the three floors up to her flat. She put the lights on, crossed to the window, and moved the curtains so that Barty could see her. The Rolls-Royce purred into action and moved along the darkened road.

Joy waited five minutes and then raced back down the stairs, ran along the street and round the corner to her parked car. She drove at speed to Holland Park, praying all the way that Charles would be sound asleep and that she would be able to slip into bed without him realising what the time was.

Once in the house, she took off her shoes, and, not bothering with any lights, tiptoed up the stairs. Gingerly she opened the bedroom door. She stood a moment, listening for the safe sound of his regular breathing. There was silence. She crossed to the bed and looked down. It was empty. With a feeling of mounting sickness she switched on the bedside light. The bed had not been slept in. Perfect, unrumpled sheets told her everything.

*

Gloria was elated. It did not matter how often she told herself she was being stupid, the feeling of excitement kept bubbling up and most of the time she knew she had a silly smile on her face that she could not control either.

She was elated because she knew she was in love. She was excited because she was strangely confident that Peter was falling in love too. She told herself it was stupid to think this way because she had nothing to base it upon. They had enjoyed a pleasant evening together, they had talked – nothing more.

Reason could tell her one thing but emotions told her another. There had been an undercurrent between them that evening. There had been more to their unburdening themselves to each other than reason could explain. She had analysed why she had confided her past to him. Now she understood. She had told him everything, even the worst, so that he knew all there was to know about her, so that there was nothing about her that someone could surprise him with in the future. Clearing the emotional deck for him was the best way she could describe it.

Oddly she was not afraid of her honesty. She felt he had accepted it, as if knowing himself her reasons for doing it. And if she needed further proof it was the way he had said goodnight. The way he had not presumed she would invite him into her bed. That's what nearly every man expected these days, but not Peter. He *was* different, he was a gentleman, he would court her, she knew! She knew!

And if she really delved back into her memory she could remember feeling exactly like this about him all those years ago, when she had had that hopeless crush on him, a married man. But now he was separated and it seemed all she had to do was to uncork the memories, those old feelings she had had for him. It was as if she had been waiting for him, that all the other lovers had meant nothing to her because she had put her love on hold for him.

In love she might be but she had work to do. Her new job at Westall's did not begin until Monday, but she already had plans. First she called Julius to check with him that, although she was not yet officially employed by him, she could start negotiations with an author. He laughed at her enthusiasm, and wished her luck. Her next call was to Primrose Cooper to tell her Shotters had turned her novel down but that she was in the happy position of being able to offer her a contract with Westall's, the details of which they would discuss next week.

That done, and after a light lunch, she began something which had once given her pleasure and which she had not done for months – she cleaned her house from top to bottom. She knew why she was doing it, she had a purpose now. There was someone who cared for her, someone to share it with.

She hoped he would telephone soon and then she would take the initiative, she would suggest he came to dinner. If her plan worked out he would stay the weekend. And then – she felt almost breathless at the idea – within a week or two she would suggest he need not bother to look for a house, he was welcome to move in with her.

Perhaps thinking this way was proof, if proof were needed, of her feelings for him. In all other previous relationships she had never countenanced the idea of anyone moving in with her. She had been happy to have them stay for the odd weekend, occasionally for a week. But always she had begun to feel restless, wanting them away, wanting her privacy back. Not this time.

As she worked she wondered what they would do this weekend. Perhaps if the weather held they could go to the country. Maybe he would like to go to the theatre, the opera. On the other hand perhaps she should go shopping and get food in just in case he preferred to stay at home. She could just imagine them, eating, drinking, listening to music, making love. Yes, come to think of it, a weekend at home would be best of all.

The house cleaned and shining, Gloria drove to Sainsbury's and trundled round with the trolley, light-headed with euphoria. No more prepacked meals. She would cook for him. Good gracious, she thought, stopping dead in the shopping aisle, she had never wanted to do that for any of her other lovers, either. She began to run through possible menus in her head, selecting the necessary items. At the drink shelves she bought his favourite whisky – strange she should remember, from all those years back, how much he had liked Highland Park. Carefully she selected a dozen bottles of wine – six red, six white. And happily she paid the huge bill, enlarged because of the cantaloupe melons, the out-of-season asparagus and the side of smoked salmon, none of which she had meant to buy but had, because she was certain he would enjoy them.

She drove home singing, the prospect of a full and wonderful weekend ahead of her. Of course, she should have returned the car, but now there was not such a rush to do so. They could return it together tomorrow, then she would have a lift back home instead of having to take a taxi.

She pulled up in front of her house at the same time as a florist's van. She signed for the huge bouquet of flowers, a grin on her face of such happiness that she made the delivery man laugh. She decided to unpack the car first and then open the flowers, knowing full well who they were from.

She forced herself to pack away the last item of groceries, delaying the pleasure of opening the bouquet, enjoying in a masochistic sort of way the wait to see what message he had sent her. At last she allowed herself to pick up the scissors and attack the gaudy ribbon and the Cellophane encasing her flowers.

'Look what a lucky girl I am, Elephant.'

She slid the card from its tiny envelope.

'Oh, no!' she said aloud. The message slipped from her fingers.

Sorry. I won't bother you again. Peter was written on it. Nothing else.

chapter **fourteen**

'Welcome to Westall's, Gloria,' Julius said, beaming at her as she stood in his office on her first day with the firm.

'Thanks, I got here at last,' she said, and smiled. But Julius was quick to note it was not her normal big and happy smile.

'Are you all right, my dear? You look tired,' Julius said with concern.

'I'm fine, Julius,' she lied. 'I cleaned my house over the weekend – I think I'm past such violent activity.' She attempted to laugh but it only made her head feel worse. She felt dreadful. Over the weekend, that awful lonely desert of a weekend, she had managed to drink too much of the wine and too much of the whisky she had bought for Peter. She was left feeling a complete fool and was only glad she had not told anyone of her stupid feelings and dreams.

'I'm glad you brought the little dog with you. What's he called?' Julius asked, bending down to stroke it.

'Elephant. He's why I'm here. They suddenly banned him at Shotters.'

'No risk of that here.' He laughed. 'But I don't think it was just the treatment of the dog – it was only a matter of time. You're not a corporate creature, Gloria, or I don't know you very well.'

'You're probably right, Julius. This suits me better, this is a *real* publisher's.'

'Grimly hanging on by the skin of our teeth, but surviving – just. Ah, Crispin, come in. I'm glad you could make it. Of course you know Gloria.'

'We've met a couple of times at book fairs and whatever, haven't we?' She held out her hand to Crispin.

'And this is another new member of staff, Crispin. He's called Elephant, aren't you, old boy?' Julius said, grinning broadly.

Crispin neatly sidestepped the little dog with as much speed as if it were a Rottweiler. He smiled in a sickly way – another indication of his uncle's senility, thought Crispin, who regarded anyone who anthropomorphised a dog as mentally unstable. Elephant, upon sensing that here was someone who did not like him, immediately sat down as close to his feet as he could get.

'Is it too early to hear of your plans, Gloria? I've mapped out what I think will be a reasonable budget for you. As you will see, you have almost complete autonomy. Only if you should want to buy in some mega-seller I feel we should have a wider discussion. I trust your judgement entirely, otherwise.' Julius handed Gloria a folder with all the financial details she would need to run her department. 'I think it's only fair that we tell you from the start that Crispin is not too happy with this new plan.' Crispin looked up, a pained expression on his face. That might be so but he did not think it necessary for his uncle to trumpet it from the rooftops. He decided to say nothing at this juncture. 'So I suggest,' Julius continued, 'that being the case, it would be difficult for you both to liaise as you would normally. So I, for this imprint, shall take the role of financial director. Fairer all round, wouldn't you say, Crispin?'

Crispin wanted to say no it certainly was not fair all round, but then, he thought, if it was a total disaster – as it was likely to be – the less he had to do with it the better.

'That's fine by me, Uncle,' he said.

'So, Gloria, what plans do you have thus far?'

For the next hour, she was able to forget Peter as Gloria did what she liked best – talked books. She told them of Primrose Cooper. She reported on the gossip, straws in the wind which might lead to them picking up several authors. She said how she planned to get in touch with the secretary of the Red Rose Society.

'The what?' Crispin said with disdain.

'It's an organisation of women writers. Most of them write for Wallers and The Paradise Club.' At mention of these two publishing houses, Crispin snorted. 'But they do have quite a few members who write mainstream books and a lot, I know, would like to cross over. I thought, perhaps, we could arrange a competition with them, the winner to be published by us. It shouldn't cost much. I'd rather delay doing this until the present chairperson steps down – in May I think. She's one of Shotters' writers and might let them know a little too much of our business. Tatiana might like the idea and pinch it for themselves.'

'I like the idea of a competition, Gloria. We could pick up quite a bit of useful publicity that way.'

'And free, too.'

'Crispin?'

Crispin laughed a slightly maniacal laugh. 'Whatever you say, Uncle. Who am I to object?'

'Fine,' said Julius, completely ignoring the sarcasm.

'Didn't you edit Bella Ford?' Crispin asked. 'Wouldn't it make more sense if you tried to get her and others like her to move over with you?' He would like to have added that doing so would make a lot more sense of her appointment, but he refrained.

'I intend to, but not Bella. She's more trouble than she's worth. There's a lot of disaffection at Shotters as you know, but I think some will prefer to go to Tudor's or Pewter's – more established in their genre, you see.' She smiled sweetly at Crispin. 'But I'll do my best.' Just before she left she asked about a secretary.

'I presumed you would want to find your own. Until then you could borrow Crispin's?'

After the satisfactory meeting Gloria ran down the stairs from Julius's first-floor office to her own.

'Miss Catchpole,' the receptionist called out to her as she passed. 'You've a visitor.'

Standing at the desk was a woman in a mackintosh, with a scarf on her head for it was raining heavily outside. She was familiar but for the life of her Gloria could not put a name to her.

'Yes?' Gloria said hesitantly.

'Kate Howard,' the woman said, holding out her hand. 'We had lunch . . .'

'Kate, forgive me. It's the light in here,' she said quickly, though it was true. 'Plus I've got a filthy hangover. But, you know, you look different. What have you done to yourself?'

'I haven't got my specs on, it's raining so hard out there I couldn't see through them. And, well, actually, I've lost some weight.' Kate blushed at this.

'You're telling me you have. It suits you, how much?'

'Over a stone.'

'Wonderful! And, you know, you have such pretty eyes,: you should wear contact lenses, the specs hid them.'

'I've made an appointment to have some fitted next week.' Kate was not used to compliments and those from another woman meant more, in a way.

'Good. So, Kate, it's lovely to see you again. What can I do for you? Come through to my office.'

She led the way along the downstairs corridor to the back of the beautiful building. Gloria's new office was on the ground floor, with french windows opening on to a wrought-iron balcony and steps leading down into a pretty courtyard garden which would be a delight to sit in when the summer came. The room was furnished with a chesterfield sofa, two fine wing chairs and a large mahogany desk. Between the bookcases, as yet unfilled, which lined the walls, the paintwork was a pretty Adam green and Gloria shuddered to think how valuable was the carpet at her feet. Compared to Shotters this was paradise.

'Tea, coffee?'

'No, thanks, but do you mind if I smoke?'

'Not at all. There must be an ashtray here somewhere.' Gloria rootled among the papers on her desk which she had been in the process of sorting when she was called to see Julius. 'Forgive the muddle, it's my first day here,' she said, emerging triumphantly with a large glass ashtray which she was pretty sure was crystal.

'How are things with Shotters?' Gloria asked calmly, but her heart was lifting, for she knew something must be wrong for Kate to be here.

'I know I've been incredibly lucky and everything and I know this might sound dreadfully ungrateful and everybody is going to think I'm mad but – well, I can't let Shotters publish my book.' Haltingly at first and then picking up more confidence as the memory of last week's humiliation came rushing back into her mind, Kate told of her experience.

'Oh dear,' said Gloria, when she had eventually finished. She nearly said she was not surprised but her professionalism saved her in the nick of time.

'There's one thing I have to find out, Gloria – for my own peace of mind. Would you have insisted on those alterations?'

'No, I would not have done any of those things. Your book

would stand as it is. It needed tightening up here and there, and you repeat yourself a little bit too often but they were all simple editing jobs. The trouble these days is that too many publishers don't give the readers credit for any intelligence. You get one book that hits the best-seller list, then they're all rushing about like lemmings to try to find one similar. Publishing to me is trying to find new talent with a new way of telling a tale and, with luck, a new tale to tell, not a constant repetition of the old. That's what attracted me to your book. It follows no rules, no clichés. Why, look at the ending – it's sad but it's the only logical ending to have. I agree with you, Kate, don't let them touch your book, they'll destroy it. Over-edited and they could lose your author's voice. Gracious, what a lecture.' She laughed at herself and the passion with which she had been speaking.

'I've told Joy. Did she speak to you about me?'

'No, not yet.' Gloria frowned, puzzled that Joy hadn't if Kate had asked her to. 'Maybe she's been too busy,' she added kindly.

'I've asked her to get me out of my contract, I'll pay them back. I did mention you to her but she said this firm wouldn't be interested in me.'

'She can't have heard of our plans when she spoke to you. But it's only a matter of time and she will.' Gloria laughed. 'Gossip travels fast in publishing. Look at these . . .' She pointed at a pile of manuscripts on her desk. 'I only left Shotters last week, yet the news had begun to filter out and these submissions were waiting for me this morning.' She smiled at Kate who looked worried. 'It's all right, Kate, we'd love to publish your book. You know how strongly I felt about it. But my hands are tied until you extricate yourself from Shotters. I couldn't make any moves – it would be unprofessional and would look as if I was poaching and that would never do. Do you see?'

'But all is not lost?'

'No. You might have difficulties with Shotters but it doesn't sound as if they were too keen on my choice, anyway.' She smiled.

'Thank you, Gloria, you've been a big help.'

'Any time, and keep up the diet.'

As soon as Kate had gone Gloria was on the telephone to

Joy. She sounded slightly harassed and a little irritated that Kate had approached Westall's.

'I think she just came in for a shoulder to cry on,' Gloria reassured her. 'But, Joy, she means it, she won't let them touch it. Get her out of it and I promise you Westall's will pick her up.'

After her call to Joy, Gloria telephoned her secretary Rachel at Blades to invite her to come and join her at Westall's. Rachel needed no time to consider the offer and it was she who told Gloria that Blades was no more. So I was right, she thought, as she replaced the receiver. But being right did not make her happy. She had liked Blades, been proud of it. She had created it, if truth be told.

Throughout the day Gloria found that if she kept busy she could keep her feeling of depression at bay. It did not go away, but lurked, waiting for an empty moment when it would hit her. She'd allowed herself to hope and had ended up feeling a complete fool.

It was finally time for her to return home with an empty evening stretching before her. She just hoped to God there was something decent on television; if not she would read the submissions she had pointed out to Kate.

Elephant leapt ahead of her along the passage which was her hall, barking excitedly at the noise of Pink Floyd blaring out of the CD player. She walked into the sitting room to find Clive, whom she had not seen in weeks, lying on the sofa, idly reading a book. Gloria crossed the room and switched it off.

'What you do that for?'

'I don't feel like listening to it,' she said, putting on some Mozart instead. She crossed to the drinks tray, neatly stacked with bottles, and poured herself some tonic water.

'Don't I get a drink?' he demanded.

'Tonic water?'

'Hell, you ill or something? Don't be silly. Vodka straight, if you don't mind.'

'Actually, I do mind.'

She walked through to the kitchen, he followed.

'What's the matter, Gloria?'

'Nothing.'

'Oh, come on. When a woman says that it means all hell's about to break loose.'

'Nothing's the matter. I just wish you weren't here, that's all.'

'I beg your pardon?' he said, having the audacity to look surprised.

'I don't see you for weeks. I don't know where you are, what you're doing, who you're with even, and in this day and age that matters more than anything else. And then you swan in as if nothing has happened.'

'You never used to mind.'

'Is that what you thought? Oh, I minded, Clive. I minded very much. I was stupid. But everything has changed. Now I don't care a damn what you do so long as it's not with me. I've been down your road once too often.'

'You've met someone else?' he asked.

Gloria laughed. 'Christ, what conceit. You think the only possible reason I don't want to see you any more is because there's someone else. Well, for your information, there isn't. I've just had you up to here.' She tapped the underside of her chin with the flat of her hand as she spoke.

'No one, eh? So who's this from? And why are those far from dead flowers in the rubbish bin?' He was waving Peter's card at her. She steeled herself not to swoop on it thus alerting him to the fact that it was important to her, that he had caught her at a particularly vulnerable time.

'It's from my boss, Peter Holt, we had a misunderstanding at work. It's his way of apologising.'

'Oh.' Clive dropped the card on to the table, evidently disappointed he had not found her out. She wondered if she might have acted differently if for one moment she had thought he was feeling jealous. As it was she looked at his handsome but vacuous face, the over-greased hair, the trendy clothes and she despised herself for ever having found him attractive. So, she thought with satisfaction, maybe if he had been jealous it would not have made one iota of difference.

'Look, Clive, you'll have to go. I've got friends coming for dinner.'

'You? Entertaining? I don't believe it.'

She opened the refrigerator which was bulging with the food she had bought for her imagined weekend with Peter. 'See for yourself.' She shrugged her shoulders as if not caring whether he believed her or not.

'Oh, I see. Well, I'll be getting along. Shall I be seeing you again?'

'No, Clive. I don't think so. And, if you don't mind, I'd like my key back.'

He dropped the key on the table and it landed on top of the card from Peter.

'As you wish,' he said with a shrug. 'Bye, Gloria.'

'Bye,' she replied vaguely, for she was staring at the key and the card and fighting tears. In an ideal world she would have been giving Peter that key.

She heard the front door slam, heard Clive's footsteps echo on the pavement outside. She poured herself a large vodka ignoring the tonic water. She raised the glass, toasting herself for the first sensible action she had made in her personal life for a long time.

chapter **fifteen**

Kate had an appointment with Joy. When Joy had called, it was with the good news that she was out of her contract with Shotters and that Kate was to bring a cheque with her to pay her advance back. Then they were both going to see Gloria to discuss the book. That was the plan. Instead she stood in the outer office of the agency and was worried.

'You don't seem to understand,' she was saying to the young girl in the office. 'I have an appointment with Mrs Trenchard. Please let her know I'm here.'

'I'm afraid I can't.'

'Of course you can.' Kate realised she was beginning to sound irritated. She must stop, it was hardly the girl's fault. 'Look, I'm sorry, but I've come a long way for this appointment.'

'Please, Mrs Howard . . .' The girl looked close to tears.

'What on earth's the matter?'

'It's Mrs Trenchard. I haven't seen her yesterday or today. I don't know where she is.'

'Have you tried her home number?'

'I didn't bother her at first. It was slack here yesterday and she's been so tired I thought she was resting. But today when I tried no one answered the telephone at first and then a child answered, but I couldn't get any sense out of her. I've been so worried and didn't know what to do.'

'Didn't you think to go round?'

'I don't know where she lives and she's ex-directory.'

'Did you try Sir Barty?'

'Yes, but he's away.' And the young woman finally burst into tears. 'Mrs Howard, I'm frightened.'

Kate searched in her handbag for the card, now rather bent, which Joy had given her all those months ago at Barty's. She picked up the telephone and quickly dialled Joy's number. She was frowning – something must be really wrong: Joy would not leave the poor girl to manage on her own. She let the telephone ring for quite some time and was just about to replace it, when she heard it being answered.

'Joy?'

'Yes,' a weak voice answered.

'It's Kate.'

'Kate, how nice to hear from you.' Joy's voice had a strange rasping quality to it.

'Joy, are you all right? You sound strange.'

'Oh, Kate, what day is it? Oh God, our appointment – I'm so sorry . . . Can we make it another day? Can't talk, not now.' And before Kate could say any more the line went dead.

Kate did not like the sound of Joy's voice. She must be ill. She reassured Joy's secretary, collected her things and was lucky to find a cab cruising outside. She gave the address in Holland Park.

Once there she rang the bell several times but no one answered. Perhaps she had acted precipitously, maybe Joy was simply taking a few days off. But then, she thought, if she was, how dare she treat her as if she did not matter? She rang the bell again. Kate was about to turn away when she was sure she heard a child. She lifted the letterbox flap and peered in. A small girl was sitting on the black and white marbled floor crying.

'Hello,' Kate called through the gap. 'Hallo-ooo . . .' The child looked up towards the door. 'Come here, sweetheart.' Slowly the little girl stood up and approached the door. 'Don't cry, darling. Is your mummy there? I'm a friend of hers.'

'She's upstairs,' the child said, wiping her tears with the back of her hand.

'Will you go and tell her Kate's here and I'd love a cup of tea?'

'She won't come.'

'Please, be a pet, go and ask her.'

'She's asleep.'

'Is anyone else in the house with you?'

'No, my nanny's gone. My mummy shouted at her and now she's gone – ' And she burst into tears again and moved back into the hall, where she disappeared from Kate's narrow field of vision.

Kate tried to stay calm which, in the circumstances, was

335

difficult. One thing the little girl had said kept echoing in her mind. 'She's asleep.' What if she had taken an overdose? She had sounded distraught enough. Something was desperately wrong: Joy was not the sort of woman to leave a young child unattended like that.

She ran up the road, and round the corner. These houses often had a mews and a large garden, she reasoned. She was right. Twenty yards along the road, she saw the entrance to a mews. She stopped outside the house she was certain was Joy's. The black gate set in the wall was locked. Kate looked about her and saw a large dustbin; she pushed it against the wall. She was not designed for shinning over walls and had to huff and puff to pull herself up. Then she hung from the top of the wall and carefully lowered herself down the other side. There was still a small drop and she landed on her backside in a rose bush. She picked herself up, dusted her coat down, saw the damage she had done to the plants and prayed she was in the right garden. She ran up the garden path. There were steps down to a basement kitchen. She pushed at the door praying it was not locked, and it gave. She stepped in and found herself in a downstairs passage. She called out immediately.

'Is there anybody there?' She wished she could remember the child's name, but in her panic she had forgotten it. She climbed the stairs out of the basement. 'Hello,' she kept saying. Suddenly the child appeared at the head of the stairs.

'Have you come to see my mummy?'

'Yes, lovie, can you take me to her?' She held out her hand and the little girl put her small one into Kate's and led her up the long flight of stairs to the second floor.

'She's in there.' They had stopped outside a white-painted door.

Kate's heart was thumping so loudly as she pushed open the door that she was sure it was audible. The curtains were pulled and only one bedside light was on but Kate could see Joy sprawled across the bed. She rushed across the room.

'Joy,' she said loudly and then again even louder. 'Joy, wake up, it's Kate.'

'Kate? What the hell are you doing here?' To her relief, Joy opened her eyes and tried to focus on her.

'Joy, listen to me.' Kate was patting her hands urgently. 'Joy, have you taken anything? Answer me, do.'

'Taken anything? Me? Don't be bloody silly,' she said, slurring her words and trying to laugh. Then, she drifted off to sleep again. As her head flopped back on the pillow for the first time Kate noticed a large bruise on the side of her face.

Either she was very drunk or she had taken an overdose, Kate concluded. She looked at the bedside table but there were no empty bottles. Perhaps she should telephone for a doctor to be on the safe side? She looked around but could find no address book. She listened to Joy's breathing, which sounded normal enough, then crossed the room and out on to the landing where the child stood, looking wide-eyed and wan.

'What's your name?'

'Hannah.'

'Of course it is. Tell me, Hannah, do you know the name of your doctor?'

'He's called Doctor.'

'Yes, of course.' Kate stood biting her lip, thinking. 'Is there another telephone I can use? I don't want to wake Mummy, she's tired.'

'This way.' Hannah led her to another room and pointed to the instrument.

Quickly Kate dialled Westall's number.

'Why, hello, Kate,' said Gloria. 'Aren't we meeting later?'

'Gloria, I'm sorry to bother you but I didn't know who else to contact. I'm at Joy's, I'm afraid she might have done herself a mischief.'

'A mischief? What on earth are you talking about, Kate?' Gloria laughed at such an antiquated turn of phrase.

'Hannah's with me,' Kate said pointedly. 'I can't find her doctor's number.'

'Oh my God. I'll be right over. What happened?'

'I don't know what happened. Come quickly, please.'

She replaced the receiver and smiled encouragingly at the small child.

'My mummy and daddy had a row and my daddy hit her and she's been crying all night – I heard her. Then my nanny said it served her right and they were horrible to each other and my nanny went.'

'Well, what a busy time you've had. You know what would be a good idea, if we made your mummy some coffee. Shall we do that?'

She checked Joy again, forcing her to wake up before going to the kitchen and making a large pot of black coffee.

Sitting her up in a more comfortable position Kate managed to get nearly a cup of the hot liquid down a complaining Joy.

'Why you doing this to me?'

'I'm afraid you've taken some pills.'

'Pills? Don't be silly, Kate. I took two, to sleep, that's all promise,' Joy said slowly and emphatically. 'And I wish to Christ you'd let me. I'm so tired.'

'And booze, how much booze with the pills?'

'Dear Kate . . . so worried. I've a hangover. OK?' And she pushed the second cup of coffee away and slumped back on the pillows.

Kate stationed herself, for what seemed an age, at the window waiting for Gloria's taxi. The doorbell rang and she ran downstairs to answer it.

'I'm sorry I took so long, it was the damn traffic, I should have taken a taxi instead of driving. How is she?'

'Gloria, I'm sorry dragging you here, I think I overreacted. I think she's drunk.' Kate led the way back up the stairs.

'Don't worry, I wasn't busy. You did the right thing, I would want to know.' They entered the gloomy bedroom.

'Hello, Gloria, just like old times.' Joy giggled from the bed.

'You pissed?'

'Yes. And how!'

'Oh, Joy, what about Hannah?' Gloria said shocked.

'Hannah, is she all right?' At mention of her daughter Joy sat bolt upright in bed.

'No thanks to you. She was all alone downstairs. Thank God Kate came over and had the sense to break in.'

'But the nanny . . .?'

'Gone,' said Kate.

'Oh God.' Joy ran her hands through her hair. 'The bitch, the out-and-out bitch.'

'What happened, Joy?' Gloria sat on the edge of the bed and took hold of her hand.

'The usual, he's up to his old tricks, he didn't like it when I complained.' She stroked the ugly bruise on her face.

'And now? Haven't you had enough? Are you going to leave him, finally?'

'I know I've got to, Gloria, this time, I really have.'

'You need a shower, my girl. Kate and I will throw some lunch together, then I'll run you over to the flat.'

'Thanks, both of you.' Joy's eyes brimmed with tears.

chapter **sixteen**

'Why does she stay with him?' Kate asked Gloria as they sat in the flat over the literary agency, sharing a bottle of wine; while Joy and Hannah were asleep in the bedrooms above.

'She loves him, I suppose, poor cow.' Gloria topped up their glasses. 'God, I'm tired, aren't you?'

'Exhausted. How many trips did we make between here and Holland Park?'

'It must have been half a dozen but it feels more like twenty.' Gloria rubbed her aching shoulders. 'She had so much stuff.'

'Still you could see why she wanted to get it out if he's violent.'

'At least she's got the kid with her. Last time Joy left without her, and Charles wouldn't let her see Hannah. That's how he managed to get her back, I reckon.'

'What a bastard.'

'Yes, and apparently he's charm itself. Everyone thinks he's a really super bloke, only he tortures his wife behind the bedroom door. She wouldn't drink in such a self-destructive way if it wasn't for him.'

'Talking of which I shouldn't be drinking this. What about my diet?' Kate grimaced at the glass in her hand.

'We've earned this, Kate. You can go back on the diet tomorrow.'

Kate looked at her watch. 'I think I'll have another go at calling my husband, he should be home by now. He's not going to be pleased that I'm late – again.'

'We can't leave her though, can we? I mean, what if he came over here? If only the kid wasn't asthmatic and allergic to dogs, I'd stay.'

'Is she?'

'It's why they have no pets, Joy told me. I can't leave Elephant, you see. I've never left him alone all night.' Gloria looked questioningly at Kate.

'I don't know. Tony will be livid if I stay...' Kate said doubtfully. 'Let's see what she says when she wakes up.'

There were times with Tony when Kate wondered why she bothered to call, his reaction was so predictable. She explained about the problem with Joy but he was in no mood to hear explanations.

'You're still there?'

'Yes. She's asleep. Look, Tony, she's a frightened woman. I think I should offer to stay the night.'

'Sod the lot of you,' he yelled and the line went dead.

'Trouble?' Gloria said, half grinning, half anxious.

'Husbands!'

'Some days I'm glad I haven't got one.'

'Days like today I envy you. Actually I think I will have some more wine.'

'Atta girl.' Gloria laughed.

'At least I've escaped from Shotters.'

'That was wonderful news. I've been going to discuss the book with you. I can let you into a secret now. I still had a copy of your typescript, and I sent it round to Panda – you know, the paperback company. Jill Ravenscroft, the senior editor there, is a good friend of mine and I was able to swear her to absolute secrecy. Anyhow, she read it over the weekend, she loves it and they're interested. We should be able to do a joint campaign with them.'

'What's that?'

'It's better for you, is what it means. We shall offer together and we share the expenses of promotion, publicity, all that sort of thing. Panda is one of the biggest paperback houses. If they decide to back you you should get a first print run of more than forty thousand. Honestly, Kate, it's wonderful news for you.'

Kate looked deeply into her glass, biting her lip, a great lump in her throat.

'What's the matter?' Gloria asked with concern.

'Everything's so wonderful and yet I've no one to share it with. My husband doesn't give a damn, in fact he's irritated by the whole business. My daughter is never at home and, in any case, thinks only of herself. My son, the one who has shown the most interest, is working in Yorkshire. And, to top it all, my best friend and I seem so distant with each other and I miss her.'

'How did that happen?'

'The book. I don't know if you understand this, but once I'd started I just couldn't stop. Paradise to me would be someone to run my home so that I could write all the time. My husband resents the inevitable domestic changes. And my friend? I keep thinking I've sorted it out with her, but she seems . . . well, if I'm honest – jealous of my success. It sounds a horrible thing to say.'

'Poor Kate. You're not alone, you know. I've lost count of the number of times I've heard this story. You can't do it all. You can't be creative and a success and still be as you were – but some families, I gather, don't understand this. You can't do what you've done – and don't forget it's a massive achievement – without changing. And you will change more, success does that, you'll become more confident, make other friends. You're paying a price at the moment, but if they can't accept what is happening to you, they risk paying an even bigger price later when you don't want to know any more.'

'It's all so confusing, Gloria. I mean, I was happy, I'm sure I was, a bit bored with the routine, but then who isn't? Tony's a good husband, he provides well, he's faithful, not a drunkard, not a wife-beater . . .' She thought of Joy. 'We've a beautiful home. And yet this one thing, my writing, and he's shut his mind to me, apart from resentment. When I see him now, all we seem to do is row. Oh, Gloria, I'm getting so fed up with it.'

'Of course you are, and it gets in the way of your writing. With your talent you mustn't let that happen, and that's your publisher speaking.'

'What's the alternative? Say I did give it up, wrote no more, how would I feel? I know – frustrated and bitter at what might have been.'

'Don't give up. Let him adjust, I bet *you*'ve had to enough times. Be yourself, he'll probably come round. And I hate to say it, but quite quickly when the money starts coming in. If I'm right about *Winter Interlude*, I rather think it will.'

'You are kind – ' she began to say when the telephone rang. 'Shall I answer it?'

'Yes, if it's her husband she's not here.'

'Hello?' Kate said uncertainly into the telephone.

'Joy?'

'No, it's Kate Howard.'

'Not little Kate of "Sod off, Tony," fame?' A deep voice chuckled.

'I beg your pardon?' Kate felt embarrassed even though she did not recognise the voice.

'It's Barty Silver here. I remember you well.'

'Oh, Sir Barty!' she laughed. Gloria was pulling frantic faces at her; she shrugged her shoulders, not understanding what she wanted.

'Is Joy there?'

'She's asleep, tired out, poor dear. We had to move her out of her house to this flat – it took it out of all of us.'

Gloria put her head in her hands.

'Is she all right?' Barty asked anxiously.

'Yes, she's fine, just tired,' Kate said.

'Right, ta.'

Gloria picked up the bottle of wine and topped up the glasses again. 'Oh, Lord, that's done it.'

'What do you mean?'

'It's a long story and too complicated to tell right now. Just that he thinks she was living here all the time.'

'I wish you'd told me.'

'So do I. Do you fancy something to eat? I'm starving.'

In the kitchen they inspected the few groceries that Joy had brought with her. They had to settle on bread, cheese and some pickled gherkins.

'Isn't it odd the things people pack in an emergency?' Gloria said, spearing one of the gherkins.

'Yes, and they usually leave the most important. Me, I'm sure I'd grab my pruning shears and forget the silver.'

'I don't know what I'd grab, the tin-opener probably, otherwise Elephant would never speak to me again.'

'You love that dog, don't you?'

'Best friend in the world,' she said, suddenly looking sad. 'He never lets me down.'

'And someone else has?' Kate asked gently.

'You could say that. I should be used to it by now, but I'm not. I thought this was different.'

'Do you want to talk?'

'Not particularly, I'd probably end up howling.'

'It might be the best thing for you.'

'I don't think so,' Gloria said, and then, despite herself, despite her vaunted independence, she found herself telling this woman she barely knew the sad little there was to tell of Peter, the pathetic amount to which she had pinned so many dreams. She did not cry as she feared – oddly, she felt better for finally letting it all out.

'You should give him a call.'

'I couldn't. What if he refused to speak to me?'

'Then write him a letter.'

'I'm too proud.'

'Don't be, Gloria. It can be such a destructive emotion, pride. What's the point of being alone with just your pride intact? Go and see him.'

Gloria smiled at her, a smile that completely transformed her attractive face to one of beauty. 'Do you think I should? All right I will, I'll call him.'

'Who on earth's that?' Kate clasped her throat with worry at the sound of the doorbell. Gloria dived for the window and peered out.

'Oh, crikey, it's Barty in person.'

It was a sombre-faced Barty who entered the room a minute later when Gloria had let him in.

'What happened?' he asked, dispensing with any niceties.

'We don't know, Barty. They had a row. Kate found her a bit the worse for wear.'

'She got the little girl with her?'

'Yes.'

'That's good. You got some of her gear out, then.' He looked around the cluttered room where cases and cardboard boxes stood waiting to be unpacked.

'Yes, as much as we could.'

'I feared this. Silly girl.'

'She loves him, Barty. Some women will put up with a lot,' Gloria explained.

'No, I can't believe that. She went back for the kid.'

'I'm sure you're right, Sir Barty,' Kate said gently.

'She can't stay here alone. She ought to come back with me, my house is big enough.'

'She's too distraught and tired to move again, Barty. Kate has said she'll stay overnight.'

'That's kind of you, Kate. I shan't forget that.'

344

'It's the least I can do.' She looked down at the floor with embarrassment.

'Can I see her?' he suddenly asked.

Gloria led the way to the door and the stairs.

Joy was awake, sitting up in bed, gazing sadly into the distance as if unaware that Barty and Gloria were in the doorway. She looked wan, the darkening bruise on her cheek vivid against the pallor of her skin. Barty stood silent. He was angry, though it would have been impossible to tell. An intimate friend might have recognised the signs, but then Barty had no such friends. His family might have seen the same sign, but he had no family. The slight pulse, throbbing high on his temple, was the small indication that Barty Silver was bleak with anger.

Joy looked up to see them.

'Barty, it's you.' She smiled bravely.

'My poor little love,' Barty said, as soft as a sigh, and he crossed the room to the bed. Gloria turned on to the landing and quietly shut the door.

'I've been so stupid, Barty,' Joy said, close to tears.

Barty sat on the side of the bed and he then did something he had never done in his whole life: he leant forward and took Joy into his arms and held her to him. He could smell the sweetness of her hair, felt the smoothness of her skin as her cheek lay against his, was aware of how fragile and thin her body was. And then a strange thing happened. He felt a glow spread through him as if his blood had turned to warm honey.

'There, there,' he said suddenly feeling awkward as he patted her and was not sure what to say. 'There, there. Don't upset yourself . . .'

She looked at him closely and sighed and then leant back from his embrace against the pillows, now glancing everywhere but at him and Barty sat, hands in his lap, feeling inept.

'I've something to tell you,' she said eventually.

'Not now.'

'No, I must.' She sat upright. 'I went back to him, Barty. I promised you and I broke the promise I made to you.'

'I know, my dear. You needed to see Hannah, didn't you?'

She stared at him, she should tell him everything, be honest with him and explain it wasn't just Hannah.

'Yes,' she said, no more.

'You couldn't help yourself, a good mum like you. But I know.'

She frowned. 'How did you know?' she said abruptly.

'Gloria and Kate just told me,' he said hurriedly, realising from her reaction that she would not like the fact that he had always known – the friend he had put in the basement flat had reported to him, as he had asked him to. Joy would not like the idea of being spied on, no one would. 'Kate's offered to stay the night.'

'How kind, but not necessary. I'm all right now. I got drunk but I was so sad and he hurt me . . .' She put her hand to the bruise on her face.

'I hate him,' Barty said his voice full of anger. 'I'll look after you.'

'Barty, you're so kind to me, why?'

'I think I . . . I want to ask you something, Joy . . .' And then he stopped speaking and looked into the corner of the room, an embarrassed expression on his face.

'What?'

Barty shook his head. 'No, not now. It's the wrong time . . . later.' And he scooped her into his arms again because he felt a great need to and he wondered if he would experience that pleasant sensation again. He did.

chapter **seventeen**

Having been reassured by Joy that she was fine and not afraid, but, rather, feeling ashamed for her drunkenness, Kate had caught a mid-evening train home. She was no longer too concerned about seeing an angry Tony.

Before she had left Joy's flat, Barty had taken her on one side. 'Kate, I can't thank you enough for your kindness to Joy. You're not to worry. I'll keep an eye on her for all of us.'

'It was nothing, Sir Barty.'

'Barty, please. No, you need not have bothered, I'm grateful. I'd appreciate it if you could tell your husband I've got some more business I can put his way.'

Kate hoped that the message from Barty would put Tony in a sufficiently good mood that he would want to hear all her interesting news – she had discussed ideas for the cover with Gloria and planned a launch party. She hoped he was happier because she was going to have to tell him that Gloria needed her in London next week for a whole day to discuss the editing of the book. This time she was not concerned, she was sure that any suggestions Gloria had would be constructive ones.

It was therefore something of a let-down to find that Tony was not at home. She waited until almost midnight for him to return but tiredness finally overtook her and she went to bed.

He was not beside her when she woke in the morning.

She found him in the kitchen. He was taciturn in the extreme. Kate made herself sound cheerful but it did not last and soon they were arguing – about her trips to London, about money, about anything, it seemed, that he could dredge up which had annoyed him in the past. And, most ludicrous of all, he seemed to be hinting that she had met someone else.

'Dear God, Tony, I'm getting so fed up with this. Can't we have a reasonable conversation these days?' she shouted in exasperation. 'I've been with my agent. I don't know anyone else. Please stop this endless carping.'

'The choice is yours,' he answered coldly.

'I'm not staying here for this,' she said crossing to the door. There she turned to face him.

'Oh, by the way, Tony, Barty says to tell you he might have some more business to put your way.' She noticed his eyes light up with interest. 'But since you are so uninterested in my work I'm not sure I want him to help you. Barty's very grateful to me for helping out with Joy. And you know what, Tony? I reckon one word from me and he'll forget all about it – so think on that, husband dear.' And she slammed the door shut behind her.

She went upstairs, dressed quickly and, with coat on, was about to return downstairs when she met Lucy on the landing, returning from sleeping at her best friend's house.

'So, you're back,' her daughter said.

'Same could be said of you,' Kate snapped back.

'Sorry I spoke,' Lucy said with equal spirit. 'Where are you going now?'

'Pam's. Your father will tell you why,' Kate said, running down the stairs.

As she drove along, she wondered why she was going there. What was the point? It was not as if she and Pam were close any more. But some of that friendship must remain or why did she instinctively run to her, to cry on her shoulder?

Pam was surprised to see her so early. It was the only explanation for her seeming reluctance to let her in.

'Do I have to stand here all day?' Kate forced a laugh.

'Sorry, come in.' Pam held the door open for her. 'I'm in the kitchen. I was just having some coffee.' She led the way through the green baize door from the main hall along a long corridor to the kitchen, which was so perfect it looked like an advertisement for a kitchen-unit supplier. 'Why such an early visit?'

'I was in the dumps. I need advice. I need to talk to you. Doug here?' she asked, hoping he wasn't about to interrupt them.

'No, he's away for a few days,' Pam replied as she took a mug from the long dresser. 'What's up?' She sat down opposite Kate.

As Kate related her problems with Tony she began to feel uncomfortable. The bickering, the hurt, the rows they had had when told like this sounded like one great moan on her part.

She knew she was not explaining well – she didn't need the somewhat cynical expression on Pam's face to tell her that. She finally finished.

'Well, if you want the truth, Kate, I feel sorry for Tony.'

'You what?' Kate sat bolt upright. She might have been expressing herself badly but not *that* badly, she thought.

'You must see it from his point of view. One day he wakes up and his perfect wife has changed. You *have* changed and I don't think you're even aware of how much.'

'Don't be silly! How have I changed? All right, maybe the house has gone to pot and I'm not jam-making and whatever else I used to do. But for God's sake, Pam, there's more to life than all that.'

'I'd agree with you. I always thought you were too perfect for your own good. No, it's more than that. You're more confident, you've gone away from us all just as I said you would. Poor Tony feels lonely.'

'Well, I never thought to hear you of all people talk like this.'

'I'm sorry. But that's how I see it. You've found something in your life, Kate, something more important than anything else. And good luck to you. You can't go back but you've got to learn to compromise a bit.'

'You don't understand what I'm trying to tell you. He's trying to stop me, he's still sneering at the book even now when it's to be published. That's spite.'

'That's an SOS.'

'Oh, really, Pam! You don't know what I've put up with.'

'Then leave him,' Pam said bluntly.

'Pam!' Kate was shocked.

'No good looking at me like that. If it's so intolerable, you'd no doubt be doing both of you a favour.'

Kate drained her coffee and picked up her handbag.

'I'd better be going.'

Pam laughed. 'Sorry, but you wanted advice and I can't help it if you don't like what I give you.' She followed Kate into the hall and opened the front door. 'By the way, what about my book? What does Joy say? Or have you not given it to her?'

'Pam, I don't think she can possibly have looked at it yet, the poor woman is in a mess – she's left her husband. I promise I'll nag her as soon as she has sorted herself out.'

'Maybe she can advise you,' Pam said laconically.

'I'm sorry I bothered you, Pam. It's not fair of me when you and Doug are friends to both of us. I won't bring it up again. But there is one thing. I'm going to need some new clothes soon. Will you help me choose?'

'I'd love to.' Suddenly Pam stepped forward and kissed her on the cheek. 'I really am your friend, you know. I do care,' she said abruptly.

'I know you do,' Kate said as she slid behind the steering wheel of her car.

A long-faced Lucy was sitting in the kitchen when she returned home.

'Mum.' As Kate entered the room she immediately crossed to her and put her arms about her mother. 'Mum, I'm so sorry, I can't tell you how furious I am with Dad.'

'You spoke to your father?'

'We had a row, Mum, I'd no idea he could be such a male chauvinist pig. I couldn't believe what I was hearing.'

'Where is he now?' she asked warily.

'Gone out. Gone to see Fred, I think. Coffee?'

'No. Blow the coffee, Lucy. Let's have some wine.' Kate stood up and went out to the pantry to the small fridge emblazoned with stickers saying, 'Tony's, keep out'. They had been a joke once, it was she who had bought them for him. She did not see the funny side today as she opened the door and deliberately chose the most expensive bottle she could find. 'Pouilly Fuissé,' she announced to her daughter, waving the bottle on high.

'I've got to apologise to you, Mum. I haven't taken your writing seriously enough either.'

'Lucy, you've your own life to lead, I didn't expect you to. Lots of people write but who could have guessed I would have the luck to get this far?'

'That's no excuse. I should have been encouraging you, been pleased for you. I think, in a way, I was afraid of losing you as a mum, that you wouldn't have time for us any more. That was stupid of me. Mind you, I'm proud as punch now. Everyone at school is fed up with the subject of my mum and her book.'

'Bless you.' Kate poured the wine. 'It's bloody hard being a woman, Lucy. Take all this as a warning. Equal opportunity, my eye. It doesn't work that way in our circle. I've given twenty-five years to running this family, his life. Is it wrong of me to want to do something else now? I don't think I've been a bad manager –'

'You've been the best.'

'But you see, Lucy, it's *my* time now. It's *my* turn to do something. It's no longer enough for me to be a homemaker – those things are no longer important to me. I was happy doing that once, I couldn't be happy just doing that again.' She sipped at the wine. 'You know you used to tease me about being menopausal? It's true, I am. But, you know, it's as if that was a sign to me to get off my arse, to stop mooning about feeling sorry for myself, to *do* something. And since I have, I've found so much more energy. I've felt better, I'm alive for the first time in years.'

'Can I read it?'

'I'd love you to.'

'You don't think Dad's jealous, do you?'

'That I'll find another man? Well, evidently.'

'No, I meant the book. I wonder if he's afraid you're going to succeed, that you're going to be famous. Maybe he doesn't think he can handle it.'

'Steve said something similar. Oh, no, Lucy, that's too silly. No, he thought I'd found a fellow. Me? Laughable, isn't it?'

Barty had had the telephone numbers both at the flat and Joy's office changed to ex-directory. This was fine except that he had not told her. Nor did Gloria know.

She had been trying to contact Joy for a couple of days and was concerned when she could not get through and could not prise the number out of the exchange. She hoped Joy was not going to pieces. She could sympathise with her problems: they were horrendous. But what woman in business did not at some time or other have personal problems? No professional woman worth her salt could afford the luxury of showing she was upset, let alone give in to her problems by not turning up for work at all. Gloria knew that shows of weakness played right into the hands of those men who were always waiting for such opportunities. Men who would then be able to say, 'See, women can't have positions of power, their emotions get in the way.' It would be unforgivable if Joy was to let her own sex down.

Luckily Gloria was busy. The best thing to keep her mind off

Peter, and what might have been, was work. She had still not taken Kate's advice to contact him. A couple of times she had even picked up the telephone to dial his number, but when it came to it, she found she could not. She resisted being the one who made the advances.

Gloria's new list at Westall's was to have an autumn launch, a whole season earlier than Julius had anticipated. She had been lucky in buying in two American novels, and she wanted Kate's book as the lead title. She wanted to launch it in time for the Christmas market, which was a risky thing to do. Christmas was not the best time to publish a first novel: with so many other books released with gift-buying in mind a first novel could so easily sink without trace. But it was a strong novel, different from many others and, if she was honest, Gloria had to admit that she found the risk involved exciting.

She had already spoken to the Red Rose Society. At the party for the opening of yet another shop in the Cavendish book chain, she had bumped into Olive West, chairperson-designate of the society. She had known Olive for years although never published her, but gave a hint or two that this was a situation which might be changing. Olive was a sweet woman, very intelligent, a highly professional writer. She was easy to swear to total secrecy, so that Shotters would not find out, since she loathed Tatiana Spence perhaps even more than Gloria did. Gloria had floated her idea of a competition to run concurrent with Kate's promotion. Writers would be invited to submit the first chapter and a synopsis of a novel suitable for the women's market. The Red Rose Society would administer it, doing the first readings and choosing a short list to be judged by Gloria and a personality, yet to be chosen. The winner, apart from getting a cash prize, would have their completed work seriously considered for publication by Westall's. The society always had a banquet just before Christmas, which would be the ideal time to announce the winner. Best of all for Westall's, the organisation had a huge mailing list and a good press officer. Media coverage was sure to follow, which, while helping Kate's sales, would give Westall's valuable free publicity.

It was all very neat and Gloria was pleased and excited by the plan. To get the ball rolling in time it would have to be announced in the next Red Rose newsletter which was going out in June – next month.

The speed with which Gloria was working was making Julius sceptical. He did not like things to be rushed, especially books. If a book was good enough to be published then it was good enough to have time spent on it to make it perfect.

'Look, Julius, this list has to be got going as soon as possible, you said yourself we need the money. The sooner the better. I've got these two books from America – they'll sell in well, I'm sure, they're both established authors I've managed to poach.'

'Who from?'

'Dawn-Rose is from Pewter's and Reena from Tudor's.'

'Well done,' he smiled. 'It makes such a change – everyone normally poaches from me.'

'Those two need no editing – we can offset from the American editions – artwork is no problem either, we can use the existing jackets. That means we only have Kate to worry about and if we bring her out in October that gives us six months to do it in. The main problem with a totally unknown writer like Kate is the publicity angle. I've been talking to Val. She's very excited at the news angle of Kate – having started writing and then been published in under a year. It's unheard of. It's like a fairy story. If Kate and I work like the clappers we'll do it. Your art department say they can foresee no problems – we'll go for a simple, dramatic cover that can be done in-house. What's more, Panda are very keen we do – they want Kate for their lead title the following October.' Gloria took a long sip of water, she was so keyed up she wished it was a vodka.

'That good?'

'That good, Julius.'

'Well, it's your decision and I promised you total control . . . Good luck with it, I hope you make it.'

Kate had not resolved anything with Tony when she went for her editorial meeting with Gloria. She could not believe how in tune they were. Parts of the book, she knew, were flat, or had not turned out as she had wanted. Without fail Gloria had picked them out. She made suggestions as to what should be done and Kate could not imagine why she had not seen the solutions herself.

'It's all so obvious. Why didn't I think of that?' She smiled across the desk at Gloria after scribbling down yet another answer to a plot problem.

'Because you're too close to it. Every book needs new eyes to look at it.'

'I'm really enjoying this. It's like a polishing process, getting it perfect.'

'Let's hope you always think like that.' Gloria laughed, thinking of the arguments she had with some of her authors. 'We've got a publication date pencilled in. Last Thursday in October – Westall's always publish on a Thursday.'

'October?' Kate said. 'Gracious, so soon?'

'We wanted to do it then so it's under a year from the novel's conception to being published. First books are notoriously difficult to place but let's keep our fingers crossed and hope that you prove everyone wrong. It could be a wonderful month for you.'

'Shotters told me February was.' Kate could not help but laugh.

'You'd be amazed at the lies we have to tell to assure authors that any month is perfect. You should hear some of my fibs,' Gloria replied, also laughing.

Gloria should not have worried about Joy. She called full of apologies that Gloria had not been informed of her change of number.

'I do hope you haven't been going mad trying to get hold of me?'

'Good heavens no.' Gloria laughed as she lied. 'Just yelled at British Telecom. How are you?'

'Fine. I'm having a bit of a problem getting a nanny for Hannah – they turn their nose up at this little flat. But otherwise I'm OK – work, that's the solution.' She laughed and at the other end Gloria frowned. It sounded a rather false and brittle laugh.

'Don't do too much, will you? You've been through a lot,' said Gloria completely forgetting her own emotional problems.

'Don't worry about me. I feel wonderful, especially now I've got both Kate and Barty's contracts almost finished and am rid of my husband.' The strange laugh rang out again.

Charles was not having a good time either. Finding Joy's telephone number changed and unable to contact her, his anger with her deepened. He had been burgled, his car broken into twice and vandalised. He shut up the house and moved in with Penelope. Once there he gave vent to his paranoia. There was nothing she could say to persuade him that the burglary and trouble with his car were nothing to do with Barty Silver.

During this period Barty worked on his autobiography, made a million pounds from various businesses, and bided his time.

chapter **eighteen**

Joy was tired, which she could not admit to anyone. Undoubtedly it was this tiredness which had led her to shout at her secretary – something she had never done before. The young woman, having struggled into work despite a very heavy cold, understandably took umbrage and walked out. This left Joy with a word processor she did not understand, a telephone system she could not work, and a filing system which took time for her to find anything.

After two days of frustration in the office she employed her first temp who only lasted one day. Something to do with the buses, she had explained, but Joy felt it was because she was bored, alone in the office. She was now on her third temporary member of staff. She was getting weary of having to explain everything anew and was determinedly sweet with this one in the hope she might stay, if only for a week. Her search for a new permanent secretary was taking up too much time and her over-flowing ashtray indicated the strain she was beginning to feel.

Hannah, as if sensing all was not well, began to play up. If Joy cooked her a boiled egg for breakfast she demanded it scrambled. Each morning there was a fight over which clothes the child would condescend to wear. Normally quiet and placid, she had now begun to play games which involved much stomping, shouting and throwing things.

The search for a suitable nanny continued but so far the accommodation was not good enough for any of them. They all expected an *en suite* bathroom, a private sitting room, a car and their own colour television and video recorder, none of which Joy could supply.

With no nanny Joy was relying on Universal Aunts to supply her with a child-minder so that she could get on with some work. The problem was that each day a different woman turned up to care for Hannah and such lack of continuity was exacerbating the problem. But when Joy telephoned the company to ask them to send only those willing to work on a semi-permanent basis, they prevaricated so much that Joy was forced to conclude that the 'aunts' were refusing to return for another day with the fractious and difficult child.

Temporary staff of any description did not come cheap and Joy was becoming worried about money but was loath to bother Barty with her problems. A long consultation with her lawyer had not helped her equilibrium. Having finally left Charles for good, Joy hoped for a quick divorce before she could change her mind again. She was horrified to hear that to achieve this before the period of two years' separation was up, she would have to sue him for his adultery or unreasonable behaviour.

'Luckily you have photographs of your injuries and Sir Barty's doctor's report,' her solicitor said encouragingly.

'But that would mean everything coming out in court,' Joy said, horrified at the prospect.

'Unfortunately, yes. But people soon forget . . .'

'No, no, I couldn't do that,' Joy said emphatically.

To all her other problems was added the knowledge that she would be trapped in this marriage for a further two years. To escape these worries Joy worked even harder but, with Hannah to care for and no decent help, she was having to fit it in as and when she could. Most of her reading and paperwork she did late into the night when Hannah was at last asleep. And so her tiredness intensified.

There were evenings when she had to go out. Knowing what was going on in the publishing world was essential and one sure way of finding out was to attend the numerous parties that were part and parcel of the industry.

To save money she had begun to use the *au pair* of one of her friends as a baby-sitter – she cost less than the professional ones.

This particular evening she was due at an awards dinner, when her friend called to say that her *au pair* was ill and could not come. She gave Joy the number of another Italian girl who would be willing to sit. Not knowing the girl or anything about her, Joy was worried. But this function was important and, even more important, Tatiana Spence would be there. Joy needed to build bridges with Tatiana who was annoyed at Kate moving to Westall's and was too important in publishing for Joy to have anything but a good working relationship with her.

Joy called the new girl and made the arrangements. She cooked Hannah's supper, then took nearly an hour to persuade her to eat it. Hannah's bath over and her story read, she was put to bed and finally fell asleep. Joy was left with less than half an hour to bath and change – everything she did these days seemed to be in a rush.

The Italian girl was pleasant and spoke reasonable English. Joy set off content that Hannah would be well looked after.

It was as well she went. She found herself at the same table as Tatiana who was charming to her and Joy wondered why on earth she had been so worried. Best of all, she talked to a well-established writer who was looking for a new agent and they made an appointment to talk. When she returned to her flat she felt better than she had for weeks.

It was past midnight when she ran up the stairs.

'Sorry, I'm so late,' she called gaily as she entered her sitting room, 'I got held up; – ' She stopped in the doorway. In the centre of the room, a deep frown on his face, stood Charles.

'Who let you in?' she demanded.

'No one. I walked in. The front door was open.'

'Where's the *au-pair* girl?'

'I sent her packing *when* she came back.'

'Came back, what do you mean?'

'I arrived here hoping to see you, hoping to talk some sense into you, since you won't answer my letters and I did not have your telephone number. The front door was on the latch. I rang the bell, no one answered, so I came in. The baby-sitter you had thought good enough to care for my daughter was out – '

'Hannah, is she . . .?' She turned to leave the room.

'Hannah is fine, no thanks to you. The baby-sitter claimed she had only popped out for a minute to get some fags. How was I to know how long she had been out? She could have been out all evening. You're irresponsible, Joy, totally so.'

'I'm not. Hannah is never left alone.'

'She was tonight,' he said shortly.

'I'll speak to the girl. That was very wrong of her even if she was only out for a minute.'

'Did you know this person?'

'She was recommended by a friend.'

'You'd no right to leave her with someone you did not know.'

'I'm sorry, Charles. But no harm was done.'

'Wasn't it? I've removed Hannah. You are unfit to look after her and obviously too busy.'

'Removed her? What the hell do you mean? What are you saying?' She ran from the room, racing up the stairs with a thumping heart to her daughter's bedroom. The bed was bare, Hannah's clothes had been packed, her toys taken. 'Oh, no – ' She stumbled back down the staircase. 'How dare you, Charles? You've no right to take her. Where is she?'

'I'm going to court tomorrow, I'm applying for temporary custody.'

'How dare you?' she repeated. 'I've managed on my own for a month well enough. Where is she? You have to tell me. She can't stay with you and that whore, Penelope, I won't allow that.'

'I don't think the choice will be yours to make, Joy.'

'Is she with her?'

'No, she's at my mother's. Penelope took her there.'

'In the middle of the night? Are you mad? You must have scared her half to death.'

'Don't be silly, Joy. It was hardly the middle of the night – nine to be exact. Of course she was not scared. She was pleased to see me – she does love me, you know. And she knows Penelope well. She'll be happy at my mother's until I can make other arrangements.'

'You talk as if it had all been decided. It hasn't. I shall fight you.'

'Oh yes, and how? With what? Going to go running to Daddy to help you?'

'Barty will help me.'

'He won't want to get involved with any nasty publicity, and I'd make it nasty if he sticks his nose in, I can assure you.'

'He loathes you, Charles. He'll help me.'

'You should choose your friends with a lot more care, Joy,' Charles said coldly. 'It won't look good in court when the judge finds out that your protector is a raving homosexual.'

'He isn't, that's malicious gossip. It would be beyond the comprehension of someone as obsessed with sex as you to understand that not everyone is like you. Barty isn't homosexual, bisexual or heterosexual, he's not interested in sex at all. Nor is he my protector, he's a friend.'

'My dear Joy. I can assure you by the time I've finished the judge will have no doubt what role he plays in your life. You will be found to be a most unsuitable person to care for my daughter. That's a promise.' He smiled at her as he walked towards the door. She couldn't believe that she had once lived for him to smile at her just like that.

She heard the front door slam. She poured herself a large drink. She was about to drink it, then suddenly slammed it down. No, that was no solution. She dialled a number which would connect her with Gervase on his mobile telephone, and where Gervase was there would be Barty.

'Barty, I'm sorry, I know it's late but can I see you?'

Barty was waiting for her in the hall of his mansion. He stepped forward immediately, hands held out in greeting, smiling gently. On the way here she had been full of anger and indignation but now inside Barty's house with him holding her hands, with the feeling of safety he always gave her, Joy broke down.

Barty led her to his private sitting room, a room she had never been in before and one which now, with tears cascading, she could not see. Barty sat her on the sofa and fussed about pouring her a drink, finding her a cigarette.

'When you're ready, Joy, tell Barty,' he said settling himself beside her, waiting patiently while, between sobs, she told him what had happened.

'First thing tomorrow we'll get the lawyers to slap an injunction on him. Don't you worry, he can't take your little girl away from you, a good mum like you.'

'It's not right using her like this.'

'Of course it isn't. The law can be dumb but not that dumb. The judge'll see through his nasty games.'

'Do you really think so, Barty?'

'Would I say it if I didn't?'

'There is one thing – he's going to use my friendship with you as grounds for showing I'm unfit.'

'Consorting with undesirables?' Barty laughed almost as if he was delighted with the accusation.

'Yes, I mean . . . it's too awful, Barty. I won't have you dragged into this mess, it's just not fair.'

'But I am involved and honoured to be so.'

'Oh, Barty.' Joy looked up at him, her blue eyes blurred with tears. 'Why are you so kind to me?'

''Cause I love you, girl. That's the truth.'

Joy stopped crying, stopped wiping her eyes with his handkerchief. She looked at him with amazement. She did not say anything, she was too stunned.

'Bit of a shock, isn't it?' Barty laughed a small, rather embarrassed laugh. 'Took me by surprise, I can tell you.' He looked at her anxiously, his large round face devoid of any smiles. 'It's not what I expected, I thought all that had passed me by.' He paused as if waiting for her to say something, but she did not. 'I didn't mean to say anything. I thought, best to let it lie, tell no one, including you. After all, why should a lovely lady like you want someone like me? That's what I thought, but then I saw you looking so sad and crying and all . . . I couldn't bear to see you like that. I want to protect you from feeling as you do, for ever. And, well, the words just sort of popped out. I'm sorry.' Barty hung his head so as not to see the expression on her face.

'Barty, my dear, what can I say?' She put her hand out and touched his gently. She was surprised, but deeply moved. Nothing had prepared her for such a conversation.

'Don't say anything, I'd rather you didn't. I know what you're going to say.' He was still looking down.

'Do you really know what I'm going to say?'

Barty was staring intently at where her hand rested on his. Joy's mind was racing. She was safe with Barty. She always felt a great blanket of security when in his company. There was no violence here. 'What am I going to say, then?' she said, softly.

Barty mumbled.

'I'm deeply honoured, Barty. More than I think you'll ever realise,' she said quietly.

He looked at her then with an expression of disbelief.

'Could you say that again?' He spoke in barely a whisper.

She laughed but it was gentle. 'I think you heard, Barty.'

'Perhaps you don't understand, Joy. I mean I love you and I would like to marry you.'

'I didn't for one moment think that you of all people, Barty, would be thinking of anything else.'

'You mean you would be willing to marry me, once you are free?'

'Barty – I need time. I'll have to think about it.'

'Oh my God!' Barty floundered for words. 'Of course. You take all the time in the world. Oh, Joy. I do love you. Not just words . . . not that I've ever said them to a living soul before . . . but, well, you know.' He looked at her.

'Yes, I know, Barty. It's not something that's easy to explain.'

Then Barty hung his head again. 'You won't want to go through with it when you've heard me out. I say I want to marry you, but it wouldn't be a marriage like other people's I mean, I wouldn't want to bother you, if you know what I mean.'

'Sleeping together, you mean?'

'Well, yes . . .' Barty's voice emerged strangled with many different emotions.

'I know, Barty, and I understand. But you see that's one of the things I'd need time to think about.'

'You understand?' Barty repeated, fully aware that he sounded like an idiot.

'Maybe it is possible to love without sex, I don't know. Perhaps it might even be better. What has all that ever brought me? Much unhappiness.' She spoke with conviction, she spoke the truth. They liked each other, they respected each other, it seemed the most logical thing in the world to do, it might work, she thought. And unfortunately she found herself thinking also of how annoyed it would make Charles.

chapter **nineteen**

Tony was speaking to Kate, but it was in a formal and rigid manner, as if he hardly knew her; there was certainly no conversation between them. She would not have been human had she not felt a certain smugness when he came to tell her she was wanted on the telephone and that it was Barty. She picked up the receiver, puzzled as to why he should wish to speak to her.

'Kate, I see you've an appointment with Joy on Wednesday. I thought I ought to put you in the picture. Joy's had a bit more trouble from that husband of hers.'

'Oh, no. What?'

'He's nicked the kid. Don't worry, my lawyers are working on it. Thing is, Kate, she's tired, poor little thing's had a lot on her plate.'

'I know, Barty. The office, looking after Hannah, she would have managed – '

'Exactly, this bit of bother is the last straw. I've insisted she has a complete rest. I've popped her into a nursing home I've an interest in – she's not ill, you realise,' he said hurriedly.

'No, of course not. Just needs a good sleep.'

'Right on, Kate. Thing is, the business. Joy has recommended another agent, a Faith Cooper, to help her out. We have every intention of expanding and this matter has brought things to a head sooner – Faith'll be looking after you until Joy gets back.'

'Give her my love, tell her not to worry. She's lucky to have you as a friend, Barty.'

'Oh no, Kate, it's me what's lucky to have her. And while we're on the phone maybe it's a good time for me to have a natter with that husband of yours, shall I?'

'Yes, Barty, that would be very kind of you.'

Kate was peeling potatoes when Tony came back into the kitchen.

'Thanks, Kate.'

'Thanks for what?'

'You know, not letting on to Barty that I've been a bit of a berk.'

'Have you, Tony?' She glanced down at the potatoes in the bowl. Was this a good time to mention she was off to London again? She felt resentful that this situation had arisen, making a prisoner of her again. She was going, there was no doubt about that. So perhaps it was best to get it over with. She felt he was trying to apologise; it was as close to an apology as she was likely to get from Tony.

'Tony, there's just one thing. I have to go to London again. I'm sorry, but there it is.' She said this with a finality that would brook no argument. 'My agent has a lot of personal problems and she wants me to meet her new partner. And Gloria, my editor, wants to see me to talk about publication plans.' She stated it, she did not ask him, she was not apologising. It was the best, the only way, to handle him, she had decided.

During their period of hostility, Kate had rationalised many things. The situation with Tony was not something she enjoyed, nor one she wanted to continue. When they had rowed after Barty's party and Tony had said he had had enough, she had faced the prospect of his leaving her with a sense of freedom, almost excitement. It was a feeling that she could not recapture. Now, when she thought of separation, she found herself afraid of the loneliness it might entail.

She now felt that if only he would accept her new career with grace, she would be content. She realised that one of her main problems had been boredom, she had solved that. These days there were not enough hours in the day.

She knew she no longer loved her husband, not as she presumed she once had – it still puzzled her why she had such difficulty remembering their early days together – but she was fond of him, and still grateful for all he had given her. She did not want her marriage to end. But if it was not to finish, something had to be done to save it.

It was so easy to fall into the trap of thinking that only her own viewpoint was right. She could see now that when Tony had called her selfish he had also been right. They had both been selfish, and that must stop.

If one looked at it in the fairest light Pam had also spoken the truth. The change her new career had made to this family had been momentous. And what husband would accept his routine being upset? She could acknowledge that she had allowed her book to become so important as to exclude everything else. While unfair to the family it was not a good idea for her. She had not read a paper, watched anything on TV, taken an interest in anything else for months. If she was not careful she was heading towards a trap even more demanding and restrictive than the one she had found herself in before.

She made several resolutions, even to the extent of writing them down and pinning them to the side of her word processor so she would not forget. She was determined, while writing her second novel, to restrict herself to set hours of work – she must make time for family and friends. The money she earned could and should be used to help make the house run as it once had, so that her family did not suffer from her absences. While the writing had become a joy to her she did not want to see it become a burden to others. Compromises were going to be made, and not just on Tony's side.

This time before she went to London she cleaned the house, did a wash and iron that left nothing dirty, shopped for provisions and cooked Tony's favourite meal for Lucy to heat up for him.

Kate went to her first appointment with Joy's new associate, Faith Cooper. And as at their first meeting at the writers' weekend, she was unsure whether she liked her. There was nothing wrong in the warm welcome she received. And Faith remembering her was gratifying, as was the fulsome praise for Kate's book she generously gave. Of course, Kate admitted to herself, she did feel embarrassed. After all, it had been Faith who had seen the spark in her and had asked to see her work. But Faith made no mention of this which, if anything, made Kate feel even more uncomfortable.

The only things that Kate could pin down were the somewhat brusque manner and a super-professionalism and efficiency which bothered her. There was a steeliness to Faith, a harshness, a feeling that she probably lacked humour. Kate sat opposite her and realised she felt more than a little afraid of her.

Faith had her new contract with Westall's, and a list of

details in relation to it, to discuss. Kate's head was soon reeling, assaulted by percentages and fractions of percentages which Faith rattled off at speed. Since she had been hopeless at maths at school, she had to confess she did not understand a word Faith was saying and that she would rely on her good judgement. By the merest lift of an eyebrow, Kate was left in no doubt what Faith thought of women who could not understand the mathematics of business.

However, unrelaxed as she was, Kate could not fault the deal Faith had finally worked out for her. It was to be a two-book joint deal with Westall's and Panda Books, the paperback house. Kate was bowled over by this news, and said so, for Panda was a household name.

'Imagine them wanting to buy my book,' she said, amazed at the very idea.

'To make it into the big-time as an author you need to be bought by one of the big two paperback houses. If you think of any of the bookshops you go to, which paperbacks are most prominently displayed? Panda and Eagle. Had you stayed with Shotters they would have insisted that their new paperback imprint – Sabre – should publish you. But how long will it take them to build up to the sales levels and profile of the other two? Years. So many paperback books are produced each year that it's a continuous battle, requiring endless negotiations between the sales managers and the multiple bookshop chains, to get the optimum shelf positions and their co-operation to promote you in-store. And you can't get much better than the sales team at Panda. So, for you, this is all very satisfactory.' Faith paused only long enough to light a cigarette and to offer one to Kate. 'Westall's probably won't sell the number of hardbacks that Shotters, with its huge sales team and reputation in your genre, could have sold. But, on the other hand, this is a new venture for them – they have to make it work, so money and enormous effort will be put behind you. It's a rare book that becomes a bestseller without help, Kate. No, it's the publishers *deciding* who they are going to push into making a bestseller that is relevant – and, lucky old you, they've decided to put the loot behind you.' Faith dragged deeply on her cigarette and chuckled, a delightful deep, bubbling noise so infectious that it made Kate wonder if she had not been judging her harshly. 'And we've still got the American and foreign rights to sell.' Faith rubbed her hands with satisfaction.

'America? Gracious, I hadn't even given it a thought,' Kate said, finally getting a word in.

'You should do – it can be a very lucrative market. Even if you don't get a huge advance, the country is so vast that their print-runs are enormous compared with ours, so royalties from that source can be considerable. Foreign rights – the advances are small, but when you think of the number of countries you can sell to – it all adds up, Kate. But don't set your heart on America. It's an incredibly difficult market to break in to. For instance, Bella Ford still hasn't made it and I could name you a dozen others. But I'll put myself on the line. I've got a funny feeling about yours, it could have a universal appeal. I think we might just be lucky.'

'Really?' Kate had thought with the acceptance of her book the excitement was over. It seemed it was only just beginning.

'I've discussed it with Joy and I've sent the typescript to an agent in New York we've decided to use. It means higher commission for you, unfortunately. I know that Joy was hoping to deal with America herself, but quite honestly, Kate, we've decided we need an agent on the spot, talking to the editors every week, knowing exactly what they're looking for. Unless you're on the spot with an ear to the gossip you can easily come a cropper. I know of one author who was taken on by a new publisher and they turned out to be fly-by-nights who had set up an office with a couple of editors. They offered the moon and six months later they were shutting up shop. The author was left with nothing, and the big New York publishers don't want to know her. Our agent will be aware who's financially secure or not. Barty agrees with us.'

'Have you been an agent long?'

'Too long.' She chuckled again. 'I was an editor, loads of us were, but I prefer the cut and thrust of the marketplace to editing – more exciting. I've been with Ambert's – one of the biggest agencies, I expect you've heard of them – but it was getting too big and boring.'

'You sound like Gloria talking about the publishing conglomerates.'

'Exactly, and I think the agencies are next. We'll see take-overs and amalgamations there as well, you mark my words. I was fed up with all the committees and discussions. I wanted the challenge of a small operation again. Barty and Joy appeared at just the right time.'

'And you could leave at such short notice?'

'Barty is a wonder, he can always get whatever he wants. He's connected to Ambert's in a way I haven't yet worked out, so he could get me out of my contract, wham bam.' She lit yet another cigarette. For every cigarette Kate smoked, Faith smoked three – it made her feel much better about her habit. 'My coming here is an advantage to this agency since most of my authors will follow me, you see. So everyone is happy – you included, I hope.' She flashed Kate a huge encompassing smile.

'Of course.' Kate smiled back. 'Do you know when Joy's coming back full time?' she asked in all innocence.

'No, I've no idea,' Faith said stiffly. 'If you've any worries about my ability perhaps you should discuss it with Barty.' She sat bolt upright behind her desk, no smile, the expression of her grey eyes suddenly hard. She was bristling with indignation, Kate realised.

'Good gracious no. I was only enquiring about Joy. I heard about the problems with her husband, and Hannah.'

'Ah, I see.' Faith relaxed in the chair, indignation mollified – for the time being, thought Kate. 'So, if you're satisfied about this contract, I suggest you sign it here and now and everyone at Westall's will sigh with relief.'

'Where?' Kate picked up a pen.

Faith watched her signing. 'I suppose your contract with Shotters was the exciting one?'

'Not really. My husband was away, the kids were out, my best friend didn't answer my calls, so the cat watched me sign.' She could laugh now; it was not so funny at the time. She picked up her handbag from the floor, ready to leave.

'By the way, Kate, before you go. This stuff from Pam Homerton, Joy asked me to read it. Is she anything to do with you? Only there's no address.'

'Yes, she's my friend, actually. I hoped Joy would write to her about her work.'

'Could you give me her address, better still her telephone number? I'd like to talk to her. It's wonderful writing.'

'You think so?' Kate tried to keep the surprise out of her voice.

'Oh, yes. You must have heard of Sappho, the women's imprint? They'll kill for it.'

'Wonderful, thanks, Faith,' said Kate, mentally making a note never to do any reviewing or criticism, assuming she was ever asked. Never, it was all too subjective.

'No, we should be thanking you for introducing her. Of course, she won't make the sort of money you will make but she'll get the prizes and plaudits. You can't have everything in life, can you?' She chuckled again, inhaled deeply on her cigarette, and had a coughing fit.

At Westall's Kate met more of the team. Val from publicity, Ben from design, John in marketing. The first thing that struck her was how normal everyone's clothes were, and the second was that there were no outlandish names. She could not help but wonder why. But the biggest contrast of all was the enthusiasm she met. They talked as if *Winter Interlude* was the only book that mattered. She knew this was not so, but it did not stop her basking in their compliments. They loved her writing, they did not want this, that and the other changed. Incredibly they appeared to care as much about it as she did. She apologised for her ordinariness, fearing it would prove a liability in publicising her.

'Gracious, no,' enthused Val. 'We shall use that very fact to our advantage. Every other writer these days is a celebrity of sorts – you're a refreshing change. You prove everyone wrong. It can be done – that first book accepted and successful. And to embark on a new career in your middle years, why, Kate, you'll be an inspiration to thousands.' Val was grinning at her, her keenness infectious, and Kate thought how much nicer 'middle years' sounded to 'middle-aged' – less leaden.

She was shown the artwork for the jacket and could have hugged Ben, could have cried. It was just as she had envisaged it, how she would have drawn it if she had the talent: simple, eye-catching yet still dignified. It was a very special moment.

'This is one of those days when I'm afraid that if I pinch myself I might wake up and find it all a dream,' she said, thanking them all for their hard work.

'It's no dream, Kate, you're on your way.' Gloria smiled at her. 'There's just one other thing. It's dreadfully short notice but we were wondering if perhaps you could get to our sales conference next month? It would help the teams so much if you could meet them. It's easier for them to sell a new author if they've met you. Then they can tell the bookshop people what a lovely person you are. It all helps. Of course, your husband's invited as well. The team from Panda will be there too.'

'I should love to, how kind of you to ask. I'm not sure about Tony, though, he's so busy these days,' she lied. 'And, anyway, I'm not at all sure he'd want to come,' she added, which was the truth.

chapter **twenty**

'I want something in red, an outfit for the sales conference,' Kate told Pam as they entered the exclusive dress shop.

'Why red particularly?'

'I don't know, I suppose because when we went on the writers' weekend every other writer was in red, it seemed to me. My book jacket's primarily red too, with gold lettering.'

'Then I can't think of a better reason.'

Kate had forgotten there had been a time, less than a year ago, when she had found shopping in Bristol impossible, but those dreadful feelings of doom and panic had now disappeared completely from her mind.

They finally settled on a scarlet silk dress with a dramatic jacket of red, gold and black sequins. In truth, Pam decided, Kate would never have had the courage to choose it herself.

'You know, Kate,' said Pam, as they left the dress shop, 'I'd no idea you'd lost so much weight.'

'Great, that's just what every dieter wants to hear. What's the point if no one notices?'

'I never think of weight.'

'You don't need to,' said Kate with feeling.

'You need a new face. Let's go into Dingle's and play with the make-up.'

Two hours later, with the back seat of Pam's car covered in carrier bags, Kate with a stunning new make-up applied *gratis* by one of the beauty consultants in Dingle's, they were about to set off home.

'What a day!' Kate sighed, leaning back on the comfortable leather of the seat. 'God knows what I spent, and it's all been paid for by me. No guilt, no apologies, no lying. Bloody wonderful!'

'And I just love that blue suit on you, it looked stunning. And the green blouse with it, that's sheer genius.'

'I didn't need that suit.'

'Of course you didn't, that's the joy of it.' Pam laughed.

'Nor did I need three pairs of shoes – two of them identical.'

'Of course you did. Red suede can scuff – you've got to look your best.'

'You're sure I'm not going to look like mutton dressed as lamb?'

'Don't talk such rubbish. But you've got to get your hair cut and streaked, I insist. It'll take years off you. And when do you say your contact lenses will be ready?'

'I've got them, I'm wearing them for a bit longer every day. By the time of the conference I'll be up to full-time wearing.'

'Do they hurt?' Pam shuddered.

'Not much, the odd prick. I had them once before, don't you remember?'

'You'd never get me putting things in my eyes. Horrible thought!' Pam turned round and took something from the back seat. 'There's just one other thing.' Pam handed Kate a small gift-wrapped parcel.

'What's this?'

'It's for you, because I doubted you. It's me saying sorry for masses of things.'

Mystified, Kate opened it. Inside was a gold fountain pen.

'For signing all your books and contracts,' Pam said shyly.

'What a lovely idea. What a thoughtful gift.' Kate leant over and kissed her friend. 'But what did you mean, that you doubted me?'

Pam looked embarrassed and looked all ways but at Kate. 'Silly of me, I suppose, but I just thought you'd drop everyone when you started meeting new people.'

'Yes, it was silly of you. Why should I do a thing like that?'

'And I thought you were becoming so obsessed with it all that you wouldn't have time or inclination to help anyone else, and I was wrong on that too.'

'Oh, go on . . .' It was Kate's turn to feel embarrassed.

'It's true. You bothered even when you didn't really like what I had written.'

'What gives you that idea?' Kate said, probably a shade too quickly.

'It's true, though, isn't it?' Pam smiled at her.

'Not exactly. More like I didn't understand what you were doing – that's nearer the truth.'

'Ha! Don't fib to me. Honest, I don't mind. I thought it was a load of old cobblers myself.' And she laughed and Kate joined in, but she was not too sure that Pam was necessarily speaking the truth.

'Well, you're on your way, just like I said. It'll be me helping you choose an outfit next year, for your sales conference.'

'Felicity says that not many authors are invited to the conferences, she said you had been honoured.'

'Felicity said that? That was nice.'

'Is Tony going with you?'

'He still hasn't made up his mind. In a way, I hope he doesn't.'

The hotel, in its own park with a herd of deer grazing and a river flowing through the grounds, was large, crenellated, turreted and opulent.

'It looks like something out of a Hammer House of Horror film.' Kate giggled nervously. She was not nervous at the prospect of staying in something so grand but at the ordeal ahead.

'They obviously don't stint themselves,' said Tony. Rather grudgingly, she thought.

'Or us,' she answered pointedly.

They had not said what time they were arriving but Penny, Val's assistant at Westall's, was waiting for them at reception and insisted on accompanying them to their room. She explained the timetable, asked if there was anything they needed, and left them.

'Well, just look at all this,' Kate said, already busily inspecting the suite. 'I didn't expect all this, did you?' She fingered the flowers on the coffee table which had a welcome note attached. 'Look, champagne!' she exclaimed opening the small refrigerator, cased in mahogany and disguised as a cupboard.

'I'm glad I'm not a shareholder in either company,' Tony said, loosening his tie, throwing off his jacket and sitting down in a large, beautifully upholstered wing chair. He began to read the complimentary copies of the newspapers left for them beside a stack of glossy magazines.

'I think I'll take a bath and get myself organised. I'd love a gin and tonic with loads of ice to drink in the bath.' She smiled brightly.

'Not champagne?'

'Oh, hardly, I don't think we should open that, do you? No, gin will be fine.' She would have loved the champagne but felt it would be a bit cheeky, and what if they were supposed to pay for their own drinks? Tony would have a heart attack at the price a hotel like this was likely to charge.

'Bit early to start, isn't it?' he said.

'We've two hours before we go to the pre-dinner drinks reception. I need something to bolster me up and a drink in the bath is such a treat.'

She ran the bath, poured the complimentary bath oil into it, noting with satisfaction that it was expensive. She wondered if she dared pinch the remaining sachets of it, and the shampoo, soap and conditioner? Or would people laugh at her? She carefully bound her newly styled hair in a scarf, accepted her drink from Tony and sank with contentment into the warm water. Now this, she thought, was real luxury, no supper to worry about, the next two hours just to pamper herself. She could get used to a life like this.

Half an hour later she was wondering what to do next. She had painted her nails, her make-up was complete, her hair was combed out as the hairdresser had taught her, she was in her underclothes powdered and scented, her dress was on the hanger, covered with a muslin bag to protect it, ready to be slipped on. She sat on the bed and looked about her. Pam said it always took her a minimum of two hours to get ready to go out. What on earth did she do that took so long? Mind you, she thought, the end result was worth it with Pam. She picked up the remote control for the television and flicked through the channels. It was not like the one at home: not only were there the normal channels, plus Sky, but three film channels too. The first one was showing a children's film – must be pampered children whose parents brought them here, she thought, clicking over to the next which had a film she had already seen. She switched to the last one. On the screen, filling it, were two of the largest breasts she had ever seen and certainly with the biggest nipples. Two hands, hairy and male, suddenly appeared and began to fondle the nipples which stood to attention like organ stops. Kate sat forward transfixed. Five minutes later she was rolling on the bed laughing – if this was porn they could keep it! She'd never seen anything so limp or pathetic, in all senses of the words, as this. Tony put his head round the door.

'What's the joke?'

'Tony, you've simply got to come and watch this. It's so funny. I've never seen such a lifeless penis in my whole life!' She shrieked with laughter. 'He's going to have to beat it to get anywhere with it.'

Tony was across the room in a second and the screen went black.

'What did you do that for? I was enjoying myself – it was a good laugh.'

'Don't be stupid, you have to pay to watch the porn channel. That's not going to look good on the bill, is it?'

'Tony, no!' Kate looked aghast.

'Yes, look.' He handed her the card which had been on top of the set and which she had not noticed. 'You pay for all the movie channels.'

'Can we pay quietly at reception so that no one will know? You do it, I'm too embarrassed.'

'It registers automatically, it will have already. Honestly, Kate, I'm surprised at you even wanting to watch such smut.'

'I was curious, I'd never seen anything like that before. I don't think I'll bother again,' she said, subdued now. 'But . . . How do you know so much about it?' She sat up with interest. 'Is that what you get up to on your business trips? Is that it? Watching movies like that?'

'Don't be childish, Kate.' He was kicking off his shoes.

'I'm not being childish. I'm interested. I mean, if you like them then we could watch one together.'

'Kate, really!' He was removing his socks.

'No, I'm serious, Tony. If that's your bag . . . I mean I don't mind.' She was kneeling up on the bed now. 'It might help . . .'

'What's that supposed to mean?' he said, looking up sharply.

'It might make it more . . . Oh, Tony, it's difficult to explain.'

'More interesting? Is that what you meant? Quite honestly, Kate, I'm appalled. I had no idea that you were interested in perversions of any description.' He was struggling with the zip on his trousers. 'Isn't it wonderful? First you were dissatisfied with your home life and now it's your sex life. I begin to think nothing will ever be enough for you ever again, Kate.' He strode towards the bathroom and slammed the door.

Oh dear, thought Kate, she had only been trying to help. She could think of nothing worse than Tony making love to her with something as ludicrous as she had just watched going on in the background, but she had heard that pornography could be a stimulus. How sad if he really was satisfied with their sex life as it was. She sighed, and then she smiled at how impossible it was for a man to look dignified in his shirt tails.

She slipped into her new red dress and shoes and admired herself in the long mirror. It looked good, she looked good. She fluffed her hair. Pam had been right, the shorter style did make her look younger, and she loved the highlights. Why had she not had them done years ago instead of creeping around looking like a mouse?

She wandered through to the sitting room and poured herself another drink. She picked up the notes she had made for her speech and practised them in front of the mirror.

'What on earth have you got on?' Tony asked when he eventually joined her.

'It's my new dress, Pam helped me choose it.' She twirled around the better for him to see it.

'And how much did it cost?'

'You? Nothing. I bought it myself with my own money,' she said with marked satisfaction.

'You look like a Christmas tree with all those vulgar sequins. Have you seen my cuff-links?'

'I'll get them,' she said, going back into the bedroom with head held high. That was spiteful of him. She supposed he was getting back at her over her remarks about the film. Well, she was not going to fall for it, not this time. She knew better now. The dress was dramatic and suited her. She looked better than she had in years, probably better than she had ever looked.

'You are going to change, aren't you?' He had followed her into the room.

'No, I like this dress and sequins aren't vulgar – they're all the rage. Here are your links.' And she sailed out and did not bother to offer to help him put them in.

There was a knock at the door. She opened it to find Val with someone she had not met before.

'Kate, you look wonderful!' Val kissed her on both cheeks. 'What a stunning dress, you'll put us all to shame. This is Jill Ravenscroft, your editor at Panda. Jill, meet Kate, our favourite author.' Kate had hated that expression when those at Shotters had said it, but Val saying it was different. When she said it Kate felt it was true.

'Hello.' The two women shook hands. Jill looked as young as Lucy, Kate thought.

'I loved the book, Kate. We're going to do big things with it.' Jill smiled. Kate relaxed – it was a genuine smile.

'Come in. Drink?'

'Lovely,' the two young women said in unison. Kate crossed to the small refrigerator.

'What would you like?'

'Any champagne?' They both said instantly.

'Yes, there is. Anyone any good at opening bottles?'

'Me.' Jill stepped forward. 'You can't work at Panda and not learn how to open champagne bottles.' And with amazing dexterity she had the bottle uncorked in a flash.

'Tony, let me introduce you.' Kate smiled broadly at her husband as he entered the room, willing him not to show he was in a mood. The introductions were made, the drink poured.

'You must be so proud of your wife, Mr Howard,' Val said, taking her glass.

'Yes, of course,' Tony said, happily enough, Kate thought, and he handed a glass to Jill.

There was an awkward silence and the two women looked at their glasses as if waiting for something and then at Tony and then at each other.

'I think we should toast the book's success, don't you?' Val looked about her.

'*Winter Interlude*,' she and Jill said, raising their glasses. 'Good luck to it, with mega-sales.'

Kate thought the book was so much part of her that she should not drink the toast, it might be unlucky.

'The book,' said Tony raising his glass. Kate wished he had not taken so long to do so.

'Kate's managed such a great achievement, Mr Howard. So few books get selected. You should see the number of manuscripts we reject in a month, and Westall's is one of the smaller houses. Imagine what it's like at, say, somewhere like Shotters,' Val said politely.

'I always say you stand as much chance of winning the

football pools.' Jill laughed a loud, gutsy laugh totally at odds with her heart-shaped face and slim prettiness.

'I didn't realise publishing was a lottery,' Tony said.

'I didn't mean that, Mr Howard. I just meant that statistically the odds must be about the same.' Jill had stopped laughing and spoke rapidly.

'Did you like the book, Mr Howard?' Val asked.

'I haven't read it,' Tony admitted.

'No?' both women said, wide-eyed with surprise.

'What if I hadn't liked it? What if I found myself in it, and in an unfavourable light? That could have led to the most appalling friction *chez* Howard. I'll wait for the hardback to be published.' Then he laughed and Kate realised she was not the only woman in the room who relaxed. They don't like him, she thought. Why won't he ask them to call him Tony? Why's he being so stiff?

'Of course, understandable,' said Val, looking about for somewhere to put her glass.

'I can recommend it thoroughly,' said Jill, putting hers on top of the TV set and Kate wondered whether to confess about the blue movie or not.

'Well, if you don't mind, Kate, Mr Howard?' Val looked at her watch. 'Perhaps we should be making a move. There's a whole army of people out there longing to meet you, Kate.'

'Kate! It must be Kate.' A large ginger-haired man wearing red spectacles which clashed dramatically with his colouring, a large cigar between clenched teeth, encompassed Kate in a bear hug of welcome. 'I'm Sherpa Tensing.' He laughed loudly, not just at his odd joke but at the look of total astonishment on Kate's face. 'Teddy Fletcher, sales director of all you survey.' He swung his arm and cigar expansively to include everyone in the crowded room. 'And you must be Tony?' He held out a large hand. 'You must be a proud man, Tony my lad. Right, Kate. Everyone wants to meet you. You come with Uncle Teddy now.' He grabbed hold of her hand and they lunged into the crowd, which parted briefly and then closed around them again like a satiated sea anemone.

For the next half-hour Kate found herself becoming more muddled and perplexed by every introduction. There were too many people, too many names, and too many grand-sounding titles to too many jobs.

'Confused?' Teddy grinned at her, and putting his arm about her waist he gave her a comforting squeeze.

'Very.'

'Don't worry, you'll get us all sorted out eventually. I'm the most important person here, so provided you remember me, you're home and dry, petal. Isn't that right?' he said to someone over Kate's shoulder.

'Don't you listen to a word he says, Kate, it's all blarney.'

She swung round. 'Mr Westall,' she said, with marked relief at seeing a face she knew.

'Julius, please. What did I say at Barty's party? Writers' circles are a good way to start, aren't they?'

'You remembered?' Kate said, and hoped he did not also remember her passing out on Barty's rug.

'Of course. And didn't I say how well the name will look? Have you seen the proofs? Teddy, have you got a spare copy?'

'I didn't know they had been done.' Kate was surprised at the speed of everything.

'It was an unholy rush and Gloria is frightened the mistakes in it will be horrendous, but we needed it for my chaps to read to sell on, you see, petal. Charlie,' he bellowed, making all those around him jump in the air. 'Proof over here for my favourite author Kate, chop, chop.'

When she held the copy in her hands she touched it gently. 'I think I want to cry.'

'Ah,' said Teddy, looking sentimental.

'Wait until you see the hardback, then you really will. I've yet to meet an author who doesn't want to cry their eyes out when that first copy is finally in their hands.' Julius smiled at her.

'There seem to be so many high spots in this business. I keep coming across them convinced that's the last and then something else lovely happens.' Kate blew into her handkerchief as dinner was announced. 'My husband?' she said, suddenly remembering Tony and looking about the room for him.

'He's fine, he's over there with the MD of Panda,' Julius assured her. He took her arm, and with Teddy on her other side she was escorted into dinner.

She barely ate a thing, she was far too nervous and she did

not dare drink fearing that, with the gin, the champagne and the wine at the reception, she had already had far too much. She wished the meal would go on for ever but inexorably it came to an end.

Others made speeches and Kate sat bright red with confusion at the fulsome compliments paid to her. And then it was her turn. Kate, who had once given a talk to the Women's Institute on jam-making, and one impassioned plea for better sex education to the other committee members of the Middle School PTA, got to her feet. She looked at the expectant faces turned her way and longed to make a dash for it, but took a deep breath and began.

When she sat down everyone in the large room was standing and clapping. She had made them laugh, she really had. They had enjoyed it! And the first thing she did was to pick up her glass and take the largest swig of wine she had ever swallowed in one gulp.

'Let's go into the bar, everyone wants to buy you a drink.' Teddy stood up, collecting the large bouquet of flowers that had been presented to Kate.

'I'd like to put them in water,' she said.

Immediately Teddy signalled to Penny who happened to be passing. She took the flowers and Kate's room key and went off to do it for her.

'Can't have you getting tired out, petal.' Teddy fussed over her and Kate, not used to such consideration, glowed with happiness at the novelty of it all.

'You coming, Tony?' She looked at her husband appealingly. He had said little through dinner and was the only one not to congratulate her on her speech.

'I suppose so,' he said, getting to his feet. 'But if one more person says how proud I should be feeling, I'll hit them.'

'You must be feeling so proud tonight, Tony me lad,' said Teddy, grinning from ear to ear. He turned and winked broadly at Kate, who had to stifle a grin herself. Tony at least had the grace to look disconcerted.

In the bar it was impossible to buy anyone a drink. Tony tried several times but each time was refused and another round came their way. At last Gloria fought her way through the mass to where Kate was sitting.

'You look fabulous. What a dress. And you were wonderful.

My table were in stitches. Did that really happen to an editor? Locked in the loo with hordes of rampaging fans? It rings a bell . . .'

'I exaggerated a bit. There were only five but two dozen sounded better. Was I really all right?'

'You were a star! I couldn't believe that you weren't used to public speaking every day of your life. Wasn't she wonderful, Mr Howard?'

'Wonderful,' Tony replied in an expressionless voice.

'You must be so proud of her, I know I am.' Gloria patted Kate's arm. Kate looked anxiously at Tony but he gazed fixedly at the drink in his hand.

'Don't be so formal, Gloria. You don't mind if she calls you Tony, do you?'

A grunt was the only description for her husband's reply.

At this point Teddy appeared with a bevy of men – sales manager of this, of that, promotions director, promotions manager, special projects director . . .

'Here we go again.' Kate laughed. 'I can't imagine what it is you all do.'

'We shall explain,' Teddy said grandly, shooing away those he deemed had sat at Kate's table long enough and launching into a noisy explanation of how useless everyone but him really was.

More champagne arrived. Kate realised she was becoming squiffy but it was all so pleasant. All the compliments and enthusiasm were giving her such a lift that when another bottle arrived it seemed the most natural thing to allow her glass to be refilled. It was half-way through this bottle that she realised Tony was no longer at the crowded table.

'Anyone seen my husband?'

Teddy, in his role of court jester, made a great play of looking for Tony under the table and then, to her acute embarrassment, stood on the table, clapped his hands for silence and asked if anyone had seen a lost husband, '. . . five foot eleven, dark-haired, with a hump, and wearing spectacles . . .'

'He doesn't wear spectacles.' Kate pulled at his trouser leg, giggling.

'But he's got a hump?' Teddy leaned down to speak to her.

'I think I'll go to bed.' Everyone looked up to see Tony

standing at the side of the table looking at Teddy with dislike. 'You coming?' he asked, clutching a bottle of Perrier water to him like a shield.

'No, I don't think so, Tony. I'm enjoying myself.'

'I'm glad somebody is,' he said, before turning smartly on his heel and marching away.

'Whoops, have we upset him?' Teddy clambered off the table.

'He's very tired, he works hard,' Kate said loyally.

'Yes, I'm sure he does,' Teddy said quietly, suddenly serious.

Kate was glad she had not gone to bed with Tony. There might be a lot of horseplay down here but there was serious talk too. She learnt a lot that night, and not just about the plans for her book; she learnt that she had acquired responsibilities. In the past it had just been her and her novel; now there was a whole army of people to whom the success or failure of her book was an important issue. She was no longer alone as she had thought. They asked after her second book and she knew she owed it to them to make a go of that one too. It was not a game any more, it was serious business.

Kate had always enjoyed a good gossip, never more so than now – especially the most interesting snippet about Bella Ford. Her latest book had been rejected by Shotters and Bella was busily searching out a new publisher.

'Know what she did?' Teddy asked, eyes shining with mischief. 'She was booked into this swishy hotel. You know, one of those with shops in the hall? She bought a ton of stuff – Waterford crystal, a watch, handbags, underwear, you name it, Bella bought it. She put the whole lot on the bill and left Shotters to pick up the tab.'

'She didn't?' Kate said, shocked.

'Yes, she did. That's why they turned her down. Then Peter Holt telephoned everyone and told them what she had done. No one will pick her up now.'

'Oh, the poor silly woman,' said Kate.

'I shouldn't waste your sympathy on her, Kate. It was Bella who shopped you to Tatiana. My secretary Rachel was still there when it happened,' Gloria explained.

'Did they call the police?' Kate asked, full of indignation now that her suspicions about Bella had been confirmed.

'No, but that's my girl.' Gloria laughed at the change in Kate.

'Pity,' she said, emboldened by the champagne. 'I inadvertently watched a blue movie tonight and I see you have to pay extra for that. I'll pay of course.' She managed to say all this without blushing once.

'Inadvertently, you say? I should bloody cocoa!' Teddy roared with laughter, and Kate realised this was something she was never going to live down.

The next morning she awoke to a very bad hangover and no sympathy from Tony.

'You were drinking like a pig, serves you right,' he said, too loudly for comfort.

'I needed to relax, I'm not used to making speeches.'

'Is that what it was?'

She looked at him, a weary expression on her face. 'Why do you have to put down everything I do? Why can't you be happy for me?'

'I'd be happy for you if you weren't so intent on making a spectacle of yourself. Letting those men fawn all over you, giggling at that idiot in the red glasses with his fatuous jokes. I can tell you one thing, Kate, I'm not coming to another of these dos and that's a promise.'

'Good, I wouldn't ask you. What did you contribute last night? Bugger all. You sulked, you couldn't even put yourself out to talk to people. God knows what they thought of you.'

'Quite honestly, Kate, I don't give a damn what they thought of me.'

'Oh, Tony, listen to us, here we go again. I thought we were going to get on better. What more do you want?'

'I want you to give up all this nonsense.'

She sat back on the pillows and looked at him with astonishment. 'You can say that after last night? Didn't you hear what my print run is to be? It's wonderful! I'm going to be read by hundreds of thousands of people. I want to give people pleasure –'

'You want to be famous, isn't that it?' He sneered.

'Fine, what if I do? Is there anything wrong in being acknowledged for what you achieve? They respect me. They've made me see I've a talent not everyone has. I can make us a fortune.'

'Come down to earth, Kate. If it wasn't your book there are a dozen others out there they could have published.'

'That's where you're wrong – ' But she stopped, what was the point? It wasn't only that he did not understand, he didn't want to.

'One book doesn't make a writer,' he said.

'I know what the trouble was last night. You couldn't take me being the centre of attention, could you? All the dinners and dances we've been to, it's always been you who people wanted to talk to. I was just the wife in the background. Well, now, Tony, you're getting a taste of what it's like to be the little woman. And it seems you are sadly lacking in the maturity required to deal with the role.' They were arguing, she knew they were, but to anyone else it would have sounded like a conversation, so normal was the tone of their voices.

'Sometimes, Kate, you talk a load of crap.'

'To your ears probably, but then you never have enjoyed listening to what you don't want to know.'

'We can't go on like this,' he said, so matter-of-factly that at first she wondered if she had heard him correctly.

'No, we can't.'

'And you won't give up this nonsense?'

'No, I can't.'

'Then I suggest we put the house on the market, divide the proceeds down the middle. Mind you, if you're right about your earnings, then I shall be coming to you for a divorce settlement. I'm not going to hold my breath, though. I think I'll go for a walk. Shall I see you at breakfast?'

'No, I don't think so, I'm not hungry,' she said, as he walked to the door.

Kate got off the bed, opened the refrigerator door and found some orange juice. She could hardly believe what was happening to her. Marriages did not break up with polite questions like 'Shall I see you at breakfast?' Marriages broke up with grand fights and screaming matches. Didn't they?

She sat on the bed in the luxurious hotel and knew that he was right. Neither of them could go on like this. Funny old world, she thought. She had come to help promote a book and was leaving with her marriage over and divorce a serious possibility.

She wished she had not debased herself by offering to watch porn movies with him. That was annoying.

part three

chapter **one**

Crispin's divorce was made final in August and two weeks later, in September, he married Bee-Bee. The unseemly haste was intentional for he felt, more than anything, that it showed the contempt with which he now regarded Charlotte. He had given her everything she had asked for, which he also felt indicated his disdain. But he could afford to enjoy such little triumphs now, such as not arguing about the Regency chest-on-chest, or the framed set of eighteenth-century flower engravings.

'Have whatever you want,' he had said with magnificent scorn as if he were above such haggling, and had walked out of the house leaving a surprised and even more huffy Charlotte behind him.

He had explained to the other shareholders and his cousin at every available opportunity the madness of Julius employing Gloria to launch his new list – doomed to failure and inevitably more debts – and ensuring that everyone was keener than before to sell – if and when. Ah, when? He had taken trouble to consult medical friends and had purchased several medical textbooks. Now he watched Julius with all the care of a diagnostician. He was certain that there was a slight blueness about Julius's mouth that had not been there before, and he was convinced of a marked breathlessness.

Even Crispin could not fault the wedding arrangements. The Benton family's country house was in deepest Berkshire – a better county socially there could not be. The old house, which was huge and rambling and stuffed with valuable antiques, was perfect. The gardens were a by-word in horticultural circles. The local vicar, while initially opposed to a divorcé marrying under his church's Saxon roof, had a remarkable change of heart when a cheque from Mr Benton covering all the repairs to that precious roof and then some over was wafted under his nose.

It had been a happy time. Not only were they to be given a London house but they had the use of the dower house on Benton's estate – not that Crispin could see himself spending much time there, the pleasures of the countryside were an ongoing mystery to him. A new house in Chelsea was chosen and with furniture, wallpapers, curtains and carpets to be selected for it, many joyous hours were filled.

He had a new mistress, Cleo. Crispin had solved the problem of his sexually less than enthusiastic wife-to-be, and the problem of young mistresses desperate for marriage, in one go. Cleo was forty, rapacious for the sex her millionaire banker husband was disinclined to supply her with and, best of all, she was so socially prominent and domestically comfortable that the last thing she wanted was to be found out, let alone divorced. He was well set up.

So it was that as Bee-Bee, looking like an aristocratic virginal shepherdess in a Watteau painting, dress low cut and prettily panniered, with a gorgeously luxuriant headdress of fresh flowers from her family garden, swayed down the aisle towards him, he was able at the same time to see Cleo, sophisticated and elegant, standing in the congregation. At sight of both women he thought of the two things he adored – sex with Cleo, and money in the shape of Bee-Bee – and had such an erection that he had to approach the altar with both hands clutched firmly in front of his crotch, looking like a small boy caught scrumping apples.

Near the front of the church Gloria, stunning in a lemon-yellow and black fine linen suit with a large matching hat trimmed with black satin, stood and feared she would cry. She loathed weddings for that reason. She never knew why she cried. Was it because the brides invariably looked so beautiful? Or because she knew, like most people there, that statistically the likelihood of most marriages lasting was abysmal – and the thought of all that lost hope made the tears flow? Or because, and this she feared was the most likely reason, she had never been a bride and longed to be one.

She had taken great pains to look right today for she was sure that Peter Holt would be a fellow guest. As she had paid the horrendous bill for her outfit, even as she dressed this morning, she had assured herself she wanted to look her best just to show him she did not care, that she could get on just fine without him. But a nasty niggling thought would keep popping up and asking her if she thought he would find her beautiful.

They should have met before now and it was a miracle they had not. Publishing was such a small world that it was unusual not to see everyone on a regular basis at parties, launches and the like. Gloria had attended many and Peter's absence could mean only one thing: he was avoiding her. He would not be able to do that today, though. Everyone who was anyone in publishing was present. He must be here even if she had not yet seen him.

She wished that avoiding him was simply a matter of not seeing him. But it was more than that. Every day she thought of him and longed for him. Every night before she went to sleep she ached for him. She had tried to fill this void in her life but no man she met interested her. She still thought often of telephoning him, but then she always decided, To hell with him, and slammed the receiver down. Perhaps worst were the nights when she dreamt of him, and it was always so perfect that upon awakening she felt desolate that it was only a dream.

What would happen today? She did not know. Did she want him to see her and rush up to claim her? She smiled at the juvenile notion. Did she fear him ignoring her? No, he would not do that, he was too kind and gentle a man for that. Gentle? After the way he had behaved that was an odd word to choose. No, she just wanted to be near him, in the same room as him, breathing the same air, able to watch him, that's what she wanted. But to do that, she had to look her best, she thought, as she picked up her hymn book.

Julius stood in the family pew with his wife and felt sorry for the poor little girl who was marrying his nephew. He looked across at her father who was smiling with such pride and contentment. Julius was amazed that someone so obviously successful and, presumably, astute should have been taken in for one moment by Crispin. He could not be as intelligent as he looked otherwise he would be paying the boy a large sum not to marry his daughter. As it was, he was apparently lashing out a fortune to bless the union.

He took a handkerchief out of his pocket and mopped his brow. It was hot in here, he thought, too many people. He held the hymnal up but found difficulty in seeing the words. Must get my eyes checked, he thought.

Mike Pewter, taking up enough room for two in his pew, could, from his massive height, see everyone. He was astonished to note Peter here with Hilary. To his surprise, he had been pleased when Peter had confided to him that he was getting divorced. Surprised because he had not until then realised the extent of his dislike for Hilary. Now they seemed to be together again and he wished he had not been so open with Peter, congratulating him on his decision and unwisely mentioning that he had never had time for the stuck-up cow. He should have known better, should have waited for the divorce before opening his big mouth. Shotters must be turning the fellow mad. He'd advised him time and again to get out, that such an organisation was not for him. Why, he would be happy to set up something himself with Peter if he wanted a partner. Odd that Peter did nothing about it. Not like he used to be at all.

He caught sight of Gloria standing in the next aisle. Now there was an attractive woman, spirited too – he liked them with plenty of originality and vivacity. He had often noticed her, not that he had ever done anything about it. For a start he had heard she preferred young men to mature studs such as himself. What's more, he always avoided affairs with anyone connected with the business – it made things too complicated if anything went wrong, which it invariably did. If he had been Peter she was the one he would have gone for. He knew that. Peter fancied her – he'd confessed as much once when in his cups. But there he was with Hilary. Rather him than me. He rubbed his chin with his large hand; of the two, he knew which one he'd prefer in his bed. He snorted with amusement, a little too loudly, so that Lady Lily found it necessary to give him a sharp dig with her elbow. Mike gave his concentration to the proceedings once more and bellowed out the hymn lustily.

Peter stood beside his wife and wished he had not come. He found weddings depressing affairs, reminding him of the day he had taken the vital step himself. It did not help to find himself placed beside his estranged wife by an officious usher who had refused to seat him elsewhere. He wondered if Gloria would be here. He wanted her to be so that he could talk to her, find out why, even when he had sent her flowers, there had been this silence from her. But then he also hoped she wasn't, unsure of what he would hear, what he would say.

The hymn soared about him but Peter's mind was on other things. He must stop thinking of Gloria. He switched to work. Once he had thought about work non-stop because it was the best thing in his life. Now he thought about it because it was the worst. The figures were bad. Important authors were leaving in a haemorrhage which did not seem capable of being staunched and new authors were proving elusive to find. Sales were down. The economies made were not sufficient. And, to cap it all, Costas was coming next week and Peter still did not know how he was going to explain everything to him. He wished he could get into a car, a boat, a plane, he did not mind which, and just take off into the blue and not let anyone know where he had gone. That would be bliss.

Barty Silver stood a proud man with Joy beside him. Not that they were engaged, Joy had still to make up her mind, but as each day passed he felt her moving closer to that decision as their friendship, always good, deepened. He was hopeful that by spring he and Joy would be enjoying just such a ceremony.

He had planned it all. He had a house in the Bahamas: they would marry there, in the gardens beside the sea. He would charter a couple of Boeings to bring all his friends. He would take over the local hotel – he made a mental note to get Gervase to find out from his solicitor when he could hope for everything to be finalised.

Thinking of his house in the Bahamas made him decide that it would be a good idea if he took Joy out there next week, he would like her to see his other homes. Perhaps a holiday away from England and the lawyers would help her decide. He felt for her hand and gave it a little squeeze. She looked up at him and smiled wanly. She was not happy, he knew that; it did not matter what he did or what he gave her. She could never be happy when that bastard had her little girl. Barty had failed her there. His lawyers were good but Charles was better: he had temporary custody. Barty hated to fail in anything. Somehow he had to succeed, to see to it that that evil bastard would never keep Hannah, not while Barty Silver lived. The small pulse in his temple pounded.

Joy wished she could have smiled more warmly at him. No man could have been kinder than Barty had been and in return what did she give him? She was being a dismal companion, it wasn't fair. She tried hard but the emptiness inside her, the longing she felt for Hannah, made happiness elusive.

She knew what he must be thinking, weddings did that to people, they thought of their own – past or future. He would be planning theirs now. She still had not given him her answer and she did not know why. She had decided she wanted to marry him, knew that she loved him – if not like a lover then more than a friend. So why didn't she? Fear, perhaps, that by marrying him she would never get Hannah back. Fear that if that happened she would never know happiness again.

Now she was concentrating on translating the Latin wording on the monuments about her, anything to take her mind off one particular wedding, all those years ago when she had been happy and so beautiful. She dared not think of it for if she did she thought of Charles, and when she did that she felt guilty, for in doing so she felt she was betraying Barty.

'Dearly beloved, we are gathered together . . .' the vicar began and the congregation rustled with anticipation.

The wedding reception was in the great hall of the Bentons' large Tudor house where florists had worked through the night so that now it was like standing in a summer garden. Crispin was pleased: not many people had a hall of such magnitude that it could take the three hundred wedding guests. There was a marquee in the garden, but that was for the five hundred expected for the dance in the evening. Crispin was particularly delighted with the marquee, which he had had a hand in designing so that it was reminiscent of Brighton Pavilion. He had just the waistcoat to wear to the dance tonight, Regency in style, white silk with scarlet and gold birds-of-paradise embroidered upon it. He stood on the receiving line very much at peace with his world.

Invariably at any such function it was only a matter of minutes before Julius, Peter and Mike deserted their wives and found each other. This occasion was no different, and soon they were deep into the gossip that was so much part of their work and which they would, all three, have insisted was 'business talk'.

Roz approached Gloria and asked if she could stick with her.

'I don't know many people here – they're all too top drawer for me. He only invited me because he didn't think I would come.'

'Who?' asked Gloria, shuffling slowly along the long receiving line.

'Crispin, the creep!'

'Am I to take it you don't much like our financial director either?' Gloria laughed.

'Of course, you wouldn't know. We had an affair for ages. I thought I was going to marry him, more fool me.'

'You'd have been more of a fool if you had married him.'

'That's true.' Roz laughed this time.

'Is that why you left Westall's?'

'Yes. I thought I'd be able to stick it out, but I couldn't, especially when he got engaged. He seemed to gloat then instead of showing any embarrassment.'

'Bet Julius misses you.'

'I think he must. He telephoned me last night to see if I was coming. He wants to talk to me about something urgent. I'm to meet him in the bar of the hotel.'

'Maybe he's going to offer you your job back.'

'No, thank you, I'm happy at Pewter's. You don't know why he wants to see me?'

'No, sorry. Here we are, best foot forward, Roz, I'm right behind you.'

Both women passed along the receiving line, shaking hands, smiling, muttering inanities.

'How pretty you look, Roz,' Crispin said, almost with regret, Gloria thought.

'I always do, Crispin. Always.' Roz tossed her head and swept on.

From the other side of the marquee Peter saw Gloria. He felt a surge of excitement. With heart thumping he weaved his way across to her.

'Gloria, hallo.'

She had her back to him but she recognised the voice immediately. She turned slowly, delaying the moment when she had to see the polite expression on his face.

'Peter.' She faced him, smiling brilliantly, all charm, all self-possession, and then she looked at him and there was no expression of polite friendliness, instead he was looking at her with longing . . .

'Peter . . .' she said, feeling confused.

'I've got to talk to you, Gloria. I must. But not here. Are you staying at the big hotel? Sod, I can't remember its name – ' He was speaking quickly, urgently.

'The Deer Park Hall?'

'Yes, that's it. Later, when we've got away from here. About six, I'll ring your room.'

'Yes . . . I'll look . . .'

'Gloria, long time no see.' Hilary had chosen that precise moment to join them. 'Peter, there's some people over there I want you to meet.' She put a proprietorial arm through his. 'Excuse us, Gloria.'

Peter turned round, pointing furiously at his watch. But Gloria did not see, her eyes were brimming with tears.

'I'm getting out of here,' she burst out.

'Gloria, what's happened?' Roz called out, trailing behind her.

'Bloody men, that's what.' And she was running to get to her car, and to get away, right away.

Elephant, never a dog for strange hotel rooms, was beside himself with joy to see her back so soon. She was packed in a trice. Within minutes, bill paid and suitcase in the boot, Gloria and Elephant were ready to go.

'Where to, Elephant? I've a week off. Where shall we go? My mother's?'

Elephant sneezed.

'All right, then, not my mother's – it's too far, anyway.' The dog had made her laugh. 'Let's go to Oxford, I haven't been there for ages.'

Expertly she manoeuvred her car out of the crowded car park and was soon on the main road, her foot down, putting as much space between her and Peter as quickly as possible. What a complete fool she was. She had this week's holiday and no plans made. And why not? She had pretended, even to herself, that she wanted to act on impulse. It was not true. She knew why she had made no arrangements. She had hoped to see him, prayed something would happen between them, longed to get away – just with him.

'Fool!' She pressed down hard on the accelerator, Elephant

yapped, he liked speed. 'I've got to get him out of my mind, Elephant. This is hopeless.'

Julius was waiting for Roz in the bar before dinner. Later they would have to return for the infernal wedding dance. He knew he would hate it but Jane was insisting they attend. He ordered a double whisky and the Buck's Fizz which he knew was Roz's favourite.

'Roz, my dear. Thank you for giving me your time.'

'It's entirely my pleasure, Mr Westall.'

'Didn't enjoy the wedding?'

'Not a lot. I might have if Crispin hadn't been there.' She giggled.

Julius's smile turned to a frown as he saw Peter Holt enter the bar, looking about him. He did not want anyone to join them or even sit nearby – he did not want to be overheard. He frowned even more as Peter approached their table.

'Sorry to disturb you, but you haven't seen Gloria, have you? I arranged to meet her and reception says she's checked out.'

'She left in a hurry. She was upset,' Roz said, looking at Peter with a loathing that Julius noticed, though he did not know the reason for it.

'Oh, I see. You don't know where she's gone?'

'No. I don't.'

'Thanks. I'll try her home.' And with a distracted air he left them.

'Something I've missed?' Julius asked.

'Gloria was talking to him and then she began to cry and ran out of the marquee. It must have been something he said to her.'

'Ah, young people.' Julius nodded, even more perplexed. 'Roz, I've asked you here because I want you to do me a favour. I need someone I can trust and I think I can trust you again, can't I? I need someone who does not like Crispin.' He smiled kindly at her. She blushed at the thought that he was trusting her after all she had done to him.

'I want to explain some things to you.' And he began. Ten minutes later he had finished. 'Do you think you would mind doing that?'

'Of course not, not for you. It gives me the creeps, though, just thinking about it.' Roz shuddered.

'You know how it is with me, Roz. You're one of the few people I have told.'

'Yes, but I don't like to dwell on it. I can't bear to think of you dying.' Roz fought not to cry.

'I don't mind so much, you know.'

'Oh, please, Mr Westall . . .' Roz produced a handkerchief.

'Sorry. Here it is, then. You'll look after it?' He handed her a large white envelope.

'Yes. As soon as I hear anything has happened to you, I'm to give this to Gloria.'

'That's right.'

'Excuse me asking, but why could your lawyer not do it?'

'I've learnt about office staff and their indiscretions once before . . .' He laughed gently so as not to hurt her too much.

'Oh, Mr Westall. You can trust me this time. You don't know how much this means to me, after what I did. I promise you, Lepanto is safe with me.' And this time she did not bother to fight the tears but let them flow. Julius glanced about the bar uncomfortably, afraid people would think he had been unkind to her.

chapter **two**

Oxford held little interest for Gloria, which was indicative of her state of mind. This city was normally one of her favourites. The following day she went to Stratford where Elephant enjoyed barking at the swans, but she felt she could not face sitting through a Shakespeare play on her own. Cheltenham failed to amuse her and so she pressed on to Bristol. The Unicorn had the universality of a modern, purpose-built hotel and was not the type she would normally have chosen, but it was ideal in her present mood, for anonymity was hers for the taking. In a smaller, more intimate establishment she might have been forced into talking to strangers.

From her bedroom window the following morning she could watch the crowds of people ambling about the dockside looking at the ships, the houseboats, the sleek, elegant four-masted schooner moored below. Were they, like her, dreaming of stepping aboard, upping anchor and away – it did not matter where?

She took Elephant for a walk along the Watershed, window shopping, and they stopped for coffee and a cake. She persuaded Elephant to stay in the car, something he was not normally keen on, but she wanted to go to the Arnolfini to see the latest art exhibition. After taking a drink on the dockside, and Elephant for another walk, she did not know what else to do. She returned to the hotel and leafing idly through her address book realised that Kate lived in the area. Perhaps Kate would like to join her in Bristol for lunch tomorrow? she asked on the telephone. Instead she found she had been invited to stay overnight with Kate.

She pulled up outside Kate's house and envied her. The house and the village were perfect, almost ridiculously so. This place was everyone's dream of what an English village should be. She felt she had stepped into a jigsaw puzzle picture.

'Why the for-sale sign? This must be anyone's ideal. You

couldn't let this go, surely?' Gloria asked after the hellos were over and Kate had welcomed her. The inside of the house was exactly as one would imagine it to be from the outside – comfortable furniture, the odd antique, gleaming copper, pot-pourri and the tantalising smell of baking in the background.

'Sadly so,' Kate said, taking Gloria's coat and fussing over Elephant who, with snout in the air, had also got a whiff of something interesting in the kitchen. 'It will be a wrench,' she said in a tight-sounding voice as she led the way into the drawing room.

'Then why sell?' Gloria asked practically.

'It's too big now, my son's away in Yorkshire and my daughter goes to Cambridge this term. She's there now, sorting things out. I shall miss – Oh, hell!' She tossed her head. 'Why am I lying to you? I'm getting divorced. We have to sell if both of us are to have roofs over our heads. Neither of us wants to lose it, but there it is. Drink? Sherry? Gin?'

'Kate, I'm so sorry,' said Gloria. Kate picked up the bottle of Gordon's and waved it at her with a questioning look. 'Yes, please. This is dreadful news, Kate. I thought there was something wrong at the sales conference, it was as if your husband didn't really approve. Everybody felt it, they all said so after you had left. Teddy was beside himself, he felt he might have gone too far and offended him – he's very sensitive, you know, even if it isn't at first apparent.' She laughed at the thought of their ebullient and noisy sales director who was famous for putting his foot in it.

'Good gracious, no. Do reassure him. Tony didn't really want to come and, if I'm honest, I didn't want him to either. I suppose we both thought he *should* go – better to go by instinct, isn't it?'

'Then it did have something to do with it?' Gloria said aghast, as she took the glass of gin and tonic.

'All it did was bring things to a head which had been bubbling madly for months.'

'Is it the writing?' Gloria asked.

'I suppose that's symptomatic of things. I started because, to be honest, I was so bloody miserable. No, saying it was the writing that broke up our marriage would be the same as saying another woman did. It's never one thing, it's a vast pyramid of petty things. And then something happens, there's an alteration in the routine. For us it was my taking up writing – and the whole edifice collapses.'

'Are you all right?' Gloria asked anxiously.

'I'm fine. A bit scared, of course. I've never lived alone in my whole life. It's a challenge really to see if I can.'

'Move to London.'

'I don't think so.' Kate shuddered at the thought. 'I'm sorry, I don't have your love for the city. I'm a country soul. No, I thought I'd get a cottage, in a village but nearer London.'

'Won't you miss your friends?'

'Most of those we have are Tony's by inclination. My one and only friend is Pam – do you remember, I told you about her? She's gone odd on me again, I can't keep up with her. I think, Gloria, that I might be reaching that point in life when one begins to think that old friends are more trouble than they're worth. They always seem to think they know what is best for you and that time has given them the right to tell you.' She smiled ironically but she did not say how when she had told her she was getting divorced Pam had said, in no uncertain terms, that it was all her fault, and since she had done nothing but moan about Tony for years it was not surprising the poor man had had enough. 'Would you be insulted if I suggested we lunch in the kitchen?'

'I'd regard it as an honour.'

Half an hour later she was trying to persuade Kate to write a cookery book.

'I couldn't. I wouldn't know where to begin.'

'You probably said that about writing a novel before you wrote one.' Gloria smiled.

'That's true. I did. Cooking, though?' She paused as if thinking about the project. 'No, I'm too slapdash a cook for that, I can't be doing with weighing and measuring. I just throw things together and pray they work.'

'Well, that lot certainly did,' Gloria said, patting her stomach with satisfaction. 'Joy needs some of your cooking. I saw her at a wedding over the weekend. She looks thinner than ever. She's going to marry Barty when her divorce comes through – she told me that in strictest confidence, she hasn't even told him and I probably shouldn't have told you.'

'I won't breathe a word. It's a surprise, though. Barty doesn't seem the marrying kind; does he? Is she in love with him?'

'I don't know. It's not something you can ask. I mean, normally you automatically assume people are in love. But I felt she was anxious when she told me, as if expecting me to be censorious.'

'And were you?'

'Me? Good gracious, no. I can't think of a nicer bloke, can you? It's rubbish about him being gay, you know.'

'But is he interested in sex at all? If he isn't, then she's in for a difficult time. You can't be a normal woman and live with a man you love and not have sex, it would be so sad. Let's hope she's just enormously fond of him, then it won't matter so much. More apple pie?'

'Heavens, I couldn't manage another bite.'

'Did you get in touch with Peter Holt?' Kate asked, taking Gloria completely off guard.

'No. I thought about what you had said for ages, but in the end I just couldn't. I must have picked up the phone a hundred times and always chickened out. I told you what a proud old hen I am.' She laughed, but Kate noted how hollow it was. 'Just as well I didn't. He was at the same wedding with his wife, he's obviously gone back to her. I think he might at least have told me.'

'Are you sure?'

'Saw them with my own eyes. In fact, I cleared off when I did. I was a bit upset,' she said with masterly understatement.

'Maybe they were together just by accident. If they knew the same people . . .? Hold on – ' Kate leapt up from the table, opened the door of the pantry and began to rootle in a pile of old newspapers 'Here it is.' She returned to the table. 'Look this is only last Wednesday's.' She opened the page at the gossip diary. 'See,

Will beautiful Hilary Holt take even more interest in horses now she is so often in the company of Pinkers Flynn, 45, roistering bloodstock agent and filly fancier? Successful publisher, Peter Holt, 45, Hilary's little-seen husband, does not share her interests it would seem . . .

'Look, there's a photo.'

'Let me see that.' Gloria leant over for the page. She reread the piece Kate had just read out. And studied the faces of Hilary and a stranger in the photograph. 'This could be an old picture, you know what these columns are like – they need to fill a space, they dig in the archives.'

'It was taken last week at a charity ball in London. Look at the caption under the photo.'

'This Pinkers bloke wasn't at the wedding.'

'Well, hardly. You don't trot your fancy man along to weddings and things like that, do you? What's more, everyone around here says they're getting divorced. Peter lives near here, you know – or used to.' She added meaningfully, 'His estate is up for sale,' and began to make the coffee.

'Oh, Kate, what if it's true?' Gloria looked at her with eyes shining with hope.

'It might be a good idea if you found out if it was true or not, don't you think? There's the telephone,' she said briskly, and pointed to it.

'Shall I?'

Kate doubted if Gloria really required an answer so she continued with the coffee preparations.

'Em? It's Gloria Catchpole. Might I have a word with Peter?'

'Gloria, lovely to hear from you. Are you well?'

'Fine, thanks.' Gloria rolled her eyes with exasperation as Em prattled on about how she missed her and what was she doing, and who at Shotters was pregnant and who was having it away with whom. Gloria felt that if Em did not put her through to Peter soon she would lose her nerve.

'Em, it's lovely to hear all the news but I am in a bit of a rush. If I might be put through . . .?'

'Sorry, Gloria. Peter's in New York. Mr Carras was coming here this week, supposedly, and then changed his plans and sent for him. It's not right the way they make poor Peter run around after them, is it, Gloria?'

'When did he go?' Gloria asked, ignoring Em's impassioned defence of her boss.

'Monday night. He was trying to get hold of you all day Monday. Should I take a message? He'll be calling later, I expect.'

'Yes, tell him I called, would you. Tell him I'll be back home tomorrow, Friday. Thanks, Em.' She replaced the receiver. 'He'd been trying to get hold of me,' she said to Kate, eyes shining.

'There then, isn't that nice?' Kate beamed, and poured out

the coffee. When the telephone rang she answered it. From the rigid way she stood and the rather stiff responses she made, Gloria wondered if she was speaking to her husband. She was.

'That's that, then. We've sold the house,' she said bleakly when she had rung off. She looked close to tears. 'It's really silly to feel upset. I expected it. They're very nice people – he's something in computers. They've got three young children. It will be nice for the house to have youngsters running about it again – makes a house alive, don't you think?' All the time she was talking, Kate was rearranging the lumps of sugar in the bowl, piling them up, then knocking them down. Suddenly she stopped and looked at Gloria. 'Oh, Gloria, it's so awful. This place has been my whole life . . .' and she began to cry. Gloria held her close. 'I'm sorry,' Kate said, grabbing for some kitchen paper and blowing her nose.

'I'm so sorry, crying all over you like that.'

'Why not? What are friends for?'

'It's just, I don't know how I'll cope . . .' She sat at the kitchen table, looking small and vulnerable as she systematically tore the paper in her hands to pieces.

'You'll cope, you're a gutsy lady. Remember in Barty's loo? You were bored. You'll never be bored again, not now you've got your writing.'

'God, yes, Gloria, imagine this happening and nothing to fall back on.' She shook her head as if pulling herself together. 'I'm being bloody stupid. I know Tony and I can't go on together, that it's a relationship that lost its way a long time ago – it was simply that neither of us was aware of it. And everything has happened so fast. I wish he wasn't so bloody laid-back about it. It's somewhat insulting.' She managed a weak laugh.

'Is there anyone else?'

'I don't think so.'

'Would you mind if there was?'

'I don't know, I doubt it. I don't feel like that about him any longer. It's fear of the unknown that's hard at my age. And not living here. I don't want to lose my home. I really think I feel worse about losing the house than my marriage ending. And what does that make of all those years? Wasted time?'

'Tell you what, why don't we do the washing up, get in the car and go and look at possible places for your cottage? We could go to some agents, get a few details. Maybe we could even view a couple. I love doing that – snooping about in other people's lives.'

'I had thought of the Thames valley, I like it there.'

'Then that's where we'll go, have a look-see.' Gloria began to stack the dishes.

chapter **three**

Julius's morning had been very satisfactory. The first quarter of Barty's autobiography was finished and had been sent to Julius to reassure him as to its progress. He had read it and found it moving and riveting. It was early days but that morning he had a verbal agreement with the editor of the *Sunday Times* to buy the first serial rights of the book for a very hefty sum – a sum that would make the accountants happy for a change. Julius even allowed himself the pleasure of contemplating a trading-account balance sheet in the black again, something he had not dared to dream of for some time.

He had walked through the offices, which he always liked to do, seeing the various departments beavering away. But today was special, for today he had made his tour with good news to impart instead of lying about bad.

Lunch had been with Mike Pewter at his club. This had become almost a weekly ritual ever since the weekend at Peter's when he had turned down their offer of assistance. It was as if Mike and Peter were keeping a friendly eye on him. It amused him while he was touched by their concern. This lunch had been without Peter – away in New York with his masters.

'I don't like it, Julius. I don't like to see a good publisher going to rack and ruin as he is. It's not Peter's style to be at the beck and call of others. He should get out. Start up again if necessary. I keep telling him.'

'Maybe Costas's contract with him is watertight.'

'No, it isn't. I know. He told me his lawyers had found a loophole, should he want to jack it in. So why doesn't he?'

'A broken marriage and the inevitable divorce are probably problems enough for him at the moment without all the drama of resigning and starting again.'

'He hasn't even got a woman. It's unhealthy, an attractive man like him. He rarely goes out socially, just moons about that flat in the Barbican – like an expensive mausoleum, Lily described it.'

'I'd have thought another woman was the last complication he needed for the time being.'

'I thought he'd go for Gloria, you know. She'd suit him down to the ground – intelligent, attractive, as much in love with the business as he is. There's a woman who can raise the pulses if ever I saw one. Why doesn't he?'

'Really, Mike, I don't know. And if I did, I wouldn't dream of interfering.' Julius smiled with affection at the huge man opposite him who, being happy, like a child, wanted everyone else to be happy with him. 'I think I'll have the steak and kidney pudding, Mike. There's a definite nip in the air today – time for puddings, don't you think?'

'Always trust a man who likes his fodder, Julius, it's always been a rule of mine. Never fails. How about the Château Petrus? A marriage made in heaven, wouldn't you say?' He guffawed heartily and ordered for them both.

After his long, heavy lunch Julius walked in Hyde Park for an hour, in sunshine that had already lost its summer power, watching the nannies with their charges, enjoying seeing lovers entwined in each other's arms on the grass.

He had an appointment for tea with Sally Britain and, after signing his letters at the office, took a taxi to the Basil Street Hotel where Sally always stayed when in London. Women never failed to amaze Julius. Sally looked exactly as she had years ago. She must have aged, for sixteen years had passed since they were lovers. But to his eyes she was still the same, still as pretty, still as feminine. He enjoyed seeing her for in doing so he was able to capture, for just a little while, a whisper of the happy past.

It was September, so she was about to deliver to him her next book. It was a ritual they always indulged in. Tea with tiny finger sandwiches, Earl Grey, and then a cake or two. At that point Sally always said she should not eat one for the sake of her figure. And he always said what nonsense and how perfect she was. Then, laughing, from her briefcase she would present him with the perfectly typed manuscript, always wrapped in pretty paper and ribbons, like a present. That was the moment he always ordered champagne.

Two hours later, he kissed her goodbye.

'I'll read this tonight, and look forward to it,' he said, as he stepped into his taxi.

He collected his car and, hoping to avoid the worst of the traffic, decided not to bother with the motorway but to take the long route home. He had already called Jane to say he would be an hour late. The drive home was pleasant. The golden early autumn sun always seemed more beautiful than the white of the summer one. And as he motored along he noted the leaves beginning to change. Odd how some people found the autumn a sad time of year, he looked forward to it, loved it best of all.

Dinner was a light meal after such a lunch. Jane knew better than to prepare a rich one when he had been with Mike. That was an indication of advancing age, he had joked. Once he could have eaten two huge meals in a day, but the consommé and the sole were just perfect. He thanked her. He had reached the high spot of his day when he could go to the peace of his study, pour himself a large whisky and settle down to read Sally's manuscript.

At midnight, half-way through, he set the papers down. Wonderful, he smiled. Clever Sally, she never let them down. He had read this far and he still did not know who the murderer was. It was amazing that someone so sweet and feminine could produce such horror. He poured a small nightcap and climbed the stairs to bed.

He opened his window, sniffed appreciatively at the air, liking the hint of autumnal decay.

He climbed into bed and read for another hour. He puffed up his pillows to his liking and turned out his light at about one. He was quickly asleep for Julius never had trouble sleeping. At about three he died.

chapter **four**

Crispin was very annoyed. He slammed the telephone down.

'Isn't that just bloody typical?' he said to Bee-Bee who was reclining on the bed in their suite, still breakfasting off a tray. 'Typical! He never liked me and then he ruins my honeymoon by dying.'

'Who died?'

'My uncle Julius.'

'Darling, what super news! Now you'll be so rich and Daddy will be so pleased for you.' Bee-Bee beamed at him.

He crossed to the wardrobe and pulled down a case. He opened a drawer and began to hurl underpants and socks into it.

Bee-Bee set her tray on the floor and sat up on the bed. 'Why are you packing? You're not going back to England?' she asked anxiously.

'Sweetheart, I'm sorry, I have to. I know it's rotten for you. But there's so much for me to see to back home, I dare not risk being here.'

'But no one will expect you to miss your honeymoon for a silly old funeral.'

'I'm not just going back for the funeral. I've got things to do, wheels to set in motion,' he said with a pompous air. He looked at his watch, eleven, local time. With luck he could be back by three. His stomach was churning with excitement. At long last, he thought.

Mike Pewter had been in the office for an hour when his secretary buzzed him to say his wife was on the telephone. She had heard the news on the radio.

'Oh, Lily, no!' he groaned.

'I'm afraid so, my darling. But it was in his sleep, he didn't suffer. Think. Perhaps this is for the best, Julius of all people would have hated to be an invalid.'

'I bought him a huge lunch yesterday. Maybe it was too much for him. He'd hinted once or twice that his quack had told him to ease up a little.'

'Mike, no one could stop Julius enjoying his food and drink, it would be the same as someone trying to stop you.'

'Even so, Lily, I feel bad about it. It could be my fault. We did have two bottles of the Château Petrus, it seemed such a good idea,' he said sadly.

'I doubt if it made any difference. I've thought for some time that there was an air of resignation about Julius, as if he knew his time was short.'

'Oh, Lily. I feel so sad, I loved that man.'

'And he knew you did, that's important to remember.'

When he replaced the telephone Mike laid his large head on his arms and cried like a baby.

Barty Silver was informed as he sat under a large beach umbrella conducting business on three telephones and two fax machines. Gervase had come to him the moment he had picked the news up from the wire service. It was seven in the morning, local time. Barty would never dream of being up at such an hour at home, but when in the Bahamas he often worked this early, it was one of the reasons he was beginning to think seriously of spending more time here. 'Now that is sad,' he said. Barty hated it when people he knew and respected died and the older he became the worse it was. At his age, there wasn't time to replace these people in his life, was how he thought, and such people were becoming less and less in evidence.

By eleven he wondered if Joy was up. She spent too much time in bed, lying in late, and retiring soon after dinner. It was unhealthy, he thought, but he had not said as much to her, not really understanding the ways of women. But he did wonder if all this insisting on solitude and taking long walks on the beaches was a good idea. He had hoped this break would help her stop fretting about Hannah. Barty still had not resolved the problem for her and was frustrated he hadn't but her sadness over her daughter only made him all the more determined to succeed.

He summoned her maid and asked her to ask Mrs Trenchard

to join him by the pool at her earliest convenience. Barty asked, he never ordered.

An hour later Joy appeared.

'Sad news, Joy, my girl. I didn't want anyone else to tell you.'

'Hannah?' she said immediately, clutching at her throat and going even paler than she was already.

'Hannah's fine. No, it's poor old Julius, went to sleep and passed on. What a way to go! I've got to go back for the funeral. Do you want to come, or would you rather stay here and rest?'

'I didn't know you were such great friends.'

'Oh, yes, Julius and I go back a long way. And in any case he was my publisher.' He smiled affectionately at her. 'Got to go, girl, show willing. And I've a thing or two to sort, know what I mean?' And he tapped the side of his nose with his finger, a gesture that irritated her. Her own reaction worried her.

'If you don't mind I think I'd rather stay here. It's harder in London, knowing Hannah's in the same city. Faith can go to the funeral in my place. There's sure to be a memorial service later, I'll go to that.'

'Of course, you stay and rest. I'll be back as soon as I can.' He patted her hand and wished he had the courage to lean over and kiss her. He did not for he was not certain of her reaction. He sensed that Joy was struggling with herself, reaching conclusions that he might not like.

Upon arrival in London, Crispin hired a chauffeur-driven car and made straight for Julius's house where, rightly, he guessed the family would have gathered. His mother was crying. Now that was odd, thought Crispin. She had despised her brother, and certainly never had a good word to say about him. Everyone knew that, so why the tears? He was quite shocked by Uncle Simon who looked as if he had aged ten years overnight. He seemed not to know where he was. But it was only nine months since he had been capable of screwing extra money out of him; he had been bright enough then, thought Crispin maliciously. Crispin could only conclude he must be drunk as he blundered about with Dulcett in anxious pursuit. His aunt Jane was a picture of composure but that was what one would have expected from her. John was stridently in evidence with his wife Poppy, who was already seriously bored at having to be in the country. Cousin Caroline, dry-eyed and steely, had appeared with her chinless husband, who appeared only able to talk about the weather and farm subsidies, subjects of stunning boredom to Crispin. It was a truly awful family he belonged to; thank God it was only necessary to see them at times like this. It was another indication of how inconsiderate Julius was – it was only last Saturday that he had had to endure them at his wedding. He could not wait to get away from his family. Diffidently he suggested that perhaps they should have a meeting to discuss the business.

Even he was surprised at the alacrity with which they had agreed; he had quite expected to have to wait until after the funeral.

He painted the gloomiest picture yet of the fortunes of Westall and Trim, neatly avoiding the coup of Barty's first serial rights. As financial director it was his sad duty to report that he felt the only possible solution was the sale of the firm to the highest bidder, even though it broke his heart, pained him, saddened him, all this said in as mournful a voice as he could muster and one which, to his surprise, he almost believed himself.

There was no hesitation from anyone; all agreed that the sale should proceed as quickly as possible. Perhaps Crispin could put out some feelers for them within the trade, they asked. Only Simon objected, wittering on that it was not what Julius would have wanted, and dabbing his eyes with a paint-stained handkerchief. To Crispin there was something obscene in having to witness old men crying, as if their bodily fluids were leaking. The others began to shuffle in their seats and look guilty. Crispin quickly pointed out that Simon had sold his interest, and with an expressive shrug of his shoulders implied that therefore his opinion was not worth listening to, let alone relevant.

Crispin declined his aunt's invitation to stay overnight, mumbling something about problems in London with his new house. He summoned his chauffeur and was driven rapidly back to London to the ever-open arms and thighs of his mistress Cleo.

*

Gloria had enjoyed her stay with Kate. She had insisted on taking Kate out to dinner the previous night in Graintry. Apart from wanting to repay her hospitality, Gloria had suggested the meal out for she dreaded Tony returning home, imagining how stilted the evening would be. She need not have worried, she did not even see him. He returned after they were both in bed and had gone by the time she was up in the morning.

'He eats out most evenings. I've offered to cook for him but he refuses. It's rather childish really, as if he's sulking,' Kate explained over breakfast.

Or as if he's got a bit on the side, thought Gloria, as she agreed with Kate.

They had spent most of that day in house-hunting again. They had found three possibles and Gloria felt she had left Kate in better spirits than she had found her.

It was six before she arrived home in London. Even though Elephant was telling her patiently enough that he wanted his supper she listened to her answering machine first. There was no call from Peter. And she had allowed herself to hope. Stupid of her. She turned on the television for the six o'clock news but she was in the kitchen feeding her dog when the report of Julius's death was repeated.

She poured herself a drink and wondered what to do with herself. She had been so convinced he would call that she had turned down Kate's invitation to stay another night – that would have been more fun than the prospect of an interminable evening alone. She supposed she could have a bath; after all, that was what she usually did when at a loose end.

She was half-way up the stairs when the front-door bell rang. Peter was on the doorstep.

'Peter! I expected you to telephone from New York. Not to turn up. What a wonderful surprise. Come in . . .' She was full of exuberance but it began to wane as she saw the serious expression on his face. Wrong again, Gloria, she told herself. He had come to tell her why he had returned to his wife – it was patently obvious. She led the way into her sitting room, glad to be in front of him so he could not see the bleakness on her own face.

He stood awkwardly, it seemed to her, in the middle of the room. She dived for the television and turned it off.

'Drink?' she asked brightly, anything to delay him telling her he was back with Hilary.

'You haven't heard?' he said.

'Heard what? Got some good gossip?' She forced herself to laugh.

'It's Julius. Last night ... Gloria, I'm sorry there's no easy way to tell you this. He died.'

She stood there unable to take in what he was saying. 'Julius?' she asked, registering only that Peter was not speaking about himself and Hilary.

'In his sleep, apparently. I didn't know until I got off the plane an hour or so ago and picked up an *Evening Standard*.'

'You didn't get the message I left at the office? You came straight here?' Her voice was rising with excitement at the implication.

'I wanted to see you and be with you. I knew how desperately upset you would be. I knew you loved Julius too.'

It was then it hit her. It was then she realised what he had been saying. She felt self-repugnance that she should have reacted the way she did, thinking only of herself. 'Oh, no. Not Julius.' She began to cry, and he took her in his arms to comfort her.

It was some time before Gloria calmed down. Even as she cried she was unsure if all the tears were for Julius or if she was crying for something else. Was she also weeping with relief that Peter had come to her?

'We need a drink,' Peter finally said, when he was sure the storm of emotion was over.

'In the fridge,' she said. While Peter collected the wine, Gloria inspected herself in the mirror over the fireplace, dabbing with a Kleenex at the streaks of mascara around her eyes.

'Better?' he asked.

'Much. I'm sorry.'

'Don't even say it.' He smiled at her as he handed her a glass of white wine.

They sat reminiscing about Julius and the old times and had soon opened a second bottle.

They had both already had far too much to drink so it was a mistake to open yet another and she couldn't remember whose suggestion it was.

Nor, the following morning, did she have a clear recollection of who had suggested that he stay. When she awoke to find him sleeping beside her she had no idea if they had made love or not. She hoped not and yet at the same time . . . ?

As she watched him in his sleep, the strain from yesterday having completely disappeared, he looked young again. She would have liked to touch him, feel the stubble of his morning beard, touch his eyelids, but she stopped herself and contented herself with looking at him. He stirred, and then, as if her stare had woken him, he opened his eyes, blinked and then smiled a long lazy smile.

'Sorry about last night,' he said.

'Don't be silly, there's nothing to apologise for.'

'I was pissed. That's why I was so useless.'

'So was I,' she said, relieved that she had not let stupid, unthinking sex get in the way of this particular friendship, but wishing she could remember what had happened more clearly.

'I'm not now,' he said quietly, and she felt his hand under the cover tentatively search for her body. She felt a jolt of pleasure as his hand found her breast, she felt her nipples stiffen, felt that melting charge slide down through her body as if there was a hot line from her breasts to her pussy. Involuntarily, she moaned with pleasure. She did not want this, this was wrong, she would regret it, she must stop him. But then his mouth was at her breast and he was sucking her and she was lost.

He made love to her and she found herself responding to him in a way that was strange to her. She wanted to hold him, she wanted to give him happiness. His happiness was all that mattered. She did not think of taking from him, she forgot, so absorbed had she become in his contentment.

He was gentle, he was sensuous, he was rough, he was unkind, he was gentle. She had no idea what he would be doing to her next, all she knew was that she wanted him inside her – deep within her, safe, for ever.

Eventually she slumped back on the pillows, satiated and exhausted.

'Stupid old Hilary,' she chuckled.

'Lucky old me,' he grinned, and he was making love to her again and to her horror Gloria found she was crying. Tears were falling from her eyes, down her cheeks, damp on her body. They would not stop. He wiped them away gently.

'My darling, what's the matter?'

'I don't know. I'm sorry. It's so stupid. I think it's because I'm just so happy.'

'I didn't realise I was so good.'

'Oh, Peter . . . ' she said, and started laughing.

'I'm rather chuffed – after all, you must know what you're talking about.' He laughed with pleasure at what he thought was a good joke. Gloria froze inside. She looked away from him. He put his arm around her, she stiffened at his touch. He knew he should apologise, realised that his words could be so easily misinterpreted, but as so often with unfortunate remarks, they had slipped out before he had time to think. He opened his mouth as if to say something, and then changed his mind, afraid he might make matters worse. Instead he nuzzled her neck, and she turned to him and held him to her almost with desperation.

Roz had taken a long weekend break. Seeing Crispin the previous Saturday had upset her more than she had realised at the time. It was easy to pretend she still hated him when others were around but it was impossible to deceive herself. She knew he was selfish, cruel and self-seeking but he still had a hold over her.

She had borrowed an isolated cottage, belonging to a friend, near Brancaster beach in Norfolk. There was no radio and no television but Roz did not mind. She had come here for peace and quiet and to think. Her thoughts were concentrated on the thick envelope Julius had given her, realising it bestowed a considerable amount of power – enough to get Crispin back into her bed.

Roz slept in a bedroom with sloping ceiling and gingham curtains and the sound of the sea swishing on the sand. She slept, unaware that Julius was dead. At the foot of the bed was her handbag and in it, for safe-keeping, the letter from Julius to Gloria.

chapter **five**

On the following Monday, Crispin was, to say the least, rather hurt by the unfriendly way in which both Peter Holt and Mike Pewter spoke to him when he called to say that, acting for the rest of the family, he wanted to talk about the sale of Westall and Trim.

'Good God, man! Have you no respect? You haven't even buried Julius yet,' Peter had snarled at him.

'Ghoul!' Mike had bellowed before slamming down the telephone.

If that was how they wanted it they could lump it, he said to himself. Tudor's had been very willing to talk and, what was more, he had an intriguing invitation from Barty Silver. Barty had made an appointment to see him, once Julius was interred. All this old-fashioned insistence on burial first was a waste of time as far as Crispin was concerned. Still, if that was what Barty wanted, he would go along with it.

He set about compiling figures for Tudor's. He knew they expected a snap decision, but they were not going to get it. He would let them dangle, certainly until he had seen Silver. And since Mike and Peter had been so rude, he would cast his net further afield. He made a call to a company chairman in Germany and planned what to say to his contacts in America, later in the day, when they were awake.

Mike and Peter met for lunch.

'What are we going to do about Westall's, Peter?'

'The way I snapped at Crispin, I shouldn't think Shotters is in the running.'

'The decision is not entirely his, is it? I don't have much time for Julius's son, but he's a good businessman, I hear. He'll want the best price and in the end the rest of the family will defer to him, the banker, not the publisher.'

'I don't know. I doubt if Shotters will be interested. Costas is screaming for retrenchment, not expansion. I had a rather sticky interview with him last week.'

'And . . .?'

'Oh, come on, Mike. I work for the man, you don't expect me to tell you the ins and outs of Shotters.' He laughed at Mike's hopeful cheek.

'Worth a try.' He bowed his head in mock shame. 'Did you know Barty is snooping about?'

'No. But then I'm not surprised. Ever since that party last year when the place was alive with publishers I've wondered what he's up to – he gave me a rare old grilling. And then, shortly after that, he started up that agency with Joy Trenchard. He's been flirting on the edges for some time.'

'Yes, and then allowing his memoirs to go to Westall's when sense will tell you that they must have been the underbidders by thousands. Now why do that? Unless he intended one day to own it and reap the benefit for himself. I tell you, Peter, Barty in the business is not something I look forward to. The man seems to attract success like a fly-paper. What about you?'

'Sorry, what about me?' Peter put his head on one side, wondering what Mike had up his sleeve now.

'Why don't you bid for it? Get out of Shotters, have your own company again. You could afford it, they'll never sell for the amount Crispin is hoping for.'

'Me? No, thanks. For a start I could never work with Crispin and if I did do something – and I'm not saying I will . . .' He waggled his finger at Mike, laughing at him as he did so. 'If I did, I think I'd like to start again from scratch.'

'Crispin is the last thing to worry about. He isn't staying in publishing. He wants an academic life in Oxford or Cambridge and he's been sniffing around there like a weasel for months, sounding people out – so I've been told.'

'God help either university, then,' Peter said with feeling.

'What's Gloria going to do, I wonder?'

'For the time being she says she's staying put – she has her new list, which is important to her. She wants to see who buys before deciding anything.'

'Does she now?' Mike was grinning from ear to ear. 'So you've seen her again? Good.' He sat back with a contented expression, amused to see the discomfort on Peter's face.

'I had to see her about Julius.'

'Of course.' Mike folded his arms over his expansive chest.

'I knew how upset she would be.'

'Of course.'

'It isn't like that, Mike.'

'Oh no?'

'If we weren't in such civilised surroundings, I'd fling a bread roll at you.'

'You do that, Peter. You can't lie to me, my boy. I'm delighted.'

The atmosphere at Westall's was grim. Most of the women had been crying. No one could believe that Julius was not coming back – he had been so happy on Thursday, everyone was at pains to tell each other.

Little work was being done; instead people were meeting in offices in whispered huddles, wondering what was to happen to them all. This concern for their future in no way detracted from their genuine grief for the man and Julius would undoubtedly have approved of their concern for the future of his 'house'. Rumours were flying around.

By ten a strong rumour, emanating from the publicity office, was circulating that Julius's son was giving up banking and would be running everything. This news did not meet with any approval. They all had a reasonable and logical pessimism about those who entered publishing knowing nothing about it.

By eleven someone in the postroom said that one of the telephonists had overheard a conversation revealing that Crispin had bought out the family. This was met with feelings bordering on despair, for Crispin was one of the least popular members of staff. At that there was much bravado and talk of resignations.

Some felt that the family would never sell, that their sense of loyalty would be too great. These opinions tended to be held by the older members of staff – Liz, who had been an editor here for twenty-eight years, Effie, who had started as an accounts clerk twenty-seven years ago, and in any other firm by now would have been retired. And old Stan who burrowed away in the basement postroom and would never say how long he had worked for Westall's in case someone managed to work out that he was getting on for eighty.

'I hate to interrupt this conference, but we do have books to get out,' Gloria said, standing in the door of the publicity office where Val, Penny and several of the editors had been drinking copious amounts of coffee and smoking themselves silly. 'We've a week to *Winter Interlude*'s launch, or have you forgotten? I don't see over much in the publicity schedule for Kate yet. So, Val, if you don't mind?'

'Hard cow,' Penny said when Gloria had gone. 'How can she even think about the bloody book on a day like this?'

'No, she's right,' Val said. 'This endless debate is getting us nowhere. Mr Westall would not want the books to suffer in any way. Come on, Penny, have you spoken to the *Express* yet?'

The door to Julius's office was open, just as it always had been. Crispin had toyed with the idea of using it himself now he had so much checking to do, and so many telephone calls to make. But even Crispin was sensitive enough to know that it would not be popular, so he restricted himself to collecting some papers he needed for his calculations and congratulated himself that, with his cousin inheriting Julius's shares, he need not worry ever again about the identity of the Lepanto Trust – for whoever they were, their measly two per cent of the shares could not stop the sale, for millions, of Westall and Trim.

Gloria was trying to work but finding it increasingly difficult. She would have liked time to herself to think about last night and Peter but instead she was continually interrupted by the telephone. Those authors who had heard the news at the weekend were first to call and somehow someone, she did not know who, had delegated Gloria to deal with them and their worried enquiries. Then it seemed that all the authors had been calling each other, for a second wave of calls came from those who never bothered with newspapers or television but had been told by those who did. And so the reassurances had to be repeated all over again. Some of the calls were hard to take and Gloria felt as though she had spent the whole day in tears. The one from Sally Britain had been the hardest – she was beside herself with grief, and she and Gloria wept copious tears together.

By mid-afternoon she could take no more. She picked up a strangely subdued Elephant – he had been like that all day as if he had sensed that something was very much amiss – and called Crispin.

'Crispin, I'm going home. I'm sorry, but the telephone calls are getting me down. I've asked the switchboard to put them through to you. I'll see you tomorrow.'

'Fine, Gloria. Thank you for all your wonderful support today. By the way, the funeral is fixed, Thursday at eleven at his local parish church. I know I speak for the rest of the family when I say I hope you will be there,' he said, unctuously. Gloria longed to hit him.

Back home she began to prepare dinner. Peter had said he would come. She wanted him to come and she didn't. Part of her was longing to be in his arms and have him make love to her. Another, more logical, part was telling her it would be better not to see him and so avoid making a fool of herself by jumping to too many conclusions too quickly.

He had explained the note on the flowers. They were meant as an apology for boring her with his problems, something he would not repeat. The florist must have misheard him on the telephone and written 'bother' instead. When Gloria had not telephoned he had taken it as an indication that he had presumed on her friendship and had bored her to tears. His words had been music to her ears, but perhaps it was the siren song. It might be the truth, she told herself, but she was not willing to accept it entirely. She had been badly hurt, far worse than any other man had managed to hurt her. And like a person wary of fire because once badly burnt, she was not going to let it happen again. She still felt cold inside when she thought of his joke. Did he think that all she wanted was to be in bed with him? She realised men could and did sometimes say crass things when they had just made love – a form of shyness, she supposed. But, still, such reasoning did not help her. Last time, he had come here because he was upset: Gloria had left the firm that day, and he was still adjusting to the shock of his wife's adultery. This time he had come because Julius had died. She would believe him when both their lives were on an even keel, not now.

All the same, when he arrived she was pleased – even if she managed to disguise just how pleased.

'You seem distant, Gloria,' he said, as they sat eating the meal she had prepared.

'Do I? I'm sorry, I don't think I am.'

'You were so warm before.'

'Aha, well, things happen, don't they, Peter?'

'I don't understand, Gloria. What things? I've explained as best I can.'

'When I didn't call I don't understand why you didn't telephone me.'

'How could I? I presumed that I had offended you – as I had feared.'

'I want to believe you, Peter, but I'm not what you think I am.'

'And what's that?' He smiled, puzzled.

'I'm not interested in a one-night stand.'

'Nor am I.'

'I'm afraid of being hurt again.'

'I'd never hurt you, not intentionally.'

'I need time, Peter. My trust went wobbly.' She attempted to smile.

'Then you don't want to see me again?'

'Yes, of course I do,' she said quickly, and then immediately kicked herself for sounding so eager. 'At the moment, with the shock of Julius's death, we are both so upset that our emotions may not be reliable. We have to get over this before we can honestly look at each other and know how we truly feel.'

'Then you don't want me to stay tonight?'

'No, Peter. I can't risk it.' She was lying, she longed for him to stay, but she could not let him know. 'In a little while perhaps,' she said smiling at him, hoping he could understand her muddled logic.

Roz should have returned to work on the Monday. Instead she had telephoned in to say she was unwell but the secretary had not mentioned Julius's death. She wasn't ill, but she was enjoying the isolation. She took long walks on the beach debating what to do. Finally she had made a decision. It would be pointless to use the letter to try to get Crispin back in her bed. Nor could she bring herself to betray Julius's trust again – how would she ever face him? It would be better if she waited until he died. Then, hopefully, she would feel no guilt. Before giving the letter to Gloria, she could steam it open, photocopy it and then decide whether to invite Crispin round for dinner.

It was not until Tuesday evening that Roz set out in her ancient Mini for the drive back to London. Despite the car's age and rather dilapidated state, she sped along making good time, for the traffic was light. It seemed to Roz almost as if she was the only person awake in the world – there were so few lights on in the cottages and villages she passed. Her decision made, she felt quite lighthearted.

On the straight approach to Newmarket, she leant forward to fiddle with the radio, just as a front tyre blew. The car slewed across the road as she fought to gain control. She went for the brake but in her panic hit the accelerator. The small car slammed into a tree and burst into flames with an explosion that could be heard for miles. It was two days before her body was identified.

chapter six

Publishers, authors, booksellers, friends, they were all there, filling the small church to overflowing, some having to stand outside in the drizzle, which everyone agreed was fitting weather. Julius would have been proud at the turn-out, they also acknowledged to themselves.

Gloria had travelled down with Peter and was glad she had for she loathed funerals, not as most people disliked them, no, more than that. She dreaded them, for invariably she disgraced herself by getting a fit of the giggles.

'I am the Resurrection and the Life saith the Lord . . .' The vicar appeared at the head of the procession intoning the words in a voice so sepulchral that Gloria longed to laugh. As Peter took hold of her hand and held it tight, she smiled a thin-lipped, desperately controlled smile at him.

She also knew that no matter how hard she tried she couldn't think holy thoughts. She never did. Somehow her thought patterns always went off at a silly tangent despite her efforts to order them otherwise. Today she found herself thinking she never wanted a funeral like this for herself. And she found herself wondering about being buried at sea. Which was also fine. But then she remembered her mother telling her that that was not such a good idea unless one took great care of the winds and tides – bodies were forever washing up at Mount's Bay, Penzance, so distressing to all concerned. This made her want to giggle so she hung on to Peter harder, which luckily he took as evidence of her grief. Such irreverence had nothing to do with her true feelings about Julius, it was how she was. Churches had that effect upon her.

The family were feeling pleased with everything. The turnout, the flowers, all had gone well. Sheltering under large umbrellas, which caused rather than prevented drips down the collar, John conducted his mother away from the graveside, followed by the family. Uncle Simon had been too poorly to attend; Dulcett had come but none of them regarded her as family so they all studiously ignored her.

One of the first to reach the family group was their lawyer, who scurried up with a young woman, dressed fittingly from head to toe in black. None of them recognised her.

'Mrs Westall, John . . .' Tristan Kemp said breathlessly, mopping not rain but sweat from his brow, unusual since the day was chilly. 'Is there somewhere private we can talk? It's rather urgent.'

'Now, Tristan? Hardly,' Jane Westall said, irritated with the epicene man she had never really liked but with whom Julius had insisted on dealing. Kemp's firm had always dealt with the Westalls' affairs.

'Yes, now, I'm afraid. This is Miss MacPherson from London.'

'How do you do?' Jane said in her most dismissive manner, and offered a limp handshake.

'I'm sorry to interrupt you now, Mrs Westall, at such a time,' Miss MacPherson said in the clear accents of the Home Counties and not the Highlands. 'It is necessary, I am afraid, for I am acting on the express instructions of your late husband. You see, Mr Westall made another will and – '

'He did what?' John interrupted.

'Christ!' Crispin added.

'He left strict instructions that it was not to be mentioned until his funeral was over – he said he did not want any prior unpleasantness.'

'Have you seen this so-called will, Tristan?'

'Yes, Mrs Westall.'

'And?'

'I can see nothing wrong with it. Julius made it back in December. He wasn't ill or anything,' Tristan said lamely, aware that he was about to be the centre of a God-awful family row and wishing he was somewhere else.

'We shall see about that. Back to the house, everyone, and hurry – some of these people are coming back. You . . .' Jane pointed imperiously at the young woman. 'Have you a car? Then follow us.'

At which the family streaked for their limousines, leaving the congregation somewhat nonplussed as they stood waiting to make their condolences. Unsure what to do, the majority returned to their study of the many wreaths that lay on the grass which, incongruously, was scattered with confetti.

When a decent enough interval had elapsed, those guests considered sufficiently important by Jane Westall returned to the house to find Dulcett the only family member present. The rest were in heated conference in the library observed by a lachrymose Simon, who had not waited for their return before starting on the whisky.

Miss MacPherson was made of sterner fibre than Tristan Kemp. She moved not an inch in her deliberations despite being shouted at by the grieving family.

'I realise this must be most distressing for you, Mrs Westall, but the fact is that your husband made this will while of sound mind. It was duly drawn up, correctly witnessed. It is a valid will, Mrs Westall,' she said with such patent patience that Jane was doubly offended.

'You need not speak to me as if I were a five-year-old. Tristan, don't just stand there looking pathetic, tell us what we should do.' In her anger, Jane turned on the family advisor, who spoke hesitantly.

'I'm afraid there is nothing I can say. This is a proper will. I must say, I'm a little hurt he did not come to us, but no doubt Julius had his reasons.'

'Stop whimpering, Tristan. Of course, my mother will contest this will,' John said, pouring himself half a tumbler of whisky.

'I'm sure Mr Kemp's advice would be the same as mine, Mr Westall. It would be an expensive and futile exercise. Your mother has been most generously provided for – this house, and a considerable insurance policy. You and your sister have both been left a large amount of money from the sale of his paintings. A court would regard these legacies as fair and honourable. But apart from that there is this clause that your father insisted upon. I'm afraid if any of you do contest this will, or block the transfer of shares, then his instructions are quite clear, he wishes that his shares and proceeds from his paintings should go to the Battersea Dogs' Home. No, thank you, Mr Westall, I won't have a drink, I must be getting back. I've left a copy of the will with Mr Kemp. Thank you all,' she said, with more than a hint of irony, packed up her briefcase and left them.

'Kemp, get us out of this.' Crispin's voice had risen an octave with emotion.

'There's nothing to be said. Miss MacPherson has said it all.'

'I don't believe this.' John had slumped in a chair, his head in his hands in despair.

'This trust my husband has set up for his employees, is that legal? Could he do that?' Jane asked Tristan.

'Perfectly legal, Mrs Westall. A man may do as he wishes with his estate.'

'Well, it's wrong. This is just typical of Julius, he always was a vindictive man.'

'He bloody wasn't! How dare you say that of him.' Simon had leapt to his feet, tears of grief replaced by a scowl of anger. 'A better man there never was. His tragedy was ending up with you lot as a family. I'm not surprised he did this. He loved the firm, he must have known what you all planned. You know what? I'm glad, good for Julius!' And he suddenly roared with laughter.

'Oh, shut up, you senile old fool,' Crispin shouted.

'I wish you lot would stop caterwauling, I've got to think,' John said with irritation. 'Look, Kemp, if my memory serves me right, the terms of the Westall's articles are that shares have to be offered to the existing shareholders first. If no one wants to buy, then the new shareholders have to be agreed by a majority?'

'That is certainly so.'

'Then there's no problem. My mother, aunt and Crispin refuse to have the employees as shareholders.'

'We would have to buy them out,' Crispin said, but cheering up immeasurably. 'You could arrange the finance for that, John. We'd recoup the moment we sold out.'

'Hang on, where would that leave Caroline?' It was her husband Bertie speaking, a rare occurrence. 'It doesn't help her or John. They would lose out. All that would mean is that you existing shareholders would reap everything.'

'You'd have to trust us, Bertie, old chap.' Crispin flashed one of his biggest smiles, but Bertie looked very doubtful.

'No, that's no good. Bertie's right, there's too much at stake,' John said, having second thoughts and no intention of trusting any of them.

'Miss MacPherson has told you what would happen should

any of you block the transfer of the shares to a trust for the employees. Mrs Westall would still benefit from the insurance policy, but this house would be sold and Mrs Westall would live in a cottage to be retained for her on the estate. And John and Caroline would not benefit at all. Now we don't want that do we?' Tristan smiled, he was feeling less in awe of them now. In fact, he was rather enjoying watching them squirm.

'I'm not losing out on the paintings as well,' John said with feeling.

'Aren't you all panicking unnecessarily? Everyone has done very well – even you, Caroline. Jane will be left most comfortably. And if it's what my brother wanted ... It would be typical of Julius that even if the company is sold – and I do believe he thought that inevitable himself – that his employees should benefit.' It was Marge speaking up for the first time.

'Mother! I don't believe you're saying this.' Crispin faced Marge. 'You always said you loathed him.'

'Did I? I don't remember,' she said dismissively to her son. 'I may not have agreed with everything he did,' Marge looked pointedly at her sister-in-law, 'but he was my brother and I loved him. And, if you must know, I find this haggling over poor Julius's wishes unseemly in the extreme. I should most certainly vote in favour of the employees' trust.'

'I'm sorry, Crispin, but this house means too much to me and I cannot risk ending my days in a poky cottage. I think it is all grossly unfair and spiteful. I shall never forgive Julius, but I would vote for the employees' trust with Marge. You'd be outvoted, Crispin,' said Jane with a finality that brooked no argument.

'Good show!' Simon clapped.

'There's one thing you all seem to have forgotten.' Crispin drawled, proud he was able to conceal his seething anger. 'There's the little matter of the Lepanto Trust and its decisive two per cent. We have to find out who this wretched trust is, approach them, buy them out. All right, we lose half, but at least the employees' trust could not stop us selling the whole lot, for then we should be in the majority. And I'm sure that, after this fiasco, the less we have to do with the company in the future, the better.' There was a murmur of agreement to this.

'That bloody Lepanto Trust,' said John. 'I've tried many times to find out who it is. Have you had any luck, Crispin?'

'No, but then I was looking with my hand tied behind my back. I had no access to his study here, his safe ... I'm sure now that it will be easy enough.' He smiled. He could afford to: whatever happened, it did not alter his share in the pay-out when the business was sold.

'Who is this Gloria Catchpole?' Jane asked, pronouncing the name as if it was something indescribable.

'She's an editor, she worked for Julius years ago,' said Crispin.

'And he wishes her to be the new managing director. Would she be capable?'

'Very, I fear.'

'And why make Peter Holt and that mountain of a man Pewter this trust's trustees?'

'Mischief, I should think. He knows they would fight tooth and nail to keep it as it is and never sell,' Crispin explained.

'Then we have to find out who or what the Lepanto Trust is before this unholy trinity do, don't we? Then we shall sell and that will be an end to all this nonsense. Now, if everyone will excuse me, I have guests to attend to.' Jane stood up and regally left the room, the others trailing along behind her.

Gloria could not understand why Mrs Westall was so rude to her when she offered her condolences. She had met her once or twice, but only fleetingly, and nothing she had ever done could justify the way the woman had swept past her ignoring her completely.

'What did you do?' Peter grinned at her.

'A difficult woman, I shouldn't let her upset you,' Mike consoled her.

'Well, well. What a clever little group we have here.' Crispin had sidled up to them. 'I really think that in the circumstances it would be more tactful if you all left my aunt's house, don't you?'

'What the hell are you going on about, Crispin?'

'Oh, come, Mike. You and my uncle were as thick as thieves. You're not going to tell me that you don't know what the old bastard has done?'

'Not the foggiest,' Mike said puffing a large amount of cigar smoke in the direction of Crispin, who ignored the smoke and looked at him with cynical disbelief.

'What did you have to do, Gloria, to gain such an advantage?

Screw the old roué? No, I suppose at his age that was probably out. Little bit of the old fellatio? Was that it?'

'Crispin, you'll apologise for that.' Peter squared up to him.

Gloria said nothing but her hand swished out and slapped him hard across the cheek. It failed to remove his smile however, he merely stood rubbing his cheek where the blow had fallen.

'What other conclusions are we to come to?' Crispin sneered.

'I wish you would get it into your fat head, Crispin, none of us has an inkling what the hell you are going on about,' Mike growled.

'Julius's will. He's left the whole of his shares to an employees' trust – me excluded, of course, but that's what I would expect from my loving uncle. He has decreed that sweet Gloria here is to be managing director and you and Peter are to be the trustees. And you tell me you knew none of that?' At the expressions of total shock on their faces he began to wonder if they had spoken the truth after all. 'It doesn't matter, though. I'll tell you now, in your new capacity. You only have forty-nine per cent of the shares and the family intend to sell – but, I hasten to add, not to Pewter's or Shotters. Sorry about that.' He bowed and left the three standing, glasses in hand, looking at each other with total amazement.

'Good God, I'd no idea. You, Peter?'

'Not a word.'

'Nor me,' added Gloria.

'Good old Julius. He was always a fighter. Well, we can't let them sell, can we? Nor stay here. Need a lift?'

And without saying the customary goodbyes, they left, unsure still that it was true, and even more unsure how they were to stop the family.

chapter **seven**

As the day for the launch of her book came nearer, Kate felt herself being swept along by events.

Never confident of how she looked, she had taken a severe knock when, in Graintry, she had sat in the studio of the one and only local photographer.

'I hate having my photograph taken,' she laughed, feeling awkward, as the man fiddled with the lights and equipment. 'Hope I don't break your camera,' she giggled but seeing the bored expression on his face realised she was probably repeating a cliché he had heard a million times before.

'You sure you want black and white?' he asked.

'Yes, that's what I was told.'

'Most people want colour these days, the lighting has to be different for black and white.'

'Sorry,' she said and wondered what it was about her that made her feel she had to apologise for everything.

'What did you say this was for?'

'It's an author photo, for promotions, posters and book jackets, that sort of thing,' she said, brightening up, presuming he would be complimented by her choosing him to take something so important.

'Well, there's not much point in trying to make you look glamorous then, is there?' he had replied.

That had been a couple of months ago, now she held her book in her hand, the photograph on the back cover. He had been right, she certainly did not look glamorous, far from it, she looked ordinary – mumsy, if she was honest. But the book, that was something else. Julius had been right, she did cry when she saw it. She could not leave it alone, but kept picking it up, admiring it, stroking it, unable to believe that it had really come about. She wished she could tell him of her reaction to the book and thank him. She had been saddened to hear of his death; she did not know enough about publishing to know that it might mean her own future was at stake.

She was waiting, hair freshly shampooed and blow-dried, made up and smartly dressed in a red skirt and black sweater, for her first interview. Never having done such a thing before she did not know what to expect, but at least it was for the local paper, she consoled herself, which might be an easier baptism than the national who had asked to interview her next week.

Dee Masters was young, with too much make-up, dressed in a black leather miniskirt and a bright green cotton sweater so tight her nipples protruded. She played constantly with the dangling earrings she wore and which kept getting tangled in her long hair. She was evidently proud of her peroxided mane, for she played with that constantly too, brushing it out of the way, flicking it back, tossing her head so it swished from side to side. Kate was not impressed, merely hoped that with all that flicking, tossing and swishing she did not have dandruff.

Since the interview was to be about her and the book she was somewhat nonplussed when Dee blithely announced she had not read it.

'Ah, I see,' said Kate, though she longed to say, Why not?

'So many books land on my desk it's just impossible to read them all,' Dee said cheerfully as if reading her mind. 'In any case, it might be a bad idea. What if I hated your book? It might colour how I react to you as a person and so make for a bad interview. That's what I've found in the past.'

Knowing nothing about journalism there was no way Kate felt she had the right to argue with Dee, even though she found her argument somewhat weak. She felt that the more probable explanation was that Dee was too lazy and could not be bothered.

'Far better if you tell me what your book's about.' Dee produced a small tape-recorder from the copious bag she carried. 'You don't mind, do you?'

In fact Kate did mind: if having her photograph taken was agony, listening to her own voice played back on a tape-recorder was her idea of hell. She only had to catch sight of one of the machines and her voice changed its key, she sounded stilted and could only speak with a ludicrously exaggerated accent. 'That's fine,' she said, despising herself for not objecting. Diffidently, she began to talk. Writing it had been easier, she concluded, than having to explain it. The plot, when described as now, seemed weak and rather pointless.

'Sounds riveting,' said Dee, but still did not say she would read it. 'Right, now I want to hear all about you.'

Kate began the monologue of her ordinary life and, as she always did, ended up apologising for it. 'Not a lot for you to write about, is there?'

'Amazing achievement, though, I envy you. I'd love to write a novel.'

'Really? Why don't you? I'm sure that with all your writing you could,' Kate said encouragingly.

'Oh, I could do it easily enough,' Dee said confidently. 'It's finding the time, that's the problem. If I had the time, I would.' Dee flicked her hair for the umpteenth time. Kate, remembering how she had fitted in her writing around home and family, made no comment. 'Why do you think you suddenly decided to write?'

'I don't think I could have done it at an earlier age. I'd always been a full-time mother, you see. Bringing up a family requires a lot of energy – mental I mean, not just physical. But there comes a time when the children don't need you quite so much and you're left with this great reservoir of mental energy and what do you do with it? That's a dangerous time for a woman – she can go on tranquillisers or she can *do* something. I was lucky, I found writing.'

'So you would say you were impelled by the menopause into writing?' Dee leant forward with interest.

'That's not exactly what I said. No.'

'Do you think that women like you write these books because they are disappointed in their own lives? That you create a fantasy world as an escape, where the men are perfect, the sex divine?' Dee chortled.

'No, I don't,' Kate said, offended, but more, she felt uncomfortable that Dee might be a little too close to the truth for comfort.

'What is more to the point, do you think you are really being fair to your own sex, Kate?'

'I'm sorry, I don't understand.'

'You write of a fantasy world with fantasy men and women – let's face it, I've never met anyone remotely like these heroes and heroines. Have you? It's all impossibly unattainable to a woman trapped in a council flat with three kids under five, it could make her even more bitter with her lot in life. Wouldn't you agree?' Dee smiled expansively, exposing overlarge teeth and swishing her hair over her shoulder with a confident jerk of the head.

Kate felt herself bridling. 'I don't see why women can't have a degree of escapism. No one criticises thriller writers – do men become frustrated because they're not 007? But, in any case, if you had taken the trouble to read my book you would have found out it isn't like that.' Kate wished she had the courage to ask this patronising woman to leave. But if she did, what would she write about her? 'It's all a matter of opinion, isn't it?' she added and loathed herself for being so wimpish.

'And your husband – Tony, isn't it?' Dee continued to smile as if she had not even noticed that Kate had been sharp with her. 'How does Tony feel about it all? He must be very proud of you.'

Kate made a fatal mistake. She laughed a small bitter laugh which Dee swooped on with all the instincts of a vulture.

'He's not proud?'

'I didn't say that. Of course he is ... I don't know ... I mean, he never said, he's not like that. And I didn't ask ...' Her voice trailed off lamely.

Dee leant forward and pointedly switched off the tape-recorder. 'There that's better, there are some things best not taken down on tape.' She smiled, a small sympathetic one this time, and patted Kate's hand. 'There. Quite honestly, Kate, I sense you are not totally happy with your success. I've turned the machine off, you can talk to me if you like.'

'No, really. I'm more than pleased.'

'It's not always easy is it, being a career woman? I know. You can't imagine the trouble I've had with my husband. He wants it to be like it was with his father and mother – me at home, cooking his meals, always there waiting for him. He hates me working, can't understand my ambition.'

'Really?' Kate said with interest. She made some sandwiches and opened a bottle of wine, and for the next hour she had a wonderful time talking to this woman who understood her problems. They talked of the impossibility of men, and how hard it was to be a successful woman in a man's world.

By the time the newspaper photographer came Kate felt she had made a new friend, and she could not understand why she had been suspicious of her. Dee even understood how she hated to be photographed. She fussed about, checking Kate's make-up, rearranging her hair, advising her where to sit and stand for the best results. Pictures were taken of her in the kitchen, drawing room, at her desk, in the garden. When it was time for Dee to go it was with promises that they would meet up again and soon.

During this period Kate felt intensely lonely. She was approaching so many new and exciting experiences and yet there was no one to share them with, no one to reassure her she was doing all right. She hardly ever saw Tony, he left early and returned late. At weekends he had taken to going away. She had initially asked where but he was obviously loath to tell her so she stopped asking. Lucy had been walking in the Lake District and was now involved with her imminent departure to university. Pam, following Faith's interest in her work, had embarked on a schedule of writing so strict that she did not have time to see Kate, she said.

As the date for the completion of the house sale approached she viewed it with increasing alarm. She knew she should be beginning to pack yet could not bring herself to do anything about it. That would be too final. Until the contract was signed there was always the chance that they might sort something out between them – if only she could get Tony on his own to speak to. It was all made worse when Lucy finally went and Kate had to cope with the peculiar emptiness of a house when a child had grown up and left. She had herself driven Lucy to Cambridge.

'You are sure you're going to be all right, aren't you, Mum?' Lucy had asked as they drove along.

'Of course,' Kate replied brightly. She could not tell her daughter the truth and spoil these first important and exciting days in a new environment.

'Will you be lonely when you move?'

'Good gracious, no. I'm getting used to being alone. What do I see of your father now?'

'Yes, but you've had me pottering in and out during the past weeks and what about leaving Pam and all your friends? Don't you think you should have stayed in the area?'

'No, that's one thing I could not do. Being the odd one out at dinner parties when once I'd been part of a couple. Perhaps meeting Tony at a function, which would be so embarrassing for everyone else. It's best to make a clean break, I think.'

'But you've never had to live alone before.'

'I've my writing, you can't be lonely when you've got dozens of characters in your head all longing to be let out.'

'Are you *sure* you're doing the right thing?'

'The decision has been taken out of my hands, Lucy. Your father doesn't appear to want to talk to me about it.'

'What do you want to do?'

'I'd like to stay just the way I am but with your father understanding and accepting my writing. Since there seems to be fat chance of that, I don't have much alternative, do I?' She shrugged her shoulders.

'Do you love Dad?'

'You know, Lucy, I don't think I know what love is any more. I might write about it but as for myself and your father, who the hell knows? I'm fond of him. But is that enough?'

'You might meet someone else.'

'Me? You must be joking.' Kate laughed.

'I don't know. You're very attractive, you know, especially now you've lost weight, and Pam was so right about your hair.'

'Me? Attractive?' Kate showed she was amused by her daughter's assessment, but secretly she was more than pleased. And on the drive back oddly she found herself thinking of Stewart Dorchester, the reporter she had met at Barty's party, all that time ago and who, she often found, popped into her thoughts for no apparent reason. She wondered if they might bump into each other again.

The tabloid papers were due in the shape of Sybil Cavay from the *Daily News*. She had been nervous enough waiting for Dee from the *Graintry Echo*, this day she felt physically sick. Sybil Cavay was known as the Shrew of Shrews. She was proud of the title and she honed her sarcasm carefully to retain it. It was a rare interview where Sybil did not lash out with her pen. The problem she set for publicity departments was that she was read by millions. On the days when her interview appeared sales of the *News* were larger than any other day. But occasionally someone took her fancy and then no one could be kinder or heap more praise. So risks were taken but, to protect Kate, Val had volunteered to be present.

Kate made herself up and not liking the effect cleaned it all off and started again, trying hard to remember all the tips the woman on the make-up counter in Dingle's had given her. She dressed and then decided the blue dress she had on made her look dowdy. She changed into a red one, which she thought made her look flighty. Eventually she chose a pair of black silk trousers and a baggy white lawn shirt she had just bought. She put on two long chains that looked gold even though they weren't, tucked a red scarf in the collar and laughed at herself that she had to have something red about her. Would this do? She looked at her reflection in the mirror, twisting round to try to see how she looked from the back, and hoping the girl in the shop had not lied when she had reassured Kate that her bottom was not too big for trousers, for Sybil of all people would write about it if it was. She glanced at her watch. She would have to do, the reporter would be here in five minutes. She took one last look at herself. Once on her own she would no longer be able to buy garments like these. She supposed she would be back to watching the pennies – still, it had been fun while it lasted.

She fussed about in the drawing room wondering where on earth had Val got to. And then the doorbell rang.

Kate opened the door with a smile on her face which she was sure looked as false as it was. But the smile changed into one of genuine pleasure.

'Stewart!' she exclaimed.

'Hope you're not disappointed it's me rather than Sybil?' He grinned.

'Disappointed? Relieved, more like!' she said, holding the door open wide and welcoming him.

'Sybil sends her apologies, she was held up and I volunteered to take her place.' He laughed the rich laugh that so attracted her when they had met at Barty's. He was not about to tell her that as soon as he had heard who was to interview her he had pulled rank and insisted he do it himself. There was no way he was going to allow Sybil loose on someone like Kate.

'I thought you concentrated on politicians and world leaders?' She showed him into the drawing room.

'Not always. I need some treats.' He smiled at her and she felt suddenly shy.

'I have to tell you straight away, Kate, I liked your book enormously. I read it in one sitting. Is it really a first novel? I'm amazed.'

From such a beginning Kate feared it could only get worse. It did not; talking to Stewart about her writing and the book was like talking to an old friend, one who understood instinctively what she was trying to say. Unlike Dee he did not seem to be particularly interested in her private life.

His photographer arrived when they were only half through and the ritual was repeated all over again – photos in every room, with the last in the garden.

The photographer collected his gear and left.

'Fancy lunch?' Stewart asked her.

'You're hungry? I could rustle up something for us.'

'You don't want to do that. Let me take you out.'

'Oh, I could hardly . . .' she began, flustered.

'It's on expenses,' he said, as if in explanation.

'That would be lovely,' she answered feeling that that would be perfectly correct, a professional lunch, no more no less. And she drove them into Graintry.

She didn't know why but when they entered the restaurant she wanted someone she knew to be there, to see her with this man. She felt strangely proud to be with him.

He insisted she had a drink and she accepted even though she had resolved she wouldn't. And when she began to decide what to eat, choosing carefully the less fattening dishes, he insisted she had the lobster as he was going to.

'But my diet . . .' she protested.

'I think you're perfect,' he said and she felt herself blushing. And he ordered sauté potatoes as if to confirm his opinion.

He looked after her, that was what was so strange and pleasant about this lunch. He seemed to want to please her, to try to anticipate whatever she wanted. Several times his hand brushed against hers and she wondered if she dared think it was not an accident.

She could not remember ever talking so much to someone who, after all, was a virtual stranger. But then she began to discover they had far more in common than she had realised.

Stewart had been divorced for two years and he understood totally her feelings of confusion and fear.

'It's the sense of failure, that's the worst thing to bear, I found,' he said.

'Isn't it?' she answered with feeling. 'Wondering if all the past years have been a waste.'

'They're not, you know, that's what you'll learn eventually. And the guilt will go, one person doesn't cause a break-up.'

'That's what I keep trying to tell myself,' she said a shade woefully. He put his hand across the table and laid it on hers. She was struck by the warmth of his touch.

'Poor Kate, I feel for you. But I promise you, the guilt will go and the fear. There are advantages, too. Being able to do what you want, meeting new people. It's been an exciting time for me, finding myself again, if you like.'

'Do you really think so?' she asked, willing him to keep his hand on hers and feeling ridiculously disappointed when he removed it and offered her a cigarette instead.

They lingered over coffee and were reluctant to go but finally even they could not ignore the exasperated expressions of the waiters.

Shyly she asked him if he would like to come back to tea. He said he would love to but he had an appointment in London he could not miss. She covered up her regret and drove him to the station.

On the way home she wished she hadn't invited him. How foolish of her, too forward. He had just been friendly, nothing more. It was probably her loneliness that made her imagine and long for something more.

Unexpectedly Tony was at the house when she arrived.

'Had guests?' He nodded at the coffee cups she had forgotten to clear up in the drawing room before going out.

'A reporter from the *Daily News* and his photographer.'

'My, my. The big time,' he said.

She looked up, but he was smiling, he had not meant it unpleasantly.

'Yes. Apparently I'm very lucky, not many first-time novelists get much media attention.'

'Why you, then?'

'I think they're interested that I've taken it up in middle age – you know, there's so much fuss these days about the forty-

and fifty-year-olds, with families away and with oodles of money and no mortgages to pay.'

'Then we're hardly typical of them, are we?' He was laughing.

'Would you like me to cook you supper tonight?' she asked, emboldened by his good humour.

'That would be very nice, thanks. I need to sort out some papers in my study. And, Kate, we should get down to thinking about who's having what, shouldn't we?'

She agreed even though it was the last thing she wanted to do. As she began preparing the meal she wondered if tonight she should talk to him, grab at this opportunity of him being there especially as he was in a good mood. At some point, before it was too late, she had to try to explain that this was not really what she wanted – that somehow circumstances had just seemed to scoop them up and rush them into making idiotic decisions.

They sat in the dining room. Kate had laid the table with special care and had even lit candles. She had cooked his favourite meal – duck breasts in an orange and brandy sauce with mangetout peas, and had asked him to select one of the better wines to go with it.

'I've made a list of the things that I would really rather have – my mother's bureau, the bookcase in my study and that picture of boats we bought in St Ives . . . those sort of things.' He handed her a list of items, neatly typed, across the table.

'I haven't even begun to think about what I want to take.'

'How big's the cottage you've decided on?'

'Minute, compared with this. It's got three bedrooms but most of the bedroom furniture will be too big for it. And the sitting room's half the size of the one here.'

'We'll have to sell what's left over and divide the proceeds,' he said with uncharacteristic reasonableness.

'Tony . . .' she looked at him a wistful expression on her face. 'Look, I don't want any of this. I never meant it to happen.'

'I thought you were bored to tears with me.'

'No, not you. I was bored with myself – an entirely different thing altogether. I know we haven't been getting on, but that's happened in the past and we've weathered it. Why can't we weather it this time?'

'Too much has changed, you especially. I don't think even now you're aware of how much you have altered, Kate. You're not my Kate any more.'

'That's silly, Tony. Of course I am. All right, I've a career now, but that's the only difference. And I've been thinking, with both children off our hands, I shall have so much more time that my writing isn't going to affect you nearly as much as it has done.'

'It's more complicated than that, Kate. It isn't just what has happened to us. It's what has happened to me.' He looked down at the book beside his plate for what seemed an inordinate time. 'There's someone else, Kate. I want a divorce because I want to marry again.'

'Oh, I see,' she said politely, while she felt her skin tauten, her stomach lurch, her mind rejecting such an unlikely idea. 'Well, that's that, then, isn't it?' She smiled bravely.

'Yes, I suppose so,' he replied, picking up his book as he always did between courses.

'I made a lemon mousse, you like that, don't you?' She escaped to the kitchen to fetch the pudding so that he could not see how close to tears she was. But she did not cry: the tears stayed locked inside her. They were not so much for losing him to another woman, but that her marriage had ended. It was marriage she wanted, not necessarily him. It was his picking up his book at such a critical moment in both their lives that told her that.

chapter **eight**

Prior to the meeting of the shareholders of Westall and Trim, when the employees' trust's shareholding was to be voted upon, Gloria in her capacity of acting managing director called all the staff together. Her position as a director was also to be voted on at the same meeting.

They gathered in Julius's office. For some, it was the first time they had been in there since he had died. The room was exactly the same, except the walls were bare where his pictures had once hung. Otherwise it was as if he had just popped out of the room for a moment. It even smelt of him. Gloria had chosen this room on purpose: with such important decisions to be made she wanted to feel his presence, wanted to try to be close to him, and instinctively she felt it was what the others wanted also.

'I'm not sure, but I think the family are likely to announce that they wish to sell the company.' Consternation and cries of 'Shame' followed this information. She held up her hand to silence them. 'Obviously we ourselves are going to have to vote on this issue. Our trustees Peter Holt and Mike Pewter have asked me to discuss it with you. Apparently, the decision whether to vote our shares for selling or not is theirs to make. They feel that it would not be fair for them to act without prior consultation with you. I gather that they would act on a majority consensus.'

'It would be wicked to sell. Mr Westall left us the shares to preserve the company not to let it go to the highest bidder the moment he is dead,' Effie from accounts looked upset and flustered as she spoke.

'I know, Effie, but we have to accept that there is a lot of money at stake. If it is sold, everyone in this room stands to benefit.'

'You sound as if you want it to go,' Ben from design said a little belligerently.

'Gloria hasn't been with us long,' Liz said with an audible sniff. 'It's not the sacred trust to her that it is to some of us.'

Gloria loathed emotional talk such as that and felt it could only cloud the issue. 'We all care, Liz, probably as much as you do. For some of us how the voting goes can affect our future careers,' she said pointedly. Liz was not only on the brink of retirement, but Gloria knew she had been one of the first to complain about the advent of Gloria's new list. 'You've obviously forgotten that my first job was with Westall's. I love this firm. And, in any case, as one of the newer members of staff now, I don't stand to get much money in the event of a sale. As you well know, Mr Westall made sure in the terms he drew up that those with the longest service in the firm benefit the most. I want everyone to know the facts and to know what they might be voting for.'

'What sort of sums are they expecting to get?' Ben asked. 'After all, let's face it, the poor firm hasn't been doing too well recently.'

'Peter says that Crispin is hoping for a ludicrous sum, but that between five and six million pounds is probably more realistic and even that, given the present market and our trading figures, is a long way from being guaranteed. Like everything that's for sale, it would depend on how desperate someone is to buy the name of Westall. So you see why we have to consider the facts. There are thirty-five of us. Those ten of you who have worked here the longest stand to reap a small fortune. Even for the rest it would be a considerable windfall.'

There was a lot of shuffling and whispered conversations between the group.

'Perhaps you would all like a little more time to think? Say you all sleep on it and we'll vote tomorrow.'

'When's the meeting?'

'Tomorrow afternoon.'

'I don't think we need time, Gloria. I think most of us have made up our minds. Maybe we should first vote on whether we should vote,' said Ben, who seemed to have taken on the role of spokesman.

There was a show of hands: the vast majority wanted to vote now. 'Let's get it over with,' someone shouted from the back of the room.

'Fine, then the vote is – should we ask our trustees to vote for or against the sale of this company?' Gloria said with sinking heart. 'I suggest we do a paper vote and that way no one will feel intimidated one way or the other.' She asked Rachel to cut up pieces of paper. 'A simple "yes" or "no" will suffice.'

'Do you honestly think the trustees will act on our decision if they don't have to?' Ben asked in the sort of sceptical voice that implied a lifetime of being overriden by those in authority.

'I think they will. Why else would they request that we discuss it and vote on it ourselves?'

Gloria felt tired. She had spent most of last evening arguing with Peter and Mike about the fate of Westall's. She felt strongly that Julius had made them trustees to ensure that this very situation did not happen. It seemed to her that if they let it go ahead they were no better than Crispin and the others. It was obvious, she argued, which way the employees would vote. Salaries in publishing were not high – Peter and Mike should know better than most since they paid them, she had said rather acidly. The workforce at Westall's was no different from any other – they had mortgages, children to educate and how many could afford to turn their backs on ready money like this?

'Don't you see what you're doing?' she had asked them angrily. 'By letting the staff decide the firm's fate you're ignoring Julius's wishes.'

'Gloria, we hear what you're saying.' Mike had spoken patiently. 'But Julius has put us in an invidious position. He did not make his intentions clear and there is no way we wish to be accused of mishandling the employees' affairs.'

'Legally it could be dodgy, too, Gloria. We could end up by being sued if we're not careful. There's no other way,' Peter had said firmly. Gloria had fallen silent but had looked at Peter amazed. How could they be lovers and have such different views? If she had been a trustee she would have taken the risk for the sake of the firm, she knew she would.

Rachel handed out the papers. Some preferred to go away and vote in private. It was an hour before Rachel had collected all the papers and placed them on Gloria's desk. She began to unfold them and to place them in piles. There were two spoilt papers with 'don't know' written on them. But Julius would

444

have been proud: on the other thirty-three was written 'No'. He obviously knew his employees better than Gloria did.

The following day the shareholders met in the boardroom. There was an atmosphere of animosity as if Gloria and the other two had somehow engineered the whole thing. She was glad that she had the moral support of both Peter and Mike. As they walked in Peter took her hand and squeezed it encouragingly. She smiled gratefully. Everyone took their places around the table at the appointed time. Marge, as largest shareholder and senior family member, took the chair. No one objected.

'Who is Lepanto?' Peter asked pointing to the empty chair beside him.

'Ah, who indeed?' Crispin smiled superciliously, unpleasantly. 'The important thing is, they own two per cent of the shares.'

'So, a decisive interest.' Peter looked thoughtful.

'Exactly,' Crispin smirked.

'In the past, Julius always had their proxy,' Marge explained.

'So who has it now?' Peter asked.

'No one.'

'Were they informed of this meeting?' Peter was being very serious.

'They were,' Crispin said smugly.

'So where are they?'

'They'll be here.' Crispin spoke with confidence. He had written at length to the trust, care of the bank, explaining the reason for this meeting and its importance. He had outlined the amount of money that would be at stake if the company was sold and, using his figures, what Lepanto's share would be. He was confident that no one would miss such a meeting in the circumstances.

'How long do we give them, Crispin?' Marge asked.

'The meeting was convened for three. It is already five past,' Mike said authoritatively.

Crispin looked put out by this even if he did quickly compose his features. 'Should we not wait?' he said.

'I don't think so,' said Mike, in the voice of someone who was used to not being argued with.

'You're not even shareholders yet. Strictly speaking you shouldn't even be here,' Crispin said, more to annoy than anything else. He was not unduly worried that Lepanto, yet again, was not present. It was obvious which way the voting would go. Julius had slipped up, he had not made it a condition of the trust that they should not sell.

'Crispin, don't be tiresome. This is a mere formality, we agreed they might just as well be here,' Jane snapped with irritation at her nephew.

The vote to include the trust was carried by Marge and Jane voting for, their twenty-nine per cent of the votes being larger than Crispin's twenty per cent vote against. Gloria's position as managing director was grudgingly ratified and she could not help but wonder how long she would be able to work with these people who so resented her and her position.

'There is only one piece of business to be discussed and that is the sale of Westall and Trim,' Marge said in a businesslike manner. 'Those for?'

Crispin, Jane and Marge held up their hands.

'Those against?'

Peter raised his hand for the trustees.

'Oh, come on, Peter, you can't do that,' Crispin objected.

'We just have,' Peter smiled pleasantly.

'You've no right to cheat those poor people out of a small fortune,' Jane said crossly.

'We're not cheating anyone out of anything – ' Peter began.

'Julius only asked you to act as trustees because he knew how pig-headed you would be,' Jane added for good measure.

'On the contrary, the workforce had a vote of their own yesterday to decide what they wanted to do. What were the figures, Gloria?'

'Two spoilt papers and thirty-three in favour of the firm continuing.'

'I don't believe this.' Crispin was on his feet, staring angrily at them.

'You better had,' Mike said, laconically.

'Of course, it doesn't depend on us,' Marge said smoothly. 'There is the Lepanto Trust to be considered. They must be contacted again and another meeting arranged.'

'Exactly!' Crispin said with a confidence he was far from feeling and he looked shiftily at his aunt and mother and then down at the papers in front of him.

Soon after the meeting ended, Mike, Peter and Gloria were huddled together in Gloria's office over a bottle of wine.

'We look like the three witches.' Gloria smiled at the other two. Peter put his arm round her; she leant forward to pour the wine, away from his touch.

'I always think best with a drink in my hand,' Mike explained. 'I'm glad you've got a fridge installed, Gloria. I once heard of an author turning down a large offer from a publisher trying to poach her, purely and simply because they did not have a fridge in the MD's office, and she thought they might not be her sort of people and that they might be mean in other ways too.' He bellowed with laughter. 'She came to us instead.'

'Has her liver survived?' Gloria grinned.

'Right, to business,' said Peter, concerned that discussions should begin before Mike suggested another bottle of wine. He was finding it difficult to concentrate on business with Gloria so close. The meeting had been bad enough and he had forced himself to take the initiative when all he wanted to do was to sit and enjoy looking at her. She, as if reading his thoughts, smiled a warm intimate smile, and then looked away. She was maddening, he thought. He coughed, and sat up straight as if telling himself to pull himself together.

'You've never heard of this Lepanto Trust, Gloria?'

'First time today, Peter. I've racked my brains but I'm sure Julius never said a word about it to me.'

Again she smiled at him; she knew she was perplexing him, one minute encouraging him with a look, and then shying away from him. She wished she could explain her confusion to him, but how could she when she barely knew herself?

'It's odd that he didn't. The two per cent the trust owns in shares is critical – he knew that. Why did he not tell you or at least make arrangements that you would be told in the event of his death? Through his lawyer or someone.'

'Or a friend he could trust,' Mike added.

'Oh my God, no!' Gloria exclaimed. 'I wonder. Do you remember his secretary Roz – a rather quiet, shy girl? She went to work for one of your editors, Mike. She was at Crispin's wedding. She told me Julius wanted to see her to discuss something urgently. She asked me if I knew what he wanted, but I didn't. But . . .' She looked aghast.

'No problem then, we'll give her a call,' Peter said moving to pick up the telephone.

Mike put out his hand to stop him. 'No point, Peter. The poor kid was killed in a car crash last week.'

'God, how awful,' Peter said, but then, not knowing Roz well, added, 'There might be something, a note or whatever, she might have left.'

'If she had it with her then we've lost it – the car was a burnt-out shell, Peter,' Gloria explained.

'Oh, Lord, poor girl.' He looked into his wine glass. 'Do you think Crispin and Co. know who Lepanto is?'

'They must do,' Gloria said mournfully. 'And that's it. They'll persuade whoever it is to vote with them. Poor Julius, why on earth did he not make it a condition of the trust not to sell?'

'Because he thought there was no need,' Mike said mournfully. 'He obviously believed the Lepanto people or person wouldn't vote with Crispin. I can't imagine Julius leaving himself uncovered, like this. He must have told Roz, or given her something that would ensure Westall was safe. It's obvious – not in a million years would he have thought that a young woman like Roz would die at the same time as himself.'

'I don't think they do know,' Peter said. 'Didn't you see Crispin at the end of that meeting? He looked really shifty, as if he had promised them he knew when he didn't.'

'Then we have to find out before they do,' Mike announced. 'It's as simple and as hard as that.'

They sat silent, each trying to remember something from the past that might point them in the right direction.

'Who's using Julius's office?' Peter asked.

'No one, no one has liked to. His son and daughter came and took the pictures – or, rather, they supervised the Sotheby's people removing them. And the odd personal things from his desk have gone. Otherwise it's just as he left it.'

'Selling the bloody pictures he loved with him hardly cold in his grave,' Mike moaned lugubriously.

'Then you've got to move into it, Gloria, and quickly.'

'I don't think I could, Peter.' She shuddered. 'It would be disrespectful somehow. That's Julius's office.'

'Nonsense, Peter is right. Julius would expect you to move in there, and with office space at a premium you can't afford to waste it,' Mike said practically. 'And if you're there . . .?' He looked questioningly at Peter.

'Exactly. If you're there, Gloria, you can see how much snooping Crispin is up to. And, what's more, it gives you the opportunity to look yourself.'

'But what am I looking for?'

'Use your imagination, Gloria, for goodness sake,' Mike barked. 'Go through the bookcases, the ledgers, his safe. Look for anything that has anything to do with Lepanto. It must be in that room somewhere.'

'Let's do it now.' Peter stood up.

'Do what? Begin the search?' Gloria looked up at him, and thought how tall and how handsome he was, how enchanting his smile, and then stopped herself. She had vowed not to look at him in that way, not for the time being. For when she did her body reacted, her pulse raced, she wanted him – it could not be, not yet.

'We'll give you a hand.'

Together they began to pack her books and papers into boxes which Gloria found in the postroom. It was a strange sight, she thought, as she watched Peter and Mike laden with cardboard boxes staggering up the stairs. The two most important men in British publishing working as removal men.

Once everything had been moved Peter looked at the books in one of Julius's bookcases and Mike the other. They climbed the library steps – even though Gloria feared for them under Mike's weight – and carefully checked the spine of each book.

'Anything?' she called.

'No sign of the word Lepanto here,' Mike bellowed down from the top of the steps.

'I wonder what it means?' she asked.

'God knows, but we're going to find out,' said Peter emphatically, looking down at her and wishing Mike would go and leave them alone. It was agony being with her and not able to touch her, caress her, love her. But that was wishful thinking on his part, he thought, as he returned to checking the books. Last night had been wonderful, they had been so close. But when he began to kiss her, first she melted in his arms, then suddenly she drew away from him and her wonderful body felt rigid to the touch.

'But why, Gloria?' he had asked, desire frustrated again.

'I don't know . . . it's so difficult to explain.'

And he had done what he did too frequently these days he had slammed into the night, his body aching with longing for her.

'There's nothing here,' he said, descending the library steps.

chapter **nine**

It was Joy's idea that Kate's launch party should be held at Barty's and he was quite happy to oblige for several reasons, not least that he would agree to almost anything that Joy asked. Gloria was overjoyed to accept the invitation on behalf of Westall's. Launch parties were notoriously difficult to arrange and many a publicity manager had sleepless nights over them. So many were held in London that the journalists had become blasé about attending them. They had become so picky that unless an author was a celebrity, it was a notorious book, the publishers came up with an original idea for a party, or loaded them with freebies, they frequently did not bother to show up at all. What was left was a handful of people rattling about a large room, hired to take far more. Instead of a throng, there was the handful of staff from the publisher's, the author, her friends and relations, all gamely wading through the canapés ordered for dozens and pretending they were having a wonderful time and that no one was in the least bit disappointed by the poor press turn-out. Launch parties were held more to impress an author the house particularly wanted to keep than to reap publicity. But with Barty's as the venue, the magic of his name would create an altogether different problem, that of keeping the numbers of the press to within reasonable limits.

Barty and Joy had arrived from the Bahamas two days before the launch of *Winter Interlude*. Crispin's appointment with Barty had been scheduled for the day before the party. Barty had met Crispin only a couple of times and had not been overly impressed. He was cynically suspicious of people who thought themselves as charming as Crispin evidently did. And he was equally suspicious of those with a superiority complex, for life had taught him they rarely had anything to be superior about.

'No doubt you realise why I've asked to see you, Mr

Anderson,' Barty said, once Crispin had been welcomed and seated in front of his awe-inspiring desk.

'Not really, Sir Barty.' Crispin smiled, presuming it would be appreciated. It was not.

'I wish to buy Westall and Trim,' Barty announced baldly.

'Really?' said Crispin, hoping he did not look too surprised. 'I had no idea you were interested in publishing, Sir Barty.' He put on his gently quizzical face but Barty did not answer. 'Of course, it might be for sale and it might not be.'

'Oh, come, Mr Anderson. Have you not already approached every major British publishing firm? Not to mention Schubert's of New York, Tiffel of Munich and my friend Costas?'

'I might have put out the odd feeler.'

'Quite so, and I assume you just happen to have the figures there with you.' Barty indicated the smart Hermès briefcase on the floor beside Crispin.

'Oddly enough, I have.' He smirked and dug deep into the case for the folder.

'I shall wish to be informed of the bids offered by Tudor's, Pewter's, Shotters and whoever else you have begun negotiations with. For such a co-operation on your part I shall, of course, show my appreciation to you personally.' Barty spoke so matter-of-factly that it was several moments before Crispin realised he was being bribed.

'How very kind of you, Sir Barty,' he said smoothly. 'I can assure you I shall not be dealing with either Shotters or Pewter's – I'm not too pleased with Peter's or Mike's attitude,' he said pompously.

'I see,' said Barty, thinking what a stupid man he had sitting in front of him. Did he seriously imagine he was superior in any way to those two? And how unprofessional to allow personal animosity to get in the way of a deal, something Barty would never do. 'Should you approach other firms I wish to be informed who they are.'

'Of course, Sir Barty.'

'You would be well advised to tell me for I shall know, you realise. You act straight with me, I'll do likewise.'

'Surely. I can foresee no difficulties whatsoever.'

'You've solved who Lepanto is then, have you?'

At this, had Crispin been drinking, he would have choked.

'A mere formality, Sir Barty,' he said with an airy wave of the hand, while wondering how the hell Barty knew so much.

'I have to be straight with you, Mr Anderson, and tell you I should not wish you to remain with the firm. It rarely works, a member of the family remaining.'

'I'm desirous of leaving in any case,' Crispin said, with, he congratulated himself, a marked degree of dignity, while deeply insulted that there should be someone who did not wish him to remain.

'And I do not wish Miss Catchpole's life, within the firm, to be made difficult during this period of negotiation. I don't want her leaving in a huff. Know what I mean?'

'You would want Miss Catchpole to stay?' Crispin said, surprised that anyone should want to retain someone as difficult as Gloria, while at the same time wishing to get rid of him. Barty must be the same as his uncle, he thought – silly where beautiful women were concerned.

'I would. Thank you for calling, Mr Anderson. Gervase will see you out.' And Barty returned to the study of his papers, an obvious and insulting form of dismissal. Crispin was furious. We'll see about you, smart-arse, he thought as he stalked, head held high, the long length of Barty's study. It would be hard to turn down Barty's back-hander but, then, with the amount of money he would be getting, what would such a small sum matter? And this interview proved one thing to him: Westall's was a desirable acquisition. There would be no shortage of buyers, so the sky was the limit in money terms. Who needed Silver? He took the opportunity of slamming the door of the study shut with a satisfying bang.

Barty's next appointment was with the barrister dealing with Joy's divorce.

'I want this resolved, and quickly, Burrows.'

'We are up against one of the finest minds in law with Charles Trenchard.'

'Then if you're not up to him find me someone who is,' Barty said sharply. 'I don't see the problem. The man is a known wifebeater – we've got the photos and the doctor's report for that. Who's to say that he won't beat his daughter too?'

'But Mrs Trenchard won't allow us to use that evidence against him. She's worried about the effect of adverse publicity on her daughter.'

'I know, understandable. But maybe it's in her best interests to pretend you wouldn't dream of using it and then do so. She's hardly likely to stand up in court and make a scene, is she? I keep telling her that today's news is forgotten tomorrow.'

'But it would be unethical to act in such an underhand manner.'

'Ethics? Ethics? What's that, all of a sudden? How do you spell it? Don't give me that old cobblers.'

'He is being most objectionable about you, of course,' Burrows said with a discreet cough, not wishing to mention the allegations of homosexuality in actual words, but wanting very much to change the subject.

'Nearly every bishop in the land has given me a glowing reference, what more do you want, the Queen? What about the private detectives, have they come up with anything?'

'Mrs Trenchard finds the use of them distasteful.'

'And I don't. I'm employing them, not her. Get them back on the job – and fast – and don't let her know.'

'Yes, Sir Barty.'

'And next time you come here I would appreciate some good news for the fees I'm paying you.'

'Yes, Sir Barty.' The barrister hastened from the room, relieved to be escaping.

Barty was a different person when dealing with Joy as they sat over their lunch. Gone was the ruthlessness. Instead, he coaxed and cajoled her, trying to persuade her that every weapon in their armoury should be used.

'Look, my darling. I know it's hard for you, but divorce always is unpleasant and you do want your little girl back, don't you?'

'Oh, I do. And I know you're doing your best for me. But, Barty, you don't know Charles as I do. If he thinks we'll use his beating me as evidence, or gets wind of our using private detectives, it will make matters worse. I'd much rather stick with suing him for his adultery.'

'And Hannah?'

'Surely the judge will let me have her? It's nearly always the mother who wins, isn't it?' She said this anxiously: she was worried and finding it difficult to sleep. She was having to face the unpleasant fact that Charles was capable of anything and would use her friendship with Barty against her. She could imagine the slanderous innuendo of which Charles was capable – Barty's lifestyle, the young male aides, the question mark over his sexuality which he had never bothered to respond to, seeming instead to bask in the conjecture.

What would a judge think? If Barty was deemed unsuitable, then what would she do? Which would she choose? Hannah, of course, but what of Barty? She was not *in* love with him, but she loved him.

Those nights when she could not sleep a traitorous thought often slipped into her mind, demanding attention. Was she refusing to co-operate with the barrister because she did not want to alienate Charles too much? Because if she was reasonable with him he might see the error of his ways and return to her? And what sort of fool did that make her even to think it? And if she was thinking it, what was she doing stringing Barty along? Joy felt she was in a vortex of conflicting emotions.

The launch was in full swing. Dozens of journalists had come: an opportunity to see inside Barty's house was not one to let pass by. And they were even more intrigued to find out why this unknown author had such an influential patron. Barty was always good copy. As each one took their turn to talk to Kate, Val stood protectively close, like a nanny, Kate thought. A television producer from the *Goodly Hour* was there and, having talked to Kate, arranged with Val that Kate should be on the show tomorrow evening. Kate felt light-headed with the excitement of it all and everyone's satisfaction with how things were going.

'Hallo, Kate.'

She swung round to find Stewart Dorchester standing behind her.

'Oh, Stewart, how wonderful to see you,' she said excitedly, and standing on tip-toe kissed him full on the lips. She stepped back hand over her mouth, aghast at her behaviour. 'I'm sorry. I shouldn't have done that. I'm tipsy.'

'Be my guest.' He smiled at her and touched his mouth. Kate felt a surge of excitement.

'I wonder . . .' she began.

'Sorry, Stewart, you've done your interview. I need Kate over here.' It was Val taking her by the arm and with smooth, smiling professionalism, sweeping her away to talk to another reporter. When she had finished with him it was to see Stewart in the corner in deep conversation with a very pretty young woman. Stupid me, she thought despondently and turned to the next person demanding her attention.

It did not take the journalists long to find out the connection between Barty and Joy and two and two were put together and fantastic sums reached. The morning papers would be full of her liaison with Barty. This was exactly what Barty had intended to happen. He knew Joy far better than she realised and felt that the more established they were as a couple in the eyes of the media, the harder it would be for her to back away.

Kate, having apparently spoken to everyone who wanted to speak to her, was desperately in need of a cigarette. At the first opportunity, she slipped out to the ladies' for a quick smoke. She thought she would never stop laughing when she found Gloria and Joy already ensconced in there, sitting at the coffee table, a bottle of wine between them.

'We should have a reunion in here every year,' Gloria said, laughing too. 'Drink, Kate?'

'It's the only place in this damn house to get any privacy,' said Joy. 'Cigarette, Kate?' She proffered her case.

'From that remark are we to conclude that all is not well *chez* Silver?' Gloria asked, archly.

'Gracious, I must sound so ungrateful, but I feel almost smothered with attention.'

'Sounds lovely, don't you think, Kate?'

'I felt smothered with it out there but I have to confess I rather liked it.' Kate grinned. 'On the home front I think I could do with some of it at the moment.'

'Kate's getting divorced too, Joy.'

'Kate, I didn't know, I'm sorry. What happened?'

'I don't know to be quite honest, everything has happened so quickly. I thought we might be able to sort something out but Tony's found someone else, so there doesn't seem much point in trying any more. Best bow out with dignity.'

'You really think that?' Joy leant across the low table, clutching her glass of wine and looking earnestly at Kate.

'Yes, I do. What's the point of hanging on in if someone doesn't want you any more? You've got to keep your self-respect, haven't you?'

'Yes, but sometimes it's so hard.' Joy smiled weakly.

'At least you've got Barty,' Gloria said softly.

'Oh, yes, poor Barty. Honestly I don't know what I'm up to. One thing I do know, I'm not being fair to him. I know if I can sort out the custody of Hannah I should stay with him, but I keep thinking of Charles,' Joy said with a sigh.

'Joy, you must be mad,' Gloria said with exasperation.

'I know, I know, but I can't help it.'

'I expect you keep remembering the good times and have forgotten the bad. Bit like having a baby, isn't it? You forget the pain. I'm doing the same. I know it's best for Tony and me to split and then I think, it wasn't that bad . . .'

'Do you honestly?'

'Yes, but I'm fighting it.' Kate laughed. Joy did not join in the laughter.

'God, I'm in such a mess again. I just don't think I can go through with it with Barty and yet I'm too fond of him to tell him.'

'Why did you agree to in the first place?' asked Kate.

'At first I think I genuinely wanted to but I'm beginning to wonder if it was not to get back at Charles. I thought the idea of me as Lady Silver with all this wealth would infuriate him.'

'What, and he'd come running? Oh, Joy, really.' Gloria looked at her in horror.

'Well, not exactly,' Joy lied.

'Quite honestly, Joy, you appear to be on a hiding to nothing. At this rate, you'll lose everything, Barty included, then where will you be?' Kate said quite crisply. 'Barty's no fool, he'll work it out before long – if he hasn't already. I think you have to be straight with him, see what sort of solution you can work out.' Kate helped herself to another glass of wine. 'And what about you, Gloria? We always seem to land up using this loo as a confessional, what's been happening to you?'

'Not a lot.' Gloria pulled a face. 'Not strictly true. Peter Holt's back in my life, only I'm being ultra cautious this time.'

'Why? I thought you were crazy about him.'

'I am, but I'm so scared of getting hurt. All the other times men have been bastards to me I've bounced back but this time, I don't think I would, that's the problem.'

'You mean you're not seeing him?' Kate looked perplexed.

'No, we go out regularly – dinners, the theatre. It's rather nice, really, like old-fashioned dating. He brings me home, we'll have a drink, he kisses me and goes.'

'Sounds lovely.' Joy sighed.

'How long before he gets fed up?' Kate queried, wondering why it was so easy to see other people's problems while one battled through a morass of misunderstanding of one's own. 'What's the point in letting happiness pass you by because you might, just might, get hurt? That's about the silliest thing I've heard in years.'

'Joy, cast your mind back to about a year ago. Remember a quiet little mouse got herself locked in the loo because she was too scared to let us know she was there? Dominated by hubby, wouldn't say boo to a goose. Where's she gone? Who's this?' Gloria laughed at Kate.

'Oh dear, am I being terribly bossy?'

'No, actually you're talking a lot of sense, isn't she, Joy? Problem is, will we listen?' Gloria grinned. 'But what's all this with you and Stewart Dorchester, Kate?'

'I'm sorry?' Kate said almost spilling her wine with surprise.

'You remember Sybil Cavay was going to interview you?'

'Yes.' Kate felt uncomfortable, sure she was about to blush.

'Well, publicity were poleaxed when Stewart telephoned to say he was doing it – he doesn't normally interview popular fiction authors. And he hinted, like a sledge-hammer, that Val need not be there to protect you. Well, I ask you?' Gloria rolled her eyes archly. 'We've been agog ever since.'

'He was very pleasant. It was just an interview, that's all,' Kate said quickly. She would have loved to talk to them of how she was beginning to feel about Stewart, but she didn't. They would probably laugh. After all, wasn't Stewart out there now talking to an attractive young woman? A romantic dreamer, that's all she was.

'But are you enjoying your launch, Kate?' It was Joy asking as if she sensed Kate's discomfort at the question from Gloria.

'It's wonderful, I've had the most marvellous time. It does one a power of good in the sort of situation I'm in to be so spoilt. It's going to help me get through the whole catastrophe, I know it is. That's what you should do, Joy, really throw yourself into your work – don't be dependent on a man, ever again. Whoops, there I go again, bossing. Sorry. I'll change the subject. Can you two help me? I've been invited on the *Goodly*

Hour show, tomorrow. I feel sick with terror already. Why can't books just sell themselves? Why do we have to do things like this?' she complained. 'And what do I wear?' she pleaded.

'Sheena Goodly is very nice, she's only bitchy to know-alls.' Gloria advised. 'And you'll love it once you get going. You forget the cameras are there, you know. You'll be a trouper before you know where you are.'

'You'll be fine, Kate. But the clothes are important. Don't wear anything too fussy and don't wear red – it can "bleed" on the screen and make you look fuzzy. And don't wear white, it's too bright, they'll only make you change. And don't be scared, just be yourself,' Joy added.

chapter **ten**

In the hotel she had been booked into by Westall's, Kate had ordered every newspaper she could think of. They had been delivered with her early-morning tea. She had not wanted breakfast for she knew she would be too nervous to eat a thing all day. She leafed quickly through them. There was plenty of coverage but it was mainly about Joy and Barty – all the photographs were of them – though two papers had mentioned the party was for the launch of her book. She read Stewart Dorchester's feature on her and when she had finished hugged the paper to her. The dear man, it was wonderful. She turned to the book pages. She had only one review.

> From the prestigious publishers of Sir Gerald Walters – Nobel Prize winning author and the greatest living writer in the English language, we now have *Winter Interlude* by Kate Howard, a housewife by profession and a profession she would be wise to return to. The reader's stomach will churn at this tale of, less an interlude, but more an interminable nauseous saga . . .

She could read no more for tears prevented her seeing the writing on the page. She did not feel anger, instead real misery swamped her. Until now, all she had heard was praise and enthusiasm for her work and nothing had prepared her for such a cruel and unthinking review as this. She was about to bury her head under the pillow and try to pretend she had not read it when the telephone rang.

'Yes?' she said hoping her voice would not betray that she was crying.

'Kate? It's Gloria. Have you see the review by James Oaktree?'

'Yes,' was her muffled reply.

'Don't take any notice. He's a spiteful toad – he's got acne, too, which does not help his personality problems.' Gloria laughed and waited for Kate to do so also. When she did not she began again. 'Julius turned down his first novel last year and he's finally having his nasty revenge. It's Westall's he's getting at, not you.'

'It's kind of you to say that, Gloria, but at the moment I'm afraid it doesn't help much.'

'You must listen to me, Kate. He's unimportant, a failed writer venting his spleen.'

'I didn't expect anything quite like this. I mean, I don't pretend to be a literary writer, so why attack me?'

'Believe me, a bad review is better than no reviews. It'll help your sales, honestly. At least the book was reviewed, your genre so rarely is and when it is they usually attack. Invariably either the reviewer's own novel has been rejected or it has earned peanuts. They're jealous of the sales and the advances writers like you get. Come on, cheer up. Get your hair done, it's a big night tonight.'

'Can you come?'

'Kate, I'd love to, and I will if I can, but I'm snowed under here. Val will be with you. If I don't see you, good luck.'

Kate forced herself to reread the review. It did not make her feel better but she vowed one thing: she would never read another review ever again.

Gloria was surrounded by papers and ledgers. Elephant liked this game and was jumping from one pile of papers to another like stepping stones. She sat on the floor in Julius's office and scratched her head. Nowhere was there a reference to the Lepanto Trust. She also had a shrewd idea that Crispin had been snooping about in here last night when she had been at the party. She had made a point of locking the door but then common sense told her that someone like Crispin was sure to have had a key made, probably long ago. The papers felt as if they had been touched by someone. It was not evidence, it was a feeling she had that he had been in here, and that was not proof enough to accuse him. But, then, she supposed, he had as much right to be going through everything as she had – and, as a member of the family, more so. The safe was still locked but that would not have helped him either, there was nothing in there.

Where now? She picked up her notepad and began to make a list. *1. Books – check backlists of publications.* She sucked her pencil. Everyone had always presumed that Julius had a copy of every book he had ever published in here in the large mahogany bookcases, but maybe he did not. 2. *List books in bookcase*. They had better be put in alphabetical order, too, for simplicity – she would get Rachel to do that and to check off against the lists of books published. But how far was she supposed to go back? The year when Julius took control would seem logical. She'd have to find that out from someone who had worked here the longest. 3. *Ask Mrs Westall if she could check Julius's library at home?????* She stabbed at the paper as she added the row of question marks. That was a hope! Why should Mrs Westall help what she would see as the opposition? 4. *Have the royalty ledgers sent up from accounts*. She had already spoken to Effie about payments to the trust.

'I've already told Crispin, dividends were paid to the bank. I know nothing else about Lepanto,' she had snapped. 'I've work to do, if you don't mind.'

Effie was normally testy, people in accounts often were. They were always being harassed by someone. It was they who fielded the endless queries from paranoid authors convinced they were being cheated on their royalty statements, and dealt with belligerent agents when advances were a day late. It was not a happy department, but Effie was edgy even by accounts department standards. Gloria felt that she was not telling her everything but, on the other hand, that could have been because, Gloria sensed, the woman did not like her. She would ask for the royalty statements when Effie had gone to lunch – her assistant was a lot more helpful. After that she really had no idea which way she was going to turn.

In his office at Shotters Peter sat doodling at his desk. He spent a lot of time doing that these days. As more and more key men were being shipped over from New York he was finding less and less to do. Nothing had been said, or even hinted, that Costas wanted him out but the signs were becoming unmistakable. He supposed they would prefer him to resign out of boredom or a fit of pique but he had no intention of doing any such thing. If he did so, under the terms of his contract, he could end up paying to leave the firm he had created. They would have to terminate his contract and pay him compensation. It was a giant cat-and-mouse game, really – and Peter was not sure if he was the cat or the mouse.

He was waiting for the arrival of Drew Wincanton III, the head of Costas's American publishing arm, whom he had met once on a trip to New York. He did not much like the man. It had been an odd meeting: at the time, Peter had felt he was not supposed to like him, as if Wincanton was going out of his way to be antagonistic. Perhaps, he wondered now, the animosity had been deliberately created because Wincanton was likely to be his replacement here, and part and parcel of the plan to get him to resign. Well, he smiled to himself, they were going to have to wait.

He had had his daily row with Hilary. She telephoned most mornings at about eleven. He expected the calls now and felt he would be quite lost without them. This morning's had been typical – a list of bills that had arrived, and which she considered were his responsibility and he did not. There was usually a tiff about the ownership of something: today's had been about a painting which she said had been given to her as a wedding present when he could distinctly remember writing the cheque for it. He would probably let her have it in the end, but he had no intention of making it easy for her – not that he cared, just the principle of the thing.

He looked at the list of thoughts he had written about Lepanto. Once he had finished with Wincanton he would pop over to Westall's and use the mystery of Lepanto as an excuse. Anything to see Gloria again.

He sighed. He did not know where he was with her. She seemed to enjoy being with him, certainly she never turned down an invitation, and they had fun together. But when he took her home, convinced each time that this was it, that she would ask him to stay, she seemed to shy away from him like a frightened animal. He felt as perplexed as an adolescent boy having to learn how to deal with girls and with no experience to fall back on. It was ridiculous. The odd thing was that he had not wanted to go out with anyone else. He had had no sex for weeks now, but he did not want to sleep with just anyone, only Gloria. As each day passed, frustrated as he was, he was more and more convinced that he was in love. He wondered if he should tell her, or was that what she was frightened of – total commitment? If he blurted it out, would she run a mile?

And if he didn't, would she continue to keep him at arm's length? God, it was all so complicated, he thought.

Ten minutes later he was angry and his voice was raised.

'No, Drew, I won't do that and that's flat.'

'I'm afraid you're going to have to, buddy.'

'I wish you would not call me your buddy when I'm not. I will not con my authors in this way and that's an end to it. Go back and tell your master that.'

'Look, Peter, Costas is fully aware that you would not like this proposal and he has given me authorisation to go over your head. It's been decided. As our authors reach the end of their seven-year contracts with other paperback houses, the licences will not be renewed. They will revert to us and those books will be reissued by Sabre. I don't see what you're getting so het up about. They're our authors, it's just good business sense.'

'It's lousy publishing ethics. Those paperback houses invested heavily in those authors and renewal has always been automatic. Losing their biggest earners in this way could ruin them.'

'Exactly, and Sabre benefits. Good heavens, man, you set Sabre up, don't you want it to succeed?'

'Of course, but honourably. This stinks. Why you're not even consulting with the authors. You're just going to face them with it, *fait accompli*. They're not going to like this.'

'They won't have any choice, if you read their contracts.'

'Christ! I just don't believe this is happening.'

'You'd better believe.'

'I won't do it.'

'Then there's no alternative.'

'I'm not resigning.'

'We're not asking you to. If you could be out of here within the hour? Thank you, Peter.' As Drew stood up to leave, he slapped an envelope on the desk. 'Severance of your contract, cheque inside. Oh, and by the way, Costas was not too happy that you had not opened negotiations for Westall and Trim when you were one of the first approached.'

'It's not even for sale yet.'

'It's only a matter of time but we gather you were most unpleasant to the firm's principal – we expect better from our executive management than that, Peter.'

'Crispin – the principal! That'll be the day.' Peter laughed.

'Anyhow, it's all on line now, I've seen to that. So, Peter, I don't think there's anything else. Have a nice day.'

The door slammed shut and Peter sat at his desk for a moment as if poleaxed. Then he was suddenly galvanised into action. He buzzed for Em.

'I've just had the chop, Em.'

'Peter, no!' Em's hand flew to her mouth, her eyes filled with tears. 'Not you, you *are* Shotters.'

'Don't worry, Em. Do you know it's odd but I'm quite pleased, really. I've not been happy since I sold up. I want to issue a press statement. I'll dictate that to you and then if you could get hold of the MDs of all these paperback houses, I need to speak to them.'

The press release, unlike the usual '. . . parting by mutual and amicable agreement . . .' lies, told the truth. The morning papers would be full of Costas's plan. Authors and their agents would be on the rampage. Hopefully one of the richer ones would take up the cudgels for the rest. The managing directors of the paperback houses he contacted were duly grateful and within five minutes of his calls meetings were set up and lawyers were being consulted.

He was being underhand. He did not care, he felt no loyalty to this Shotters. It had long ceased to be the firm he had started. It was a money factory now and the authors expendable workhorses. To Peter this was not publishing.

An hour later, with help from his staff most of whom were in tears, he had packed the contents of his desk, the bookcases were emptied, his paintings wrapped in brown paper, his ornaments in boxes and his shower room stripped. The security men were carrying everything down to the basement where a van, hurriedly summoned, was waiting for them. Peter had thought of calling a meeting of heads of department and then decided not to bother. Most of his old staff were long gone, none of those remaining had been with him initially. He felt sad for Shotters and what he had allowed to happen to it but he did not feel sorry for himself.

Once out on the street he hailed a cab and set off for Westall and Trim. He tapped on the door to Julius's office.

'Any jobs going?' He grinned as he poked his head round to see Gloria sitting on the floor, surrounded by papers. Gloria's heart lurched as it always did when she saw him.

465

'Peter, what a lovely surprise. What do you mean?'

'I've been sacked.'

'No! Oh, my poor darling.'

'Yes, and for a devious reason.' But he was smiling, she had called him darling. 'They're reverting the paperback licences of our bestselling authors and reprinting them with Sabre,' he said, thinking what wonderful eyes she had.

'They're not! Hell, what will that mean to publishing?' she asked, noting, as usual, how elegantly he moved across the room to her.

'There won't be a paperback house that will feel safe to invest in an author hardbacked by a publisher with its own paperback arm, that's for sure. Paperbacks are going to have to buy into hardback houses or be bought by one and offer an author the whole package.'

Certainly her mouth was one of the sexiest he had ever seen, he thought. God, how he'd love to kiss her now, this minute.

'But that way there would be fewer publishing houses acquiring books. And authors scrabbling around for those few left – it's hard enough for first-time writers now. Who will pick them up then?' she said, wishing he would kiss her instead of talking business. He couldn't care for her as she did him otherwise he would, surely?

'It'll take time to shake down. But on the way over here, I was thinking in the end it might be for the good – everyone should be safer in the long run, publishers and authors alike. It's just that I think the existing contracts should stand. Authors feel intense loyalty to their paperback houses, more so, often, than to the hardback publisher. But that's Costas for you.' He watched her as she stood up, admiring her figure and her long shapely legs. As always she was wearing the sheer black stockings which made them even more stunning.

'What will you do?'

'Take a holiday.' He grinned. 'Fancy coming?' he joked but longed for her to agree.

'I can't think of anything nicer. But I've got to sort out Lepanto first if I'm to keep my job,' she said regretfully. How wonderful, she thought, to go away, just the two of them. Then she wouldn't be able to resist – but perhaps that was a good reason not to go. In any case, he had probably asked her as a joke.

'Have you come up with anything?' he asked politely. What had he expected? Of course she would refuse.

'I think I have, as a matter of fact – not that it gets us any further on, just deepens the mystery.' Gloria stood up straight, she was being silly letting her mind wander in this way. She must concentrate. It was Lepanto he had come about, not her. 'Effie seemed a bit shifty to me when I asked her about payments to the trust. While she was out at lunch I got the royalty statements going back fifteen years. And look,' she hauled a ledger towards her. 'See, here, each year there's a payment to Lepanto and it goes up a little each time. Here, you see, when accounts went over to computers, it's still there. But it just says the name of the trust, there's no book title mentioned as there usually is. Well, what book earns royalties for that number of years, and further back still if we get the relevant ledgers? I mean, someone like Gerald Walters does, but then we would know which book it was, there would always be copies around, we'd have them in the warehouse. It's a mystery.'

'Have you looked in the bank paying-in books, in the record of payments ledgers? Is there anything in them?'

'What would they tell us?'

'I don't know, but perhaps there's a discrepancy or something. It would be worth checking them.'

Gloria crossed to her desk and buzzed Rachel to go to accounts and ask Effie for the relevant ledgers for the past fifteen years. 'I can't go myself.' She giggled. 'Effie frightens me – you know, one of those slightly shrewish ladies who lie about their age and always think you're up to something sexually exciting in the next room.'

'Would that we were,' said Peter with feeling. Gloria looked up. Rachel quickly arrived with the pile of ledgers.

'I don't know what she's got to hide but Effie didn't want me to have these and she's very huffy.'

Gloria and Peter looked at each other, eyebrows raised.

'I'll take these and you those. The dates are easy enough, March and September are normal time for royalty payments. Make us some tea, Rachel, there's an angel.' Gloria sat back on the floor where it was easier to spread out the ledgers. There was silence for five minutes while both went through them. Elephant sat quietly, watching.

'Peter?' She looked up at him.

'I think I might have found the same thing. Here, in the paying-out book, a payment to Lepanto, and then in the bank paying-in book, the same date always, a payment to Westall and Trim from Julius Westall.'

'For the same amount.'

'Every time.'

'So what was he playing at?'

'God and Effie apparently know. Get her up here, Gloria, scared of her or not.'

A few minutes later an anguished-looking Effie had joined them.

'Perhaps you know what this is all about, Effie?' Gloria smiled encouragingly at her.

'Mr Julius wasn't doing anything wrong,' Effie said defensively, folding her arms over her small breasts.

'Of course he wasn't, we know that, but we're trying to solve the puzzle. It is for everyone's good, Effie, honestly.'

'Each year, as you see, he had me send out a royalty statement and cheque to the Lepanto Trust, it went straight to the bank. Then Mr Julius gave me a cheque for the same amount written on his personal account, which I banked in the company's account.'

'Do you know why he was doing this, Effie?'

'No. He never said and I never asked. I didn't think it was my place.'

'Of course not, Effie. But perhaps you had a theory?' Peter smiled at her kindly.

'Well, it's just my idea, I've no proof of course, but Mr Julius was such a kind man I always presumed it was to an author who didn't have much money.'

'But if that was the case why pretend there were royalties due?' Gloria asked.

Effie looked at her as if she was half-witted. 'It was obviously someone who would not dream of accepting charity. This way Mr Julius could help and yet the person would think that they had earned the money.'

'And you've no idea who it could be?'

'No. The system was already in operation when I came twenty-seven years ago. Mind you . . .' she paused and took a small handkerchief from an inside pocket, and dabbed at her eyes as if she was stopping any tears that might have the temerity to fall. 'I've often thought it must be a lady friend of Mr Julius. He would look after someone he had cared for, don't you think?' And she trumpeted into the handkerchief and made rapid excuses that she had work to do.

Over their tea Peter and Gloria discussed how far they had got, which, they both agreed, was not very far. They had an author, probably female, probably an ex-mistress, who had written a book published by Westall's which had disappeared, for they had no title. And why should that book not be here when every other book was? Because Julius did not want anyone to know who the author was, because he or she had the controlling shares. They had gone full circle. But at least the detective work had given them a brief respite from their longing for each other.

'Will you have dinner with me tonight? I think we've done enough here for one day.'

Gloria looked at her watch. 'I'd love to but I really should go to the television studios. Poor Kate's doing her first show and she's terrified. I said I would if I could.'

'Can I come?'

'Please, I'd love you to.' Gloria's heart lifted with relief. Because of the stupid way she was behaving she would not be surprised if he stopped asking her out. She packed the ledgers into one neat pile, switched off the light and they left the office.

Gloria should really have locked the relevant documents in the safe for within an hour of her leaving Crispin had let himself into the room. He was a little slower than they had been but by the end of the evening he had reached much the same conclusion.

'Bet it was one of his bits of crumpet,' he said to himself as he restacked the ledgers in the same order in which Gloria had left them.

chapter **eleven**

'I'm going to be sick.

'No, you're not, it's just your imagination.'

'You want to bet?' A frightened Kate looked up at Val. 'I can't do it, Val. I'm sorry if I'm letting everyone down but I can't go through with it and that's that.'

'Everyone feels like that first time, you'll be fine.'

'Have you been on television?'

'Well, no –'

'Then you don't know what the bloody hell you're talking about,' Kate said, fear making her irritable.

'Would you like a drink? Would that help?' Val asked, unperturbed – this was par for the course with most authors racked with nerves.

'Gin and tonic, a big one.'

There was a tap on the dressing-room door and Gloria appeared. She had left Peter outside, certain that too many people would only make Kate more nervous.

'Hello, how are you?'

'She's fine, aren't you, Kate?' Val said in the over-bright manner of a nurse in the presence of a terminally ill patient. 'Situation normal,' she whispered in an aside to Gloria.

'What are you two whispering about? What are you saying about me?' Kate asked in the rising tones of paranoia.

'I was just asking Gloria if she'd like a drink, that's all.'

The door closed behind Val.

'She's like a broody hen, she's making me nervous,' Kate complained.

'Shall I tell her to go away, then?'

'Oh no, we can't do that, I don't want to offend her. Oh, Gloria, I feel dreadful. What's my hair look like? It's a mess, isn't it? It cost me a small fortune and then they made it look dreadful.' Kate appeared to be unable to stop talking.

'It looks very pretty, honestly. Why would I lie to you?'

Gloria said when Kate looked at her disbelievingly. She hated these stints in television studios holding the hands of nervous authors. She felt for them – it was a wretched ordeal which none of them ever seemed to get used to. It always reminded her of having to wait in hospitals with relatives whose loved ones were undergoing brain surgery – not that she ever had, but this is what she imagined it must be like. 'Have you been to Make-up yet?'

'Oh, my God! If you can't tell I have, then they must have made an awful job of it.' Kate twisted round and anxiously scrutinised her face in the mirror.

'On the contrary, it shows what an excellent job they've done.' Gloria tried to keep any hint of amusement out of her voice. 'Is that your dress?' She nodded at a particularly pretty peach-coloured two-piece hanging up. 'Lovely colour.'

'It was the nearest I could get to red – red's my lucky colour you see. But I've got a red petticoat instead.' Kate opened the towelling robe she was sitting in to show Gloria. 'Oh, Gloria, what the hell am I doing here?' Kate sighed audibly. 'I wish I could put the clock back. Last October I was married, a housewife, normal. Look at me now, a wreck. I don't want to be a success, I want to go back to my mundane life, I really do. You know what's happening? God's punishing me for being bored and discontented with my life, that's why I'm here. I wish I could go home!'

'You're here, my love, because inside you there is a great hunger to succeed. That's what you have and it's like gold dust. That's the difference between you and thousands of other women who want to write and don't make it. You've worked so hard to be here, now enjoy it. You've earned it.'

'Can I come in?' Joy's head appeared around the door. 'How're you feeling, Kate?'

'If anyone else asks me that I'll scream!' Kate said, sounding as if she was verging on hysterics.

'Sorry. Hallo, Val, what have you got there? I do hope that's not for Kate, it wouldn't be wise.'

'It won't hurt, Joy. It's just what Kate needs, isn't it?' Gloria said soothingly.

Yet another knock on the door and Sheena Goodly appeared.

'Hallo, Kate, just popped in to see how you are – feeling terrified no doubt. Don't worry, you'll forget the cameras once

471

we start. Just one thing, don't look directly into them, will you? Is that what you're wearing? Perfect.'

Sheena had on twice the amount of make-up that Kate had, and looked half the size she normally appeared on Kate's television screen at home. Did this mean Kate was going to look insipid and as large as a house? Sheena smiled brightly at her, but it was the professional smile of a performer, an instant let's-be-best-friends smile that, try as she might, Kate could not respond to.

'Who else have you got on?' Gloria asked.

'Barry Filmour – he's divine. Do you know him, Kate? I'll talk to him for a few minutes and then I've got that boring old trout Dame Fiona Martingale rabbiting on about abortions – not that I should think any man ever got close enough to her to impregnate her in the first place. Then last of all it's Kate with Sebastian Trumpington, and that'll be a wow!' Sheena spoke with exaggerated enthusiasm, just like Kate's games mistress had when she was trying to convince the hockey team they could win, thought Kate. If it was supposed to fire her up, then Sheena was failing, just as the games teacher had.

'Sebastian who? Who's he?' Kate demanded.

'He's a literary editor with rather strong views about women's fiction.'

'I can't talk about women's fiction. I'm not an expert. I've only written one book. I don't even have any views on the subject.' Kate's voice was rising in panic.

'Don't worry, Kate, I have. I'll lead you and you'll be surprised what opinions you do have when it comes to it. There,' she looked up at the intercom as it crackled and her name was called, 'I must fly. See you in approximately twenty minutes, Kate. Good luck.'

The small dressing room was overcrowded and becoming uncomfortably hot. Kate began to fantasise about locking herself in the lavatory, pretending she was stuck, and by the time they got her out the programme would be over.

When a young man with earphones and a clipboard eventually came to collect her she could vaguely remember everyone kissing her and then she was racing along endless corridors with anonymous doors, trying to keep up with the floor manager, as he turned out to be, in his Nike trainers, who said nothing to her except to repeat that she was not to look directly at the cameras. The senior floor manager said the same as she arrived at the side of the set and repeated it as he gently pushed her forward. Her legs felt leaden as she began to walk.

The lighting on the set was blinding. The roar of welcome from the audience as she was announced was out of all proportion. Why should they be cheering her when none of them could possibly know who she was?

When Sheena spoke to her she was amazed that she answered and sound emerged. But how the hell was she supposed to ignore the cameras with their large black blank eyes which seemed to be nosing everywhere. She felt her answers were dull, sensed the audience becoming restless and was not surprised that Sheena was concentrating on her fellow guest, the tall and rather languid Sebastian Trumpington. And then luck was with her.

'One of the scandals of modern-day publishing is the effort spent, ludicrous advances paid and paper wasted on popular and commercial fiction – the publishers have very many expressions to describe it.' Sebastian was speaking, slowly, pontificatingly. 'I have a better word for it. Now what was it?' Sebastian paused looking up at the lights overhead in an exaggerated play of searching for the lost word. 'To publish schlock, that's it. Schlock pure and simple, there's no defence for it.'

'I beg your pardon?' Kate suddenly sat up straight.

'Rubbish pandering to the common denominator, that's what this kind of fiction is. Like the worst television, like the worst of the gutter press. From my experience one cannot even say there is good and bad schlock, there isn't, it's all rubbish.'

'And who are you to say that?' Kate demanded.

'Because I've read some of it. I don't read it on a regular basis. I have too great a respect for my brain to do that. But what I have read has made me positively nauseous.'

'Just because you don't like it doesn't necessarily make it rubbish. Thousands would disagree with you. Look at the number of people who buy popular fiction.'

'That's no excuse for it.'

'That's every excuse for it. If people want to read these books then good luck to them. They entertain, they allow people to relax and escape the harsh realities of life. Who are you to be saying that they shouldn't?' Kate leant forward, audience, lights, cameras, nerves all forgotten.

'They would be better off spending their time reading Jane Austen, Proust.'

'Proust!' The word exploded from Kate like a gun retort. 'Are you joking? It might be hard for you but try to imagine – you've got two kids under five, a husband who drinks and gambles, you're trapped in your house all day, the debt collector's due and you're lonely, scared and with no hope. Or you're a middle-class woman whose husband bores her and she him; their life will go on in the same rut as it has for years and she knows it. And you're telling me they'll be made happier reading Proust. Oh really, Mr Trumpington. You're probably one of those people who sneer at Tchaikovsky just because everyone can hum the *Nutcracker*. People like you make me sick. You're nothing but a pseud, Mr Trumpington.'

The audience went wild. Sheena glowed. Kate beamed with a sense of triumph and Mr Trumpington was silent. By sheer chance Kate had the last word. The closing music began, the titles rolled, Sheena made her ending remarks, they were off the air. Then perfect strangers bounded up to Kate, kissing her, telling her how good she had been. 'You're a star!' they all exclaimed.

'You were a star!' Gloria hugged her as she came off the set.

'I was very rude.'

'He deserved it. How do you feel?'

'Wonderful. I could climb Mount Everest right now, run a marathon, write a dozen books.'

'You're on an adrenalin high. Come on, we're all going out to dinner. You joining us, Joy?'

'If you don't mind, Kate, I wanted to have a long talk with Barty tonight and it's one of the few evenings he's free.'

'Of course I don't mind. Do you know what you're going to say to him?' Kate asked.

'No.' Joy laughed nervously. 'But I've been thinking about what you said, I've got to be straight with him.'

In the restaurant, Kate thought she had never felt so elated in her life. 'What did you say was happening to me – an adrenalin high? This must be how you feel on speed – I think I could learn to like it.' Kate laughed loudly, bubbling with excitement. Throughout the meal she could not sit still; she drank too much too quickly and stayed sober, and she felt she wanted to talk and talk and never stop. If only one other person was here. Every time there was a flurry of new arrivals in the restaurant she looked up hoping one would be Stewart.

Joy felt nervous as she waited for Barty to return from a reception he had been to at the Swedish Embassy. It was all very well saying she was going to be straight with him, but where and how to start were occupying her mind.

'You look very pretty.' He kissed her cheek when he joined her in the little sitting room they used when they were alone. 'How was Kate? I hope Gervase videoed it for me.'

'She was wonderful, a natural, everyone said so.' She lit a cigarette, aware her fingers were trembling. 'I wondered if I could have a word with you before dinner, Barty?'

''Course you can.' He sat down beside her on the sofa. 'Why are you looking so serious?'

'I want to be honest with you, Barty. I don't think I can go ahead with our plan to get married.' She sat stiffly, not looking at him, hating herself for saying it and knowing she loved him too much not to.

'And why not?' he asked calmly.

'Because although I love you as a friend, I don't think I'm in love with you, and so it would not be right.'

'I'm fully aware of that. It's good enough for me.'

'But it's more complex than that Barty. What if the courts object to you as stepfather to Hannah? How on earth can I choose between you?'

'You wouldn't have to. We'll win her back.'

'But you can't be sure of that.' Joy sighed and looked intently at her hands. There was nothing for it, she was going to have to tell him everything. 'It's like this, Barty. I should hate Charles – but I don't. And – I'm loath to admit this – there are times I find myself wondering if we can't get back together again.' There, she had said it. She did not look at him but continued the study of her hands, twisting the wonderful ring that Barty had given her and which, until she was free, was on her right hand.

'I think I can wear that.'

'I'm sorry?' Joy asked, not sure if she had heard correctly.

'I'm not totally stupid, Joy.' He took her hand in his. 'There's always been the risk that you think you're still in love with Charles. But note I said "think". What you are in love with is the few good times you had with him – memories can be a sod of a thing. You're beginning to forget the bad times – but I won't forget. Never.'

'That's strange. That's what Kate said.'

'Kate's a wise woman. I'll be straight with you, Joy. I think that perhaps you agreed to think about marrying me so quickly in the hope that it might bring him to heel?' He glanced quizzically at her, a gentle smile on his round, bland face. Joy felt herself begin to blush. 'But he didn't come to heel, did he, Joy? And that's the point. I'm willing to gamble he won't in the future either. And also that the feelings you have for him are because you are confused and that they will fade too. And I love you, nothing has altered that. I told you what I could and could not give you, the offer remains.'

'But, Barty, I'm being unfair to you. I've been so hypocritical.'

'How come? It can't have been easy to say what you just have to me. I respect your honesty. I might be wrong, you might go back to him. If so, don't worry about me – I'd be sad but I'd recover. I can't say fairer than that now, can I?'

'Barty, I don't deserve you.'

'Don't be silly,' Barty smiled bashfully but resolved to get on to the barrister. This problem had to be resolved quickly.

Gloria lay in bed unable to sleep. It had been a lovely evening. Kate had been such fun, bubbling with excitement and sheer joy. She had not taken her car to the studio so Peter drove her home. She had felt so relaxed with him tonight, had felt so happy and, for once, sure of him. She had decided that tonight she would ask him to stay.

When they had arrived back at her house he had leant across to her and kissed her on the cheek.

'You look tired, Gloria, it's been a long day. No need to feel you have to be polite and ask me in for a drink. I'm ready for bed myself.'

'Thank you, Peter,' she had said, feeling as if a bucket of cold water had been poured over her. 'Thanks for the lift,' she had added politely.

Now she lay alone when he should have been with her. Just

her and Elephant snoring gently in his basket at the end of her bed. She feared she might have been too cautious. She felt he had become bored with her and her stupidity.

Kate lay wide-eyed in the dark in her hotel room and thought she had never felt more lonely. She had experienced two of the most wonderful days of her life. She had been fêted and fussed and now, suddenly, she felt lower than she could ever remember. She looked at the empty pair of pillows beside her and felt sad. She wanted the success, the acclaim, but she also wanted to be loved. She did not want to be alone. She was afraid. And when she closed her eyes it was the image of Stewart, large and shambling, with his kind smile, that filled her mind.

chapter **twelve**

Kate opened the door of her house and the minute she entered it she knew that something was different. She stood for a moment in the hall and told herself not to be so stupid. She listened but all she heard was the rumble of the central-heating boiler, the tick of the clock in the hall, the swish of tyre wheels on the damp road outside. All normal sounds. Why, then, was she imagining this silence to be leaden with something else, with anger, disruption?

She looked in the drawing room but everything was as she had left it. She pushed open the kitchen door and the cat mewed to her in welcome while the Aga burbled sibilantly. She crossed the room, pulled the kettle on to the hob and leant against the bar of the cooker. She felt depressed and yet last night she had been flying. In the run-up to her launch the telephone had never stopped ringing but this morning, at her hotel, it had not rung once. She had telephoned Gloria, who was not in the office, and spoken to Val who was polite but sounded distracted. Reason told her that they had moved on to the next book to be published, but it was hard to accept. For so long it was as if only her book existed for them too. She felt as if she was yesterday's news. Nothing was happening and she felt bereft.

She had been away for nearly a week and a pile of mail awaited her, mostly dull bills but among them, excitingly, was a note from Stewart Dorchester with an invitation to the *Daily News* best book of the year award, at the Café Royal, no less. It was in a couple of days, no time to write – she would telephone him to let him know she would love to go. It was also an excuse to hear his voice again.

She made her mug of coffee and walked to the pine table. On its surface was a copy of the *Graintry Echo* opened at a page where her face loomed up at her. They had used a photograph of her in this very kitchen standing by her Aga. She smiled, at least the photograph was a good one. Kate sat down and looked for the article.

Writing Ruins Local Author's Marriage

The words did not jump out at her, they careered from the page. There it all was, her confidential talk with Dee. She had written of Tony's disinterest, was he jealous? And a long section on men's inability to cope with their women's success. She covered her face with her hands. Even the menopause was mentioned . . . 'Oh, God . . .' she groaned. No wonder she had sensed anger in the air. What must Tony have thought? The telephone made her jump. She let it ring, not wishing to answer it, not wanting to talk to anyone, she felt so humiliated. It stopped. Five minutes later it rang again. This time she made herself get up to answer it.

'So you're back?' Tony greeted her.

'Tony, I've just seen the newspaper. I'm sorry, it wasn't like that . . . the woman has written things wrongly. It's not fair – '

'It certainly isn't fair, making me a laughing stock in my own town. How dare you discuss our problems with a total stranger?'

'But I didn't realise that I was.'

'Don't give me that crap, Kate. I haven't the patience to discuss anything with you any more. I've moved my stuff out, I've rented a cottage for a month until the house sale is finalised. By the way, saw you on television, nice to see you ripping into some other poor sod for a change.'

The line went dead. She walked slowly back to the table and her now tepid coffee. Was that how he saw her, a raving termagant? Well, one thing had come out of the whole fiasco: she had learnt a salutary lesson that nothing was off the record with certain elements of the press.

Still, she thought, there were other members of the press. She telephoned Stewart and while she waited for the connection to be made realised she had butterflies in her stomach. If she had any doubts about anything, that call from Tony had changed her mind.

'Stewart? Thanks for your note. I'd love to come.'

'Oh, great. I missed you at Barty's the other night. I looked for you but I presumed you had left early.'

'No,' she said, not liking to tell him she had been in the loo with Gloria and Joy.

'Never mind, we can make up for it at the awards. I'll leave your invitation at the desk for you. I might be a bit late, I've an interview with the Home Secretary in the morning.'

'I see,' she said, impressed. When she finally rang off she felt ridiculously excited, like a young girl, and immediately began to plan what to wear. She was putting the kettle back on when the front-door bell rang. What now? she thought, as she went to answer it.

'Doug? Good gracious, what a surprise!' She forced herself to sound welcoming, though the thought of entertaining Pam's husband right now did not appeal. But she had not seen him for months and it would be churlish not to invite him in.

'Saw you on the telly last night, Kate. You were a smash.'

'Thanks. Coffee? I've just put the kettle on.' She led the way into the kitchen.

'I'm sorry to bother you, Kate, you must be a busy woman these days – what with the book and everything. But I had to talk to someone or I thought I'd go mad.'

'Of course, what on earth's the matter? Sit down, you don't look well,' she said, for in the better light of the kitchen she saw he looked grey with fatigue.

'You don't know, do you?'

'Know what?'

'Pam, she's done a bunk . . .'

'Pam? Dear God, Doug, I'm sorry. I'd no idea, I haven't seen her in weeks, why we hardly even talk on the telephone these days. When did she go, where's she gone?' She had sat down, forgetting the coffee in her concern for the man.

'With your Tony. She's done a bunk with your husband.'

The familiar walls of her kitchen appeared to move inward as if made of rubber. She was aware that Doug was still talking and forced herself to listen.

'She told me about it last week – give her her due, she was ashamed and all. And then I got home from work last night and she'd gone.'

'You're not joking, are you?' She knew she was staring at him with amazement.

'No, sorry, I'm not.'

'He told me the other day he had met someone else, but, not

in a million years . . .' Her voice trailed off as her brain tried to assimilate this information.

'It's been going on for over a year.'

'Over a year? Surely not.'

'Oh yes, a year ago last August apparently. She didn't want to tell me but I made her.'

'But how?'

'Remember Pam went to visit her sister in Harrogate? She'd flown back from Australia for a holiday . . .'

'Yes, yes, and Tony was at a conference on . . .' she laughed, a mirthless sound. 'Rather apt actually, a conference on children in divorce, if I remember.'

'Right. Well, they met, had a drink and the rest is history, as they say.' He smiled wanly. 'I tried to give her everything she wanted but it wasn't enough. It's my fault, but one thing and another, I wasn't much cop at, well, you know, sex,' he said with discomfort.

This time when Kate laughed it was with genuine amusement. Doug, in his misery, looked at her perplexed.

'I'm sorry, Doug, I know it's not really funny. But you see, poor Pam – she won't get much joy there either. Tony's useless in bed.'

'That's not what she said, made him sound like the stud of the century,' he said mournfully.

'She didn't? Oh, that was cruel of her. And it can't be true, not unless he's had a dose of hormones or something. Bloody hell, Doug, this is lousy, isn't it? One's marriage breaking up is bad enough but the deception?' She shook her head, not able to take in fully all the implications of this news. 'What about her writing?'

'She's given that up, said Tony didn't want her to do it. She said his happiness was more important to her.'

'That rings true,' she said with feeling.

'I want her back, Kate. I can't live without her, I know I can't.' And to Kate's horror the large, burly man began to cry.

'There, there, she'll be back. If he bores her half as much as he bored me, she'll soon come running home.'

She sat patting his hand, murmuring words of comfort and thought she had come full circle. She had confessed to his being boring that night she had met Gloria and Joy. Then, just speaking the words had been like a liberation to her. For the past year she had swung as if on a see-saw, first wanting him gone, then trying to save her marriage. Now she had said it again – he was boring, and once again the simple word had made her feel free of him. Nothing had changed in those twelve months where he was concerned and nothing would. But Pam? How could Pam have deceived her? They had gone on the writers' weekend together, shopped, nattered on the telephone as if everything was the same when it wasn't. She had thought she knew Pam better than any other woman, and she hadn't. She had put her occasional strangeness down to jealousy over her writing but it probably wasn't that at all – that was when Pam had shown her true colours. She had not liked what was going on, she had been embarrassed in Kate's company. Such a defence of her old friend cheered her a little and Kate felt no anger towards her, only puzzlement. 'Oh, Pam, you fool,' she said aloud.

That lunchtime Barty received a visit from the private detective he had hired. The man had a selection of photographs with him. They had been taken the night before in a brothel, one with a special room for 'correction'. There, smiling straight at the camera, was the face of Charles Trenchard, dressed from head to toe in black leather, a whip in his hand, a large erection and about to beat a woman trussed up in shackles like a chicken.

'Love a duck,' said Barty. 'The things people do!'

'The rest are even better, sir.'

'How did you get them, for God's sake? Why, the man hasn't even had the sense to wear a mask.'

'There's a viewing gallery, sir, behind a two-way mirror ... Simple. He wouldn't have twigged. The flash can be a bit dodgy sometimes but, as you see, he had other things on his mind. Fair old dick he's got on him, hasn't he?' The detective grinned at him.

'I wonder if he goes there often?' Barty said more to himself than to the man.

'He's booked in for tomorrow, if that should be of any help to you, sir.'

'Immeasurable help. See Gervase on the way out. He'll see you right.'

As soon as the detective had left, Barty telephoned an old friend of many years' standing.

'Gloria? I've the most wonderful book for you, it's so readable, I couldn't put it down. I'm having it biked over straight away.' Joy's voice bubbled down the telephone.

'You're working again, that's wonderful news.'

'I had a long talk with myself. I've been behaving stupidly and selfishly. Kate was right, work is wonderful for sorting oneself out. I'm going to stick to it now, and with Barty. Even if I don't get Hannah back I've got to learn to carry on and Barty's the best person to teach me. He's so calm, so sensible and kind. I would have to look a long while ever to find someone who cares as much for me as he does.'

'I'm glad. Will Faith stay on?' Gloria asked.

'Yes. Most of her authors are coming with her and with Kate's success and getting Barty's book, the work is pouring in, and it's going to need the two of us. I've done it, Gloria. The agency is a success!' She was laughing. 'Just one other thing, it's dreadfully short notice, but it's my birthday tomorrow. You and Peter don't fancy coming to dinner? Barty wanted to give me a party but I said I'd prefer just a quiet dinner with friends.'

'I'll have to check with Peter but I'm sure it'll be fine.'

Gloria was smiling when she replaced the receiver. Life with Barty was unlikely to be a bed of roses or a sea of passion but, Joy was right, kindness went a long way in a relationship. Look at the mess she had been making of her own life with her preoccupation with sex or no sex.

The telephone rang again.

'Gloria, I've an Ulrika Talbot-Blaize, for you,' said Rachel.

'Who?'

'She says she's one of our authors. Wants to arrange to have a manuscript picked up.'

'Picked up?'

'I know, sounds a bit potty, doesn't she?'

'You'd better put her on.'

The line deadened, then clicked as Rached rerouted the call.

'Is this Miss Catchpole?' a deep, gin-soaked voice, so husky it would be difficult to tell if it was a man or woman speaking, asked. 'I was so pleased to hear of your appointment, not enough women in positions of power these days despite women's liberation or whatever it is they call it. Just look at the Cabinet – it really is too bad the lack of women there after those poor suffragettes went through so much, wouldn't you agree?'

'Mrs Talbot-Blaize?'

'Miss, actually. I was never one for the fetters of the marriage vows myself, too restraining.' A chuckle as deep and rich as the voice burbled along the telephone lines.

'Your manuscript?' Gloria tried to keep the amusement she was feeling out of her voice.

'Yes, so sad, I had hoped to finish it in time for Julius to read it, but silly man curled up his toes before I'd finished. Of course I'm disastrously late with it, about twenty years, in fact, but time does fly so, don't you find? And I did get so bored writing the thing. I find that too, don't you? Memories are so turgid, one wants to be up and fornicating not writing about it. But it's done now, so could someone come and fetch it, please?'

'Can you not post it?' Gloria had difficulty controlling her laughter.

'Post it? Well, there's a novel idea. No, I don't think so, my dear. I don't want to risk it in the post, it's the only copy I've got. Better you pop in and collect it. That's what Julius did.'

'Well, of course, if that's what Julius did. Your address?' She picked up her pen. Miss Talbot-Blaize was someone she very much wanted to meet.

'Just pop into the pub, the Old Success in Sennen, they'll direct you. So nice talking to you, Miss Catchpole. Come for lunch, we'll sink a gin or two.'

'Sennen, did you say? How extraordinary, my parents live near there. I could come when I next visit them.'

'Capital. Give me a buzz, I'm always here. If not, Jago is.'

'Miss Talbot-Blaize, your book, what's it called?'

'This one? I thought *Last and Lingering Troubadour* ties in rather well with the other one, don't you think?'

One of the delights of publishing, Gloria thought as she rang off, was the differing characters of the authors. Certainly, there were the difficult ones like the Bellas of this world, but there were some lovely eccentrics, too, like this one, and they made up for all the horrible carping ones.

'Rachel, could you look on the computer to find out the

name of the novel or memoirs – I'm not sure which – of Ulrika Talbot-Blaize. What a character!'

Gloria returned to the work she had been doing. She was managing, contrary to her original fears, to do some editing and was working on a new book by Grace Bliss, fitting it in between the now inevitable administrative chores.

'Can't find her, Gloria. Sorry, there's no one of that name on the computer and no one's heard of her,' Rachel reported half an hour later.

'That's odd. She sounded potty enough to have got the wrong publishers. Never mind, it doesn't matter. I'm to see her next time I go home. I'll find out before then.'

The next morning Gloria was in the postroom attempting to retrieve a letter she had sent down last night. She had written rejecting a manuscript, but last night, when she could not sleep, she had had second thoughts and decided she would publish it after all.

The postroom was in the basement. Shelves lined the walls. On one side were those for incoming mail. There were pigeon holes with the names of all employees above the table where letters were sorted and then delivered about the building by Stan, the old postman who had been employed here longer than anyone else. Several parcels and Jiffy bags were waiting to be dealt with. Those addressed to a specific person were left unopened and would be delivered later but the date of their arrival and the addressee were logged in a large book that stood on a central table, and which the recipient signed when they accepted the package. Those parcels addressed merely to Westall and Trim were opened and their contents, name of sender and date of arrival were entered, plus a given number, into another book on which was written Unsolicited Manuscripts. These were placed on the shelves on the other wall, under a number pinned to the shelf. This neat orderly row of typescripts was what was known as the slush pile, even if there was no pile. Although, like every other publishers, they accepted no responsibility for the safety of a manuscript, it would be a dreadful thing to lose one. This system and Stan had ensured that nothing was ever lost from here, even if there were often panics in the offices upstairs.

Gloria stood anxiously while Stan checked the post on the

shelves on the remaining wall where post to be sent out was held.

'Sorry, Gloria, it would have gone out last night if you put it out to be collected before four-thirty.'

'I did. Never mind, Stan. We've probably lost the best book since what? *Gone with the Wind*. My fault, I shouldn't be a ditherer.' She turned to go and then had an idea. 'By the way, Stan, does the name Ulrika Talbot-Blaize mean anything to you?'

'Ulrika? Most certainly does. There was a woman for you.' He sighed at what was evidently a happy memory. Gloria stood by the door waiting patiently. 'Wonderful creature. Beautiful? There was never anyone like her, nor has been since, in my opinion. Like a film star. She walked down the street and heads turned. Racy she was, very fast, but charming with it. Oh, yes.' He nodded. 'She had charm and no side to her. "Hello, Stan how are you?" she'd say, just like I was important. One of Mr Julius's ladies, if you know what I mean. Bishop's daughter she was, they often are the raciest, so I'm told.'

'She wrote a book?'

'That she did.' He laughed. 'That caused a stir and no mistake. The lawyers had to labour over that one, her memoirs they were, you see. The people she had known in a very special way . . .' He raised one eyebrow. 'Half the Cabinet, actors, royalty, they were all in it. Scandalous it was. But what a read!'

'She's written a sequel.'

'Never? Good God, I'd have thought she'd be dead by now what with the amount of booze she packed away. Mr Julius had given up on ever receiving that book, I can tell you. I often mentioned it to him, but he said he doubted if she would ever finish it.'

'What was the first book called, do you remember?'

'Like yesterday. Lovely title. *To Whom the Bird Has Sung*. Some bird, some song.' The old man laughed.

chapter **thirteen**

Kate walked rather tentatively into the crowded reception room of the Café Royal. The noise was so loud it was like walking into solid sound. She took a glass from a hovering waiter and looked about her among the groups intent on their conversations, hoping to see Stewart and, if not him, then someone she knew. She stood to one side and watched. Every other face was that of someone famous. Some writers she admired and others she did not. A sprinkling of actors. And a few of that strange breed of person who was merely famous for being famous.

'Hallo, should I know you?' She turned to find a woman about her own age, smartly dressed and clutching a glass as if it was a life-raft.

'I shouldn't think so, my name's Kate Howard.'

'Kate Howard? No, name doesn't ring a bell, I'm afraid.'

'I write fiction – for women mainly.'

'What are you doing here, then?'

'I'm not sure.' She smiled. 'I was just invited.'

'I won my ticket. Every year the paper runs a competition, you get a copy of the winning book as well.'

'That's nice.'

'Not that they're my sort of book, a bit too literary for me. I like a good read myself.'

'Me too,' Kate said with more feeling than the woman realised.

'It was once for the most popular book – now they're too highbrow for me. Still it's a day out, isn't it? Oh, excuse me, I must go. Look, do you see? It's Gerald Walters over there! Now his books I do like.' And Kate was left alone again.

'Kate. Lovely to see you, what on earth are you doing here?' It was Sheena Goodly. 'Gracious, that sounds awful!' She laughed. 'It's just after the other night – well, this is such a literary turnout, isn't it?'

'I was invited.' Kate forced herself to smile.

'You should see the postbag we got about you. I'll send them on. Whoops! Look who's here, your biggest fan, Sebastian Trumpington.'

'Good God, my favourite author,' Sebastian drawled sarcastically. 'But what on earth are you doing at a turn-out like this – thought you regarded us as pseuds?'

'Not all of you,' Kate corrected him. 'I was invited.' But this time she was not smiling.

Although the room was crowded, she did not feel like trying to speak to anyone. She felt certain that if another person asked her what she was doing here, she might just hit them with her handbag. She was relieved when the master of ceremonies announced that luncheon was served. She was first at her table. She peeked at the place names either side of her. The one on her left meant nothing. But on her right she saw Stewart's name.

'Glad you could make it.' She looked up to see a smiling Stewart taking his seat.

'Stewart. At last, a friendly face. Could you answer a question that's been bothering me? What *am* I doing here?' She laughed.

'You're here because I loved your book and your writing – you should be one of the finalists in my opinion. But there you go – I'm not in charge of the selection. And the other reason?' He put his hand out and took hold of hers. 'Because I think you're a lovely person and I found I wanted to see you again. Do you mind?' He was looking at her with a serious expression.

'No, I don't mind at all,' she said, but she could not look at him for fear he might see the excitement that he had sparked.

Late that afternoon there was a police raid on a brothel in central London. Certain people were arrested. The male customers, as is so often the case, were given a warning at the police station, and sent on their way. The madame of the brothel and the prostitutes, as is so often the case, were charged.

As he let himself into his mistress's house, Charles Trenchard was feeling enormously relieved at the understanding attitude of the police.

'Darling, you have a visitor.' Penelope met him in the hall.

Charles entered the sitting room to find Sir Barty Silver with an impassive Gervase awaiting him.

'Charles, long time no see.' Barty rose and smiled warmly.

'What are you doing here, Silver? We've nothing to say to each other that can't wait for the courts.' Charles crossed to the drinks tray and poured himself a whisky, pointedly omitting to extend the courtesy to others.

'Ah, Charles, that's where you could be wrong. If you wouldn't mind,' he smiled quizzically at Penelope.

'No, darling, don't leave, I'd rather you stayed. In fact, with the divorce proceedings as far advanced as they are, and my wife domiciled at your address, I don't think you should even be here, Silver.'

'Oh, I don't know about that, Trenchard. And if you take my advice, I think it would be better if the young lady did leave us.'

There was something in the way he spoke that persuaded Penelope that she did not wish to remain in the room. 'I've some work to do,' she said as an excuse.

'Well?' Charles looked at Barty with loathing.

'It's Joy's birthday today. I fancy giving her a really nice present.'

'So?'

'Like her daughter – Hannah.'

'No way, Silver.'

'I'm not so sure about that. Gervase . . .' Barty flicked his fingers at the young man who clicked open a briefcase and removed an envelope. Before taking it from Gervase's outstretched hand, Barty with slow deliberation took a pair of chamois-leather gloves from his coat pocket and slipped them on.

'Now, what have we here? Holiday snaps? No, Trenchard, we've got very nasty dirty pictures.' He shook the envelope so that the photographs scattered out on to the table. 'Of you.' Barty waved the envelope at Charles.

Charles did not even have to look at the contents of the package, he had already turned white.

'Not a pretty picture, as they say, is it?' Barty smiled a small, private smile. 'Now, we have one or two things to consider here, Trenchard. You come with me now and collect Hannah to return her to her mother, or, I'm sorry to say, copies of these photographs will be delivered, within the hour, to the other members of your chambers, and, I regret, the Lord Chancellor himself.'

'This is blackmail.'

'Yes, you would be correct in that.'

'You can't get away with blackmail, not in this country.'

'Can't you? So now, since these rather mucky photos have found their way into my hands, you'll stop blackmailing me, won't you? I know what you're implying about Joy and me – we'll see that the little lady is well chaperoned and make no mistake. And you've been lying about me, slandering me, making out I'm some sort of queer, so Joy can't have her little one with her. I'm not the pervert around here, Mr Trenchard – you are. And I'll make sure all those who should know, do know – including that rather pretty lady out there.'

'I demand the negatives.'

'And why not, Mr Trenchard?'

Charles picked up his car keys. 'Very well, then, but you haven't heard the last of this, Silver.'

'Oh, I think I have.'

'I suppose you were responsible for the raid this afternoon?'

'What a thing to say, Mr Trenchard! Whatever next?' Barty wagged his finger at him as he laughed.

By the time Gloria and Peter arrived for dinner, Hannah was installed in the nursery Barty had had decorated and he and Joy had filled with expensive toys. Several copies of the photographs of Hannah's father were installed in Barty's safe.

Joy was almost incoherent with excitement. 'The best birthday present ever,' she said, looking at Barty with adoration, the look Gloria had waited to see her give him. 'We should be able to get married in three months.'

'That's marvellous. Will you stop working?'

'Oh, no, remember what dear agony aunt Kate had to say. We women need our independence.' She laughed, taking hold of Barty's hand and squeezing it, laughing with the confidence of a woman secure with her man.

The dinner was sublime but Gloria was not surprised. With both Barty and Joy being such perfectionists, it was inevitable. In truth, they were a lot better suited than one at first thought.

'So, Gloria, are you enjoying Westall and Trim?' Barty asked.

'Very much so.'

'Brian's almost finished my book. It's good, very good.'

'That will be a launch and a half.' Gloria grinned. 'We're hoping for a summer publication for that one.'

'I've seen Crispin Anderson. I've told him I would be interested in acquiring the firm.'

'But, Barty, it's not for sale,' Gloria said, not sure of her ground.

'That's a shame,' he said noncommittally. 'We could have worked well together, you and I, I think. You come highly recommended,' and he smiled across the table at Joy.

'If anyone buys it I think it should be Peter,' Joy stated firmly.

'Me? Why me?' Peter looked puzzled.

'Because it's a wonderful firm, and not one that the conglomerates should be allowed to get their hands on. You'd keep it as Julius wanted it. And you need something to do, you'll go mad doing nothing.' Joy shrugged her shoulders. 'And, I think you and Gloria together would take Westall's into the twenty-first century and make it a force to be reckoned with.'

'Why thank you, Joy, that's a lovely thing to say.' Gloria looked with gratitude across at Joy. What a wonderful dream that would be, she thought.

'But what hope would I have of acquiring it with Barty in the bidding?' Peter said.

'Are you interested, Peter, seriously?' Barty asked.

'I don't know. I could be.'

'Oh, Barty, then you've got to drop out, that would be awful if you were fighting each other – and Peter needs it more than you. Please.' Joy was pleading.

'I can see marriage is likely to ruin me if I allow myself to listen to my wife too often.' He smiled indulgently at her. He sat thinking a moment, looking around the table, all faces looking at him expectantly 'All right, against my better judgement, I'll pull out. But I warn you, Peter, I'm in the market. The next opportunity that presents itself, I buy. Then we'll be rivals.'

'That's a horrendous thought, something Mike Pewter and I dread,' Peter said laughing.

'Mind you, I think it would be better if I didn't tell Crispin

Anderson. I could be of use to everyone if he thinks I'm still interested – get my drift?' He winked. 'So, Gloria, you've solved the mystery of Lepanto, then?'

'How on earth did you know about that? And what makes you ask?'

Barty tapped the side of his nose. 'I know lots of things.' Joy watched him and with relief found the action did not irritate her. 'The only way you could confidently say it was not for sale was if the employees' trust had control of the Lepanto shares, that's all. So it's a mystery no more?'

'I wouldn't say that.' Gloria shook her head. 'Up to yesterday I thought we were getting nowhere. Then an author contacted me out of the blue. And I've got this feeling she might be the key to it. I'm going to see her and try to find out though I don't know how to approach the subject when it's only a feeling.'

'Feelings usually have reasons,' Barty interrupted.

'She wrote a book years ago and we can't find a copy. That's odd, you see. We think Julius had copies of everything, so why not this one?'

'What was the book called?' Joy leant forward with interest.

'A lovely title, it sounds like poetry, but I've never heard it. *To Whom the Bird Has Sung*.'

From the end of the table, Barty coughed. 'Allow me,' he said. Everyone looked in his direction.

> *'The last and lingering troubadour,*
> *To whom the bird has sung,*
> *Who once went singing southward*
> *When all the world was young.'*

Barty sat back with a wide grin.

'Barty, that was lovely. What a wonderful poem.'

'We learnt a lot at Barnardo's, you know.' His grin had become mischievous.

'Who's it by?'

'G. K. Chesterton.'

'No one knows any Chesterton, these days.'

'More's the pity. But I do, Gloria, I do.' Barty was laughing now.

'What? Why are you laughing at me? What is it, Barty?'

'Do you want to know, really?'

'Barty, come on, don't be horrible to poor Gloria.'

492

'Want to know the title, Gloria?'

'Of course.'

'"Lepanto", Gloria, that's what it's called. What about that, then?'

chapter **fourteen**

During the afternoon of Barty's dinner party, Crispin had been busy. Since the identity of Lepanto was not at the office, he reasoned it must be at Julius's house in the country. He had telephoned his aunt and requested that he be allowed to do a thorough search of the library there. They had searched it once but not well enough for Crispin's satisfaction. He arrived mid-afternoon and after a pleasant chat and a cup of Earl Grey with his aunt, he settled into the library-cum-study that had been Julius's domain.

It was rather creepy being alone in the room for Julius's presence was very strong, and Crispin had the uncomfortable feeling that at any moment the door might open and his uncle walk in and demand to know what the hell Crispin was doing rummaging through his desk.

The desk held no clue, nor did a bureau which was stuffed with papers. Crispin had quite an amusing time with some letters he had found there. They were from various women, some so old the ink had faded. The sentimental old fool must have been keeping them for years. Odd he should keep them here where his wife might find them but, then, maybe the man did not care. Of course, if Jane found them she might burn them so he stuffed them in his briefcase. Archives should never be destroyed, he told himself. He would keep them, one never knew. Some person some day might wish to write a biography of Julius and he might be able to sell them.

He sat for some time at the desk, trying to get into the man's mind, wondering where he could have left a clue or made a slip. Only the books were left. He crossed to the large bookcase opposite: at least he had kept the books published by Westall's together. But he had been through these at the office. And then his eye saw one book. He frowned. A vague memory stirred. He took it down from the shelf, and, professional that he was, studied the cover, removed it, inspected the hard covers, the gold printing on the spine. Nice work. But it was the title that bothered him. He was sure he had not seen this book in the office, and that someone had mentioned it – recently. *To Whom the Bird Has Sung*. Sir Gerald Walters, that was it, he'd wanted to call a book by this title. He flipped the book open – dedicated to Julius himself. Now that was interesting. And then he saw the poem, saw who it was by, saw the title. He dived for the telephone, dialled directory enquiries and rang the number he had been given. Five minutes later he had an appointment for the following morning with Ulrika Talbot-Blaize, who, most satisfactorily, had said she had been expecting to hear from him. He telephoned British Rail and booked on the overnight sleeper to Penzance; it arrived just before eight in the morning. He went in search of his aunt to tell her all was solved.

Once everyone at the dinner party had realised the full potential of what Barty had said, pandemonium broke out. Barty, who had always claimed he did not like personal contact, was engulfed in hugs and kisses from both Joy and Gloria. Their excitement was infectious and Barty relinquished himself to the onslaught. Though he would never have dreamed of admitting it to anyone, he rather enjoyed it.

'I want to cry,' Gloria said, looking very much as if she was about to.

'Well, cry, my darling.' Peter put his arm about her.

'I just don't believe we've solved it. This nutty Ulrika woman – she simply has to be Lepanto, doesn't she?' Gloria looked at the faces around her as if pleading with them to agree with her.

'Telephone her, ask her,' Joy suggested practically.

Gloria looked at her watch. 'I can't, it's gone ten, she's old and probably in bed.'

'We could drive down through the night, and telephone her at a more civilised hour,' Peter said.

'Would you come?'

'You're not driving all that way on your own.'

Gloria, unused to being looked after by anyone, became quite fluttery with pleasure. 'If we leave about midnight we'd be at my parents between six and seven depending on the traffic.'

'What on earth will they say if we turn up at such a God-awful hour?'

'It isn't, to them. My father is always up by six. We could bath and change and call Ulrika about ten. What do you think?'

'We'll do that.'

'That settled, how about more coffee and a brandy?'

'No, whoever's doing the driving no more booze,' Barty ordered. And since they were sharing the driving they both had coffee.

'What a birthday!' Joy smiled contentedly.

Kate lay in the hotel bed and listened to the unfamiliar sounds of London outside the building. She lay on her back, looking at the ceiling, conscious of a wonderful feeling of lethargy as if she had been asleep for a hundred years and would need another hundred to wake up fully. There was no going back. Tony had said she had changed, now that change was complete. Writing her book had freed her mentally but now she was freed physically. She looked down at the man cradled in her arms and could have wept with happiness. The unimaginable had happened, someone she had found attractive had wanted her also. Where would it lead? Where did she want it to lead? She did not know. All her life she had wondered what the future held. Worried about it, if she was honest. Now she did not care. It was this moment that mattered, this contented minute of lying holding a man who had given her a pleasure she had not imagined existed. If it never happened again, so be it, she had experienced joy untold, she had memories now, real, worthy memories.

It had been wonderful. Being here with him had been the most natural thing in the world. After the awards, they had spent the afternoon together going to the zoo. They had talked and talked. She had told him things about herself, dreams and hopes, fears from the past that she had never told a living soul, never thought to put into words and certainly not to Tony. They had dined and as the meal progressed their physical need for each other became so strong that neither said anything, suggested it nor hinted at it – it was not necessary for both knew what the other wanted. They had left the restaurant and walked until they had found this hotel. He had looked down at her, a gentle smile on his face, and she had nodded, even then had not spoken.

He had undressed her, slowly, so slowly that her longing was intensified into a great ache inside her. She was embarrassed he should be looking at her – the second man in her life to do so. She wanted to cover herself, hide her body from his gaze. He had stroked her sensuously and had kissed her body with soft caressing kisses. He had knelt before her and she found she was no longer embarrassed but a woman hungry for her man.

He stirred and, as if aware that new arms were holding him, woke quickly. He sat up and looked down at her, smiling gently.

'Why so serious?' he asked.

'I'm angry, if you must know. Angry that all my adult life I've been cheated of the pleasure you gave me last night.'

He leant forward and kissed her. 'It was something wonderful and different for me, too, you know.'

She put up her hand and gently caressed his face. 'I just can't believe it happened. I mean, at my age you don't expect this.'

'Speak for yourself.' He laughed. 'I'm older than you!'

'Yes, but you're a man.'

'I gathered that. I'm glad you did, too!'

'No, you know what I mean.' She smiled shyly. 'It's different for a man. Your grey hair is distinguished, mine is an indication that I'm over the hill. I'm overweight, that's middle-age spread, a man's overweight and he's a fine figure of a man.'

'I think you're beautiful.'

'Please don't say things you don't mean. It's not fair.'

'I never would. I do think you're beautiful. I don't know what has happened to you in the past, Kate, that makes you feel you must knock yourself, but I intend to put a stop to it. No more putting yourself down, right?'

'I'll try.' She was laughing now, feeling a confidence so new to her she did not even recognise it.

'So where do we go from here?'

'I don't know, Stewart.'

'You don't regret last night?'

'Don't be silly.'

'I want to see you again and again, Kate.'

'Good. I do, too.'

'I never expected anything like this to happen to me again in my life.' He sighed. 'I have to go to Edinburgh today, a big book launch. How about the weekend?'

'That would be lovely.'

'Shall we meet here, in this hotel?'

'No. Come to my house. We'll be more comfortable, more private there.'

It was early still when Kate drove into her driveway. Pam's car was parked outside.

'Pam? You're an early visitor,' she said with no rancour.

'I was just about to drive off. I need to see you, Kate.' Pam's face, pink with embarrassment, looked up at her.

'Of course, come in.'

In the kitchen Kate did what she always did, put the kettle on even before she had taken off her coat.

'I had to talk to you, Kate, tell you how sorry I am. I've hardly slept worrying what you must think of me. I know it's unlikely but I still want to be your friend. I know what you must be thinking of me.'

'I doubt if you do, Pam.' Kate was smiling at her. 'I was a bit shaken at how long it has been going on, I thought that was a bit tacky.'

'I know.' Pam hung her head in shame.

'But I do understand why it happened. You were lonely.'

'But my best friend's husband? It's all so shitty. I can't believe I did it.'

'You've gone back to Doug, haven't you?'

'Yes. I was mad to leave. But when Tony said you and he had split up and were getting a divorce, I felt responsible in a way. And then when he phoned to say he had found us a house to rent, I thought I had to see it through. I realise now I was playing a game. It was the excitement when it was illicit, it was like a drug. Now it's in the open . . .' she shrugged, 'I found I wanted Doug.'

'He does love you, you know, desperately. Tony would have been so wrong for you. There are people who suck other people dry of their personality and he's one of them.'

'Can we still be friends?'

'I don't know if we will ever be the same again, with each other.'

'You'll feel you can't trust me? What a fool I've been.' Pam was close to tears.

'I'm trying to be honest, Pam. I don't know, but I don't blame you for taking away from me something that had already disappeared. It wouldn't be fair. I would just be blaming you for something that Tony and I had caused to happen.'

'I wanted to see you and patch it up, but you being so reasonable is making me feel worse,' Pam said contrarily.

'I don't feel like screeching at you, that's all. Coffee or tea?' She smiled at the ordinariness, the mundane question.

'Coffee, please. But are you going to be all right? Tony said you'd found a cottage, but you've never lived alone in all your life.'

'Now's my chance. I've found a place, near Henley, but I'm not sure about it any more. This morning I've been wondering whether to get a flat in London.' She paused and wondered if to continue, and thought, what did it matter? She was a free agent now. 'I've met someone, you see.' She heard herself saying the words and shook her head in amazement that she, of all people, could be saying them.

'No! How exciting.' Pam was leaning over the table, red hair falling round her pretty face, eyes sparkling with interest – just like old times. 'Tell me all.'

'Don't pinch this one.' Kate laughed, shocked by what she was saying – it was all right for Pam to take her husband, not her lover. If she needed anything to show her the futility of continuing with her marriage, then that comment did.

But as she spoke of Stewart she wondered, if she had not found him, would she have been quite so understanding with Pam?

On the long car journey west, driving through the night, for the first time Gloria felt totally relaxed with Peter. Whether it was the pleasant evening they had enjoyed, solving the Lepanto riddle or simply being so close in the confines of the car, she did not know. But as she sat beside him occasionally glancing at him as the lights from oncoming cars lit his face, she felt safe, just as she had that first night in the restaurant. She snuggled down into the seat of his large BMW and sighed.

'That sounds like a very contented sigh.' He took one hand off the steering wheel and touched her gently.

'Don't laugh at me, but I suddenly feel secure with you.'

'And you haven't before?'

'No.'

'What's changed?' he asked and glanced across at her, his hopes rising.

'I don't know. I haven't been playing games with you, you know.'

He did not answer but turned off the motorway and into the brightly lit parking area of a service station. He stopped the car and turned to her. It was now or never, he thought.

'Look, Gloria. I don't think we've been straight with each other,' he began.

'I know,' she said, her heart sinking.

'The point is. Well, I think I've been stupid but what with Hilary and then Julius . . .'

Gloria looked straight ahead, her mind screaming, don't say it. She had been right, then. He had turned to her for comfort, nothing else. Fool again, she thought bitterly.

'What I should have done, right at the beginning, was tell you.'

'Yes,' she said, in a small and miserable voice.

'Tell you how much I love you and can't live without you and . . . honestly, Gloria, I can't go on like this.'

She turned to face him.

'What did you say?'

'I love you.'

'Oh, Peter. I love you, too.'

'But then why?'

'Because I was afraid that you didn't. I couldn't bear it, loving you and you not loving me.'

'What idiots we've been,' he said, taking her in his arms.

'No. What an idiot I've been,' she managed to say before his mouth was covering hers. And a couple of long-distance lorry drivers cheered them as they ambled by.

Mrs Catchpole was none too happy with Gloria for bringing a guest unannounced. Her annoyance was somewhat mollified when she discovered who he was. She fussed about them, cooking bacon and eggs and making proper coffee rather than the instant she and her husband usually drank. But Mrs Catchpole was no fool. She sensed a closeness between her daughter and this man, and what an improvement he was on some Gloria had brought home to introduce to them. This one was worth making an effort for.

'Do you know this Ulrika woman?'

'Slightly. She's quite mad, of course, not someone one would invite for sherry. A somewhat racy past I've heard,' Mrs Catchpole added in a whisper which, since they were the only ones present, seemed extreme. 'What's more . . .' This time the whisper was accompanied by a quick glance over her shoulder to check she was not being overheard. 'It's rumoured that her gardener – an appallingly rude man – is rather more than a gardener, if you know what I mean. It's disgusting at her age! And she smokes.' This last was Mrs Catchpole's final statement of disapproval.

'Jago Arscott isn't that bad,' Gloria's father said. 'He's just not one for the small talk.'

'What did you say his name was?' Gloria spluttered behind a wedge of toast.

'Arscott – it's a common enough name in the West Country. He's more of a handyman.' Her father winked at her and Gloria and Peter collapsed with laughter leaving Mrs Catchpole quite nonplussed.

Crispin was feeling disgruntled. He had hardly slept a wink all night, what with the noise of the wretched train, the way it had kept stopping and inconsiderate railway people shouting at each other on stations. Now he had arrived at Penzance and it was cold and raining. If Crispin loathed the countryside there was something he loathed even more and that was the seaside. An out-of-season seaside was even worse – depressingly so.

The buffet was closed and, in any case, railway station buffets were not his idea of places to eat. He found a taxi and asked to be taken to the best hotel for breakfast.

'They'm all closed. Out of season you see,' the man muttered at him. 'There's a Little Chef up Hayle way, that there'll be open.'

So Crispin found himself eating the American breakfast in the sort of fast-food outlet he would never normally be seen dead in. That he enjoyed the meal was neither here nor there; he was just relieved that there was no chance of anyone he knew seeing him.

The taxi returned for him at nine-thirty and he ordered the man to drive him to Sennen. At least the driver was of the silent variety, which Crispin regarded as a blessing. The truth was that the man was not speaking to him for, in his velvet-collared cashmere coat, with his arrogance, he epitomised all the taxi-driver loathed most about 'they' who lived the other side of the Tamar.

They had had to ask directions of a fisherman, who was leaning on a railing studying the sea with an expression of terminal doom. Crispin could not understand one word of what he said, but luckily his driver could.

Crispin eventually found himself standing on the top of a cliff in the teeming rain. He entered a gate and started on a vertiginous descent of steep steps cut into the rock. Below him he could see a granite house, perched like the poop deck of a man-o'-war on a wide shelf half-way down the cliff. The sea was pounding ominously close on the rocks below. And the wind was howling around him as if spitefully trying to pluck him off the cliff. The creeper on the house was lashed by the wind, which screeched as if in a tantrum or as if complaining that it could not gain entrance to the house. By the time Crispin battled to the front door he was soaked and bitterly cursing his dead uncle for such self-indulgent mysteries.

The door was opened by what Crispin could only describe as a horny-handed churl, who looked at him with the same suspicion as the driver and the fisherman. So much for merry peasants and sons of the soil. Did no one with any charm live in these parts? He sighed inwardly.

'I've an appointment with Ulrika Talbot-Blaize. Crispin Anderson.' He smiled more out of habit than conviction. The man did not speak but held the door open, not wide, but a measly foot more which just allowed Crispin to slither in. 'Such a storm,' he said, mopping the rain from his face.

'Storm! This? Nonsense, a little light wind.' A deep voice, bubbling with laughter, called from the doorway into another room. The owner stepped forward. 'Crispin? I've been expecting you. I'm Ulrika Talbot-Blaize.' Crispin found himself shaking hands with a woman of gargantuan proportions in a loose-fitting dress of shimmering green silk. He did not like shaking the hand: Crispin did not like people who were over-large for to him it showed a lamentable lack of self-discipline. 'Jago my handsome, don't just stand there, take the man's coat, and get the port. This way, Crispin.' She held up her hand to guide him through a low doorway and smiled at him. Crispin, half-way through the door, stopped and looked at her with a puzzled expression. For the smile transformed the woman's face. It was like the moon shining on a romantic ruin, softening its lines, and for a short moment the ruin was again the beautiful building it once had been. And then she stopped smiling, the illusion was gone and she was a fat old lady again. But she laughed as if she was fully aware of the effect her smile had had upon him, as if it was something that was frequent in her life.

chapter **fifteen**

As Gloria and Peter drove up to the cliff-top, having followed her mother's directions, they saw a taxi standing waiting. They parked behind it and as they were getting out of the car the gate opened and Crispin appeared.

'What a pleasant surprise seeing you two here. Now, I wonder what on earth could bring you to this neck of the woods?' He smiled superciliously. Gloria felt her heart plummeting. They were too late, he had beaten them to it. No doubt, in that over-smart briefcase, he already had the signed power of attorney over that precious two per cent of votes.

'My parents live here,' she said, not wanting him to see how upset she was. Peter took hold of her hand.

'Of course, you're wasting your time. You do realise that, don't you?' Crispin said as he slid into the back of the car. 'Bloody awful weather and you say your people actually *live* here? Extraordinary! Any chance of a lift back to London?'

Gloria felt like exploding with rage at the audacity of the man.

'Sorry,' Peter said for her. 'We'll probably stay on a few days and meander back.'

'Oh, quite.' Crispin smirked. 'Not much point in rushing back is there, Peter, now you've no job. Right, driver. The station. See you two.' He slammed the taxi door shut and waved. Peter made the V-sign at him.

'Sorry, but I can't stand that creep,' he said.

'He's beaten us, hasn't he? What lousy luck. Is there any point our going in?'

'Of course there is. Don't you have her new manuscript to pick up?' He held the small gate open for her and gingerly, clinging to the handrail, they made their way down the cliff. Half-way down, Peter paused. 'What a position! I'd give anything for a house like this, wouldn't you? From the road no one would even know it was here.'

'Prefer it to a Cotswold manor house?'

'You bet. Shall we look for somewhere like this? A bolt-hole. The train only takes five hours.'

'That would be nice,' she said, her heart jolting at the implication.

This time the door was flung open wide and Ulrika stood waiting for them. 'At last, you've come. I've been waiting for you, nearly gave you up. Come in out of the rain, get by the fire, have a drink.' Ulrika busily ushered them into the small but beautifully furnished hallway. 'This way, my dears.' Despite her large size, Ulrika was fluttering about them as if excited to see them. They entered a long beamed room. It was far bigger than one would have expected, for from the outside the house looked quite small. The room was cluttered with furniture, wonderful oak, and the chairs covered with ancient tapestry. The walls were in need of paint, but it did not matter since they were covered with paintings of all shapes, sizes and periods. They were pictures that, because of their random age and content, one felt had been collected with love rather than an eye to investment. There were bowls of gold and bronze chrysanthemums, their distinctive scent filling the air. And in the fireplace a log fire crackled; in front of it lay a snoring bulldog who did not even open one eye in greeting, and beside her a large, tailless grey cat. From a big window all one could see was the sea and sky – nothing else was visible.

'My God, it's wonderful, like being on the bridge of a ship.'

'Fun, isn't it? My great-grandfather built it. There was a cottage here, and he added on and then my grandfather and father added, too. That's why it's called Bishop's Rock – nothing to do with the actual rock, no, they were all bishops, you see. You'd never get away with it, these days, what with planning officers and miserable little farts like that. Get by the fire, Gloria, my dear, you're soaked. Jago!' Ulrika yelled in her deep husky voice, making both of them jump. A small very dark man, looking more Spanish than English, appeared. 'Drinks, please, Jago. What would you like? I'm having port myself, warms the cockles.'

'Any wine? That would be lovely,' said Peter, thinking what a dreadful hour to be drinking but sensing she would be hurt if they refused.

'Jago, did you hear?' she said, so loudly that Gloria felt only the dead would not. 'There's a darling, get some for us, will you?' She smiled at the man and both Peter and Gloria were taken aback by the magical change in her face when she did. She was no longer old, no longer fat, her face was alive, animated and beautiful still. The man shuffled out. 'He's as thick as two short planks, but hung like a donkey.' She guffawed loudly and neither of the other two knew quite where to look.

'What happened to the cat's tail?' Gloria asked hurriedly to cover her confusion.

'Bloody mink got it. Poor Rupert was nearly a goner.' She bent down and stroked the animal who rolled lazily on its back. 'I'd given up fur coats, felt they were wrong. But after that verminous creature got hold of my cat I went straight out and bought one – Rupert's revenge, you see. I'm just waiting for one of those animal liberation people to nobble me. I'll tell them about mink, that I will.'

And Gloria thought, yes, she would, and God help them.

When the drinks had been poured and the fire was beginning to thaw them out Gloria asked after the manuscript.

'Oh, my dear, that was a ruse. I'm afraid it's still not finished but one of these days I'll get around to it, I will. No, I called you because you had not contacted me and Julius had told me you would as soon as he had curled his toes up. Well, you didn't so I thought I had better call you and drop a few hints. I couldn't tell you all, you see, because Julius had made me swear on the Bible that I never would let on about the trust to a living soul – except Jago, of course. He was so afraid of that frightful family finding out – oh, that's funny, did you notice the alliteration there?' She stopped to have a chuckle. The others waited patiently. 'Well, I was not sure if my vow still counted now he was dead. But I thought I had better not, just to be on the safe side. I hoped you would work things out yourself and come and find me. And you did, so clever of you.'

'But Julius's nephew worked it out too, and got here before us,' Gloria said with a sad expression.

'What, that little shit? Dreadful man. But doesn't he fancy himself? Last Christmas, or thereabouts, Julius telephoned me and warned me. He told me about his nephew and his plans to harm my darling's company. No, no. I told Crispin I hadn't the foggiest notion what he was talking about. I said I'd never heard of a trust. He didn't believe me, of course, but I said it must be a coincidence – the Lepanto poem in my book must have given Julius the idea of using that name. He seemed to swallow that.'

'So you didn't give him power of attorney?' The question tumbled out of Gloria and she was almost afraid to hear the answer.

'Good God, no. I've the papers here, all ready – been here for weeks, waiting for you. My lawyer in Penzance drew them up for me.'

'And it was Julius set the trust up for you?'

'No, that was my father, after the book came out. It did rather well you see, and he thought I was rather wayward – I can't imagine why. And when he died he added my inheritance to it as well. Mind you, that's worth bugger all these days. When Julius gave me the shares in Westall's we just added them to the existing trust for safety – he thought I was somewhat wayward, too.' She chuckled, a wonderful dark and happy sound.

'Julius gave you the shares?' Peter asked, entranced by this strange but very feminine woman.

'Bless him, yes. We had a wonderful summer once. I love summer affairs best of all, don't you, dear?' She smiled at Gloria. 'It's something about the sun, I think, makes one more lustful than in the winter. I've always said it was a good job I didn't live in the tropics, I'd have been flat on my back all my life.' She laughed and then stopped abruptly and gazed into the fire as if at ghosts from the past. They waited for her to speak for it was a silent moment, a very private one. 'I suppose I shouldn't have accepted them really, but then, I thought, why not? I'd made him happy and he me, and if he wanted to give me a little present, then why should I spoil his pleasure in giving? So I took them. He was such a wonderful man and the only one I ever really loved, and I like to think that I was something special to him too.'

'Oh, I'm sure you were,' Gloria said with a lump in her throat.

'And then each year he paid me royalties I knew I had not earned, and I took them, too. He thought he had hoodwinked me, but he hadn't. But, you see, it made him so happy to give them to me – a link with the past, I suppose. I could not have let him know I had guessed and take away his joy in giving. And, I'll be quite honest, these last few years it has helped enormously.' She suddenly sat upright in her chair. 'Still, to business or you'll be bored rigid with my rattling on. But it's so lovely to have people here who knew him too, you see, such a dear man.' She sighed. 'We'll get my cleaning lady to witness the signatures and everything – she'll be here soon.'

'Can't Jago witness?' Peter asked.

'Good Lord no, my dear. He's my trustee.' She laughed very loudly at their surprised expressions. 'I beat father and Julius, come the end. Jago's ideal, he can barely read but adores me and does just what I tell him. More wine, dear hearts?'

It was long past lunchtime when Gloria and Peter eventually left Ulrika. They were laden with presents – a small watercolour of the view that Gloria had admired and which Ulrika insisted she take. A bottle of the wine for Peter after he had said how good it was. Some of the pickle they had had with their ham at lunch after both had said how delicious it was, and a signed copy of *To Whom the Bird Has Sung*.

'What are we going to do about her royalties?' Gloria asked as Peter drove very carefully back to her parents' cottage. 'You heard what she said about them coming in handy.'

'We'll have to keep them on. But, if she wants to sell her shares, I'll happily buy them, then she'll be set up for life. I didn't mention it to her, I think she should have advice from someone not involved, don't you?'

'That's why I love you, you're such a kind, sensitive, man.' Gloria smiled at him.

They had reached her parents' cottage. But instead of going in Peter suggested they walk awhile in the rain. They walked to the Great Carn, an outcrop of rocks perched on the top of a cliff overlooking the Atlantic. Peter sat on one of the boulders and patted the space beside him for Gloria to join him.

'Bit more romantic than a service station, isn't it?' He smiled, gesturing to the great sweep of sky and sea, the Longships lighthouse wailing a warning of incoming fog.

'You could say that.' She snuggled close to him.

'I wanted somewhere special. I want to ask you to marry me, Gloria, once I'm free.'

'Peter . . .' It was all she could say, she was too happy for words to come.

'Is that yes?'

'A million of them.'

'I love you,' they both said in unison and they sealed their promises with a kiss.

He looked at her a long time as if to memorise this moment. 'Did you notice Ulrika called us dear hearts? That's what I'm going to call you from now on, my dear heart.'

'She was a magic lady. No wonder Julius loved her, what a character.'

'Like someone else I know.' He nuzzled the side of her neck.

If things were to be resolved, there had to be more meetings. Peter and Gloria talked long into the night about his buying the family's shares in Westall. He had delayed making this decision for, unsure as he had been of Gloria's feelings for him, he did not want her to think he was rushing her, and also he had been worried that perhaps she would not want him involved in what was increasingly *her* publishing house. Now everything had changed, but still he wondered if maybe marriage to each other should be enough. He need not have had such fears and doubts for, as they talked and planned the future of the company, both were bubbling over with ideas and schemes. They could not wait to work together and they couldn't wait to be man and wife.

When they finally went to bed it was to separate rooms. Gloria felt too intimidated by the close proximity of her mother even to contemplate their sleeping together. She was relieved that Peter made no suggestion that he slip into her room when her parents were asleep.

They had planned to set off the following morning but Mrs Catchpole insisted they stay for lunch, and then for tea, so it was almost midnight before they drove up to Gloria's house. She felt oddly shy as she invited him in for a drink. But still he said nothing, made no move towards her. He stood to go as he was now used to doing. Gloria had not expected this, not now he had said he wanted to marry her.

'Peter . . . this is difficult . . . I hate making the advances, but please stay,' she said, feeling ridiculously gauche.

Laughing he bent forward and kissed her. 'I was only teasing,' he said, taking her by the hand and leading her towards the stairs. As they ascended he put his arm about her as if afraid she would escape. He pushed open the bedroom door and slammed it shut and they were in each other's arms.

There was a soft whimpering from the landing.

'Excuse me,' Peter said. He crossed the room and opened the door. 'Hallo, Elephant. Left all alone? We can't have that, can we?'

With great dignity Elephant stalked into the room, tail held high. He crossed to his basket, turned round five times and lay down, and immediately his eyes were closed.

'Oh, Peter, I love you more for that.' Gloria laughed at him.

In his basket Elephant was not asleep, just pretending. He settled further into his blanket. He had always liked this particular gentleman the most.

In the past few months, Gloria had dreamt often of Peter making love to her again, but nothing in her dreams was to match the reality. His hunger for her matched her own need for him. They tore their clothes in their haste to be rid of them and their desperate longing to feel the flesh of each other. He knelt in front of her admiring her naked body and then, with deliberate slowness, pulled off her black silk stockings, looking at her all the time, which was enough for her to be ready for him. His hands held her hips, and his mouth found her and his tongue was finding every secret place. Gloria felt her body jolt rigid, her legs buckle from the ecstasy he was giving her. She screamed with joy as she climaxed and fell back on the bed, but still he held her hips, still continued to pleasure her, and she lost count of the times her body arched in passion. Then he was upon her and thrusting into her, and she felt his flesh, his sweat and her love for him.

Mike was overjoyed on two counts – that Peter and Gloria were at last together and that his old friend had decided finally to bid for the family's shares in Westall. But if he was to do so, it was not proper that he remain a trustee and so another one had to be found. Barty Silver was approached and agreed to replace Peter. If he could not own the company, he reasoned, then the next best thing would be to be a trustee of the employees' trust.

Everyone reluctantly agreed that no matter how much they all loathed Crispin he had done a good job of whipping up interest in the sale. The offers began to come in and it soon transpired that Peter would be the under-bidder by quite a large sum. He would either have to borrow heavily – and how long would it be before, like Julius, he found himself in difficulties? – or he would have to take a partner, which he was most reluctant to do.

Then a very strange thing happened. One by one the other publishing houses who had shown interest began to withdraw their bids. A week later, only Peter's offer remained. Crispin was beside himself with anger and fury. He telephoned, he wrote, but suddenly people were not in for his calls and his letters went unanswered. Everyone had their suspicions, but nobody liked to ask – only Joy. Barty confessed to her that, yes, his tentacles were broad and far-reaching. He had done nothing wrong, he said, wide-eyed and innocent. All he had done was to ask a few people who owed him favours to repay them by withdrawing from a deal he had an interest in. He was only making sure that Julius's wishes were fulfilled.

Peter now owned the shares. Lepanto remained. Both Mike and Barty had decided that perhaps it was better if Lepanto shares were not owned by either Peter or the employees – the buffer of two per cent in the middle might be as good a thing in the future as it had been in the past. That was the plan until Gloria received a telephone call from Dulcett. She and Simon had married and as a wedding present he had given her a lump sum of money. They were both wondering if any shares were available that she might buy. Simon had agonised over selling his shares against Julius's wishes and late in the day he wanted to make amends. He felt he was too old but would like Dulcett to be involved with the firm. And her name was now Westall.

'How romantic,' Ulrika had said, with marked satisfaction, when she was asked if she would like to sell her shares to Dulcett.

The day that everything was finally signed they planned to celebrate. That afternoon, Kate, in London to see Stewart, called into the office with the first three chapters and a synopsis of her next book, *Autumn Fever*.

This was always a worrying time for author and publisher alike. Many people could write one book, but did they have it in them to write a second? Gloria would like to have read it there and then. Instead she controlled herself and placed it on one side.

'You look pleased with yourself.' She smiled at Kate, who looked particularly attractive in a cherry-red suit and black leather boots.

'I'm very excited. Joy's sold my American rights. I couldn't believe her when she said for how much. I had to sit down, I must have smoked a whole packet of cigarettes in five minutes.' She laughed.

'That's absolutely wonderful news. Joy hadn't told me, but I'm seeing her tonight for dinner. Why don't you join us? Are you free?' Gloria asked.

'I am, if I might bring someone?' she said, knowing she was blushing.

'Kate! No! How wonderful, who is it?'

'Stewart Dorchester,' Kate said feeling ridiculously embarrassed and proud at the same time.

'So there was something between you two! I knew it!' Gloria was beaming with pleasure. 'He's a sweetie. Oh, I do approve. No wonder you look so stunning. There's nothing like love, is there?'

As soon as Kate had left, Gloria settled down with the manuscript she had brought with her. Half an hour later she sat back with a satisfied smile. It was wonderful. Kate was a real writer, no question.

So it was that at the celebration dinner which followed the three women were together – a little over a year from the day they first met.

'How everything has changed,' Kate said. 'I still can't believe the new path my life has taken.' She looked proudly at Stewart.

'And we're all happy, aren't we?' said Joy, thinking of Hannah peacefully asleep, and smiled at Barty.

Gloria leant her head against Peter's shoulder. 'And for a change,' she laughed, 'we're not in Barty's loo!'

available from
THE ORION PUBLISHING GROUP

———————

☐ **Advances** £5.99
ANITA BURGH
0 75280 931 8

☐ **Avarice** £5.99
ANITA BURGH
0 75281 641 1

☐ **Breeders** £5.99
ANITA BURGH
0 75280 691 2

☐ **Clare's War** £5.99
ANITA BURGH
0 75284 290 0

☐ **The Cult** £5.99
ANITA BURGH
0 75280 929 6

☐ **Distinctions of Class** £5.99
ANITA BURGH
0 75281 066 9

☐ **Exiles** £5.99
ANITA BURGH
0 75284 409 1

☐ **The Family** £5.99
ANITA BURGH
0 75282 772 3

☐ **Lottery** £5.99
ANITA BURGH
0 75281 640 3

☐ **On Call** £5.99
ANITA BURGH
0 75281 695 0

☐ **Overtures** £5.99
ANITA BURGH
0 75281 684 5

☐ **The Azure Bowl** £6.99
ANITA BURGH
0 75283 744 3

☐ **The Golden Butterfly** £6.99
ANITA BURGH
0 75283 758 3

☐ **The Stone Mistress** £6.99
ANITA BURGH
0 75283 759 1

All Orion/Phoenix titles are available at your local bookshop or from the following address:

> Mail Order Department
> Littlehampton Book Services
> FREEPOST BR535
> Worthing, West Sussex, BN13 3BR
> *telephone* 01903 828503, *facsimile* 01903 828802
> *e-mail* MailOrders@lbsltd.co.uk
> (Please ensure that you include full postal address details)

Payment can be made either by credit/debit card (Visa, Mastercard, Access and Switch accepted) or by sending a £ Sterling cheque or postal order made payable to *Littlehampton Book Services*.
DO NOT SEND CASH OR CURRENCY.

Please add the following to cover postage and packing

UK and BFPO:
£1.50 for the first book, and 50p for each additional book to a maximum of £3.50

Overseas and Eire:
£2.50 for the first book plus £1.00 for the second book and 50p for each additional book ordered

---

BLOCK CAPITALS PLEASE

name of cardholder ....

address of cardholder ....

delivery address
(if different from cardholder)
....

postcode ....   *postcode* ....

☐ I enclose my remittance for £.............................

☐ please debit my Mastercard/Visa/Access/Switch (delete as appropriate)

card number ☐☐☐☐☐☐☐☐☐☐☐☐☐☐☐☐

expiry date ☐☐☐☐   Switch issue no. ☐☐

signature ....

prices and availability are subject to change without notice